THE
TOWER
OF FOOLS

ANDRZEJ SAPKOWSKI

Translated by
DAVID FRENCH

This paperback edition published in 2021

First published in Great Britain in 2020 by Gollancz
an imprint of The Orion Publishing Group Ltd
Carmelite House, 50 Victoria Embankment
London EC4Y 0DZ

An Hachette UK Company

1 3 5 7 9 10 8 6 4 2

Published by arrangement with the Patricia Pasqualini Literary Agency.

A CIP catalogue record for this book is
available from the British Library.

ISBN (Mass Market Paperback) 978 1 473 22614 2
ISBN (eBook) 978 1 473 22615 9

Typeset by Input Data Services Ltd, Somerset

Printed and bound in Great Britain by Clays Ltd, Elcograf S.p.A.

MIX
Paper from
responsible sources
FSC® C104740

www.gollancz.co.uk

Prologue

*The end of the world did not occur in the Year of Our Lord 1420,
although much had indicated that it would.*

*The chiliasts' dark prophecies that predicted the End quite precisely
– on the Monday after Saint Scholastica's Day in the month of February of the year 1420 – did not come true. Monday came and went,
Tuesday, too, then Wednesday: still nothing. The Days of Punishment
and Vengeance preceding the coming of the Kingdom of the Lord never
arrived. Although a thousand years had passed, Satan was not loosed
from his prison, nor did he go out to deceive the nations in the four
quarters of the Earth. No sinners or foes of God perished from sword,
fire, hunger, hailstones, fangs of beasts, stings of scorpions or venom of
snakes. The faithful waited in vain on the peaks of Tábor, Beránek,
Oreb, Sion and the Mount of Olives, and in the* quinque civitates,
*the five chosen cities, for the second coming of Christ, as foretold in
the Prophecy of Isaiah. The end of the world did not come to pass. The
world neither perished nor went up in flames. Not all of it, at least.*

But things certainly weren't dull.

*My, but this pottage is truly delicious. Thick, spicy and creamy. I
haven't eaten soup like this for ages. Thank you, noble gentlemen, for
the repast, and thank you, young miss innkeeper. What would I say to
beer, you ask? Yes. By all means.* Comedamus tandem, et bibamus,
cras enim moriemur.

*Where was I? Ah, yes – time passed, and the end of the world still
did not occur, and events transpired according to their rightful order.
Wars were waged, plagues proliferated,* mors nigra *raged, hunger
abounded. Neighbour robbed and killed neighbour and lusted after his*

wife, and men behaved like wolves towards one another. The Jews were treated to a little pogrom from time to time and the heretics to a bit of burning at the stake. Other notable events included skeletons cavorting around burial grounds, Death roaming the Earth with his scythe, an incubus forcing its way between the trembling thighs of sleeping maids, and a striga alighting on the back of a lone rider in the wilds. Clearly, the Devil was involving himself in Earthly affairs, wandering around like a roaring lion considering who to devour next.

Plenty of esteemed people died during that time. Plenty were also born, of course, but dates of birth aren't written down in chronicles and no one ever remembers them, with the possible exception of mothers, and in cases when a babe is born with two heads or two cocks. But deaths? Such things are carved in stone.

Wherefore in 1421, on the Monday following Laetare Sunday, Jan apellatus *Kropidło, Piast duke and* episcopus wloclaviensis, *died in Opole, having attained a well-deserved three score years. Before his death, he had made a donation of six hundred grzywna to the city of Opole. It is said that part of the sum, representing the dying man's last will, went to Red-headed Kundzia's, a celebrated Opole brothel. The bishop had availed himself of the services of that establishment, located at the rear of the Franciscan monastery, right up until his death – though towards the end he was more voyeur than active participant.*

In the summer of 1422 – I do not recall the exact date – Henry V, King of England and victor at Agincourt, died in Vincennes. Charles VI, King of France, having been quite mad for five years, outlived him by a mere two months. The madman's son, Charles the Dauphin, laid claim to the crown, but the English refused to recognise him. The Dauphin's mother, Queen Isabelle, had, after all, much earlier proclaimed him a bastard, conceived some distance from the marital bed and with a man of sound mind. And since bastards don't ascend the throne, an Englishman, little Harry, the son of Henry V, became the rightful ruler of France aged only nine months. Harry's uncle, John of Lancaster, Duke of Bedford, became Regent of France. He, together with the Burgundian faction, held northern France – including Paris – while the south was controlled by the Dauphin Charles and the

Armagnac faction. And dogs howled among the corpses on battlefields between the two demesnes.

At Pentecost in 1423, Pedro de Luna, the Avignon antipope, an anathematized schismatic, entitling himself Benedict XIII – contrary to the resolutions of two ecumenical councils – died in Pensicola Castle, not far from Valencia.

Other men passed during this time. The Habsburg, Ernest the Iron, Duke of Styria, Carinthia, Carniola, Istria and Trieste. Jan of Racibórz – a duke of both Piast and Přemyslid blood – also dead. Wacław, dux *Lubiniensis, died young; Duke Henryk, Lord of Ziębice with his brother Jan, died. Henryk* dictus *Rumpoldus, Duke of Głogów, died in exile. Mikołaj Trąba, Archbishop of Gniezno, an upright and judicious wise man, died. Michael Küchmeister, Grand Master of the Teutonic Knights, died in Malbork. Jakub Pęczak known as 'Fish', a miller from near Bytom, also died. I admit he was a mite less famous and celebrated than the above-mentioned men, but he had the advantage over them that I knew him personally and used to drink with him, which I never did with the others.*

Meanwhile, important cultural developments were also taking place. Bernardino of Sienna, John Cantius and John Capistrano preached, Jean Gerson and Paweł Włodkowic taught, Christine de Pisan and Thomas Hemerken à Kempis wrote eruditely. Laurentius of Březová was writing his exquisite chronicle. Andrei Rublev painted icons, Tommaso Masaccio painted, Robert Campin painted. Jan van Eyck, Duke John of Bavaria's artist, painted the Adoration of the Mystic Lamb altarpiece for Saint Bavo's Cathedral in Ghent. It is a most gorgeous polyptych, now adorning Jodocus Vijd's chapel. In Florence, the master Pippo Brunelleschi finished building the marvellous dome over the four naves of the Cattedrale di Santa Maria del Fiore. And we in Silesia were not to be outdone – here, Piotr of Frankenstein completed a most impressive church dedicated to Saint James in the town of Nysa. It's not far from here in Milicz, so you should take the chance to see it if you haven't yet been.

In that year of 1422, at Shrovetide, King Władysław II of Poland, born Jogaila of Lithuania, held his nuptials with great pomp in the city of Lida, wedding Sophia of Halshany, a blushing young maid of seventeen – more than half a century younger than he. It was said that the maid was more famous for her looks than her morals, which would cause many a problem later. For Jogaila, forgetting his duty to satisfy a young wife, set off to fight the Prussian lords – I mean the Teutonic Knights – in early summer. Thus the new Grand Master of the Order, Paul von Rusdorf, Küchmeister's successor, met the full force of the Polish army soon after taking office – and felt it keenly. You may hear nothing of his prowess in Sophia's bedchamber, but Jogaila was still spry enough to give the Teutonic Knights a sound thrashing.

At that time, a host of important events also took place in the Kingdom of Bohemia. There was great unrest there, with much bloodletting and unceasing war. About which I can in no way speak . . . Please forgive an old man, m'lords, but to fear is human, and I've felt the rod too often for rash words. After all, gentlemen, I see on your tunics the Polish Nałęcze and Habdanki arms, and on yours, noble Czechs, the cockerels of the lords of Dobrá Voda and the arrows of the knights of Strakonice . . . And you, grim sir, are a Zettritz, judging by the bison's head on your escutcheon. Though I'm unable even to place your slanting chequerboard and gryphons, m'lord. Neither can it be ruled out that you, a friar of the Order of Saint Francis, won't inform to the Holy Office, which one can be certain about in your regard, friars of Saint Dominic. Given such diverse and international company, you may see for yourselves why I can't breathe a word about Czech matters, not knowing who among you supports Albrecht, and who the Polish king and heir. Who among you supports Meinhard of Hradec and Oldřich of Rožmberk, and who supports Hynce Ptáček of Pirkštejn and Jan Kolda of Žampach. Who here supports Count Spytko of Melsztyn, and who is a partisan of Bishop Oleśnicki. I have no desire for a flogging, but I know I'll get one, because I often have. Why so, you ask? Why thus: if I say that during these years the valiant Czech Hussites trounced the Germans, crushing three successive papist crusades, before I know it, I'll get it in the neck from one side. But if I say instead that the heretics clobbered the crusaders at the battles of Vítkov Hill, Vyšehrad, Žatec and Německý Brod with the help of the Devil, the others will seize

4

and flog me. Wherefore I prefer to keep my counsel, and if I'm to say anything, to do so with the impartiality of an envoy – reporting, as they say, sine ira et studio, *concisely, to the point and adding nothing.*

Thus I'll say in short: in the autumn of 1420, Jogaila, the King of Poland, refused to accept the Bohemian crown that the Hussites had offered him. It had been decided in Kraków that the Lithuanian dux *Witold, who had always wanted to reign, would take it. However, so as not to vex the Holy Roman Emperor Sigismund or the Pope, Witold's nephew, Sigismund, son of Korybut was sent to Bohemia. Sigismund, commanding a force of five thousand Polish knights, arrived in Golden Prague in 1422, on Saint Stanisław's day. But around Epiphany of the following year, the prince had to return to Lithuania – Sigismund of Luxembourg and Otto Colonna, at that time Holy Father Martin V, being so enraged by that Bohemian succession. What do you say to that? Then in 1424, on the eve of the Visitation, Korybut's son was back in Prague. This time, though, against the will of Jogaila and Witold, against the wishes of the Pope and of the Holy Roman Emperor. Meaning as an outlaw and an exile. At the head of outlaws and exiles like himself. And not numbering thousands, as previously, but only hundreds.*

In Prague, the uprising devoured its own children like Saturn, as faction battled faction. Jan of Želiv, executed on the Monday after Reminiscere *Sunday in 1422, by May of that year was being mourned in every church as a martyr. Golden Prague also proudly stood up to the Tábor, but finally met its match in the shape of that great warrior, Jan Žižka. Žižka gave the Praguians a good hiding in the Year of Our Lord 1424, on the second day after the June Nones, at Malešov by the River Bohynka. There were many, many new widows and orphans in Prague after that defeat.*

Who knows, perhaps it was the orphans' tears that caused Jan Žižka of Trocnov – and later of the Chalice – to die soon afterwards in Přibyslav, near the Moravian border, the Wednesday before Saint Gall's Day. As before, some wept because of him and others wept at his passing, as at the loss of a father. Which is why they called themselves the Orphans . . .

But surely you remember these details, for it was not so long ago. And yet it all feels like . . . history.

And do you know, noble lords, how you can tell that a time is historical? Because much happens, and happens quickly.

Although the world did not end, other prophecies were fulfilled, bringing down great wars and great misfortunes on Christian folk, and many men fell. It was as though God wanted the dawning of the new order to be preceded by the extinction of the old. Many believed that the Apocalypse was nigh. That the Ten-Horned Beast was emerging from the Abyss. That the dread Four Horsemen would soon appear amid the smoke of fires and blood-soaked fields. That any moment, trumpets would sound and seals be broken. That fire would tumble from the heavens. That the Wormwood Star would fall on a third part of the rivers and the fountains of waters. That a madman, when he espied the footprint of another man on the ashes, would, weeping, kiss that footprint.

At times, it was so dreadful, it made your – if you'll pardon me, m'lords – arse go numb with fear.

It was an iniquitous time. Evil. And if you wish, m'lords, I'll tell you about it, in order to allay the boredom, before the rains that keep us in the tavern relent. I shall tell you about the folk who lived then, and about those who also lived then but were by no means folk. I'll tell how the former and the latter struggled with what that time brought. With fate. And with their very selves.

This story begins agreeably and delightfully, dreamily and fondly – with pleasurable, tender lovemaking. But may that not delude you, good sirs.

May that not delude you.

Chapter One

In which the reader makes the acquaintance of Reinmar of Bielawa, called Reynevan, and of his better features, including his knowledge of the *ars amandi*, the arcana of horse-riding, and the Old Testament, though not necessarily in that order.

Through the small chamber's window, against a background of the recently stormy sky, could be seen three towers. The first belonged to the town hall. Further off, the slender spire of the Church of Saint John the Evangelist, its shiny red tiles glistening in the sun. And beyond that, the round tower of the ducal castle. Swifts winged around the church spire, frightened by the recent tolling of the bells, the ozone-rich air still shuddering from the sound.

The bells had also quite recently tolled in the towers of the Churches of the Blessed Virgin Mary and Corpus Christi. Those towers, however, weren't visible from the window of the chamber in the garret of a wooden building affixed like a swallow's nest to the complex of the Augustinian hospice and priory.

It was time for Sext. The monks began the *Deus in adjutorium* while Reinmar of Bielawa – known to his friends as 'Reynevan' – kissed the sweat-covered collarbone of Adèle of Stercza, freed himself from her embrace and lay down beside her, panting, on bedclothes hot from lovemaking.

Outside, Priory Street echoed with shouts, the rattle of wagons, the dull thud of empty barrels and the melodious clanking of tin and copper pots. It was Wednesday, market day, which always attracted large numbers of merchants and customers.

Memento, salutis Auctor
quod nostri quondam corporis,
ex illibata Virgine
nascendo, formam sumpseris.
Maria mater gratiae,
mater misericordiae,
tu nos ab hoste protege,
et hora mortis suscipe . . .

They're already singing the hymn, thought Reynevan, lazily embracing Adèle, a native of distant Burgundy and the wife of the knight Gelfrad of Stercza. *The hymn has begun. It beggars belief how swiftly moments of happiness pass. One wishes they would last for ever, but they fade like a fleeting dream.*

'Reynevan . . . *Mon amour* . . . My divine boy . . .' Adèle interrupted his dreamy reverie. She, too, was aware of the passing of time, but evidently had no intention of wasting it on philosophical deliberations.

Adèle was utterly, completely, totally naked.

Every country has its customs, thought Reynevan. *How fascinating it is to learn about the world and its peoples. Silesian and German women, for example, when they get down to it, never allow their shifts to be lifted higher than their navels. Polish and Czech women gladly lift theirs themselves, above their breasts, but not for all the world would they remove them completely. But Burgundians, oh, they cast off everything at once, their hot blood apparently unable to bear any cloth on their skin during the throes of passion. Ah, what a joy it is to learn about the world. The countryside of Burgundy must be beautiful. Lofty mountains . . . Steep hillsides . . . Vales . . .*

'Ah, aaah, *mon amour,*' moaned Adèle of Stercza, thrusting her entire Burgundian landscape against Reynevan's hand.

Reynevan, incidentally, was twenty-three and quite lacking in worldly experience. He had known very few Czech women, even fewer Silesians and Germans, one Polish woman, one Romani, and had once been spurned by a Hungarian woman. Far from impressive, his erotic experiences were actually quite meagre in terms of both quantity and quality, but they still made him swell with pride and conceit. Reynevan – like every testosterone-fuelled young man – regarded himself as a great seducer and erotic connoisseur to whom the female race was an open book. The truth was that his eleven trysts with Adèle of Stercza had taught Reynevan more about the *ars amandi* than his three-year studies in Prague. Reynevan hadn't understood, however, that Adèle was teaching him, certain that all that counted was his inborn talent.

Ad te levavi oculos meos
qui habitas in caelis.
Ecce sicut oculi servorum
In manibus dominorum suorum.
Sicut oculi ancillae in manibus dominae suae
ita oculi nostri ad Dominum Deum nostrum,
Donec misereatur nostri.
Miserere nostri Domine . . .

Adèle seized Reynevan by the back of the neck and pulled him onto her. Reynevan, understanding what was required of him, made love to her powerfully and passionately, whispering assurances of devotion into her ear. He was happy. Very happy.

Reynevan owed the happiness intoxicating him to the Lord's saints – indirectly, of course – as follows:

Feeling remorse for some sins or other – known only to himself and his confessor – the Silesian knight Gelfrad of Stercza had set off on a penitential pilgrimage to the grave of Saint James. But on the way, he decided that Compostela was definitely too far, and that a pilgrimage to Saint-Gilles would absolutely suffice. But Gelfrad wasn't fated to reach Saint-Gilles, either. He only made it to Dijon, where by chance he met a sixteen-year-old Burgundian, the gorgeous Adèle of Beauvoisin. Adèle, who utterly enthralled Gelfrad with her beauty, was an orphan, and her two hell-raising and good-for-nothing brothers gave their sister to be married to the Silesian knight without a second thought. Although, in the brothers' opinion, Silesia lay somewhere between the Tigris and the Euphrates, Stercza was the ideal brother-in-law in their eyes because he didn't argue too much over the dowry. Thus, the Burgundian came to Heinrichsdorf, a village near Ziębice held in endowment by Gelfrad. While in Ziębice, Adèle caught Reinmar of Bielawa's eye. And vice versa.

'Aaaah!' screamed Adèle of Stercza, wrapping her legs around Reynevan's back. 'Aaaaa-aaah!'

Never would those moans have occurred, and nothing more than surreptitious glances and furtive gestures have passed between them, if not for a third saint: George, to be precise. For on Saint George's Day, Gelfrad of Stercza had sworn an oath and joined one of the many anti-Hussite crusades organised by the Brandenburg Prince-Elector and the Meissen margraves. The crusaders didn't achieve any great victories – they entered Bohemia and left very soon after, not even risking a skirmish with the Hussites. But although there was no fighting, there were casualties, one of which turned out to be Gelfrad, who fractured his leg very badly falling from his horse and was still recuperating somewhere in Pleissnerland. Adèle, a grass widow, staying in the meanwhile with her husband's family in Bierutów, was able to freely tryst with Reynevan in a chamber in the complex of the Augustinian priory in Oleśnica, not far from the hospice where Reynevan had his workshop.

The monks in the Church of Corpus Christi began to sing the second of three psalms making up the Sext. *We'll have to hurry*, thought Reynevan. *During the* capitulum, *at the latest the* Kyrie, *and not a moment after, Adèle must vanish from the hospice. She cannot be seen here.*

> *Benedictus Dominus*
> *qui non dedit nos*
> *in captionem dentibus eorum.*
> *Anima nostra sicut passer erepta est*

de laqueo venantium . . .

Reynevan kissed Adèle's hip, and then, inspired by the monks' singing, took a deep breath and plunged himself into her orchard of pomegranates. Adèle tensed, straightened her arms and dug her fingers in his hair, augmenting his biblical initiatives with gentle movements of her hips.

'Oh, oooooh . . . *Mon amour* . . . *Mon magicien* . . . My divine boy . . . My sorcerer . . .'

Qui confidunt in Domino, sicut mons Sion
non commovebitur in aeternum,
qui habitat in Hierusalem . . .

The third already, thought Reynevan. *How fleeting are these moments of happiness . . .*

'*Revertere*,' he muttered, kneeling. 'Turn around, turn around, Shulamith.'

Adèle turned, knelt and leaned forward, seizing the linden-wood planks of the bedhead tightly and presenting Reynevan with her entire, ravishingly gorgeous posterior. *Aphrodite Kallipygos*, he thought, moving closer. The ancient association and erotic sight made him approach like the aforementioned Saint George, charging with his lance thrust out towards the dragon of Silene. Kneeling behind Adèle like King Solomon behind the throne of wood of the cedar of Lebanon, he seized her vineyards of Engedi in both hands.

'May I compare you, my love,' he whispered, bent over a neck as shapely as the Tower of David, 'may I compare you to a mare among Pharaoh's chariots.'

And he did. Adèle screamed through clenched teeth. Reynevan slowly slid his hands down her sides, slippery with sweat, and the Burgundian threw back her head like a mare about to clear a jump.

Gloria Patri, et Filio et Spiritui sancto.
Sicut erat in principio, et nunc, et semper

et in saecula saeculorum, Amen.
Alleluia!

As the monks concluded the Gloria, Reynevan, kissing the back of Adèle of Stercza's neck, placed his hand beneath her orchard of pomegranates, engrossed, mad, like a young hart skipping upon the mountains to his beloved . . .

A mailed fist struck the door, which thudded open with such force that the lock was torn off the frame and shot through the window like a meteor. Adèle screamed shrilly as the Stercza brothers burst into the chamber.

Reynevan tumbled out of bed, positioning it between himself and the intruders, grabbed his clothes and began to hurriedly put them on. He largely succeeded, but only because the brothers Stercza had directed their frontal attack at their sister-in-law.

'You vile harlot!' bellowed Morold of Stercza, dragging a naked Adèle from the bedclothes.

'Wanton whore!' chimed in Wittich, his older brother, while Wolfher – next oldest after Adèle's husband Gelfrad – did not even open his mouth, for pale fury had deprived him of speech. He struck Adèle hard in the face. The Burgundian screamed. Wolfher struck her again, this time backhanded.

'Don't you dare hit her, Stercza!' yelled Reynevan, but his voice broke and trembled with fear and a paralysing feeling of impotence, caused by his trousers being round his knees. 'Don't you dare!'

His cry achieved its effect, although not the way he had intended. Wolfher and Wittich, momentarily forgetting their adulterous sister-in-law, pounced on Reynevan, raining down a hail of punches and kicks on the boy. He cowered under the blows, but rather than defend or protect himself, he stubbornly pulled on his trousers as though they were some kind of magical armour. Out of the corner of one eye, he saw Wittich drawing a knife. Adèle screamed.

'Don't,' Wolfher snapped at his brother. 'Not here!'

Reynevan managed to get onto his knees. Wittich, face white with fury, jumped at him and punched him, throwing him to the floor again. Adèle let out a piercing scream which broke off as Morold struck her in the face and pulled her hair.

'Don't you dare ...' Reynevan groaned '... hit her, you scoundrels!'

'Bastard!' yelled Wittich. 'Just you wait!'

Wittich leaped forward, punched and kicked once and twice. Wolfher stopped him at the third.

'Not here,' Wolfher repeated calmly, but it was a baleful calm. 'Into the courtyard with him. We'll take him to Bierutów. That slut, too.'

'I'm innocent!' wailed Adèle of Stercza. 'He bewitched me! Enchanted me! He's a sorcerer! *Sorcier! Diab—*'

Morold silenced her with another punch. 'Hold your tongue, trollop,' he growled. 'You'll get the chance to scream. Just wait a while.'

'Don't you *dare* hit her!' yelled Reynevan.

'We'll give you a chance to scream, too, little rooster,' Wolfher added, still menacingly calm. 'Come on, out with him.'

The Stercza brothers threw Reynevan down the garret's steep stairs and the boy tumbled onto the landing, splintering part of the wooden balustrade. Before he could get up, they seized him again and threw him out into the courtyard, onto sand strewn with steaming piles of horse shit.

'Well, well, well,' said Nicolaus of Stercza, the youngest of the brothers, barely a stripling, who was holding the horses. 'Look who's stopped by. Could it be Reinmar of Bielawa?'

'The scholarly braggart Bielawa,' snorted Jentsch of Knobelsdorf, known as Eagle Owl, a comrade and relative of the Sterczas. 'The arrogant know-all Bielawa!'

'Shitty poet,' added Dieter Haxt, another friend of the family. 'Bloody Abélard!'

'And to prove to him we're well read, too,' said Wolfher as he descended the stairs, 'we'll do to him what they did to Abélard when he was caught with Héloïse. Well, Bielawa? How do you fancy being a capon?'

'Go fuck yourself, Stercza.'

'What? What?' Although it seemed impossible, Wolfher Stercza had turned even paler. 'The rooster still has the audacity to open his beak? To crow? The bullwhip, Jentsch!'

'Don't you dare beat him!' Adèle called impotently as she was led down the stairs, now clothed, albeit incompletely. 'Don't you dare! Or I'll tell everyone what you are like! That you courted me yourself, pawed me and tried to debauch me behind your brother's back! That you swore vengeance on me if I spurned you! Which is why you are so ... so ...'

She couldn't find the German word and the entire tirade fell apart. Wolfher just laughed.

'Verily!' he mocked. 'People will listen to the Frenchwoman, the lewd strumpet. The bullwhip, Eagle Owl!'

The courtyard was suddenly awash with black Augustinian habits.

'What is happening here?' shouted the venerable Prior Erasmus Steinkeller, a bony and sallow old man. 'Christians, what are you doing?'

'Begone!' bellowed Wolfher, cracking the bullwhip. 'Begone, shaven-heads, hurry off to your prayer books! Don't interfere in knightly affairs, or woe betide you, blackbacks!'

'Good Lord.' The prior put his liver-spotted hands together. 'Forgive them, for they know not what they do. *In nomine Patris, et Filii—*'

'Morold, Wittich!' roared Wolfher. 'Bring the harlot here! Jentsch, Dieter, bind her paramour!'

'Or perhaps,' snarled Stefan Rotkirch, another friend of the family who had been silent until then, 'we'll drag him behind a horse a little?'

'We could. But first, we'll give him a flogging!'

Wolfher aimed a blow with the horsewhip at the still-prone Reynevan but did not connect, as his wrist was seized by Brother

Innocent, nicknamed by his fellow friars 'Brother Insolent', whose impressive height and build were apparent despite his humble monkish stoop. His vice-like grip held Wolfher's arm motionless.

Stercza swore coarsely, jerked himself away and gave the monk a hard shove. But he might as well have shoved the tower in Oleśnica Castle for all the effect it had. Brother Innocent didn't budge an inch. He shoved Wolfher back, propelling him halfway across the courtyard and dumping him in a pile of muck.

For a moment, there was silence. And then they all rushed the huge monk. Eagle Owl, the first to attack, was punched in the teeth and tumbled across the sand. Morold of Stercza took a thump to the ear and staggered off to one side, staring vacantly. The others swarmed over the Augustinian like ants, raining blows on the monk's huge form. Brother Insolent retaliated just as savagely and in a distinctly unchristian way, quite at odds with Saint Augustine's rule of humility.

The sight enraged the old prior. He flushed like a beetroot, roared like a lion and rushed into the fray, striking left and right with heavy blows of his rosewood crucifix.

'*Pax!*' he bellowed as he struck. '*Pax! Vobiscum!* Love thy neighbour! *Proximum tuum! Sicut te ipsum!* Whoresons!'

Dieter Haxt punched him hard. The old man was flung over backwards and his sandals flew up, describing pretty trajectories in the air. The Augustinians cried out and several of them charged into battle, unable to restrain themselves. The courtyard was seething in earnest.

Wolfher of Stercza, who had been shoved out of the confusion, drew a short sword and brandished it – bloodshed looked inevitable. But Reynevan, who had finally managed to stand up, whacked him in the back of the head with the handle of the bullwhip he had picked up. Stercza held his head and turned around, only for Reynevan to lash him across the face. As Wolfher fell to the ground, Reynevan rushed towards the horses.

'Adèle! Here! To me!'

Adèle didn't even budge, and the indifference painted on her face was alarming. Reynevan leaped into the saddle. The horse neighed and fidgeted.

'Adèèèèle!'

Morold, Wittich, Haxt and Eagle Owl were now running towards him. Reynevan reined the horse around, whistled piercingly and spurred it hard, making for the gate.

'After him!' yelled Wolfher. 'To your horses and get after him!'

Reynevan's first thought was to head towards Saint Mary's Gate and out of the town into the woods, but the stretch of Cattle Street leading to the gate was totally crammed with wagons. Furthermore, the horse, urged on and frightened by the cries of an unfamiliar rider, was showing great individual initiative, so before he knew it, Reynevan was hurtling along at a gallop towards the town square, splashing mud and scattering passers-by. He didn't have to look back to know the others were hot on his heels given the thudding of hooves, the neighing of horses, the angry roaring of the Sterczas and the furious yelling of people being jostled.

He jabbed the horse to a full gallop with his heels, hitting and knocking over a baker carrying a basket. A shower of loaves and pastries flew into the mud, soon to be trodden beneath the hooves of the Sterczas' horses. Reynevan didn't even look back, more concerned with what was ahead of him than behind. A cart piled high with faggots of brushwood loomed up before his eyes. The cart was blocking almost the entire street, the rest of which was occupied by a group of half-clothed urchins, kneeling down and busily digging something extremely engrossing out of the muck.

'We have you, Bielawa!' thundered Wolfher from behind, also seeing the obstruction.

Reynevan's horse was racing so swiftly there was no chance of stopping it. He pressed himself against its mane and closed his eyes. As a result, he didn't see the half-naked children scatter with the speed and grace of rats. He didn't look back, so nor did he see a peasant in a sheepskin jerkin turn around, somewhat stupefied, as he hauled a cart into the road. Nor did he see the Sterczas riding broadside into the cart. Nor Jentsch of Knobelsdorf soaring from the saddle and sweeping half of the faggots from the cart with his body.

Reynevan galloped down Saint John's Street, between the town hall and the burgermeister's house, hurtling at full speed into Oleśnica's huge and crowded town square. Pandemonium erupted. Aiming for the southern frontage and the squat, square tower of the Oława Gate visible above it, Reynevan galloped through the crowds, leaving havoc behind him. Townsfolk yelled and pigs squealed, as overturned stalls and benches showered a hail of household goods and foodstuffs of every kind in all directions. Clouds of feathers flew everywhere as the Sterczas – hot on Reynevan's heels – added to the destruction.

Reynevan's horse, frightened by a goose flying past its nose, recoiled and hurtled into a fish stall, shattering crates and bursting open barrels. The enraged fishmonger made a great swipe with a keep net, missing Reynevan but striking the horse's rump. The horse whinnied and slewed sideways, upending a stall selling thread and ribbons, and only a miracle prevented Reynevan from falling. Out of the corner of one eye, he saw the stallholder running after him brandishing a huge cleaver (serving God only knew what purpose in the haberdashery trade). Spitting out some goose feathers stuck to his lips, he brought the horse under control and galloped through the shambles, knowing that the Oława Gate was very close.

'I'll tear your balls off, Bielawa!' Wolfher of Stercza roared from behind. 'I'll tear them off and stuff them down your throat!'

'Kiss my arse!'

Only four men were chasing him now – Rotkirch had been pulled from his horse and was being roughed up by some infuriated market traders.

Reynevan darted like an arrow down an avenue of animal carcasses suspended by their legs. Most of the butchers leaped back in alarm, but one carrying a large haunch of beef on one shoulder tumbled under the hooves of Wittich's horse, which took fright, reared up and was ploughed into by Wolfher's horse. Wittich flew from the saddle straight onto the meat stall, nose-first into livers, lights and kidneys, and was then landed on by Wolfher. His foot was caught in the stirrup and before he could free himself, he had smashed a large number of stalls and covered himself in mud and blood.

At the last moment, Reynevan quickly lowered his head over the horse's neck to duck under a wooden sign with a piglet's head painted on it. Dieter Haxt, who was bearing down on him, wasn't quick enough and the cheerfully grinning piglet slammed into his forehead. Dieter flew from the saddle and crashed into a pile of refuse, frightening some cats. Reynevan turned around. Now only Nicolaus of Stercza was keeping up with him.

Reynevan shot out of the chaos at a full gallop and into a small square where some tanners were working. As a frame hung with wet hides loomed up before him, he urged his horse to jump. It did. And Reynevan didn't fall off. Another miracle.

Nicolaus wasn't as lucky. His horse skidded to a halt in front of the frame and collided with it, slipping on the mud and scraps of meat and fat. The youngest Stercza shot over his horse's head, with very unfortunate results. He flew belly-first right onto a scythe used for scraping leather which the tanners had left propped up against the frame.

At first, Nicolaus had no idea what had happened. He got up from the ground, caught hold of his horse, and only when it snorted and stepped back did his knees sag and buckle beneath him. Still not really knowing what was happening, the youngest Stercza slid across the mud after the panicked horse, which was still moving back and snorting. Finally, as he released the reins and tried to get to his feet again, he realised something was wrong and looked down at his midriff.

And screamed.

He dropped to his knees in the middle of a rapidly spreading pool of blood.

Dieter Haxt rode up, reined in his horse and dismounted. A

moment later, Wolfher and Wittich followed suit.

Nicolaus sat down heavily. Looked at his belly again. Screamed and then burst into tears. His eyes began to glaze over as the blood gushing from him mingled with the blood of the oxen and hogs butchered that morning.

'Nicolaaaaus!' yelled Wolfher.

Nicolaus of Stercza coughed and choked. And died.

'You are dead, Reinmar of Bielawa!' Wolfher of Stercza, pale with fury, bellowed towards the gate. 'I'll catch you, kill you, destroy you. Exterminate you and your entire viperous family. Your entire viperous family, do you hear?'

Reynevan didn't. Amid the thud of horseshoes on the bridge planks, he was leaving Oleśnica and dashing south, straight for the Wrocław highway.

Chapter Two

In which the reader finds out more about Reynevan from conversations involving various people, some kindly disposed and others quite the opposite. Meanwhile, Reynevan himself is wandering around the woods near Oleśnica. The author is sparing in his descriptions of that trek, hence the reader – *nolens volens* – will have to imagine it.

'Sit you down, gentlemen,' said Bartłomiej Sachs, the burgermeister of Oleśnica, to the councillors. 'What's your pleasure? Truth be told, I have no wines to regale you with. But ale, ho-ho, today I was brought some excellent matured ale, first brew, from a deep, cold cellar in Świdnica.'

'Beer it is, then, Master Bartłomiej,' said Jan Hofrichter, one of the town's wealthiest merchants, rubbing his hands together. 'Ale is our tipple, let the nobility and diverse lordlings pickle their guts in wine ... With my apologies, Reverend ...'

'Not at all,' replied Father Jakub of Gall, parish priest at the Church of Saint John the Evangelist. 'I'm no longer a nobleman, I'm a parson. And a parson, naturally, is ever with his flock, thus it doesn't behove me to disdain beer. And I may drink, for Vespers have been said.'

They sat down at the table in the huge, low-ceilinged, whitewashed chamber of the town hall, the usual location for meetings of the town council. The burgermeister was in his customary seat, back to the fireplace, with Father Gall beside him, facing the window. Opposite sat Hofrichter, beside him Łukasz Friedmann, a sought-after and wealthy goldsmith, in his fashionably padded doublet, a velvet beret resting on curled hair, every inch the nobleman.

The burgermeister cleared his throat and began, without waiting for the servant to bring the beer. 'And what is this?' he said, linking his hands on his prominent belly. 'What have the noble knights treated us to in our town? A brawl at the Augustinian priory. A chase on horseback through the streets. A disturbance in the town square, several folk injured, including one child gravely. Belongings destroyed, goods marred – such significant material losses that *mercatores et institores* were pestering me for hours with demands for compensation. In sooth, I ought to pack them off with their plaints to the Lords Stercza!'

'Better not,' Jan Hofrichter advised dryly. 'Though I also hold that our noblemen have been lately passing unruly, one can neither forget the causes of the affair nor its consequences. For the consequence – the tragic consequence – is the death of young Nicolaus of Stercza. And the cause: licentiousness and debauchery. The Sterczas were defending their brother's honour, pursuing the adulterer who seduced their sister-in-law and besmirched the marital bed. In truth, in their zeal they overplayed a touch—'

The merchant stopped speaking under Father Jakub's telling gaze. For when Father Jakub signalled with a look his desire to express himself, even the burgermeister himself fell silent. Jakub Gall was not only the parish priest of the town's church, but also secretary to Konrad, Duke of Oleśnica, and canon in the Chapter of Wrocław Cathedral.

'Adultery is a sin,' intoned the priest, straightening his skinny frame behind the table. 'Adultery is also a crime. But God punishes sins and the law punishes crimes. Nothing justifies mob law and killings.'

'Yes, yes,' agreed the burgermeister, but fell silent at once and devoted all his attention to the beer that had just arrived.

'Nicolaus of Stercza died tragically, which pains us greatly,' added Father Gall, 'but as the result of an accident. However, had Wolfher and company caught Reinmar of Bielawa, we would be dealing with a murder in our jurisdiction. We know not if there might yet be one. Let me remind you that Prior Steinkeller, the pious old man severely beaten by the Sterczas, is lying as if lifeless in the Augustinian priory. If he expires as a result of the beating, there'll be a problem. For the Sterczas, to be precise.'

'Whereas, regarding the crime of adultery,' said the goldsmith Łukasz Friedmann, examining the rings on his manicured fingers, 'mark, honourable gentlemen, that it is not our jurisdiction at all. Although the debauchery occurred in Oleśnica, the culprits do not come under our authority. Gelfrad of Stercza, the cuckolded husband, is a vassal of the Duke of Ziębice. As is the seducer, the young physician, Reinmar of Bielawa—'

'The debauchery took place here, as did the crime,' said Hofrichter firmly. 'And it was a serious one, if we are to believe what Stercza's wife disclosed at the Augustinian priory – that the physician beguiled her with spells and used sorcery to entice her to sin. He compelled her against her will.'

'That's what they all say,' the burgermeister boomed from the depths of his mug.

'Particularly when someone of Wolfher of Stercza's ilk holds a knife to their throat,' the goldsmith added without emotion. 'The Reverend Father Jakub was right to say that adultery is a felony – a *crimen* – and as such demands an investigation and a trial. We do not wish for familial vendettas or street brawls. We shall not allow enraged lordlings to raise a hand against men of the cloth, wield knives or trample people in city squares. In Świdnica, a Pannewitz went to the tower for striking an armourer and threatening him with a dagger. Which is proper. The times of knightly licence must not return. The case must go before the duke.'

'All the more so since Reinmar of Bielawa is a nobleman and Adèle of Stercza a noblewoman,' the burgermeister confirmed with a nod. 'We cannot flog him, nor banish her from the town like a common harlot. The case must come before the duke.'

'Let's not be too hasty with this,' said Father Gall, gazing at the ceiling. 'Duke Konrad is preparing to travel to Wrocław and has a multitude of matters to deal with before his departure. The rumours have probably already reached him – as rumours do – but now isn't the time to make them official. Suffice it to postpone the matter until his return. Much may be resolved by then.'

'I concur.' Bartłomiej Sachs nodded again.

'As do I,' added the goldsmith.

Jan Hofrichter straightened his marten-fur calpac and blew the froth from his mug. 'For the present, we ought not to inform the duke,' he pronounced. 'We shall wait until he returns, I agree with you on that, honourable gentlemen. But we must inform the Holy Office, and fast, about what we found in the physician's workshop. Don't shake your head, Master Bartłomiej, or make faces, honourable Master Łukasz. And you, Reverend, stop sighing and counting flies on the ceiling. I desire this about as much as you do, and the same goes for the Inquisition. But many were present at the opening of the workshop. And where there are many people, at least one of them is reporting back to the Inquisition. And when the Inquisitor arrives in Oleśnica, we'll be the first to be asked why we delayed.'

'So I will explain the delay,' said Father Gall, tearing his attention away from the ceiling. 'I, in person, because it's my parish and the responsibility to inform the bishop and the papal Inquisitor falls on me. It is also for me to judge whether the circumstances justify the summoning and bothering of the Curia and the Office.'

'Isn't the witchcraft that Adèle of Stercza was screaming about at the Augustinian priory a circumstance?' persisted Jan Hofrichter. 'Isn't the workshop itself? Aren't the alchemic alembic and pentagram on the floor? The mandrake? The skulls and skeletons' hands? The crystals and looking glasses? The bottles and flacons containing the Devil only knows what filth and venom? The frogs and lizards in specimen jars? Aren't they circumstances?'

'They are not,' said Father Gall. 'The Inquisitors are serious men. What interests them is *inquisitio de articulis fidei*, not old wives' tales, superstitions and frogs. I have no intention of bothering them with that.'

'And the books?' said Hofrichter. 'The ones we have here?'

'The books ought first to be examined,' replied Jakub Gall calmly. 'Thoroughly and unhurriedly. The Holy Office doesn't forbid reading. Nor the owning of books.'

'Two people have just gone to the stake in Wrocław,' Hofrichter said gloomily, 'for owning a book, or so the rumour runs.'

'Not for owning books,' the parish priest countered dryly, 'but for contempt of court, for an impertinent refusal to renounce the content propagated in those books, among which were the writings of Wycliffe and Huss, the Lollard *Floretus*, the Articles of Prague and numerous other Hussite pamphlets and tracts. I don't see anything like that here, among the books confiscated from Reinmar of Bielawa's workshop. I see almost exclusively medical tomes. Which, as a matter of fact, are mainly or even entirely the property of the Augustinian priory's *scriptorium*.'

'I repeat,' Jan Hofrichter stood up and went over to the books spread out on the table, 'I repeat, I am not at all keen to involve either the bishop or the papal Inquisition – I don't wish to denounce anyone or see anyone sizzling at the stake. But this concerns our arses and ensuring that we aren't accused of possessing these books, either. And what do we have here? Apart from Galen, Pliny and Strabo? Albertus Magnus, *De vegetabilis et plantis* . . . Magnus, ha, a nickname right worthy of a wizard. And here, well, well, Shapur ibn Sahl . . . Abu Bakr Muhammad ibn Zakariya al-Razi . . . Pagans! Saracens!'

'The works of these Saracens are taught at Christian universities,' Łukasz Friedmann calmly explained, examining his rings, 'as medical authorities. And your "wizard" is Albert the Great, the Bishop of Regensburg, a learned theologian.'

'You don't say? Hmmm . . . Let's keep looking . . . See! *Causae et curae*, written by Hildegard of Bingen. Undoubtedly a witch, that Hildegard!'

'Not really,' Father Gall said, smiling. 'Hildegard of Bingen, a visionary, called the Sibyl of the Rhine. She died in an aura of saintliness.'

'If you say so ... But what's this? John Gerard, *A Generall ... Historie ... of Plantes* ... I wonder what tongue this is. Hebrew, perhaps. But he's probably another saint. And here we have *Herbarius*, by Thomas of Bohemia—'

'What did you say?' Father Jakub lifted his head. 'Thomas of Bohemia?'

'That's what is written here.'

'Show me. Hmmm ... Interesting, interesting ... Everything, it turns out, remains in the family. And revolves around the family.'

'What family?'

'So close to home, it couldn't be closer.' Łukasz Friedmann still appeared to be utterly absorbed by his rings. 'Thomas of Bohemia is the great-grandfather of our Reinmar, the lover of other men's wives, the man who has caused us such confusion and trouble.'

'Thomas of Bohemia ...' The burgermeister frowned. 'Also called Thomas the Physician. I've heard of him. He was a companion of one of the dukes ... I can't recall which ...'

'Duke Henry VI of Wrocław,' Friedmann the goldsmith calmly offered in explanation.

'It is also said,' Hofrichter interrupted, nodding in confirmation, 'that he was a wizard and a heretic.'

'You're worrying that sorcery like a bone, Master Jan,' the burgermeister said with a grimace. 'Let it go.'

'Thomas of Bohemia was a man of the cloth,' the priest informed them in a slightly harsh voice, 'a canon in Wrocław and later a diocesan suffragan bishop and the titular Bishop of Zarephath. He knew Pope Benedict XII personally.'

'All sorts of things were said about *that* pope,' added Hofrichter, not letting up. 'And witchcraft occurred among *protonotaries apostolic*, too. When in office, Inquisitor Schwenckefeld—'

'Just drop it, would you?' Father Jakub said, cutting him off. 'We have other concerns here.'

'Indeed,' confirmed the goldsmith. 'And I know what they are. Duke Henry had no male issue, but three daughters. Our Father Thomas of Bohemia took the liberty of a dalliance with the youngest, Margaret.'

'The duke permitted it?' Hofrichter asked. 'Were they such good friends?'

'The duke was dead by then,' the goldsmith explained, 'so Duchess Anne either didn't see it or chose not to. Although not yet a bishop, Thomas of Bohemia was on excellent terms with the other nobles of Silesia. For imagine, gentlemen, somebody who not only visits the Holy Father in Avignon, but is also capable of removing kidney stones so skilfully that after the operation, the patient doesn't just still *have* a prick – he can even get it up. It is widely believed that it is thanks to Thomas that we still have Piasts in Silesia today. He aided both men and women with equal skill. And couples, too, if you understand my meaning.'

'I fear I do not,' said the burgermeister.

'He was able to help married couples who were unsuccessful in the bedchamber. Now do you understand?'

'*Now* I do.' Jan Hofrichter nodded. 'So, he probably bedded the Wrocław princess according to medical principles, too. Of course, there was issue from that.'

'Naturally,' replied Father Jakub, 'and the matter was dealt with in the usual way. Margaret was sent to the Poor Clares convent and the child, Tymo, ended up with Duke Konrad in Oleśnica, who raised him as his own. Thomas of Bohemia grew in importance everywhere, in Silesia and at the court of Charles IV in Prague, so the boy had a career guaranteed from childhood onwards – an ecclesiastical career, naturally, all dependent on what kind of intelligence he displayed. Were he dim, he'd become a village priest. Were he reasonably bright, he'd be made an abbot in a Cistercian monastery somewhere. Were he intelligent, a chapter of one of the collegiates would be waiting for him.'

'How did he turn out?' Hofrichter asked.

'Quite bright. Handsome, like his father. And valiant. As a

young man, the future priest fought against the Greater Poles beside the younger duke, the future Konrad the Elder. He fought so bravely that nothing was left but to dub him a knight and grant him a fiefdom. And thus, the young priest Tymo was dead, and long live Sir Tymo Behem of Bielawa. Sir Tymo, who soon became even better connected by wedding the youngest daughter of Heidenreich Nostitz, from which union Henryk and Tomasz were born. Henryk took holy orders, was educated in Prague and until his quite recent death was the scholaster at the Church of the Holy Cross in Wrocław. Tomasz, meanwhile, wedded Boguszka, the daughter of Miksza of Prochowice, who bore him two children, Piotr and Reinmar, this Reynevan who is causing us so much trouble.'

Jan Hofrichter nodded and sipped beer from his mug. 'And this Reinmar-Reynevan who's in the habit of seducing other men's wives ... what is his position at the Augustinian priory? An *oblatus*? A *conversus*? A novice?'

'Reinmar of Bielawa,' Father Jakub said, smiling, 'is a physician, schooled at Charles University in Prague. Before that, the boy attended the cathedral school in Wrocław, then learned the arcana of herbalism from the apothecaries of Świdnica and the monks of the monastery of the Hospital of the Holy Ghost in Brzeg. It was those monks and his uncle Henryk, the Wrocław scholaster, who placed him with the Augustinians, who are skilled in herbalism. The boy worked honestly and eagerly in the hospital and the leper house, proving his vocation. Later on, he studied medicine in Prague, again benefitting from his uncle's patronage and the money his uncle received from the canonry. He clearly applied himself to his studies, for after two short years he was a Bachelor of Arts. He left Prague right after the ... erm—'

'Right after the Defenestration,' the burgermeister said, undaunted. 'Which clearly shows he had nothing in common with Hussite heresy.'

'Nothing links him with it,' Friedmann the goldsmith calmly

confirmed. 'Which I know from my son, who also studied in Prague at the same time.'

'It was also very fortunate,' added Burgermeister Sachs, 'that Reynevan returned to Silesia, and to us, in Oleśnica, and not to the Ziębice duchy, where his brother Piotr serves Duke Jan as a knight. Reynevan is a good and bright lad, though young, and so able at herbalism that you'd be hard-pressed to find his equal. He treated the carbuncles that appeared on my wife's ... body, and cured my daughter's chronic cough. He gave me a decoction for my suppurating eyes, which cleared up as if by magic ...' The burgermeister fell silent, cleared his throat and shoved his hands into the fur-trimmed sleeves of his coat.

Jan Hofrichter looked at him keenly. 'Now all is clear to me about this Reynevan,' he finally pronounced, 'I know everything. Misbegotten, albeit, but of Piast blood. A bishop's son. A favourite of dukes. Kin of the Nostitz family. The nephew of the scholaster at Wrocław Collegiate Church. A friend of rich men's sons at university. On top of that, as if that weren't enough, a conscientious physician, almost a miracle worker, capable of winning the gratitude of the powerful. And of what did he cure you, Reverend Father Jakub? From what complaint, out of interest?'

'The complaint,' the parish priest said coldly, 'is no subject for discussion. Let's just say that he cured me.'

'It's not worth the worry of executing somebody like that,' added the burgermeister. 'It'd be a shame to let such a lad perish in a family feud, just because his head was turned by a pair of beautiful ... eyes. Let him serve folk. Let him treat folk, since he is skilled—'

'Even by using a pentagram drawn on the floor?' snorted Hofrichter.

'If it works,' said Father Gall gravely, 'if it helps, if it eases the pain, why not? Such abilities are divine gifts; the Lord gives them according to His will and according to designs known only to Him. *Spiritus fiat, ubi vult*, it's not for us to question His ways.'

'Amen,' concluded the burgermeister.

'In short,' Hofrichter kept pushing, 'someone like Reynevan cannot be guilty? Is that it? Eh?'

'He who is without guilt,' Father Gall replied inscrutably, 'let him cast the first stone. And God will judge us all.'

For a while, such a pregnant silence reigned that the rustle of moths' wings striking the window could be heard. The long-drawn-out and melodious call of the town guard was audible from Saint John's Street.

'Wherefore, to summarise,' said the burgermeister, sitting up straight at the table so as to rest his belly against it, 'the brothers Stercza are to blame for the disturbance in town. The brothers Stercza are to blame for the material damage and bodily injuries. The brothers Stercza are to blame for the grave injury to and – God forbid – the death of the Very Reverend Prior. They, and they alone. And what happened to Nicolaus of Stercza was a ... mishap. Thus shall we present it to the duke on his return. Agreed?'

'Agreed.'

'*Consensus omnium.*'

'*Concordi voce.*'

'But were Reynevan to appear anywhere,' Father Gall added a moment later, 'I advise seizing him quietly and locking him up here, in our town-hall gaol. For his own safety. Until the matter blows over.'

'It would be well to do so swiftly,' added Łukasz Friedmann, examining his rings one last time, 'before Tammo of Stercza gets wind of the damnable business.'

As he left the town hall and headed straight into the darkness of Saint John's Street, the merchant Hofrichter glimpsed a movement on the tower's moonlit wall, an indistinct, moving shape a little below the windows of the town trumpeter, but above the windows of the chamber where the meeting had just finished. He stared, shielding his eyes from the somewhat blinding light of the lantern carried by his servant. *What the Devil?* he thought and crossed himself. *What's creeping across the wall up there? An owl? A swift? A bat? Or perhaps...*

Jan Hofrichter shuddered, crossed himself again, pulled his marten-fur calpac down over his ears, wrapped his coat around him and set off briskly home.

Thus he didn't see a huge wallcreeper spread its wings, fly down from the parapet and noiselessly, like a nightly spectre, glide over the town's rooftops.

Apeczko of Stercza, Lord of Ledna, didn't like visiting Sterzendorf Castle. There was one simple reason: Sterzendorf was the seat of Tammo of Stercza, the head and patriarch of the family – or, as some said, the family's tyrant, despot and tormentor.

The chamber was airless. And dark. Tammo of Stercza didn't let anyone open the windows for fear of catching cold, or the shutters, because light dazzled the cripple's eyes.

Apeczko was hungry and covered in dust from his journey, but there was no time either to eat anything or to clean himself up. Old Stercza didn't like to be kept waiting. Nor did he usually feed his guests. Particularly members of the family.

So Apeczko was swallowing saliva to moisten his throat – he hadn't been given anything to drink, naturally – and telling Tammo about the events in Oleśnica. He did so reluctantly, but he had no choice. Cripple or not, paralysed or not, Tammo was the family patriarch. A patriarch who didn't tolerate defiance.

The old man listened to the account, slumped on a chair in his familiar, bizarrely twisted position. *Misshapen old fart*, thought Apeczko. *Bloody mangled old bugger.*

The cause of the condition of the Stercza family's patriarch was neither fully understood nor common knowledge. One thing wasn't in doubt – Tammo had suffered a stroke after a fit of rage. Some claimed that the old man had become furious on hearing that a personal enemy, the hated Konrad, Duke of Wrocław, had been anointed bishop and become the most powerful personage in Silesia. Others were certain the ill-fated outburst was the result of his mother-in-law, Anna of Pogarell, burning Tammo's favourite dish – buckwheat kasha with fried pork rind. No one would ever know what really happened, but the outcome was evident and couldn't be ignored. After the accident, Stercza could only move his left hand and foot – and clumsily at that. His right eyelid drooped permanently, glutinous tears oozed ceaselessly from his left, which he occasionally managed to lift, and saliva dribbled from the corner of his mouth, which was twisted in a ghastly grimace. The accident had also caused almost complete loss of speech, giving rise to the old man's nickname: Balbulus. The Stammerer-Mumbler.

The loss of the ability to speak hadn't, however, resulted in what the entire family had hoped for – a loss of contact with the world. Oh, no. The Lord of Sterzendorf continued to hold the family in his grasp and terrorise everybody, and what he wanted to say, he said. For he always had to hand somebody who could understand and translate his gurgling, wheezing, gibbering and shouts into comprehensible speech. That person was usually a child, one of Balbulus's countless grandchildren and great-grandchildren.

This time, the interpreter was ten-year-old Ofka of Baruth, who was sitting at the old man's feet and dressing a doll in colourful strips of rag.

'Thus,' Apeczko finished his account, cleared his throat and moved on to his conclusion, 'Wolfher asked me through an emissary to inform you that he will deal swiftly with the matter. That Reinmar of Bielawa will be seized on the Wrocław road and punished. But for the present, Wolfher's hands are tied because the Duke of Oleśnica is journeying with his entire court and diverse eminent clergymen, so there is no way to pursue him. But Wolfher vows to seize Reynevan and claims he can be entrusted with the family's honour.'

Balbulus's eyelid twitched and a dribble of saliva trickled from his mouth.

'Bbbhh-bhh-bhh-bhubhu-bhhuaha-rrhhha-phhh-aaa-rrh!' reverberated through the chamber. 'Bbb . . . hrrrh-urrrhh-bhuuh! Guggu-ggu . . .'

31

'Wolfher is a bloody moron,' Ofka of Baruth translated in her high, melodious voice. 'An idiot I wouldn't even trust with a pail of puke. And the only thing he's capable of seizing is his own prick.'

'Father—'

'Bbb ... brrrh! Bhhrhuu-phr-rrrhhh!'

'Silence,' translated Ofka without raising her head, busy with her doll. 'Listen to what I say. To my orders.'

Apeczko waited patiently for the wheezing and croaking to finish and then for the translation.

'First of all, Apecz,' Tammo of Stercza ordered via the little girl's mouth, 'you will establish which of the women in Bierutów was charged with supervising the Burgundian. She obviously didn't realise the true aim of those charitable visits to Oleśnica or alternatively was in league with the harlot. Give that woman thirty-five sound lashes with a birch on her naked arse. Here, in my chamber, in front of my eyes, that I might at least have a little diversion.'

Apeczko of Stercza nodded. Balbulus coughed, wheezed and slobbered all over himself, then grimaced dreadfully and gaggled.

'I order the Burgundian, meanwhile, to be taken from the Cistercian convent in Ligota, where I know she is in hiding,' translated Ofka, tidying her doll's oakum hair with a small comb, 'even if you have to storm it. Then imprison the trollop among monks favourably disposed towards us, for example—'

Tammo abruptly stopped stammering and gobbling, his wheezing caught in his throat. Apeczko, pierced by the old man's bloodshot eye, saw that he had noticed his embarrassed expression. That he understood. That it was impossible to hide the truth any longer.

'The Burgundian escaped from Ligota,' he stammered. 'In secret ... No one knows whither. Busy with the pursuit of Reynevan ... they – we – allowed her to escape.'

'I wonder,' Ofka translated after a long, pregnant silence, 'I wonder why this doesn't surprise me at all. But since it is so, let it be. I won't bother myself with the whore. Let Gelfrad deal with the matter on his return. He can handle it himself, whether or not he's a cuckold. It's nothing new in this family, actually. It must have happened to me, for it can't be possible that such fools sprang from my own loins.'

Balbulus coughed, wheezed and choked for a while. But Ofka didn't translate, so it couldn't have been speech, just ordinary coughing. The old man finally took a breath, grimaced like a demon and struck his cane against the floor, then gurgled horribly. Ofka listened, sucking the end of her plait.

'But Nicolaus was the family's hope,' she translated. 'Was of my blood, the blood of the Sterczas, not the dregs of the Devil knows what mongrel couplings. So the killer will have to pay for Nicolaus's spilled blood. With interest.'

Tammo banged his cane against the floor again. It fell from his shaking hand. The Lord of Sterzendorf coughed and sneezed, spraying saliva and snot around. Hrozwita of Baruth, Balbulus's daughter and Ofka's mother, who was standing alongside, wiped his chin, picked up the cane and pressed it into his hand.

'Hgrrrhhh! Grhhh ... Bbb ... bhrr ... bhrrrllg ...'

'Reinmar of Bielawa will pay me back for Nicolaus,' Ofka translated unemotionally. 'He will pay, as God and all the saints are my witnesses. I will lock him up in a dungeon, in a cage, in a chest like the one the Duke of Głogów cast Henry the Fat into, so small he won't even be able to scratch himself, with one hole for food and another directly opposite. And I'll keep him like that for half a year. And only then go to work on him. And I'll bring a torturer all the way from Magdeburg, because they have excellent men there, not like the ones here in Silesia, where the rascal expires on the second day. Oh, no, I'll get hold of a master who'll devote to Nicolaus's killer a week. Or two.'

Apeczko Stercza swallowed.

'But to do that,' Ofka continued, 'we must seize the adulterer. Which demands intelligence. Wits. Because the adulterer is no fool. A fool wouldn't have graduated from Prague, or ingratiated himself with the Oleśnica friars, or have so ably seduced Gelfrad's French wife. With a crafty one like that, it's not enough to chase up and down the Wrocław road like an idiot, making a fool of oneself. Giving the affair renown that will serve the rake – and not us.'

Apeczko nodded. Ofka looked at him and sniffed and wiped her little snub nose.

'The adulterer,' she translated on, 'has a brother, residing on an estate somewhere near Henryków. It's quite likely he'll seek shelter there. Perhaps he already has. Another Bielawa, before he died, was a priest at the Wrocław Collegiate, so it's conceivable the rascal will want to hide with another rascal. I mean to say with His Excellency, the Most Reverend Bishop Konrad, that old soak and thief!'

Hrozwita of Baruth once again wiped the old man's chin, which was covered in snot after his furious outburst.

'Furthermore, the rake has acquaintances among the monks of the Monastery of the Holy Ghost in Brzeg, in the hospice. Our sly boots may have headed there, to surprise and mislead Wolfher. Which isn't too difficult, in any case. Finally, the most important thing. Listen carefully, Apecz. It's certain that our adulterer will want to play the *trouveur*, pretend to be some sort of Lohengrin or Lancelot. He will want to contact the Frenchwoman. And we will most likely catch him there, in Ligota, like a dog with a bitch in heat.'

'Why in Ligota?' Apeczko dared to ask. 'For she—'

'Has fled, I know. But he doesn't.'

The old fart's soul, thought Apeczko, *is even more twisted than his body. But he's as cunning as a fox. And, to give him his due, he knows a great deal. Knows everything.*

'But to achieve what I have just ordered,' Ofka translated into comprehensible language, 'you're not much bloody use to me – you, my sons and nephews, blood, apparently, of my blood and bone of my bone. Therefore, you will hasten as quickly as you can to Niemodlin, and then to Ziębice. When you get there ...

Listen carefully, Apecz. You will find Kunz Aulock, called Kyrie-eleison. And others: Walter of Barby, Sybek of Kobylagłowa and Stork of Gorgowice. You will tell them that Tammo Stercza will pay a thousand Rhenish guilders for the capture of Reinmar of Bielawa alive. A thousand – remember.'

Apeczko swallowed at each name, for they were the names of the worst thugs and killers throughout Silesia, scoundrels with neither honour nor faith. Prepared to murder their own grand-mothers for three skojeces, never mind the astonishing sum of a thousand guilders. My *guilders*, thought Apeczko crossly. *Because that ought to be* my *inheritance when that damned cripple finally kicks the bucket.*

'Do you understand, Apecz?'

'Yes, Father.'

'Then begone, off with you. Out of here, to horse, carry out my orders.'

First, thought Apeczko, *I'll head towards the kitchen, where I'll eat my fill and drink enough for two, you stingy old bugger. And then we'll see.*

'Apecz.'

Apeczko Stercza turned around. And looked. But not at Balbulus's contorted, flushed face, which seemed to him, for the first time here in Sterzendorf, to be unnatural, out of place. Apeczko looked into little Ofka's huge, nut-brown eyes. At Hrozwita, standing behind his chair.

'Yes, Father?'

'Do not let us down.'

But perhaps it isn't him at all? The thought flashed through his mind. *Perhaps it's a corpse sitting on this chair, a half-dead carcass with its brain utterly eaten up by paralysis? Perhaps . . . it's them? Perhaps it's the women – girls, maidens and matrons – who rule at Sterzendorf?*

He quickly drove away the preposterous thought.

'I won't, Father.'

*

35

Apeczko Stercza had no intention of hurrying to carry out Tammo's orders. He walked briskly to the castle kitchen, murmuring angrily, where he demanded everything the said kitchen had to offer. Let the cripple lord it in his chamber upstairs; outside, executive power belonged to somebody else. Outside the chamber, Apeczko of Stercza was master, and he demonstrated it as soon as he entered the kitchen. A dog earned a kick and bolted, howling. A cat fled, deftly dodging the large wooden spoon thrown at it. The maids flinched as a cast-iron cauldron slammed down on the stone floor with a dreadful bang. The most sluggish maid was hit on the back of the neck and called a whorish clod. The serving boys learned all sorts of things about themselves and their parents, and several made the close acquaintance of their master's fist, as hard and heavy as a lump of iron. A servant who needed to be told twice to bring wine from the master's cellar received such a kick that he lurched forward onto hands and knees.

Soon after, Apeczko – *Sir* Apeczko – was sprawled on his chair, greedily chewing great mouthfuls of roast venison, fatty pork ribs, a huge ring of blood pudding, a hunk of dried Prague ham and several pigeons boiled in broth, accompanied by a whole loaf of bread as large as a Saracen's buckler. Washed down, naturally, with the best Hungarian and Moldavian wines, which Balbulus kept for his own personal use. He tossed bones on the ground like a lord of the manor, spitting, belching and glowering at the fat housekeeper, just waiting for her to give him an excuse.

The old bugger, the old fart, the paralytic orders me to call him 'father' when he's only my uncle, my father's brother. But I must put up with it. For when he finally turns up his toes, I, the eldest Stercza, will at last become head of the family. The inheritance, of course, will have to be divided up, but I shall be head of the dynasty. Everybody knows it. Nothing will hinder me. Nothing will stop me . . .

What might hinder me, thought Apeczko, swearing under his breath, *is this furore with Reynevan and Gelfrad's wife. What may hinder me is a family feud making me fall foul of the Landfriede laws governing family feuds. Hiring thugs and killers may hinder me, as*

36

might the noisy pursuit, incarceration in a dungeon, ill-treatment and torture of a lad who's kin of the Nostitzes, related to the Piasts and a vassal of Jan of Ziębice. And Konrad, Bishop of Wrocław – whose dislike of Balbulus is mutual – is just waiting for the first opportunity to give the Sterczas what for.

Not good, not good, not good.

And to blame for all of this, Apeczko suddenly decided, picking his teeth, *is Reynevan, Reinmar of Bielawa. And he shall pay for it. But not in a way that would incite the whole of Silesia. He shall pay in an ordinary way, quietly, in the dark, with a knife in the ribs. When – as Balbulus guessed right – he appears in secret at the Cistercian sisters' convent in Ligota, beneath his lover's window. One thrust of a knife and he'll land plop in the Cistercians' carp pond. And hush! The carp won't let on.*

On the other hand, one cannot utterly ignore Balbulus's instructions, if only because the Mumbler usually checks whether his orders are executed by giving the same orders to not one, but several persons.

What to do, by the Devil?

Apeczko thrust a knife into the table with a thud and drained his beaker in one draught. He looked up and met the gaze of the fat housekeeper.

'What are you staring at?' he growled.

'The senior master has recently stocked up with some excellent Italian wine,' said the housekeeper calmly. 'Shall I have it drawn, Your Grace?'

'Indeed.' Apeczko smiled in spite of himself and felt the woman's calm soothing him, too. 'Indeed, please do, I shall taste what has been maturing in Italy. And please send a boy to the watchtower, have him bring me a half-decent horseman with his wits about him. Someone who's capable of delivering a message.'

'As you wish, Your Grace.'

Hooves thudded on the bridge. The messenger hastening away from Sterzendorf looked back and waved at his woman, who was bidding him farewell from the embankment with a snow-white kerchief. And suddenly caught sight of movement on the moonlit wall of the watchtower, a vague moving shape. *What the Devil?* he thought. *What's creeping about there? An owl? A swift? A bat? Or perhaps . . .*

The messenger muttered a spell to protect him from magic, spat into the moat and spurred on his horse. The message he was carrying was urgent, and the lord who had sent it cruel.

So he didn't see a huge wallcreeper spread its wings, fly down from the parapet and noiselessly, like a nightly spectre, glide over the forests eastwards, towards the Widawa Valley.

Sensenberg Castle, as everybody knew, had been built by the Knights Templar, and not without reason had they chosen that exact location. Looming above a jagged cliff face, its summit had been a place of worship to pagan gods since time immemorial, where, so the stories said, the people of the ancient Trzebowianie and Bobrzanie tribes offered the gods human sacrifices. During the twelfth century, when the circles of round, moss-covered stones hidden among the weeds were all that remained of the pagan temple, the cult continued to spread and sabbath fires still burned on its summit in spite of several bishops' threats of severe punishments for anyone who dared celebrate the *festum dyabolicum et maledictum* at Sensenberg.

But in the meantime, the Knights Templar arrived. They built their Silesian castles, menacing, crenellated miniatures of the great Syrian Templar fortresses, erected under the supervision of men with heads swathed in scarves and faces as dark as tanned bull's hide. It was no accident that they always located their strongholds in the holy places of ancient, vanishing cults like Sensenberg.

Then the Knights Templar got what was coming to them. Whether it was fair or not, there is no point arguing over it; they met their end, and everybody knows what happened. Their castles were seized by the Knights Hospitaller and divided up between the rapidly expanding monasteries and the burgeoning Silesian magnates. Some, in spite of the power slumbering at their roots, very quickly became ruins. Ruins which were avoided. Feared.

Not without reason.

In spite of escalating colonisation, in spite of settlers hungry for land arriving from Saxony, Thuringia, the Rhineland and Franconia, the mountain and castle of Sensenberg were still surrounded by a strip of no man's land, a wilderness only entered by poachers or fugitives. And it was from those poachers and fugitives that people first heard stories about extraordinary birds and spectral riders, about lights flashing in the castle's windows, about savage and cruel cries and singing, and about ghastly music which appeared to spring up from nowhere.

There were those who did not believe such stories. Others were tempted by the Templar treasure that was said still to lie somewhere in Sensenberg's vaults. And there were downright nosy and restless individuals who had to see for themselves.

They never returned.

That night, had some poacher, fugitive or adventurer been in the vicinity of Sensenberg, the mountain and castle would have given cause for further legends. A storm was approaching from far beyond the horizon and flashes of lightning flared in the distance, so far away you couldn't even hear the accompanying rumble of thunder. And suddenly, the bright eyes of the windows blazed in the black monolith of the castle, framed against the flashes in the sky.

For inside the apparent ruin stood a huge, stately hall with a high ceiling. The light from candelabras and torches in iron cressets accentuated the frescos on the bare walls portraying religious and knightly scenes. There was Percival, kneeling before the Holy Grail, and Moses, carrying the stone tablets down from Mount Sinai, and Jesus, falling beneath the cross for the second time. Their Byzantine eyes gazed down upon the great round table and the knights in full armour and hooded cloaks sitting around it.

A huge wallcreeper flew in through the window on a gust of wind.

The bird wheeled around, casting a ghastly shadow on the frescos, and alighted, puffing up its feathers, on one of the chairs. It opened its beak and screeched, and before the sound had died away, not a bird but a knight was sitting on the chair, dressed in a cloak and hood, looking almost identical to the others.

'*Adsumus*,' the Wallcreeper intoned dully. 'We are here, Lord, gathered in Your name. Come to us and be among us.'

'*Adsumus*,' the knights encircling the table repeated in unison. '*Adsumus! Adsumus!*'

The echo spread through the castle like a rumbling thunderclap, like the sound of distant battle, like the booming of a battering ram on a castle gate. And slowly faded among the tenebrous corridors.

'May the Lord be praised,' said the Wallcreeper, after the echo fell silent. 'The day is at hand when all His foes will be reduced to dust. Woe betide them! That is why we are here!'

'*Adsumus!*'

'My brothers, providence is sending us another chance to smite the Lord's foes and to beset the enemies of the faith,' the Wallcreeper intoned, lifting his head, his eyes gleaming with the reflected light of a flame. 'The time has come to deliver the next blow! Remember this name, O brothers: Reinmar of Bielawa. Reinmar of Bielawa, called Reynevan. Listen . . .'

The hooded knights leaned in, listening. Jesus, falling beneath the cross, looked down on them from the fresco, and there was endless human suffering in his Byzantine eyes.

Chapter Three

In which there will be talk of things having apparently little in common with each other, such as hunting with falcons, the Piast dynasty, cabbage and peas, and Czech heresy. And also of a dispute about whether one should keep one's word. And if so, when and regarding whom.

The ducal retinue made a long stop on a hillock above the River Oleśniczka, which wound its way among black alder wetlands, a copse of white birches and bright green meadows, looking down on the thatched roofs and smoke of the village of Borów. Not in order to rest, however, but rather to tire themselves out by indulging in lordly pursuits.

As they approached, flocks of birds of many breeds flew up from the marsh. On seeing this, Duke Konrad Kantner of Oleśnica instantly ordered the procession to stop and asked for his favourite falcons. The duke passionately adored falconry, and the whole world could wait while he watched his favourite Motley rend the plumage from mallards and witness Silver intrepidly battling a heron in the air.

So the duke galloped through the rushes and wetlands like a man possessed, accompanied fearlessly by his eldest daughter Agnieszka, Seneschal Rudiger Haugwitz and several careerist pages.

The rest of his retinue waited at the edge of the forest but did not dismount, since no one knew when the duke would weary of his play. The duke's foreign guest was yawning discreetly. The chaplain was muttering – probably a prayer; the bailiff was counting – probably money; the minnesinger was composing – probably rhymes; Agnieszka's ladies-in-waiting were gossiping – probably about other ladies-in-waiting; and all the while, the young knights were killing time by riding around and exploring the nearby undergrowth.

'Ciołek!'

Henryk Krompusz reined in his horse abruptly and turned, trying to determine which bush had just quietly called him by his nickname.

'Ciołek!'

'Who's there? Show yourself!'

The bushes rustled.

'By Saint Jadwiga . . .' Krompusz's mouth fell open in astonishment. 'Reynevan? Is it you?'

'No, it's Saint Jadwiga,' replied Reynevan in a voice as sour as a gooseberry in May. 'Ciołek, I need help . . . Whose retinue is it? Kantner's?'

Before Krompusz worked out what was happening, two other Oleśnica knights had joined him.

'Reynevan!' groaned Jaksa of Wiszna. 'Christ Almighty, what do you look like!'

I wonder how you'd look, thought Reynevan, *if your horse had given up the ghost just outside Bystre. If you'd had to wander all night through the bogs and wildernesses by the River Świerzna, and just before dawn exchange your wet, muddy rags for a smock swiped from the fence of a peasant's cottage. I wonder how you'd look after something like that, you foppish dandy.*

Benno Ebersbach, the third Oleśnica knight to ride up, was probably thinking the same thing.

'Instead of gawping,' he said dryly, 'give him some raiment. Off with those rags, Bielawa. Come on, gentlemen, take whatever you have from your saddlebags.'

'Reynevan,' said Krompusz, still unable to believe what he was seeing. 'Is it truly you?'

Reynevan didn't reply. He put on a shirt and jerkin one of

them threw him. He was so angry, he was close to tears.

'I'm in need of help,' he repeated. 'In great need.'

'We see that,' Ebersbach confirmed with a nod, 'and also concur that your need is great. Great indeed. Come on. We must present you to Haugwitz. And the duke.'

'Does he know?'

'Everybody knows. Everybody's talking about it.'

If Konrad Kantner, with his oval face made longer by a deeply receding hairline, his black beard and the piercing eyes of a monk, did not overly resemble a typical member of the dynasty, his daughter Agnieszka was a veritable chip off the Silesian–Mazovian block. The princess had the flaxen hair, bright eyes and small, blithe retroussé nose of a Piast, immortalised by the now famous sculpture in Naumburg Cathedral. Agnieszka, Reynevan quickly calculated, was around fifteen, so must already be promised in marriage. Reynevan couldn't recall the rumours as to whom.

'Stand up.'

He stood up.

'Know,' said the duke, fixing him with forbidding eyes, 'that I do not approve of your deed. In fact, I consider it ignoble, reprehensible and opprobrious, and frankly advise remorse and penance, Reinmar of Bielawa. My chaplain assures me that there is a special enclave for adulterers in Hell. The devils sorely vex the miscreants' instruments of sin. I shall forego the details owing to the presence of the maid.'

Seneschal Rudiger Haugwitz snorted angrily. Reynevan said nothing.

'How you will make amends to Gelfrad of Stercza is a matter for you and him,' continued Kantner. 'It is not for me to interfere in this issue, particularly since you are both vassals of Duke Jan of Ziębice. I ought to simply wash my hands of the matter and send you to him.'

Reynevan swallowed.

'But,' continued the duke after a moment of dramatic silence, 'out of respect for your father, who laid down his life at Tannenberg at my brother's side, I shall not allow you to be murdered as part of a foolish family feud. It is high time we put an end to such feuds and live as befits Europeans. You may journey with my entourage all the way to Wrocław. But stay out of my gaze, for the sight of you does not please me.'

'Your Ducal—'

'I said begone.'

The hunt was definitely over. The falcons were hooded, the mallards and herons they had caught already hanging from the bars of the wagon. The duke was content, his entourage, too, because the potentially interminable hunt had been brief. Reynevan noticed several clearly grateful glances – the rumour had already spread through the retinue that the duke had curtailed the hunt and resumed the journey because of him. That probably wasn't the only rumour doing the rounds, and his ears burned as though all eyes were on him.

'Everyone,' grunted Benno Ebersbach, who was riding alongside him, 'knows everything . . .'

'Every*one*, yes,' confirmed Henryk Krompusz, quite sadly. 'But, fortunately for you, not every*thing*.'

'Eh?'

'Are you playing the fool, Bielawa?' asked Ebersbach, without raising his voice. 'Kantner would certainly drive you away, and perhaps also send you in chains to the castellan, if he knew somebody had dropped dead in Oleśnica. Yes, yes, don't goggle at me. Young Nicolaus of Stercza is dead. Cuckolding Gelfrad is one thing, but the Sterczas won't ever forgive you for killing their brother.'

'I never . . .' Reynevan said after a series of deep breaths. 'I never laid a finger on Nicolaus, I swear.'

Ebersbach was clearly unimpressed by Reynevan's oath. 'And to complete the set, the lovely Adèle has accused you of witchcraft, saying you bewitched and took advantage of her.'

'Even if she did,' replied Reynevan after a short pause, 'she was compelled to. On pain of death. She is in their grasp, after all—'

'No, she isn't,' countered Ebersbach. 'The lovely Adèle fled from the Augustinian priory, where she publicly accused you of devilish practices, to Ligota and the safety of the Cistercian nuns' convent.'

Reynevan sighed with relief. 'I don't believe those accusations,' he repeated. 'She loves me. And I love her.'

'Beautiful.'

'If you only knew *how* beautiful.'

'That's as may be,' said Ebersbach, looking him in the eyes, 'but it got quite ugly when they searched your workshop.'

'Ah. I was afraid of that.'

'You ought to be. In my humble opinion, the only reason the Inquisition isn't on your back already is because they still haven't finished cataloguing the devilry they found there. Kantner may be able to protect you from the Sterczas, but not, I fear, from the Inquisition. When news of that sorcery gets out, he'll hand you over to them himself. Don't come to Wrocław with us, Reynevan. Take my advice – split off before we get there and flee, hide somewhere.'

Reynevan didn't reply.

'And by the by,' Ebersbach threw in casually, 'are you indeed versed in magic? Because, you see, I recently met a maiden . . . And . . . How can I put it . . . ? An elixir would come in handy . . .'

Reynevan didn't reply.

A cry sounded from the head of the entourage.

'What is it?' asked Ebersbach.

'Byków,' guessed Ciołek Krompusz, urging on his horse. 'The Goose Inn.'

'And thanks be to God,' Jaksa of Wiszna added in hushed tones, 'because I have a dreadful hunger after that sodding hunting.'

Reynevan still said nothing. The rumbling coming from his guts was all too eloquent.

The Goose was roomy and probably famous, for there were plenty of guests, both locals and visitors, judging by the horses, servants and soldiers bustling about. When Duke Kantner's retinue rode into the courtyard with great flourish and noise, the innkeeper, who had been forewarned of their imminent arrival, dashed out through the doorway like a ball from a bombard, scattering poultry and splashing muck around. He hopped from foot to foot, bowing and scraping.

'Welcome, welcome, you're most welcome,' he panted. 'What an honour, what an honour it is that your enlightened graciousness—'

'It's thronged here today.' Kantner dismounted from his bay, helped by his servants. 'Who are you putting up? Who is emptying your pots? Will there be sufficient for us, too?'

'Most definitely, most definitely,' assured the innkeeper, struggling to catch his breath. 'And it isn't at all thronged now ... I drove the lesser knights, bards and free peasants outside ... I only just saw m'lords on the highway. There's room in the chamber now, in the snug, too, only—'

'Only what?' Rudiger Haugwitz raised an eyebrow.

'There are guests in the chamber. Important and clerical personages ... Emissaries. I dared not—'

'And well you didn't,' interrupted Kantner. 'You would have slighted me and the whole of Oleśnica had you dared. Guests are guests! And as I am a Piast, not a Saracen sultan, it is no offence to me to eat alongside other guests. Lead on, gentlemen.'

The partially smoke-filled chamber perfused with the smell of cabbage was indeed not crowded. In truth, only one table was occupied. Two of the three tonsured men seated there wore clothing typical for journeying clergy, but so opulent that they couldn't have been ordinary priests. The third was wearing the habit of a Dominican.

At the sight of Kantner entering, the clergymen stood up from the bench. The one with the most sumptuous costume bowed, but without undue humility.

'Your Grace Duke Konrad,' he said, showing that he was well informed. 'This is indeed a great honour for us. I am, with your permission, Maciej Korzbok of the Poznań Diocese, on a mission to Your Grace's brother in Wrocław, and my travelling companions are Master Melchior Barfuss, curate to the Bishop of Lubusz, and Reverend Jan Nejedlý from Vysoké, *prior Ordo Praedicatorum*.

The Brandenburgian and the Dominican lowered their tonsured heads, and Konrad Kantner responded with a faint tilt of his.

'Your Eminence, Your Excellencies,' he said nasally, 'it will be delightful to sup in such company. And to converse, both here and on the road, if it doesn't tire you, Reverends, since I also ride to Wrocław. With my daughter . . . Over here, Anežka . . . Curtsy before Christ's servants.'

Anežka curtsied and bowed her head, intending to kiss Maciej Korzbok's hand, but he stopped her, blessing her with a swift sign of the cross over her flaxen fringe. The Czech Dominican put his hands together, leaned over and muttered a short prayer, adding something about *clarissima puella*.

'And this,' continued Kantner, 'is Seneschal Rudiger Haugwitz. And these are my knights and my guest . . .'

Reynevan felt a tug on his sleeve. He obeyed Krompusz's gestures and hisses and followed him out into the courtyard where the commotion caused by the duke's arrival continued. Ebersbach was waiting there.

'I asked around,' he said. 'They were here yesterday – Wolfher of Stercza and five other men. Those Greater Poles over there, they said the Sterczas had stopped them but didn't dare try anything with these clergymen. They are clearly searching for you on the Wrocław highway. In your shoes, I'd flee.'

'Kantner,' Reynevan mumbled, 'will defend me . . .'

Ebersbach shrugged. 'It is your decision. And your neck. Wolfher is proclaiming loudly and in detail what he'll do to you when he catches you. If I were you—'

'Firstly, I love Adèle and I will not abandon her!' Reynevan burst out. 'And secondly . . . Where do you suppose I could escape to? To Poland? Or perhaps Samogitia?'

'Not a bad idea. About Samogitia, I mean.'

'Bugger!' said Reynevan, kicking a hen that was bustling around his legs. 'Very well. I'll think about it. And make a plan. But first I'll eat something. I'm dying of hunger, and the smell of cabbage is killing me.'

Had they delayed any longer, the young men would have ended up with nothing. Pots of kasha and cabbage with peas and bowls of meaty pork bones had been placed on the high table, before the duke and his daughter. The dishes only headed to the other end of the table after the three clergymen sitting closest to Kantner – who, it turned out, were good trenchermen – had eaten their fill. On the way, to make matters worse, was Rudiger Haugwitz, who was no slouch, either, and the duke's foreign guest. The black-haired knight's face was so swarthy he might have only just returned from the Holy Land, and he was even broader-shouldered than Haugwitz. Thus, by the time the bowls reached the lower-ranking and younger men, there was almost nothing left in them. Fortunately, a moment later, the innkeeper gave the duke a huge board of capons, which looked and smelled so tasty that the cabbage and pork fat lost some of their appeal and reached the end of the table almost intact.

The Duke's daughter Agnieszka nibbled a capon leg with her little teeth, trying to stop the grease from dripping on the fashionably slashed sleeves of her dress. The men discoursed about this and that. It was the turn of one of the clergymen, the Dominican Jan Nejedlý of Vysoké.

'I am,' he sermonized, 'or rather *was* the prior of Saint Clement's in Prague Old Town and a Master at Charles University. Now, though, as you see, I am an exile, dependant on someone's else's generosity. My monastery was plundered, and I fell out of favour at the academy with apostates and scoundrels like Jan of Příbram and Křišťan of Prachatice, may God strike them down—'

'There is among us,' Kantner interrupted in mid-sentence, catching Reynevan's gaze, 'a student from Prague.'

'Then I would advise you to keep a close watch on him.' The Dominican's eyes flashed above his spoon. 'Loth as I am to make accusations, heresy is like soot, like pitch. Like dung! Whoever comes close to it must be fouled.'

Reynevan quickly lowered his head, once again feeling his ears burn and the blood rushing to his cheeks.

'Whatever next!' laughed the duke. 'Our scholar a heretic? Why, he's from a decent family and is studying to be a priest and a physician at the Prague Academy. Am I right, Reinmar?'

'By Your Grace's leave,' Reynevan said, swallowing nervously, 'I no longer study at Prague. On my brother's advice, I left the *Carolinum* in 1419, soon after Saints Abdon and Sennen's Day . . . I mean, right after the Defenestra— You know when. Now I'm thinking of studying in Krakow . . . Or in Leipzig, where most of the Prague masters fled . . . I won't return to Bohemia while the unrest endures.'

'The unrest!' the Dominican spat, strands of cabbage flying from his mouth onto his scapular. 'A nice little word, indeed! You here, in this peaceful land, cannot even imagine what heresy is afoot in Bohemia, what monstrosities that hapless land is witness to. Fomented by heretics, Wycliffites, Waldensians and other servants of Satan, the mob has directed its unthinking fury at faith and the Church. In Bohemia, God is being destroyed and His temples burned. God's servants are being slaughtered!'

'Truly dreadful tidings reach us,' confirmed Melchior Barfuss. 'One doesn't want to believe—'

'But one must!' the Dominican insisted, his voice growing ever louder. 'Because none of the accounts are exaggerated!'

The beer in his mug splashed around and Agnieszka shrank back involuntarily, shielding herself with the capon leg.

'Do you desire examples? I can oblige. The massacres of friars and chaplains in Český Brod, of Cistercians in Zbraslav, of Dominicans in Písek, of Benedictines in Kladruby and of Premonstrant nuns in Chotěšov. Monasteries looted and burned down, priests burned alive, altars and holy pictures desecrated . . .

Sacrilege not even the Turk would stoop to, atrocities at the sight of which even Saracens would tremble! O God, how long will You refrain from avenging our spilled blood?'

The silence that followed, in which only the murmured prayers of the Oleśnica chaplain could be heard, was interrupted by the deep, resonant voice of Duke Konrad Kantner's guest, the swarthy, broad-shouldered knight.

'It didn't have to be like that.'

'I beg your pardon?' The Dominican raised his head. 'What do mean by that, sir?'

'It could all easily have been avoided. Had Jan Huss not been burned at the stake in Constance.'

'You defended the heretic then,' said the Dominican, squinting, 'by shouting, protesting, submitting petitions, I know you did. And you were as wrong then as you are now. Heresy spreads like a weed and the Bible orders the weed destroyed by fire. Papal bulls decree it—'

'Leave bulls for conciliar quarrels,' the swarthy man interrupted. 'They sound risible in a tavern. But I was right in Constance, whatever you say. King Sigismund had given his royal word and guaranteed Huss safety. He broke his word and his oath, thus besmirching royal and knightly honour. I could not gaze on that unmoved, and did not wish to.'

'A knightly oath,' growled Jan Nejedlý, 'should be given in the service of God, whoever made the vow, whether squire or king. Do you call keeping one's word and promise to a heretic divine service? Do you call that honour? I call it a sin.'

'If I give my knightly word, I give it before God. Which is why I keep my word even to Turks.'

'One may keep it to Turks,' said Jan Nejedlý, 'but not heretics.'

'Verily,' said Maciej Korzbok, the Poznań curate, very gravely. 'The Moor or the Turk is a heathen from ignorance and savageness. He can be converted. A dissenter or schismatic turns away from faith and the Church, derides them, blasphemes against them, which is why he is a hundredfold viler to God. And however heresy is fought is right. Why, no one of right mind who goes to kill a wolf or a rabid dog talks of honour or the knightly parole! All things are permitted against a heretic.'

'In Krakow,' Kantner's guest turned his weather-beaten face towards him, 'Canon Jan Elgot cares not for the sanctity of confession when trying to ensnare a heretic. Bishop Andrzej Łaskarz, whom you serve, orders the same from priests of the Poznań Diocese. All things are permitted indeed.'

'You do not hide your sympathies, sir,' Nejedlý said sourly, 'so neither shall I. Huss was a heretic and had to burn at the stake. The Holy Roman Emperor Sigismund, King of Hungary and Bohemia, acted correctly by not keeping his word to a Czech heretic.'

'Which is why the Czechs love him so much now,' retorted the swarthy man. 'For that reason, he fled Vyšehrad with the Czech crown under one arm. And he now rules Bohemia, but from Buda, because he won't be allowed back into Hradčany in a hurry.'

'You dare to sneer at King Sigismund,' observed Melchior Barfuss, 'and yet you serve him.'

'One doesn't rule out the other.'

'Or perhaps for another reason?' the Czech retorted scathingly. 'For you, sir, fought with the Poles on King Jogaila's side at Tannenberg against the Knights Hospitaller of the Virgin Mary. Jogaila – a neophyte king who openly abets Czech heresy and bends a willing ear towards schismatics and Wycliffites, while Polish knights slaughter Catholics and plunder monasteries in Bohemia. Jogaila pretends all this occurs without his will and consent, yet he does not ride against the heretics himself. Were he to ally with King Sigismund in a crusade, they would be done with the Hussites in a trice! Why, then, does Jogaila not do that?'

'Indeed.' The swarthy man sneered knowingly. 'Why not? I wonder.'

Konrad Kantner cleared his throat loudly. Barfuss pretended that all his attention was taken up with cabbage and peas while Maciej Korzbok bit his lip and nodded grimly.

'It is true,' the swarthy man admitted, 'that the Holy Roman Emperor has more than once shown he is no friend of the Polish kingdom. Yet I can vouch that every Greater Pole will come to the defence of the faith – but only if Sigismund guarantees that no Teutonic Knights or Brandenburgians will attack us as we march south. And how can he give such a guarantee if he is scheming with them to divide Poland up? Am I right, Duke Konrad?'

'Why are we prattling on about this?' Kantner's smile lacked sincerity. 'We politick unduly, and politics is an ill partner for vittles. Which, incidentally, grow cold.'

'But we ought to talk of this,' protested Jan Nejedlý, to the delight of the younger knights, whom two pots had reached almost untouched by the loquacious magnates. Their delight was premature, however, for the magnates proved they could talk and eat simultaneously.

'Please observe, m'lords,' the prior from Saint Clement's continued while devouring the cabbage, 'it is not only a Czech matter, this Wycliffite plague. The Czechs – whom I know – are liable to come here, too, as they did to Moravia and Austria. They may come after you, gentlemen. All of you, sitting here.'

'Pshaw.' Kantner pouted, poking his spoon around in the bowl in search of scraps of meat. 'I don't believe that.'

'I even less,' said Maciej Korzbok, snorting beery foam. 'It would be a long march to Poznań to find us.'

'And to Lubusz and Fürstenwalde,' said Melchior Barfuss, his mouth full. 'Blow that, I fear them not.'

'And rightly so,' added the duke with an unpleasant sneer, 'given that the Czechs will be receiving guests before they can pay anyone else a visit. Particularly now they've lost Žižka, I think the Czechs can expect their guests any day.'

'A crusade?' Korzbok said. 'You know something, Your Grace?'

'Not at all,' replied Kantner, while his expression suggested quite the opposite. 'I'm simply pondering. Innkeeper! Ale!'

Reynevan slipped noiselessly out into the courtyard, from there behind the pigsties and then into some bushes beyond the vegetable patch. After relieving himself and before returning to the chamber, he went outside the gate and gazed for a while along the highway, which was vanishing in a blue haze. He felt reassured not to see the Stercza brothers galloping towards him.

Adèle, he suddenly thought, *Adèle is not at all safe with the Cistercian nuns in Ligota. I ought . . .*

I ought. But I'm afraid. Of what the Stierczas might do to me. Of what they are talking about doing in such detail.

Returning to the courtyard, he was amazed to see Duke Kantner and Haugwitz emerging from behind the pigsties. *But why should it surprise me?* he thought. *Even princes and seneschals go behind pigsties to see a marshal about a hound.*

'Listen carefully, Bielawa,' said Kantner bluntly, washing his hands in a pail that a serving wench had hurriedly brought him. 'You will not ride with me to Wrocław.'

'Your Grace—'

'Shut your trap and don't open it until I give the word. I'm doing this for your own good, idiot boy, for I am certain that in Wrocław my brother the bishop will lock you in a tower quicker than you can say *benedictum nomen Iesu*. Bishop Konrad the White is very hard on adulterers, no doubt because he doesn't like the competition. Instead, you will take the horse I've lent you and ride to the headquarters of the Knights Hospitaller in Mała Oleśnica. You will tell the commander, Dietmar of Alzey, that I have sent you there for a penance. Then you will sit there quietly until I summon you. Clear? And here is a pouch for the journey. I know it is meagre – I would give more, but my bailiff advised me against it. This inn has unduly eaten into my expense account.'

'You are too kind,' Reynevan muttered his thanks, although the weight of the pouch by no means deserved them. 'Many thanks for your generosity. It is just that—'

'Fear not the Stierczas,' interrupted the duke. 'They won't find you in the house of the Knights Hospitaller, and you won't ride there alone. It so happens that my guest is travelling that way, towards Moravia. You must have seen him at table. He agreed that you may accompany him. He didn't agree immediately, truth be told, but I convinced him. Do you wish to know how?'

Reynevan nodded.

'I told him your father fell in my brother's company at Tannenberg, for my guest was also there. Except he calls it "Grunwald" because he was on the other side. Cheer up, laddie, cheer up. I have helped you as best I can. You have a horse and some coin. And safe passage guaranteed.'

'In what way guaranteed?' Reynevan plucked up the courage to mutter. 'Your Grace ... Wolfher Stercza is riding with five men, and I with one knight. Even if he has an esquire, Your Grace – he is but a single knight!'

Rudiger Haugwitz snorted. Konrad Kantner pouted condescendingly.

'Oh, you dolt, Bielawa. Supposedly a learned bachelor and you didn't recognise a man of such renown? For that knight, believe me, six is but a trifle.'

And seeing that Reynevan still hadn't understood, he explained: 'He is Zawisza the Black of Garbów.'

Chapter Four

In which Reynevan and Zawisza the Black of Garbów talk about this and that on the Brzeg highway. Then Reynevan cures Zawisza's flatulence and Zawisza repays him with valuable lessons from recent history.

Slowing his horse a little, Zawisza the Black of Garbów raised himself up in the saddle and let out a prolonged fart. Then he gave a great sigh, pressed both hands down on his pommel and farted again.

'It's that cabbage,' he explained as he drew level with Reynevan once more. 'One can't eat so much cabbage at my age. On the bones of Saint Stanisław! When I was young, I could eat a half-gallon of the stuff in no time and it didn't bother me as long as there was plenty of caraway seed. But now, I barely take a bite and it gurgles in my guts, and the gases – you can see for yourself, lad – are almost rending me asunder. Age is a heavy burden.'

His horse, a mighty black stallion, broke into a thundering run as though raring to charge. The stallion was covered, from tail to nostrils, in a black caparison adorned on its withers with Sulima, the knight's coat of arms. Reynevan was surprised not to have recognised the famous emblem sooner, the design of which was unusual in Polish heraldry.

'Why so silent?' Zawisza suddenly asked him. 'We ride and ride and you've spoken barely a dozen words, at best, and then only when pressed. Have I offended you? It's about Grunwald, isn't it? Know what, lad? It would be easy for me to say that I couldn't have killed your father or even crossed swords with him, but I shall not, for t'would be an untruth. That day, on the Dispersion of the Apostles, I killed many men in the utter pandemonium. For it was a battle, and that's that.'

'My father,' said Reynevan, clearing his throat, 'bore on his shield—'

'Coats of arms I do not remember,' Zawisza interrupted bluntly. 'In battle they mean nothing to me. What matters is which way a horse's head is facing. If it's pointing at mine, I smite, even if the fellow has the Virgin Mary herself on his shield. In any case, when blood sticks to dust, and dust to blood, you can see bugger all anyway. I repeat, Grunwald was a battle. And a battle is a battle. Let's leave it at that. Don't take umbrage with me.'

'I am not.'

Zawisza reined in his stallion a little, raised himself in the saddle again and farted. Frightened jackdaws took flight from roadside willows. Garbów's retinue, consisting of a grizzled esquire and four armed servants, maintained a prudent distance some way back. Both the esquire and the servants had splendid mounts and their costumes were rich and spotless, as befitted the retainers of the Starosta of Kruszwica and Spiš who was said to collect rent from around thirty villages. However, neither the esquire nor the servants looked like sleek, lordly pages. On the contrary, they looked like cruel killers, and the weapons they carried were no parade-ground trinkets.

'So if you are not taking umbrage,' Zawisza went on, 'why, then, are you so silent?'

'Because it appears,' Reynevan plucked up the courage, 'that you are more offended by me than I by you. And I know why.'

Zawisza the Black turned in his saddle and looked long at him. 'Thus speaks sorrowfully wronged innocence,' he said at last. 'Know this, son, it is foolish to bed other men's wives, and I consider it a base practice worthy of punishment. Frankly speaking, in my eyes, you are no better than a cutpurse or a chicken thief. Worse, even, for the latter are but wretched knaves who have seized an opportunity out of desperation.'

Reynevan made no comment.

'Ages ago, it was customary in Poland,' Zawisza the Black continued, 'for a seducer of other men's wives to be taken to a bridge and his ball sack fastened to it with an iron hobnail. And a knife was laid beside him. "You wish for freedom? Then cut yourself free."'

Reynevan didn't comment this time, either.

'It is no longer practised,' the knight admitted, 'and that's a pity. My Lady Barbara is by no means flighty, but when I think that a dandy, a pretty boy like you, lad, might take advantage of her in Krakow in a moment of weakness . . . what can I say?'

The ensuing lengthy silence was again interrupted by the cabbage the knight had consumed.

'Aaaye.' Zawisza grunted with relief and looked up at the sky. 'But know that I do not condemn you, laddie, for let he who is without sin cast the first stone. And having summed it up thus, let us talk no more about it.'

'Love is a wonderful thing and has many names,' said Reynevan, a little pretentiously. 'After hearing songs and romances, no one carps about Tristan and Isolde or Lancelot and Guinevere. But a no less great, impassioned or sincere love binds Adèle and me together. And damn it, everybody seems to have it in for me—'

'If that love is so great,' Zawisza replied, feigning interest, 'why then are you not with your lady? In order to be with Isolde, Tristan disguised himself – if my memory serves me right – in the rags of a shabby beggar. In order to rescue his Guinevere, Lancelot took up arms against the massed ranks of the Knights of the Round Table.'

'It's not so simple.' Reynevan blushed like a beetroot. 'What will she gain if they catch and kill me? Or I, for that matter? But I shall find a way, never fear. Even if I have to disguise myself as Tristan did. *Amor vincit omnia.*'

Zawisza raised himself up in his saddle and broke wind. It was hard to tell if it was a comment or just the cabbage.

'One profit of this dispute,' he said, 'is that we've begun to talk, for it is mournful to ride in silence with head hanging. Let's talk on, my young Silesian. On any subject.'

Reynevan plucked up the courage to ask: 'Why do you ride this way, sir? Isn't it quicker to get to Moravia from Krakow via Racibórz? And Opava?'

'Perhaps it is,' agreed Zawisza. 'But I, you see, cannot bear the Lords of Racibórz. The recently deceased Duke Jan, may the Lord keep him in His care, was a whoreson who sent assassins to dispatch my comrade Přemysl. Jan's young lad, Mikołajek, follows boldly in his father's footsteps, so they say. Furthermore, I chose a roundabout route because I had things to discuss with Kantner in Oleśnica and am to report what Jogaila had said about him. On top of that, the route through Lower Silesia usually abounds with . . . attractions. Although I see that opinion is something of an exaggeration.'

'Ah!' Reynevan guessed astutely. 'That is why you ride in full armour, and on a war horse! You are looking for a fight. Am I right?'

'You are,' Zawisza the Black calmly agreed. 'They said that Silesia teems with Raubritter robber knights.'

'Not here. It's safe here. That's why it's so thronged.'

Indeed, they couldn't complain of a lack of company, for the road was busy with traffic heading in the opposite direction, from Brzeg to Oleśnica. They'd already passed several merchants on heavily laden wagons cutting deep ruts, escorted by a dozen or more armed men with thuggish faces, and a column of pitch makers weighed down by full goatskins, their presence announced in advance of their arrival by the sharp smell of their wares. A knight rode by with a lady and a small retinue. His Bavarian armour was opulent, and the fork-tailed lion rampant on his shield declared his membership of the Unruh family. Recognising Zawisza's coat of arms at once, the knight greeted him with a proud bow which clearly indicated that the Unruh didn't consider themselves the Zawiszas' inferiors. The knight's companion, wearing a pale mauve dress, was riding side-saddle on a gorgeous dark bay mare. Surprisingly, she wore no headdress, and the wind was freely playing in her golden hair. As she rode alongside, the woman raised her head, smiled delicately and granted Reynevan, who was staring at her, such an intense come-hither look that the young man trembled.

'Oh my,' said Zawisza soon after. 'You won't die of natural causes, my lad.'

And farted. With the force of a medium-calibre bombard.

'In order to prove,' said Reynevan, 'that I don't begrudge you your spitefulness or taunts, I'll cure you of your flatulence.'

'How, pray tell?'

'You will see. What we need is a shepherd.'

A shepherd appeared quite soon, but on seeing some horsemen turning from the highway towards him took panicked flight, plunged into the thicket and vanished like the morning mist. Only his bleating sheep remained.

'We should have laid a trap for him,' observed Zawisza, standing up in his stirrups. 'We won't catch up with him over that bumpy ground. Judging by the speed he set off at, he's probably crossed the Odra by now.'

'And the Nysa, too,' added Wojciech, the knight's esquire, demonstrating both a ready wit and a knowledge of geography.

Reynevan was unmoved by the teasing. He dismounted and walked purposefully over to the shepherd's hut, from which he emerged a moment later holding a large bunch of herbs.

'I didn't need a shepherd,' he calmly explained. 'Just these. And a dash of boiling water. Any chance of a cooking pot?'

'Whatever you need,' said Wojciech dryly.

'If you have to boil water, we'll make a stop.' Zawisza looked up at the sky. 'And a lengthy one, for night approaches.'

Zawisza the Black leaned comfortably against his sheepskin-covered saddle, looked into the mug he had just drained and sniffed.

'In truth, it tastes like sun-warmed moat water and stinks of tomcat,' he announced, 'but it works. My gratitude, Reinmar. It is a falsehood, I see, that universities teach a young man naught but drunkenness, lewdness and vulgar speech.'

'A whit of knowledge about herbs, nothing more,' replied Reynevan modestly. 'What really helped you, Lord Zawisza, was casting off your armour and resting in a more comfortable position—'

'You are too modest,' interrupted the knight. 'I know my own limits, know how long I'm capable of enduring in the saddle and wearing armour. Indeed, I often journey at night with a lantern rather than resting – it shortens the journey, and there's always the chance that somebody might accost me in the dark, which provides a welcome diversion. But since you claim this is a peaceful spot, why weary the horses? Let us sit by the fire until dawn and tell tales . . . That is also amusement, after all. Perhaps not as good as disembowelling a few Raubritters, but still.'

The fire crackled merrily, lighting up the night. An appetising aroma drifted up from the grease dripping from sausages and chunks of bacon sizzling on sticks grilled by Esquire Wojciech and the servants. Zawisza's retinue kept their silence and a suitable distance, but Reynevan could still see the gratitude in the glances they were casting him. They clearly didn't share their master's fondness for riding through the dark hours by lantern light.

The sky above the trees twinkled with stars. The night was cool.

'Yeees . . .' Zawisza rubbed his belly with both hands. 'Your potion has eased me, truly – what was that magical herb, some kind of mandrake? And why did you seek it in a shepherd's hut?'

'After Saint John's Day,' explained Reynevan, glad to be able to show off, 'shepherds gather various herbs known only to them and dry them in their huts. And they make from them a decoction, which—'

'Which is given to their flock,' Zawisza calmly interrupted. 'You mean you treated me like a bloated ewe. Well, if it helped—'

'Don't mock me, Sir Zawisza. Folk wisdom is prodigious, and

none of the great physicians or alchemists scorned it. Medicine has benefitted greatly from the common folk, shepherds in particular, for they have vast knowledge about herbs and their medicinal – and other – powers.'

'Indeed?'

'Indeed.' Reynevan nodded, moving closer to the fire to be more visible. 'You'd not believe, Sir Zawisza, how much power is hidden in this bundle, in this bunch of dry herbs from a shepherd's shack, which isn't worth a brass farthing. Infusions made from them work miracles, yet few physicians know how effective they are. One must also invoke the patron saints of shepherds when giving these herbs to one's flock.'

'What you were mumbling over the cooking pot wasn't about saints.'

'It wasn't,' Reynevan confessed, clearing his throat. 'I told you, folk wisdom—'

'That wisdom reeked of the stake,' Zawisza said, his tone serious. 'In your shoes, I'd be careful who I treated and with whom I spoke. I'd be careful, Reinmar.'

'I will.'

'While I,' Esquire Wojciech spoke up, 'think that if witchcraft exists, it's better to be versed in it than not. I think—'

He fell silent, seeing Zawisza's menacing look.

'And *I* think,' the knight said sharply, 'that all the evil of this world comes from thinking. Particularly among people who have no inclination at all towards it.'

Wojciech leaned even lower over the harness he was cleaning and greasing. Reynevan waited a little longer before speaking again.

'Sir Zawisza?'

'Aye?'

'In the tavern, during the dispute with that Dominican, you didn't conceal . . . How should I put it . . . ? That you support the Czech Hussites. Or that you're more for them than against, at least.'

'And what, you immediately label such thoughts as heresy?'

'Among others,' Reynevan admitted a moment later. 'But I'm more intrigued by—'

'By what?'

'By what happened at the Battle of Německý Brod in twenty-two, when you were taken captive. For legends are already circulating—'

'Such as?'

'That the Hussites captured you because you felt it beneath you to flee but couldn't fight, being an emissary.'

'Is that the rumour?'

'It is. But also that . . . That King Sigismund shamefully fled and left you in the lurch.'

Zawisza said nothing for a time.

'And you would like to know the truth?' he finally said.

'If,' Reynevan replied hesitantly, 'it would not inconvenience you—'

'Why would it inconvenience me? Conversation passes the time agreeably. Why not then converse?'

Despite his declaration, the knight from Garbów again fell silent for a long time and played with the empty mug. Reynevan wasn't sure if Zawisza was waiting for a question, but he didn't hurry to ask one. Rightly, as it turned out.

'Methinks I ought to begin at the beginning,' said Zawisza, 'when Jogaila – sorry, I should say the Polish King Władysław II – sent me to the King of Hungary on a sensitive mission pertaining to his marriage to Queen Euphemia-Sophia, King Sigismund's sister-in-law and widow of the late Czech King Wenceslaus. Nothing came of it, of course, for in the end King Władysław preferred Sophia of Halshany, but that wasn't known then. King Władysław ordered me to make the necessary arrangements with Sigismund, mainly with regard to the dowry. So off I went. Not to Pressburg or Buda, though, but to Moravia, from where Sigismund was just setting out on another crusade to deal with his disobedient subjects, with the firm intention of capturing Prague and rooting out Hussite heresy in Bohemia once and for all.

'When I arrived on Saint Martin's Day, Sigismund's crusade was advancing quite satisfactorily, although his army was somewhat weakened. Most of the Lusatian forces commanded by Komtur Rumpold had returned home, content with having ravaged the lands around Chrudim. The Silesian contingent, which included our recent host Duke Konrad Kantner, had also returned home. Consequently, King Sigismund's march to Prague was only supported by Albrecht's Austrian knights and the Moravian army of the Bishop of Olomouc. Even so, Sigismund's Hungarian cavalry alone numbered more than ten thousand . . .'

Zawisza fell silent for a time, staring into the crackling fire.

'Like it or not,' he continued, 'I had to take part in the crusade in order to negotiate Jogaila's marriage with Sigismund, and consequently witnessed all sorts of terrible things, including the capture of Polička and the slaughter that followed it.'

The servants and the esquire sat motionless. Maybe they were sleeping – Zawisza's voice was soft and monotonous, perhaps soporific for people who knew the story already or had experienced these events themselves.

'After Polička, Sigismund set off for Kutná Hora. General Žižka barred his way and repelled several charges by the Hungarian cavalry, but when word of the city being taken by treachery got out, he retreated. The king's men entered Kutná Hora, intoxicated by their triumph – they had defeated Žižka. Žižka himself had fled from them! And then Sigismund committed an unforgivable error, although I and Filippo degli Scolari tried to dissuade him—'

'You mean Pippo Spano? The celebrated Florentine condottiere?'

'Yes, but don't interrupt, lad. Against the advice of myself and Pippo, King Sigismund, convinced that the Czechs had fled in panic and wouldn't stop till they reached Prague, let the Hungarians scour the area for winter quarters, because the frost was bitter. So, the Magyars dispersed and spent Christmastide pillaging, assaulting womenfolk, burning down villages and murdering anyone they considered heretics or their supporters. Which meant anybody they came across.

'Fire lit up the night sky, smoke filled it during the day, and in Kutná Hora, King Sigismund feasted and held trials. And then, on the morning of the Epiphany, the news arrived that Žižka was approaching. Žižka hadn't fled but merely fallen back, regrouped and gained reinforcements, and was now heading for Kutná Hora with the full force of the Tábor and Prague behind him. "He's in Kaňk, he's in Nebovidy!" And what did the valiant crusaders do on hearing that? Seeing there was too little time to gather the men dispersed around the countryside, they ran away, leaving plenty of arms and goods and burning down the town behind them. For a while, Pippo Spano brought the panic under control and halted the forces halfway between Kutná Hora and Německý Brod.

'And then, from a distance ... Laddie, I'd never seen or heard anything like that before, and I've seen and heard plenty. The Taborites and Praguians marched on us, bearing standards and monstrances, in a splendid, disciplined array, their songs booming like thunder. On rolled their infamous battle wagons, from which handgonnes, cannons and trestle guns leered at us ...

'And what did those brave crusaders do then? Before the Hussites were even within range, Sigismund's entire army fled headlong in utter panic to Německý Brod. To a man, they ran screaming from a crowd of peasants in bast shoes whom they had jeered at not long before, casting down weapons they had mainly raised against unarmed men during this entire infernal crusade. They fled before my astonished eyes, laddie, as though they were scared of ... the truth. Of the slogan *VERITAS VINCIT* embroidered onto the Hussite standards.

'Most of the Hungarians and armoured lords managed to flee to the left bank of the frozen Sázava. Then the ice broke. I advise you, lad, with all my heart, if you have to fight in winter, never flee across ice wearing armour. Never.'

Reynevan vowed to himself that he never would.

Zawisza puffed and cleared his throat. 'As I was saying,' he went on, 'the knights, though they had lost their honour, saved their skins. Mostly. But the foot soldiers were caught by the Hussites and bludgeoned, and the snow on the road was stained red for two miles, from the village of Habry to the outskirts of Německý Brod.'

'And you, sir? What—?'

'I didn't flee with the king's knights, nor when Pippo Spano and Jan of Hardegg fled – and I must salute them, for they were some of the last to flee and put up a fight as they did so. Contrary to the tales you've heard, I also fought, and fought hard, emissary or not. And I didn't fight alone, for there were a few Poles and Moravian lordlings at my side, men who didn't like running away any more than I did. All I'll say of that battle is that we fought, and many are the Czech mothers who weep because of me. But *nec Hercules—*'

The servants, it turned out, were not asleep. For one suddenly jumped to his feet, as though stung by a viper, a second cried in a stifled voice, and a third drew a short sword with a grating sound as Esquire Wojciech seized a crossbow. Zawisza's harsh voice and imperious gesture quietened them all.

Something emerged from the gloom.

At first, they thought it was a fragment, a swirl of darkness limned by anthracite blackness in the flickering murk of the night, lit up by flashes of fire. When the flame burned more fiercely, that cloud of darkness, although losing none of its blackness, assumed a shape, and a form. A stocky, plump form, but not that of a bird ruffling up its feathers, nor a beast bristling its fur. The creature's head, pulled into its shoulders, was topped by a pair of large, pointed feline ears, sticking up straight and unmoving.

Without taking his eyes off the creature, Wojciech slowly put the crossbow down. One of the servants appealed for the intercession of Saint Kinga, but he was also quietened by a gesture from Zawisza. Not violent, but charged with power and authority.

'Greetings, stranger,' said the knight from Garbów,

astonishingly calm. 'Fear not and take your seat by our campfire.'

The creature moved its head and Reynevan saw a fleeting flash of large eyes reflecting red flame.

'Fear not and take a seat,' repeated Zawisza in a voice that was kindly and hard at the same time. 'You need not fear us.'

'I fear you not,' said the creature hoarsely, to everyone's utter astonishment. Then the creature held out a paw. Reynevan would have sprung back had he not been too afraid to move. He suddenly realised in astonishment that the paw was pointing at the arms on Zawisza's shield. Then, to his even greater astonishment, the creature pointed at the cauldron with the herbal infusion.

'Sulima and a herbalist,' the creature croaked. 'Rectitude and knowledge. What is there to fear? I fear not. My name is Hans Mein Igel.'

'Greetings to you, Hans Mein Igel. Be you hungry? Or thirsty?'

'No. It came to sit down. And listen. For it heard their words. And came to listen.'

'Please, be our guest.'

The creature approached the campfire, bristled up into a ball and stopped moving.

'Aaaye.' Zawisza's composure was truly astonishing. 'Where was I?'

'You were . . .' Reynevan swallowed, regaining his speech. 'You were saying *nec Hercules*.'

'That is so,' croaked Hans Mein Igel.

'Aye,' said the knight freely, 'that I was. *Nec Hercules*, the Hussites overcame us. Indeed, we were fortunate to be attacked by the cavalry, for the Tábor flailmen do not know the words "mercy" or "ransom". When they finally hauled me from the saddle, one of the knights remaining with me managed to shout out who I was, that I had fought at Grunwald with Žižka and Jan Sokol of Lamberk.'

Reynevan gasped softly on hearing the distinguished names. Zawisza was silent for a long time.

'You probably know the rest,' he said finally, 'for the rest cannot differ much from the legend.'

Reynevan and Hans Mein Igel nodded in silence. It was a good while before the knight took up the story again.

'Now I feel I have brought a curse on myself in my old age,' he said. 'For when my ransom was paid and I returned to Krakow, I told King Władysław everything I had seen at Epiphany at the Battle of Německý Brod, and everything I saw the following day after the town was captured. I told all but gave no advice, imposed not my opinions, was circumspect in expressing my judgements or conclusions. I simply talked, and he – the cunning old Lithuanian – listened. And knew. And never, laddie, you may be certain, will that cunning old Lithuanian ever send Polish or Lithuanian knights to fight the Czechs, no matter that the Pope weeps over the endangered faith, and Sigismund does rage and menace. And that is my fault, because of my account. And the only right conclusion that can be drawn from it is that the Polish and Lithuanian knighthood are needed to fight the Teutonic Knights, and it would be foolish, utter nonsense, to drown them in the Sázava, the Vltava or the Labe. Jogaila, having also heard my account, will never join an anti-Hussite crusade, either. Which is why I'm riding to Hungary against the Turks, before they excommunicate me.'

'You are jesting, sir,' said Reynevan. 'Excommunication? A knight of your renown . . . You must be jesting.'

'Indeed,' said Zawisza with a nod. 'Indeed, I jest. But I do fear it.'

For some time, they said nothing. Hans Mein Igel panted softly. The horses snorted restlessly in the darkness.

'Would that mean the end of knighthood?' Reynevan risked asking. 'And chivalry? Can the infantry, tight-knit and serried, shoulder to shoulder, not only stand up to armoured cavalry, but even defeat it? Is this the end of . . . an era? Perhaps the age of knighthood is ending?'

'A war without knights or chivalry,' Zawisza the Black replied a moment later, 'will eventually become sheer slaughter, a massacre. I would want no part of something like that. But I probably won't live to see it. Between us, I wouldn't want to.'

Silence reigned for a long time. The campfire died down, the logs glowing scarlet, occasionally exploding with a bluish flame or a geyser of sparks. One of the servants snored. Zawisza wiped his forehead with a hand. Hans Mein Igel, as black as a wisp of darkness, moved his ears. When the flames reflected in his eyes once again, Reynevan realised that the creature was looking at him.

'Love has many names,' said Hans Mein Igel suddenly, 'and it will determine your fate, young herbalist. Love. It will save your life when you won't even know that it is love. For the Goddess has many names. And still more faces.'

Reynevan was dumbstruck. Zawisza reacted first.

'Well, well,' he said. 'A prophecy. Obscure like every prophecy, suiting everything and nothing at the same time. No offence, Master Hans. Do you have anything for me?'

Hans Mein Igel moved his head and his ears.

'A city stands on a hill by a great river,' he finally said in his indistinct, hoarse voice. 'On a hill with a river winding around it. And it is called the Town of Doves. An evil place. Do not go there, Sulima. An evil place for you, the Town of Doves. Ride not there. Turn back.'

Zawisza said nothing for a long time, plunged into a deep reverie. He was silent for so long that Reynevan presumed he would brush off the strange nocturnal creature's words. He was wrong.

'I am a man of the sword,' Zawisza interrupted the silence. 'From the moment I first picked up a sword some two-score years ago, I've known what fate awaits me. But I will not look back at the *hundsfelds*, the graves, the royal betrayals, the wickedness, the baseness, the mean-spiritedness I've left behind me. I'll not turn back from my chosen path, Master Hans Mein Igel.'

Hans Mein Igel didn't say a word, but his large eyes flared.

'All the same,' Zawisza the Black added, wiping his forehead,

'I'd prefer you prophesy me love, as you did Reynevan. Not death.'

'I, too, would prefer that,' said Hans Mein Igel. 'Farewell.'

The creature suddenly grew in size and bristled even more. And vanished, dissipating into the same gloom from which it had emerged.

The horses snorted and stamped in the darkness. The servants snored. The sky was growing lighter, the stars fading above the treetops.

'Uncanny,' said Reynevan finally. 'That was uncanny.'

The knight jerked up his head, woken from his slumber.

'What? What was uncanny?'

'That . . . Hans Mein Igel. Do you know, Sir Zawisza, that . . . Well, I have to confess . . . I was full of admiration for you.'

'Why?'

'When it emerged from the darkness, you didn't even flinch. Why, your voice didn't even tremble. And when you talked to it afterwards, my admiration . . . For it was . . . A night creature. Something . . . alien.'

Zawisza the Black of Garbów looked long at him.

'I know many people,' he finally replied, very gravely, 'who feel much more alien to me.'

The dawn was foggy and damp; drops of dew hung in great garlands on cobwebs. The forest was silent, but as menacing as a sleeping beast. The horses started at the haze creeping towards them, snorting and shaking their manes.

A stone cross stood at the crossroads, beyond the forest. One of Silesia's numerous reminders of crimes past and very belated remorse.

'Here we part,' said Reynevan.

The knight looked at him, but refrained from commenting.

'Here we part,' the boy repeated. 'Like you, it's not to my liking to look back at *hundsfelds*. Like you, I find the thought of baseness and mean-spiritedness revolting. I'm returning to Adèle – never mind what that Hans said, my place is beside her. I won't flee like a coward, like a petty thief. I shall face what I have to face, like you did at the Battle of Německý Brod. Farewell, noble Sir Zawisza.'

'Farewell, Reinmar of Bielawa. Watch your back. *Adieu.*'

'You, too. Who knows, perhaps we shall meet again.'

Zawisza the Black of Garbów looked long at him.

'I doubt that,' he finally said.

Chapter Five

In which Reynevan experiences what a wolf feels like being hunted in a forest. Then meets Fair Nicolette. And then sails off downstream.

A stone penitentiary cross stood at the crossroads, beyond the forest. One of Silesia's numerous reminders of crimes past and very belated remorse.

The arms of the cross were clover-shaped and on the base was carved a battleaxe. That was the weapon the penitent had used to send his neighbours to the next world.

Reynevan examined the cross carefully and uttered a foul oath.

It was the very same cross beside which he had said farewell to Zawisza a good three hours earlier.

To blame was the fog, creeping since dawn like smoke over the fields and forests; to blame was the drizzle slanting small drops into his eyes. And when it stopped, the fog became thicker. To blame was also Reynevan himself, his fatigue and his lack of sleep, his distraction caused by obsessive thoughts about Adèle of Stercza and his plans to free her. And besides, who knew? Perhaps to blame were the sprites, imps, will-o'-the-wisps and other spirits that lived in great numbers in the Silesian forests, the decidedly less benevolent friends and relatives of Hans Mein Igel who were fond of leading people astray.

Searching for the culprit made no sense and Reynevan knew it. One had to assess the situation judiciously and act accordingly. He dismounted, leaned against the penitential cross and began to think hard.

Instead of being about halfway to Bierutów, he had returned to his starting place, not more than a mile from the town of Brzeg.

Or perhaps, he thought, *perhaps destiny guided me? Gave me a sign? I could ride to Brzeg and ask for help from my brethren at the Monastery of the Holy Spirit. Or maybe I should stick with the original plan and ride straight towards Bierutów, to Ligota, and to Adèle.*

I ought to avoid the town, he concluded after some thought. His good relationship with the Brzeg monks was known to everybody, including the Sterczas. Additionally, Brzeg was on the road to the Knights Hospitaller Commandery, where Duke Konrad wanted to imprison Reynevan until the trouble blew over. In spite of the duke's good intentions, Reynevan had absolutely no desire to spend years doing penance with the Knights Hospitaller, plus somebody from Kantner's entourage might have let slip or been bribed to reveal the duke's plan to the Sterczas, who would be lurking outside Brzeg by now.

And so, he thought, *I'll ride to Adèle, to rescue her. Like Tristan to Isolde, like Lancelot to Guinevere. A fool's errand straight into the lion's den, perhaps, but my pursuers might not be expecting such a risky gambit. Most importantly, Adèle is in need and must be missing me, so I cannot keep her waiting.*

As his mood brightened, so did the sky, as though touched by Merlin's wand, and the overwhelming greyness began to take on colour. The birds, gloomily silent until then, began to timidly call, finally to chirp loudly. Dewdrops shone silver on the cobwebs and the mist-shrouded roads looked like a scene from a fairy tale.

Angry at himself for being too cocksure to think of it earlier, Reynevan called to mind another means of countering misleading spells. Clearing away the weeds covering the base of the cross, he quickly found what he was looking for: feathery caraway, red bartsia covered in pink flowers and spurge. After he'd stripped the leaves from the stems and placed them together, it took him a moment to recall how to wind them and on which fingers, how to plait them and how to make the node, the knot. And how the spell went.

One, two, three
Wolfsmilch, Kümmel, Zahntrost
Binde zu samene
Semitae eorum incurvatae sunt
Thus, my road is straight.

A moment later, one of the branches of the crossroads became brighter, friendlier, inviting. Without the talisman, Reynevan would never have guessed it was the right path. But Reynevan knew that talismans didn't lie.

After riding for a few minutes, he heard the barking of a dog and the loud, excited gaggling of geese. Soon after, his nostrils were pleasantly tickled by the smell of smoke from a smokehouse where something delicious was being cured. Reynevan succumbed to the aroma so utterly that he was oblivious to everything around him, and found himself riding through a wattle gate into the courtyard of a roadside inn. A dog barked at him, more from a sense of duty than in warning. The smell of baking bread mingled with the aroma of the smoked meats, masking even the stench of a great cesspool besieged by geese and ducks.

Reynevan dismounted and tied his grey to a stake. A stableman grooming some horses nearby was so busy, he didn't even acknowledge his arrival. But something else had caught Reynevan's attention. On one of the posts of the porch hung a hex: three twigs tied into a triangle and entwined by a garland of wilted clover and marsh marigold on a messy tangle of colourful threads. Reynevan pondered on it, but was not especially surprised. Magic was everywhere, and people used magical symbols not even knowing what they meant or what purpose they really served. Most crucially in this instance, although inexpertly tied, the hex might have confused his talisman.

That's why I ended up here, he thought. *Bugger. Ah well, since I'm here . . .*

He entered, stooping to pass beneath the low lintel.

The fish skins covering the small windows barely let in any

light, casting the room in semi-darkness lit only by flashes of fire from the hearth. From time to time, a cauldron suspended above the fire overflowed, generating more smoke and further reducing visibility. Only one table in the corner was occupied: four men, probably peasants. It was difficult to tell in the gloom.

Reynevan had only just sat down on a bench when an aproned serving wench placed a bowl in front of him. He had intended to buy some bread and ride on, but the dumplings in the bowl smelled so enticingly of melted pork fat that he put one of the few coins Kantner had given him down on the table.

The serving wench leaned over slightly, handing him a linden-wood spoon. A faint odour of herbs emanated from her.

'You're in hot water,' she murmured softly. 'Sit tight. They've seen you. Move from the table and they'll have you. So, sit still and don't budge.'

She went towards the hearth and stirred the contents of the steaming, bubbling cauldron. Reynevan, worried, sat still and stared at the bits of fried meat in the dumplings. His eyes were now sufficiently accustomed to the gloom to see that the four men at the corner table had too many weapons and too much armour to be peasants. And that all four had their eyes fixed on him.

He cursed his stupidity under his breath.

The serving wench returned.

'There are too few of us left in this world,' she murmured, pretending to be wiping the table, 'for me to let you be caught.'

When she stilled her hand, Reynevan saw a marsh marigold on her little finger similar to the ones on the hex on the post. The stem had been tied so that the yellow flower formed the gem of a ring. Reynevan gasped, involuntarily touching his own talisman of knotted spurge, red bartsia and caraway fastened to the button of his jerkin. The wench's eyes flashed in the semi-darkness. She nodded.

'I saw as soon as you entered,' she whispered, 'and knew that they were after you. But I won't let them catch you. Too few of us remain, and if we don't help each other, we shall vanish for good. Eat, take no notice.'

He ate very slowly, feeling shivers running down his back under the gaze of the men in the corner. The serving wench clanged a frying pan, shouted something to somebody in the other room, threw a log on the fire and returned. With a broom.

'I've had your horse taken to the threshing floor behind the pigsty,' she murmured as she swept. 'When it all starts, flee through that door at the back beyond the straw mat. Once past the threshold, be heedful of this.'

Still sweeping, she picked up a long stalk of straw and furtively but quickly tied three knots in it.

'Don't worry about me.' Her whisper dispelled his qualms. 'No one will pay me any attention.'

'Gerda!' yelled the innkeeper. 'The bread needs taking out! Move, slattern!'

The girl went away. Stooping, plain, inconspicuous, no one paid any attention to her. No one except Reynevan, to whom she tossed a parting glance as fiery as a flaming brand.

The four men at the table in the corner moved and stood up. They approached, spurs jingling, leather creaking, chainmail clanking, their fists resting on the hilts of swords and daggers. Reynevan once again cursed his lack of good sense under his breath, this time more crudely.

'Sir Reinmar of Bielawa. Look, boys, see for yourself how experienced hunters work. The quarry well tracked, the forest well surveyed, just a little fortune needed to bag something. And fortune has verily smiled on us today.'

Two of the characters were flanking him, one to the right, the other to the left. The third took up a position behind Reynevan. The fourth, the one who had spoken, moustachioed, dressed in a densely studded brigantine, stood opposite. Then, without waiting for an invitation, sat down.

'You won't put up a fight,' he didn't ask, but rather stated, 'make any trouble or brouhaha. Eh? Bielawa?'

Reynevan didn't reply. He held the spoon between his mouth and the edge of the bowl, as though not knowing what to do with it.

'You won't,' the moustachioed character assured himself. 'Because you know, don't you, that would be most foolish. We have nothing against you, it's just another job, but we prefer our work easy. If you begin to kick and yell, we'll make you docile in a trice. We'll break your wrist on the edge of this table, and after that we won't even have to tie you up. Did you say something, or am I hearing things?'

'I didn't say anything.' Reynevan overcame the resistance of his numb lips.

'Very good. Eat up. It's quite some way to Sterzendorf, why should you ride hungry?'

'Particularly since they definitely won't feed you right away at Sterzendorf,' drawled the character on the right, who was wearing a mail shirt and iron vambraces on his forearms.

'And even if they do,' snorted the one behind him that he couldn't see, 'it surely won't be anything to your liking.'

'If you release me . . . I'll pay you . . .' Reynevan stammered out. 'I'll pay you more than the Sterczas.'

'You're insulting professionals,' said the moustachioed man. 'I am Kunz Aulock, called Kyrie-eleison. You can hire me, but you can't bribe me. Get those dumplings down you, double-quick!'

Reynevan ate, but the dumplings had lost their flavour. Kunz Aulock stuck the mace he had been holding into his belt and pulled on his gloves.

'You ought not to have lain with other men's women,' he said. 'Not long ago,' he added, not expecting a response, 'I heard a priest drunkenly reading a letter. To the Hebrews, I believe. It went like this: every transgression will receive a just reward. Put simply, it means that if you do something, you must be aware of the consequences of your deeds and be ready to suffer them. You have to be able to accept them with dignity. Why, for example, look to the right. This is Lord Stork of Gorgowice. Having penchants similar to yours, quite recently, he and some comrades committed a misdeed on an Opole townswoman, for which, if they catch him, they'll rend his flesh with pliers and break him on the wheel. And so? Look and admire how Lord Stork bears his fate with dignity, how clear are his countenance and gaze. Let him be an example.'

'Let me be an example,' croaked Lord Stork, distinguished by a pockmarked face and a rheumy gaze. 'And stand up. Time we went.'

Right then, the hearth exploded with a roar and spat fire, sparks and clouds of smoke and soot into the chamber. The cauldron shot up and clattered onto the floor, spilling its boiling contents. Kyrie-eleison leaped forward, but Reynevan propelled the table at him with a powerful shove. The unfinished bowl of dumplings smacked Lord Stork straight in his pimply face as Reynevan kicked the bench backwards and dived towards the door leading to the threshing floor. One of the thugs managed to seize him by the collar, but Reynevan had studied in Prague and had his collar felt in most of the inns of the Old Town and the Lesser Quarter. He twisted, elbowed him hard in the face, wriggled away and made a break for the door. He recalled the warning and nimbly dodged the tied-up straw lying just beyond the threshold.

Kyrie-eleison, who was pursuing him, naturally didn't know about the magical straw and measured his length on the doorstep, sliding headlong through pig muck. Right afterwards, Stork of Gorgowice tripped over the talisman and the third thug fell onto Stork, who was cursing vehemently. Reynevan was already in the saddle of the waiting horse, already spurring it to gallop, straight ahead, across the gardens, through cabbage beds and gooseberry hedges. The wind whistled in his ears and he heard curses and the squealing of pigs behind him.

He was among the willows by a drained fishpond when he heard the tramping of hooves and the yelling of his pursuers. Instead of avoiding the fishpond, he skirted around it along the very narrow causeway. His heart missed a few beats each time the causeway subsided beneath the horse's hooves. But he got away.

His pursuers also hurtled onto the causeway but were less fortunate. The first horse didn't even make it halfway but slid off neighing and sank up to its girth in sludge. The second horse recoiled, churned up the embankment with its hooves and slid up to its rump in the sticky mud. As the riders yelled and cursed furiously, Reynevan took advantage of the circumstances and the time he had gained. He jabbed his heels into the grey and galloped across the moors towards the tree-covered hills, beyond which he hoped were forests and safety.

Aware that he was taking a risk, he forced the heavily wheezing horse to gallop hard uphill. He didn't allow the grey to rest at the top, immediately urging it down the sparsely forested hillside. And then, quite unexpectedly, his way was blocked by a rider.

The frightened grey reared up, neighing piercingly. Reynevan somehow managed to stay in the saddle.

'Not bad,' said the horseman. Or rather the Amazon. For it was a young woman, tall, dressed in male attire with a tight velvet jerkin with the ruffled collar of a white shirt spilling out at the neck. A thick, fair plait fell down to her shoulder from beneath a sable calpac decorated with a plume of heron's feathers and a golden brooch with a sapphire worth probably as much as a fine horse.

'Who's after you?' she shouted, skilfully controlling her skittish horse. 'The law? Speak!'

'I'm not a criminal—'

'For what reason?'

'For love.'

'Ah! I thought so at once. See that row of dark trees? The Stobrawa runs that way. Ride there as quickly as you can and hide among the swamps on the left bank while I draw them away from you. Give me your mantle.'

'What do you mean, m'lady . . . ? How can—?'

'Give me your mantle, I said! You ride well, but I ride better. Oh, what an adventure! Oh, there'll be a story to tell! Elżbieta and Anka will faint with envy!'

'M'lady ...' mumbled Reynevan. 'I cannot ... What will happen if they catch up with you?'

'Them? Catch up with me?' She snorted, narrowing eyes as blue as turquoises. 'You must be jesting!'

Her mare, coincidentally also grey, tossed its shapely head and danced again. Reynevan was compelled to admit the strange maiden was right. That noble, unmistakably fleet steed was worth considerably more than the sapphire brooch in her calpac.

'It's madness,' he said, tossing her his mantle. 'But thank you. I'll return the favour—'

The cries of his pursuers echoed up from the bottom of the hill.

'Don't waste time!' called the maid, covering her head with the hood. 'Ride on! Across the Stobrawa!'

'M'lady ... Your name ... Tell me ...'

'Nicolette. My Aucassin, pursued for love. Faaareweeell!'

She urged her mare into a gallop, but it was more flying than galloping. She rode down the hillside like a hurricane, in a cloud of dust, showed herself to the pursuers and crossed the moor at such a crazy gallop that Reynevan immediately lost his pangs of remorse. He understood that the fair-haired Amazon wasn't risking anything. The heavy horses of Kyrie-eleison, Stork and the rest, carrying two-hundred-pound fellows, couldn't compete with the grey full-blooded mare laden only with a girl and a light saddle to boot. And indeed, the eye couldn't even track the maid as she dashed out of sight behind the hill. But the pursuers followed her, resolute and relentless.

They might wear her down with a steady pace, thought Reynevan fearfully. *Her and that mare of hers. But,* he salved his conscience, *she surely has her attendants somewhere close at hand. On such a horse, thus attired, she's clearly a maid of noble birth, and such as her don't ride alone*, he thought, galloping on in the direction she had indicated.

And there's no doubt, he thought, gulping wind as he rode, *she is surely not called Nicolette. She was mocking me, poor Aucassin.*

Hidden among the alder marshes on the Stobrawa, Reynevan took a breather, even allowing himself to feel a little proud and scornful, a veritable Roland deceiving the hordes of Moors on his trail. But his pride and good mood abandoned him when something completely unknightly occurred that never – if you believe the ballads – happened to Roland.

His horse went lame.

Reynevan dismounted at once on sensing the horse's jarring, broken rhythm. He examined the grey's leg and horseshoe but was unable to diagnose anything, much less palliate it. He could only walk, leading the limping animal by the reins. *Marvellous*, he thought. *One horse worn out, another lame in a matter of days.*

To make matters worse, whistles, neighing and curses shouted by the now-familiar voice of Kunz Aulock suddenly resounded from the right-hand bank of the Stobrawa. Reynevan dragged his horse into some denser bushes and covered its nostrils to stop it neighing. The cries and curses faded away in the distance.

They've chased down the lass, he thought, and his heart sank, both out of fear and remorse. *They've caught up with her.*

They haven't, his good sense reassured him. *At most, they've found her entourage and realised their error. And 'Nicolette' has ridiculed and mocked them, safe among her knights and servants.*

So they've returned and are circling, tracking. Like hunters.

He spent the night in the undergrowth, shooing away mosquitoes, his teeth chattering. He must have fallen asleep at some point and dreamed, because how else could he have seen that wench from the inn, that plain girl, the one with the marsh marigold ring on her finger, unnoticed by anyone? How else, if not as an apparition in a dream, could she have come to him?

So few of us are left, so few, said the lass. *Don't let them catch you, don't let them track you down. What doesn't leave tracks? A bird in the air, a fish in the water.*

A bird in the air, a fish in the water.

He wanted to ask her who she was, how she knew talismans and how she'd caused the fireplace to explode – because it wasn't gunpowder. He wanted to ask her many things.

He didn't manage to. He awoke.

He set off before dawn, following the river downstream. He had been walking for about an hour, sticking to the high beech forest, when all of a sudden, a broad river spread out below him. Only one river in the whole of Silesia was that broad.

The Odra.

A small launch was sailing against the current, bobbing gracefully like a grebe and nimbly gliding along the edge of a bright shoal. Reynevan watched keenly.

You're so crafty, he thought, observing the wind filling the launch's sail, the water foaming before the bow. *Such great hunters, are you, Master Kyrie-eleison et consortes? You tracked me down after combing the forest, but just wait, I'll outwit you. I'll slip from your snare so skilfully, with such panache, that pigs will fly before you pick up my trail again. Because you'll have to ride as far as Wrocław to search for it.*

A bird in the air, a fish in the water . . .

He pulled the grey towards a rutted road leading to the Odra. To be safe, he stayed among the osiers until he confirmed that he had guessed right: the road ran towards a river jetty.

From some way off along the jetty, he heard men's irate, raised voices. He couldn't tell if it was a quarrel or passionate haggling. However, he easily recognised the language they were speaking. For it was Polish.

Before he left the osier grove and saw the jetty from the hillside, Reynevan knew to whom the voices and the small vessels moored to stakes belonged. They were Water Poles, Odra rafters and fishermen, who were more of a clan than a guild. The Water Poles controlled a large slice of fishing in Silesia, a considerable stake in floating timber and an even more significant one in ferrying, in which line of work they rivalled the Hanseatic League. The Hanseatic League hadn't got further up the Odra than Wrocław, while the Water Poles shipped goods as far as Racibórz and beyond the mouth of the Warta.

The smell of fish, mud and pitch drifted over from the jetty.

Reynevan struggled to lead the limping horse down the slippery clay of the hillside. They passed between shacks, huts and drying nets, heading towards the sound of feet thudding and slapping on the jetty as goods were loaded and unloaded under the watchful eye of a bearded merchant. A bull lowed and stamped on its way to one of the punts, making the entire jetty shake. The rafters swore in Polish.

Things soon calmed down as the wagons carrying hides and barrels trundled off, but not for long as the bull tried to destroy the cramped enclosure it had been driven into. The Water Poles began their customary quarrelling. Reynevan knew enough Polish to understand it was an argument about nothing.

'Is anyone sailing downstream, may I ask? To Wrocław?'

The Water Poles stopped bickering and examined Reynevan with a none too friendly gaze. One of them spat in the water.

'And if so, what then?' he grunted. 'Honourable master?'

'My horse is lame, and I have to get to Wrocław.'

The Pole bridled, hawked and spat again.

'Well,' said Reynevan, not giving up. 'What's it to be?'

'I don't take Germans.'

'I'm not German. I'm Silesian.'

'Aha?'

'Aha.'

'Then say: She sells seashells on the seashore.'

'She sells seashells on the seashore. And you say: red leather, yellow leather.'

'Red leather, le . . . lello . . . yellow leather . . . Jump aboard.'

Reynevan didn't need to be told twice, but the boatman bluntly curbed his enthusiasm.

'Hey! Not so fast! Firstly, I'm only going as far as Oława.

Secondly, it costs five skojeces. And another five for the horse.'

'If you don't have it,' another Water Pole interjected with a cunning grin, seeing Reynevan looking abashed and rummaging in his pouch, 'I'll buy the horse off you. For five . . . Very well, let it be six skojeces. Twelve groschen. Leaves you with just enough for the trip. And as the horse is no longer yours, you won't have to pay to transport it. Clear profit.'

'This horse,' observed Reynevan, 'is worth at least five grzywna.'

'That horse isn't worth shit,' observed the Pole acutely, 'because you can't ride it to where you're headed. So, what'll it be? Selling?'

'If you throw in another three skojeces for the saddle and harness.'

'One skojec.'

'Two.'

'Done.'

Horse and money changed owners. Reynevan bade farewell to the grey by patting its neck and stroking its mane, sniffing a little as he said goodbye to a friend and companion in misfortune. He grabbed a rope and jumped on board. The sailor unhitched the painter from a stake. The punt shuddered and slowly joined the current. On the jetty, the Water Poles examined the grey's leg and argued about nothing.

The punt sailed downstream. Towards Oława. The Odra's grey water lapped and foamed against the sides.

'M'lord.'

'What?' Reynevan started and rubbed his eyes. 'What is it, skipper?'

'Oława's ahead of us!'

A punt sailing with the current and making no stops can cover the five miles from the mouth of the Stobrawa to Oława in less than ten hours. The punt's skipper had much business to conduct at many stops along the way, and Reynevan spent a day and a half and two nights on the punt instead of ten hours. He had few complaints, however, as he was reasonably safe, travelling comfortably, resting, sleeping well and eating his fill. He even managed to converse a little with the skipper.

Although the Water Pole didn't give his name or ask for Reynevan's, he was essentially a friendly, easy-going person, simple but by no means stupid, somewhat taciturn but never brusque or rude. The punt weaved between river islands and shoals, calling at jetties now on the left bank, now on the right. The four-man crew were rushed off their feet and the skipper swore and drove them on. The Water Pole's wife, a woman considerably younger than her husband, steered with a steady hand. In order not to abuse their kindness, Reynevan did his best not to stare at her sturdy thighs, visible beneath her rolled-up skirt, and to look away when her shirt clung to breasts worthy of Venus during manoeuvres with the steering oar.

Travelling on the punt, Reynevan had many new experiences and gained a little knowledge of life on the river. He learned the difference between hand nets and cast nets, and between weirs and dams. He ate things he'd never eaten before, like grilled fillets from a catfish measuring five cubits and weighing in at a hundred and twenty pounds. He also learned how to ward off a vodnik, a nix and a virnik. And he heard a lot of very bad words about German lordlings who oppressed the Water Poles with swingeing tariffs, tolls and taxes.

The following day turned out to be Sunday, when the Water Poles and the local fishermen didn't work. They prayed long at roughly carved figures of the Virgin Mary and Saint Peter, then feasted, then had something like a moot, then drank and fought.

So, although the journey was lengthy, time didn't drag at all. And now it was dawn or rather morning, and the city of Oława was around the next bend. The Water Pole's wife pressed herself against the steering oar and her breasts pressed against her blouse.

'In Oława, I'll need one – at most two – days to deal with various things,' said the skipper. 'If you can wait that long, I'll take you to Wrocław, young Master Silesian. Without further dues.'

'Thank you.' Reynevan shook the skipper's proffered hand,

aware he had been honoured with friendship. 'Thank you, but during the journey I've had time to think over a few matters, and now Oława suits me better than Wrocław.'

'As you wish. I'll set you down wherever you want – on the left bank or the right?'

'I need the Strzelin road.'

'So the left. Am I correct in thinking you'd rather steer clear of the town?'

'I would,' Reynevan admitted, astonished by the Water Pole's perspicuity. 'If it doesn't put you out.'

'How could it? Turn to port, Maryśka. Make for Drozd's Weir.'

A vast oxbow lake spread out beyond Drozd's Weir, entirely covered with a carpet of yellow-blooming water lilies. Through the fog shrouding the lake came the distant sounds of Oława's suburbs: crowing cockerels, barking dogs and the clanging of a church bell.

At the skipper's signal, Reynevan jumped out onto a rickety jetty. The punt brushed against a stake, parted some weed with its prow and languidly swung around into the current.

'Don't leave the causeway!' called the skipper. 'And keep the sun on your back until the bridge over the Oława, then turn towards the trees. There'll be a stream and beyond it the Strzelin road. Can't go wrong!'

'Thank you! Godspeed!'

The punt began to vanish in the fog rising from the river. Reynevan threw his meagre bundle of possessions over his shoulder.

'Young Master Silesian!' came a voice from the river.

'Aye?'

'Red leather, yellow leather!'

Chapter Six

In which Reynevan is first given a thrashing and later sets off for Strzelin in the company of four people and a dog. The tedium of the journey is enlivened by a dispute about heresies, which we are told are spreading like weeds.

Reynevan was following a merrily burbling stream along the edge of a forest as it meandered among green knotgrass and through an avenue of willows. In a clearing up ahead, a road crossed the stream over a footbridge of sturdy timbers so black and moss-covered that it might have been built during the reign of Henry the Pious. On the bridge was a wagon, pulled by a bony bay nag. The wagon was tilting sharply. It was clear why.

'Looks like you have a problem with that wheel,' stated Reynevan, walking closer.

'It's worse than you think,' replied a young woman, ginger-haired and pretty though somewhat plump, smudging tar on her sweaty forehead. 'The axle has broken.'

'Ah. Nothing to be done without a blacksmith, then.'

'Oy vey,' cried the other traveller, a bearded Jew in modest but neat and by no means shabby raiment, clutching a fox-fur hat. 'O, God of Isaac! Disaster! Woe betide us! What to do?'

'Were you making for Strzelin?' Reynevan asked, guessing from the way the shaft was pointing.

'Correct, young sir.'

'I shall help you in exchange for a ride, for I am heading that way, too. And I also have troubles—'

''Tis not difficult to discern.' The Jew's beard moved as he spoke, and his eyes flashed cunningly. 'You're a nobleman, young sir, that is apparent. So where, then, is your horse? But let it be. You have a kind look in your eyes. I be Hiram ben Eliezer, rabbi of the Brzeg Qahal. Travelling to Strzelin—'

'And I be Dorota Faber,' the ginger-haired woman cheerfully interrupted in mid-sentence. 'Travelling the wide world. And you, young sir?'

'My name is . . .' Reynevan decided after a moment's thought, 'Reinmar of Bielawa. Listen. Here's what we'll do. We'll pull the wagon off the bridge somehow and unhitch the mare, then I'll ride her bareback to the suburbs of Oława and take that axle bearing to a blacksmith. If necessary, I'll bring him back here with me to finish the job. Let's get to work.'

It turned out not to be so easy.

Dorota Faber wasn't much use, the old rabbi none at all. Although the scrawny mare doggedly beat her hooves on the rotten timbers and leaned into the collar, they barely shifted the wagon two yards. Reynevan was unable to lift the conveyance by himself. They finally sat down by the broken axle and stared panting at the gudgeon and lamprey teeming at the bottom of the stream.

'So where do your world travels take you?' Reynevan asked the ginger-haired woman.

'I'm looking for work,' she replied freely, rubbing her nose with the back of her hand. 'For now, since Master Jew graciously took me aboard, I'll go with him to Strzelin, and then, who knows, maybe even to Wrocław itself. In my line of work, I can find employment anywhere, though I'd prefer the best . . .'

'In your . . . line of work?' Reynevan began to twig. 'You mean . . .'

'Exactly. I am, as you would say, a strumpet. Until recently employed at the Crown whorehouse in Brzeg.'

'I understand.' Reynevan nodded seriously. 'And you are travelling together? Rabbi – you took as a passenger a . . . a woman of easy virtue?'

'Shouldn't I have done so?' Rabbi Hiram opened his eyes wide.

'Well, I did. For, my young lord, I'd have looked a right prick if I hadn't.'

Footsteps boomed on the moss-covered timbers.

'Problem?' asked one of the three men who had set foot on the bridge. 'Do you need some help?'

'It would come in handy,' admitted Reynevan, although he didn't like the look of the potential helpers' disagreeable faces and shifty eyes one little bit. With good reason, it turned out, as soon as several pairs of powerful hands had made quick work of pushing the wagon into the meadow beyond the bridge.

'There!' said the tallest of the characters, chin covered in stubble, shaking a stout stick. 'Job done, now it's time to pay. Unhitch the horse from the wagon, Jew boy, take off your coat, give me your purse. And you, lordling, off with your jerkin and boots. And you, my lovely, off with everything, you'll be paying in kind. Strip!'

His comrades guffawed, baring rotten teeth. Reynevan stooped over and grasped the stake he had used to lever the wagon.

'Look at the bold young master.' The unshaven man pointed his stick at him. 'Life still hasn't learned him that when someone orders you to hand your boots over, you do it. Because you can walk barefoot, but not on broken legs. Come on! Let's 'ave 'im!'

The thugs nimbly dodged the stake Reynevan was swinging. One ran up from behind and knocked him to the ground with a skilful kick to the backs of his knees, then himself cried out and staggered, shielding his eyes from the fingernails of Dorota Faber, who was clinging to his back. Reynevan shielded himself from kicks and blows and tried to intervene when he saw one of the thugs punching the Jew. And then he saw a demon.

The thugs began yelling. In terror.

Whatever had set upon the thugs was not, of course, a demon. It was a huge, pitch-black mastiff with a spiked collar around its neck. The dog rushed the thugs like a bolt of black lightning, attacking like a wolf rather than a mastiff. It bit deeply and repeatedly. On the calves. On the thighs. On the crotch. And when the men fell over, on their arms and faces. The men's cries became horribly high-pitched. Spine-chilling.

A piercing, modulating whistle rang out. The black mastiff immediately sprang away from the thugs and sat motionless, ears pricked up, like a figure made of anthracite.

A horseman appeared on the bridge. He was wearing a short grey cloak fastened with a silver clasp, a tight doublet and a chaperon with a long liripipe draped over one shoulder.

'When the sun appears above that spruce,' said the stranger in a powerful voice, straightening his modest frame in the saddle atop a black stallion, 'I shall set Beelzebub on you, you blackguards. Since time is short and Beelzebub swift, I suggest speed. And advise against rest breaks.'

The rogues didn't need to be told twice. They fled into the forest, limping, groaning and glancing back fearfully. Beelzebub, appearing to know how to scare them even more, didn't look at them, but at the sun and the top of the spruce.

The horseman gently urged on his mount, and from the height of his saddle examined Hiram ben Eliezer, Dorota Faber and Reynevan, who was getting to his feet, feeling his ribs and wiping blood from his nose. The horseman scrutinised Reynevan particularly closely – which didn't escape the lad's notice.

'Well, well,' their rescuer finally said. 'A classic situation, straight from a fairy tale – a bog, a bridge, a wheel and a problem, and help arrives right on cue. You didn't summon me, did you? Aren't you afraid I'll take out a devilish pact and make you sign it?'

'No,' said the rabbi. 'It's not that particular fairy tale.'

The horseman snorted.

'I am Urban Horn,' he announced, looking straight at Reynevan. 'Whom have my Beelzebub and I helped?'

'Rabbi Hiram ben Eliezer from Brzeg.'

'Dorota Faber.'

'The Knight of the Cart.' Reynevan, in spite of everything, didn't trust him.

Urban Horn snorted again and shrugged.

'I expect you're heading towards Strzelin. I overtook another traveller on the road heading there. I suggest you beg a lift from him rather than hang around over a broken wheel till nightfall. It would be better. And safer.'

Rabbi Hiram ben Eliezer gave his conveyance a last, lingering look, but nodded in agreement.

'And now farewell.' The stranger's gaze shifted to the forest and the top of the spruce. 'Duty calls.'

'I thought,' Reynevan offered, 'it was only to frighten them . . .'

The horseman looked him in the eyes, and his eyes were cold. Icy.

'It was,' he admitted. 'But I, Lancelot, never make idle threats.'

The traveller Urban Horn mentioned turned out to be a priest, a fat man with a high tonsure, wearing a cloak trimmed with polecat fur, driving a large wagon.

The priest reined in his horse, listened to their account from the box seat, examined the wagon with the broken axle, scrutinised each of the three people standing imploringly before him, and finally understood what they were asking.

'You want a ride?' he finally said in great disbelief. 'To Strzelin? On my wagon?'

The three of them struck even more imploring poses.

'I, Filip Granciszek of Oława, parish priest of Our Lady of Consolation, a good Christian and Catholic, am to invite onto my wagon a Jew, a whore and a vagabond?'

Reynevan, Dorota Faber and Rabbi Hiram ben Eliezer looked at each other bashfully.

'Oh, get on,' the priest finally announced dryly. 'I'd look a right twat if I didn't.'

Not an hour had passed before Beelzebub, shining with dew, ran up beside the dun gelding pulling the priest's wagon. And a little later, Urban Horn appeared on the road on his black horse.

'I'll ride with you as far as Strzelin,' he announced. 'If, naturally, you have nothing against it.'

No one did.

No one asked about the fate of the rogues. And Beelzebub's wise eyes gave away nothing.

Or everything.

They rode along the Strzelin highway, along the Oława valley, now among dense forests, now across moors and vast meadows. The mastiff Beelzebub ran in front like a footman, patrolling the road, occasionally vanishing into the forest where he ferreted around in the undergrowth. The black dog didn't chase or bark at hares or jays, however, since that was clearly beneath him. Urban Horn, the mysterious stranger with the cold eyes riding alongside the wagon on his black horse, never had to call or rebuke the dog.

Dorota Faber drove the priest's wagon, which was being pulled by a dun gelding. The red-haired harlot from Brzeg begged the parish priest to let her and evidently regarded it as a kind of payment for the ride. And she drove splendidly, with great skill. Thus, Father Filip Granciszek, who was sitting beside her on the coachman's seat, could doze or converse without worrying about the conveyance. Reynevan and Rabbi Hiram ben Eliezer sat on sacks of oats and dozed or chatted.

The Jew's scrawny mare shambled at the rear.

Thus, they rode, dozed, conversed, took breaks, conversed and dozed. They ate this and that. They downed a clay pitcher of vodka that Father Granciszek found among his chests. They drank another that Rabbi Hiram pulled from his overcoat.

It quickly came to light that the parish priest and the Jew were travelling to Strzelin for almost the same reason: an audience with the canon of the Wrocław Chapter, who was visiting the city and the parish. While Father Granciszek had been summoned to present himself, the rabbi was visiting uninvited, hoping to be granted an audience. The parish priest was doubtful of his chances.

'The reverend canon,' he said, 'has a great deal of work there, cases and trials and endless audiences. Most trying times are upon us.'

'As though they were ever easy,' said Dorota Faber, tugging on the reins.

'I'm talking about trying times for the Church,' stressed Father Granciszek. 'And for those of real faith, since the evil of heresy is spreading. You meet somebody, he greets you in God's name, and you can't tell if he's a heretic. Did you say something, Rabbi?'

'Love thy neighbour,' muttered Hiram ben Eliezer, possibly in his sleep. 'The prophet Elijah may appear with any face he wants.'

'Jewish philosophy.' Father Filip waved a contemptuous hand. 'But I say: vigilance, work and prayer. For Saint Peter's rock trembles and sways, and the evil of heresy is spreading.'

'You've already said that, Pater.' Urban Horn reined in his horse to ride beside the wagon.

'For it is the truth,' said Father Granciszek, now fully awake. 'However many times it is said, it is the truth. Heresy is spreading, apostasy is multiplying. False prophets are springing up like mushrooms, ready to distort Divine Law with their false teachings. Verily, the apostle Paul wrote prophetically to Timothy: "For the time will come when they will not endure sound doctrine; but after their own lusts shall they heap to themselves teachers, having itching ears; And they shall turn away their ears from the truth, and shall be turned unto fables." And they will claim, Christ have mercy, that they do what they do in the name of truth.'

'Everything in this world,' Urban Horn observed casually, 'occurs under the banner of the fight for truth. And though it usually concerns all sorts of truths, one truth benefits from it. The real truth.'

'What you've said sounds like heresy,' the priest replied, frowning. 'If I may say so, regarding the truth, I agree more with what Master Johannes Nider wrote in his *Formicarius*, where he compares heretics to ants living in the Indies. They pick grains of gold out of the sand and carry them back to their anthill, although of course they have no use for it. Heretics, Master Nider writes in his *Formicarius*, are just the same, rummaging in the Holy Bible and searching for grains of truth, although of course they know not what to do with that truth.'

'That was very nice,' Dorota Faber sighed, urging the gelding on. 'The bit about the ants, I mean. Oh, truly, when I listen to someone that wise, it gets me right in the belly.'

The priest ignored both her and her belly, launching into a lengthy diatribe about various heretical enemies of the faith, the Church and the Pope.

'To make it even more amusing,' Urban Horn interjected with a smile, 'all the sects you named consider themselves righteous and all the others as enemies of the faith. As far as the Pope is concerned, you must admit, Father, that it's sometimes difficult to choose the one true sect among the many. While as far as the Church is concerned, to a man they appeal for reform, *in capite et in membris*. Doesn't that make you wonder, Reverend?'

'I don't really understand your words,' confessed Filip Granciszek. 'But if you mean that heresy is growing in the very bosom of the Church, you are right. They who err in their faith, arrogantly exaggerating their piety, are extremely close to that sin. *Corruptio optimi pessima!* Consider the well-known self-mortifiers or Flagellants. As early as 1349, Pope Clement VI had pronounced them heretics, excommunicated them and ordered them punished, but did it help?'

'It didn't help at all,' pronounced Horn. 'They continued to roam throughout Germany, causing delight since plenty of maids travelled with them, who flogged themselves, naked to the waist with their tits out. The last Vatican Council has condemned them again, but it won't change anything. Some pestilence or other calamity will occur and self-scourging processions will begin again. They must simply enjoy it.'

'A certain learned master in Prague proved that it's an affliction.' Reynevan joined the discussion a little dreamily. 'That certain women find bliss in flogging themselves naked, in front of everybody's eyes. Which is why there are so many women among the Flagellants.'

'I advise against making reference to Prague masters at the present time,' suggested Father Filip caustically. 'Nonetheless, there is something in it. The Order of Preachers show that much evil comes from corporeal intemperance, which is insatiable among women.'

'Better leave women alone,' Dorota Faber said unexpectedly, 'for you aren't without sin yourselves.'

'In paradise,' Granciszek glared at her, 'the serpent chose Eve, not Adam, and he must have known what he was doing. So, too, must the Dominicans. I never meant to denigrate women, but simply to show that lust and promiscuity lie at the heart of many of the present heresies, probably owing to some sort of gleeful perversity. The Church forbids it? Let's do it out of spite. The Church demands humility? Very well, let's show our bare arses! Does it call for moderation and decorousness? Very well, let's fornicate like cats in March!'

'Fascinating,' Urban Horn said, lost in reverie.

Reynevan blushed and Dorota snorted, showing that they weren't unfamiliar with the matter, either.

The wagon bounced so hard on one pothole that Rabbi Hiram woke up, and Father Granciszek, who was about to begin another lecture, almost bit his tongue off. Dorota Faber clicked at the gelding and flicked the reins. The priest adjusted his position on the coachman's seat.

'There were others,' he continued, 'who sinned, like the Flagellants, with excessive piety, which is only a step away from degeneration and heresy. I'm talking about the Beghards from Świdnica and Nysa.'

Reynevan, although he had a somewhat different view of the Beghards and Beguines, nodded. Urban Horn did not.

'The Beghards,' he said calmly, 'also known as the "willingly poor", could be an example for plenty of priests and monks. They also rendered considerable services to society. Suffice it to say that the Beguines curbed the plague in their hospitals in 1360 and prevented the epidemic from spreading, which saved thousands of people from death. The Beguines received a fine reward for that: accusations of heresy.'

'There were indeed many devout, pious men among them,' agreed the priest, 'but there were also apostates and sinners. Many Beguinages, including those hospices you mentioned, turned out to be hotbeds of sin, blasphemy, heresy and sordid lasciviousness. Much vice also occurred among the wandering Beghards.'

'You are free to think thus.'

'Me?' Granciszek bristled. 'I am but a parish priest from Oława, what do I matter? The Beghards were condemned at the Council in Vienne and by Pope Clement, almost a hundred years before my birth. I wasn't yet born when, in 1332, the Inquisition revealed practices as dreadful as the exhumation and desecration of corpses among the Beguines and Beghards. I wasn't yet born when, in 1372, the Inquisition was reopened in Świdnica on the strength of fresh papal edicts. The Beghards and Beguines—'

'The Beghards and Beguines,' Urban Horn continued, 'were baited and dogged throughout Silesia. But you'll probably wash your hands of that, too, O Oława priest, because it was also before your time. Know that it was also before mine, which doesn't stop me knowing what really happened. That most of the Beghards and Beguines when captured were tortured to death. Those who survived the torture were burned at the stake. And quite a large group, as is customary, saved their skin by denouncing others, turning in their companions, friends and even family to be tortured and killed. Some of the traitors later donned Dominican habits and displayed a veritable neophyte's enthusiasm in the fight against heresy.'

'Is that wrong?' The parish priest looked hard at him.

'To denounce?'

'To zealously fight against heresy. You judge that to be wrong?'

Horn turned around suddenly in the saddle, and his face had changed.

'Don't try tricks like that on me, Pater,' he hissed. 'What will you gain by catching me out with a trick question? Look around. We aren't in a Dominican priory, but in the Brzeźmierz Forests. If I feel in danger, I'll simply whack you on the head and toss you under a bush. And in Strzelin, I'll say you died on the way from overheating of the blood and an influx of fluids and humours.'

The priest paled.

'Fortunately for us all,' Horn finished calmly, 'it will not come to that, because I am not a Beghard, nor a heretic, nor a member of the Brethren of the Free Spirit. But don't try any more Inquisitors' tricks, Oława priest. Agreed?'

Filip Granciszek didn't reply, but nodded several times.

When they stopped to stretch their legs, Reynevan couldn't resist. He took Urban Horn to one side and asked what had caused his sharp reaction. Horn didn't want to talk at first, limiting himself to a few oaths and grunts about sodding amateur Inquisitors. Seeing, however, that Reynevan wanted more, he sat down on a fallen tree and called his dog.

'I don't give a damn about any of their heresies, Lancelot,' he began quietly. 'Even though only a halfwit – and I don't consider myself one – would fail to notice that perhaps something ought to change, or be reformed. And I can understand that it piques the Church when they hear there's no God, that no one cares about the Ten Commandments, and that we ought to worship Lucifer. I understand why they'd start yelling "heresy" on hearing that kind of *dictum*. But what then? What infuriates them the most? Not apostasy and godlessness, not the denial of the sacraments. It is the call for evangelical poverty that enrages them the most. For humility. For sacrifice. For service to God and the people. They go into a frenzy when anybody asks them to renounce power and money. That's why they attack the heretics so ferociously. Dammit,

I consider it a miracle that Poverello, Francis the Pauper, wasn't burned at the stake! But I fear that every day some anonymous Poverello, unknown and unrecognised by anyone, is thrown on the pyre.'

Reynevan nodded.

'That's why it annoys me so much,' finished Horn.

Reynevan nodded again. Urban Horn scrutinised him.

'Well, well, I've gone on a little,' he said, yawning, 'and such talk can be dangerous. Many a man has cut his own throat with his own wagging tongue ... But I trust you, Lancelot. You don't even know why.'

'Oh, but I do.' Reynevan smiled affectedly. 'If you suspected that I would denounce you, you'd whack me on the head and say in Strzelin that I died of a sudden influx of fluids and humours.'

Urban Horn smiled. Very evilly.

'Horn?'

'Yes, Lancelot.'

'It's easy to see that you're a worldly wise and shrewd fellow. You wouldn't by any chance know which noble family has estates in the vicinity of Brzeg?'

'And where does your curiosity — so dangerous nowadays — come from?' Urban Horn's eyes narrowed.

'Where it usually comes from: curiosity.'

'How could it be otherwise?' Horn raised the corners of his mouth in a smile, but the suspicious gleam didn't leave his eyes. 'Oh well, I shall satisfy your curiosity as far as I am able. In the vicinity of Brzeg, you say? Konradswaldau belongs to the Haugwitzes. The Bischofsheims own Jankowice, Hermsdorf is the property of the Galls ... While Schönau, from what I know, is the seat of Cup-Bearer Bertold of Apolda ...'

'Does one of them have a daughter? Young, fair-haired—'

'My knowledge doesn't extend that far,' Horn cut him off, 'and I don't usually let it. And I advise you against it, Lancelot. Noblemen can tolerate ordinary interest, but they dislike it greatly when anybody shows too much interest in their daughters. Or wives ...'

'I understand.'

'Good for you.'

Chapter Seven

In which Reynevan and company arrive in Strzelin on the Eve of the Assumption, just in time for a burning. Then those who ought to do so listen to the teachings of the Canon of Wrocław Cathedral. Some more willingly than others.

Outside the village of Höckricht, near Wiązów, the previously empty highway was a little busier. Aside from peasants' carts and merchants' wagons, there were also horsemen and soldiers, hence Reynevan considered it advisable to put his hood up. Beyond Höckricht, the road, winding among picturesque birch woodland, became empty again, and Reynevan heaved a sigh of relief. A little prematurely.

Beelzebub once again demonstrated his impressive canine intelligence. Up until then, he hadn't even growled at the soldiers passing them, but now he gave a short, sharp warning bark, unerringly sensing the intentions of some knights who unexpectedly emerged from the birch woodland on both sides of the road. The mastiff also snarled ominously when one of the servants attending them took a crossbow from his back on seeing him.

'Hey, you there! Stand still!' yelled one of the knights, as young and freckled as a quail's egg. 'Stand still, I say! Don't move!'

The mounted servant riding next to the knight slipped a foot into the stirrup of the crossbow, nimbly cocked it and mounted a bolt. Urban Horn walked his horse forward a little.

'Don't you dare shoot at the dog, Neudeck. Take a good look at him first and you'll recognise him.'

'Zounds!' The freckled knight shielded his eyes with a hand

against the flickering confusion of birch leaves being tossed around by the wind. 'Horn? Can it truly be you?'

'In person. Order your man to put the crossbow down.'

'Yes, yes. But hold the dog. As to our business here, we're a search party tracking somebody. Thus, I must ask you, Horn, who rides with you?'

'Let us first be specific,' said Urban Horn coldly. 'Who are my noble lords pursuing? If it's cattle thieves, for instance, that rules us out for plenty of reasons. *Primo*: we don't have any cattle. *Secundo*—'

'Very well, very well.' The freckled knight had already looked over the priest and the rabbi and contemptuously waved a hand. 'Just tell me: do you know them all?'

'I do. Will that suffice?'

'It will.'

'We beg your forgiveness, Reverend.' Another knight, in a sallet and full armour, bowed slightly before Father Granciszek. 'But we do not incommode you for sport. A crime has been committed and we are pursuing a murderer on the orders of Lord Reideburg, the Strzelin starosta. This is Sir Kunad of Neudeck, while I am Eustachy of Rochow.'

'What crime was it?' the priest asked. 'For God's sake – has somebody been killed?'

'Aye. Not far from here. Sir Albrecht Bart, Lord of Karczyn.'

There was silence for some time, finally broken by Urban Horn's voice. And his voice was altered.

'What? How did it happen?'

'It was most strange,' Eustachy of Rochow replied slowly, after a moment, which he spent looking at Horn suspiciously. 'Firstly, it was at high noon. Secondly, it was in combat. Were it not impossible, I'd say it was a duel. One man, mounted and armed, killed Lord Bart with a skilful sword thrust to the face, between nose and eye.'

'Where did this happen?'

'A quarter of a mile from Strzelin. Lord Bart was returning

from visiting a neighbour.'

'Alone? With no escort?'

'Such was his custom. He had no enemies.'

'Eternal rest,' muttered Father Granciszek, 'grant him, Lord. And light—'

'He had no enemies,' repeated Horn, interrupting the prayers. 'But are there any suspects?'

Kunad of Neudeck rode closer to the wagon, examining Dorota Faber's breasts with evident interest. The courtesan flashed him a charming smile. Eustachy of Rochow also rode closer, grinning. Reynevan was very pleased, for no one was looking at him.

'There are a few suspects.' Neudeck tore his gaze away from Dorota. 'Some suspicious individuals were loitering in the area – Kunz Aulock, Walter of Barby and Stork of Gorgowice. A rumour is circulating that some youth bedded a knight's wife, and that knight is now hunting the seducer, hell-bent on catching him.'

'It cannot be ruled out,' added Rochow, 'that the same libertine, chancing upon Lord Bart, panicked and killed him.'

'If so,' said Urban Horn, cleaning his ear out with a finger, 'you'll easily catch that "libertine", as you call him. He must be at least seven foot tall and four foot across the shoulders. It'd be difficult to hide someone like that among ordinary folk.'

'True,' admitted Kunad of Neudeck gloomily. 'Lord Bart was no weakling; not just any old runt could have done it ... But it may be that spells or witchcraft were used. They say that the fornicator is also a wizard.'

'By the Blessed Virgin!' squawked Dorota Faber, and Father Filip crossed himself.

'In any case, all will be revealed,' Neudeck finished. 'For when we catch up with that philanderer, we shall find out the details, oh yes, we shall ... And it won't be difficult to spot him, in any case. We know he's handsome and is riding a grey horse. Should you encounter him—'

'We shall not hesitate to inform the authorities,' Urban Horn calmly promised. 'Handsome youngster, grey horse. Can't be missed. Or confused with anything else. Farewell.'

'Gentlemen,' asked Father Granciszek, 'perhaps you know whether the Canon of Wrocław is still residing in Strzelin?'

'Indeed. He's passing judgements at the Dominican priory.'

'Is it His Eminence Notary Lichtenberg?'

'It is not,' countered Rochow. 'He is called Beess. Otto Beess.'

'Otto Beess, Provost at Saint John the Baptist's,' muttered the priest, once the knights had set off again and Dorota Faber had urged on the gelding. 'A severe man. Most severe. Oh, Rabbi, you have but faint hopes of an audience.'

'Actually, no,' said Reynevan, who had been beaming for some time. 'You will be received, Rabbi Hiram. I promise you.'

Everybody looked at him, but Reynevan only smiled mysteriously. After which, still extremely cheerful, he jumped down from the wagon and walked alongside. He hung back a little and Horn caught up with him.

'Now you see, Reinmar of Bielawa,' he said softly, 'how quickly notoriety sticks. Hired thugs are abroad, scoundrels like Kyrie-eleison and Walter of Barby, but if they kill anyone, the suspicion will fall on you first. Do you see the irony of fate?'

'I observe two things,' murmured Reynevan in reply. 'The first, that you *do* know who I am and probably have all along.'

'Probably. And the second?'

'That you knew the victim. This Albrecht Bart of Karczyn. And I'd swear you're riding to Karczyn right now. Or you were.'

'Well, well,' said Horn a moment later, 'how acute you are. And so confident. I even know where your confidence derives from. Wonderful to have friends in high places, eh? Wrocław canons? A fellow feels better at once. And safer. But that feeling can be illusory, oh, it can.'

'I know,' said Reynevan, nodding. 'I'm keeping in mind those bushes you mentioned. The humours and the fluids.'

'And so you should.'

*

The road led up a hill at the top of which was a gallows bearing three hanged men, all dried out like stockfish. And down below, Strzelin spread out before the travellers, with its colourful suburbs, city wall, castle from the times of Bolko the Stern, ancient rotunda of Saint Gotthard, and the more modern spires of the monasterial churches.

'Hey,' remarked Dorota Faber, 'something's going on down there. Is it a holiday today or something?'

Indeed, quite a large crowd had gathered outside the city wall, and a line of people were heading from the gate to join them.

'Looks like a procession of some kind,' Dorota guessed.

'A Mystery, more likely,' stated Granciszek, 'for today's the fourteenth of August, the Eve of the Assumption. On we go, Miss Dorota. Let's see it close up.'

Dorota Faber clicked her tongue at the gelding. Urban Horn called his mastiff to heel and put him on a leash, clearly aware that in a crowd even a clever dog like Beelzebub might forget himself.

The procession, approaching from the city, came close enough to their vantage point for them to make out clergymen in their vestments, monks in the habits of their orders and a number of burghers in fur-lined coats that almost touched the ground. Also present were several mounted knights in tunics decorated with coats of arms, and a dozen or so halberdiers in yellow jerkins and dully gleaming kettle hats.

'The bishop's men,' Urban Horn quietly informed them. 'And that huge knight on the bay there, with the chequerboard emblem, is Henryk of Reideburg, the Starosta of Strzelin.'

The bishop's soldiers were frogmarching three people, two men and a woman. The woman was dressed in a white shift, and one of the men was wearing a pointed, brightly painted cap.

Dorota Faber flicked the reins and yelled at the gelding and the crowd of townspeople who were reluctantly parting in front of the wagon. After descending the hill, the travellers were too low to see anything. When the throng became too dense to push through and the wagon stopped moving, they stood up for a better view.

Reynevan could now see the heads and shoulders of the three people, and the stakes they were tied to rising above their heads. The piles of brushwood stacked up around the stakes were out of his line of sight, but he knew they were there.

He heard a voice, loud and thunderous but indistinct, so muffled by the sounds of the crowd that Reynevan had difficulty making out any words.

'Crimes directed against the social order ... *Errores Hussitarum ... Fides haeretica* ... Blasphemy and sacrilege ... *Crimen* ... Proved during interrogation ...'

'It would appear,' said Urban Horn, standing up in the stirrups, 'that our dispute on the road regarding the punishment of heretical acts will soon be summarised before our very eyes.'

'It does.' Reynevan swallowed and asked the nearby townsfolk: 'Hey, friends – who are they executing?'

'Erratics,' explained a man in beggar's rags. 'They've caught some erratics. They say they're hussies or something—'

'Not hussies, horse sons,' corrected another, similarly ragged, with an identical Polish accent. 'They're going to be burned for sacrilege. For giving communion to horses.'

'Hey, you ignoramuses!' said a pilgrim from the other side of the wagon with shells sewn onto his cloak. 'They know nothing!'

'And you do?' Reynevan asked.

'Aye ... Jesus Christ be praised!' The pilgrim noticed Father Granciszek's tonsure. 'The heretics are called Hussites, from the name of their prophet Huss, not from horses. The Hussites say there's no Purgatory, and they take communion *sub utraque specie*, which means under both kinds. So they're also called Utraquists—'

'Don't lecture us,' interrupted Urban Horn, 'because we've all been educated. My companion asked you why those three are being burned at the stake.'

'That I don't know. I'm not from around here.'

'That one there,' said a local, a brickmaker judging by his

clay-spattered jacket. 'That one in the cap of shame is a Czech, a Hussite envoy, an apostate priest. He travelled here from Tábor in disguise, inciting people to revolt and burn churches down. His own countrymen recognised him, the same ones who fled Prague after 1419. And the other is Antoni Nelke, a teacher at the parish school, a local accomplice of the Czech heretic. He hid him and passed around Hussite writings.'

'And the woman?'

'That's Elżbieta Ehrlich. She's a different kettle of fish. She and her lover poisoned her husband together. The lover fled, otherwise he'd be bound to a stake, too.'

'The cat's out of the bag now,' interrupted a thin fellow with a felt cap clinging closely to his skull. 'Because it were Ehrlich's second husband they murdered. Probably poisoned the first, too, the hag.'

'Maybe she did, maybe she didn't, who can say?' A fat towns-woman in a short embroidered sheepskin jacket joined the discussion. 'They say the first one drank himself to death. He was a shoemaker.'

'Shoemaker or not,' the thin man stated, 'she poisoned him, no two ways about it. Must have dabbled in witchcraft, too, if she's upset the Dominican court—'

'If she poisoned him, it serves her right.'

'It certainly does!'

'Quiet!' called Father Granciszek, craning his neck. 'The priests are delivering the verdict and I can't hear a thing.'

'Why bother listening,' sneered Urban Horn, 'when every-thing's already been decided? The people at the stake are *haeretici pessimi et notorii*. And the Church, which abhors bloodshed, is handing the punishment of the guilty over to the *brachium saecu-lare*, the secular arm—'

'Silence, I said!' snapped Father Granciszek.

'*Ecclesia non sitit sanguinem.*' A voice, fragmented by the wind and muffled by the murmur of the crowd, reached them from the stakes. 'The Church does not wish for blood and shies away from it . . . May thus the justice and punishment of the secular arm be meted out. *Requiem aeternam dona eis . . .*'

The crowd cried out in a powerful voice. Something was happening by the stakes. Reynevan stood on tiptoe, but too late. The executioner was now behind the woman, possibly adjusting the rope around her neck. Her head lolled on her shoulder, softly, like a cut flower.

'He throttled her.' The priest sighed quietly, as though he had never seen anything like it before. 'Broke her neck. He did the same to that teacher, too. They must have shown remorse during the interrogation.'

'And turned someone in,' added Urban Horn. 'The usual story.'

The rabble howled and protested, displeased with the mercy shown to the teacher and the poisoner. The shouting grew louder when flames burst from the bundles of brushwood and suddenly exploded, in the blink of an eye engulfing the faggots, the stakes and the people tethered to them. As the fire roared and shot upwards, the crowd recoiled from the heat, making the crush even greater.

'A botch-up!' yelled the brickmaker. 'Shoddy workmanship! They used dry bloody brushwood! It's just like straw!'

'Verily, a botch-up,' said the thin man in the felt cap. 'The Hussite didn't even make a sound! They don't know how to burn. Back home in Franconia, the Abbot of Fulda knew his stuff! Supervised the burnings himself. He had the logs arranged so that first only the legs fried, then the knees, then higher, to the stones, and then—'

'Thief!' A woman hidden in the crowd began to shriek. 'Thiiieeef! Stop, thief!'

The fires roared, radiating waves of fierce heat. The wind blew towards the travellers, carrying the foul, choking, cloying smell of burning corpses. Reynevan covered his nose with his sleeve. Father Granciszek coughed, Dorota choked and Urban Horn spat, grimacing horribly. Rabbi Hiram, however, astonished everyone. The Jew leaned out from the wagon and vomited violently and copiously – on the pilgrim, the brickmaker, the townswoman, the Franconian and everybody else in the vicinity. People quickly dispersed.

'Please forgive me . . .' the rabbi managed to mumble between spasms. 'It isn't a political statement, just ordinary puking.'

Canon Otto Beess, the Provost of Saint John the Baptist's, made himself comfortable in his chair, straightened his skullcap and examined the claret swilling around in a goblet.

'Please make sure,' he said in his usual grating voice, 'that the site of the fire is thoroughly tidied and raked. All the remains – even the smallest – are to be gathered and tossed into the river. There has been an increase in the gathering of charred bones and the worshipping of them as relics. Honourable councillors, please take good care. And Brothers, see that they do.'

The Strzelin councillors present in the castle chamber bowed their heads in silence, and the Dominicans and the Friars Minor lowered their tonsured pates. Everyone present knew that the canon usually made requests rather than giving orders. They also knew the difference was only a formality.

'I ask the Predicant Friars,' continued Otto Beess, 'to please continue, in keeping with the directives of the *Inter cunctas bull*, to monitor all symptoms of heresy and the activities of Taborite emissaries, and to report the smallest, even apparently insignificant details involved with those activities. I am also counting on help from the secular arm, which I ask of you, noble Sir Henryk.'

Henryk of Reideburg bowed his head, but only slightly, then immediately straightened up his mighty frame, resplendent in a chequered paltock. The Starosta of Strzelin didn't conceal his pride or disdain, made no pretence at being humble or compliant. It was clear that he tolerated the visit of the Church hierarchy because he had to, but couldn't wait for the canon to finally leave his territory.

Otto Beess was aware of that.

'Also, noble Starosta Henryk,' he added, 'please take greater pains than hitherto in solving the murder of Sir Albrecht of Bart committed in Karczyn. The chapter is anxious to identify the perpetrators of that crime. Lord Bart, in spite of a certain peevishness and some controversial views, was a noble gentleman, a *vir rarae dexteritatis*, a great benefactor of the Henryków and Krzeszów Cistercians. We demand that his murderers be suitably punished – by which I mean the *actual* murderers. The chapter will not be content with blame being placed on a scapegoat. We do not believe that Lord Bart died at the hands of those heretics burned today.'

'Those Hussites may have had accomplices—' Reideburg said, clearing his throat.

'We do not rule that out,' said the canon, staring fixedly at the knight. 'We aren't ruling anything out. Sir Henryk, impart greater urgency to the investigation. Request, if necessary, the help of the Starosta of Świdnica, Lord Albrecht of Kolditz. Indeed, ask anyone you wish for aid, as long as there are results.'

Henryk Reideburg bowed stiffly. The canon returned the bow, but carelessly.

'Thank you, noble knight,' he said in a voice like a rusty cemetery gate creaking open. 'I shan't keep you any longer. I also thank you, gentle councillors, and you venerable friars. I won't interfere with your duties, of which, I imagine, you have plenty.'

The starosta, councillors and monks exited, shuffling their poulaines and sandals.

'You, worthy seminarists and deacons, are also aware of your duties, I don't doubt,' the Canon of Wrocław Cathedral added a moment later, 'so please attend to them. Forthwith. Our brother secretary and father confessor will remain. As will ...'

Otto Beess raised his head and fixed Reynevan with a piercing gaze.

'As will you, my lad. We have something to discuss. But first of all, I will receive the supplicants. Please call the parish priest from Oława.'

Father Granciszek entered, his face paling and flushing by

turns in an extraordinary fashion, and immediately genuflected. The canon didn't ask him to get up.

'Your problem, Father Filip,' he began, his voice grinding, 'is a lack of respect and trust towards your superiors. To possess individuality and one's own opinion is, indeed, laudable, considerably more praiseworthy than dull, ovine obedience. However, there are certain matters where one's superiors are absolutely right and infallible. Some believe they can interpret the Holy Father's decisions according to their own whims. But that is not the way! *Roma locuta, causa finita*. Which is why, my dear Father Filip, if the Church superiors tell you what you should preach, you are to comply. Even if your individuality protests and screams, you are to comply. I see you wish to speak. So speak.'

'Three-quarters of my parishioners,' mumbled Father Granciszek, 'are rather slow-witted, I'd say, *pro maiori parte illiterati et idiote*. But to the other quarter, I cannot say what the Curia instructs in my sermons. I do say that Hussites are heretics, murderers and degenerates, and that Žižka and Koranda are devils incarnate, criminals, blasphemers and iconoclasts who face eternal damnation and infernal agony. But I can't say they eat babes in arms, or that they share their wives among them. Or that—'

'Do you not understand?' the canon interrupted him sharply. 'Do you not understand my words, Father? *Roma locuta!* And for you, Wrocław is Roma. Preach what you are told to, about their common wives and their sodomy, how they eat babes and boil monks alive, and tear out the tongues of Catholic priests. If you receive such a directive, you will teach that when Hussites take communion from a goblet, hair sprouts from the roofs of their mouths and dogs' tails from their backsides. I'm not joking – I've seen the relevant documents in the bishop's chancel. As a matter of fact,' he added, looking with slight sympathy at Granciszek cowering before him, 'how do you know they don't grow tails? Have you been to Prague? To Tábor? To Hradec Králové? Have you received communion *sub utraque specie?*'

'No!' The parish priest almost choked on his breath. 'The very thought!'

'Excellent. *Causa finita*. And this audience. In Wrocław, I'll say that a reprimand sufficed, that you won't cause any more problems. And now, so you won't have the impression of a vain peregrination, you will say confession and do the penance the confessor demands of you. Father Felicjan!'

'Yes, Reverend?' replied the canon's secretary.

'Prostration before the high altar in Saint Gotthard's Church for the entire night, from Compline to Prime. The rest I leave to your own discretion.'

'May God keep you—'

'Amen. Farewell, Father.'

Otto Beess sighed and held out an empty goblet towards a seminarian, who immediately poured claret into it.

'No more petitioners today. Come with me, Reinmar.'

'Reverend Father ... Before ... I have a request ...'

'Yes?'

'I was accompanied on my journey by a rabbi from Brzeg—'

Otto Beess gestured an instruction. A moment later, a seminarian led in Hiram ben Eliezer. The Jew bowed low, sweeping the floor with his fox-fur cap. The canon scrutinised him attentively.

'What can the representative of the Brzeg Qahal want from me?' he grated. 'What brings him here?'

'You ask what brings him here, Reverend Father?' Rabbi Hiram lifted his bushy eyebrows. 'And I answer: the truth. The evangelical truth.'

'The evangelical truth?'

'And no other.'

'Speak, Rabbi Hiram. Don't make me wait.'

'When the Reverend Father commands, why then would I not speak? I say: various noble gentlemen walk around Brzeg, Oława, Grodków and the neighbouring villages, calling for the reprehensible murderers of Jesus Christ to be beaten, in order to plunder their homes and outrage their wives and daughters.

Those ruffians quote prelates to prove that the beatings, pillage and rape are the will of God and the bishops.'

'Go on, friend Hiram. I am a patient man.'

'What else can I say? I, Rabbi Hiram ben Eliezer from the Brzeg Qahal, entreat you, Reverend Father, to observe evangelical truths. If you must beat and pillage the murderers of Jesus Christ, please do so! But, by Father Moses, beat the ones who actually crucified him – by which I mean the Romans!'

Otto Beess said nothing for a long time, scrutinising the rabbi through half-closed eyes.

'Yeees,' he finally said. 'And do you know, friend Hiram, that you can be locked up for talk like that? I speak, naturally, of the secular authorities. The Church is forbearing, but the *brachium saeculare* can be harsh when it comes to blasphemy. No, no, don't say anything, friend Hiram. I shall speak now.'

The Jew bowed. The canon didn't change his position on his chair, didn't move a muscle.

'Holy Father Martin, the fifth of that name, following his enlightened predecessors, has deigned to declare that Jews, in spite of appearances, were created in God's image and some of them, albeit a small number, will attain salvation. In that case, persecution, discrimination, victimization, oppression and all other mistreatment, including forced baptism, are improper. You surely cannot doubt, friend Hiram, that the Pope's wishes are considered commands for every priest. Or perhaps you do?'

'How can I doubt it? Why, he's probably the tenth pope in a row to say the same thing . . . Thus it doubtless is the truth—'

'If you don't doubt,' interrupted the canon, pretending not to hear the mockery, 'you must understand that accusing clergymen of inciting attacks on Israelites is calumny. Unforgivable calumny.'

The Jew bowed in silence.

'Of course,' Otto Beess narrowed his eyes slightly, 'the laity knows little or absolutely nothing about papal directives. And they're pretty ignorant about the Bible, too, since they are, as somebody quite recently said, *pro maiori parte illiterati et idiote.*'

Rabbi Hiram didn't even budge.

'While your Israelite tribe, Rabbi,' continued the canon, 'stubbornly and with great pleasure, lavishes the rabble with pretexts. Here you start an epidemic of the plague by poisoning wells; there you torture an innocent little Christian girl to death; there you let a child's blood to make matzoh. You steal and desecrate sacramental bread. You engage in shameful usury and cut hunks of raw flesh from debtors who cannot afford your outrageous interest. And you earn your living from diverse other vile practices, I believe.'

'What should one do, I ask you, Reverend Father?' said Hiram ben Eliezer after a tense moment. 'What to do, to avoid such things? I mean poisoning wells, torturing little girls, letting blood and desecrating the host? What, I ask, to do?'

Otto Beess said nothing for a long time.

'Any day now,' he finally said, 'a special tax payable by all will be proclaimed, to raise funds for an anti-Hussite crusade. Every Jew will have to pay one guilder. Beyond what the Brzeg commune must give, it will also freely add ... A thousand guilders. Two hundred and fifty grzywna.'

The rabbi nodded, making no attempt to haggle.

'That money will serve our common good,' the canon said, without special emphasis, 'and, I would say, a common cause. The Czech heretics endanger us all. Mainly righteous Catholics, of course, but you Israelites have no reason to love the Hussites, either. On the contrary, in fact. It will be an opportunity, Hiram, to play a part in the vengeance, at least by making a donation.'

'Vengeance is mine,' replied Hiram ben Eliezer a moment later. 'Thus says the Lord, Adonai. Recompense to no man evil for evil, says the Lord. And our Lord, as the prophet Isaiah testifies, is generous in forgiving.

'Besides,' the rabbi added quietly, seeing that the canon had fallen silent, hands pressed against his forehead, 'the Hussites have only been murdering Jews for six years. What is six against a thousand?'

Otto Beess raised his head. His eyes were as cold as steel.

'You'll come to a sticky end, friend Hiram,' he said, grinding his teeth. 'I fear for you. Go in peace.

'Now,' he said after the Jew had closed the door, 'it's finally your turn, Reinmar. Let us talk. You mustn't worry about the secretary or the seminarian. They can be trusted. They are present, but it's as if they weren't.'

Reynevan cleared his throat, but the canon didn't let him speak.

'Duke Konrad Kantner arrived in Wrocław four days ago, on Saint Lawrence's Day, with an entourage of ghastly gossipmongers. Nor is the duke himself especially discreet. Hence, not only me, but almost the whole of Wrocław is aware of the intricacies of your affair with Adèle, Gelfrad of Stercza's wife.'

Reynevan cleared his throat again and lowered his head, unable to endure the piercing look. The canon put his hands together in prayer.

'Reinmar, Reinmar,' he said, with exaggerated dismay. 'How could you? How could you so offend the law of God and man? For, after all, it is said: marriage is honourable in all, and the bed undefiled, but God will judge whoremongers and adulterers. All too often, however, betrayed husbands consider God's justice to be too tardy and mete it out themselves – and viciously.'

Reynevan cleared his throat even louder and lowered his head even more.

'Aha,' guessed Otto Beess. 'Are they after you already?'

'They are.'

'Are they hard on your heels?'

'They are.'

'O, young fool!' said the priest a moment later. 'You ought to be locked away at once in the Narrenturm, the Tower of Fools! You would fit in perfectly with its residents.'

Reynevan sniffed and made a face which he hoped was remorseful. The canon nodded, sighed deeply and interlaced his fingers.

'You couldn't resist temptation?' he asked with the tone of an expert. 'And you dreamed about her at night?'

'I could not,' admitted Reynevan, blushing. 'And I did.'

'I know, I know.' Otto Beess licked his lips and his eyes suddenly flared wide. 'I know that forbidden fruit is sweet, as is the desire to experience a stranger's embrace. I know that the lips of a strange woman drop as a honeycomb, and her mouth is smoother than oil. But in the end, the Proverbs of Solomon teach us wisely: she is bitter as wormwood and sharp as a two-edged sword. Beware, my son, that you don't burn up like a moth in a flame. That you do not follow her to death and fall into the Abyss. Listen to the wise words of the Bible: remove thy way far from her, and come not nigh the door of her house.

'Come thee not nigh to her door,' repeated the canon, and then the preacher's exultant cadence vanished from his voice as though blown away by the wind. 'Listen carefully, Reinmar of Bielawa. Note well the words of the Bible and mine. Etch them into your memory. Listen to my advice: stay well away from the person concerned. Don't do what you intend or what I read in your eyes, young man. Stay well away from her.'

'Yes, Reverend Father.'

'The scandal will somehow ease with time. The Sterczas will be threatened with the Curia and the Landfriede, placated with the customary fee of twenty grzywna, and the standard penalty of ten grzywna will also have to be paid to Oleśnica town council. All told, it's little more than the price of a good thoroughbred horse – you'll manage to raise that with your brother's help, and if necessary, I'll pay the rest. Your uncle, the scholaster Henryk, was a good friend and teacher of mine.'

'May my thanks—'

'But I'm helpless,' the canon interrupted sharply, 'if they catch you and club you to death. Do you understand, you hot-headed fool? You must get Gelfrad of Stercza's wife out of your head once and for all, along with any thoughts of clandestine visits, letters, messengers and the like. You are to vanish. Leave the country at once. I recommend Hungary. Do you understand?'

'First I'd like to go to Balbinów . . . To visit my brother—'

'I absolutely forbid it,' Otto Beess cut him off. 'The men who hunt you no doubt expect that, as they did your visit here. Remember: when you flee, flee like a wolf. Never along well-trodden paths.'

'But my brother . . . Peterlin . . . If I really must flee—'

'I myself will inform Peterlin about everything using trusted envoys. But I forbid you from going there. Do you understand, madcap boy? You may not travel roads that your enemies know. You may not appear in places where they may be waiting for you. Which means under no circumstances go to Balbinów. Or Ziębice.'

Reynevan sighed, and Otto Beess swore.

'You didn't know,' he drawled. 'You didn't know she was in Ziębice. And I, old fool that I am, have revealed it to you. Oh well, it has happened. But it means nothing. It matters not where she is – be it Ziębice, Rome, Constantinople or Egypt, you will not go near her, son.'

'I shall not.'

'You cannot even know how much I'd like to believe you. Listen to me, Reinmar, and listen carefully. You will receive a letter; I shall ask my secretary to write it in a moment. Fear not, the document will be written in such a way that only the addressee will understand it. You will take the letter and conduct yourself like a hunted wolf. You will travel by roads you have never trodden, on which you will not be sought, to the Carmelite priory in Strzegom. You will give my letter to the prior, and he will introduce you to a certain individual. And you will say to him, when you find yourselves alone together: the eighteenth of July, 1418. He will then ask you: where? You will reply: Wrocław, the New Town. Have you got that? Repeat it.'

'The eighteenth of July, 1418. Wrocław, the New Town. What's it all for? I don't understand.'

Ignoring his question, the canon explained calmly, 'If it becomes truly dangerous, I will not save you. The only way I could protect you for certain would be to shave you a tonsure and lock you up in a Cistercian monastery, hidden from sight. But that, I expect, you would prefer to avoid. In any case, I'm unable to spirit you off to Hungary. The man I'm commending to you can. He will guarantee your safety and, if necessary, defend you. He is a fellow of quite dubious character, oftentimes of rude manner, but you must suffer it, because in certain circumstances he is indispensable. Thus, remember: Strzegom, the priory of the friars of the Order of *Beatissimae Virginis Mariae de Monte Carmeli*, outside the town walls, on the road to the Świdnica Gate. Have you got that?'

'Yes, Reverend Father.'

'You will set off without delay. Too many people have already seen you in Strzelin. As soon as you receive the letter, you will be gone.'

Reynevan sighed, for he still had a heartfelt desire to chat with Urban Horn somewhere over a mug of beer. Horn aroused great esteem and admiration in Reynevan, and had grown in his eyes at least to Sir Yvain, the Knight of the Lion. Reynevan was absolutely itching to ask Horn for his assistance in a knightly quest – the freeing of a certain oppressed maiden. He was also thinking about saying goodbye to Dorota Faber. But one didn't treat the advice and orders of Canon Otto Beess lightly.

'Father Otto . . .'

'Yes?'

'Who is the man in the Carmelite priory?'

Otto Beess said nothing for a time.

'Somebody,' he said finally, 'for whom nothing is impossible.'

Chapter Eight

In which things start splendidly, but later go downhill.

Reynevan was cheerful and happy. He was overflowing with joy, and everything around him enraptured him with its beauty. The valley of the Upper Oława, carving its meanders into the green hills, was glorious. His stocky bay colt – a gift from Canon Otto Beess – trotted nimbly along the road beside the river. A zephyr blowing from the hills bore with it heady scents – now of jasmine, now of bird cherry. And now of shit – apparently, there were human settlements in the vicinity.

Reynevan was cheerful and happy. He had every reason to be.

He hadn't managed, in spite of his efforts, to say goodbye to his erstwhile travelling companions, which he regretted, and Urban Horn's mysterious disappearance in particular had greatly disappointed him. But it was the memory of Horn that had prompted him to act.

In addition to the bay stallion with the white arrow on its forehead, Canon Otto had also given him a pouch for the road, much heavier than the one he had received a week earlier from Duke Konrad Kantner. Weighing the pouch in his hand and guessing that it contained at least thirty Prague groschen, Reynevan was once again convinced of the superiority of the priestly estate over the knightly one.

That pouch had changed his destiny.

In the Strzelin tavern he visited searching for Horn, he had come across the canon's factotum, Father Felicjan, greedily eating thick slices of fried sausage from a saucepan and washing down the grease with heavy local beer. Reynevan knew at once what to do, and he didn't even have to try too hard. The priest licked his lips at the sight of the pouch and Reynevan handed it over without a trace of regret. And without counting how much it actually contained. Naturally, he immediately obtained all the information he needed. In addition, Father Felicjan was prepared to reveal several secrets he'd heard during confession, but Reynevan politely declined since the names of the penitents didn't ring any bells, and thus their sins and peccadillos held no interest for him.

He set off for Strzelin in the morning. Almost without a farthing to his name. But cheerful and happy.

Although by no means heading in the direction the canon had instructed him to go. Rather than taking the main road westwards, towards Świdnica and Strzegom, quite contrary to the categorical ban, Reynevan rode southwards, up the Oława, along the road to Henryków and Ziębice.

He sat up straight in the saddle, smelling the pleasant fragrances borne on the wind. Little birds tweeted and the sun was shining. Ah, how beautiful was the whole world. Reynevan felt like shouting for joy.

The comely Adèle, Father Felicjan revealed to him, had managed to escape and shake off her pursuers in spite of being surrounded by her brothers-in-law in the Cistercian monastery in Ligota. She fled to Ziębice, to seek refuge in the Poor Clares convent. Indeed, the priest said, licking clean the saucepan, when Duke Jan of Ziębice found out, he unequivocally ordered the nuns to hand over his vassal's wife. He put her under house arrest until the matter of the alleged adultery was cleared up. 'But,' and here Father Felicjan belched heartily and beerily, 'although the sin demands a punishment, the woman is safe in Ziębice and is not now under threat of mob violence or harm from the Sterczas. Duke Jan,' and here Father Felicjan blew his nose, 'emphatically warned Apecz Stercza, even shook a finger at him during the audience. No, the Sterczas cannot now do any evil to their sister-in-law. Not a chance.'

Reynevan urged the bay through a meadow yellow with mullein and violet with lupins. He felt like laughing and shouting for joy. Adèle – his Adèle – had outwitted the Sterczas. They thought they had her cornered in Ligota, but she had deceived them and fled, at night, on a grey mare, with her plait flowing in the wind . . .

Just a moment, he reflected. *Adèle doesn't have a plait.*

I must control myself, he thought soberly, spurring his stallion on. *For Nicolette, the Amazon with a tunic as bright as straw, doesn't mean a thing to me. Indeed, she saved me, confused my pursuers, and I shall repay her when the occasion arises – why, I'll fall at her feet. But I love Adèle and only Adèle, the lady of my heart and my thoughts. I am definitely not enthralled by that fair plait, nor those azure eyes under that sable calpac, nor those cherry lips, nor those shapely thighs, gripping the sides of her grey mare . . .*

I love Adèle. Adèle, from whom all of three miles separate me. Were I to ride at a gallop, I'd reach the gates of Ziębice before the clock strikes noon.

Easy does it. Keep a cool head. First of all, I must visit my brother, as he is on my way. Once I've freed Adèle from her prison we shall flee to Bohemia or Hungary and I might never see Peterlin again. I have to say farewell to him, explain things. Ask for his brotherly blessing.

Canon Otto forbade me. Canon Otto ordered me to slink like a wolf, avoiding well-trodden paths. Canon Otto warned me that my pursuers might be lying in wait for me in the vicinity of Peterlin's estate . . .

But Reynevan had a solution to that, too.

Reynevan headed up a stream, hidden among the bulrushes and barely visible beneath the canopy of alders, until it joined the Oława. He knew a way that led not to Balbinów, where Peterlin lived, but to Powojowice, where he worked.

The first sign that he was close to Powojowice came from the very stream Reynevan was riding beside. First, it gave off a faint smell, then a more intense one and finally began to stink. At the same time, the water changed colour to a dirty red. Reynevan left the trees and saw the reason – some way off stood several huge wooden frames with lengths of cloth hanging from them. The colour red predominated – indicating that day's production – but there was also sky blue, navy blue and green fabric.

Reynevan knew those colours, currently associated with Piotr of Bielawa more than the hues of his family's coat of arms. He had made a tiny contribution to those colours by helping his brother obtain the dyes. The deep, vivid red came from a secret mixture of cochineal, alkanet and madder. All the shades of blue were created using a mixture of bilberry juice and woad, which he cultivated himself – a rarity in Silesia. Woad mixed with saffron and safflower gave a sumptuous, intense green.

The wind was blowing towards him, carrying with it a stench that made his eyes water and seared the little hairs in his nostrils, which emanated from components of the dye: the white lead, lye, acids, potash, white clay, ash, suet and spoiled whey used in the final stage of the bleaching process were pretty foul-smelling, but none of them rivalled the odour of the vital agent used in Powojowice – stale human urine. The urine matured for around two weeks in large vats and was then used copiously during the fulling process. The result was that the Powojowice fulling mill and its surroundings reeked to high heaven of piss, and with a favourable wind, the stench even reached the Cistercians in Henryków.

Reynevan rode along the bank of the little river, coloured red and smelling like a latrine. He could already hear the fulling mill – the relentless clatter of water-powered drive wheels, the rattle and creaking of ratchets and the grinding of gears. To that was soon added a deep, earth-shaking thudding – the banging of fulling hammers, striking the cloth in the fulling mill. Peterlin's fulling mill was modern. In addition to several traditional stations, he also possessed water-powered hammers that fulled more quickly, efficiently and evenly. And were louder.

Lower down, beyond further drying racks and a row of pits, he saw buildings, sheds and the canopy of the fulling mill. As usual, a good twenty wagons of various sizes and types were standing there, some belonging to suppliers – Peterlin imported large quantities of potash from Poland – and others belonging to weavers bringing cloth to be felted. Powojowice's reputation was such that weavers travelled there from all over. He saw master weavers crowding around the fulling mill and supervising the work, could even hear their shouts above the clatter of the machine. As usual, they were arguing with the fullers about the methods of arranging and turning the cloth on the fulling frames. He noticed among them several monks in white habits with black scapulars, which was also nothing new since the Cistercian monastery in Henryków manufactured substantial quantities of cloth and was one of Peterlin's regular customers.

But absent from all this activity was Peterlin himself. For his brother, who was very prominent in Powojowice, usually rode around the area looking dignified. Piotr of Bielawa was a knight, after all.

Even stranger was that the tall, thin figure of Nicodemus Verbruggen, a Fleming from Ghent and a great master of fulling and dyeing, was also nowhere to be seen.

Recalling the canon's warning just in time, Reynevan rode into the estate furtively, hidden behind the wagons of other customers. He lowered his hat over his nose and hunched down in the saddle to avoid drawing attention to himself.

The building, usually noisy and heaving with people, appeared quite empty. No one reacted to his shout or was alerted by the slamming of the door. There wasn't a living soul in the long entrance hall, or the servants' quarters. He entered the main chamber.

On the floor in front of the hearth sat master Nicodemus Verbruggen, grey hair cut short like a peasant's but dressed like a lord. A fire was roaring in the grate, and the Fleming was tearing up sheets of paper and throwing them into the flames. He was almost finished – a scant few sheets remained on his knees, while a whole pile was blackening and curling up in the flames.

'Master Verbruggen!'

'*Jesus Christus* ...' The Fleming raised his head and threw another sheet in the fire. '*Jesus Christus*, young Master Reinmar ... O, misfortune, Young Master ... O, dreadful misfortune ...'

'What misfortune, good sir? Where's my brother? What are you burning?'

'*Mynheer* Piotr ordered me to. He showed me a trunk and spake thus: "Nicodemus, if anything should happen, God forbid, remove the documents from this trunk and burn them, fast. But the fulling mill is to work on." Thus spake *Mynheer* Piotr. *En het woord is vlees geworden* ...'

'Master Verbruggen ...' Reynevan felt a terrible presentiment lifting the hairs on the back of his neck. 'Master Verbruggen, tell me! What are these documents? And what word has become flesh?'

Fleming pulled his head into his shoulders and threw the last sheet of paper into the fire. Reynevan leaped forward, scorching his hand as he pulled it from the flames and waved the fire out. Partially.

'What is it?'

'Killed,' Nicodemus Verbruggen said softly. Reynevan saw a tear rolling down the grey bristles on his cheek. 'Good *Mynheer* Piotr dead. They killed him. Murdered him. Young Master Reinmar ... O, misfortune, *Jesus Christus*, O, woe ...'

The door slammed shut. The Fleming looked around and realised that no one had been listening to his last words.

Peterlin's face was white. And full of pores. Like cheese. In spite of being washed, there were traces of congealed blood in the corners of his mouth.

The older knight of Bielawa lay on a bier in the middle of the village hall, among twelve burning candles. Two gold Hungarian ducats had been placed on his eyes; under his head had been laid spruce branches, whose smell, mixed with the scent of melting wax, filled the village hall with the sickly, morbid stench of death. The bier was draped with a red cloth. *Dyed with cochineal from his own dyeing works*, thought Reynevan nonsensically, feeling tears pricking his eyes.

'How ...' He stuttered with a lump in his throat. 'How ... could it ... have happened?'

Gryzelda née Der, Peterlin's wife, looked at him. Her face was flushed and swollen from weeping. Her two children, Tomasz and Sybilla, were clinging to her skirts, snivelling. But her gaze was unfriendly – downright malicious, in fact. Peterlin's father-in-law and brother-in-law, old Walpot of Der and his ungainly son Krystian, were also looking at him in a none-too-friendly way.

No one deigned to answer his question. But Reynevan had no intention of giving up.

'What happened? Will somebody just tell me?'

'Some characters killed him,' mumbled Peterlin's neighbour, Gunter of Bischofsheim.

'God will punish them for it,' added the parish priest from Wąwolnica, whose name Reynevan couldn't recall.

'He was stabbed with a sword,' said Matjas Wirt, a local land-owner. 'His horse came home riderless. At high noon.'

'At high noon,' repeated the parish priest, putting his hands together in prayer. '*Ab incursu et daemone meridiano libera nos, domine ...*'

'His horse came home,' repeated Wirt, slightly disorientated by the priestly interjection, 'with a bloodied saddle and shabrack. We began to search and found Master Piotr in the forest, at the roadside just outside Balbinów ... He must have been riding from Powojowice. The ground was churned up by hooves, evidently a band fell on him—'

'Who?'

'No one knows,' said Matjas Wirt, shrugging. 'Brigands, no doubt—'

'Would brigands have left his horse?' said Reynevan. 'That's impossible.'

'Who knows what's possible and what's not?' said Gunter of

Bischofsheim. 'Master Der and my men are scouring the forest, perhaps they'll catch somebody. We also sent word to the starosta. His men will come and investigate, find out who had reason to murder him and who would benefit from it.'

'Perhaps it was a usurer, disgruntled about an unpaid loan?' said Walpot of Der. 'Perhaps a rival dyer, wishing to rid himself of a competitor? Perhaps a client, cheated out of three broken groschen? That's how things turn out when you betray your birthright and mingle with the hoi polloi. Play at being a merchant. Judge a man by the company he keeps. Urgh! I gave you in marriage to a knight, daughter, and now you're the widow of a—'

He suddenly fell silent and Reynevan realised Der had seen his expression. Despair and fury were wrestling fiercely inside him. Reynevan fought to control himself, but his hands were trembling, as was his voice when he spoke.

'Were four horsemen seen, perchance?' he said with difficulty. 'Four armed men? One tall, moustachioed, in a studded jacket . . . One short, with a pimply face—'

'Aye, there were,' said the priest unexpectedly. 'Yesterday, in Wąwolnica, near the church. Just as the angelus was tolling . . . They looked like stern swordsmen. Four of them. The horsemen of the Apocalypse, in sooth.'

'I knew it!' screamed Gryzelda in a voice hoarse and strained from crying, shooting a look worthy of a basilisk at Reynevan. 'I knew as soon as I saw you, you scoundrel! It's because of you! Because of your trespasses and misdeeds!'

'Another Bielawa.' Walpot Der emphasised the title with a sneer. 'Also a nobleman. But this one dabbles in leeches and enemas.'

'Scoundrel, ne'er-do-well!' Gryzelda's screams grew louder and louder. 'Whoever orphaned these children was on your trail! Nothing but woe do you cause! All you ever brought your brother was shame and distress! What do you want here? Sniffing around for an inheritance, you vulture? Begone! Begone from my house!'

Reynevan barely succeeded in controlling his trembling hands, but he couldn't find his voice. He was seething inside with rage and fury, fighting a great urge to tell the Ders what he thought about their entire family, who were only able to play at being lords and ladies thanks to the money Peterlin earned from the fulling mill. But he restrained himself. Peterlin was dead. He lay, murdered, with Hungarian ducats on his eyes, in his own village hall, among smoking candles, resting on a red cloth, on a bier. Peterlin was dead. It was revolting to quarrel and bicker in the presence of his corpse. The very thought sickened him. Furthermore, Reynevan feared that he would collapse into tears if he opened his mouth.

He left without a word.

Mourning and dejection hung over the village of Balbinów. It was empty and silent, the servants having made themselves scarce, prudently staying out of the way of the grief-stricken mourners. Not even the dogs were barking. There were no dogs to be seen. Apart from . . .

He rubbed his tear-filled eyes. The black mastiff sitting between the stable and the washhouse was no apparition. Nor did it have any intention of vanishing.

Reynevan glanced quickly around the courtyard and entered the building via the coach house. He walked beside a trough – the building was simultaneously a cowshed and a pigsty – and reached the horses' stalls. Kneeling in the corner of the stall usually occupied by Peterlin's horse, on straw he had swept aside, jabbing a knife into the clay floor, was Urban Horn.

'What you're searching for isn't here,' said Reynevan, amazed at his own calmness. Horn, surprisingly, didn't look at all nonplussed. He met Reynevan's eyes, staying where he was.

'What you're searching for was concealed somewhere else. But it doesn't exist any longer. It was destroyed by fire.'

'Indeed?'

'Indeed.' Reynevan pulled from his pocket a charred piece of paper and threw it carelessly down onto the clay floor. Horn still didn't stand up.

'Who killed Peterlin?' Reynevan took a step forward. 'Did the Sterczas hire Kunz Aulock and his gang? Did they also kill Lord Bart of Karczyn? What have you to do with this, Horn? Why are you here in Balbinów, barely half a day after my brother's death? How do you know his hiding place? Why are you looking for the documents that went up in smoke in Powojowice? And what were those documents?'

'Flee from here, Reinmar,' drawled Urban Horn. 'Flee from here, if you value your life. Don't even wait for your brother's funeral.'

'Answer my questions first, beginning with the most important: what links you to the murder? What links you to Kunz Aulock? Don't even try lying!'

'I won't try,' replied Horn, without lowering his gaze, 'either to lie, or to answer. For your own good, actually. It may surprise you, but that is the truth.'

'I'll make you answer.' Reynevan took another step and drew a dagger. 'I'll make you, Horn. By force, if necessary.'

The only sign that Horn had whistled were his pursed lips, for the sound was inaudible. But only to Reynevan, for a moment later, something struck him in the chest with tremendous force, slamming him onto the dirt floor. Pinned down by the weight, he opened his eyes to see Beelzebub's full set of huge teeth bared in front of him. The mastiff's saliva dripped down onto his face, the stench making him nauseous. A malevolent, throaty growl paralysed him with fear. Urban Horn appeared in his field of view, putting the charred paper into his jerkin.

'You won't make me do anything, my lad,' said Horn, straightening the chaperon on his head. 'But listen to what I'll tell you out of kindness. Beelzebub, stay.'

Beelzebub stayed. Although it was clear he was itching to move.

'Out of kindness do I advise you, Reinmar,' repeated Horn. 'Flee. Vanish. Listen to the advice of Canon Beess. Because I wager my life that he gave you some advice, some guidance on how to get out of the quandary you find yourself in. Don't disregard the counsel and instructions of people like Canon Beess, lad. Beelzebub, stay.

'I am truly sorry about your brother. You have no idea how much. Farewell. And beware.'

When Reynevan opened his eyes – which he had kept tightly shut before Beelzebub's menacing muzzle – neither the dog nor Horn were in the barn.

Reynevan crouched on his brother's grave, huddled up and trembling with fear. He sprinkled all around himself a mixture of salt and hazel ash and repeated a charm in a trembling voice, believing less and less in its effectiveness with every repetition.

> *Wirfe saltze, wirfe saltze*
> *Non timebis a timore nocturno*
> *Neither a plague, nor a guest from the darkness*
> *Nor a demon*
> *Wirfe saltze, wirfe saltze . . .*

Monsters seethed and murmured in the darkness.

Aware of the risk and the time he was wasting, Reynevan had waited for his brother's burial. Despite the efforts of his sister-in-law and her family, he would not be discouraged from keeping vigil over the corpse, and he took part in the exequies and funeral mass. He was there, with the sobbing Gryzelda, the parish priest and a small cortège when Peterlin was buried in the cemetery behind the small, old Wąwolnica church. Only then did he depart. Or rather – pretend to depart.

When dusk fell, Reynevan hurried back to the cemetery. On the freshly dug grave, he arranged his magical instruments, which he had assembled with surprisingly little difficulty. The oldest part of the Wąwolnica cemetery adjoined a ravine hollowed out by a small river; the ground had subsided there, offering easy access to the ancient graves, so Reynevan's magical arsenal even included a coffin nail and a skeleton's finger.

Nothing helped, however, not the finger bone, nor the monks-hood, sage and chrysanthemum picked near the cemetery, nor the charm whispered over an ideogram furrowed in the soil with a crooked coffin nail. Peterlin's soul, in spite of the assurances in the magic books, did not rise up over the grave in ethereal form. It didn't speak. Or give a sign.

If only I had my books here, thought Reynevan, resentful and disheartened by his repeated failures. *If I had* The Lesser Key of Solomon *or the Necronomicon ... A Venetian crystal ... A little mandrake ... If I had access to an alembic and could distil an elixir ... If ...*

It wasn't to be. His grimoires, the crystal, the mandrake and the alembic were far away, in Oleśnica. In the Augustinian priory. Or – more likely – in the Inquisition's possession.

A storm was swiftly approaching beyond the horizon. The rumbling of thunder accompanying the flashes of lightning intensified. Then the wind dropped completely and the air became as lifeless and heavy as a shroud. It must have been close to midnight.

And then it began.

Another flash of lightning lit up the church. Reynevan saw in horror that the entire bell tower was teeming with spider-like creatures. In front of his very eyes, several stone crosses moved and slumped over, and in the distance, one of the graves visibly bulged. The crunching of coffin planks followed by a loud squelching resounded from the darkness over the ravine. And then came a howling.

His hands were jumping as if he were feverish as he sprayed more salt around, and his lips barely let him mutter the formulae of the spell.

Most of the movement was occurring in the ravine, in the oldest part of the cemetery covered in alders. Fortunately, Reynevan couldn't see what was going on there; not even the lightning revealed anything more than vague shapes and contours in the gloom. But the sounds provided intense impressions – the throng rooting around among the ancient graves stamped, roared, wailed, whistled, cursed, snapped their jaws and gnashed their teeth.

Wirfe saltze, wirfe saltze ...

A woman laughed shrilly and spasmodically. A baritone voice mockingly parodied the liturgy of the Mass, accompanied by wild cackling. Somebody was banging a drum.

A skeleton emerged from the gloom. It pottered around a little, then sat down on a grave and stayed there, skull bent forward and resting in its bony hands. A moment later, a shaggy creature with huge feet sat down beside it and began to frantically scratch them, grunting and moaning. The pensive skeleton paid no attention.

A death cap mushroom passed by on spidery legs, followed by something resembling a pelican, but with scales instead of feathers and a beak full of pointed fangs.

An enormous frog hopped onto an adjacent grave.

And Reynevan was aware of another presence, something utterly hidden in the darkness, invisible even in the flashes of lightning. But he knew it was staring at him, and closer examination revealed eyes shining like rotting wood. And long teeth.

'*Wirfe saltze.*' He sprinkled the last of the salt in front of himself. '*Wirfe saltze ...*'

Suddenly, a bright, slow-moving spot caught his attention. He tracked it, waiting for another flash of lightning. When it came, he saw to his amazement a girl in a white shift, picking large, spreading nettles and laying them in a basket. The girl saw him, too. After a moment's hesitation, she put the basket down. She paid no attention whatsoever to either the sorrowful skeleton or the shaggy creature still poking between his huge toes.

'Pleasure?' she asked. 'Or duty?'

'Errr ... duty ...' he said, overcoming his fear and understanding what she meant. 'My brother ... my brother was killed. He's buried here ...'

'Aha,' she said, brushing aside strands of hair from her forehead. 'And as you see, I'm here picking nettles.'

'To sew a blouse,' he said with a sigh a moment later. 'For your brothers, magicked into swans?'

She was silent for a long while.

'You're odd,' she finally said. 'The nettles are for cloth, to be sure. For shirts. But not for my brothers. I don't have any brothers. And if I had, I'd never let them wear these shirts.'

She laughed throatily on seeing his expression.

'Why are you even talking to him, Eliza?' said the toothy something, still mostly invisible in the darkness. 'Why bother? The rain will come just before dawn and wash his salt away. Then his head will be bitten off.'

'It's not right,' said the sorrowful skeleton, not raising its skull. 'It's not right.'

'Of course it isn't,' the girl addressed as Eliza replied with a nod. 'He's Toledo. One of us. And few of us are left.'

'Wanted to talk to a stiff,' declared a dwarf with buck teeth, appearing out of nowhere. He was as plump as a pumpkin, his bare belly shining beneath a short, frayed waistcoat.

'Wanted to talk to a stiff,' he repeated. 'With his brother, what's buried here. Wanted answers to his questions. But he didn't get any.'

'Then it behoves us to help,' said Eliza.

'It does,' said the skeleton.

'Sure,' croaked the frog.

Lightning flashed; thunder boomed. A wind sprang up, whispered in the dried stalks, whipping and spinning clouds of dry leaves. Without hesitation, Eliza crossed the salt and shoved Reynevan hard in the chest. He fell over onto the grave, banging the back of his head on the cross. He saw stars, then everything went dark, then saw flashes again, but this time from the lightning. The earth beneath him trembled and whirled around. Two rings of shadowy, dancing shapes cavorted, spinning in opposite directions around Peterlin's grave.

'Barbelo, Hekate, Holda!'

'*Magna Mater!*'

'Eia!'

The ground beneath him rocked and tipped so steeply that Reynevan had to spread out his arms to stop himself from sliding as his feet scrabbled vainly for purchase. But he didn't fall. Sounds and singing filled his ears. Apparitions filled his eyes.

'Veni, veni, venias,'
ne me mori, ne me mori facias!
Hyrca! Hyrce! Nazaza!
Trillirivos! Trillirivos! Trillirivos!

Adsumus, says Percival, kneeling before the Holy Grail. *Adsumus*, repeats Moses, stooped beneath the weight of the stone tablets brought down from Sinai. *Adsumus*, says Jesus, falling beneath the weight of the cross. *Adsumus*, repeat the knights gathered around the table with one voice. *Adsumus! Adsumus!* We are here, O Lord, gathered in Your name.

An echo runs through the castle like booming thunder, like the sound of a distant battle, like the thudding of a battering ram against a castle gate. And slowly vanishes among the dark corridors.

'Viator, the Wanderer, will come,' says a young girl with a vulpine face and dark circles under her eyes, adorned in a garland of verbena and clover. 'Someone departs, someone comes. *Apage! Flumen immundissimum, draco maleficus* ... Ask not after my name, it is secret. Out of the eater came forth meat, and out of the strong came forth sweetness. And who is to blame? The one who will tell the truth.

'They shall be gathered together, as prisoners in the pit, and shall be shut up in the prison, and after many years shall they be punished. Beware the Wallcreeper, beware the bats, beware the demon that wasteth at noonday, and beware the one that walketh in darkness. *Love*, says Hans Mein Igel, *love will save your life. Do you regret it?'* asks the girl smelling of sweet flag and mint. *'Do you regret it?'* The girl is naked, yet innocent, *nuditas virtualis*. She is barely visible in the gloom, but so close Reynevan can sense her warmth.

The sun, the serpent and the fish. The serpent, the fish and the sun set in a triangle. The Narrenturm falls, the *turris fulgurata* crumbles away, the tower is struck by lightning. The poor fool falls from it, tumbles down, towards destruction. *I am that fool*, a thought flashes through Reynevan's head, *a fool and a madman, I am the one falling, tumbling into the abyss.*

A burning man runs screaming across a thin cover of snow from a burning church.

Reynevan shook his head to drive away the apparitions. And then, in the glare of another flash of lightning, he saw Peterlin.

A spectre, motionless as a statue, suddenly glowing with an unnatural light. Reynevan saw that the light, like beams of sunlight through the cracks in a shed, was shining through numerous wounds – in his breast, his neck and his belly.

'Oh, God, Peterlin . . .' he groaned. 'How terribly they . . . They will pay for this, I swear! I will avenge you . . . I will avenge you, dear brother . . . I vow . . .'

The spectre made a vigorous gesture. Clearly opposing, forbidding. Yes, it was Peterlin, for no one but their father gestured like that when he opposed or forbade something, when he reprimanded little Reynevan for japes or madcap ideas.

'Peterlin . . . Dear brother . . .'

The same gesture, even more vehement and emphatic. Leaving no room for doubt. The hand, pointing south.

'Flee,' said the spectre in the voice of Eliza of the nettles. 'Flee, little one. Far away. As far away as you can. Beyond the forests. Before the dungeon of the Narrenturm claims you. Flee, leaping across the mountains, bounding over the hills, *saliens in montibus, transiliens colles.*'

The ground whirled furiously. And everything ended in darkness.

The rain awoke him at dawn. He was lying on his brother's grave on his back, motionless and numb, raindrops splashing on his face.

*

'Permit me, young man,' said Otto Beess, canon of Saint John the Baptist's and provost of the Wrocław Chapter. 'Permit me to succinctly recapitulate what you've told me and what has made me stop believing my own ears. Thus, Konrad, Bishop of Wrocław, having the opportunity to tan the Sterczas' hides, who genuinely hate him and whom he genuinely detests, does nothing. Having almost irrefutable proof that the Sterczas are embroiled in a family feud and murder, Bishop Konrad is taking no steps to deal with this matter. Is that right?'

'Precisely so,' replied Gwibert Bancz, the Bishop of Wrocław's secretary, a young seminarian with a pretty face, faultless skin and soft velvet eyes. 'It has been decided. No measures against the Stercza family. No interrogations. Not even a reprimand. The bishop decreed it in the presence of His Excellency Bishop Suffragan Tylman. And in the presence of the knight to whom the investigation was entrusted. The one who rode to Wrocław this morning.'

'The knight,' repeated the canon, staring at a painting portraying the martyrdom of Saint Bartholomew, the only decoration on the chamber's severe walls apart from some shelves holding candlesticks and a crucifix. 'The knight who came to Wrocław this morning.'

Gwibert Bancz swallowed. The situation was embarrassing and always had been. And there was nothing to suggest it would ever change.

'Precisely.' Otto Beess drummed his fingers on the table, focusing all his attention on the saint being tortured by the Armenians. 'Precisely. Who is that knight, my son? Name? Family? Arms?'

The seminarian cleared his throat. 'Neither name nor family were mentioned . . . He wore no coat of arms, was entirely attired in black. But I have seen him with the bishop before.'

'So what did he look like? Must I drag it out of you?'

'Youngish. Tall, slim . . . Black, shoulder-length hair. Long nose, almost a beak ... *Tandem* a gaze that is almost ... bird-like ... Piercing ... *In summa*, difficult to call him handsome ... But manly—'

Gwibert Bancz suddenly broke off. The canon didn't turn his head, didn't even stop drumming his fingers. He knew Bancz's concealed erotic predilections, and that knowledge had allowed him to turn the young seminarian into his informer.

'Go on.'

'So, this unknown knight – who, incidentally, evinced neither humility, nor reticence of any kind in the bishop's presence – reported on the investigation into the case of the murders of Lords Bart of Karczyn and Piotr of Bielawa. And it was such a report that His Excellency the bishop suffragan could not restrain himself at one point and began to laugh ...'

Otto Beess raised his eyebrows.

'That knight said the Jews were to blame, since near the place of both crimes one could smell *foetor judaicus*, the typical stench of Jews ... In order to remove that odour, Jews drink Christian blood, as is commonly known. Thus, the killings, the stranger continued – heedless of the fact that the Reverend Tylman was splitting his sides laughing – bore the marks of a ritual murder and the culprits should be sought in the local qahals, particularly in Brzeg, since the rabbi of Brzeg had just been seen in the vicinity of Strzelin, in the company, to boot, of the young Reinmar of Bielawa, who, as Your Excellency knows—'

'I know. Go on.'

'Hearing such a *dictum*, the Reverend Bishop Suffragan Tylman declared it all poppycock, saying that both had been murdered with swords. Added that the said Albrecht of Bart was a strongman and a born swordsman. And that no rabbi – not from Brzeg or anywhere else – could have overcome Lord Bart, even if they had chosen to fight with Talmuds. And began to laugh again.'

'And the knight?'

'He said that if the Jews hadn't killed the noble gentlemen Bart and Piotr, then the Devil must have. So, in essence it's all one.'

'And what was Bishop Konrad's response?'

'His Eminence,' the seminarian cleared his throat, 'glared at Reverend Bishop Tylman, evidently displeased by his merriment, and spoke at once, most sternly, seriously and officially, and ordered me to note it down—'

'He discontinued the investigation,' interrupted the canon, very slowly pronouncing the words. 'He simply discontinued the investigation.'

'It is as if you had been there. And the Reverend Bishop Suffragan Tylman didn't say a word, but his expression was strange. Bishop Konrad noticed that and said, angrily, that the argument was in his favour, that history would testify to it, and that it was *ad maiorem Dei gloriam*.'

'He said that?'

'Using those very words. For that reason, Reverend Father, don't take this matter to the bishop. I guarantee it won't change anything. Furthermore—'

'Furthermore what?'

'The stranger told the bishop that if he invoked anyone, submitted any petitions or demanded further investigation, he insisted on being informed about it.'

'He insisted,' repeated Otto Beess. 'And how did the bishop respond?'

'He nodded.'

'Well, well – Konrad, an Oleśnica Piast – nodded.'

'He did, Reverend Father.'

Once again, Otto Beess looked at the painting, at the torture of Bartholomew, from whom the Armenians were flaying long strips of skin using enormous pliers. *Were one to believe the* Golden Legend *of Jacobus da Varagine*, he thought, *the sweet scent of roses hung over the place of his martyrdom. Like hell. Torture stinks. A stench hangs over all places of torment and torture, as it did over Golgotha. I swear there weren't any roses there, either. There was, how aptly,* foetor judaicus.

'Please, my boy. Take it.'

The seminarist, as usual, first reached for the pouch, then abruptly withdrew his hand as though the canon had offered him a scorpion.

'Reverend Father . . .' he mumbled. 'I don't do it for . . . for a few paltry pennies . . . but because—'

'Take it, my son, take it,' interrupted the canon with a condescending smile. 'I've already told you on other occasions that an informer must receive payment. One most despises those who inform for nothing. For idealistic reasons. Out of fear. Out of anger and envy. I've told you before: Judas deserves contempt less for his betrayal and more for doing it so cheaply.'

The afternoon was bright and warm, a pleasant change after several days of rainy weather. The spire of Mary Magdalene's Church and the roofs of houses gleamed in the sun. Gwibert Bancz stretched. It had been freezing at the canon's. The chamber was in shade, the walls were cold.

Aside from his premises in the chapter house on Cathedral Island, Provost Otto Beess had a house in Wrocław in Shoemakers Street, not far from the town square, where he usually received people whose visits ought to go unnoticed, and Gwibert Bancz's was one of those. So Gwibert Bancz decided to make use of the opportunity. He didn't feel like going back to the island, for it was unlikely the bishop would need him before Vespers, and from Shoemakers Street it was a short distance to a certain beer cellar he knew just past the Poultry Market. He could spend some of the money he had received from the canon there. Gwibert Bancz firmly believed he was ridding himself of sin by ridding himself of the money.

Nibbling a pretzel purchased at a stall he had just passed, he took a shortcut by ducking into a narrow alley. It was quiet and deserted there; so deserted that rats, alarmed by his appearance, scurried away from his feet.

Hearing the rustle of feathers and the flapping of wings behind him, he looked back and saw a large wallcreeper perching ungainly on a frieze above a bricked-up window. Bancz dropped the pretzel, stepped back and recoiled.

Before his very eyes, the bird slid down the wall, scraping it with its claws. It became blurred. Grew in size. And changed shape. Bancz wanted to scream but not a sound emerged from his constricted throat.

Where the wallcreeper had been a moment before, now stood the knight the seminarist knew. Tall, slim, black-haired, dressed in black, with the piercing eyes of a bird.

Bancz opened his mouth again, and again could utter nothing except a soft croak. The Wallcreeper moved fluidly towards him. Now quite close, he smiled, winked and pursed his lips, blowing the seminarist a very erotic kiss. Before the seminarist knew what was happening, he glimpsed the flash of a blade as he was stabbed in the belly and blood spurted onto his thighs. He was stabbed a second time in the side, the knife crunching on his ribs. His back slammed against the wall as a third blow almost pinned him to it.

Before Bancz could find it in himself to yell, the Wallcreeper leaped forward and slit open his throat with a sweeping slash.

Some beggars found the corpse curled up, lying in a black puddle. Before the town guard appeared, merchants and stallholders had sped over from the Poultry Market.

A ghastly, choking, gut-wrenching air of dread hung above the scene of the crime.

A dread so terrible that while the crowd waited for the guard to arrive, no one dared to steal the pouch protruding from the victim's slashed-open mouth.

'*Gloria in excelsis Deo,*' intoned Canon Otto Beess, lowering his touching palms and bowing his head before the altar. '*Et in terra pax hominibus bonae voluntatis . . .*'

The deacons stood on either side, joining him in song with hushed voices. Otto Beess continued to celebrate the Mass, mechanically, routinely, but his thoughts were elsewhere.

Laudamus te, benedicimus te, adoramus te,
glorificamus te, gratias agimus tibi . . .

The seminarist Gwibert Bancz has been murdered. In broad day-light, in the centre of Wrocław. And Bishop Konrad, who dropped the investigation into the murder of Peterlin of Bielawa, will also likely drop the investigation into his secretary's murder. I don't know what's happening here. But one needs to take care of one's own safety. Never, under any circumstances, give a pretext or opportunity, and never allow oneself to be taken by surprise.

The singing soared up to the high vault of Wrocław Cathedral.

Agnus Dei, Filius Patris, qui tollis peccata mundi,
miserere nobis;
Qui tollis peccata mundi, suscipe deprecationem
nostram . . .

Otto Beess knelt down before altar.

I hope, he thought, crossing himself, *I hope that Reynevan made it to . . . That he's safe now. I truly hope . . .*

Miserere nobis . . .

The Mass continued.

Four horsemen galloped over the crossroads, beside a stone cross, one of Silesia's numerous reminders of crimes past and belated contrition. The wind howled, the rain lashed down and mud splashed up from hooves. Kunz Aulock swore, wiping water from his face with a wet glove. Stork of Gorgowice echoed him still more crudely under his dripping hood. Walter of Barby and Sybek of Kobylagłowa didn't even feel like swearing. *Let's ride as quickly as possible*, they were thinking, *to any old tavern, into the warm and dry for a mug of mulled ale.*

Mud splashed from the horses' hooves, muddying the already muddied, cloaked figure huddled by the cross. None of the riders paid the figure any attention.

And nor did Reynevan raise his head.

Chapter Nine

In which Scharley makes an appearance.

The prior of Strzegom Carmelite priory was as thin as a skeleton; his complexion, dry skin, carelessly shaved stubble and long nose made him resemble a plucked heron. When he looked at Reynevan, he squinted, and when he resumed reading the letter from Otto Beess, he brought the letter close up to his nose. His bony blue hands trembled relentlessly and pain kept contorting his mouth. The prior was by no means an old man, but Reynevan had seen this illness before, which ate its victim away like leprosy – but invisibly, from the inside. An illness against which all medicines and herbs were powerless, against which only the most powerful magic was effective. Even if someone knew how to treat it using magic, they didn't, because times were such that once the patient was cured, they were liable to denounce the physician.

Clearing his throat, the prior shook Reynevan out of his reverie.

'Only for this one thing did you await my return, young man?' he asked, picking up the Wrocław canon's letter. 'Four whole days? Aware that the subprior has full authority during my absence?'

Reynevan limited himself to a nod. Reference to the condition of handing the letter directly to the prior was so blatantly obvious, it didn't bear mentioning. As regards the four days spent in the village near Strzegom, there was no point mentioning them, either – they had passed God knew when, like in a dream. For Reynevan, the time since the tragedy in Balbinów felt like a dream. He was numb, distracted and befuddled.

'You waited,' the prior stated a fact, 'to hand me the letter in person. And do you know what, young fellow? It is very good that you did.'

Reynevan didn't comment this time, either. The prior returned to the letter, bringing it up almost to his very nose.

'Oh, yes,' he finally said in a slow, drawling voice, raising his eyes and squinting. 'I knew the day would come, when the reverend canon would remind me of my debt and demand repayment. With usurious interest – which, incidentally, the Church forbids the collection of. Young fellow, do you believe unreservedly in what the Church, our mother, demands?'

'Yes, Reverend Father.'

'A commendable virtue. Especially today. Especially in a place like this. Do you know where you are? Do you know what this place is? Apart from a priory?'

Reynevan did not reply.

'You either don't know,' the prior guessed from the silence, 'or are adroitly pretending not to. For this is a house of penance, with which you may also be unfamiliar or pretend to be so. Thus, shall I tell you: it is a prison.'

The prior fell silent, folded his hands together and looked intently at his interlocutor. Reynevan, naturally, had guessed the priory's purpose some time before but had kept it to himself. He didn't want to spoil the Carmelite's pleasure that conducting a conversation like this was clearly giving him.

'Do you know,' continued the monk, 'what His Excellency the canon deigns to ask of me in this letter?'

'I do not, Reverend Father.'

'Your ignorance partially excuses you. But because I know, nothing can excuse me. In the process, if I refuse the request, my own wrongdoing will be excused. What do you say to that? Doesn't my logic rival that of Aristoteles?'

Reynevan didn't reply and the prior fell silent. After a while, he used a candle to set light to the canon's letter, turned it over to allow the flame to catch hold and tossed it onto the floor.

Reynevan watched the paper curl up, blacken and crumble. *And thus, my hopes crumble to ash,* he thought. *Besides, they are untimely, senseless and vain. So, perhaps it's better things happened this way.*

The prior stood up.

'Go to the hosteller,' he said briefly and dryly. 'Have him give you food and drink, then afterwards hasten to our church where you'll meet the one you are meant to meet. Orders will be issued; you'll both be able to leave the priory without any hindrance. Canon Beess stressed in his letter that the two of you will embark on a long journey to distant places. I'll add that it's very good the journey will be long. It would, in fact, be a great error not to go far enough away. And return too soon.'

'Thank you, Your Excellency—'

'Don't thank me. And if it occurs to one of you to seek my blessing before you set off, please give up that thought, too.

The vittles at the priory were indeed like prison food. Reynevan, however, was still too distressed and apathetic to notice. Furthermore, he was simply too hungry to turn his nose up at salted herring, kasha without grease and beer which differed from water only in its colour, and then only slightly. Or perhaps it was actually a fast day? He couldn't remember.

So, he ate briskly and hungrily, which the old hosteller observed with evident satisfaction, no doubt used to much less enthusiasm from his guests. Scarcely had Reynevan dealt with the herring than the smiling monk gave him another, plucked straight from a barrel. Reynevan determined to exploit that show of friendship.

'A veritable fortress, this priory of yours,' he said with his mouth full. 'No wonder, either, for I know what purpose it serves. But I see no armed guards. Have none of the monks performing penance ever escaped?'

'Oh, my son, my son.' The hosteller shook his head at Reynevan's naive obtuseness. 'Escape? But why? Don't forget who's performing penance here. Penance will one day be over for each of them. And although none of the men here is doing penance *pro nihilo*, the end of it erases their guilt. *Nullum crimen*, everything returns to normal. But an escapee? He would be an outlaw till the end of his days.'

'I see.'

'Good, for I'm not permitted to talk about it. More kasha?'

'With pleasure. And these penitents, for what misdeeds, I wonder, are they in here for?'

'I'm not permitted to say.'

'Oh, I'm not asking about specific cases, just in general terms.'

The steward cleared his throat and glanced around apprehensively, no doubt aware that in the house of penance, even the kitchen walls, hung with frying pans and garlic, might have ears.

'Oh,' he said softly, rubbing his hands, oily from herrings, on his habit. 'They are doing penance for diverse things, my son, for diverse things. They are mainly sinful priests and monks, men whose vows bore down too heavily on them. Imagine it yourself: vows of obedience, humility, poverty, abstinence and moderation ... As they say: *plus bibere, quam orare*. And a vow of chastity, regrettably ...'

'*Femina*,' guessed Reynevan, '*instrument diaboli?*'

'If it were only *femina* ...' The steward sighed, raising his eyes. 'Oh, boundless sins, boundless, it cannot be denied. But here there are graver matters – much graver ... But I'm not permitted to talk about that. Eaten your fill, my son?'

'I have. Many thanks. It was delicious.'

'Come whenever you wish.'

Inside the church, it was extremely gloomy. The glow of candles and the light from the narrow window fell only in the region of the altar itself, the tabernacle, the crucifix and a triptych depicting the Lamentation. The rest of the chancel, the entire nave, the wooden galleries and the choir stalls were plunged in murky semi-darkness. *Perhaps it's intentional*. Reynevan couldn't rid himself of the thought. *Perhaps it's so that during prayers, the penitents can't see each other's faces and don't guess at other men's sins and offences. And compare them with their own.*

'I'm here.'

The deep, resonant voice that boomed from an alcove hidden between the choir stalls had a depth of gravity and dignity. But it was probably only an echo from the domed vault, moving around the stone walls. Reynevan moved closer.

A picture of Saint Anne with the Virgin Mary on one knee and Jesus on the other towered over the confessional, which exuded a faint aroma of incense and linseed oil. The painting was lit by a cresset, which had the effect of plunging the surroundings into an even dimmer gloom, hence Reynevan could only see the outline of the man sitting inside the confessional.

'So, I ought to thank you for the chance of regaining my freedom of movement,' said the man, setting off more echoes. 'Thus, I thank you. Although it seems to me that a certain Wrocław canon is the person I ought to be more grateful to, perhaps? And an event that took place ... Well, say it for form's sake, so I can be completely certain I'm talking to the right person. And that this isn't a dream.'

'The eighteenth of July, 1418.'

'Where?'

'Wrocław. The New Town ...'

'Of course,' confirmed the man a moment later. 'Of course, it was Wrocław. Where else, if not there? Very well. Now come closer and assume the required position.'

'I beg your pardon?'

'Kneel.'

'My brother has been killed,' said Reynevan, not moving, 'and my life is threatened. I'm being pursued and must flee. But first I have to take care of a few things, and settle a few scores. Father Otto assured me you'd be able to help me. You and no other, whoever you are. But I have no intention of kneeling before you ... How should I address you? Father? Brother?'

'However you like. Uncle, if you wish. I couldn't care less.'

'I'm not in the mood for jokes. I told you: my brother's been killed. The prior said we can get out of here. So, let's leave this sorrowful place. And on the way I'll tell you what needs doing. You'll know enough, but nothing more.'

'I asked you to kneel.' The echo of the man's voice rumbled still more deeply.

'And I told you: I have no intention of confessing to you.'

'Whoever you are,' said the man, 'you can choose one of two ways. One leads to me, on your knees. The other leads through the priory gate. Without me, naturally. I'm not in anyone's pay, laddie, nor a thug hired to take care of your affairs and settle your scores. It is I, take careful note, who decides how much and what information I need. In any case, it is all about mutual trust. You don't trust me, so how am I to trust you?'

'The fact that you're leaving prison is down to me,' Reynevan snapped back pugnaciously. 'And Father Otto. Take note of that and don't get too big for your boots. It's not me but you who is facing a choice. Either leave with me or rot in here. The choice—'

The man interrupted him by knocking loudly against the wood of the confessional.

'You ought to know that hard choices are nothing new to me,' he said a moment later. 'You act arrogantly, thinking it daunts me. Earlier this morning, I knew nothing of your existence, and later this evening, if needs be, I'll forget about it. I repeat – for the last time – either make your confession as an expression of trust, or be gone. Make haste with your choice, for it'll soon be Sext, and they strictly observe the liturgy of canonical hours here.'

Reynevan clenched his fists, fighting the overwhelming urge to turn and leave, go out into the sunshine, fresh air, greenery and open space. He finally swallowed his pride. Common sense prevailed.

'I don't even know if you are a priest,' he stammered out, kneeling on the polished wood.

'It doesn't matter.' Reynevan could hear something like

mockery in the man's voice. 'All I care about is a confession. Don't expect absolution.'

'I don't even know what to call you.'

'The world knows me by many names,' came back the voice from behind the grille, softly but clearly. 'Since I have the chance to be reintroduced into the world, I ought to choose something ... Willibald of Hirsau? Or perhaps, hmm ... Benignus of Aix? Or perhaps ... perhaps ... Master Scharley? What do you think, laddie: Master Scharley? Very well, don't make faces. Simply Scharley. All right?'

'Very well. Let's get on with it, Scharley.'

Barely had the massive hasp and staple lock of the Carmelite priory in Strzegom slammed behind them, barely had the two men put some distance between themselves and the beggars by the gate, barely had they entered the shadows of the roadside poplars, than Scharley astonished Reynevan.

The recent penitent and prisoner, a moment earlier intriguingly enigmatic, dour and silently dignified, now suddenly roared with Homeric laughter, leaped like a stag, threw himself down among the weeds and for a moment rolled around on his back like a colt, yelling and laughing by turns. Finally, before the eyes of the dumbfounded Reynevan, his former confessor turned a somersault, sprang up and directed an extremely insulting gesture at the gate with his right hand. The gesture was supported by a long litany of tremendously indecent curses and invective. Several applied to the prior personally, several to the Strzegom priory, several to the Carmelite Order in general, and several had a universal dimension.

'I never judged it was so hard in there,' said Reynevan, calming his horse, which had been startled by Scharley's performance.

'Judge not, that ye be not judged.' Scharley brushed down his clothes. 'To begin with. Secondly, kindly refrain from comments, at least for now. Thirdly, let's hurry to town.'

'To town? What for? I thought—'

'Don't think, either.'

Reynevan shrugged and spurred his steed down the highway. He pretended to turn his head away, but couldn't refrain from directing a furtive look at the man striding beside his horse.

Scharley wasn't particularly tall, even a little shorter than Reynevan, but that detail went unnoticed, since the erstwhile penitent was broad-shouldered, well built and no doubt strong, evidenced by the wiry, muscular forearms revealed by the rolled-up sleeves of his shirt. Scharley refused to leave the Carmelite priory wearing a habit, and the costume he had been given was slightly outlandish.

The penitent had a rugged, lively face, endlessly changing, conveying a wide gamut of expressions. His aquiline nose bore the marks of an old fracture, and the dimple in his chin vanished into a faded but still visible scar. Scharley's eyes, as green as bottle glass, were very strange. When you looked in them, your hand automatically checked to see if your purse was where it should be, and your ring still on your finger. Your thoughts anxiously ran to your wife and daughters back at home, and your faith in their feminine virtue was exposed in all its naivety. That's how you felt when you looked into Scharley's bottle-green eyes. His face definitely had more of Hermes than of Apollo about it.

They passed a large expanse of suburban gardens, then the Chapel and Hospice of Saint Nicholas. Reynevan knew that the hospice was run by the Knights Hospitaller and also that the order had its commandery in Strzegom. Recalling Duke Kantner's instruction to head to Mała Oleśnica, he began to feel anxious. People might associate him with the Knights Hospitaller, so the road he had chosen wasn't that of a hunted wolf; he doubted Canon Otto Beess would have applauded his choice, either. At that moment, Scharley proved his perspicacity for the first time. Or perhaps he really could read minds.

'No need to worry,' he said cheerfully. 'Strzegom has a population of over two thousand, so we'll vanish there like a fart in a snowstorm. Besides, you're in my care, and I made a commitment.'

'I keep wondering,' replied Reynevan after the long pause he needed in order to cool down, 'what a "commitment" like this means to you.'

Scharley flashed his white teeth at a group of linen pickers marching in the opposite direction, buxom wenches in blouses open at the neck to reveal plenty of their sweaty and dust-covered charms. There were about a dozen of them and Scharley grinned at them all in turn, hence Reynevan gave up hope of ever hearing an answer.

'The question was philosophical,' answered the penitent, surprising him, and tearing his eyes away from the rounded behind of the last linen picker, jiggling beneath a shift wet with sweat. 'I don't usually answer those sober. But I promise I'll give you an answer before sundown.'

'I don't know if I can bear to wait, or if I'll expire from curiosity before then.'

Scharley did not reply, but speeded up so that Reynevan had to urge his horse to a gentle trot. They soon arrived at the Świdnica Gate. On the other side of it, beyond a gaggle of grimy pilgrims and ulcerous beggars squatting in the shade, was Strzegom itself and its narrow, stinking, thronged, muddy streets.

Whatever the destination and purpose of their journey, Scharley strode confidently and decisively towards it. They headed down a lane filled with the noise of so many clattering looms it had to be called Weavers Street. They soon found themselves in a small square with a church spire towering over it. Their eyes and noses told them that cattle had recently been driven through it.

'Just look,' said Scharley, stopping. 'A church, an inn and a brothel, and right in the middle of them a pile of shit. Here you have the parabola of human existence.'

'I thought,' Reynevan didn't even smile, 'you didn't philosophise when sober.'

'After a long period of abstinence,' Scharley's sure steps took them into a backstreet, towards a counter laden with casks and mugs, 'just the very scent of good beer intoxicates me. Hey, good fellow! White Strzegom ale, please. Straight from the cellar. Be so kind as to pay, laddie, since as the Good Book says, *argentum et aurum non est mihi.*'

Reynevan snorted, but tossed a few halers down onto the counter.

'Will I ever find out what brought you here?'

'You shall. But only when I've downed at least three of these.'

'And then?' Reynevan frowned. 'The aforementioned brothel?'

'It can't be ruled out, laddie.' Scharley raised the mug. 'It can't be ruled out.'

'And then? A three-day bender on the occasion of your release?'

Scharley didn't reply, since he was drinking. Before tilting the mug, however, he winked, and it could have meant anything.

'This was a mistake, then,' Reynevan said seriously, staring at the penitent's Adam's apple bobbing up and down. 'Perhaps the canon's. Or perhaps mine, for obeying him and agreeing to associate with you.'

Scharley drank, ignoring him.

'Fortunately,' Reynevan continued, 'everything can easily be resolved.'

Scharley took the mug away from his mouth, breathed out and licked the froth from his upper lip.

'You want to tell me something,' he guessed. 'So, speak.'

'The two of us,' said Reynevan coldly, 'simply don't suit each other.'

The penitent nodded a request for another beer, and for some time thereafter was only interested in his second mug.

'We do differ a little, it's true,' he admitted after taking a gulp. 'I, for example, don't fuck other men's wives. And were we to have a good look, we'd probably find a few other differences. That's normal. While we may have been created in His likeness, the Creator made sure there are individual differences. And may He be praised for that.'

Reynevan brandished a hand, growing ever angrier.

'I'm wondering,' he blurted out, 'whether to say farewell to you in the name of the Creator, right here, right now, so we can go our separate ways. For I truly don't see how you can help me. I fear you cannot.'

Scharley looked at him over his mug.

'Help?' he repeated. 'With what? We can easily find out. Just shout: "Scharley, help!" and help will come.'

Reynevan shrugged and turned around, intending to leave. He bumped into somebody. And that somebody struck his horse so hard, the horse squealed and kicked, throwing him to the ground.

'Watch where you're walking, dimwit. Where are you going with that nag? This is a city, not your shitty village!'

The person who had thumped him and dressed him down was one of three young men, sumptuously, fashionably and elegantly attired. They were almost identical – dressed in similar fanciful fezzes atop hair curled using irons, and padded jerkins with such thick quilting that their sleeves resembled huge caterpillars. They were also wearing fashionable tight Parisian hose called *mi-parti*, with legs in contrasting colours. They were all carrying turned canes with knobs.

'Jesus Christ and all the saints,' said the dandy, whirling his cane around. 'What churlishness in this Silesia, what a vulgar wilderness! When will anyone teach them manners?'

'It will be necessary,' said a second, with an identical Gallic accent, 'to undertake that task ourselves. And bring them into Europe.'

'Correct,' echoed the third fop, in red and blue *mi-parti*. 'To begin with, we'll tan the hide of that peasant in the European style. Come on, gentlemen, your canes! And may none of us shirk!'

'I say!' yelled the owner of the beer stall. 'There'll be no brawling here, sirs, or I'll summon the guard!'

'Shut your trap, you Silesian oaf, or you'll get a hiding, too.'

Reynevan tried to get to his feet, to no avail. A cane thudded on his shoulder, another fell on his back with a dry thump and a third slapped him on the buttocks. He decided there was no point waiting for further punishment.

'Help!' he yelled. 'Scharley! Help!'

Scharley, who had been observing the incident with moderate interest, put down his mug and ambled over.

'That's enough merriment.'

The dandies looked around – and roared with laughter in unison. Indeed, Reynevan had to admit that in his scant, motley attire, the penitent didn't look especially dignified.

'Christ the Lord,' snorted the first dandy, clearly devout. 'What hilarious characters one can meet at the end of the world!'

'It's a local jester,' concluded the second. 'You can tell by his ridiculous costume.'

'Handsome is as handsome does,' replied Scharley coldly. 'Get out of here, gentlemen. Double quick.'

'Whaat?'

'M'lords,' repeated Scharley, 'if you'd kindly move away. I mean, move a long way from here. It doesn't have to be Paris – the other end of the city will do.'

'Whaaaat?'

'M'lords,' repeated Scharley, slowly, patiently and emphatically as though speaking to a child. 'If you wouldn't mind taking your leave, m'lords, and engage in something you are familiar with. Like sodomy. Otherwise you'll receive a damned good thrashing before any of you gentlemen have time to say *credo in Deum patrem omnipotentem.*'

The first fop swung his cane. Scharley nimbly dodged the blow, seized the stick and twisted. The fop turned a somersault and landed in the mud. The penitent used the cane to hit the second dandy over the head, sending him into the beer stall, and quick as lightning rapped the third one's knuckles. Meanwhile, the first one had sprung up and lunged at Scharley, roaring like a wounded bison. Without visible effort, the penitent stopped the charge with a blow that folded the dandy in two. Then Scharley elbowed him powerfully in the kidney and kicked him nonchalantly in the ear as he fell. The man curled up like a worm and didn't try to stand.

The other two looked at each other and drew daggers in unison. Scharley wagged a finger at them.

'I advise against that,' he said. 'Knives can cut!'

The fops ignored the warning.

Reynevan thought he'd been watching the incident closely, but he must have missed something because he couldn't comprehend what happened next. Juxtaposed against the dandies rushing at him and whirling their weapons like windmills, Scharley appeared almost motionless, and the movements he made when they fell on him were subtle, almost too quick to apprehend. One of the fops dropped to his knees, lowering his head almost to the ground, wheezed and spat teeth out into the mud one after another. His companion was sitting, screaming unremittingly in a thin, high ululation, mouth wide open like a very hungry infant. He was still holding his own dagger, but his comrade's knife was plunged up to its gilded guard into his thigh.

Scharley looked up at the sky and spread his arms as if to say, *What did I tell you?* He took off his ridiculous, over-tight tunic and went over to the man spitting teeth. He nimbly caught him by the elbow, jerked it up, grabbed a sleeve and ejected the dandy from his quilted jerkin with several well-aimed kicks. Then donned it himself.

'Handsome is as handsome does,' he said, stretching luxuriously. 'But only when a man is well attired does he feel true dignity.'

Then he leaned over and tore an embroidered pouch from the fop's belt.

'Wealthy city, this Strzegom,' he said. 'Wealthy indeed. Money's lying around in the streets, just look.'

'In your shoes . . .' said the owner of the beer stall in a trembling voice. 'In your shoes, I'd make myself scarce, sir. They're wealthy merchants, guests of His Lordship Guncelin of Laasan. They had it coming to them, for the brawls they keep starting . . . But you ought to flee, for Lord Laasan—'

'Runs this town,' finished Scharley, removing the pouch from the third dandy. 'Thanks for the beer, good fellow. We'll be off, Reinmar.'

They went. The dandy with the knife in his thigh bade them farewell with his despairing, unremitting, infantile howling.

Chapter Ten

In which both Reynevan and the reader have the chance to get to know Scharley better, the opportunity afforded by a shared perambulation and various accompanying events. Finally, three classically iconic and absolutely anachronistic witches make an appearance.

Lounging comfortably on a moss-covered stump, Scharley observed the coins he had tipped from the pouches into his cap. He couldn't conceal his disappointment.

'Judging by their dress and manner,' he grumbled, 'you'd have said they were wealthy parvenus. But what penury in their pouches. See for yourself, laddie. What dross! Two ecu, a few clipped Parisian solds, fourteen groschen, some half-groschen, Magdeburg pfennigs, Prussian skojeces and szelągs, denarii and wafer-thin halers and some other shit I don't even recognise – counterfeit, no doubt. The bloody pouches with their silver thread and pearls are worth more. But pouches aren't cash. Where can I sell them now? And the coins won't even suffice for an old nag, and I need a sodding horse. Dammit, the garb on those fops was also worth more than the contents of their purses. I should have stripped them naked.'

'Then,' Reynevan observed tartly, 'Lord Laasan would surely have sent a hundred men after us and not a dozen. And not down one, but all the roads.'

'But he only sent twelve, so don't harp on.'

Indeed, no more than a half-hour after they had left Strzegom via the Jawor Gate, a dozen horsemen in the livery of Guncelin of

Laasan, magnate, Lord of Strzegom Castle and the city's actual ruler, burst from the gate and thundered down the highway. But Scharley, soon after leaving the city, demonstrated his cunning by ordering Reynevan to turn into the forest and hide in the undergrowth. There they waited to make sure their pursuers didn't double back.

Reynevan sighed and sat down next to Scharley.

'The result of our acquaintance so far is as follows,' Reynevan said. 'If, this morning, I was only being hunted by the Stercza brothers and their hired thugs, come this afternoon, Lord Laasan and a squad of armed men from Strzegom are also hot on my heels. I dread to think what'll be next.'

'You asked for help.' The penitent shrugged. 'And I have pledged to protect you. I told you as much, but you refused to believe me, Doubting Thomas. Didn't the first-hand evidence convince you, or do you have to touch the wounds?'

'If the guard had arrived sooner,' Reynevan pouted, 'or the comrades of the men you beat up, then there'd be something to touch. I'd be dangling from a noose by now. And you, my guardian and defender, would be hanging right beside me.'

Scharley didn't reply, just shrugged again and spread his hands. Reynevan smiled in spite of himself. He still didn't trust the strange penitent or understand where Canon Otto Beess's trust in him came from. He was no closer to Adèle, and only seemed to be getting further away. Strzegom had been added to the list of places where he couldn't show himself. But Scharley, he admitted, had impressed him a little. Reynevan could already envision Wolfher Stercza kneeling and spitting his teeth out one after another. Morold – who had tugged Adèle by the hair in Oleśnica – sitting and howling like a baby.

'Where did you learn to fight like that? In the monastery?'

'Indeed,' Scharley calmly agreed. 'Believe me, laddie, monasteries are full of teachers. Almost everybody there can teach you something. All you need is the desire to learn.'

'Was it the same in the penitent house at the Carmelite priory?'

'Even better regarding learning, of course, as we had a lot of time on our hands. Especially if Brother Barnabus wasn't your cup of tea, for while he's as plump and pretty as a girl, he's not actually a girl, which bothered some of us a touch.'

'Spare me the details, please. What shall we do now?'

'Following the example of the Four Sons of Aymon,' Scharley stood up and stretched, 'we will both mount your Bayard and ride south, towards Świdnica. Avoiding main roads.'

'Why?'

'In spite of acquiring those three pouches, we still suffer from a lack of *argentum et aurum*. I'll find a solution to that in Świdnica.'

'I meant why avoiding main roads?'

'You rode to Strzegom along the Świdnica road. There's every chance we'll come face-to-face with the men who are pursuing you.'

'I lost them. I'm certain—'

'They're also counting on that certainty,' interrupted the penitent. 'It appears from your account that you're being tracked by professionals. It's not easy to lose men like that. Let's go, Reynevan. It would be wise to get as far away from Strzegom and Lord Laasan as possible before nightfall.'

'On that, we can agree.'

The evening found them in a forest near a settlement. Smoke crawled over the thatched roofs of the cottages, mingling with the mist rising from the meadows. At first, they planned to spend the night in a hay barrack, buried in warm straw, but some dogs sniffed them out and barked at them so fiercely they gave up the idea. Now, almost groping their way in the darkness, they stumbled on a derelict shepherd's hut at the edge of the forest.

They heard rustling, scraping, squeaking and growling, and every few moments, the pale lights of animals' eyes flashed in the gloom. They were most probably martens or badgers, but just to be sure, Reynevan tossed onto the campfire the remains of the monkshood picked in the Wąwolnica cemetery and some stonecrop he'd gathered before dusk, muttering a spell to himself as he did so. He wasn't quite certain if they were the right spells or if he'd remembered them correctly.

Scharley looked on with interest.

'Go on,' he said. 'Tell me more, Reinmar.'

Reynevan had already told Scharley about all his difficulties during the 'confession' in the Carmelite priory, when he had also presented his plans and intentions in broad outline. The penitent hadn't commented then, so his interest in discussing the details was even more unexpected now.

'I wouldn't like the very start of our acquaintance to be soured by misunderstandings and insincerity,' he said, poking a stick around in the fire. 'So, I'll tell you frankly and bluntly, Reinmar, that your plan is only fit to be stuck up a dog's arse.'

'What?'

'A dog's arse,' repeated Scharley, modulating his voice like a preacher. 'That's what the plan you presented me with earlier is fit for. Being a judicious and educated young man, you can't fail to see that, or expect me to take part in it.'

'Canon Otto Beess and I got you out of prison,' said Reynevan, without raising his voice even though he was seething with fury. 'Not from love, by any means, but so – and only so – you could assist me. As a judicious penitent, you can't have failed to see that. And now you choose to inform me that you won't participate. So I shall also speak frankly and bluntly: go back to prison in the Carmelite priory.'

'I am still in prison in the Carmelite priory. Officially, at least. But you probably don't understand that.'

'I do.' All of a sudden, Reynevan recalled his conversation with the Carmelite hosteller. 'I also understand perfectly that what matters to you is to atone for your sins, because after your *nullum crimen* penance, you'll be back in grace and privilege. But I understand, too, that Canon Otto has you by the balls, for all he has to do is announce that you've fled from the Carmelite priory and you'll be an outlaw to the end of your days. There'll be no return to your order and your warm little monastery. Incidentally, which order and which warm little monastery would that be, may one ask?'

'No, one may not. Indeed, Reinmar dear, you understand things perfectly. I was released from the priory unofficially and I'm still performing my penance. And it's true that owing to Canon Beess I'm performing it at liberty, for which I praise the canon, since I love liberty. Why, though, would the pious canon take away from me what he gave me? After all, I'm doing what he obliged me to do.'

Reynevan opened his mouth, but Scharley immediately interrupted him, and quite bluntly, too.

'Your tale of love and crime, although enthralling and truly worthy of Chrétien of Troyes, didn't enthral me. You won't convince me, laddie, that Canon Otto Beess commended you to my care to assist in saving oppressed womenfolk and to be an accomplice in a family feud. I know the canon. He's a wise fellow. He sent you to me in order for me to rescue you, not for us both to put our heads on the block. Thus, I shall do what the canon expects of me: I'll save you from your pursuers and deliver you safely to Hungary.'

'I won't leave Silesia without Adèle, or without avenging my brother. I don't deny that I could use some help and that I'm counting on it – counting on you. But if you won't help me, too bad. I'll cope by myself, and you can act according to your will. Go to Hungary, to Ruthenia, to Palestine, wherever you want. Enjoy the freedom you so love.'

'Thanks for the suggestion,' Scharley replied coldly, 'but I shan't avail myself of it.'

'Oh? And why not?'

'You clearly won't cope. You'll lose your head. And then the canon will demand mine.'

'Aha. If your head matters to you, you don't have a choice.'

Scharley said nothing for a long time. Now that Reynevan knew him a little, he didn't expect it to end there.

'Regarding your brother,' Scharley said after a time, 'I'm going to be firm, if only because you can't be certain who killed him. Don't interrupt! A family feud is a grave matter. And you, as you divulged, have neither witnesses nor proof, just speculation and conjecture. I said, don't interrupt me! Hear me out. Let's get away, wait, gather information, acquire proof and raise some funds, then put a force together. I'll help you. If you obey me, I promise you'll taste revenge as it is best served. Cold.'

'But—'

'I haven't finished yet. Regarding your sweetheart Adèle, the plan is still a load of cobblers, but I suppose stopping in Ziębice won't prolong our journey much. And a great deal will be explained in Ziębice.'

'Are you implying something? Adèle loves me!'

'Is anyone denying that?'

'Scharley?'

'Yes.'

'Why do you and the canon insist on Hungary?'

'Because it's far away.'

'But why not Bohemia? It's also far away. And I know Prague, I have chums there—'

'What, don't you go to church? Don't you listen to sermons? Prague and the whole of Bohemia is now a cauldron of boiling pitch, and one can get one's fingers badly scalded. And it might get even livelier soon. The Hussites' effrontery has gone too far; neither the Pope, nor Sigismund, nor the Elector of Saxony, nor the landgraves of Meissen and Thuringia will put up with such insolent heresy. The Hussite apostasy is a thorn in Europe's side. Any moment, the whole of Europe will mount a crusade against Bohemia.'

'There have already been anti-Hussite crusades,' Reynevan observed sourly. 'The whole of Europe marched on Bohemia and received a sound beating. I recently heard about that beating from an eyewitness.'

'A credible one?'

'Absolutely.'

'But what of it? Europe got a hiding and learned some lessons. Now it's preparing itself better. I say again: the Catholic world will not tolerate the Hussites. It's only a matter of time.'

'They've tolerated them for seven years now. Because they have to.'

'The Albigensians lasted a hundred years, but where are they now? It's only a matter of time, Reinmar. Bohemia will be bathed in blood, just like the Languedoc of the Cathars. And using the methods tried and tested in Languedoc, they will wipe out everyone in Bohemia, leaving it to God to identify the innocent and the faithful. That's why we're not going to Bohemia, but to Hungary. In Hungary, we only need fear the Turks, whom I prefer to the crusaders. When it comes to slaughter, Turks are no match for crusaders.'

The forest was quiet, nothing rustled or squeaked; the creatures had either taken fright at the spells, or – more likely – were simply bored of them. Just to be sure, Reynevan tossed the last of the herbs onto the fire.

'We ride to Świdnica tomorrow, I hope?' he asked.

'Absolutely.'

Avoiding main roads had its pitfalls. Namely, when they left the wilderness to rejoin the road, it was very difficult to work out where the roads led.

Scharley stood bent over some tracks in the sand and examined them, cursing softly. Reynevan let his horse graze in the roadside grass and looked up at the sun.

'The east is over there,' he ventured, 'so we ought to go that way—'

'Don't be clever,' Scharley interrupted. 'I'm examining the tracks and discerning which way the main traffic goes. And I declare that we should go . . . that way.'

Reynevan sighed, since Scharley was pointing exactly where he had. He tugged his horse and set off after the penitent, who was marching briskly in the chosen direction. After a short time, they came to a crossroads. Four absolutely identical-looking roads led off in four different directions. Scharley muttered angrily and once again stooped over the hoofprints. Reynevan sighed and began to search around for herbs, for it was looking as though a magical talisman would be necessary.

The bushes rustled, his horse snorted and Reynevan jumped.

An old beggar emerged from the thicket, hauling up his breeches. A wandering beggar, one of hundreds roaming the highways, scrounging at doorways and porches, seeking alms outside convents and sustenance from taverns and peasant cottages.

'Jesus Christ be praised!'

'For ever and ever, amen.'

The beggar was typical of his kind. His peasant's homespun coat was mottled with many-hued patches, while his bast slippers and crooked stick had witnessed numberless roads. A red nose and unkempt beard peeped out from under his ragged cap, made mainly from rabbit and cat hide. The beggar had a long sack slung over one shoulder and a tin pot hanging from his neck.

'May Saint Wacław and Saint Vincent come to your aid. May Saint Petronilla and Saint Jadwiga, patron of—'

'Whence do these roads lead?' Scharley asked, interrupting the litany. 'Which way's Świdnica, Grandfather?'

'Whaaat?' The beggar put a hand to his ear. 'Come again?'

'Which way do the roads lead?'

'Ooh . . . The roads . . . Aha . . . I know! That 'un goes to Olszany, and that 'un to Świebodzice, and that 'un . . . Bugger . . . I forget where—'

'Never mind.' Scharley waved him away. 'I know everything now. If Świebodzice's that way, then Stanowice's the opposite way, on the Strzegom road. So that road goes to Świdnica, via Jaworowa Góra. Farewell, Grandfather.'

'May Saint Wacław—'

'If anyone asks about us,' Reynevan interrupted him this time, 'you never saw us. Got it?'

'What have I got? May Saint—'

'To help you remember what was asked of you,' Scharley rummaged in his pouch, 'here's a penny, Grandfather.'

'Good gracious! Thankin' you! May you be—'

'And you, too.'

Before they'd ridden far, Scharley looked back. 'See, Reinmar, how elated he is, how joyfully he's feeling and sniffing the coin, delighting in its thickness and weight. Indeed, a sight like that is true reward for a benefactor.'

Reynevan didn't reply, too busy watching the flocks of birds that had suddenly flown up from the trees.

'Verily,' Scharley went on with a grave expression as he strode beside the horse, 'one must never indifferently and callously pass by human poverty. One must never turn one's back on a pauper. Mainly because a pauper might smack you in the back of the head with his staff. Are you listening to me, Reinmar?'

'No. I'm looking at those birds.'

'What birds? Oh, bugger! Into the trees! Into the trees, quick!'

Scharley gave the horse a hard slap on the rump, then set off after it at such speed that the horse, frightened into a gallop, only caught him up beyond the treeline. Once in the forest, Reynevan dismounted and led his steed into the undergrowth, then joined the penitent watching the highway from the thicket. For a while, nothing happened, the birds stopped shrieking, and it was so quiet and peaceful that Reynevan was about to mock Scharley and his excessive timidity. He wasn't quick enough.

Four horsemen appeared at the crossroads and surrounded the beggar with a thudding of hooves and wheezing of horses.

'They aren't the Strzegom troops,' muttered Scharley. 'So it must be . . . Reinmar?'

'Yes,' Reynevan confirmed dully. 'It's them.'

Kyrie-eleison leaned over from the saddle and asked the beggar something in a loud voice, while Stork of Gorgowice pushed his horse against him. The beggar shook his head and put his hands together, undoubtedly entreating Saint Petronilla to help them.

'Kunz Aulock,' said Scharley, pointing him out to an astonished Reynevan, 'or Kyrie-eleison. A right thug, although he's actually a knight from a notable family. Stork of Gorgowice and Sybek of Kobylagłowa, rare scoundrels both. And the one in the marten cap is Walter of Barby. Anathematised by the bishop for his raid on a farm in Ocice, the property of the Racibórz Dominican nuns. You never mentioned that you're being tracked by such celebrated men, Reinmar.'

The beggar fell to his knees, hands still joined in prayer, cried out and beat his breast. Kyrie-eleison, still in the saddle, lashed him across the back with a knout. Stork and the others also made use of their whips, crowding and impeding each other, while their horses began to shy and thrash around. Stork and the anathematised Walter of Barby dismounted and began to punch the beggar, and when he fell over, took to kicking him. The beggar was screaming and wailing pitifully.

Reynevan swore and punched the ground. Scharley looked askance at him.

'No, Reinmar,' he said coldly. 'Nothing of the kind. They aren't the French dandies from Strzegom. They are four crafty, heavily armed brigands and butchers. Not even I could cope with Kunz Aulock in a duel. So abandon your foolish thoughts and hopes. We'll sit here as quiet as mice.'

'And look on as they kill a completely innocent man.'

'Indeed,' the penitent replied a moment later, still watching. 'Because if I have to choose, my life is dearer to me. And apart from owing my soul to God, I also owe money to several people. It would be unethical, foolish recklessness to deprive them of the chance of repayment. Besides, we're talking needlessly. It's all over. They've lost interest.'

Indeed, Barby and Stork treated the beggar to several parting kicks, spat on him, mounted their horses, and a moment later all four of them were galloping, whooping and raising dust, towards Jaworowa Góra and Świdnica.

'He didn't betray us,' sighed Reynevan. 'They gave him a sound beating, but he didn't turn us in. Despite your derision, the alms we gave the pauper saved us. Mercy and munificence—'

'Had Kyrie-eleison given him a skojec rather than a thrashing, the beggar would have betrayed us at once,' commented Scharley coldly. 'Let's be off. Unfortunately, once again through the trees. Someone, if I remember rightly, was recently bragging about throwing off his pursuers and erasing his tracks.'

'Oughtn't we to ...' Reynevan ignored the sarcasm and watched the beggar searching on all fours in the ditch for his cap. 'Oughtn't we repay that? Compensate him? After all, you possess a little money from pillaging the dandies, Scharley. Show more mercy.'

'I cannot.' Mockery lit up the penitent's bottle-green eyes. 'Out of mercy. I gave him a counterfeit coin. If he tries spending one, they'll just give him a beating. If they catch him with a few more, they'll hang him. So I'm mercifully sparing him such a fate. Into the forest, Reinmar, into the forest. Let's not waste time.'

After a brief shower of warm rain, the wet forest began to vanish in the mist. The birds weren't singing. It was quiet as a tomb.

'Your deathly silence appears to indicate something,' said Scharley at last as he walked beside the horse. 'Disapproval, perhaps. Permit me to guess ... It's about that beggar?'

'Indeed it is. You behaved shabbily. Unethically, to put it mildly.'

'Aha. A person who's accustomed to bedding other men's wives is teaching me morals.'

'Would you mind not comparing incomparable things?'

'You only think they're incomparable. Furthermore, what you call a reprehensible misdeed was motivated by concern for you.'

'That's difficult to comprehend, I confess.'

'I'll explain at a suitable occasion,' Scharley said, stopping. 'In the meantime, though, I suggest we address a slightly more pertinent matter. Namely, that I haven't got a clue where we are. I've lost my way in this lousy fog.'

Reynevan looked around and then up at the sky. Indeed, the pale disc of the sun peeping through the fog, which a moment before had been visible and acting as a signpost, had vanished completely. The thick fog hung so low that even the tops of the tallest trees were disappearing in it. At ground level, the blanket of fog was so thick that the ferns and bushes seemed to be protruding from an ocean of milk.

'Instead of being distressed regarding the fate of poor beggars and having moral dilemmas,' the penitent said, 'why don't you use your talents to find the road?'

'I beg your pardon?'

'Stop playing the innocent. You know exactly what I'm talking about.'

Reynevan also thought that talismans would be indispensable, but he didn't dismount, prevaricating. He was cross at the penitent and wanted him to know it. The horse snorted, tossed its head, and stamped its forehooves, and the sound of the stamping spread through the fog-shrouded forest.

'I can smell smoke,' Scharley suddenly announced. 'A fire's burning somewhere around here. It's either woodcutters or charcoal burners. We can ask them for directions and save your magical talismans for another day. And your moods.'

He set off so swiftly, Reynevan could barely keep up with him. His horse shuffled about constantly, resisting, snorting nervously, crushing toadstools under its hooves. The ground, lined with a thick carpet of rotten leaves, suddenly began to incline downwards, and before they knew it, they were in a deep ravine. The walls of the ravine were covered with sloping, misshapen trees shrouded in lichen, their roots – exposed by the subsiding earth – like monstrous tentacles. Reynevan felt shivers running down his back and huddled in the saddle. His horse snorted.

He heard Scharley cursing in the mist in front of him. The

penitent was standing at a point where the ravine divided into two branches.

'That way,' he finally said with conviction, resuming his march.

The ravine kept dividing; they were in a veritable labyrinth of ravines, while the smell of smoke, Reynevan thought, was coming from every direction at the same time. Scharley walked straight ahead and confidently, then speeded up and even began to whistle. And stopped as soon as he had begun.

Reynevan understood why. As bones began to crunch under his horse's hooves.

The horse neighed nervously as Reynevan dismounted and took the bridle firmly in both hands. Just in time, as the bay, snorting in panic and anxiously glaring at him, stepped back, stamping heavily, crushing skulls, pelvises and shinbones. Reynevan's foot was caught between the broken shards of a human ribcage. He shook it off with panicky swings of his leg. He was trembling in disgust. And fear.

'The Black Death,' said Scharley, now standing beside him. 'The plague of 1380. Entire villages were wiped out, people fled into the forests, but the plague caught them there, too. The corpses were buried in ravines, like these. Then wild animals tore them up and scattered the bones around . . .'

'Let's go back,' said Reynevan, clearing his throat. 'Let's turn back right away. I don't like this place. I don't like this fog. Or the smell of that smoke.'

'You're as timid as a wench,' sneered Scharley. 'The corpses—'

He didn't finish. A sudden swish, whistle and snigger made them duck. A human skull shot above the ravine, trailing sparks and a ribbon of smoke behind it. Before they had time to calm down, another flew over, whistling even more horrifyingly.

'Let's turn back,' said Scharley dully. 'Right away. I don't like this place.'

Reynevan was absolutely certain they were retracing their steps, returning the way they'd come. But a moment later, the steep side of a ravine rose up right in front of their noses. Without a word, he turned into another ravine. After a few paces, they were also stopped by a vertical wall bristling with a tangle of roots.

'Bugger this,' panted Scharley, turning back. 'I don't understand—'

'And I'm afraid,' groaned Reynevan, 'that—'

'We don't have a choice,' growled the penitent, when once again they ended up in a blind alley. 'We have to go back and cross the boneyard. Quick, Reinmar. Look lively.'

'Wait.' Reynevan stooped and looked around, searching for herbs. 'There's another way—'

'Now?' Scharley interrupted harshly. '*Now* you're deciding to use your skills? There's no time now!'

Another skull whistled above the forest like a comet and Reynevan agreed with the penitent's plan. They passed through the heap of bones. The horse snorted, tossed its head and shied, and it took all of Reynevan's strength to pull it along. The smell of smoke grew stronger. There seemed to be a scent of herbs in it. And something else, something elusive and sickly. Terrifying.

And then they saw the campfire.

The fire was smoking near a pit, under a huge fallen tree trunk. A blackened cauldron hung above the fire, belching forth clouds of steam. Beside it towered a pile of human skulls. A black cat was lying on top of the pile in a typically languorous feline pose.

Reynevan and Scharley stood paralysed. Even the horse stopped snorting.

Three women were sitting around the fire.

Two of them were obscured by the smoke and steam pouring from the cauldron. The third, sitting on the right, looked quite old. Although her dark hair was densely shot with grey, her face – tanned by the sun and rainy weather – was a little misleading; the woman could have lived three dozen years as easily as six. She was sitting in a carefree pose, swaying and turning her head around unnaturally.

'Greetings,' she croaked, then belched thunderously and long. 'Greetings, O Thane of Glamis!'

'Stop talking nonsense, Jagna,' said the second woman, the one in the centre. 'You're drunk again, dammit.'

A gust of wind dispersed the smoke and steam a little, allowing them to see things more clearly.

The woman sitting in the middle was tall and quite well built, with wavy, flame-red hair tumbling around her shoulders from beneath a black hat. She had prominent cheekbones flushed bright red, a shapely mouth and very bright eyes. A dirty green woollen scarf was draped around her neck. Her stockings were knitted from the same material – the woman was sitting with legs casually sprawled apart and her skirt raised quite freely, allowing them to admire not only her stockings and calves but also an impressive eyeful of things normally kept covered.

The third one, sitting on her right, was the youngest, barely a girl. She had sparkling eyes with dark rings under them and a thin, foxy face with a sallow complexion. Her fair hair was adorned with a garland of verbena and clover.

'Well, just look,' said the red-haired one, scratching her thigh above the green stocking top. 'There was nothing to eat, and blow me, the grub's turned up all by itself.'

The swarthy one addressed as Jagna belched and the black cat meowed. The feverish eyes of the wench in the garland lit up with an evil flame.

'We request forgiveness for the intrusion,' Scharley said, bowing. He was pale, but working hard to keep control. 'We apologise to you, dear and honourable ladies. But let us not disturb you. We wish no trouble. We're here by accident, and we'll be off immediately. If we may, dear ladies—'

The red-haired witch picked up a skull from the pile, lifted it high and loudly chanted a spell. Reynevan thought he could make out Chaldean and Aramaic words in it. The skull snapped its jaws, shot upwards and whistled over the pine tops.

'Grub,' repeated the red-haired witch in a voice devoid of emotion. 'And talking grub to boot. There'll be a chance to chat before our meal.'

Scharley swore under his breath. The woman licked her lips suggestively and fixed him with her gaze. There was no time to delay. Reynevan inhaled deeply.

He touched the top of his head, then bent his right leg at the knee, raised it, crossing his other leg behind him, and seized the tip of his boot with his left hand. Although he'd only done it twice before, it went extremely smoothly. It was enough to concentrate and murmur the spell.

Scharley swore again. Jagna burped. The eyes of the red-haired witch widened.

And Reynevan, just like that, slowly rose from the ground in the same position. Not very high, just three or four spans. And not for long. But it sufficed.

The red-haired witch picked up a clay demijohn, took a long drink from it, then another. She didn't offer it to the girl, and put the vessel out of range of Jagna's claw-like fingers, who held her hand out greedily. She didn't take her eyes off Reynevan, and her pupils looked like two dark points in her bright eyes.

'Well, well,' she said. 'Who'd have thought it? Mages, true mages, Toledo. Here, in the presence of a simple witch. What an honour. Come closer. Have no fear! Surely you didn't take the jest about grub and cannibalism seriously?'

'No, not at all,' Scharley eagerly assured her, so eagerly it was obvious he was lying. The red-haired witch snorted in laughter.

'What, then, do you seek in my poor nook, my dear sorcerers?' she asked. 'What do you wish for? Perhaps—'

She broke off, laughing.

'Or perhaps you're simply lost, dear sorcerers? Forgetting magic in your male pride? And now that same pride won't let you admit it, especially before womenfolk?'

Scharley regained his poise.

'Your intelligence goes hand in hand with your beauty, madam,' he said, bowing courteously.

'Just look, Sisters,' said the witch, flashing her teeth, 'what a courteous fellow he is, what pleasant compliments he regales us with. He knows how to delight a woman. A veritable troubadour. Or bishop. It's truly a shame that so rarely . . . For womenfolk and wenches, indeed, often risk this path through the backwoods and wilderness, since my reputation spreads far and wide. Few know how to remove a foetus so elegantly, safely and painlessly as I. But men . . . Why, they come here much more seldom . . . Such a pity . . .'

Jagna laughed throatily and the wench sniffed. Scharley blushed, but probably more from desire than embarrassment. Reynevan, meanwhile, also recovered his composure. He had discerned certain fragrances in the steam from the bubbling cauldron and had a good look at the bunches of herbs, both fresh and dried.

'Your beauty and acuity,' he said, straightening up, a little over-bearingly but aware he was making an impression, 'are matched only by your humility, for I am certain that countless visitors come here, and not just for medical services. I see burning bush, and devil's trumpets. And there's squill, and there ragweed, an oracular herb, and henbane, which calls forth prophetic visions. And there is money to be made from predictions and prophesies, if I'm not mistaken?'

Jagna belched. The wench gave him a piercing look. The red-haired witch smiled enigmatically.

'You aren't in error, O fellow adept,' she said finally. 'There is great demand for fortune-telling and prophecies. A time of change and transformation approaches, and many would know what that time will bring. And you also want knowledge of what fate will bring you. Am I not right?'

The red-haired witch tossed some herbs into the cauldron and stirred them around. But it was the young wench with the face of a vixen and feverishly bright eyes who was to prophesy. Soon after drinking the decoction, her eyes grew cloudy, the dry skin on her cheeks tightened and her lower lip revealed her teeth.

'*Columna veli aurei*,' she suddenly mumbled. 'The Column with the Golden Veil. Born in Genazzano, will depart this life in

Rome. In six years. The place vacated will be taken by a she-wolf. On *Oculi* Sunday. In six years.'

The silence, only disturbed by the crackling of the fire and the cat's purring, lasted so long that Reynevan began to doubt there was more to come. Wrongly.

'Before two days pass,' said the wench, holding out a trembling hand towards him, 'before two days pass, he will be a renowned poet. His name will be celebrated far and wide.'

Scharley shook slightly with suppressed laughter, but quietened down at once under the harsh gaze of the red-haired witch.

'The Wanderer will come,' said the prophetess, exhaling loudly several times. 'The *Viator* will come, the Wanderer, from the sunlit side. An exchange will occur. Someone leaves us and the Wanderer comes to us. The Wanderer says: *Ego sum qui sum*. Ask not the Wanderer his name, it is obscure. For who will guess what it is? Out of the eater came forth meat, and out of the strong came forth sweetness.'

The dead lion, the bees and the honey, thought Reynevan, *the riddle that Samson gave the Philistines. Samson and the honey ... What does it mean? What does it symbolise? Who is the Wanderer?*

'Your brother calls,' came the soft voice of the medium, electrifying him. 'Your brother calls: Go and come. Go, leaping across the mountains. Do not delay.'

He listened eagerly.

'Isaiah says: gathered, imprisoned in a pit, shut up in prison. An amulet ... And a rat ... An amulet and a rat. Yin and yang, Keter and Malkuth. The sun, the serpent and the fish. They will open, open the gates of Hell, then the tower will tumble, *turris fulgurata* will fall, the tower struck by a thunderbolt. The Narrenturm will crumble into dust, and bury the fool under the rubble.'

Narrenturm, Reynevan repeated in his head. *The Tower of Fools! By God!*

'*Adsumus! Adsumus! Adsumus!*' screamed the wench suddenly, tensing up powerfully. 'We are here! From the arrow that flieth in the day, *a sagitta volante in die*, beware it, beware it! Beware the terror by night, beware the pestilence that walketh in darkness; beware the demon that wasteth at noonday! And that which calls: *Adsumus!* Beware the Wallcreeper! Fear night birds, fear silent bats!'

Taking advantage of the inattention of the red-haired witch, Jagna noiselessly snatched the demijohn and took several deep gulps. She coughed and hiccoughed.

'And beware,' she cackled, 'of Birnam Wood ...'

The red-haired witch silenced her with a poke in the ribs.

'And people will burn,' the prophetess sighed piercingly, 'running all in flames. Erroneously. Owing to a semblance of names.'

Reynevan leaned over towards her.

'Who killed ... ?' he asked quietly. 'Who will shoulder the blame for my brother's death?'

The red-haired witch hissed angrily in warning, shaking a large wooden ladle at him. Reynevan was aware that what he was doing was forbidden, that he was risking the irreversible rupture of the prophetic trance. But he repeated the question. And received the answer immediately.

'The blatant liar is guilty.' The girl's voice dropped a tone and became hoarser. 'The liar or the one that tells the truth. Tells the truth. Lies or tells the truth. And that depends on what beliefs are held in this regard. Scorched, charred, burned. Not burned, because dead. Buried when dead. Disinterred anon. Before three years pass. Ejected from the grave. *Buried at Lutterworth, remains taken up and cast out* ... The ash from burned bones flows down the river ... The Swift to the Avon, the Avon to the seas, from the seas to the oceans ... Flee, flee, save your lives. So few of us remain.'

'A horse,' Scharley suddenly rudely interjected. 'To flee I need a horse. I'd like to—'

Reynevan quietened him with a gesture. The girl looked on with unseeing eyes. He doubted whether she would answer. He was mistaken.

'Chestnut ...' she mumbled. 'It will be a chestnut.'

'And on top of that I'd like—' Reynevan began, but broke off, seeing that she had finished. The girl's eyes closed; her head drooped limply. The red-haired witch held her up and then gently laid her down.

'I won't stop you,' she said a moment later. 'Ride along the ravine, turning only to the left, always to the left. There'll be a beechwood, then a glade and in it a stone cross. Directly opposite the cross will be a clearing. It'll lead you to the Świdnica road.'

'Thank you, Sister.'

'Heed yourselves. So few of us remain.'

Chapter Eleven

In which the convoluted prophecy begins to come true in a convoluted way, and Scharley meets a friend. And reveals new, previously unrevealed talents.

A penitential cross, one of Silesia's numerous reminders of crimes past and belated contrition, stood among the high grass beyond the beechwood, where the track met the clearing. Judging from the traces of erosion and vandalism, the crime happened long ago, was perhaps older even than the settlement, the ruins of which were still visible nearby in the form of hillocks and hollows densely overgrown by weeds.

'A very belated penance,' commented Scharley, now riding behind Reynevan on his bay horse. 'Passing literally down the generations. Inherited, I'd say. Carving a cross like that takes quite some time, so it's erected at the earliest by a son, who wonders whom his deceased father killed and what brought on remorse in his old age. What do you think, Reinmar?'

'I don't.'

'Are you still angry with me?'

'No.'

'Aha. Let's ride on, then. Our new friends weren't lying. The clearing right opposite the cross, though it must date back to Bolko the Courageous, will surely lead us out onto the Świdnica road.'

Reynevan urged on his horse. Still saying nothing, although it didn't bother Scharley.

'I must confess you impressed me, Reinmar of Bielawa. With

the witches, I mean. Let's face it, any old folk healer or wise woman can toss a handful of herbs on a fire, mutter an incantation and spell, even make a talisman. But that levitation of yours, why, that's no joke. Come clean, where did you study in Prague? At the Charles University or with Czech sorcerers?'

'The former doesn't rule out the latter,' said Reynevan with a smile.

'I see. You mean everybody levitated during lectures?'

Without waiting for an answer, the penitent made himself more comfortable on the horse's rump.

'But it astonished me that you're simply running away, hiding from your pursuers in the undergrowth in a manner more befitting a hare than a mage. If mages ever have to run away, they do it with more class. Medea, for example, fled from Corinth in a chariot pulled by dragons. Atlantes flew away on a hippogryph. Morgan le Fay used mirages to confuse her pursuers. Viviane . . . I can't recall what Viviane did.'

Reynevan made no comment. He couldn't recall, either.

'You don't have to answer,' continued Scharley, mockery even more evident in his voice. 'I understand. You have too little knowledge and skill; you're but a novice of the secret arts, barely a sorcerer's assistant. A fledgling of magic who will one day grow into an eagle, a Merlin, an Alberich or a Maugris. And thus, woe betide—'

He broke off, seeing on the road what Reynevan was seeing.

'Our friends the witches really weren't lying,' he whispered. 'Don't move.'

In the clearing, head bowed and nibbling grass, stood a horse. A fine saddle horse, a light palfrey with slender cannons, chestnut coat and darker mane and tail.

'Don't move,' Scharley repeated, dismounting gingerly. 'This might be an unrepeatable opportunity.'

'That horse is somebody's property,' said Reynevan firmly. 'It belongs to somebody.'

'Indeed. To me. As long as you don't frighten it. So don't.'

Seeing the penitent approaching very slowly, the horse raised its head high, shook its mane and gave a long snort, but didn't take fright and allowed him to grasp its bridle. Scharley stroked its muzzle.

'It's someone else's property,' repeated Reynevan. 'Not yours, Scharley. You'll have to give it back to its owner.'

'Good people . . .' Scharley muttered softly. 'I say, whose horse is this? See, Reinmar? No one's coming forward. So *res nullius cedit occupanti.*'

'Scharley—'

'Very well, calm down, don't trouble your fragile conscience. We'll give the horse back to its rightful owner. On condition that we meet them. And may the gods save us from that, I entreat.'

His entreaties clearly didn't reach their addressees or were ignored, for the clearing suddenly teemed with men on foot, panting and pointing at the horse.

'Is this your chestnut?' asked Scharley, smiling benignly. 'Are you looking for it? You're in luck. He was heading north at full gallop. I barely managed to stop it.'

One of the visitors, a large bearded man, observed him suspiciously. Judging from his dishevelled clothing and repugnant appearance, he was – like the others – a peasant. And like the others, he was armed with a stout stick.

'You stopped him, so you deserve credit,' he said, jerking the bridle tether from Scharley. 'And now be on your way.'

The others approached, surrounding him in a tight ring and the chokingly unbearable stench of agriculture. They weren't free peasants, but the rural poor: landless tenants, labourers and shepherds. Arguing with people like that about a reward made no sense, which Scharley understood at once. He forced his way wordlessly through the crowd. Reynevan followed him.

'Hey.' A stocky, foul-smelling shepherd suddenly seized the penitent by the sleeve. 'Friend Gamrat! Just letting them go? Without asking who they be? P'raps they're them outlaws? Those two what the Strzegom lords are seeking? And promising a bounty for seizing them? Ain't it them?'

The peasants murmured. Friend Gamrat moved closer, resting on his ash staff, as gloomy as a wet All Saints' Day.

'Perhaps they be,' he grunted ominously. 'And perhaps they bain't ...'

'They bain't, they bain't,' a smiling Scharley assured them. 'Didn't you know? Those two have been caught, and the bounty's been paid.'

'Methinks you're a-lyin'.'

'Leave go of my sleeve, fellow.'

'And what if I don't?'

The penitent looked him in the eyes for a moment. Then threw him off balance with a hard shove and spun to kick him in the shin just below the knee. The shepherd dropped to his knees and Scharley broke his nose with a short punch from above. The peasant grabbed his face and blood gushed through his fingers, decorating the front of his smock with a vivid patch.

Before the peasants had overcome their surprise, Scharley snatched Friend Gamrat's stick from him and struck him in the temple with it. Friend Gamrat's eyes rolled up and he slumped into the arms of the peasant behind him, whom the penitent also walloped. Scharley spun around like a top, aiming blows to every quarter.

'Flee, Reinmar!' he yelled. 'Run for it!'

Reynevan dug his spurs into the horse's side, jostling the throng, but didn't manage to get away. The peasants leaped on him like dogs from both sides and grabbed the harness. He struck out feverishly with his fists, but they dragged him from the saddle. He fought as hard as he could, kicking like a mule, but blows were raining down on him, too. He heard Scharley's furious yelling and the dry crack of the ash staff falling on skulls.

The peasants overwhelmed Reynevan and pinned him down. The situation was desperate. He was no longer fighting a band of peasants, but a terrible many-headed monster, a hydra with a hundred legs and a hundred fists, slippery with filth and stinking of muck, urine and rancid milk.

Over the cries of the mob and the swoosh of blood in his ears, he suddenly heard battle cries, thudding and neighing, and the ground trembled from the pounding of horseshoes. Bullwhips whistled, cries of pain resounded, and the many-armed beast smothering him disintegrated. The peasants – a moment earlier meting out violence – were now on the receiving end. The horsemen rampaging around the clearing ran them down and thrashed them mercilessly with their whips. Some of the peasants fled into the trees, but none avoided being struck.

Things soon quietened down a little. The horsemen were calming their snorting horses and combing the battlefield, looking for anyone they could still thrash. It was quite a colourful company. It was obvious at once that it was a party to be respected rather than joked with, not only from their apparel and gear, but also from their faces, which even a mediocre physiognomist would have found little difficulty classifying as shady and thuggish.

Reynevan stood up. And found himself face-to-face with a dapple-grey mare, on which sat a stout, fair-haired woman in a man's doublet and beret, flanked by two riders. A pair of piercingly shrewd hazel eyes looked out from beneath the plume of bee-eater's feathers adorning the beret.

Scharley, who appeared not to have suffered any serious injuries, stood alongside and discarded the remains of his ash staff.

'By the spirits,' he said. 'I don't believe my eyes. But this is no mirage – it's the Honourable Dzierżka Zbylut in the flesh. The proverb is apt: it's a small world . . .'

The dapple-grey mare shook its head, jangling the rings on its bit. The woman patted its neck in silence, measuring the penitent up and down with her piercing gaze.

'You've let yourself go, Scharley,' she finally said. 'And your hair's a little grey these days. Greetings. And now let's get out of here.'

*

They were sitting at a table in a large, whitewashed corner room at the back of the inn. One window looked out onto an orchard, some crooked pear trees, blackcurrant shrubs and hives droning with bees. The other window gave onto a paddock filling up with horses which were being gathered into a herd. Among the hundred or more steeds prevailed heavily built Silesian *dextrarii*, bred for heavy cavalry. There were also castellans, Spanish-blood stallions, Greater Poland lance horses and small cobs and nags. Among the thudding of hooves and neighing could be heard the cries and curses of grooms and stable boys, and the shady-looking men from the escort.

'You really have let yourself go,' repeated the woman with the hazel eyes, 'and silver threads have appeared in your hair since last I saw you.'

'What to do?' answered Scharley with a smile. '*Tacitisque senescimus annis.* Though the years only enhance your beauty and charm, Lady Dzierżka Zbylut.'

'Don't try to butter me up. And don't "lady" me, because I'll feel like some old dowager. And I'm not Zbylut any longer. When old Zbylut died, I went back to my maiden name, Dzierżka of Wirsing.'

'I remember now,' Scharley said, nodding. 'Zbylut of Szarada did indeed depart this life, may God keep him in His care. When was it, Dzierżka?'

'It'll be two years this Holy Innocents'.'

'How time flies. In the meanwhile, I was—'

'I know,' she interjected, and cast a piercing glance at Reynevan. 'You still haven't introduced your companion.'

'I am . . .' Reynevan hesitated for a moment, finally deciding that the Knight of the Cart might be both tactless and risky with regard to Dzierżka of Wirsing. 'I am Reinmar of Bielawa.'

The woman said nothing for a moment but continued to stare at him.

'Indeed,' she finally drawled. 'It's a small world. Would you like some beer soup, boys? They serve excellent beer soup here. I have it whenever I visit. Would you like to try some?'

Scharley's eyes lit up. 'Naturally, I would. Thank you, Dzierżka.'

When Dzierżka of Wirsing clapped her hands together, servants appeared immediately and busied themselves. Judging by the alacrity with which they came running, Reynevan surmised that she must be a regular guest here, known to have florins to spend. A moment later, the food arrived and he and Scharley were slurping soup, fishing out lumps of white cheese with lindenwood spoons, quickly but rhythmically to avoid clashing them together in the large bowl. Dzierżka tactfully kept silent, watching them and nursing a mug sweaty from the cold beer inside it.

Reynevan sighed deeply. He'd not eaten a hot meal since the lunch with Canon Otto in Strzelin. Meanwhile, Scharley was staring at Dzierżka's beer so meaningfully that he was soon brought a mug dripping with froth.

'Where is God leading you, Scharley?' she finally said. 'And why are you brawling with peasants in forests?'

'We're on a pilgrimage,' the penitent lied light-heartedly, 'to Our Lady of Bardo, to pray for the betterment of this world, and were attacked without reason. Verily, the world is full of wickedness, and you'll sooner meet a rogue on the highway than an abbess. That rabble attacked us entirely without cause, led by the sinful urge to do evil. But we forgive our trespassers—'

'I hired some peasants to search for a runaway colt.' Dzierżka interrupted his flow. 'I don't deny they are loathsome brutes, but later they were telling stories about some men being hunted and a bounty—'

'The delusions of idle and shallow minds,' said the penitent, sighing deeply. 'Who can fathom them?'

'You were locked away to do penance, weren't you?'

'I was.'

'And?'

'Nothing.' Scharley didn't twitch. 'Tedium. One day like the next. Over and over. *Matutinum*, Laudes, Prime, Terce, then *rumpus-pumpus* with Brother Barnabus, followed by Sext, Nones, then Barnabus, Vespers, *collationes*, Compline, and Barnabus—'

'Will you stop dissembling!' Dzierżka interrupted him again. 'You know what I mean, so tell me: did you escape? Are they after you? Is there a bounty on your head?'

'O God, deliver me!' Scharley appeared hurt by the implication. 'I was released. No one is after me – I'm a free man.'

'Of course, I keep forgetting,' she retorted with a sneer. 'But if you say so, I'll believe you. And if so . . . that truth leads to a simple conclusion.'

Scharley raised his eyebrows above the spoon he was licking, suggesting curiosity. Reynevan squirmed anxiously on the bench. Rightly, as it turned out.

'It leads to the simple conclusion,' repeated Dzierżka of Wirsing, scrutinising him, 'that the honourable young Sir Reinmar of Bielawa is the object of the hunt and the pursuit. The fact that I didn't guess it at once, young man, is because you rarely lose out in such matters if you count on Scharley. Oh my, you're perfectly matched, perfectly—'

She suddenly sprang up and rushed over to the window.

'Hey, you!' she yelled. 'Yes, *you*, you sodding prick! Strike that horse again and I'll have it drag you around the paddock!'

'Forgive me,' she said, returning to the table and folding her arms under her heaving bosom, 'but I have to keep an eye on things. As soon as my back's turned, they get up to no good, the wastrels. Where was I? Oh, yes. You're a perfect match, you buffoons.'

'So you know all about it?' Reynevan asked.

'I'll say! Folk talk of nothing else. Kyrie-eleison and Walter of Barby are racing around the highways, while Wolfher of Stercza is combing Silesia with five men, asking questions, making threats . . . Even so, you're fretting needlessly, Scharley, and you, laddie. You're safe with me. I don't care about your amorous adventures or family feuds; the Sterczas are no flesh and blood of mine. Unlike you, Reinmar of Bielawa. It may surprise you to learn that we are related – don't gape – for I'm *de domo* Wirsing, from the Wirsings of Reichwalde. And the Wirsings of Reichwalde are related to the Nostitzes through the Zedlitzes. And, after all, your grandmother was a Nostitz.'

'That's true,' said Reynevan, overcoming his astonishment. 'Why, m'lady, you're well versed in familial connections—'

'I know a thing or two,' she cut him off. 'I knew your brother, Piotr, well. He was a friend of my husband's. He supped oft with us at Skałka and used to ride horses from our stud.'

'You speak in the past tense, m'lady,' said Reynevan, his face darkening. 'So you know . . .'

'I do.'

Dzierżka of Wirsing interrupted the lengthening silence. 'Accept my heartfelt sympathies,' she said, and her expression confirmed her sentiments. 'The events at Balbinów are a tragedy for me, too. I knew and liked your brother. I always esteemed his good sense, his sober views, the fact that he never played the upstart lordling. No two ways about it – my Zbylut learned some gumption thanks to Peterlin. He stopped swaggering, saw how the world really works and began to breed horses. Piotr was his model, building a dyeing works and a fulling mill, making money and ignoring what other knights might say about it. And soon he was a true lord, powerful and wealthy, and the noblemen disdaining him bowed and scraped as long as he was gracious enough to lend them cash—'

Reynevan's eyes flashed. 'Peterlin used to lend money?'

'I know what you suspect,' Dzierżka looked at him keenly, 'but it's doubtful. Your brother only lent money to people he knew and trusted. One can upset the Church with usury. Peterlin added some interest, not even half what the Jews ask, but it's difficult to defend oneself against denunciation. And regarding your suspicions . . . While it's true there's no shortage of people prepared to murder for unpaid debts, the people your brother lent money to weren't that kind. So you're barking up the wrong tree, kinsman.'

'No doubt.' Reynevan pursed his lips. 'There's no point looking for new suspects. I know who killed Peterlin and why. I have no doubt in that regard.'

'Then you're in a minority,' said the woman coldly, 'because most people do.'

Another silence followed, interrupted once again by Dzierżka of Wirsing. 'Folk are talking about it,' she repeated. 'But it would be highly unwise, even downright foolish, to resort hastily to feuds and revenge on the basis of rumour. I say that in case by some chance you're not making for Our Lady of Bardo at all, but have quite different plans and designs.'

Reynevan pretended he was utterly absorbed by a stain on the ceiling. Scharley's expression was as innocent as a newborn baby's. Dzierżka kept her hazel eyes on both of them.

'But regarding Peterlin's death, there are doubts,' she continued a moment later, lowering her voice, 'and grave ones. Because a strange plague is abroad in Silesia, a mysterious pestilence that falls on tradesfolk and merchants, and not even noblemen are unscathed. People are dying mysterious deaths . . .'

'Sir Bart,' Reynevan muttered under his breath. 'Sir Bart of Karczyn . . .'

'Sir Bart, indeed.' She nodded. 'Then there's Tomasz Gernrode, master of the leatherworkers' guild from Nysa, and Herr Fabian Pfefferkorn, a lead merchant from the Niemodlin trading company. And most recently, barely a week ago, Mikołaj Neumarkt, a Świdnica cloth *mercator*. A veritable pestilence . . .'

'Let me guess,' Scharley spoke up. 'None of them died of smallpox. Or old age.'

'Correct.'

'I'll guess further: not without reason do you have a larger escort than usual, consisting of particularly heavily armed thugs. Where did you say you were going—?'

'I didn't. I only mentioned the matter so you would understand how serious it is. So you would understand that what's happening in Silesia, with the best will in the world, can't be attributed to the Sterczas. Nor can Kunz Aulock be blamed for it, because it began well before the young Master of Bielawa was caught in bed with Lady Stercza. You'd do well to remember that. I have nothing more to add now.'

'You've said too much not to finish,' Scharley said without lowering his eyes. 'Who's killing the Silesian merchants?'

'If we knew,' Dzierżka of Wirsing's eyes flashed dangerously, 'they wouldn't be doing any more killing. But fear not, we'll find out. And you stay away from it—'

'Does the name Horn mean anything to you?' interrupted Reynevan. 'Urban Horn?'

'No,' she replied, and Reynevan knew at once she was lying. Scharley shot him a glance that told him not to ask any more questions.

'Stay away from it,' repeated Dzierżka. 'It's a dangerous matter. And you have – if one is to believe the rumours – enough worries of your own. Folk are saying that the Sterczas are determined to catch you. That Kyrie-eleison and Stork are hunting you like wolves, that they're on your trail. And finally, that Sir Guncelin of Laasan has offered a bounty for two rascals—'

'Rumours,' interrupted Scharley. 'Gossip.'

'Perhaps. Still, such things have led many a man to the gallows, so I'd advise you to steer clear of the highways. And instead of Bardo, where you claim to be heading, I'd suggest you choose another, more distant town. Like Pressburg, for example. Or Esztergom. Or even Buda.'

Scharley bowed respectfully. 'Sound advice,' he said, 'and thanks for that. But Hungary is far, far away, and lacking a horse, I have to walk—'

'Don't beg, Scharley. It doesn't suit you— Bugger!'

She sprang up again, rushed over to the window and hurled more insults at a man handling a horse carelessly.

'Let's go outside,' she said, adjusting her hair, her bosom heaving. 'If I don't supervise them myself, the whoresons will cripple those colts.'

'A nice little herd,' said Scharley once they were outside. 'Even for the Skałka stud. There's a pretty penny to be made if you sell it.'

'Fear not.' Dzierżka of Wirsing gazed at her horses in delight. 'Castellans are in demand, cobs, too. Noblemen forget their miserliness where horses are concerned. You know what it's like: every man wants to be proud of his horse and his entourage on an expedition.'

'What expedition is that?'

Dzierżka cleared her throat and looked around. Then grimaced. 'For the betterment of this world.'

'Oh,' guessed Scharley. 'The Czechs.'

'Better not to talk about that too loudly.' The horse trader grimaced even more. 'The Bishop of Wrocław is said to be coming down hard on the local heretics. Many towns I passed had gibbets creaking with hanged men, often accompanied by the smoking embers from burnings.'

'But we're not heretics. So why should we be afraid?'

'Where stallions are being gelded,' said Dzierżka, 'it's best to keep an eye on your own balls.'

Scharley didn't comment. He was busy watching some soldiers pulling a wagon covered in a black, tarred tarpaulin from a shed. A pair of horses was harnessed to the wagon. And then, urged on by a fat sergeant, the soldiers carried out a large iron-bound chest and slid it under the tarpaulin. Finally, a stout individual in a beaver calpac and a cape with a beaver collar emerged from the inn.

'Who's that?' Scharley asked, his curiosity piqued. 'An Inquisitor?'

'Almost,' replied Dzierżka in hushed tones. 'He gathers taxes.'

'What taxes?'

'A special tax, for the war against heretics.'

'Czech heretics?'

'Are there any others?' Dzierżka grimaced again. 'And the tax was approved by the lords in the Frankfurt Reichstag. Anyone with a wealth of over two thousand guilders has to pay one guilder, anyone with less – half a guilder. Every squire from a noble family has to give three guilders, a knight five and a baron ten. All clergymen have to pay five from every hundred of their annual stipend, priests without stipends – two groschen . . .'

Scharley grinned, showing his white teeth.

'All the priests declared a lack of stipend, no doubt. Led by the aforementioned Bishop of Wrocław. But four burly men were needed to lift the casket, and I counted eight in the escort. It surprises me that such a hefty load is being guarded by such a small number.'

'The escort changes along the route,' explained Dzierżka. 'The knight whose estate they're passing through supplies the men. That's why there are so few at this moment.'

'I understand. Oh well, Dzierżka, it's time to say goodbye. Thank you for everything.'

'You can thank me in a moment, after I've had my men prepare you a little horse so you won't have to jog alongside your companion's mount, and will have a chance when they catch up with you. Just don't think it's out of charity and the goodness of my heart. You can pay me back on a suitable occasion. Forty Rhenish guilders. Don't give me that look – it's a bargain! You ought to be grateful.'

'And I am.' The penitent smiled. 'I am, Dzierżka. My heartfelt thanks. I've always been able to count on you. And so you won't say I only take, take, take, here's a present for you.'

'Some purses,' Dzierżka stated coolly. 'Embroidered with silver thread and pearls. They're quite pretty, even if they're fake. But why three?'

'Because I'm generous. And that's not all.' Scharley lowered his voice and looked around. 'You ought to know, Dzierżka, that the young Reinmar present here has certain . . . abilities. Absolutely remarkable, not to say . . . magical.'

'Eh?'

'Scharley is exaggerating,' said Reynevan, flinching a little. 'I'm a physician, not a magician—'

'Precisely,' the penitent interrupted him. 'Should you need an elixir or philtre . . . Like a love potion, let's say. Maybe an aphrodisiac or something for virility . . .'

'For virility,' she repeated pensively. 'Hmm . . . It could come in useful—'

'There you go.'

'—for my stallions,' Dzierżka of Wirsing finished her own sentence. 'I can cope with love myself, and manage splendidly without sorcery.'

'A quill, ink and paper, if you please,' Reynevan said after a moment of silence. 'I'll write down the recipe.'

The horse being prepared turned out to be a well-formed chestnut palfrey, the very one they had found in the clearing. Reynevan, who hadn't really given credence to the prophesies of the sylvan witches at first, now pondered deeply while Scharley leaped into the saddle and trotted briskly around the paddock. The penitent displayed another talent – a firm hand and strong knees soon had the chestnut trotting gracefully, and the stable boys and soldiers from the escort applauded Scharley's perfect riding position. Even the composed Dzierżka of Wirsing clicked her tongue in approval.

'I never knew,' she muttered, 'that he was such a cavalier. Verily, he isn't lacking in talent.'

'Indeed.'

'And you, kinsman,' she said, turning around, 'take care of yourself. Hussite emissaries are being hunted down. Strangers and foreigners are watched and anything suspicious is reported, because anyone who doesn't inform is himself suspicious. And if it wasn't enough that you're foreign *and* a stranger, your name and family have become well known in Silesia. I suggest you make something up. Best to keep your given name so you won't be constantly confused . . . Let's say you'll be . . . Reinmar of Hagenau.'

Reynevan had to smile. 'But that's the name of a famous poet—'

'Don't be fussy. In any case, times are hard – who remembers the names of poets these days?'

Scharley finished his display with a short but vigorous gallop, then brought the horse to a sliding stop, showering gravel around. He rode over, making the chestnut do some pretty dressage steps that earned him more applause.

'An elegant creature,' he said, patting the colt's neck. 'And swift. Thank you again, Dzierżka. Farewell.'

'Farewell. And may God be with you.'

'Goodbye.'

'Goodbye. See you in better times.'

Chapter Twelve

In which Reynevan and Scharley eat luncheon in a Benedictine monastery on Saint Giles's Eve, which falls on a Friday, a fast day. And after luncheon, they exorcise a devil. With an utterly unexpected result.

They heard the monastery before they saw it, because even though it was hidden in a forest, it suddenly spoke with the deep but melodic tolling of a bell. Before the sound had died out, they saw red-tiled roofs on buildings surrounded by a wall, reflected in the still waters of fishponds disturbed from time to time by ripples marking the feeding of large fish. Frogs and ducks went about their business in the rushes.

The horses walked along a reinforced causeway, down an avenue of trees.

Scharley stood up in the stirrups. 'Look at the monastery. I wonder what the rules are like. Do you fancy eating carp? Or tench? It's Friday today and the monks have rung the Nones. Perhaps they'll offer us luncheon?'

'I doubt it.'

'What do you doubt and why?'

Reynevan didn't reply. He was looking at the half-open monastery gate, from which a piebald horse was cantering, ridden by a monk. Once outside the gate, the monk spurred his mount to a hard gallop – which ended badly. The little piebald horse turned out to be wild and skittish, and the monk, clearly a Benedictine from his black habit, wasn't blessed with equestrian skill. He had also mounted the piebald wearing sandals, which just wouldn't stay in the stirrups. After galloping about a quarter of a furlong, the piebald kicked and the monk sailed out of the saddle and tumbled over and over, flashing bare calves, and finally came to rest under some willows. The horse kicked and neighed, pleased with itself, and then trotted along the causeway towards the two travellers. Scharley grabbed its reins in passing.

'Just look at that centaur!' he said. 'Rope for reins, a blanket for a saddle and rags for a girth. I don't know if the Rule of Saint Benedict of Nursia permits or forbids riding horses, I truly don't, but it ought to forbid riding like that.'

'He was obviously in a hurry to get somewhere.'

'That's no excuse.'

Like the monastery, they heard the monk before they saw him, for he was sitting among the burdock with his head on his knees, sobbing hard enough to break your heart.

'There, there,' said Scharley from the height of his saddle. 'No need to shed tears, Frater. Nothing's lost. The horse didn't run away, we have him here. And you'll learn to ride, Frater, for I see you have a great deal of time ahead of you in which to do so.'

Scharley was indeed right. The monk was but a boy, whose hands, lips and the rest of his face were shaking.

'Brother ... Deodatus ...' he sobbed. 'Brother Deodatus ... will die ... because of me ...'

'Eh?'

'It's all my fault ...'

'Were you hurrying to get a physician?' Reynevan quickly guessed. 'To treat a sick man?'

The boy sobbed, 'Brother Deodatus ... will die because of me ...'

'Collect yourself and speak more coherently, Frater!'

'An evil spirit has entered Brother Deodatus and possessed him!' shouted the monk, raising reddened eyes. 'So the abbot ordered me to ride as quickly as possible to Świdnica, to the Order of Preachers ... To fetch an exorcist!'

'Wasn't there a better horseman in the monastery?'

'No, and since I'm the youngest . . . Oh, how hapless am I!'

'I'd say happy, actually,' Scharley said gravely. 'Verily, happy. Find your sandals among the weeds and hasten to the monastery. Announce the good news to the abbot that the Lord's grace is shining on your monastery. That on the causeway you encountered Master Benignus, the veteran exorcist, whom an angel assuredly sent this way.'

'Is that you, good sir? You are—'

'I said hasten to the abbot as quickly as possible. Inform him that I approach.'

'Tell me I misheard you, Scharley. Tell me it was a slip of the tongue. That you didn't say what I think you just said.'

'Meaning what? That I'll exorcise Brother Deodatus? But of course I shall. With your help, laddie.'

'Oh, no. Don't drag me into this. I have enough problems already. I don't need any new ones.'

'Neither do I. But I do need luncheon and money. And luncheon as soon as possible.'

'That's the stupidest idea of all possible stupid ideas,' judged Reynevan, looking around the sunlit cloister. 'Do you know what you're doing? Do you know what you risk by impersonating a priest? An exorcist? Posing as some bloody Master Benignus?'

'Impersonating? I *am* a priest. And an exorcist. It's a matter of faith and I have faith. That I'll succeed.'

'I believe you're mocking me.'

'Not in the slightest. Start preparing spiritually for the task.'

'I won't take part in anything of the kind.'

'And why not? You're supposed to be a doctor. It's your duty to help the suffering.'

'He,' said Reynevan, pointing towards the infirmary, which they had just left and where Brother Deodatus was lying, 'he cannot be helped. The monk is in lethargy. In a coma. You heard the monks say they tried to rouse him by pricking his heels with a hot knife, to no avail? Thus it's an affliction of the brain, the *spiritus animalis*. Some sort of *grand mal* or "great malady". I've read about it in Avicenna's *Canon medicinae*, also in the works of Razes and Averroes, and I know it's incurable. One can only wait—'

'Indeed, one can wait,' interrupted Scharley. 'But why wait with one's arms folded? Particularly if one can act? And make money from it? Without harming anyone?'

'Without harming anyone? What about ethics?'

'I don't usually discuss philosophy on an empty belly.' Scharley shrugged. 'But later, belly full of food and beer, I'll lay out the *principia* of my ethics and astonish you with their simplicity.'

'I dread to imagine it.'

'Reynevan.' Scharley whirled around. 'For God's sake, think positively.'

'I *am* thinking – and I think this could end badly.'

'Oh, think what you want. But for now, be so kind as to shut up, because they're coming.'

The abbot was indeed approaching, in the company of several monks. The abbot was short, plump and chubby-cheeked, but his benign and good-natured appearance was contradicted by the fierce grimace of his mouth and his lively eyes, which swiftly jumped from Scharley to Reynevan and back again.

'Well?' he asked, slipping his hands beneath his scapular. 'What's wrong with Brother Deodatus?'

'The *spiritus animalis* is afflicted,' announced Scharley, pouting proudly. 'It is some kind of *grand mal* or great malady, as described by Avicenna, in brief: *tohu wa-bohu*. You ought to know, *Reverende Pater*, that things look bleak. But action shall be taken.'

'What action?'

'To drive the evil spirit from the possessed man.'

'Are you so certain that it is possession?' asked the abbot, tilting his head.

'I'm certain it's not diarrhoea.' Scharley's voice was quite cold. 'Diarrhoea has different symptoms.'

'You are not men of the cloth, however.' The abbot's voice still carried a note of suspicion.

'Oh, but we are.' Scharley did not bat an eyelid. 'I've already explained it to the brother infirmarian. We dress secularly for camouflage, to baffle the Devil, in order to take him by surprise.'

The abbot looked keenly at him. *Oh dear, this isn't good*, thought Reynevan. *He's no fool. This might indeed end badly.*

'How, then, do you mean to proceed?' The abbot kept his probing eyes on Scharley. 'According to Avicenna? Or perhaps according to the instructions of Saint Isidor of Seville, found in the work entitled . . . Oh, dear, I've forgotten . . . But you, learned exorcist, undoubtedly know—'

'*Etymologiae*.' Scharley didn't bat an eyelid this time, either. 'I make use of the lore found there, for it is elementary knowledge, and of the same author's *De nature rerum*.'

The abbot's gaze softened somewhat, but it was clear that some suspicion remained.

'You are learned, there's no denying it,' he said with a sneer, 'as you have demonstrated. And what now? Will you ask for vittles first? And beverages? And advance payment?'

'Not a word about payment,' said Scharley, straightening up so proudly that Reynevan was seized with real admiration. 'Not a word about coinage, for I am neither a merchant nor a money-lender. I shall settle for alms, a modest gift, and by no means in advance, but only after the work is complete. Regarding vittles and beverages, however, I shall remind you, Reverend Father, of the words of the Gospel: evil spirits are driven out only by prayer and fasting.'

The abbot's face lit up and the hostile severity vanished from his eyes.

'Verily,' he said, 'I see I am dealing with virtuous and pious Christians. And verily I say: the Gospel is all very well, but how can one, as the saying goes, work on an empty stomach? I invite you to *prandium*. A modest, fast-day prandium, for today is Friday. Beavers' tails in sauce . . .'

'Lead on, honourable Father Abbot,' said Scharley, swallowing loudly. 'Lead on.'

Reynevan wiped his mouth and stifled a belch. The beavers' tails, stewed in a thick horseradish sauce and served with kasha, turned out to be delicious. Until then, Reynevan had only heard of that speciality. He knew that in some monasteries it was eaten during fasts, since for some obscure reason beaver was considered to be something like fish. It was, however, quite a rare delicacy, since not every abbey had beaver lodges in the vicinity and not all of them had hunting privileges. But the great pleasure of eating this titbit was marred by anxious thoughts of the task awaiting them. *Although*, he mused, scrupulously wiping his bowl with a hunk of bread, *no one can take away what I've just eaten.*

Scharley, who had made short work of quite a small portion – it was a fast day, after all – was now pontificating.

'Various authorities have voiced their opinions regarding devilish possession,' he said. 'The greatest of them – men who are no doubt familiar to you – are both sainted fathers and Doctors of the Church such as Basil, Isidor of Seville and Gregory of Nazianzus. Surely the works of Tertullian, Origen and Lactantius are known to you?'

Some of the Benedictines present in the refectory nodded eagerly and others lowered their heads.

'But those sources of knowledge are quite general,' Scharley continued to explain, 'and thus a serious exorcist cannot restrict his learning to them alone.'

The monks nodded again, sedulously eating up the kasha and sauce in their bowls. Scharley sat up straight and cleared his throat.

'I know Michael Psellos's *Dialogus de energia et operatione daemonum*,' he announced somewhat proudly. 'I know by heart excerpts from *Exorcisandis obsessis a daemonio*, a work by Pope Leon III. I also know the *Book of the Secrets of Enoch*, but that's nothing to boast about since everybody does. While my assistant, the courageous Master Reinmar, has even deeply explored Saracen writings, keenly aware of the risks that contact with the magic of the pagan carries with it.'

Reynevan blushed. The abbot smiled benignly, taking it as a sign of modesty.

'Verily!' he announced. 'Why, I see that you are scholars and experienced exorcists. I wonder, do you have many devils to your name?'

'In truth,' Scharley lowered his eyes, as modest as a Poor Clare novice, 'I can't compete with records. The most devils I've managed to cast out of a possessed person at one time is nine.'

'Indeed,' said the abbot, clearly worried, 'that is not many. I've heard of Dominicans who—'

'I've also heard,' interrupted Scharley, 'but not seen. Furthermore, I was talking about higher devils, and it's well known that every higher devil has at least thirty lower devils in its service. However, self-respecting exorcists don't keep count, because if you cast out the leader, its followers will also flee. But were I to reckon up using the method of the Order of Preachers, then I might easily compete with those Dominicans you mentioned.'

'Quite right,' admitted the abbot, but somewhat hesitantly.

'Unfortunately,' added Scharley, coldly and a little nonchalantly, 'I cannot give written guarantees. Please keep that in mind so there won't be any grievances afterwards.'

'Eh?'

'Saint Martin of Tours,' Scharley still didn't bat an eyelid, 'took from every exorcised devil a document signed with its own devilish name, stating that the given devil would never, ever dare to possess a given person again. Many celebrated saints and bishops managed to do the same, but I, a humble exorcist, am unable to obtain a document of that kind.'

'Perhaps it's for the better!' said the abbot, crossing himself, as did the other monks. 'Holy Mother, Queen of Heaven! A parchment signed by the Evil One's hand? What an abomination! And a sin! We don't want that—'

'I'm glad you don't,' Scharley cut him off. 'But first duties and then pleasure. Is the patient in the chapel?'

'Absolutely.'

One of the younger Benedictines, who hadn't taken his eyes off Scharley for a long time, suddenly spoke. 'Nonetheless, how may it be explained, Master, that Brother Deodatus is lying like a log, barely breathing and not moving a finger, when almost all the learned books you have quoted say that the possessed person usually has an extraordinary agitation of the limbs, and that the devil endlessly jabbers and yells through him? Is there not some contradiction here?'

'All affliction,' said Scharley, looking down on the monk, 'including possession, is the work of Satan, the destroyer of God's work. Every malady is prompted by one of the four Black Angels of Evil: Mahazel, Azazel, Azrael or Samael. The fact that the possessed person isn't thrashing about or crying out but is lying lifeless proves that he has been possessed by one of the demons subordinate to Samael.'

'Christ the Lord!' said the abbot, crossing himself.

'Notwithstanding,' Scharley said, arrogantly, 'I know how to deal with such demons. They fly on the wind and possess a fellow noiselessly and stealthily, through the breath, which is called *insufflatio*. I shall command the Devil to leave the afflicted man via the same route, through *exsufflatio*.'

'How can it be,' the young monk went on, 'that the Devil is in the abbey, where there are bells, the Holy Mass, the breviary and sanctity? How can it be that he has possessed a monk?'

Scharley retorted with a stern look.

'As Saint Gregory the Great, Doctor of the Church, teaches,' he said severely and emphatically, 'a nun once swallowed the Devil with a lettuce leaf from the monastery vegetable garden because she ignored the duty of praying and crossing herself before meals. Did Brother Deodatus not commit similar misdeeds?'

The Benedictines lowered their heads and the abbot cleared his throat.

'That is indeed true,' he muttered. 'Brother Deodatus could be secular, extremely secular, and not dutiful enough.'

'It is then simple to fall prey to the Evil One,' Scharley concluded dryly. 'Lead me to the chapel, Brothers.'

'What will you need, Master?' asked the abbot. 'Holy water? A cross? Holy pictures? A benedictional?'

'Just holy water and a Bible.'

The chapel was cold and in semi-darkness, lit only by the glowing halos of candles and a slanting column of coloured light filtered through a stained-glass window. Brother Deodatus lay in the light, on a catafalque covered by a linen mortcloth. He looked as he had in the monastery infirmary an hour earlier, when Reynevan and Scharley saw him for the first time. His face was set like a wax mask and had the yellowish colour of a boiled marrowbone, his cheeks and mouth sunken, his eyes closed and his breath so shallow as to be almost imperceptible. He had been positioned with his arms – marked with wounds from bloodletting – crossed on his chest and a rosary and mauve stole entwined around his inert fingers.

A few paces from the catafalque, an immense man with shaven head, vacant gaze and the facial expression of a slow-witted child was sitting on the floor, his back resting against the wall. The giant had two fingers of his right hand in his mouth and his left hand was clutching a small clay pot to his belly. Every few seconds, the giant sniffed repulsively, peeled the dirty, sticky pot from his sticky, dirty tunic, wiped his fingers on his belly, shoved them in the pot, gathered some honey and lifted them to his mouth. Then the ritual was repeated.

'He's an orphan, a foundling,' the abbot said, anticipating the question and seeing Scharley's disgusted expression. 'Christened "Samson" by us owing to his great size and strength. He's a servant here in the monastery, a little simple . . . but he loves Brother Deodatus greatly, trots behind him like a little dog . . . So we thought—'

'Very well, very well,' interrupted Scharley. 'He may sit there as long as he stays quiet. Let us begin. Master Reinmar ...'

Reynevan, imitating Scharley, hung a stole around his neck, placed his hands together in prayer and inclined his head. He didn't know if Scharley was pretending or not, but *he* was praying earnestly and zealously. He was, quite simply, terrified. Scharley, meanwhile, looked absolutely confident, oozing imperious authority.

'Pray,' he instructed the Benedictines. 'Say the *Domine sancte.*'

He stood beside the catafalque, crossed himself and made the sign of the cross over Brother Deodatus. He gestured to Reynevan to sprinkle holy water on the possessed man. The possessed man, naturally, didn't react.

'*Domine sancte, Pater omnipotens . . .*' The murmur of the monks' prayers echoed around the star vault. '*Aeterne Deus, propter tuam largitatem et Filii tui . . .*'

Scharley cleared his throat loudly.

'*Offer nostras preces in conspectu Altissimi,*' he thundered, making even louder echoes, '*ut cito anticipent nos misericordiae Domini, et apprehendas draconem, serpentem antiquum, qui est diabolus et satanas, ac ligatum mittas in abyssum, ut non seducat amplius gentes. Hinc tuo confisi praesidio ac tutela, sacri ministerii nostri auctoritate, ad infestationes diabolicae fraudis repellendas in nomine Iesu Christi Dei et Domini nostri fidentes et securi aggredimur.*'

'*Domine,*' Reynevan joined in on an agreed sign, '*exaudi orationem meam.*'

'*Et clamor meus ad te veniat.*'

'Amen.'

'*Princeps gloriosissime caelestis militiae, sancte Michael Archangele, defende nos in proelio et colluctatione. Satanas! Ecce Crucem Domini, fugite partes adversae! Apage! Apage! Apage!*'

'Amen!'

On the catafalque, Brother Deodatus gave no sign of life. Scharley discreetly wiped his forehead with the end of the stole.

'Thus is the prelude complete,' he said, without lowering his eyes under the enquiring looks of the Benedictines. 'And we know one thing: we are not facing any old miserable devil, for one like that would already have fled. We must bring out the heavier bombards.'

The abbot blinked and shifted restlessly. The giant Samson, sitting on the floor, scratched his crotch, sniffed, hawked, farted, laboriously unstuck the pot of honey from his belly and then glanced down at it to see how much was left.

Scharley's eyes swept the monks with a look which he thought was both wise and inspired.

'As the Good Book teaches us,' he said, 'Satan is characterised by overweening pride. Nothing else but his immeasurable pride caused Lucifer to rebel against the Lord, so he was punished for his hubris by being cast into the infernal abyss. But the Devil remains prideful! The exorcist's first task is thus to pique the Devil's pride and love for himself. In short: thoroughly abuse him, curse, insult and revile him. Calumniate him and then he will flee with his tail between his legs.'

The monks waited, certain there was more to come. They were right.

'Thus we shall now insult the Devil,' continued Scharley. 'If any of you are sensitive to coarse language, you ought to leave without delay. Come here, Master Reinmar, speak in the words of the Gospel of Saint Matthew. And you, Brothers, pray.'

'"And Jesus rebuked the Devil and he departed out of him,"' recited Reynevan. '"And the child was cured from that very hour. Then came the disciples to Jesus apart and said, "Why could we not cast him out?" And Jesus said unto them, "Because of your unbelief."'

The Benedictines' murmured prayers mingled with the recitation. Scharley, meanwhile, straightened the stole around his neck, stood over the motionless Brother Deodatus and spread his arms wide.

'Vile Devil!' he yelled so loudly it made Reynevan stammer and the abbot start. 'I command you immediately to depart this body, O unclean power! Get out of this Christian, you filthy, obese, lewd hog, O beast among all the beasts and most bestial, O scum of Tartarus, O abomination of She'ol! I cast you out, you bristly Jewish swine, to the infernal pigsty, where I hope you will drown in shit!'

'*Sancta Virgo virginem,*' whispered the abbot, '*ora pro nobis . . .*'

'*Ab insidiis diaboli,*' the monks echoed, '*libera nos . . .*'

'You ravaged old crocodile!' Scharley roared, flushing red. 'You dying basilisk, you shit-covered mandrill! You tarantula, tangled up in your own web! You filthy dromedary! Hear me as I call you by your true name: *scrofa stercorata et pedicosa*, filthy and louse-ridden swine, foulest of the foul, most foolish of the fools, *stultus stultorum rex!*'

Brother Deodatus, lying on the bier, didn't even twitch. Although Reynevan sprinkled him profusely with holy water, the drops trickled impotently down the old man's hardened features. Scharley's jaw muscles were twitching powerfully. *The climax is approaching*, thought Reynevan. He wasn't wrong.

'Begone from this body!' bellowed Scharley. 'You catamite fucked in the arse!'

One of the younger Benedictines fled, covering his ears, taking the Lord's name in vain. The others were either very pale or very red-faced.

The shaven-headed giant grunted and moaned, trying to thrust his whole hand into the honey pot, which was impossible since his hand was twice as large as the pot. The giant lifted the vessel up high, tipped his head back and opened his mouth wide, but the honey didn't drip as there was simply too little of it left.

'And what about Brother Deodatus, Master?' the abbot found the courage to stammer out. 'What about the evil spirit? Has it departed?'

Scharley stooped over the possessed man and almost touched Brother Deodatus's lips with his ear.

'It is nearly at the surface,' he stated. 'We'll soon cast him out. We must simply shock him with a foul odour. The Devil is sensitive to foul odours. Come on, Fratres, bring a bucket of dung, a frying pan and a cresset. We will fry fresh dung under the possessed man's nose.'

Several brothers ran off to carry out his instructions. The hulk sitting by the wall picked his nose, looked at his finger and rubbed it on a trouser leg. Then he resumed removing the rest of the honey from the pot. With the same finger. Reynevan felt the beavers' tails he'd eaten rising up his throat on a swelling wave of horseradish sauce.

'Master Reinmar.' Scharley's stern voice brought him back to the world. 'Let us not cease our efforts. The Gospel of Mark, please, a suitable passage. Pray, Brothers.'

'"When Jesus saw that the people came running together,"' Reynevan obediently read, '"he rebuked the foul spirit, saying unto him, Thou dumb and deaf spirit, I charge thee, come out of him, and enter no more into him."'

'*Surde et mute spiritus ego tibi praecipio,*' Scharley repeated menacingly and commandingly, stooping over Brother Deodatus. 'May His power cast you out along with your entire cohort!'

The honey-guzzling hulk suddenly coughed, slobbered and snorted mucus. Scharley wiped the sweat from his forehead.

'An exacting and difficult *casus*,' he explained, avoiding the abbot's increasingly suspicious expression. 'It will be necessary to use even stronger arguments.'

For a moment, it was so quiet that all that could be heard was the insistent buzzing of a fly that had flown into a spider's web in the window alcove.

'By the Apocalypse,' Scharley's now slightly hoarse baritone sounded in the silence, 'which our Lord used to reveal things which are to come to pass, and confirmed those things through the mouth of an angel banished by him, I curse you, Satan! *Exorciso te, flumen immundissimum, draco maleficus, spiritum mendacii!*'

As before, the words had no effect. All sorts of emotions were etched on the faces of the watching Benedictines. Scharley took a deep breath.

'May Agios strike you as he struck Egypt! May they stone you to death, as the Israelites stoned Achan. May they trample you with their feet and hang you on a tree, as were the five Amorite kings! And may your tail be cut off right by your devilish arse!'

Oh, thought Reynevan, *this is going to end badly.*

'Devilish spirit!' Scharley suddenly spread his arms over Brother Deodatus, who was still showing no signs of life. 'I curse you by Acharon, Ehey, Homus, Athanatos, Ischiros, Aecodes and Almanach, by Pophiel and Phul! I curse you by the mighty names of Shmiel and Shmul! I curse you with the most abominable of names: with the name of the overpowering and terrible Semaphor!'

Semaphor was no more effective than Phul and Shmul. It couldn't be denied. Scharley saw it, too.

'Jobsa, hopsa, afia, alma!' he screamed savagely. 'Melach, Berot, Not, Berib *et vos omnes*! Hemen etan! Hemen etan! Bow! Wow! Wow!'

He's lost his mind, thought Reynevan. *And in a moment, they'll pounce. They'll soon work out that it's all nonsense – they can't be that stupid.*

Scharley, now awfully sweaty and hoarse, caught his eye and winked an extremely clear request for support, a request bolstered by an insistent though furtive gesture. Reynevan raised his eyes towards the vault. *Anything*, he thought, trying to recall the old books and conversations with friendly mages, *anything has got to be better than 'bow-wow-wow'.*

'Hax, pax, max!' he bellowed, waving his arms. 'Abeor super aberer! Aie Saraye! Aie Saraye! Albedo, rubedo, nigredo!'

Scharley, breathing heavily, glanced at him gratefully and gestured for him to continue. Reynevan took a deep breath.

'Tumor, rubor, calor, dolor! *Per ipsum, et cum ipso, et in ipso!* Jobsa, hopsa *et vos omnes! Et cum spiritu tuo!* Melach, Malach, Molach!'

They'll start beating us any moment now, he thought feverishly.

Any second now. There's nothing to be done. I'll have to go all out. In Arabic. Stand beside me, Averroes. Save me, Avicenna.

'*Kullu-al-Shaitanu-al-rajim!*' he screamed. '*Fa-anasahum Tarish! Qasura al-Zoba! Al-Ahmar, Baraqan al-Abayad! Al-Shaitan! Khar-al-Sus! Al ouar! Mochefi al relil! El feurj! El feurj!*'

The last word, as he vaguely recalled, meant 'pudenda' in Arabic and had little in common with an exorcism. He was aware of the great stupidity he was engaged in. He was even more astonished by the outcome.

He felt as though the world had stood still for a moment. And then, in utter silence, among the tableau of Benedictines in black habits frozen against the grey walls, something twitched, something disturbed the dead calm with a movement and a sound.

The vacant-looking giant sitting by the wall suddenly tossed aside the sticky, dirty honey pot in disgust and revulsion. The pot clattered against the floor and didn't break, but rolled, penetrating the silence with a dull but noisy clunking.

The giant raised his honey-covered fingers up to his eyes. He looked at them for a moment and his chubby, moonlit face showed first disbelief and then horror. Reynevan watched him, breathing heavily. He felt Scharley's urgent gaze on him, but he was unable to utter a word. *That's it*, he thought. *That's it.*

The hulk, still looking at his finger, moaned. Heart-rendingly.

And then Brother Deodatus, lying on the bier, grunted, coughed, wheezed and kicked his legs. Then he swore, extremely secularly.

'Saint Euphrosyne . . .' the abbot groaned, kneeling. The other monks followed his example. Scharley opened his mouth, but quickly and astutely closed it. Reynevan put his hands to his temples, not knowing whether to pray or run away.

'Bugger . . .' croaked Brother Deodatus, sitting up. 'My throat's dry . . . What? Did I sleep through supper? A pox on you, Brothers, I only wanted a nap. I asked you to wake me up in time for Vespers . . .'

'It's a miracle!' yelled one of the kneeling monks.

'God's kingdom is come,' said another, falling spreadeagled on the floor. '*Igitur pervenit in nos regnum Dei!*'

'*Alleluia!*'

Brother Deodatus, who was now sitting on the bier, looked uncomprehendingly from the kneeling monks to Scharley with the stole around his neck, from Reynevan to the giant Samson, still examining his hands and belly, from the praying abbot to the monks who had just run in with a pail of manure and a copper frying pan.

'Would someone kindly tell me what the hell's going on here?' asked the recently possessed monk.

Chapter Thirteen

In which, after leaving the Benedictine monastery, Scharley lectures Reynevan about his existential philosophy, which can be reduced to the theory that you only need to drop your trousers and look the other way for some unkind person to have a go at you. A moment later, life confirms his arguments in every detail. Scharley is saved from trouble by somebody the reader already knows – or, rather, thinks they know.

The exorcism in the Benedictine abbey – although in principle crowned by success – further deepened Reynevan's dislike of Scharley, which had been increasing from day one and intensified after the incident with the beggar. Reynevan now understood he was dependent on the penitent's assistance and that without him, attempting to free his beloved Adèle by himself had slim chance of success. Understanding his dependence was one thing, but the dislike remained, nagging him like a torn fingernail or a chipped tooth, and Scharley's behaviour only deepened it.

A dispute flared up the evening after they left the monastery, when they were but a short distance from Świdnica. Paradoxically, Reynevan was recalling Scharley's exorcistic mischief and reproaching him for it while they consumed gifts obtained through that very mischief. For on parting, the grateful Benedictines had given them a large bundle containing a rye loaf, a dozen apples, a dozen hard-boiled eggs, a ring of smoked juniper sausage and a fat Polish blood pudding.

Our wanderers were sitting on a dry hillside at the edge of a forest, eating and gazing at the sun, which was sinking lower and lower towards the tops of the pine trees. And arguing. Reynevan had raced on somewhat, extolling ethical norms and criticising roguery. Scharley immediately took him down a peg.

'I don't accept,' he pronounced, spitting out the shell of a badly peeled egg, 'moral teachings from someone who is in the habit of screwing other men's wives.'

'How many more times,' said Reynevan in irritation, 'do I have to repeat that it's not the same? That you can't compare them?'

'You can, Reinmar, you can.'

'Interesting.'

Scharley pressed the loaf against his belly and cut off another hunk.

'What makes us different,' he began a moment later, speaking with his mouth full, 'is experience and practical wisdom. What you do instinctively, driven by an outright childish desire to satisfy your sexual urges, I carry out deliberately, according to a plan. But the same drive lies at the heart of both behaviours. Namely, the conviction that what counts is me, my welfare and my pleasure, and the rest can go to hell if it doesn't serve my interests. Don't interrupt. To you, your dear Adèle's charms were like a sticky bun to a child. In order to taste it, you forgot everything else – all that mattered was your own pleasure. No, don't try bringing love into this, quoting Petrarch and Wolfram of Eschenbach. Love is also a pleasure, and one of the most selfish I know.'

'I will not listen to this.'

'*In summa*,' continued the penitent adamantly, 'our existential beliefs don't differ at all, since they are based on the same *principium*: everything I do should serve me. Where we do differ, though—'

'So we do differ, then?'

'—is the ability to think long term. In spite of frequent temptations, I refrain as far as I am able from bedding other men's wives, because long-term thinking suggests that in addition to not benefitting me, it will cause me problems. I don't pamper the poor with alms, not out of miserliness, but simply because such charity doesn't achieve anything. In fact, it is blatantly harmful – you lose a penny and gain the reputation of a fool. And since *numerus* fools *infinitus est*, I swindle them whenever I can, including foolish Benedictines. Got it?'

'I understand what you were imprisoned for,' said Reynevan, biting off a mouthful of apple.

'You've understood nothing. But there's time for you to learn – it's a long way to Hungary.'

'Do you think I'll make it there? In one piece?'

'What do you mean by that?'

'Because the more I listen to you, the bigger an idiot I feel. An idiot who any moment may become the victim on the sacrificial altar of his own convenience.'

'You see, you're making progress,' Scharley said happily. 'You're beginning to reason sensibly. Apart from your unwarranted sarcasm, you're now beginning to grasp the fundamental principle of life: the principle of limited trust, which teaches us that the surrounding world is ceaselessly lying in wait for us, and never passes up an opportunity to cause you insult, distress or harm. That it's only waiting until you drop your breeches to kick you in your bare arse.'

Reynevan snorted.

'From which two conclusions can be drawn,' continued the penitent, without faltering. '*Primo*: never trust or believe people's intentions. *Secundo*: if you ever cause anyone harm or distress, don't fret over it. You were simply quicker, you acted preventatively—'

'Be quiet!'

'Why? I'm telling you the honest truth and I believe in the principle of free speech. The freedom—'

'Be quiet, dammit. I heard something. Someone's sneaking up on us—'

'Probably a werewolf!' Scharley chuckled. 'A terrible manwolf, the scourge of the parish!'

As they were leaving the monastery, the thoughtful monks had warned them to be on their guard. They said that for some time, especially during the full moon, a dangerous *lykanthropos* or werewolf had been prowling the vicinity. The warning had greatly amused Scharley, who for a good few furlongs had split his sides laughing and mocked the superstitious monks. Reynevan didn't really believe in werewolves, either, but he didn't laugh along with Scharley.

'I can hear footsteps,' he said, pricking up his ears. Somebody was approaching, there was no doubt.

A jay in the undergrowth screeched in alarm. The horses snorted. A branch snapped. Scharley shielded his eyes against the setting sun.

'The Devil take it,' he muttered under his breath. 'That's all we need. Have a look, someone's arrived.'

'It might be . . .' stammered Reynevan. 'It's—'

'The colossus from the Benedictine abbey,' said Scharley, confirming Reynevan's suspicions. 'The priory giant, Beowulf the Honey-Eater. The pot-licker with the biblical name. What did they call him? Goliath?'

'Samson.'

'That's right, Samson. Pay no attention to him.'

'But what's he doing here?'

'Pay no attention and he might just go his own way, wherever that leads.'

But it didn't look as though Samson intended to go. On the contrary, it looked as though he had reached his destination, for he was lounging on a tree stump a few yards away with his chubby, gormless face turned towards them. But his face was clean, much cleaner than before, and the dried-on mucus was gone from under his nose. What's more, the smock he was wearing was freshly laundered. In spite of that, he still exuded a faint smell of honey.

'Oh well,' said Reynevan, clearing his throat. 'Politeness requires—'

'I knew it,' interrupted Scharley, sighing. 'I knew you'd say that. Hey, you there! Samson! Vanquisher of the Philistines! Are you hungry?'

Without waiting for a reaction, Scharley tossed a piece of black pudding towards the colossus, as one would a treat at a dog or cat. 'Grub! Do you understand? Grub, over here! Foodies! Yum-yum! Do you want some?'

'Thank you,' the giant replied, unexpectedly clearly and alertly, 'but I'll decline. I'm not hungry.'

'This is a strange matter,' muttered Scharley, leaning towards Reynevan's ear. 'How did he get here? Was he following us? After all, he supposedly trails after Brother Deodatus, our recent patient . . . We're at least a mile from the priory, so he must have set off immediately after us and followed our trail at a brisk pace. To what end?'

'Ask him.'

'I will. At the right moment. For now, just to be sure, let's talk in Latin.'

'*Bene.*'

The sun was sinking lower and lower over the dark forest. Cranes flying westwards gave their bugle-like calls as frogs in the swamp by the river began a raucous concert. And the dry hillside at the edge of the forest resounded with the language of Virgil.

Reynevan talked about his recent history and described his adventures. Scharley listened – or at least pretended to. The priory hulk, Samson, was staring vacantly at something or other, and his chubby physiognomy continued to be free of any noteworthy emotions.

Reynevan's tale was, naturally, only the preamble to the main thrust – another attempt to draw Scharley into armed intervention against the Sterczas. Nothing came of it, naturally. Not even when Reynevan began to tempt the penitent with the prospect of big money – without, of course, any idea where that money would be obtained from. In any case, the issue was purely academic since Scharley rejected the offer. The dispute was revived, with both parties making copious use of classical quotations – from Tacitus to Ecclesiastes.

'*Vanitas vanitatum*, Reinmar! Vanity of vanities and all is vanity! Be not hasty in thy spirit to be angry, "for anger resteth in the bosom of fools". Remember – *melior est canis vivus leone mortuo*, a living dog is better than a dead lion.'

'Come again?'

'If you don't abandon your foolish plans of revenge, you'll be dead, because those plans mean certain death to you. And even if I'm not killed, I'll be thrown in gaol again. And not for a vacation in a Carmelite priory this time, but into a dungeon, *ad carcerem perpetuum*. Or a lengthy term of *in pace* in the monastery, which they consider merciful. Do you know, Reinmar, what *in pace* is? It's being buried alive. In a cellar, in a cell so cramped and low that you can only sit, and as the amount of excrement increases, you have to stoop more and more so as not to scrape your head on the ceiling. You must be out of your mind if you think I'll risk something like that for your cause. And such a murky cause, to boot.'

'What's murky about it?' Reynevan asked indignantly. 'My brother's tragic death?'

'The circumstances around it.'

Reynevan pursed his lips and turned his head away. For a while, he looked at the giant Samson sitting on the tree stump. *He looks different in some way*, he thought. *He still has the face of a moron, but something's changed. What?*

'There's nothing unclear about the events surrounding Peterlin's death,' Reynevan continued. 'Kyrie-eleison murdered him. Kunz Aulock *et suos complices*. *Ex subordinatione* and for the Sterczas' money. So the Sterczas ought to bear—'

'Weren't you listening to what your relative Dzierżka was saying?' interrupted Scharley.

'I was. But I didn't attach any weight to it.'

Scharley took a demijohn from a saddlebag and uncorked it, releasing the smell of liqueur. The demijohn had not been among the farewell gifts from the Benedictines and Reynevan feared the worst regarding how the penitent had acquired it.

'It's a great mistake,' Scharley said, swigging from the demijohn and passing it to Reynevan, 'not to listen to Dzierżka. She usually knows what she's talking about. The circumstances of your brother's death are not clear, laddie. Certainly not clear enough to instantly undertake a bloody vengeance. You don't have any proof of the Sterczas' guilt. *Tandem*, you don't have any proof of Kyrie-eleison's guilt. Why, *in hoc casu*, there's even a lack of motives.'

'What ...' Reynevan choked on the liqueur. 'What are you saying? Aulock and his gang were seen near Balbinów.'

'*Non sufficit* as evidence.'

'They had a motive.'

'What motive? I listened carefully to your account, Reinmar. The Sterczas, your lover's brothers-in-law, hired Kyrie-eleison to capture you alive – the events at that tavern near Brzeg prove that incontrovertibly. Kunz Aulock, Stork and Walter of Barby are professionals who only do what they are paid to do. They were paid to get you, not your brother. Why would they leave a body behind them? A cadaver lying in the road is a problem for professionals: they risk being hunted, the law, revenge ... No, Reinmar. There isn't an ounce of logic in it.'

'So who, in your opinion, murdered Peterlin? Who? *Cui bono?*'

'Now you're asking the right questions – it's worth considering who benefits from his death, so you must tell me more about your brother. On the way to Hungary, naturally. Via Świdnica, Frankenstein, Nysa and Opava.'

'You've forgotten about Ziębice.'

'True. But *you* haven't. And you won't, I fear. I wonder when he'll notice.'

'Who? What?'

'Samson Honey-Eater from the Benedictine abbey. There's a nest of hornets in the tree stump he's sitting on.'

The giant sprang up. And sat back down when he realised he'd been duped.

'As I suspected,' Scharley said with a grin, 'you understand Latin, Brother.'

To Reynevan's astonishment, the giant smiled back.

'*Mea culpa*,' he replied in an accent Cicero would have found no fault with. 'But that's no sin, after all. And if it is, then who *sine peccato est?*'

'I wouldn't call eavesdropping on other people's conversations under the pretext of not understanding a language a virtue,' Scharley pouted.

'You're right,' said Samson, slightly inclining his head. 'And I've already admitted my guilt. And in order not to multiply my misdeeds, I warn you that shifting to the tongue of the Gauls will not guarantee you discretion, either, for I speak French.'

'Oh?' Scharley's voice was as cold as ice. '*Est-ce vrai?* Indeed?'

'Indeed. *On dit, et il est verité.*'

Silence reigned for some time. Finally, Scharley loudly cleared his throat.

'I don't doubt you speak the tongue of the English equally well,' he ventured.

'*Ywis*,' the giant replied without faltering. '*Herkneth, this is the point, to speken short and plain. That ye han said is right enough. Namore of this*, enough of that. Though I speak with the tongues of men and of angels, I am become as sounding brass or a tinkling cymbal. Instead of showing off our eloquence, let's get down to business, for time is short. I didn't follow you for pleasure, but was led by a pressing need.'

'Indeed? And what is that *dira necessitas* based on, might one ask?'

'Look closely at me and answer with hand on heart – would you like to look as I do?'

'No, we wouldn't,' Scharley replied with disarming frankness. 'But you harbour a grudge towards the wrong person, friend. You owe your appearance directly to your father and mother. And indirectly to the Creator, although much seems to belie that.'

'I owe my appearance to you,' said Samson, completely ignoring the mockery, 'and to your idiotic exorcisms. You've stirred up some serious trouble, boys. It's time to look truth in the eye and begin to contemplate how to correct what you've done, and to think about making amends to the one you've made problems for.'

'I still have no idea what you're talking about,' stated Scharley. 'I swear on everything dear to me, meaning my old cock, *Je jure ça sur mon coullon.*'

'Such eloquence, such oratory,' commented the giant, 'but not an ounce of acumen. Do you really not understand what happened as a result of your sodding spells?'

'I . . .' Reynevan uttered. 'I understand that . . . during the exorcism . . . something happened.'

'Well, well,' said the giant, looking at him, 'the triumph of youth and a university education – judging from your colloquialisms, probably acquired in Prague. Yes, yes, young man. The incantations and spells may have had side effects. The Bible says: "the prayer of the humble pierceth the clouds". Well, it did.'

'Our exorcisms . . .' whispered Reynevan. 'I sensed it. I sensed a sudden inflow of the Power. But is it possible—'

'*Certes.*'

'Don't act like a child, Reinmar,' said Scharley calmly. 'Don't let him beguile you. He's mocking us. He's posing as a devil accidentally called forth by our exorcism, a demon summoned from the beyond and transplanted into the bodily shell of Samson Honey-Eater, the idiot of the priory. He's pretending to be a genie freed from a lamp by our spells. What have I forgotten to mention, stranger? Who are you? King Arthur returning from Avalon? Ogier the Dane? Barbarossa coming from Kyffhausen? The Eternal Wandering Jew?'

'Why stop there?' Samson crossed his mighty forearms on his chest. 'After all, you, in your ineffable wisdom, know who I am.'

'*Certes,*' Scharley retaliated with Samson's answer. 'I know. But you, Brother, came to our camp and not the other way around. Which is why it behoves you to introduce yourself. Without waiting until you're unmasked.'

'Scharley,' Reynevan interrupted, sounding serious. 'I think he's speaking the truth. We called him forth as a result of our exorcism. Why can't you see the obvious? Why—'

'Because, unlike you, I'm not naive,' interrupted the penitent. 'And I know exactly who he is, how he ended up at the Benedictine priory and what he wants from us.'

'So who am I?' The giant smiled a not-at-all foolish smile. 'Tell me, please. Forthwith. Before I'm consumed by curiosity.'

'You're a wanted fugitive, Samson Honey-Eater. An escapee. Judging from your colloquialisms, probably a runaway priest. You hid from your pursuers in the priory, pretending to be a halfwit, assisted considerably by your appearance – no offence meant. Since you're clearly not a halfwit, you instantly saw through us ... or rather me. You weren't listening to us idly. You want to flee to Hungary and knew it would be difficult by yourself. Our company – a company of cunning and worldly men – is heaven sent for you. You'd like to join us. Am I right?'

'No, you're wide of the mark in every detail but one: I did see through you right away.'

'Aha.' Scharley stood up. 'So I'm mistaken, but you speak the truth. Go on, prove it. You're a supernatural being, a resident of the beyond, from which our exorcism accidentally extricated you. In that case, show us your power. May the earth shake. May there be thunder and lightning. May the sun rise again in the night. May the frogs in the swamp sing in unison the *Lauda Sion Salvatorem* instead of croaking.'

'I'm unable to make any of those things happen. And even if I were, would you believe me if I told you so?'

'No,' admitted Scharley. 'I'm not by nature gullible. And on top of that, the Bible says: "Believe not every spirit. Because many false prophets are gone out into the world." In short: liars, liars and more liars.'

'I don't like to be called a liar,' replied the giant, gently and calmly.

'Oh, indeed?' The penitent lowered his hands, leaning slightly forward. 'What do you do when you're lied to, then? Personally,

I dislike hearing barefaced lies so much that I've been known to break the liar's nose.'

'Don't try it.'

Although Scharley was a head shorter than Samson, Reynevan had no doubt what to expect. He'd already seen it. A kick to the shin, just below the knee, the victim receiving a punch in the nose as he fell forward, the bone breaking with a crunch and blood spurting over his clothes.

If Scharley was as fast as a cobra, then the huge Samson was like a python, moving with incredible agility. He parried the kick with a lightning-fast counter-kick, deftly blocked the punch with his forearm and jumped aside. Scharley also jumped aside, flashing his teeth. Reynevan, surprising himself, leaped between them.

'Peace!' he spread his arms. '*Pax!* Gentlemen! Aren't you ashamed of yourselves? Behave like civilised people!'

'You fight . . .' Scharley straightened up. 'You fight like a Dominican. But that only confirms my theory. And I still don't like liars.'

'He might be speaking the truth, Scharley,' said Reynevan.

'Indeed?'

'Indeed. There have been cases like this. There are parallel, invisible existences . . . Astral worlds . . . They can be communicated with, and there have also been . . . cases of visits . . .'

'What are you drivelling on about, O hope of married women?'

'I'm not drivelling. They lectured on it in Prague! *The Zohar* mentions it, Rabanus Maurus writes about it in *De universo*. According to Duns Scotus, *materia prima* may exist without a physical shape. The tangible human body is only a *forma corporeitatis*, an imperfect shape, that—'

'Stop, Reinmar,' Scharley interrupted with an impatient gesture. 'Temper your ardour. You're losing your listeners. One, at least, for I'm going to take a shit in the undergrowth before bed. Which, incidentally, will be a hundredfold more productive than what we're doing here.'

'He went off to defecate,' commented the giant a moment

later. 'Duns Scotus is turning in his grave, as are Rabanus Maurus and the rest of the Kabbalists. If such authorities don't convince him, what chance do I have?'

'Slim,' admitted Reynevan, 'because you haven't dispelled my doubts yet, either. Who are you? Where did you come from?'

'You won't comprehend who I am,' the giant calmly replied, 'or where I came from. I don't fully understand how I ended up here, either. As the poet said: "I cannot clearly say how I had entered the wood."'

Io non so ben ridir com'i' v'intrai,
tant'era pien di sonno a quel punto
che la verace via abbandonai.

'For a stranger from the beyond,' said Reynevan, overcoming his amazement, 'you have a pretty decent command of human languages. And Dante's poetry.'

'I am ...' Samson said after a moment's silence. 'I am a wanderer, Reinmar. And wanderers know much. It's called the wisdom of roads travelled and places visited. I can't say any more about that, but I will tell you who is to blame for your brother's death.'

'What? You know something? Speak!'

'Not now, I must think it through again. I listened to your story and have certain suspicions.'

'Speak, by God!'

'The mystery of your brother's death resides in that charred document you rescued from the fire. Try to recall its contents – fragments of sentences, words, letters, anything. Decipher the document and I shall identify the culprit. Regard it as a favour.'

'Why are you doing me favours? And what do you expect in exchange?'

'For you to return the favour by influencing Scharley.'

'In what respect?'

'To reverse what happened, in order that I might return to

my own form and my own world, the entire exorcism must be repeated as accurately as possible. The entire procedure—'

He was interrupted by the savage howling of a wolf in the undergrowth. And the ghastly screaming of the penitent.

They both set off at a run, and in spite of his corpulence, Samson couldn't be overtaken. They flew into the gloomy thicket, making for the screams and the crack of breaking branches. And then they saw it.

Scharley was fighting a monster.

The huge beast – anthropoid, but covered in black fur – must have attacked him unexpectedly from behind, seizing Scharley with its shaggy, clawed paws in a terrible double nelson. With his neck bent so that his chin was sticking into his chest, the penitent had stopped screaming and was only wheezing, trying to keep his head out of range of the toothy, slavering jaws. He was fighting back, but ineffectively – the monster was holding him like a praying mantis, effectively immobilising one arm and seriously limiting the other. Despite that, Scharley was thrashing around like a weasel and elbowing the beast in its lupine face. He was also trying to land kicks, but his attempts were being thwarted by his trousers hanging down below his knees.

Reynevan stood petrified, paralysed by terror and indecision. Samson, however, entered the fray without a moment's thought.

Once again, the giant moved with the speed of a python and the grace of a tiger. He reached the combatants in three bounds, punched the monster in its wolfish face, seized the astonished beast by its shaggy ears, wrenched it away from Scharley, twisted it around and kicked it, sending it flying towards the trunk of a pine tree, against which the creature slammed its head with a dull thud, showering needles all around. A human skull would have cracked like an egg from an impact like that, but the werewolf immediately sprang up, howled and launched itself at Samson. It didn't attack, as one might have expected, with toothy jaws agape, but showered the giant with a hail of lightning-fast punches and kicks. Samson, unbelievably swift and agile for his size, parried and deflected them all.

'He fights . . .' grunted Scharley, as Reynevan tried to lift him. 'He fights . . . like a Dominican.'

After deflecting a series of blows, Samson waited for a suitable moment and launched a counter-attack. A punch on the nose made the werewolf howl, a kick in the knee made it stagger and then a blow to the chest sent it flying into the trunk of the pine tree. There was a dull thud, but its skull remained intact. The monster roared and leaped, lowering its head like a charging bull, hoping to knock the giant over with its momentum. The attempt failed. Samson didn't budge with the impact, but wound his arms around the werewolf. They stood like Theseus and the Minotaur, grunting, shoving each other and digging up the ground with their feet. Samson finally prevailed. He shoved the monster back and punched it, using his fist like a battering ram. There was a dull thud as its head met the trunk of the same pine tree. This time, Samson didn't give the monster the chance to recover and attack. He leaped forward, aiming several powerful, accurate blows after which the werewolf found itself on all fours with Samson standing behind it. The creature's rump, hairless and red, was the perfect target, impossible to miss, and Samson was wearing heavy boots. He kicked, and the werewolf squealed and flew through the air, smashing head first into the trunk of the hapless pine tree. Samson allowed it to get up just enough for it to offer its rump as a target again. He kicked it even harder this time. The werewolf tumbled down the slope, splashed into the river, waded out like a stag, squelched its way through the bog, crashed through the alders and fled into the forest. It howled once, from far away. Rather woefully, Reynevan thought.

Scharley stood up. He was pale. His hands were shaking and his calves trembling, but he quickly regained control of himself. He just swore softly, rubbing and massaging the back of his neck.

Samson approached him.

'Still in one piece?' he asked.

'The whoreson took me by surprise,' the penitent said, making excuses. 'It came up from behind . . . Bruised my ribs a bit . . . But I would have handled it if not for those trousers . . .'

His companions' knowing looks made him think again.

'I was on my last legs,' he admitted. 'Almost broke my neck . . . Thanks for your help, friend. You saved me. To be honest, I could easily have lost my life—'

'Never mind your life – your arse was in greater danger,' interrupted Samson. 'That lycanthrope is well known around here. As a human being, it had perverted tendencies, which remained with it in wolfish form. Now it lies in wait for someone to drop their trousers and expose their privates. The wretch usually seizes its victim from behind, holds him fast . . . And then . . . You understand.'

Scharley clearly understood, because he visibly shuddered. And then he smiled and held out his right hand to the giant.

The full moon shone enchantingly, the stream flowing through the valley like quicksilver in an alchemist's crucible. Flames shot up and sparks showered from the campfire where logs and resinous branches crackled.

When Reynevan told Scharley what would be necessary to return their new friend to the great beyond, the penitent didn't utter a single word of mockery or disapproval, restricting himself to a shake of the head and a few sighs that demonstrated his reservations about the enterprise. But he didn't decline to participate. Reynevan took part with enthusiasm. And optimism. Premature optimism, as it turned out.

At the request of the strange giant, they repeated the entire exorcism ritual performed at the Benedictine priory in the hope that another transmogrification would occur, thereby returning Samson to his realm, and the idiot from the priory to his huge body. So they repeated the exorcism, trying not to leave anything out, including the curses and nonsense words Scharley had uttered in his desperation. Reynevan even struggled hard to recall and repeat the Arabic – or possibly pseudo-Arabic – he had cobbled together from sundry sources.

All to no avail.

Nothing happened. No vibrations or movements of the Power were felt. The only results were the squawks of birds and the snorting of the horses frightened by the exorcists' cries. Astonishingly, the least disappointed appeared to be the most interested of the parties.

'It just goes to prove the theory that in magic spells, the meaning of the words and sound in general is slight,' he said. 'The crucial factor is the spiritual predisposition, determination and strength of will. I believe—'

He broke off, as though waiting for questions or comments. They didn't come.

'I believe I have no other choice but to stay with you,' he concluded. 'I'll have to accompany you, hoping that one day, one or both of you will manage to repeat what you achieved by accident in the priory chapel.'

Reynevan look anxiously at Scharley, but the penitent said nothing. He was silent for some time, adjusting the poultice of plantain leaves that Reynevan had placed on his scratched and bitten neck.

'Oh well,' he finally said, 'I'm in your debt. Passing over the doubts you didn't completely dispel, my friend, I have no objection to you joining us on our travels. To hell with who you are – you proved that you'll do more good than harm on the road.'

The giant said nothing and bowed.

'So let us travel together in good cheer,' continued the penitent. 'Although I ask that you refrain from unduly ostentatious public declarations regarding your otherworldly origins. In fact, you ought – forgive my bluntness – to refrain from declaring anything at all, for your utterances are very disconcertingly at odds with your appearance.'

The giant bowed again.

'As I said, generally speaking I'm indifferent to who you really are, so I neither expect nor demand either confessions or disclosures. But I'd like to know what to call you.'

'Ask not after my name, it is secret,' Reynevan quoted softly, recalling the three forest witches and their prophecies.

'Indeed,' said the smiling giant. '*Nomen meum, quod est mirabile* ... Samson is as good a name as any other. And my surname, why, I can owe my surname to your ingenuity and imagination, Scharley. Although I must confess, the very thought of honey makes me nauseous. Whenever I recall waking up in the chapel, with a sticky pot in my hands ... But I'll accept it. Samson Honey-Eater, at your service.'

Chapter Fourteen

Which describes events happening the same evening as those in the preceding chapter, but in a different place: in a city about eight miles away in a north-easterly direction as the crow flies. A glance at a map of Silesia, which the author warmly encourages the reader to take, will reveal which city is being discussed.

Alighting in the church belfry, the Wallcreeper had frightened the rooks; the big black birds took flight, cawing loudly, and glided down onto the roofs of houses, whirling like large flakes of soot drifting from a fire. The rooks had a numerical advantage and couldn't easily be chased away from the spires. They would never have yielded to an ordinary wallcreeper. But the rooks realised at once that this was no ordinary wallcreeper.

A strong wind was blowing over Wrocław, driving dark clouds from Ślęża. The gusts rippled the grey water of the Odra, rocked the branches of a willow tree on Malt Island and swayed the reedbeds between the old river courses. The Wallcreeper spread its wings, squawked a challenge to the rooks circling over the roofs, soared up into the air, flew around the spire and landed on a cornice. Squeezing through the tracery of the window, it plummeted into the belfry's dark depths and flew downwards, describing a breakneck spiral around the wooden staircase. It landed on the floor of the nave and transformed into a man with black hair and clothes.

The ostiary, an old man with skin like pale parchment, clacking his sandals and muttering to himself, approached from the altar. The Wallcreeper straightened up proudly. On seeing him, the ostiary paled even more, crossed himself, lowered his head and quickly withdrew towards the vestry. However, the clacking of sandals had alarmed the person the Wallcreeper was due to meet. A tall man with a short, pointed beard, wrapped in a cloak marked with the sign of a red cross and a star, emerged soundlessly from the chapel's arcades. The Church of Saint Maciej in Wrocław belonged to the Knights Hospitaller *cum Cruce et Stella*, and their hospice was right beside the church.

'*Adsumus*,' the Wallcreeper greeted him in hushed tones.

'*Adsumus*,' the Hospitaller replied softly, bringing his hands together. 'In the Lord's name.'

'In the Lord's name,' said the Wallcreeper, his head and shoulders twitching like a bird's. 'In the Lord's name, Brother. What brings you here?'

'We are always ready,' said the Hospitaller in the same soft voice. 'People keep coming. We diligently note down whatever information they bring.'

'And the Inquisition?'

'Suspects nothing. They have opened four new denunciation points, in four churches: Saint Adalbert's, Saint Vincent's, Saint Lazarus's and Our Lady on the Sand's. They won't realise that ours is still functioning. On the same days and at the same hour, on Tuesdays, Thursdays and Sundays, from the hour of—'

'I know when,' the Wallcreeper bluntly interrupted. 'I have come at precisely the right hour. Direct me to the confessional, Brother. I'll sit down, listen and find out what vexes the people.'

Barely had a minute passed before the first suppliant knelt at the screen.

'... has no respect for his superiors, Brother Titus ... Once, God forgive him, he accused the prior himself of saying Mass under the influence, when the prior had only drunk a smidgen – I mean, what's a quart split between three? Then the prior ordered him to be watched closely, and for his cell to be searched in secret ... And it revealed books and

pamphlets hidden under the bed. Hard to believe . . . Wycliffe's
Trialogus . . . Huss's *De ecclesia* . . . Lollardist and Waldensian
writings . . . Whoever possesses and reads such things must be
a secret Beghard. And since our superiors have ordered us to
denounce Beghards, I am so doing . . . God forgive . . .'

'I humbly report that Gaston of Vaudenay, a troubadour who
has inveigled his way into the good graces of the Duke of
Głogów, is a soak, a bawd, a braggart, a heretic and a heathen.
He panders to the lowest tastes of the peasantry with his piti-
ful doggerel, when God knows what they see in him or why his
primitive rhymes are preferred to mine, written as they are by
a native. Verily, the foreigner ought to be banished and return
to his native Provence, for we have no need of his outlandish
customs here!'

'. . . hid the fact that his brother is abroad, in Bohemia. And
no wonder, for before 1419 his brother was deacon at Saint
Štěpán's in Prague. Now he also serves as a priest, but with
Prokop in Tábor, he wears a beard, preaches out of doors
without a chasuble or an alb and gives communion under both
kinds. So, I ask, ought a good Catholic to conceal the fact that
he has such a brother? And may I ask, can a good Catholic
even *have* such a brother?'

'. . . and he said that the parish priest would sooner be able to
see his own ear than receive a tithe from him, and a pox on
those dissolute papists, and that the Hussites should give them
what for and the sooner they come here the better. That's what
he said, I swear on all that's holy. And what's more, he's a thief
who pinched my goat . . . He says that's a lie, says it's his goat,
but I know my own goat by the black smudge on her ear . . .'

'I wish to complain about Magda, Reverend . . . I mean my
sister-in-law. Because she's a shameless hussy . . . At night,

when my brother-in-law mounts her in bed, she pants, moans, groans, screams and meows like a she-cat. It would be one thing if it only happened at night, but it happens during the day, too, at work, when she thinks no one's looking ... She throws down her hoe, bends over, grabs the fence and my brother-in-law lifts her frock onto her back and fucks her like a billy goat ... Urgh, disgraceful ... And my man's eyes shine, I've seen him, and he licks his lips ... Then I tell her, have some decency, you harlot, why do you turn the heads of other women's husbands? And she says: satisfy your man properly, then he won't start looking around or prick up his ears when other people have a roll in the hay. And she also said she has no intention of making love quietly, because it pleases her to moan and scream. And when the priest in the church declared that such pleasure is a sin, she said he must be a fool or insane, because pleasure can't be a sin, since the Lord God created such things. When I told that to my neighbour, she said talk like that is naught but herizee and that I should inform on the harlot. So I am ...'

'... he said that it can't be the body of Christ on the altar in the church, because even if Jesus was a big as this cathedral, his body still wouldn't suffice for all those Masses, for the priests would have eaten it all up themselves long since. He talked such rot, those were his very words, and God strike me down if I be lying. And if they tie him to the stake and burn him, I humbly ask for those three acres down by the stream to be mine ... For they say, I hear, that services will be rewarded ...'

'... Dzierżka, the widow of Zbylut of Szarada, who changed her name to "Dzierżka of Wirsing" after her husband's death, took over his stud and trades in horses. Is it right for a woman to make her living from industry and trade? To create competition for us – honest Catholics? Why does she prosper so, eh, when others do not? Because she sells horses to Czech Hussites! To heretics!'

'. . . it was only just passed at the Council of Siena and confirmed by royal edicts that all trade with Hussite Bohemia is forbidden, and that anyone who trades with Hussites will be punished monetarily and corporeally. Even that Polish pagan Jogaila punishes anyone who consorts with heretics, or sells them lead, weapons, salt or provisions with infamy, exile, loss of office and privilege. And here, in Silesia? The proud merchant lords disdain the embargos. They say profit is the main thing, and you can trade with the very Devil if it brings a profit. Do you want names? Let's start with Tomasz Gernrode of Nysa, Mikołaj Neumarkt of Świdnica and Fabian Pfefferkorn of Niemodlin. And there were plenty of witnesses when Hanusz Throst of Racibórz accused the clergy of dissipation in the Moor's Head in Wrocław, *vicesima prima Iulii*, at eventide . . .'

'. . . and they say: Urban Horn. They know him, he's a rabble-rouser and a troublemaker, and probably a heretic and a convert. A Waldensian! A Beghard! His mother was a Beguine, they burned her in Świdnica after she confessed to vile practices under torture. She was named Roth, Małgorzata Roth. I saw that Horn, alias Roth, in Strzelin with my very own eyes. He incited the people to rebel and mocked the Pope. That Reinmar of Bielawa, a distant relative of Otto Beess, canon at Saint John the Baptist's, was travelling with him. Bad as each other, both converts and heretics . . .'

Dusk was falling when the last petitioner left the Church of Saint Maciej. The Wallcreeper exited the confessional, stretched and handed the bearded Hospitaller a piece of paper covered in writing.

'Is Prior Dobeneck any better?'

'He is still laid low with sickness,' replied the Hospitaller. 'In practice, Grzegorz Hejncze, also a Dominican, is the Inquisitor *a Sede Apostolica.*'

The Hospitaller's mouth twisted slightly, as though he could taste something unpalatable. The Wallcreeper noticed. And the Hospitaller noticed that the Wallcreeper had noticed.

'A stripling, that Hejncze,' he explained a little hesitantly. 'A formalist. Demands proof of everything, only very rarely does he send anyone to be tortured. Keeps finding suspects innocent and releasing them. He's soft.'

'I saw the remains of fires behind Saint Wojciech's.'

'Two heretics burned in all,' the Hospitaller said with a shrug. 'Over the last three Sundays. In Brother Schwenckefeld's time, there would have been twenty. Actually, a third will be burned any moment. The Reverend has caught a sorcerer. Apparently one of the Devil's own. As we speak, he is undergoing a painful interrogation.'

'At the Dominican priory?'

'In the town hall.'

'Is Hejncze present?'

'He is, surprisingly.' The Hospitaller's smile was a foul thing.

'This magician, who is he?'

'Zachary Voigt, an apothecary.'

'In the town hall, you say, Brother?'

'I do.'

Grzegorz Hejncze, interim Inquisitor for the Wrocław Diocese, was very young. The Wallcreeper wouldn't have given him more than thirty years, which made them the same age. When the Wallcreeper entered the town-hall cellar, the Inquisitor was taking his meal. Sleeves rolled up, he was enthusiastically wolfing down kasha and pork straight from the pot. In the light of torches and candles, the scene was harmonious: the rib vaulting, oaken table, crucifix, candlesticks festooned with wax, colourfully glazed earthenware vessels – all combined to create a pleasant ambience.

The mood was utterly destroyed, however, by the piercing cries and howls of pain coming at regular intervals from a deeper crypt, the passage leading to which was illuminated, like the gates of Hell, by the crimson flickering of flames.

The Wallcreeper stopped by the steps and waited. The Inquisitor went on eating. Only when he had eaten everything, down to the very bottom of the pot, did he raise his head. The bushy joined eyebrows above sharp eyes lent him seriousness and made him look older than he was.

'You work for Bishop Konrad, don't you?' he asked, recognising him. 'Lord . . .'

'Lord Grellenort,' the Wallcreeper reminded him.

'Indeed.' Grzegorz Hejncze reticently gestured for the serving wench to clear the table. 'Birkart of Grellenort, the bishop's confidant and advisor. Sit down, please.'

The victim being tortured in the crypt wailed, screaming wildly and inarticulately. The Wallcreeper sat down. The Inquisitor wiped some traces of grease from his chin.

'I understand that the bishop has left Wrocław? He is travelling?'

'As you say,' replied the Wallcreeper.

'No doubt to Nysa? To visit Lady Agnieszka?'

The Wallcreeper didn't react even with a flicker of his eyelid at the mention of the bishop's latest lover, which was a closely guarded secret. 'His Eminence doesn't usually inform me of such details. Neither do I enquire. Whoever pokes his nose into bishops' affairs risks losing it. And my nose is dear to me.'

'I don't doubt it. But I have only the health of His Eminence in mind, not gossip. For Bishop Konrad is not in the first flush of youth and ought to avoid an excess of feverish vexations . . . Indeed, barely a week has passed since he honoured Ulrika of Rhein with his presence. Not to mention his visits to the Benedictine sisters . . . Are you surprised, m'lord? It is an Inquisitor's job to know such things.'

A scream reverberated from the crypt, then broke off, passing into wheezing.

'It is an Inquisitor's job to know such things,' repeated Grzegorz Hejncze. 'Hence, I know that Bishop Konrad is not journeying around Silesia just to visit married women, young widows and nuns. Bishop Konrad is preparing another raid on the Broumov lands. He is trying to persuade Přemysl of Opava and Sir Albrecht of Kolditz to join him, and to gain the armed assistance of Sir Půta of Častolovice, the Starosta of Kłodzko.'

The Wallcreeper neither commented nor lowered his eyes.

'Bishop Konrad does not appear to be concerned,' continued the Inquisitor, 'that King Sigismund and the imperial princes have decided on a different course of action, in order to avoid the errors of previous crusades by forming alliances and confederations, gathering resources and winning over the Moravian lords. And to refrain from military confrontations until they are fully prepared.'

'His Eminence Bishop Konrad,' the Wallcreeper interrupted the silence, 'does not need to rely on the imperial princes, for he is their equal in Silesia – if not their superior. The good King Sigismund, meanwhile, appears busy. As the bulwark of Christianity, he is amusing himself fighting the Turks on the Danube. Or perhaps he's trying to forget other beatings, like the one he received three years ago from the Hussites at Německý Brod and his subsequent flight from the battle. But as he's in no hurry to launch another expedition to Bohemia, he's clearly not yet forgotten that humiliation. So, as God sees, the responsibility of striking fear into the heretics is being left to Bishop Konrad. For as Your Excellency knows: *si vis pacem, para bellum.*'

'I also know that *nemo sapiens, nisi patiens,*' said the Inquisitor, steadily returning the Wallcreeper's gaze. 'But enough of that. I had several issues to discuss with the bishop. A few questions. But since he is journeying ... Too bad. Because I don't imagine I can count on you to answer those questions, can I, Lord Grellenort?'

'That all depends on the questions Your Reverence deigns to ask.'

The Inquisitor said nothing for a moment, as though waiting for the person being tortured in the crypt to scream again.

'It concerns the spate of unexplained murders occurring in Silesia of late . . .' he said, when the screaming had subsided once more. 'Sir Albrecht of Bart, murdered near Strzelin. Sir Piotr of Bielawa, killed somewhere near Henryków. Sir Czambor of Heissenstein, stabbed to death in Sobótka. The merchant Mikołaj Neumarkt, attacked and killed on the Świdnica highway. The merchant Fabian Pfefferkorn, murdered on the very steps of Niemodlin collegiate church. The bishop must have heard about them. As have you.'

'This and that has reached our ears,' the Wallcreeper acknowledged indifferently. 'Neither I nor the bishop have concerned ourselves unduly with it. Since when is a murder such a sensation? People never stop killing each other. Instead of loving their neighbours, people hate each other and are liable to send them to meet their Maker for any old thing. Everybody has enemies, and there's never a shortage of motives.'

'You read my thoughts,' Hejncze declared, equally indifferently. 'The same thing applies to these unexplained murders. Apparently, there's no lack of either motives or enemies on whom suspicion quickly falls, be it neighbourly wrangles, or marital infidelity, or family feuds. You think you have the guilty within reach and that everything's clear. Then you examine the case more closely and *nothing* is clear. And that's what is sensational about these murders.'

'Is that all?'

'No. There is in addition the astonishing skill of the criminal – or criminals. In every case, the attacks occurred suddenly, literally out of the blue as they were all carried out at noon.'

'Interesting.'

'Now you begin to see why these murders are so sensational.'

'Something else is fascinating,' repeated the Wallcreeper,

'which is that you don't recognise the words of the psalm. Doesn't "from the arrow that flieth in the day" – *a sagitta volante in die* – mean anything to you? An arrow striking like lightning, a bolt from the blue bearing death? The destruction that wasteth at noonday doesn't remind you of anything? I am indeed surprised.'

'So, a demon.' The Inquisitor brought his hands with fingertips touching to his lips, but didn't manage to entirely hide a sarcastic smile. 'A demon is roaming around Silesia committing crimes. A demon and a destroying arrow. Well, well. Incredible.'

'*Haeresis est maxima, opera daemonum non credere,*' the Wallcreeper retorted at once. 'Is it fitting that I, an ordinary mortal, should have to remind the papal Inquisitor about it?'

'It is not.' The Inquisitor's gaze hardened and a dangerous tone entered his voice. 'It is entirely unfitting, Lord Grellenort. Better that you concentrate on answering my questions than on reminding me of things beyond your understanding.'

The agonised scream from the crypt was a meaningful counterpoint to his statement. But the Wallcreeper didn't even flinch.

'I am not in a position to help, Your Reverence,' he declared coldly. 'As I said, rumours about the murders have reached me, but the names of the alleged victims are unfamiliar. I don't believe it would be worth asking His Eminence the Bishop about them, either, for he would answer as I have. And ask a question I wouldn't dare to ask.'

'Oh, please do. You're in no danger.'

'The bishop would ask: do those mentioned deserve the attentions of the Holy Office?'

'And the bishop would receive an answer,' replied Hejncze at once. 'The Holy Office *did* have *suspicio de haeresi* regarding the aforementioned individuals. Suspicions of pro-Hussite sympathies and of yielding to heretical influences. Of contact with Czech apostates.'

'Aha. So they were scoundrels. If, then, they were killed, the Inquisition has no reason to mourn them. The bishop, knowing him, would undoubtedly have said one can only rejoice that somebody has already done the Office's work.'

'The Office doesn't like other people doing its work. That is how I would answer the bishop.'

'The bishop would respond that, in that case, the Office ought to act more efficiently and quickly.'

Another scream echoed from the crypt – this time much louder, more horrifying and lasting longer. The Wallcreeper's thin lips contorted into a parody of a smile.

'Oh.' He gestured with his head. 'Red-hot irons. Previously it was the standard *strappado* and screws on the fingers and toes, wasn't it?'

'An irredeemable sinner,' replied Hejncze reluctantly. '*Haereticus pertinax* . . . But let us not get off the subject, m'lord. Be so kind as to repeat to His Eminence Bishop Konrad that the Holy Inquisition observes with growing displeasure that people with delations against them are dying in mysterious circumstances. People suspected of apostasy, of shady dealings and of conspiring with heretics. Those people are dying before the Inquisition manages to interrogate them. It looks as though somebody is trying to cover their tracks. And he who covers heresy's tracks will find it difficult to defend himself against charges of heresy.'

'I'll repeat it to the bishop word for word,' the Wallcreeper replied with a derisive smile. 'But I doubt he'll take fright. He isn't the kind to. Like all Piasts.'

You would have thought, after the last yell, that the person being tortured couldn't have screamed any louder or more horrifyingly. But you would have been wrong.

'If they don't confess now,' said the Wallcreeper, 'they never will.'

'You appear to have some expertise in this.'

'Not in practical terms, heaven forbid.' The Wallcreeper smiled hideously. 'But one has read the accounts of various practitioners. I would particularly recommend the works of Jan Schwenckefeld to the attention of Your Young Reverence.'

'Indeed?'

'Absolutely. For Brother Jan Schwenckefeld rejoiced and was heartened whenever a mysterious hand put to death a scoundrel, a heretic or a heretic's henchman. Brother Jan would give silent thanks to that mysterious hand and say a prayer for him. There was simply one less scoundrel and thus Brother Jan would have more time for other scoundrels. For he considered it right and proper for sinners to live in terror, to tremble in fear both day and night, uncertain of his life, as the Book of Deuteronomy demands.'

'Fascinating, m'lord, quite fascinating. I shall ponder it, be certain.'

'You claim,' the Wallcreeper said a moment later, 'and the view has already been sanctioned by numerous Popes and Doctors of the Church, that sorcerers and heretics are acolytes in one monstrous sect, a mighty army acting according to a great plan, concocted by Satan himself, to topple God and seize control of the world. Why, then, do you so fervidly spurn the thought that in this fight, the other side of the conflict has also founded its own . . . secret organisation? Why don't you want to believe that?'

'Because,' the Inquisitor calmly replied, 'no Pope or Doctors of the Church have sanctioned that belief. God doesn't need any secret organisations when He has us, the Holy Office. I have seen too many madmen claim to be divine instruments, acting in accordance with a divine mission.'

'I envy you. You have seen much. Who would have guessed, given Your Reverence's youth.'

'Hence,' Hejncze was not swayed by the mockery, 'when I finally get my hands on that flying arrow, that self-appointed demon and divine instrument, it will by no means end in martyrdom, which that person certainly hopes for, but incarceration in the Narrenturm. For the Tower of Fools is the place for idiots and lunatics.'

Boots scraped on the stairs to the crypt, from which no cries had been heard for a long time.

Soon after, a thin Dominican entered the room. He approached the table and made a deep bow, revealing a bald pate dotted with brown liver spots over the sparse garland of his tonsure.

'Well?' Hejncze asked with visible aversion. 'Brother Arnulph? Did he finally confess?'

'Indeed.'

'*Bene*. For it was beginning to weary me.'

The monk raised his eyes. There was no aversion in them. Nor weariness. It was clear that the procedure in the crypt hadn't tired or repulsed him in the slightest. On the contrary, it was apparent he would gladly begin again. The Wallcreeper smiled at his kindred spirit. The Dominican didn't smile back.

'And?' the Inquisitor urged.

'The testimonies have been recorded. He revealed all, beginning with summoning and raising a demon, through theurgy and conjuration to tetragramation and demonomagy. He furnished the content and ritual of signing a pact. He described the persons he has seen during sabbaths and black masses ... But did not reveal, in spite of our efforts, the place where the magical books and grimoires are concealed. But we forced him to give the names of people for whom he created amulets, including lethal ones. He also confessed that he had forced a virgin to acquiesce and then seduced her with the Devil's help and the use of the Urim and Thummim—'

'What nonsense is this, Brother?' Hejncze thundered. 'This nonsense about demons and virgins? What about contacts with the Czechs? The names of Taborite spies and emissaries? The locations of hidden weapons and propaganda materials? The names of recruits? The names of Hussite sympathisers!'

'He didn't reveal any such thing,' stammered the monk.

'Then you will work on him again tomorrow,' Hejncze said, standing up. 'Lord Grellenort—'

'Give me a little more of your time.' The Wallcreeper's eyes flicked to the thin monk.

The Inquisitor dismissed the monk with an impatient wave. The Wallcreeper waited until he left.

'I would like to prove my goodwill,' he said. 'On the understanding that it will remain a secret in the case of those mysterious murders, I would advise Your Reverence—'

'Just please don't tell me that the Jews are to blame,' said Hejncze, still looking down and drumming his fingers on the table. 'Using the Urim and Thummim.'

'I would advise the apprehension – and thorough interrogation – of two individuals.'

'Names.'

'Urban Horn. Reinmar of Bielawa.'

'The brother of that murdered man?' Grzegorz Hejncze frowned, but only for a moment. 'Ah. No comment, no comment, Sir Birkart, because you're liable once again to point out my lack of knowledge of the Bible, this time with regard to the story of Cain and Abel. So those two. Can I rely on this?'

'You can.'

For a moment, they glared at each other. *I shall find both of them*, thought the Inquisitor, *and quicker than you think. I will do my utmost.*

And I will do mine, thought the Wallcreeper, *to make sure you don't find them alive.*

'Farewell, Lord Grellenort. May God be with you.'

'Amen, Your Reverence.'

The apothecary Zachary Voigt moaned and groaned. He had been thrown into a corner of the cell in the town-hall crypt, into a hollow where all the water that trickled down the walls gathered. The straw there was rotten and damp. The apothecary couldn't, however, change his location. In fact, he could barely adjust his position at all on account of his bruised elbows, dislocated shoulders, broken shins, shattered fingers and the acute pain shooting from the festering burns on his sides and feet. So he lay on his back, moaning, groaning and blinking his blood-encrusted eyelids. And was delirious.

Straight from the mould-stained wall, straight from the cracks between the bricks, a bird emerged. And immediately transformed itself into a man with black hair and clothes. Or rather, into a human-shaped form. For Zachary Voigt knew very well that it wasn't a man.

'O, my Lord . . .' he grunted, writhing on the straw. 'O, Prince of Darkness . . . Beloved Master . . . You are come! You didn't abandon your faithful servant in his hour of need—'

'I must disappoint you,' said the black-haired man, stooping over him. 'I am not the Devil. Nor an emissary of the Devil. The Devil has little interest in the fate of individuals.'

Zachary Voigt opened his mouth to scream, but only managed to croak. The black-haired man seized him by the temples.

'The hiding place of the treatises and grimoires,' he said. 'I'm sorry, but I need that information. You won't benefit from them now, and they will be very useful to me. By the way, I will save you from further torture and the stake. Don't thank me.'

'If you're not the Devil . . .'The magician's eyes opened wide in horror as he lost control of himself. 'Then you've come from . . . The other one? Oh, God . . .'

'I must disappoint you again,' replied the Wallcreeper. 'He's even less interested in the fate of individuals.'

Chapter Fifteen

In which it turns out that although the notions of 'profitable art' and 'artistic business' don't have to be a contradiction in terms, even epoch-making inventions don't easily find sponsors in the field of culture, nonetheless.

Like every town in Silesia, Świdnica threatened anybody who threw rubbish or sewage into the street with a fine. It didn't look as though the ban was enforced all that often, however – if at all. A short but heavy morning shower had soaked the town's narrow streets and the hooves of horses and oxen had quickly churned it up into a bog of shit, mud and straw. Piles of refuse rose up from the bog like enchanted isles from an ocean. Geese toddled over the muck where it was thicker and ducks swam in it where it was thinner. People moved along boardwalks made of wooden planks, often falling from them. Although allowing livestock to roam freely was also punishable with a fine, squealing pigs were scuttling down the streets in both directions, knocking down pedestrians and frightening horses.

They passed down Weavers Street, then Coopers Street – which echoed with the sound of hammers – and finally the High Street, which led to the town square. Reynevan was itching to stop at the celebrated apothecary's shop The Golden Lindworm, for he was friendly with the apothecary, Christoph Eschenloer, with whom he had once studied the basics of alchemy and white magic. But he abandoned his plan; the last three weeks had taught him much about the principles of clandestine activity. Furthermore, Scharley was hurrying him along. He didn't even slow down beside any of the beer cellars where they served the world-famous Świdnica March ale. They moved quickly through the busy vegetable market under the arcades directly opposite the town hall and squeezed past the wagons filling Kraszewice Street.

Reynevan and Samson followed Scharley under a low stone lintel into the dark tunnel of an entryway smelling as though the ancient tribes of the Ślężanie and the Dziadoszanie had been pissing there since time immemorial. The entryway exited into a courtyard, a narrow space cluttered with rubbish, scrap iron and enough cats to compete with the temple of the Egyptian goddess Bastet in Bubastis.

The courtyard ended in a horseshoe-shaped cloister with a wooden sculpture bearing faint traces of centuries-old paint and gilding, standing beside the steep steps leading up to the entrance.

'Some saint or other?'

'Luke the Evangelist,' explained Scharley, setting foot on the wooden staircase. 'The patron saint of painters.'

'But why are we visiting these artists?'

'For various items.'

'We're wasting time,' Reynevan pronounced impatiently, yearning for his beloved. 'What items? I don't understand—'

'We'll find you some new footwraps,' interrupted Scharley. 'You're in urgent need of some, believe me. And we'll also breathe more freely when you get rid of the old ones.'

Some cats reclining on the steps reluctantly moved out of their way. Scharley knocked and the solid door opened to reveal a short, scrawny, elderly gentleman with dishevelled hair and a blue nose, wearing a smock spattered with an explosion of colourful spots.

'Master Justus Schottel is absent,' he announced, narrowing his eyes comically. 'Come back later, good ... My God! I don't believe my own eyes! The honourable—'

'Scharley,' the penitent quickly interjected. 'Don't make me stand on the threshold, Master Unger.'

'Indeed, indeed ... Do come in ...'

The interior smelled strongly of paint, linseed oil and resin and work was in full swing. Several youths in greasy, blackened aprons were bustling around two curious-looking machines equipped with screw mechanisms which turned out to be printing presses. In front of Reynevan's eyes, a sheet of paper depicting the Madonna and the Infant Jesus was pulled out of a platen pressed down by a wooden screw.

'Interesting,' said Reynevan.

'Eh?' The blue-nosed Master Unger tore his gaze away from Samson Honey-Eater. 'What's that, young sir?'

'I said, it's interesting.'

'Try this.' Scharley held up a sheet of paper taken from the other machine, on which several rectangles were evenly arranged. They were piquet cards: aces, Obers and Unters in modern French patterns and in the suits of *piques* and *trèfles*.

'We can make a full pack of thirty-six cards in four days,' boasted Unger.

'They do it in two in Leipzig,' replied Scharley.

'But that's mass-produced junk!' the blue-nosed man said irritably. 'From third-rate woodcuts, painted slapdash, cut crookedly. Ours, just look, are so clearly drawn, they'll be masterpieces when they're coloured in. That's why they play with ours in castles and palaces, and those Leipzig ones are only fit for drinking dens and brothels—'

'Enough. How much does a pack cost?'

'Ex works'll cost you ninety groschen. Carriage is extra.'

'Take us through to the back, Simon. I'll wait for Master Schottel there.'

The room they passed through next was quieter and more peaceful. Three artists were sitting at easels, so absorbed by their work they didn't even turn their heads.

There was only a sketch on the first artist's board and it was impossible to guess what the painting would finally depict. The work of the second painter was considerably more advanced, showing Salome with John the Baptist's head on a plate. Salome was wearing diaphanous, flowing robes, and the artist had taken pains to ensure all the details were clearly visible. Samson Honey-Eater snorted softly and Reynevan gasped. When he glanced at the third board, he gasped even louder.

The painting of Saint Sebastian was almost finished. The subject differed quite markedly from the usual depictions of the martyr. He was still standing by a post, smiling ecstatically in spite of the many arrows piercing his belly and torso, but there the similarities ended. For this Sebastian was quite naked, sporting such a huge and impressive member that the sight of it would have shamed any man.

'A special commission,' explained Simon Unger. 'For the Cistercian convent in Trzebnica. Let me take you through to the back room, gentlemen.'

The sound of frantic clanking and clattering reached their ears from nearby Coppersmiths Street.

'They evidently have plenty of orders,' said Scharley, who had been busily writing something on a piece of paper. 'Business is booming in the copper trade. How are you doing, Simon, dear?'

'There's a slump,' replied Unger quite gloomily. 'Orders are coming in, but what's the use when there's no way of transporting the goods? You can't ride a furlong without them stopping you to ask where you're from, where you're heading. They want to know your business, rummage around in caskets and saddlebags—'

'Who? The Inquisition? Or Kolditz?'

'Both. The Inquisitor-priests reside at the Dominican monastery, a stone's throw from here, and it's as if the Devil himself has got into Starosta Kolditz. And all because they once caught a few Czech emissaries with heretical writings and declarations. When the municipal torturer gave them the red-hot irons, they revealed the names of their associates and accomplices. In Świdnica alone, eight of them were burned at the stake on the common outside the Lower Gate. But the real trouble began a week ago, when at high noon on Saint Bartholomew the Apostle's Day, someone murdered a wealthy merchant, Master Mikołaj Neumarkt, on the

Wrocław Road. It was a strange affair, most strange—'

'Strange?' Reynevan asked, suddenly taking an interest. 'Why?'

'Because, young sir, no one could understand who would have killed Master Neumarkt or why. Some said that it was robber knights, like Hayn of Czirne or Buko of Krossig. Others that it was that cut-throat Kunz Aulock. They say that Aulock is hunting all over Silesia some young blade or outlaw who dishonoured somebody's wife with rape and sorcery. Others say that the young blade Aulock's pursuing killed the merchant. And still others say that the murderers are Hussites with whom Master Neumarkt fell into disfavour. No one knows what really happened, but Starosta Kolditz is furious. He swore that when he catches Master Neumarkt's killer, he'll flay him alive. Hence, you can't deliver any goods, because someone's always searching you.'

Reynevan, who for some time had been scribbling in charcoal on a sheet of paper, suddenly jerked his head up and elbowed Samson Honey-Eater.

'*Publicus super omnes,*' he said softly, showing him the sheet of paper. '*Anne de sanctimonia. Positione hominis. Voluntas vitae.*'

'I beg your pardon?'

'*Voluntas vitae.* Or perhaps *potestas vitae*? I'm trying to recall what was written on that charred paper of Peterlin's, the one I pulled out of the fire in Powojowice. Have you forgotten? You said it was important. I was supposed to try to recall what was written on it, so I'm trying to do so.'

'Ah, indeed. Hmm ... *Potestas vitae?* Alas, it means nothing to me.'

'And Master Justus is still nowhere to be seen,' Unger said to himself.

The door opened as though a spell had been uttered and an elderly gentleman stood in the doorway, dressed in a flowing black, fur-lined coat with very wide sleeves. He didn't look like an artist. More like a burgermeister.

'Greetings, Justus.'

'By the bones of Saint Wolfgang! Paul? Is it you? At liberty?'

'Evidently. And I'm called Scharley now.'

'Scharley, hmm . . . And your . . . *compagnoni?*'

'Also at liberty.'

Master Schottel stroked a cat that had appeared from God knew where and was rubbing up against his calves. Then he sat down at the table and linked his fingers over his belly. He examined Reynevan intently, and then for a very, very long time didn't tear his gaze from Samson Honey-Eater.

'You're here for the money,' he finally said mournfully. 'I must warn you—'

'That business is very slow.' Scharley cut him off unceremoniously. 'I know. I've heard. Here's a list I drew up when I grew bored of waiting for you. I need everything on it by tomorrow.'

The cat jumped onto Schottel's knee and the printmaker stroked it pensively. He read and read. And finally looked up.

'The day after tomorrow. For tomorrow's Sunday.'

'True, I'd forgotten.' Scharley nodded. 'Oh well, we may as well celebrate the holiday. I don't know when I'll be in Świdnica again, so it'd be a sin not to visit a few cool cellars and sample this year's March ale. But the day after tomorrow, *maestro*, means the day after tomorrow. Monday, not a day later. Understood?'

A nod from Master Schottel showed he did.

'I won't ask you,' Scharley continued, 'about the state of my account, because I neither intend to dissolve the company nor withdraw from it. Just assure me that you're taking care of it. That you aren't ignoring the good advice once given to you, or the ideas that could be lucrative for the company. You know of what I speak?'

'I do.' Justus Schottel dug a large key out of his pouch. 'And I'll soon prove to you that I always take your ideas and advice to heart. Master Simon, please remove the sample engravings from the chest and bring them here. The ones from the biblical series.'

Unger quickly did as he was told.

'Here you are.' Schottel spread some sheets of paper on the table. 'All my own efforts, I didn't give them to the apprentices.

Some are ready to be printed, others need work. I believe your idea was good and that people will buy our biblical series. There you go, judge for yourself. Gentlemen, if you would.'

They all bent over the table.

'What . . . ?' Reynevan, red-faced, pointed to one of the sheets showing a naked couple in an extremely explicit position and situation. 'What is this?'

'Adam and Eve. Isn't it obvious? Eve's up against the Tree of Knowledge.'

'Aha.'

'And here, please look.' The woodcarver, full of pride in his work, directed them to another carving. 'Moses and Hagar. And here's Samson and Delilah, and Amnon and Tamar. I did a nice job, didn't I? And here . . .'

''Pon my soul . . . What's this tangle supposed to be?'

'Jacob, Leah and Rachel.'

'And this . . .' stammered Reynevan, feeling the blood about to burst from his cheeks.

'David and Jonathan,' Justus Schottel said carelessly, 'but I have to rework it—'

'Rework it into David and Bathsheba,' Scharley interrupted quite coldly, 'because all that's missing here is Balaam and the she-ass. Curb your imagination a little, Justus. The surfeit of it spoils the work, like a surfeit of salt spoils the soup. Which harms business. In general, though,' he added, to mollify the somewhat offended artist, '*bene, bene, benissime, maestro*. In brief: better than I expected.'

Justus Schottel brightened up, as vain and greedy for praise as any artist.

'So you see, Scharley, that I don't let the grass grow under my feet. I'm looking after the company. I've also established some very promising contacts that may turn out to be most beneficial for the company. For I must tell you that I met in the Ox and Lamb an extraordinary young man, a talented inventor . . . Oh, why tell you, when you can see and hear for yourself. I've invited him here – he's arriving forthwith. I guarantee that when you meet him—'

'I won't,' interrupted Scharley. 'I wouldn't want that young fellow seeing me here at all. Neither me nor my companions.'

'I understand,' Schottel said after a moment's silence. 'You're in the shit again.'

'You could say that.'

'Criminal or political?'

'Depends on your point of view.'

'Oh well.' Schottel sighed. 'Such are the times we live in. I understand you don't want to be seen here, but in this case your objections are unfounded. The young man I'm talking about is a German from Mainz, a scholar from the University of Erfurt passing through Świdnica. He knows no one here and won't meet anyone, because he's leaving soon. It would be worth making his acquaintance, Scharley, and pondering over what he's invented. He's a remarkable, enlightened mind, a visionary, I'd say. *Vir mirabilis*, in sooth. See for yourself.'

The bell of the parish church tolled deeply and resonantly, its call to the angelus prayer taken up by the bell towers of the four other Świdnica churches. The bells definitely ended the working day – even the noisy workshops in Coppersmiths Street finally fell silent.

The artists and apprentices had also left Master Justus Schottel's workshop to go home, hence when the expected guest finally appeared – that promising enlightened mind and visionary – only the master himself, Simon Unger, Scharley, Reynevan and Samson Honey-Eater greeted him in the press room.

The guest was a young man indeed, the same age as Reynevan. The two scholars soon recognised one another. On greeting, the guest bowed slightly less formally to Reynevan and his smile was a little more sincere.

The stranger was wearing high cordovan boots, a soft velvet beret and a short cloak over a leather jerkin fastened with numerous brass buckles. Slung from his shoulder was a large travelling bag. All in all, he resembled a wandering trouveur rather than a scholar – the only thing that indicated his university connections was a wide Nuremberg dagger, a weapon popular in all European academies, among both students and academic staff.

Not waiting for Schottel to introduce him, the visitor began, 'I am a bachelor of the University of Erfurt, and my name is Johannes Gensfleisch zur Laden zum Gutenberg. I know it's a little overlong, which is why I usually shorten it to Gutenberg. Johannes Gutenberg.'

'Greetings,' replied Scharley. 'And owing to the fact that I also favour shortening needlessly long things, let us get to the point at once. What does your invention do, Master Johannes Gutenberg?'

'It prints. To be more precise, it prints texts.'

Scharley casually rummaged through the prints lying on the bench, took out and presented one, which, below the symbol of the Holy Trinity, bore the inscription: BENEDICITE POPULI DEO NOSTRO.

Gutenberg blushed faintly. 'I understand your point, m'lord, but please observe that it would take a cutter two laborious days of carving in order to include even this rather short inscription on your woodcut. And should he make a mistake with one letter, all the work is fit for nothing; he'd have to start over. And were he to make an engraving for, let's say, the entire Sixty-Fifth Psalm, how long would he have to work? And if he wanted to print all the psalms? Or the entire Bible? How long—'

'All eternity, for certain,' interrupted Scharley. 'Your invention, my good sir, I imagine, eliminates the disadvantages of working in wood?'

'To a considerable extent.'

'Fascinating.'

'If you permit, I shall demonstrate.'

'Please do.'

Johannes Gutenberg opened his bag, emptied the contents

onto the table and began to demonstrate, describing his actions as he did so.

'I made hard metal blocks inscribed with the various letters,' he said as he demonstrated. 'The letters on the blocks are, as you can see, carved convexly, so I called them the patrix. By pressing the patrix into soft copper, I obtained—'

'A matrix,' guessed Scharley. 'It's obvious. The convex one fits into the concave one like a papa into a mama. Go on, Master Gutenberg.'

'I can use the art of casting to make as many casts in the concave matrix as I want to have fonts or typefaces,' the scholar went on. 'Then I arrange the typefaces, whose blocks fit perfectly next to one another, in the right order in this frame. This frame is small, for demonstration purposes, but normally it would be as large as the page in the book which is being made. As you can see, I set the length of the line thus. I put in slugs to set even margins. I secure the frame with an iron clamp so it doesn't fall apart. I apply ink, the same ink you use – would you help me, Master Unger? I put it under the press, place a sheet of paper on it – Master Unger, the screw ... And it's done, if you please.'

At the exact centre of the sheet of paper, printed clearly and legibly, they saw:

IUBILATE DEO OMNIS TERRA
PSALMUM DICITE NOMINI EUIS

'Psalm sixty-five.' Justus Schottel clapped his hands together. 'Large as life!'

'I'm impressed,' admitted Scharley. 'Greatly impressed, Master Gutenberg. I would be even more impressed were it not for the fact that it should be "*dicite nomini eius*" and not "*euis*".'

'Ha-ha!' The scholar beamed as though he'd played a prank on somebody. 'I did that deliberately in order to demonstrate how easily one can make corrections. I remove the erroneously placed type like this, and put it in the right place – the screw, Master Unger . . . And here is the corrected text.'

'*Bravo*,' said Samson Honey-Eater. '*Bravo, bravissimo*. It is indeed impressive.'

Not only did Gutenberg's mouth fall open, but also Schottel's and Unger's. It was clear they would have been less astonished if the cat, the statue of Saint Luke or the painting of Sebastian with the massive dick had spoken.

'Appearances can sometimes be deceptive,' Scharley explained after clearing his throat. 'You aren't the first to misjudge him.'

'And probably won't be the last,' added Reynevan.

'I beg your pardon,' said the giant, spreading his hands. 'I couldn't resist . . . Being a witness – when all's said and done – to an epoch-changing invention.'

'Ha!' Gutenberg beamed, like every artist glad to be praised, even if it was announced by a hulk with the face of an idiot whose head touched the ceiling. 'That's precisely it! Exactly! For just imagine, noble gentlemen, dozens of learned books, and one day, however ridiculous it sounds now, maybe even *hundreds* of them! Without arduous and interminable copying! Human wisdom printed and available! And if you, noble gentlemen, support my invention, I guarantee that your city, the splendid Świdnica, will be famous for ever as the place where the torch of enlightenment was lit. As the place whence light entered the entire world!'

'Indeed,' Samson Honey-Eater said a moment later in his soft, calm voice. 'I see it with the eyes of my soul. The mass production of paper, densely covered in letters. Each leaf in hundreds, and one day, however ridiculous it may sound, maybe even thousands of copies. All of it reproduced over and over and widely available. Lies, rubbish, libel, lampoons, denunciations, base propaganda and demagoguery pandering to the masses. Every wickedness ennobled, every villainy official, every lie the truth. Every stupidity crowned because it is all in print. It is on paper, thus it has power and is binding. It will be simple to begin it, Master Gutenberg, and to set it in motion. But to stop it?'

'I doubt it'll be necessary,' Scharley interrupted, seemingly in earnest. 'As a greater realist than you, Samson, I don't predict such popularity for this invention. And even if events were to follow the course you have prophesied, one can arrest it using a method as easy as pie. An index of forbidden books will simply be created.'

Gutenberg, beaming a moment before, had become subdued. To such a degree that Reynevan felt sorry for him.

'So you don't predict a future for my invention?' he asked in hushed tones a moment later. 'After having exposed its adverse sides with truly Inquisitorial zeal and ignoring its positive ones, just like Inquisitors. For it will be possible to print – and in the process widely popularise – the word of God. How do you respond to that?'

'We respond,' Scharley's mouth twisted into a mocking sneer, 'like Inquisitors. Like the Pope. Like Council Fathers. Why, Master Gutenberg, don't you know what the Council Fathers pronounced in this regard? *Sacra pagina* should be the privilege of men of the cloth, for only they are capable of understanding it. Keep away, secular dimwits.'

'You mock.'

Reynevan thought the same. For as Scharley went on, he didn't even attempt to hide either his sneering smile or his derisive tone.

'The secular, even those displaying vestigial understanding, can make do with sermons, lessons, the Gospels on Sunday and morality plays. And the most spiritually impoverished can make the acquaintance of the Bible at nativity and miracle plays, passion scenes and stations of the cross, by singing canticles and staring at sculptures and paintings in churches. And you want to print and give those simpletons the Bible? And maybe translated from Latin into the common tongue to boot? So that anyone can read it and interpret it in their own way? You want it to come to that?'

'I needn't want it at all,' Gutenberg replied calmly, 'because it's already happened. Quite near here. In Bohemia. And however history continues to develop, nothing can change that fact or its consequences. Whether we like it or not, we are facing reforms.'

Silence fell. It felt to Reynevan as if a cold draught had blown through the room. From the window, from the Dominican monastery a stone's throw away, where the Inquisition resided.

'When they burned Huss at the stake in Konstanz,' Unger plucked up the courage to break the long silence, 'they say a dove flew up with the smoke and ashes. They say it was an omen, that a new prophet was coming—'

'Because that's also the times we live in,' Justus Schottel suddenly exploded, 'when someone can just write out a few theses and stick the fuckers up on some church door. Shoo, Luther, off the table, you cheeky cat.'

There was another long silence in which only the contented purring of the cat Luther could be heard.

Scharley interrupted the silence.

'Blow dogmas, doctrines and reforms,' he said, 'I'd like to say that one thought pleases me greatly. If you print a load of books using your invention, m'lord, then perhaps people will start to learn to read, knowing there are things to read? After all, not only does demand create supply, but also vice versa. For in the beginning was the word, *in principio erat verbum*. Obviously, under condition that the word – meaning the book – must be cheaper than, if not a pack of cards, then at least a demijohn of vodka, since it's a matter of choice. Do you know what, Master Johannes Gutenberg? Brushing aside its flaws, after profound analysis, I'm coming to the conclusion that this invention of yours may actually be epochal.'

'You took the words out of my mouth, Scharley,' said Samson Honey-Eater. 'My thoughts entirely.'

'In that case,' the scholar's face lit up again, 'if you'd like to sponsor—'

'No.' Scharley cut him off. 'I wouldn't. It's all well and good being epochal, but I'm running a business here, Master Gutenberg.'

Chapter Sixteen

In which Reynevan, as noble as Perceval and just as stupid, hastens to somebody's rescue and defends them. As a result, the entire company has to flee. Very smartly.

'*Basilicus super omnes,*' said Reynevan. '*Annus cyclicus. Voluptas?* Yes, most certainly *voluptas. Voluptas papillae. De sanctimonia et . . . Expeditione hominis.* Samson!'

'Yes,'

'*Expeditione hominis.* Or *positione hominis.* On the charred paper. The one from Powojowice. Ring any bells?'

'*Voluptas papillae . . .* Oh, Reinmar, Reinmar.'

'I asked if it rings any bells!'

'No, alas. But I keep thinking about it.'

Reynevan did not comment, although in spite of Samson Honey-Eater's assurances, he appeared to be doing more dozing than thinking as he rode along on the sturdy, mousy gelding, the horse that Justus Schottel, the master wood carver from Świdnica, had provided on the basis of the list Scharley had drawn up.

Reynevan sighed. Assembling the equipment Scharley had ordered took a little longer than planned. Instead of three, they spent four whole days in Świdnica. The penitent and Samson didn't grumble; they were, in fact, delighted to be able to roam around the famous Świdnica cellars and thoroughly test the quality of that year's March ale. Reynevan, on the other hand, who was discouraged from wandering around drinking dens for the sake of secrecy, sat bored in the workshop accompanied by the equally boring Simon Unger, feeling cross, impatient, in love and pining. He feverishly counted the days of his separation from Adèle and not for all the world could he come up with anything less than twenty-eight. Twenty-eight days! Almost a month! He wondered if and how Adèle was able to bear it.

His wait ended on the morning of the fifth day. Having bade farewell to the wood carvers, the three wanderers left Świdnica via the Lower Gate, joining a long column of other wanderers, on horseback, on foot, with heavy loads, driving cattle and sheep, pulling carts, pushing wheelbarrows, and riding on vehicles of all sorts of construction and appearance. A foul smell and a spirit of enterprise hung over the column.

On his own initiative, Justus Schottel had come up with a good deal of varied, though clearly chaotically gathered, items of clothing that weren't on Scharley's kit list, so the three wanderers had the opportunity to put on new outfits. Scharley wasted no time and now looked grave, battle-hardened even, dressed in a quilted armoured doublet bearing the rusty imprints of a breastplate. The sober apparel also uncannily transformed Scharley himself – once rid of his clownish costume, he also rid himself of his clownish manner and quips. Now he sat erect on his beautiful chestnut, fist resting on his hip and looking down on the merchants they passed with a grim visage, bearing an appearance if not of Gawain, then at least of Gareth.

Samson Honey-Eater's appearance had also changed, although the giant had found it difficult to find anything that fitted in the parcels Schottel supplied. Finally, they managed to replace his ample smock with a loose, short journade and a cowl with fashionable serrations cut into it. It was a garment common enough for Samson to no longer stand out from the crowd – as far as that was possible. Now, all the other wayfarers in the column saw was a knight accompanied by a student and a servant. Or at least Reynevan hoped so. He also hoped that Kyrie-eleison and his band – even if they knew that Scharley was with him – would be asking about two travellers, not three.

Reynevan himself, having discarded his tattered and rather stale things, selected from Schottel's offerings a pair of tight trousers and a doublet with a fashionably padded front, giving him a slightly bird-like look. He completed his outfit with a beret of the kind worn by scholars.

The road outside the Lower Gate leading to Rychbach along the valley of the River Piława was part of the important Nysa-Dresden trade route and as such very congested. So congested, it began to irritate Scharley's sensitive nose, which led to a discussion of Gutenberg, although surprisingly not regarding his invention of printing.

'Inventors like Master Gutenberg *et consortes*,' the penitent griped, shooing flies off himself, 'might finally invent something practical. Another means of transport, let's say. Some sort of *perpetuum mobile*, something that propels itself without the need to rely on horses or oxen. Oh, I tell you in sooth, I dream of something that travels by itself, without polluting the environment at the same time. What do you say to that, Reinmar? Or you, Samson, O philosopher from the beyond?'

'Something that propels itself and doesn't stink,' wondered Samson. 'Moves by itself, but doesn't foul the road or poison the surroundings. A tricky dilemma, indeed. Experience suggests that the inventors will solve it, but only partially.'

Scharley might have intended to ply the giant with questions about the meaning of his comments, but he was disrupted by a rider, a scruffy man on a skinny nag, hurrying bareback towards the head of the column. Scharley brought his frightened chestnut under control, shook his fist at the scruff and sent a stream of invective after him. Samson stood up in his stirrups and looked back from where the scruff had galloped. Reynevan – who was quickly gaining experience – knew what Samson was looking for.

'A guilty person always behaves suspiciously,' Reynevan said. 'Somebody frightened that fugitive. Somebody coming from the city—'

'—scrutinising every traveller,' Samson completed his sentence. 'Five . . . No, six armed men. Several with emblems on their tunics showing a black bird with outstretched wings . . .'

'I know those arms—'

'So do I!' said Scharley harshly, tugging on his reins. 'To horse! After that skinny mare! Ride! Like the wind!'

Close to the head of the column, the road entered a gloomy beechwood. They rode into the trees and hid themselves in the bushes, from where they watched six horsemen ride by, on both sides of the road, examining everybody, scrupulously looking into wagons and under tarpaulins. Reynevan knew them all: Stefan Rotkirch. Dieter Haxt. Jentsch of Knobelsdorf. And Wittich, Morold and Wolfher Stercza.

'Aaaye,' Scharley drawled slowly. 'Yes, Reinmar. You thought you were wise and the whole world stupid. I regret to inform you that you were in error, for the rest of the world has already seen through both you and your naive plans. It knows you're heading to Ziębice and your sweetheart. As I said, there's no sense in going to Ziębice. None. None at all. Your plan is . . . what's the word . . .'

'Scharley—'

'Got it! Absurd.'

The argument was brief, sharp and quite pointless. Reynevan remained deaf to Scharley's logic, and Scharley unmoved by Reynevan's amorous yearnings. Samson abstained.

Reynevan, whose thoughts were mainly preoccupied by counting the days he'd been apart from his love, insisted on continuing their journey to Ziębice, either following the Sterczas or attempting to overtake them when they took a break, probably somewhere near Rychbach or in Ziębice itself. Scharley was adamantly opposed. The Sterczas' ostentatious display, he claimed, could signify only one thing.

'They've been ordered to flush you out and drive you towards Rychbach and Frankenstein,' he said. 'And Kyrie-eleison and Walter of Barby are probably lying in wait for you somewhere near there. Believe me, laddie, it's the standard means of capturing fugitives.'

'So do you have any suggestions?'

'My suggestions are limited by geography.' Scharley swept an arm in a broad gesture. 'That large thing to the east covered in clouds is Ślęża. Those things rising up over there are the Owl Mountains and that big thing is the mountain called Great Owl. Great Owl has two passes, Walim and Jugów. Taking that route, we could get to Bohemia in no time.'

'You said Bohemia was risky.'

'Right now, the greatest risk is you,' replied Scharley coldly, 'and the men who are hot on your heels. Ideally, I'd set off for Bohemia immediately, but you won't give up on Ziębice, I fear.'

'You fear correctly.'

'Then we'll have to forgo the safety the passes would have given us.'

'It would have been very dubious safety,' Samson unexpectedly interjected.

'True,' the penitent agreed calmly. 'It isn't the safest region. In that case, let's head for Frankenstein. Not by the main road, though, but skirting around the mountains, keeping to the edges of the forests of the Silesian Clearing. It's the long way around, we'll be riding a little cross-country, but what else can we do?'

'Take the highway,' Reynevan exploded. 'Follow the Sterczas! And catch up with them—'

'Haven't you heard a word I've said?' Scharley cut him off brutally. 'You really don't want to fall into their clutches, believe me.'

So they set off, at first through beech and oak forests, then along forest tracks and finally along a road winding among the hills. Scharley and Samson chatted softly. Reynevan kept quiet and brooded over the penitent's last words.

Scharley once again demonstrated that if he couldn't actually read minds, he could unerringly hypothesise on the basis of evidence. The sight of the Sterczas had awoken in Reynevan such a savage lust for revenge that he was ready to pursue them immediately, wait for nightfall, then sneak up and cut their throats as they slept. But he was restrained not only by good sense, but also by paralysing fear. He awoke several times, covered in cold sweat, from a dream in which he was captured and taken to a torture chamber in the dungeons of Sterzendorf. The dream was horrifyingly realistic regarding the instruments assembled there, and Reynevan went hot and cold by turns whenever he recalled them. Shivers also ran down his back and his heart skipped a beat whenever dark shapes loomed up at the side of the road, until careful examination revealed them to be juniper bushes rather than the Sterczas.

Things got even worse when Scharley and Samson changed the subject and began a discussion from the fields of history and literature.

'When the troubadour Guillem of Cabestany,' said Scharley, glancing meaningfully at Reynevan, 'seduced the wife of the Lord of Château-Roussillon, he had the poet killed and disembowelled, then ordered the cook to fry his heart and give it to his unfaithful spouse to eat. Then she threw herself from a tower.'

'So runs the legend, at least,' replied Samson, displaying an erudition that was stupefying when juxtaposed with his gormless expression. 'You can't always give credence to master troubadours; their verses about the amorous conquests of married ladies more often express desires and dreams than describe actual events.'

'Indeed,' Scharley agreed. 'What about Lord Saint-Gilles? He had the troubadour Peire Vidal's tongue cut out for writing a suggestive canzone about his wife.'

'According to legend.'

'And then there's Daniel Carret. As punishment for sleeping with his wife, the Baron of Faux hired thugs to kill him and then had a goblet made from his skull, from which he still drinks.'

'That's all true,' said Samson, nodding. 'Aside from the fact that he wasn't a baron but a count. And he didn't kill the poet, he imprisoned him. And he didn't have a goblet made, but a decorated pouch. For a signet ring and loose change.'

'A po—' Reynevan said, choking. 'A pouch?'

'A pouch.'

'Why have you suddenly turned blue, Reinmar?' Scharley asked, pretending to sound concerned. 'Are you perhaps unwell? After all, you've always claimed that great love demands sacrifices. And a pouch? A pouch is a trifle.'

They had just heard the sound of a bell from a nearby church – in the village of Lutom, Scharley claimed – when Reynevan stopped and raised a hand.

'Hear that?'

They were at a crossroads, beside a crooked cross and a carved figure eroded by the rain into an amorphous lump.

'They're goliards,' stated Scharley. 'They're singing.'

Reynevan shook his head. The sounds coming from a ravine disappearing into the forest in no way resembled any of the popular goliard songs. Nor did the voices he could hear resemble those of the goliards who had recently overtaken them on the road . . .

He groped for the hilt of his short sword, another of the gifts received in Świdnica, and then bent forward in the saddle and spurred his horse on. Into a trot. And then a gallop.

'Where are you going?' roared Scharley behind him. 'Stop! Stop, damn you! You'll get us into trouble, you fool!'

Reynevan ignored him and rode into the ravine. In a glade beyond the ravine, a battle was raging around a wagon covered with a black, tarred tarpaulin and drawn by two stocky horses. Beside the wagon, at least a dozen foot soldiers in brigantines, mail hoods and kettle hats, armed with pole weapons, were attacking two knights as fiercely as dogs. The knights were de-fending themselves equally fiercely, like wild boars at bay.

One knight, on horseback, was covered in plate armour from head to toe. Lance and glaive blades were glancing off his breast-plate, clattering impotently on the tassets and cuisses. Unable to reach the horseman, the assailants were taking their anger out on the horse. They weren't trying to cut it – horses were very expensive, after all – but they were poking it with their pike-staffs, hoping the frenzied horse would throw the knight. The horse really was frantic, shaking its head, snorting and biting its mouthpiece. Evidently specially trained for this kind of fighting, it was kicking out, hampering access to itself and its rider. The knight was swaying so precariously in the saddle, it was a wonder he was still in it.

The foot soldiers had managed to pull down the other knight, also in full plate, who was now defending himself resolutely, his back to the black wagon. His helmet had been knocked from his head and his long, fair, blood-spattered hair was flowing freely, his teeth flashing under a similarly fair moustache. He was driving back his attackers with blows of a two-handed sword, which, though long and heavy, was whirling in the knight's hands as though it were a small ceremonial sword. The weapon didn't just *look* dangerous – the attackers' access was already impeded by three men lying wounded on the ground, howling in pain and trying to crawl away. The remaining assailants were being wary now, trying to stab the knight from a safe distance. But even if their thrusts weren't deflected by the two-handed sword's heavy blade, the swords slid off the armour.

Reynevan took in the scene in a heartbeat: two knights in peril, being attacked by a horde of thugs. He yelled, drew his short sword from its scabbard, spurred his horse and charged to their aid, utterly heedless of Scharley's warning cries and curses.

However reckless it was, the relief came not a moment too soon, for the mounted knight had just tumbled from his horse with a crash like a copper kettle thrown from a church steeple. The fair-haired knight with the two-handed sword, pressed against the wagon by pikestaffs, could only help him with filthy words, which he was hurling lavishly at his assailants.

Reynevan rushed into the heart of the fray. He used his horse to push aside and knock over the men teeming around the fallen knight, delivering a clanging blow to the kettle hat of a man with a grey moustache. When the helmet fell off, the man turned around, scowled malevolently and hit Reynevan hard with a halberd from close quarters, fortunately only with the pole. But it was enough to knock Reynevan off his horse. The grey-moustachioed soldier leaped forward, pinned him down and seized him by the throat. And soared away. Literally. For Samson had slammed a powerful punch into the side of his head. Others jumped onto Samson at once and the giant found himself in a predicament. He seized a halberd from the ground and whacked the first attacker so hard with the flat of the blade across his helmet that the blade flew off and the man fell to the ground. Samson brandished the remaining pole, swinging it around like a reed, making room for himself, Reynevan and the knight who was getting to his feet. The knight had lost his sallet when he fell, so a young, ruddy face, a snub nose and green eyes stuck out of the bevor protecting his neck.

'Just you wait, you swine!' he yelled in a comical descant. 'I'll show you, you shit-eaters! By the skull of Saint Sabina! You won't forget me!'

Scharley came to the aid of the fair-haired knight defending himself by the wagon, who was in a lamentable situation having lost his two-handed sword in the scrum. The penitent deftly picked up an abandoned sword at full gallop and scattered the foot soldiers, hacking left and right with immense skill. The fair-haired man didn't waste time searching for his weapon in the sand, but threw himself into the fray with his fists.

The unexpected relief appeared to have tipped the scales in favour of the men being attacked, when suddenly the thud of iron-shod hooves resounded and four heavily armed men hurtled into the clearing at full gallop. Even if Reynevan had any momentary doubts regarding their identity, they were dispelled by the triumphant yells of the foot soldiers, who entered the fray with redoubled resolve at the sight of reinforcements.

'Alive!' yelled the leader of the heavily armed men from behind the visor of a helmet with three silver fish on a shield. 'Take the scoundrels alive!'

Scharley was the first casualty of the new arrivals. The penitent nimbly avoided a blow from a battleaxe by dismounting, but was overcome by the foot soldiers' superior strength. Samson rushed to his aid, wielding the halberd pole. The giant wasn't daunted by the knight coming at him with a battleaxe; he thumped the man's steed in the iron chanfron protecting its face with such force that the halberd pole shattered with a snap. But the horse squealed and fell to its knees, and the fair-haired knight dragged the rider from the saddle. They began to wrestle with each other, locked together like two bears.

Reynevan and the youngster who had been knocked from the saddle defended themselves desperately against the other armoured men, emboldening themselves with wild shouts, curses and appeals to the saints. The hopelessness of the situation couldn't, however, be denied. There was nothing to suggest that the furious attackers would remember the order to take them alive – and even if they did, Reynevan could already see himself dangling from a noose.

But fortune smiled on them that day.

'Fight, in God's name! Kill, whoever believes in God!'

Amid the tramping of hooves and pious battle cries entered more men – another three heavy horsemen in full armour and bascinets with hounskull visors. There was no doubt whose side they were on. Blows from long swords scattered the foot soldiers in kettle hats one after another across the bloodstained sand. The knight with the fish in his coat of arms swayed in the saddle after receiving a powerful blow. Another one protected him with his shield and held him up, grabbed the horse by the reins and both fled at a gallop. A third also tried to flee, but was struck in the head with a sword and trampled by hooves. The most courageous of the foot soldiers were still trying to shield themselves with their pikestaffs, but one after another they dropped their weapons and fled into the forest.

Meanwhile, the fair-haired knight knocked over his opponent with a powerful blow of his iron-gloved hand. When the man tried to stand, he shoved his foot into the man's shoulder. He sat down heavily, and the fair-haired man looked around for something to whack him with.

'Catch!' shouted one of the heavily armed men. 'Catch, Rymbaba!'

The fair-haired man addressed as Rymbaba caught the war hammer – a vicious-looking *martel de fer* – thrown to him and smashed the helmet of the man trying to get up, once, twice and then a third time so hard it rang. The man's head lolled onto one shoulder and blood gushed over the aventail, bevor and breastplate from the dented sheet metal. The fair-haired man stood astride the wounded man and struck him once again.

'Jesus Christ,' he panted. 'How I like this work . . .'

The youngster with the snub nose wheezed and spat blood. Then he sat up straight, a smile appeared on his blood-spattered face and he held his hand out to Reynevan.

'Thank you for the help, young sir knight. By the shinbone of Saint Aphrodisius, I won't forget this! I'm Kuno of Wittram.'

'And may devils flay me in Hell if ever I forget your help, m'lord,' said the fair-haired man, holding his right hand out to Scharley. 'I am Paszko Pakosławic Rymbaba.'

'Assemble,' commanded one of the men in armour, displaying a swarthy face and blue, close-shaven cheeks beneath an open visor. 'Rymbaba, Wittram, grab the horses! Quickly, dammit!'

'Blow that.' Rymbaba leaned over and cleared his nose into his fingers. 'They've fled!'

'They'll soon return,' announced another of the reinforcements, pointing at an abandoned shield with three fish, one above the other. 'Have you both lost your minds, attacking travellers right here?'

Scharley, who was stroking the chestnut's nostril, gave Reynevan a very telling look.

'Right here,' repeated the knight, 'in the Seidlitzes' lands? They won't forgive this . . .'

'They will not,' confirmed a third. 'To horse, everybody!'

The road and forest echoed with shouting, neighing and the thudding of hooves. Halberdiers were streaming among the bracken and tree stumps, and over a dozen horsemen, heavily armed soldiers and crossbowmen were rushing along the road.

'Flee! yelled Rymbaba. 'Flee if you value your lives!'

They set off at a gallop, pursued by yells and the whistles of the first crossbow bolts.

They weren't pursued for long. When the infantry fell back, the horsemen had slowed, clearly not trusting their numerical advantage. The bowmen sent one more salvo after the fleeing men, and that was the end of the pursuit.

Just to be certain, they galloped on a few more furlongs and took a roundabout route through hills and maple forests, glancing back every now and then. But no one was chasing them. They stopped near the outermost cottage of a village to rest the horses. Rather than waiting for his cottage and farmyard to be plundered, the peasant brought out a bowl of pierogi and a pail of buttermilk. The Raubritters sat, leaning against the fence. They ate in silence. The oldest, who had introduced himself as Notker of Weyrach, looked long and hard at Scharley.

'Yeees,' he said finally, licking his buttermilk-covered moustaches. 'You're decent and bold men, Master Scharley and you, m'Lord Hagenau. Incidentally, are you a descendant of the famous poet?'

'No.'

'Aha. Where was I? Ah yes, that you're bold and brave fellows. And your servant, though he looks like a halfwit, is exceptionally courageous and valiant. You came to the rescue of my boys and thus find yourselves in deep water. Trouble will come of it – you've crossed the Seidlitzes, and they are vengeful.'

'True,' agreed another knight, with long hair and a handlebar moustache, who introduced himself as Woldan of Osiny. 'The Seidlitzes are queer whoresons. The entire family. The Laasans are the same, and the Kurzbaches. All extremely nasty bastards and vengeful cunts . . . Hey, Wittram, Rymbaba, you fucked things up, a pox on you!'

'You need to think before you act,' Weyrach instructed. 'Think, both of you!'

'But we did,' mumbled Kuno of Wittram. 'We looked: a wagon's rolling by. And we thought: shall we rob it? One thing led to another . . . By the bonds of Saint Dismas! You know yourselves how it is!'

'Aye, that we do. But you still have to think it through,' said Weyrach.

'And be heedful of the escort!' added Woldan of Osiny.

'There was no escort,' said Wittram. 'Only a waggoner, some servants and a mounted man in a beaver coat, a merchant, no doubt. They fled. So we think: our luck's in. And then: fifteen grim fuckers with halberds spring out of nowhere—'

'Precisely. Hence the need for *thinking it through* before acting.'

'What times we live in!' said Rymbaba, annoyed. 'It's come to this! A stupid sodding wagon, the goods under the canvas probably only worth a few farthings, and they defended it as though it was, beg pardon, the Holy Grail.'

'It didn't use to be like that,' said the third knight, a swarthy youth not much older than Rymbaba and Wittram, called Tassilo of Tresckow, with hair cut fashionably in a style popular with the knighthood. 'You used to just call: "Stand and deliver!" and they delivered. And now they put up a fight, scrap like hell, like Venetian condottieres. Woe on us! How can we make a living in conditions like these?'

'We cannot,' Weyrach concluded. 'Our Raubritter life is becoming harder and harder. Aye . . .'

'Aye . . .' echoed the robber knights in a pathetic chorus. 'Aaaye . . .'

'Hey, there's a pig snuffling around the muck heap,' Kuno

Wittram observed, pointing. 'Do we slaughter it and take it?'

'No,' Weyrach decided after a moment's thought. 'Waste of time.'

He stood up.

'Master Scharley,' he said, 'it wouldn't do to leave you three here. The Seidlitzes hold grudges and they'll have men out already, hunting you on the roads. So, please ride with us to Kromolin, our stronghold. Our squires are there and enough comrades, too. No one will endanger or offend you there.'

'Just let them try.' Rymbaba twisted his blond moustache. 'Ride with us, Master Scharley. For let me tell you, I've taken a great liking to you.'

'Likewise to young Sir Reinmar.' Kuno Wittram slapped Reynevan's back. 'I swear on the trowel of Saint Rupert of Salzburg! So ride with us to Kromolin. Master Scharley? Agreed?'

'Agreed.'

'In that case,' Notker of Weyrach said, stretching, 'on our way, *comitiva*.'

When the procession had formed up, Scharley remained at the back and discreetly called Reynevan and Samson to him.

'That Kromolin,' he said quietly, patting his chestnut's neck, 'is somewhere in the vicinity of Silver Mountain and Stoszowice, by the so-called Czech road, a route that goes to Bohemia via the Silver Pass to Frankenstein, to the Wrocław road, so it suits our plans to ride with them. Plus it's much safer. Let's stay with them and turn a blind eye to the practice by which they earn their living. Beggars can't be choosers. Nonetheless, I advise you to be cautious and not speak too much. Samson?'

'I'll stay quiet and play the dullard. *Pro bono commune*.'

'Splendid. Reinmar, come closer. I have to tell you something.'

Reynevan, now in the saddle, rode closer, guessing what he was about to hear. He wasn't wrong.

'Listen carefully, you incorrigible ass. You constitute a lethal threat to me by the mere fact of your existence. I won't let you increase that threat by your idiotic behaviour and exploits. I won't comment on the fact that in your desire to be noble, you acted stupidly, going to the aid of brigands and helping them in their fight with the forces of order. I will not mock; God willing, you've learned something from it. But I'm warning you: do anything like that again and I'll leave you to your fate. Remember and take note, cretin: no one will come to your aid and only a fool goes to other people's. If someone calls for help, you should turn your back and move swiftly away. Play at being Percival at your own expense and risk.'

'Scharley—'

'Be quiet. And consider yourself warned. I'm serious.'

They rode through a meadow in the forest, among stirrup-high grass and herbs. The sky to the west, strewn with ragged, feathery clouds, glowed in streaks of fiery crimson. The wall of mountains and the black forests of the Silesian Clearing grew dark.

Notker of Weyrach and Woldan of Osiny, riding in the vanguard, grave and attentive, were singing a hymn, from time to time looking heavenwards from their upraised hounskull visors. Their singing, though muted, sounded dignified and severe.

Pange lingua gloriosi
Corporis mysterium,
Sanguinisque pretiosi,
Quem in mundi pretium
Fructus ventris generosi
Rex effudit Gentium.

A little further back, far enough away for their own singing not to be discordant, Tassilo of Tresckow and Scharley were singing a romantic ballad with considerably less gravity.

Sô die bluomen üz dem grase dringent,
same si lachen gegen der spilden sunnen,
in einem meien an dem morgen fruo,

und diu kleinen vogelin wol singent
in ir besten wîse, die si kunnen,
waz wünne mac sich dâ gelîchen zuo?

Samson and Reynevan followed on at a walk. Samson was listening, swaying in the saddle and humming. It was evident he knew the words of the minnesang and that – had he not been required to remain incognito – he would gladly have joined in. Reynevan was daydreaming about Adèle. He was having difficulty gathering his thoughts, for Rymbaba and Kuno of Wittram, who were bringing up the rear, were belting out lewd drinking songs one after the next. Their repertoire seemed inexhaustible.

Verbum caro, panem verum
verbo carnem efficit:
fitque sanguis Christi merum,
et si sensus deficit,
ad firmandum cor sincerum
sola fides sufficit.

The solemn tune and pious verses of Thomas Aquinas weren't fooling anyone; the knights' reputation evidently went before them. At the sight of the procession, old women gathering firewood fled in panic and adolescent girls darted away like hinds. Woodcutters ran off through clearings and horror-stricken shepherds crawled under their sheep. A tar burner fled, abandoning his cart. Three wandering Friars Minor made off, hitching their habits up above their haunches. Nor did the poetic stanzas of Walther von der Vogelweide appear to have any calming influence on them whatsoever.

Nü wol dan, welt ir die wârheit schouwen,
gen wir zuo des meien hôhgezîte!
der ist mit aller sîner krefte komen.
seht an in und seht an werde frouwen,
wederz dâ daz ander überstrîte:
daz bezzer spil, ob ich daz hân genomen.

Samson sang along under his breath. *My Adèle,* thought Reynevan, *my Adèle. Verily, when we are finally together, when our separation is over, it will be like that song of Walther von der Vogelweide's – 'The spring will come'. Or some other of that poet's stanzas . . .*

Rerum tanta novitas
in solemni vere
et veris auctoritas
jubet nos gaudere . . .

'Were you saying something, Reinmar?'

'No, Samson. I didn't say a thing.'

'Ah. But you were murmuring strangely.'

Ah, spring, spring . . . And my Adèle is comelier than the spring. Oh, Adèle, Adèle, where are you, my love? When shall I finally see you again? Kiss your lips? Your breasts . . .

'Quickly, onwards, quickly! To Ziębice!'

I wonder, too, he suddenly thought, *where the Fair Nicolette is and what she's doing?*

Genitori, Genitoque
laus et jubilatio,
salus, honor, virtus quoque
sit et benedictio . . .

Rymbaba and Wittram, hidden around a bend in the road at the back of the procession, were bellowing, frightening wild animals.

Whoremonger tanners
Tanned some arse leather.
Whoreson shoemakers
Made boots from them!

Chapter Seventeen

In which, in the Raubritter stronghold of Kromolin, Reynevan makes some acquaintances, eats, drinks, sews on ears and participates in an assembly of the Angelic Militia. Until some quite unexpected guests arrive.

From the point of view of strategy and defensiveness, the Raubritter settlement of Kromolin was located advantageously on an island created by a wide, silted-up branch of the River Jadkowa. A bridge hidden among willows and osiers provided the single access point by road, easily blocked by the barriers and *chevaux de frise* standing ready for that purpose. Even in the semi-darkness of the falling dusk, further elements of the fortifications were visible in the form of abatises and sharpened stakes stuck into the boggy bank. At the entrance to the settlement itself, the bridge was additionally barred by a thick chain which was taken down by servants even before Notker of Weyrach had managed to sound his horn, for their approach had been seen from the watchtower high above the alders.

They rode onto the island between shacks and sheds roofed with turf. The main building, similar to a fortress, was a mill, complete with a functional millrace. The glow of numerous fires beyond the mill illuminated the thatched roofs of the cottages, from which music and a hubbub of voices could be heard.

'Sounds like they're making merry,' guessed Tassilo of Tresckow.

A giggling wench in a state of undress ran out from among the cottages, her plait fluttering behind her, pursued by a fat Bernardine monk. They ran into a barn from where laughter and squeals could be heard a moment later.

'Well, well,' mumbled Scharley. 'I feel quite at home.'

They passed a latrine hidden in a thicket but revealed by its stench, then rode out into a courtyard full of people, bright with fire, noisy with music and voices. Servants and squires were soon beside them, helping the knights dismount and then leading their horses away. At a wink from Scharley, Samson sighed and went off with the servants, pulling his companions' steeds after him.

Notker of Weyrach gave his helmet to a squire but kept his sword under one arm.

'Plenty of men have come,' he observed.

'Aye,' confirmed the squire dryly. 'And they say there'll be more.'

'Come, come,' Rymbaba urged, rubbing his hands together. 'I have a hunger!'

'Indeed!' Kuno of Wittram chimed in. 'And I a thirst!'

They passed a forge belching heat, where several farriers as black as Cyclopes were bustling around, then a barn that had been converted into a slaughterhouse. Through the wide-open doors, they could see the dressed carcasses of several hogs and a great ox hanging by their legs. The entrails of the freshly butchered ox were being chucked into a bowl, while suckling pigs and rams sizzled on spits over campfires roaring outside the barn. Steam and tempting fragrances rose from blackened pots and cauldrons. Men sat alongside on benches, at tables or simply on the ground, and dogs swarmed and fought among growing piles of discarded bones. Lights shone from windows and the lamps in the porch of the tavern from which barrels rolled endlessly, to be immediately besieged by thirsty men.

The courtyard, enclosed by buildings, was bathed in the flickering light of burning torches. Peasants and merchants rubbed shoulders with Bernardine and Franciscan friars, Jews and Gypsies, and there were plenty of knights and esquires in armour with swords invariably at their belts or under their arms.

The knights' equipage defined their status and wealth. Most were in full plate, and several brazenly flaunted suits of armour made by master armourers in Nuremberg, Augsburg and Innsbruck. Others could only afford incomplete plate armour, or a breastplate, bevor, rerebraces or cuisses worn over a mail shirt.

On the steps of a granary, a group of wandering goliards hopped in time with the clamour of fiddles, flutes and horns, jangling the bells and rattles sewn onto their costumes. Close by on a wooden platform, several knights were dancing, apparently in honour of Saint Vitus given their somewhat uncoordinated jumping and hopping. Their thudding footfalls almost drowned out the music, and the clouds of dust they were kicking up made people sneeze. Wenches and Romani women laughed and squealed more shrilly than the goliards' pipes.

More masculine pursuits were being enjoyed on a large area of compacted earth in the centre of the courtyard, marked out at the corners by torches. Knights in armour were testing both each other's skills with weapons and the robustness of their armour. Blades rang, battleaxes and morning stars thudded against shields, accompanied by crude curses and the encouraging cries of spectators. Two knights, one of whom bore the golden carp of the Glaubitzes on his shield, were risking a bout without helmets. The Glaubitz was aiming blows with a sword, and his opponent, fending them off with a buckler, was trying to catch the weapon in the teeth of a swordbreaker.

Reynevan stood up to observe the fight, but Scharley tugged him by the elbow, instructing him to follow the lead of the Raubritters, who were clearly more interested in vittles and beverages than the sparring. They soon found themselves in the very centre of the feasting and merrymaking. Shouting over the hubbub, Rymbaba, Wittram and Tassilo greeted friends, exchanging handshakes and backslaps. Soon, everyone, including Scharley and Reynevan, was sitting shoulder to shoulder at the table, chewing pork and mutton chops and ribs and drinking toasts to good health, happiness and prosperity. Disdaining something as despicably small as a beaker, the sorely thirsty Rymbaba drank mead from a gallon pail, the golden fluid pouring down his moustaches and onto his breastplate.

Aside from the Glaubitz fighting in the combat circle, some others among the Raubritters wore their family crests unabashedly, clearly not believing that banditry brought shame on their houses. Near Reynevan, a beanpole in a tunic with the coat of arms of the Kottwitzes – a red bar on a silver field – was chewing on some gristle. Nearby, a curly haired knight bore the rose, the coat of arms of the Porajs. Another man, as broad-shouldered as an ox, was dressed in a lendner decorated with a golden lynx. Reynevan couldn't recall that coat of arms, but he was soon reminded.

'Sir Bożywoj of Lossow.' Notker of Weyrach did the introductions. 'Lords Scharley and Hagenau.'

'Upon my word,' said Bożywoj of Lossow, removing from his mouth a pork rib, fat dripping onto the golden lynx. 'Upon my word, welcome. Hagenau, hmm . . . Kin of the celebrated poet?'

'No.'

'Aha. Then let's drink. Your health!'

'Your health.'

'Sir Wencel of Hartha.' Weyrach continued to introduce knights as they approached. 'Sir Buko of Krossig.'

Reynevan watched with interest. Buko of Krossig, who was wearing a suit of armour edged with brass, was renowned in Silesia. Now, frowning and squinting, the celebrated Raubritter was staring at Scharley.

'Do we know each other?'

'We may have met,' replied the penitent freely. 'In church, perhaps?'

'Good health!'

'Good luck!'

'. . . council,' Buko of Krossig was saying to Weyrach. 'There will be a council. Once they all arrive. Traugott of Barnhelm. And Ekkehard of Sulz.'

'Ekkehard of Sulz.' Notker of Weyrach grimaced. 'Indeed. Sticks his nose in everywhere. What will the council be about?'

'Apparently there's an expedition in the offing,' said a knight sitting close by, regally lifting to his mouth morsels of meat he was carving with a dagger from the haunch he was holding. He had long, very grizzled hair, well-groomed hands and face, and a nobility that even some old scars couldn't mar.

'Against whom, Sir Markwart?'

Before the grey-haired knight could answer, a commotion erupted on the exercise ground. Someone swore, someone yelled, a dog was kicked and gave a short whimper. A voice called loudly for a barber-surgeon or a Jew. Or both.

'Do you hear?' The grey-haired man gestured with his head, his smile a sneer. 'Just in time. What happened? Eh? Master Jasiek?'

'Otto Glaubitz has nicked John of Schoenfeld,' panted a knight with thin moustaches drooping like a Tatar's. 'Needs a physician, but that one's scarpered. Vanished, the roguish Jew.'

'And who was threatening yesterday to teach the Jew to eat in the Christian manner? Who was forcing him to eat pig meat? Whom did I ask to leave the wretch alone? Whom did I admonish?'

'You were right, as usual, honourable Lord Stolberg,' the moustachioed knight admitted reluctantly. 'But what are we to do now? Schoenfeld is bleeding like a stuck pig, and all that remains of the barber-surgeon are his Jewish instruments ...'

'Bring me the instruments,' Reynevan said loudly and without thinking, 'and bring the wounded man here. And light, I need light!'

The wounded man, who a moment later landed with a thud of armour on the table, turned out to be one of the two from the parade ground who had been fighting without helmets. The result of his imprudence was a cheek cloven to the bone and a notched ear hanging off his head. As the wounded man cursed and struggled, blood gushed onto the lindenwood table, spattering the meat and soaking into the bread.

The physician's satchel was brought, and Reynevan got down to work by the light of several sizzling torches. He found a flacon

of Hungary water and poured the contents over the wound, causing the patient to wriggle around like a landed fish and almost
fall off the table, after which Reynevan called for help holding
him down. Reynevan quickly threaded a curved needle with stout
twine and began to suture the wounds, doing his best to keep the
stitches even. When the patient began to swear, the grey-haired
Markwart of Stolberg stopped up his mouth with a lump of pork.
Reynevan nodded his thanks and continued his work under the
fascinated gaze of the audience crowding the table. Shooing away
with his head the moths that were swarming around the torches,
he concentrated on reattaching the severed ear as close as possible
to its original location.

'Clean linen,' he asked after some time. Immediately, someone
seized a wench and ripped off her blouse, silencing her protests
with a few slaps.

Reynevan thoroughly bandaged the wounded man's head with
plenty of linen torn into strips. The patient, astonishingly, didn't
faint, but sat up, mumbled something about Saint Lucia, groaned,
moaned and shook Reynevan's hand. Immediately after, all the
others began hugging the physician and congratulating him
on his excellent work. Reynevan accepted the congratulations,
smiling and proud. Although he was aware that he could have
done better with the ear, he saw the marks of much more poorly
stitched wounds on plenty of the faces around him. The casualty
mumbled under his bandages, but no one was listening.

'Well? Quite something, isn't he?' Scharley received congratulations beside Reynevan. 'A remarkable physician!'

'He is,' agreed the culprit, the Glaubitz with the golden carp in
his coat of arms. He showed absolutely no remorse as he handed
Reynevan a mug of mead. 'And sober, which is a rarity among
quacks. Schoenfeld was lucky!'

'He was lucky,' Buko of Krossig commented coldly, 'because
it was you who smote him. Had it been me, there'd have been
nothing to stitch up.'

Interest in the occurrence suddenly dwindled, interrupted by fresh visitors riding into the Kromolin stronghold. The Raubritters murmured and an air of excitement indicated the arrival of an important individual. Reynevan watched, wiping his hands.

A cavalcade of over a dozen armed men was headed by three horsemen. In the centre rode a fat, balding man in black enamelled plate armour. To his right was a knight with a gloomy face and an oblique scar on his forehead, and to his left was a priest or monk, but with a short sword at his side and an iron bevor on a mail shirt over his habit.

'Barnhelm and Sulz are here,' announced Markwart of Stolberg. 'To the tavern, gentlemen! To the council! Summon those who are humping wenches in the hay! Awake the sleeping! To the council!'

There followed some confusion as almost every knight heading for the council got himself something to eat and drink on the way. Thunderous shouts demanded that servants roll out fresh kegs and casks. Samson was among the servants running up to answer the call. Reynevan furtively beckoned him and kept him by his side. He wanted to spare his comrade the fate of the other servants, whom the Raubritters were prodding and kicking.

'You two go to the council,' said Scharley. 'Mingle with the crowd. It will be good to know what the company is planning.'

'What about you?'

'I have other plans for now,' said the penitent, catching the flaming eyes of a comely, plump Gypsy woman milling around nearby, with gold rings plaited into her raven-black locks. The Romani woman winked at him.

Reynevan felt like commenting. But he overcame the urge.

The tavern was thronged. Smoke and the stink of men who hadn't taken off their armour for a long time mingled beneath the low ceiling. Knights and esquires grouped the benches in order to create something like King Arthur's Round Table, but there was far too little room for everybody. Many had to stand. Among them were Reynevan and Samson, trying to remain inconspicuous.

Markwart of Stolberg opened the council, welcoming the more illustrious by name. Immediately afterwards, Traugott of Barnhelm – the fat, balding newcomer with the plate armour covered in black enamel – spoke up.

'The matter before us,' he opened, clanging his scabbarded sword down in front of him, 'is that Konrad, Bishop of Wrocław, is calling soldiers to his standard. He's gathering an army to strike at the heretic Czechs. There will be a crusade. M'lord Starosta of Kolditz informed me of it through a confidant that whoever wants to, may enlist in the crusading army. The crusaders will have their sins forgiven and whatever they bag is theirs. The clergy said all sorts of things to Konrad, I don't remember what, but Pater Hiacynt, whom I picked up along the way, will explain it better.'

Pater Hiacynt, the armoured priest, stood up and cast down on the table his own weapon, a heavy, broad short sword.

'Blessed be the Lord,' he thundered as though from the pulpit, raising his hands in a preacher's gesture. 'My rock! He is preparing my hands for the fight, my fingers for the war! Brothers! Faith has vanished! In Bohemia, the heretical plague has gained new strength, and the vile dragon of Hussite heresy is raising its loathsome head! Will you, noble knights, look on indifferently as the banners of the crusade draw throngs of people from the lower orders? When, seeing that the Hussites still live, Our Lady weeps every morning? Noble gentlemen! I remind you of the words of Saint Bernard: to kill an enemy for Christ is to win him for Christ!'

'Get to the point,' Buko of Krossig interrupted gloomily. 'Be brief, Pater.'

'The Hussites are despicable to God!' Pater Hiacynt slammed both his fists down on the table. 'So, it will please God when we smite them with our swords, preventing them from luring more souls into their error and filth! The wages of sin are death! So death, death to the Czech apostates, fire and destruction on the heretical plague! Thus, I tell you and ask you, brother knights, on behalf of His Eminence Bishop Konrad – don the sign of the cross over your armour and join the Angelic Militia! Your sins and faults will be forgiven, both in this world and at the Final Judgement, and what anyone plunders is his.'

There was silence for some time. Someone belched; someone else's stomach gave a long rumble. Markwart of Stolberg cleared his throat and scratched behind his ear as his eyes swept all around.

'Well?' he began. 'What do you say, noble knights? Gentlemen of the Angelic Militia?'

'We ought to have expected it.' Bożywoj of Lossow was the first to speak. 'Cardinal Branda was residing in Wrocław with a wealthy entourage. I wondered about robbing him on the Krakow road, but the escort was too strong. It's no secret that Cardinal Branda is appealing for men to join the crusade. The Hussites have irked the Roman Pope!'

'It is also true that things are hard in Bohemia,' added Jaśko Chromy of Łubnia, the Raubritter with the moustache like a Tatar. 'The fortresses of Karlštejn and Žebrák are besieged and may fall any day. If we don't do something about the Czechs in time, they'll do something about us. We ought to consider it.'

Ekkehard of Sulz, the knight with the slanting scar on his forehead, swore and slapped his sword hilt. 'Indeed we ought!' he snorted. 'Pater Hiacynt is right: death to the heretics, fire and destruction! Whoever is virtuous must strike at the Czech! And if a chance arises, get rich, for it is right for sin to be punished and virtue rewarded.'

'It is true,' spoke up Woldan of Osiny, 'that a crusade is a large war. And it's easier to make a fortune in a large war.'

'And easier to get hit in the head,' observed the wavy-haired Poraj. 'And hit hard.'

'You grow timid, Sir Błażej Poraj Jakubowski,' called Otto of Glaubitz, the ear hacker. 'What is there to fear? You only live once! And don't we risk our necks here, making a living from pillaging? What can you grow rich on here? A merchant's purse? But in Bohemia, in a full-scale war, if you're lucky enough to take a knight alive, you can demand a ransom of six hundred score groschen. If you kill a man, take his horse and armour, that's at least twenty grzywna. And if we take a city . . .'

'Aye!' said Paszko Rymbaba, getting excited. 'The cities there are wealthy and the castles' treasuries are full. Like that Karlštejn people keep talking about. We'll capture and pillage it—'

'Oh, hark at him,' snorted the Kottwitz knight with the red bar in his coat of arms. 'Why, Karlštejn isn't in Hussite but Catholic hands. The fortress is being besieged by the heretics – the crusade is meant to bring them relief! Rymbaba, you stupid old goat, you understand nothing about politics.'

Paszko Rymbaba flushed and bristled his moustaches.

'Beware who you call stupid, Kottwitz!' he yelled, drawing a war hammer from his belt. 'To hell with politics; I know how to crack heads!'

'*Pax, pax*,' said Bożywoj of Lossow calmly, pulling the Kottwitz knight, who was now leaning across the table gripping a misericord, back into his seat. 'Peace! Both of you! You're behaving like children! All you know is boozing and brawling.'

'And Sir Hugo of Kottwitz is right,' added Traugott of Barnhelm. 'Verily, Paszko, you don't understand the mysteries of politics. We speak of a crusade – do you even know what a crusade is? Like Gottfried de Bouillon, Richard the Lionheart, Jerusalem and so on. Now do you understand?'

The Raubritters nodded, but Reynevan would have bet anything that not all of them had.

Buko of Krossig drained his mug and slammed it down on the table. 'Blow Jerusalem, Richard the Lionheart, bullion, politics and religion,' he announced soberly. 'We're going to plunder whoever we come across, and that's that, and the Devil take him and his faith. It's said that people like Fedor of Ostrog, Dobko Puchała and others are already doing that in Bohemia, and that they've lined their pockets nicely. Are we – the Angelic Militia – their inferiors?'

'We are not!' yelled Rymbaba. 'Buko's right!'

'By Christ he is!'

'To Bohemia!'

But the euphoria was brief, extinguished like a flash in the pan by the curses and dangerous looks of the sceptics.

'The aforementioned Puchała and Ostrogski,' said Notker of Weyrach, who had been quiet until then, 'feathered their nests by fighting on the winning side. So far, the crusaders have brought back more bruises than wealth from Bohemia.'

'True,' confirmed Markwart of Stolberg a moment later. 'The men who fought at Prague in 1420 described the Meissen knights of Henryk Isenburg attacking Vítkov Hill – and how they fled, leaving a mountain of corpses behind them.'

'They say that Hussite priests fought beside the soldiers, howling like wolves, striking fear,' added Wencel of Hartha, nodding. 'Even womenfolk fought there, wielding flails, as though seized by insanity . . . And those who fell alive into Hussite hands—'

'Nonsense!' said Pater Hiacynt, waving his hand dismissively. 'True, Žižka was at Vítkov, and the devilish force he sold himself to. But Žižka is dead. He's been frying in Hell for a year now.'

'Žižka wasn't at Vyšehrad on All Saints' Day,' said Tassilo of Tresckow, 'and although we had a fourfold advantage, we still took a severe beating from the Hussites. They smote us and routed us so badly, it shames me to recall how we fled – in panic, blindly, as far away as possible, until our horses began to wheeze. And five hundred men lay dead on the battlefield, the most eminent of Czech and Moravian nobility.'

Stolberg said, 'I didn't know you were at the Battle of Vyšehrad, Sir Tassilo.'

'I was. For I went like a fool with the Silesian army, with Kantner of Oleśnica and Rumpold of Głogów. Yes, yes, gentlemen, Žižka's gone to Hell, but there are other mighty warriors in Bohemia. We saw that on All Saints' Day, and you'll have to face them if you join a crusade to Bohemia.'

'Blow that.' Hugo of Kottwitz broke the silence. 'Empty threats! They beat you because you didn't know how to fight. I also fought the Hussites at Petrovice in 1421, under the command of Lord Půta of Častolovice, and we gave them a thrashing they won't forget in a hurry! And we took plenty of spoils – I got the Bavarian suit of armour I'm wearing now from there—'

'Enough talk.' Stolberg cut him off. 'Let us decide. Are we going to Bohemia or not?'

'I am!' Ekkehard of Sulz announced thunderously and proudly. 'We must root out the evil of heresy, simple as that. Burn out the leprosy before it eats everything away.'

'I'm going, too,' said Wencel of Hartha. 'I am in need of spoils – I plan to wed.'

'By the teeth of Saint Apolonia!' Kuno of Wittram leaped up. 'Some spoils could come in handy!'

'Spoils are one thing,' Woldan of Osiny mumbled, a little hesitantly, 'but I heard that whoever takes the cross will have his sins forgiven. And one has sinned greatly . . . Oh, indeed!'

'I'm not going,' said Bożywoj of Lossow bluntly. 'I won't go looking for trouble in foreign parts.'

'Me neither,' said Notker of Weyrach calmly, 'because if Sulz is going, it means the matter is dubious.'

An uproar broke out again, curses were exchanged and Ekkehard of Sulz had to be forcibly returned to his seat with his short sword half-drawn.

'Personally,' said Jaśko Chromy of Łubnia, after things had calmed down, 'I'd sooner go to Prussia to fight the Teutonic Knights with the Poles. Or vice versa, depending on who pays better.'

For a while, everybody was talking and shouting over one another, until finally Błażej, the wavy-haired Poraj, gestured for the company to be quiet.

'I won't join this crusade,' he announced in the subsequent silence, 'for I won't follow bishops and prelates like a pup. I won't be set on anybody like a cur. What is this crusade? Against whom? They're Czechs – not Saracens. They carry a monstrance with them into battle. And if they don't like Rome? Or our Bishop

277

Konrad and the other prelates? I'm not surprised. I don't like them, either.'

'You blaspheme, Sir Błażej!' roared Ekkehard of Sulz. 'Czechs are heretics! They believe in heretical teachings! Burn churches! Worship the Devil!'

'They go around naked!'

'And they want their wives to be common property!' screamed Pater Hiacynt. 'They want—'

'I'll show you what the Czechs want,' Błażej interrupted thunderously. 'And in sooth you will think about with whom and against whom you should march.'

At an obviously agreed sign, a not-so-young goliard in a red pointed hood and a doublet with an elaborately trimmed edge approached and took a rolled-up parchment from his doublet.

'May all faithful Christians know this,' he read, sonorously and resonantly, 'that the Kingdom of Bohemia continues to endure and will last for ever with God's help, to the death, according to the articles written down below. Firstly: that the word of God shall be freely expressed in the Kingdom of Bohemia and that priests may preach it unhindered—'

'What is this?' called Sulz. 'Where is it from, minstrel?'

'Let him be,' said Notker of Weyrach, frowning. 'Never mind where it's from. Go on, lad.'

'Secondly: that the Body and Blood of Christ the Lord be given under both kinds in the form of bread and wine to all the faithful. Thirdly: that the secular power of priests over wealth and worldly goods be taken from them, so that, for their own salvation, they return to the rules of the Bible and the life that Christ led with his apostles. Fourthly: that all mortal sins and other offences committed by the priesthood against divine law—'

'It's a heretical text!' shouted Pater Hiacynt. 'Merely listening to it is sinful! Do you not fear damnation?'

'Shut your trap, Pater!'

'Silence! Let him read on!'

'—be punished and condemned. Namely: simony, heresy,

taking money for baptisms, confirmations, confessions, communion, holy oil, holy water, masses and prayers for the deceased, for fasts, for ringing bells, for the parish, for buying and selling offices, benefices and prelatures, for promotions, and for indulgences—'

'Well?' Sir Błażej stood with arms akimbo. 'Is that not true?'

'Further,' continued the goliard, 'the heresies resulting from this and from shameful practices of adultery, begetting of sons and daughters out of wedlock, sodomy and other debauchery, anger, arguments, fights, backbiting, tormenting and robbing of simple folk, collecting fees, duties and donations. Every just son of his mother, the Holy Church, ought to reject that, renounce it, deplore it like the Devil and be disgusted by it—'

Further reading was disrupted by a general uproar and confusion, during which, Reynevan noticed, the goliard noiselessly slipped away with his parchment. The Raubritters yelled, swore, shoved and threatened each other, and blades began to grate in scabbards.

Samson nudged Reynevan.

'I'd say you ought to glance through the window,' he murmured. 'And fast.'

Reynevan did. And froze.

Three riders were entering the Kromolin stronghold.

Wittich, Morold and Wolfher Stercza.

Chapter Eighteen

In which modernity boldly encroaches on knightly traditions and customs, and Reynevan, as though wanting to vindicate the title of this book, makes a fool of himself. And is compelled to admit it. In front of the whole world.

Reynevan had reason to feel shame and anger, for he had succumbed to panic. At the sight of the Sterczas entering Kromolin, he was overcome by senseless, idiotic anxiety. His shame was all the greater because he was completely aware of it. Rather than assessing the situation soberly and following a sensible plan, he reacted like a frightened and hunted animal. He jumped through a window in the chamber and bolted between the sheds and shacks, towards the thicket of riverside willows that he hoped would offer him safe, dark sanctuary.

He was saved by luck and the cold that had been troubling Stefan Rotkirch for several days.

The Sterczas had set their snare well. The three brothers entered Kromolin, while the remaining three men – Rotkirch, Dieter Haxt and Eagle Owl of Knobelsdorf – had arrived unseen at the settlement some time earlier and manned the most probable escape routes. Reynevan would have run straight into Rotkirch, who was lurking behind a shed, were it not for the fact that Rotkirch sneezed so loudly his frightened horse kicked the shed with a great thud. Although panic had frozen Reynevan's brain and turned his legs to jelly, he stopped in time, doubled back, crawled on hands and knees under a fence and hid behind a pile of firewood. He was shaking so much, the entire pile appeared to be rustling as though buffeted by a strong wind.

'Psst! Psst, young m'lord!'

Beside him, behind the fence, stood a boy of about six in a felt cap and a blouse reaching halfway down his calves, tied around his waist with twine.

'Psst! To the cheese store, m'lord ... The cheese store ... Yonder!'

He looked where the boy was pointing. A stone's throw away was a rectangular wooden construction, a kind of booth with a pointed shingle roof, raised more than five yards above the ground on four sturdy posts. The structure looked more like a large dovecote than a cheese store, but above all, it resembled a trap without an exit.

'To the cheese store,' urged the boy. 'Quickly ... You can hide in it—'

'That?'

'Aye. We always hide there,' he lisped.

Reynevan didn't debate the point, particularly since someone whistled nearby, and a loud sneeze and stamp of a horse's hoof heralded the approach of the snivelling Rotkirch. Fortunately, Rotkirch rode straight into a goose shed and the birds began squawking raucously. Reynevan knew that this was the moment. He ran, bent over, beside the wattle fence and reached the cheese store. And froze. There was no ladder and no way of clambering up the smooth oaken posts.

Cursing his stupidity under his breath, he was about to continue running when he heard a soft hiss, and a knotted rope descended like a snake from an opening above him. Reynevan seized the rope with his hands and feet and climbed up it in a flash, to find himself in a gloomy, stuffy space permeated by the smell of old cheese. The person who had let the rope down and helped him climb inside was the goliard in the red jerkin and tailed hood. The same one who had just read out the Hussite declaration.

'Hush,' he whispered, putting a finger to his lips. 'Be quiet, m'lord.'

'Is it—'

'Safe here? It is. We always hide in here.'

Reynevan might have tried to ascertain why, if they hid there so regularly, they weren't regularly found, but there wasn't enough time. A sneezing Rotkirch rode right past the cheese store without giving the building a second glance.

'You are Reinmar of Bielawa,' said the goliard in the gloom. 'Brother of Piotr, who was murdered in Balbinów.'

'Correct,' Reynevan replied. 'And you are hiding here out of fear of the Inquisition.'

'Correct,' the goliard confirmed. 'What I read in the tavern . . . The Articles—'

'I know what those articles were. But the men who just arrived are not the Inquisition.'

'Could have been, though.'

'Indeed. And it looks as though you have protectors. But you hid, nonetheless.'

'And didn't you?'

The cheese store had numerous openings in it, no doubt to provide free circulation of air for the drying rounds of cheese, but they also offered a panoramic view of the entire stronghold. Reynevan pressed his eye to a hole facing the tavern and the illuminated courtyard. He could see what was happening, though it was too far away to hear anything, but it wasn't at all difficult to guess.

The council of war in the tavern was still going on, only a few men had left it. So the Sterczas were chiefly greeted in the courtyard by dogs, as well as some esquires and a handful of Raubritters, including Kuno of Wittram and John of Schoenfeld with his bandaged head. Actually, the word 'greeted' is an overstatement, since few of the knights even looked up. Wittram and the other two were still devoting all their attention to a ram's skeleton, from whose ribs they were stripping the last shreds of meat and shoving them into their mouths. Schoenfeld was quenching his thirst with malmsey, sucking it through a straw stuck between his bandages. The blacksmiths and merchants had gone to bed, the wenches, monks, goliards and Gypsies had prudently vanished, and the servants were pretending to be very busy. Which meant that Wolfher Stercza had to repeat his question.

'I asked,' he thundered from his elevated position in the saddle, 'if you've seen a young man answering to the description I just gave you. Is he or was he here? Will somebody finally deign to answer my question? Have you gone deaf, damn you?'

Kuno of Wittram spat a mutton bone straight under the hooves of Stercza's horse. Another knight wiped his fingers on his jerkin, glanced at Wolfher and slid the hilt of his sheathed sword into a better position to be drawn. Schoenfeld gurgled through the straw without looking up.

Rotkirch rode up, followed a moment later by Dieter Haxt. They both shook their heads under the enquiring stares of Wolfher and Morold. Wittich swore.

'Who has seen the fellow I described?' Wolfher repeated. 'You, perhaps? Yes, you, big man, I'm talking to you. Have you seen him?'

'No,' answered Samson Honey-Eater, who was standing by the tavern. 'I have not.'

'Whoever saw him and shows me where he is,' said Wolfher, leaning on his pommel, 'will get a ducat. Well? Here is the ducat, in case you think I'm lying. Just point out the fellow I'm searching for. Confirm he is or was here. Whoever does it gets this ducat! Come on – who wants to earn some coin?'

One of the servants reluctantly walked over, looking around hesitantly.

'M'lord, I s—'he began. He didn't finish, for John of Schoenfeld kicked him hard in the backside. The servant lurched forwards onto his hands and knees, then leaped up and fled, limping.

Schoenfeld put his hands on his hips, glared at Wolfher and mumbled something indistinctly through his bandages.

'Eh?' Stercza leaned over from the saddle. 'What did he say?'

'I'm not sure,' replied Samson calmly, 'but I think it was something about fucking Judases.'

'I believe so, too,' confirmed Kuno of Wittram. 'By the barrel of Saint Willibrord! We don't like Judases here in Kromolin.'

Wolfher flushed and then paled, clenching his fist around the handle of a whip. Wittich moved his horse and Morold reached for his sword.

'I wouldn't,' said Notker of Weyrach from the doorway of the tavern, flanked by Tassilo of Tresckow and Woldan of Osiny, with Rymbaba and Bożywoj of Lossow behind him. 'I advise you not to start, gentlemen. For I swear by God that what you start, we shall finish.'

'They murdered my brother,' panted Reynevan, his eye still pressed to the hole in the wall of the cheese store. 'Let's hope they'll start quarrelling. The Raubritters will cut them to pieces and Peterlin will be avenged.'

'I wouldn't count on it.'

He turned around. The goliard's eyes shone in the dark. *What is he suggesting?* wondered Reynevan. *That I shouldn't count on a quarrel or on revenge?*

'I don't want to fight,' said Wolfher of Stercza, softening his tone, 'and I'm not looking for trouble. See how courteously I ask. The fellow I seek killed my brother and dishonoured my sister-in-law. It's my right to seek justice—'

'Oh, gentlemen,' said Markwart of Stolberg, after the laughter had stopped. 'It was a poor choice bringing your grievance to Kromolin. I advise you to seek justice elsewhere. In the courts, for example.'

Weyrach snorted and Bożywoj of Lossow roared with laughter. Wolfher paled, aware that they were mocking him, and Morold and Wittich gnashed their teeth in frustration. Wolfher opened and closed his mouth several times, but before he managed to say anything, Eagle Owl of Knobelsdorf galloped into the courtyard.

*

'Bastards.' Reynevan ground his teeth. 'Why aren't they being punished? Why won't God flog them, send down an angel for them with a whip?'

'Who knows?' The goliard sighed in the cheesy darkness. 'Who knows?'

Eagle Owl, angry and red in the face, rode over to Wolfher, said something quickly, then pointed towards the mill and the bridge. Few words were needed. The Stercza brothers spurred their mounts and galloped across the courtyard in the opposite direction, between the shacks, towards a ford across the river. Behind them raced Eagle Owl, Haxt and the sneezing Rotkirch, eyes fixed ahead.

'Good riddance!' Paszko Rymbaba spat after them.

'They smelled a rat!' said Woldan of Osiny, laughing dryly.

'A tiger.' Markwart of Stolberg corrected him knowingly. He had been standing closer and heard what Eagle Owl had said to Wolfher.

'I wouldn't be going out just yet,' said the goliard from the darkness.

Reynevan, who was almost hanging from the knotted rope, stopped.

'I'm in no danger now,' he assured him. 'But you take heed. People are burned at the stake for what you were reading.'

The goliard drew closer, so the slit with moonlight shining through it lit up his face. 'There are things worth risking your life for. You are well aware of that, Master Reynevan.'

'What do you mean?'

'Why, you know well enough.'

'I know you,' gasped Reynevan. 'I've seen you before—'

'You have, m'lord, at your brother's home in Powojowice. But better not talk about it. Garrulousness is a perilous foible nowadays. "Many a man has cut his own throat with his own flapping tongue", as—'

'Urban Horn says,' Reynevan completed the sentence, surprising himself with his own shrewdness.

'Ssh,' hissed the goliard. 'Careful with that name, m'lord.'

The Sterczas had indeed fled the settlement in a strange panic, as though the Devil were on their heels. That sight improved Reynevan's mood a great deal. But when he saw who they were running from, it all made sense.

A man with a square jaw and shoulders as wide as a cathedral door, dressed in a sumptuous and richly gilded suit of Milanese armour, rode at the head of a troop of knights and mounted bowmen. The knight's horse, huge and black, was also armoured, its face protected by a chanfron, its neck by a criniere made of lames.

Reynevan mingled among the Kromolin Raubritters, who meanwhile had swarmed out into the yard. No one apart from Samson noticed him or paid him any attention. Scharley was nowhere to be seen. The Raubritters were buzzing around like a swarm of wasps.

Two men flanked the knight in Milanese armour: a helmetless youngster as pretty as a maiden, and a swarthy beanpole with sunken cheeks. They were both wearing full plate armour and riding fully armoured mounts.

'Hayn of Czirne,' said Otto of Glaubitz in admiration. 'Do you see that Milanese armour he's wearing? By the Devil, it's easily worth forty grzywna.'

'The youngster on the left is Fryczko of Nostitz,' panted Wencel of Hartha. 'And the one on the right is Vitelozzo Gaetani, an Italian . . .'

Reynevan gasped slightly. All around, similar gasps, puffs and soft oaths could be heard, testifying that not only he had been shocked by the appearance of one of the most famous and feared Silesian Raubritters. Hayn of Czirne, Lord of Nimmersatt Castle, enjoyed the worst possible reputation, and his name not only aroused terror in merchants and peaceful folk, but also begrudging respect in his fellow bandits.

Meanwhile, Hayn of Czirne had stopped his horse before the senior knights. He dismounted and walked over, spurs jingling and armour clanking.

'Lord Stolberg,' he said in a deep bass. 'Lord Barnhelm.'

'Lord Czirne.'

The Raubritter looked back, as though checking to see that his foot soldiers had their weapons to hand and the bowmen their crossbows at the ready. Once certain, he rested his left hand on his sword hilt and his right on his hip. He stood with legs apart and raised his head.

'I'll be brief, for I do not have time to talk long,' he thundered. 'Somebody attacked and robbed some Walloons, colliers from the mine in Golden Hill. I have decreed that the Walloons from Golden Hill are under my care and protection. So hear this and heed it: if any of you villains had a hand in it, you should own up now, because if you don't and I catch you later, I'll flay you alive, knight or not.'

It was as though a black cloud had covered Markwart of Stolberg's face. The Kromolin Raubritters murmured. Fryczko of Nostitz and Vitelozzo Gaetani didn't move, just sat on their horses like two iron statues. But the crossbowmen in the entourage bent their bows, ready for action.

'Suspicion for this misdeed,' continued Hayn of Czirne, 'falls to a large degree on Kunz Aulock and Stork of Gorgowice, so hear this, too, and heed it: if you conceal those thieving bastards in Kromolin, you'll be sorry. It is well known,' Czirne went on, ignoring the growing murmur among the knights, 'that those whoresons Aulock and Stork are in the pay of the Sterczas, the brothers Wolfher and Morold, knaves and blackguards both. Our paths have crossed in the past, but now they have overstepped the mark. If the matter with the Walloons turns out to be true, I'll disembowel the Sterczas. And while I'm at it, anyone who thinks to hide them.

'And one more thing, last but by no means any less grave, so listen carefully. Lately, *mercatores* keep being found cold and stiff,

the victims of some evil design. The matter is strange and I think
not to go into it, but I shall tell you this: the Fuggers' Augsburg
Company is paying me for protection. So if anything happens
to one of the Fuggers' *mercators* and it turns out one of you is
responsible, then may God have mercy on his soul. Understand?
Understand, you dogs?'

Among the growing furious rumbling, Hayn of Czirne suddenly drew his sword, whirling it around with a whistle.

'And if anyone opposes what I just said, or thinks that I lie, if
it might not be to someone's liking, then step forward!' he roared.
'We shall settle the matter with iron forthwith. Come on! I'm
waiting. Dammit, I haven't killed anyone since Easter.'

'Your behaviour is unseemly, Lord Hayn,' Markwart of
Stolberg said calmly.

'What I said does not apply to you, honourable Lord
Markwart, or you, noble Lord Traugott, nor any of the senior
knights. But I know my rights. I can challenge anyone from the
crowd.'

'I simply say it's not elegant,' replied Markwart of Stolberg.
'Everybody knows you, m'lord. You and your sword.'

'What then?' snorted the brigand. 'Am I to dress as a wench,
like Lancelot of the Lake did, so as not to be recognised? I said
I know my rights. And *they* know them, this gang of shitheads
with shaking calves.'

The Raubritters murmured. Reynevan saw fury drain the
blood from Kottwitz's face and heard Wencel of Hartha gnashing his teeth. Otto of Glaubitz seized his sword hilt and made a
movement as though he were about to step forward, but Jaśko of
Łubnia grabbed him by the shoulder.

'Don't,' he muttered. 'No one has ever crossed swords with him
and lived.'

Hayn of Czirne brandished his great sword again and paraded
back and forth, spurs clanking.

'Well, fart-churners?' he thundered. 'Will no one step forward?
Do you know what I think you are? I think you're wankers! Will

anyone challenge me? Will anyone dare to call me a liar? What, no one? Then all of you, to the last man, are twats and fuck-faces. And a general shame to the knighthood!'

The knight-robbers murmured louder and louder, but Hayn appeared not to notice it.

'I see only one man among you,' he continued, pointing, 'Bożywoj of Lossow over there. Indeed, I cannot comprehend what he is doing among a gathering of such cunts. He must have gone to the dogs himself, urgh, shame and disgrace.'

Lossow straightened up, crossed his arms over the lynx emblazoned on his chest and stared back fearlessly with a steady gaze. His calm clearly infuriated Hayn of Czirne. The brigand flushed and stood with arms spread wide.

'Goat shaggers!' he roared. 'Arseholes! I'm challenging you. Can you hear me, shitty-britches? Who will face me? On foot or mounted, right now, right here, on this field! With sword or battleaxe, choose your weapons! Perhaps you, Hugo of Kottwitz? Or you, Rymbaba, you shit?'

Paszko Rymbaba leaned over and seized his sword, baring his teeth under his moustaches. Woldan of Osiny grabbed his shoulder and sat him back down with a powerful hand.

'Don't be a fool,' he hissed. 'Do you have a death wish? No one can match him.'

Hayn of Czirne chuckled as though he had heard. 'Will no one come forward? Is no one brave enough? As I thought! Cowards, the lot of you.'

'Well, fuck you!' yelled Ekkehard of Sulz, suddenly stepping forward. 'Big mouth! Dickhead! Fart-face! Step onto the field!'

'I'm standing on it,' Hayn of Czirne replied calmly. 'What arms will we choose?'

'This!' said Sulz, raising a handgonne. 'You're proud, Czirne, for you're a decent swordsman and worthy axeman. But the new is coming – this is the modern world! Equal chances! Let's shoot at each other!'

Among the uproar that arose, Hayn of Czirne went over to his horse and returned a moment later with a gun. While Ekkehard of Sulz had an ordinary handgonne, a simple iron pipe on a stick, Czirne's was an artistically made harquebus, with an angular barrel set in a carved oaken stock.

'Let it be firearms, then,' he announced. 'Mark out the lists.'

Things moved quickly. Two finish lines were demarcated using spears stuck in the ground, marking a distance of ten paces between an avenue of flaming torches. Czirne and Sulz stood facing one another, each with a gun under one arm and a smouldering fuse in the other hand. The Raubritters stood aside, out of the line of fire.

'Raise your weapons!' Notker of Weyrach, who had assumed the role of herald, lifted a mace. 'Aim!'

The opponents bent forward, positioning the fuses at the height of their firearms.

'Fire!'

For a while, nothing happened. All was silent save for the fuses hissing and showering sparks around as a stink of black powder emanated from the priming pans. It looked as though it would be necessary to stop the duel in order to prime the guns again. Notker of Weyrach was already preparing to give the sign when Sulz's handgonne went off unexpectedly with a flash, a tremendous bang and a cloud of noxious smoke. Those standing closest heard the whistle of the ball, which missed the target and flew in the direction of the latrine. At almost the same moment, Hayn of Czirne's harquebus spat fire and smoke. With better effect. The ball struck Ekkehard of Sulz in the chin and tore off his head. A fountain of blood gushed from the neck of the advocate of the anti-Hussite crusade; the head slammed against the wall of the barn, fell and rolled across the field, finally coming to rest in the grass, its dead eyes watching the dogs as they sniffed it.

'Bugger,' Paszko Rymbaba said into complete silence. 'That probably can't be stitched back on.'

*

Reynevan had underestimated Samson Honey-Eater.

He hadn't even managed to saddle his horse in the stable when he felt eyes burning on the back of his neck. He turned around and stood like a pillar of salt, holding the saddle in both hands. He swore, then shoved the saddle vigorously onto the horse's back.

'Don't condemn me,' he said, pretending to be completely preoccupied with the harness. 'I have to follow them. I wanted to avoid farewells. Or actually farewell discussions that would have been a waste of time and achieved nothing except unnecessary strife. I thought it would be better . . .'

Samson, leaning against the lintel, folded his arms on his chest and said nothing, but his expression was more than eloquent.

'I must go after them,' Reynevan blurted out after a moment of tense hesitation. 'I cannot do otherwise. Understand me. I won't get a chance like this again. Providence—'

'Sir Hayn of Czirne brings many associations to my mind, too,' said Samson, 'but I wouldn't call any of them providential. Ah well, I understand you. Though I can't say it comes easy.'

'Hayn of Czirne is the Sterczas' enemy. The enemy of Kunz Aulock. My enemies' enemy and thus a natural ally for me. Owing to him, I may have the chance to avenge my brother. Don't sigh, Samson. It's neither the time nor the place for another discussion ending with the conclusion that revenge is a futile, senseless thing. My brother's murderers not only peacefully walk the Earth but are also hunting me, threatening me with death and tormenting the woman I love. No, Samson. I won't flee to Hungary, leaving them here in their pride and triumph. I have the opportunity, I have an ally, I've found an enemy of my enemies. Czirne announced that he'd disembowel the Sterczas and Aulock. Perhaps it's futile, but I want to help him do it and be there when he does. I want to watch him disembowel them.'

Samson said nothing. And Reynevan marvelled once again at how much thoughtfulness and wise concern his dull eyes and chubby idiot's face could express. And how much mute but evident reproach.

'Scharley . . .' Reynevan stammered, tightening the girth. 'It's true that Scharley helped me, did plenty for me. Why, you were a witness, more than once. But no matter how often I brought up the subject of revenge against the Sterczas, he always refused, mocking me at the same time and treating me like a stupid boy. He even makes fun of Adèle, endlessly trying to dissuade me from going to Ziębice!'

The horse stamped and snorted, as though Reynevan's agitation was affecting it. Reynevan breathed out and calmed down.

'Tell him not to bear me a grudge, Samson. Dammit, I'm not ungrateful, I'm aware how much he's done for me. But I think the best way of repaying him is by going. He said himself: I'm the biggest risk. It'll be easier for him without me. For both of you . . .'

He fell silent.

'I'd like you to come with me, but I won't ask you to. It would be base and dishonest of me. What I mean to do is risky. You'll be safer with Scharley.'

Samson said nothing for a long time.

'I won't try to dissuade you from your plans,' he said finally. 'Nor will I expose you – as you so elegantly put it – to strife and time-wasting. I'll even refrain from sharing my opinion regarding the sense of the enterprise. I don't want by any means to make things even worse and burden you with pangs of conscience. But be aware, Reinmar, that by leaving, you are thwarting my hopes of a return to my own world and my own form.'

For a long time, Reynevan said nothing.

'Samson,' he said at last. 'Tell me – truthfully, if you are able – are you really . . . ? Is what you said about yourself—'

'*Ego sum, qui sum*,' Samson interrupted gently. 'I am who I am. Let's spare each other the farewell confessions. They achieve nothing, excuse nothing and change nothing.'

'Scharley is a worldly wise and resourceful fellow,' Reynevan said quickly. 'You'll see, he'll doubtless manage to contact somebody in Hungary who—'

'It's time you left. Go, Reinmar.'

*

The entire valley was blanketed in thick fog. Fortunately, it was low-lying, right by the ground, so there was no risk – at least not for the moment – of getting lost. It was clear which way the high-way ran, for it was marked by a row of crooked willows, wild pear trees and hawthorn bushes protruding from the white shroud. Far away in the dark, a small, indistinct, dancing light – the lamp of Hayn of Czirne's troop – flickered and indicated the way.

It was very cold. When Reynevan crossed the bridge over the Jadkowa and entered the fog, he felt as though he were lowering himself into icy water. *Oh well*, he thought, *it is September after all*.

All in all, by reflecting light, the white sea of fog spreading all around offered decent visibility to the sides, but Reynevan rode in complete darkness and could barely see his horse's ears. Paradoxically, it was darkest on the highway itself, in the avenue of trees and dense bushes. More than once, the bushes' outlines were so evocatively demonic that the young man shuddered out of terror and involuntarily yanked at the reins, frightening his already timid steed. Each time, he rode on, laughing to himself at his own fearfulness. *How on earth can one be afraid of bushes?*

Two bushes suddenly barred his way, a third caught the reins and a fourth pressed what could only have been a spear blade to his chest.

Hooves stamped and the odour of horses and human sweat intensified around him. A flint and steel clanged, sparks showered around and lamps flared up. Reynevan squinted and leaned back in the saddle as one was shoved almost right into his face.

'Too pretty for a spy,' said Hayn of Czirne. 'Too young for a paid killer. But appearances can be deceptive.'

'I am—'

He broke off and cowered in the saddle as something hard struck him in the back.

'For now, I decide what you are,' stated Czirne coldly, 'and what you are not. For example, you're not a corpse torn apart by crossbow bolts lying in a ditch. For the moment, thanks to my decision. Now be quiet, because I'm thinking.'

'What is there to think about?' asked Vitelozzo Gaetani. He spoke fluent German, but his sing-song accent gave away his Italian heritage. 'Slit his throat and be done with it. And let's go, because it's cold and I want to eat.'

In the rear, hooves thudded and horses snorted.

'He's alone,' said Fryczko of Nostitz, whose young, pleasant voice gave him away. 'He's not being followed.'

'Appearances can be deceptive,' repeated Czirne.

White steam belched from his horse's nostrils. Czirne rode up close, very close, until their stirrups touched. He was at arm's length. With horrifying lucidity, Reynevan realised why. Czirne was testing him. Provoking him.

'And I still say we slit his throat,' repeated the Italian in the dark.

'Slit his throat, slit his throat,' said Czirne, losing his temper. 'Everything's simple to you people. And then my confessor will keep on at me, gnaw away at me, reproach me that it's a deadly sin to kill without reason, for you need to have an important reason to kill. Every confession, he grumbles on at me, a reason, a reason, there must be a reason. I'll end up whacking the knave over the head with a mace, for impatience is a reason, too, isn't it? But for the time being, let's do as he instructed me at confession. Well, laddie, tell us who you are,' he said, addressing Reynevan, 'and we'll see if there's a reason to kill you, or if we need to come up with one.'

'My name is Reinmar of Bielawa,' began Reynevan. And because no one was interrupting him, he continued, 'My brother, Piotr of Bielawa, was murdered. The murder was ordered by the brothers Stercza but carried out by Kunz Aulock and his gang. Thus I have no reason to like them. I heard in Kromolin that there is no love lost between you and them, either, so I'm following you to inform you that the Sterczas were in the settlement and fled on hearing of your arrival there. They rode south, across the ford. I say and do all this owing to my hatred for the Sterczas.

I'm unable to take my revenge on them by myself. My hope for that lies with your company. I don't want anything else. If I am in error . . . Forgive me and let me go on my way.'

He took a deep breath, tired by the hurried oration he had delivered. The Raubritters' horses snorted, their harnesses clanked, and the lanterns wove ghastly, dancing shadows from the darkness.

'Reinmar of Bielawa,' snorted Fryczko of Nostitz. 'Dammit, it looks as though we're distantly related.'

Vitelozzo Gaetani swore in Italian.

'On our way,' Hayn of Czirne suddenly barked. 'You, m'Lord Bielawa, by me. Close by me.'

He didn't even order for me to be searched, thought Reynevan, riding on. *He didn't check if I have a hidden weapon. And ordered me to ride beside him. It's another test. And a trap.*

A lantern had been hung up and was swaying on a roadside willow, a cunning trick to mislead any pursuers and make them believe that the troop was a long way in front of them. Czirne took down the lantern, held it up and shone it on Reynevan.

'An honest face,' he commented. 'A sincere, honest countenance. It turns out that appearances aren't deceptive and he speaks the truth. An enemy of the Sterczas, are you?'

'Yes, Lord Czirne.'

'Reinmar of Bielawa, is it?'

'It is.'

'Everything is clear. Right, seize him. Disarm him and tie him up. Put a noose around his neck. Look lively!'

'Lord Czirne . . .' stammered Reynevan, already being held by strong arms. 'What . . .? What . . .?'

'There's a bishop's *significavit* out on you, young man,' Hayn of Czirne pronounced carelessly, 'and a bounty for turning you in alive. You see, the Inquisition is hunting you. Spells or heresy, it's actually all one to me. But you'll ride to the Dominican monastery in fetters.'

'Let me go . . .' Reynevan grunted as the rope bit painfully into

his wrists. 'Please, Lord Czirne ... You're a knight, after all ...
And I must ... I am hurrying ... To the lady I love!'

'Aren't we all.'

'But you hate my foes! The Sterczas and Aulock!'

'True,' admitted the Raubritter. 'I hate those whoresons. But I,
young man, am not such a savage. I'm a European. I won't let my
likes and dislikes influence important decisions.'

'But ... Lord Czirne—'

'To horse, gentlemen.'

'Lord Czirne ... I—'

'Lord Nostitz!' Hayn interrupted forcefully. 'You say he's your
kin. Please silence him, m'lord.'

Reynevan received such a punch in the ear that he saw stars
and his head was thrown forward almost to the horse's mane.

After that he said nothing.

The sky in the east lightened, heralding the dawn. It became even
colder. Reynevan, arms bound, was shivering from cold and fear
in equal measure. Nostitz had to bring him to task several times
with a jerk of the rope.

'What are we going to do with him?' Vitelozzo Gaetani
suddenly asked. 'Must we drag him with us all the way over the
mountains? Or do we weaken the unit by giving him an escort to
Świdnica? Eh?'

'I don't know yet.' A note of impatience sounded in Hayn of
Czirne's voice. 'I'm thinking.'

'Is the bounty worth all this?' asked the Italian, continuing to
press. 'And is the bounty much less for him dead?'

'What matters to me isn't the bounty,' growled Czirne, 'but
good relations with the Holy Office. And that's enough talk! I
said I'm thinking.'

Reynevan could tell that they were now riding along a road
by the change in the sound and the rhythm of hooves hitting
the ground. He assumed it was the highway to Frankenstein, the
largest town in the locality. He had lost his bearings, though, and

was unable to deduce if they were riding towards the town or away from it. He decided not to kick himself, for the moment, or dwell on his own stupidity, and began to think feverishly, devising stratagems and plans for his escape.

'Heeeyy!' somebody screamed from the front. 'Heeeyy!'

Lanterns flashed, picking out of the darkness the angular outlines of wagons and the silhouettes of riders.

'He's here,' said Czirne quietly. 'Punctual and at the agreed place – I approve of men like that. But appearances can be deceptive. Weapons at the ready. Signore Gaetani, remain at the rear and be vigilant. Lord Nostitz, keep an eye on your kinsman. The rest follow me. Heeeyy! Greetings!'

The lantern from the opposite direction was dancing to the rhythm of a horse's steps. Three horsemen were approaching. One was stout, wearing a heavy, loose-fitting coat that also covered his steed's rump, accompanied by two crossbowmen, identical to Czirne's bowmen, wearing brigantines, kettle hats and iron collars.

'Sir Hayn of Czirne?'

'Master Hanusz Throst?'

'I like reliable and punctual men,' said the man in the coat. 'I see that our mutual friends weren't exaggerating when giving their opinion and recommendation. I'm content to see you and pleased to be collaborating. We may set off, I believe?'

'My collaboration is worth a hundred guilders,' replied Czirne. 'Our mutual friends cannot have failed to mention that.'

'Certainly, but not in advance,' snorted the man in the overcoat. 'You can't have thought, sir, that I would agree to that. I am a merchant, a man of affairs, and in business the service comes first, the payment second. Your service: to escort me safely across the Silver Pass to Broumov. If you accomplish that, you will be paid. A hundred guilders, to the haler.'

'It had better be thus,' said Hayn of Czirne, with heavy emphasis. 'Verily it had, Master Throst. Do you convey anything in the wagons, may I ask?'

'Goods,' Throst replied calmly. 'What kind is my business. As is the man who will pay for them.'

'Naturally.' Czirne nodded. 'Indeed, it is enough for me to know that you are a trader like those other men – Fabian Pfefferkorn, Mikołaj Neumarkt and the others.'

'It is probably best that you do not know more. We've conversed too much already – it's time we left. Why linger at a crossroads, tempting the Devil?'

'You are right.' Czirne reined his horse around. 'We will not stay here. Give the sign, let the wagons roll. And regarding the Devil, fear not. The demon that has recently been prowling around Silesia customarily strikes from a bright sky at high noon. Verily, as the priests say, *daemonium meridianum*, the demon that strikes at noon. But all around us, see for yourself: darkness.'

The merchant spurred his horse and caught up with the Raubritter's black.

'In that demon's shoes,' he said a moment later, 'I'd change my customs, because it has become too familiar and predictable. And that psalm also mentions the darkness. Do you not remember? *Negotio perambulans in tenebris . . .*'

'Had I known you were in such fright,' there was amusement in Czirne's dour voice, 'I'd have raised my fee to at least a hundred and fifty guilders.'

'I'll pay it,' said Throst so quietly that Reynevan barely heard him. 'One hundred and fifty guilders, cash in hand, Lord Czirne. On safe arrival. For it is true that I am afeared. An alchemist in Racibórz wrote me a horoscope, foretold from chicken's entrails . . . It revealed that death lurks above me . . .'

'Do you believe in such things?'

'Until recently – no.'

'And now?'

'And now,' the merchant said firmly, 'I'm taking my leave of Silesia. A word to the wise is sufficient; I don't want to end up like Pfefferkorn and Neumarkt. I'm going to Bohemia; no demon will get his hands on me there.'

'Indeed.' Hayn of Czirne nodded. 'Not there. Even demons are afraid of the Hussites.'

'I'm heading for Bohemia,' Throst repeated. 'And it is your task to deliver me there safely.'

Czirne didn't reply. The wagons rattled, the axles and hubs creaking on ruts.

They left the trees for open space, where it became even colder and foggier. Reynevan heard the swoosh of water over stones.

'The River Węża.' Czirne pointed. 'Less than a mile to the pass. Huzza! Drive on, driiive on!'

Pebbles clattered and grated beneath the horseshoes and wheel rims, and soon the water was splashing and foaming around the horses' feet. The little river was shallow but rapid.

Hayn of Czirne suddenly stopped in the middle of the ford, motionless in the saddle. Vitelozzo Gaetani reined his horse around.

'What is it?'

'Quiet. Not a word.'

They saw before they heard anything. What they saw was white foam splashing up from the hooves of two horses charging at them along the bed of the Węża. Only later did they see the silhouettes of two riders with cloaks billowing out like ghastly wings.

'To arms!' yelled Czirne, jerking out his sword. 'To arms! Crossbows!'

They were struck by a wind, a sudden, elemental, howling gale, lashing their faces. And then they were struck by a deranged cry.

'*Adsumus! Adsuuumuuuus!*'

The bowstrings of crossbows clanged; bolts sang. Someone screamed. And a moment later, the horsemen were splashing upon them, falling on them like a hurricane, smiting with swords, felling and trampling them. Everything swirled and seethed, the night torn apart by cries, yells, thuds and the clank of iron, the squealing and neighing of horses. Fryczko of Nostitz tumbled into the river along with his struggling steed and an esquire splashed into the water, felled by a sword blow. One of the bowmen howled and the howl turned into a wheeze.

'*Adsuuumuuuus!*'

As Hanusz Throst fled, he turned around in the saddle and screamed to see behind him a grinning horse's face, and behind it a black shape in a hood. It was the last thing he saw on this Earth. A slender sword blade stabbed him in the face between eye and nose, crunching into his skull. The merchant went rigid, his arms flapped and he tumbled onto the stones.

'*Adsumus!*' the black horseman yelled triumphantly. '*In nomine Tuo!*'

The black-clothed horsemen spurred their horses and galloped into the darkness. Hayn of Czirne gave chase, flung himself from his saddle and seized one of them. They fell into the water and leaped to their feet at once, their swords whistling and clanging together. They fought ferociously, standing knee-deep in the foaming river, streams of sparks shooting from their blades.

The black knight stumbled. Czirne, the old fox, couldn't let a chance like that go by. He swung and struck him in the head, his heavy Passau blade slicing through the hood, cleaving and lifting up the helmet. Czirne saw in front of him a visage covered in blood, as white as death, grimacing ghoulishly, and knew at once he would never forget that sight. The wounded man roared and charged, refusing to fall down, although he should have. Czirne swore, grabbed his sword in both hands and slashed once again with a powerful twist of the hips, slicing flatly into his neck. Black blood gushed out as the man's head fell onto his shoulder and lolled there, probably only held on by a scrap of skin. And the headless knight walked on, brandishing his sword and splashing gore around.

One of the bowmen screamed in terror and two others bolted in panic. Hayn of Czirne did not retreat. He swore terribly and impiously, steadied himself on his feet and smote again, this time severing the head completely and hacking off almost the entire arm. The black knight tumbled over into the shallow water by the bank, his limbs flailing, thrashing and kicking convulsively. It was a long time before he stopped moving.

Panting heavily, Hayn of Czirne pushed away from his knees the corpse of a crossbowmen in a brigantine turning in the current.

'What was that?' he finally asked. 'What by Lucifer was that?'

'May Jesus be merciful,' mumbled Fryczko of Nostitz next to Czirne. 'May Jesus be merciful . . .'

The Węża River burbled melodiously over the stones.

Meanwhile, Reynevan was fleeing, and he rode as though he'd done nothing his entire life except gallop in shackles. And he was galloping wonderfully, his bound wrists hooked firmly over the pommel, his head buried in the mane, his knees gripping the horse's sides with all his might, pounding so hard the earth trembled and the air howled in his ears. The horse – dear creature – appeared to know what was afoot, stretched out its neck and gave its all, proving that for the last five or six years it hadn't been fed on oats for nothing. Horseshoes struck the hardened ground, bushes and high grass parting while branches lashed against him. *Pity Dzierżka of Wirsing can't see this*, thought Reynevan, although he knew his equestrian skills at that moment were rather limited to managing to stay in the saddle. *But*, he thought at once, *that's still plenty*.

That thought came to him perhaps a little too soon, because at that moment, the horse decided to clear a fallen tree. And it jumped quite gracefully, except for that fact that there was a hollow beyond the tree trunk. The impact weakened Reynevan's grip and he flew into a patch of burdock which was fortunately so abundant and tall that it at least partly broke his fall. But the collision with the ground winded him and he curled up in a ball, groaning.

He had no time to uncurl himself. Vitelozzo Gaetani, who had been chasing him, dismounted.

'Trying to flee?' he wheezed. 'From me? You worm!'

He aimed a kick at him but didn't complete it. Scharley appeared as if from nowhere, pushed him in the chest and treated him to his favourite kick below the knee. The Italian only staggered, then drew his sword and gave a mighty backhand swing. The penitent nimbly dodged the blade and unsheathed his own weapon, a curved sabre. He swung it diagonally, the sabre whistling in his hand like a lightning bolt and hissing like a viper.

Gaetani wasn't frightened by Scharley's fencing skills and jumped at the penitent, wielding his sword and yelling savagely. Their weapons clanged together. Three times. The fourth time, the Italian wasn't quick enough to parry the blow from the much quicker sabre. The blade nicked his cheek and blood splashed on him. It was a small wound, and perhaps he would have fought on, but Scharley didn't give him a chance. He jumped forward and slammed him between the eyes with the pommel of his sword. Gaetani tumbled among the burdock, howling as he fell.

'*Figlio di puttana!*'

'Apparently,' said Scharley, wiping his blade on a leaf. 'But what to do – you can't choose your mother.'

'I don't want to spoil the amusement,' said Samson, emerging from the fog with three horses, including Reynevan's wheezing and foaming bay, 'but could we get out of here? And at a gallop, perhaps?'

The milky curtain fell apart as the mist rose, dispelled in the blaze of the sun shining through the clouds. The world, hitherto plunged in a chiaroscuro of long shadows, suddenly brightened up, glistening and blazing with colour like one of Giotto's frescos.

The red tiles of the towers of nearby Frankenstein glistened.

'And now,' said Samson, after feasting his eyes, 'to Ziębice.'

'To Ziębice,' Reynevan said, rubbing his hands together. 'Let's head for Ziębice. My friends . . . How can I repay you?'

'We'll think about it,' promised Scharley. 'But for the moment . . . Get off your horse.'

Reynevan did as he was told. He knew what to expect. He wasn't wrong.

'Reinmar of Bielawa,' said Scharley in a dignified and solemn voice. 'Repeat after me: I'm an ass!'

'I'm an ass—'

'Louder!'

God's creatures inhabiting the area that were just waking up – from harvest mice and fire-bellied toads to yellowhammers and pied flycatchers, crossbills and salamanders – heard Reynevan shout at the top of his voice: 'I am an ass!'

'I'm an ass,' Reynevan repeated after Scharley. 'An utter pillock, a fool, a moron, an idiot and a clown worthy of being locked up in the Narrenturm! Whatever I think up turns out to be the height of idiocy. Whatever I do exceeds those heights. I solemnly vow to improve. It is my good fortune – fortune which is utterly undeserved – to have friends who don't leave me in the lurch. I have friends I can always rely upon. Because friendship . . .'

The sun rose higher and flooded the fields in a golden blaze.

'Friendship is a great and beautiful thing!'

Chapter Nineteen

In which our heroes happen upon a very European tournament in Ziębice. For Reynevan, however, contact with Europe turns out to be very disagreeable. Painful, even.

They were already near enough to Ziębice to admire – in all their glory – the imposing walls and towers looming up from behind a wooded hill. Farmers were labouring in the fields and meadows, the pastures were dotted with sheep and the meadows around the ponds were white with geese. The hallmarks of prosperity were visible everywhere.

'A pleasant land,' said Samson. 'A hardworking, affluent region.'

'And a law-abiding one,' said Scharley, pointing at gibbets groaning under the weight of hanged men. Alongside, to the delight of crows, a dozen corpses were rotting on stakes and bones shone white on breaking wheels. 'It's clear that the law means law here and justice means justice.'

'Where do you see justice?'

'Over there,' Scharley replied, indicating the display of corpses. 'Ah, yes.'

'Which also gives rise to the affluence you rightly remarked upon, Samson,' Scharley went on. 'Indeed, such towns are worth visiting for more sensible reasons than the one we are driven by, for example, in order to fleece one of the affluent citizens of this demesne, which shouldn't be difficult since prosperity breeds masses of halfwits. But we are here to ... Never mind ... Waste of breath.'

Reynevan didn't utter a single word. He didn't feel like it. He had been listening to similar comments for a long time already.

'Christ,' gasped Reynevan as they rode out from behind the hill. 'What a lot of people! What's going on?'

Scharley reined in his horse and stood up in the stirrups.

'A joust,' he said after a moment. 'This is a joust, gentlemen. A *torneamentum*. What's the date today? Does anyone remember?'

'It's the eighth,' said Samson, counting on his fingers. '*Mensis Septembris*, of course.'

'Well I never!' Scharley said and looked at him askance. 'So you have the same calendar in the beyond, do you?'

'Generally speaking, we do.' Samson didn't react to the taunt. 'You asked for the date, so I told you. Would you like more detailed information? It's the feast of the Birth of the Virgin Mary, *Nativitas Mariae*.'

'Which is why the joust is taking place,' concluded Scharley. 'On we go, gentlemen.'

The common outside the town was full of people. Makeshift stands, covered with colourful cloth and decorated with garlands, ribbons, Piast eagles and the knighthood's escutcheons, had been erected for higher-class spectators. Beside the stands were craftsmen's booths and stalls selling food, relics and souvenirs, and above it all fluttered an extravaganza of multicoloured flags, standards, pennants and gonfalons. From time to time, the brass voices of trumpets and horns sounded over the clamour of the crowd.

They could see the lists from the hill – 250 paces long, a hundred paces wide and enclosed by a double-pole fence, especially robust on the outside and capable of holding back the weight of the commonalty. At that very moment, two knights were charging at each other, lances lowered. The crowd roared, whistled and applauded.

'This tournament, this *hastiludium* we are admiring, will make our task easier,' said Scharley. 'The whole town is gathered here. Look over there, they've even climbed up trees. Reinmar, I bet no one's guarding your beloved. Let's dismount, so as not to be conspicuous, then stroll around this vulgar pageant, mingle among the farmers and enter the town. *Veni, vidi, vici!*'

'Before we follow in Caesar's footsteps,' said Samson, shaking his head, 'we ought to check if Reinmar's beloved isn't by any chance among the spectators. If the entire town is gathered here, perhaps she's here, too?'

'But what would Adèle be doing in this company?' asked Reynevan, dismounting. 'They're holding her captive here, let me remind you. Prisoners aren't invited to jousts.'

'Probably not. But what harm does it do to check?'

Reynevan shrugged.

'Onwards, then.'

They had to walk carefully, paying attention not to step in shit since the surrounding woods had become, as they did during every tournament, a public latrine. It looked as though every inhabitant of and visitor to Ziębice had been in the bushes at least twice to defecate and urinate. It stank like hell. It was clearly not the first day of the tournament.

Trumpets sounded and the crowd yelled again in one great voice. This time, they were close enough to hear the cracks of lances breaking and the thuds of contestants colliding with one another.

'A lavish tournament,' commented Samson. 'Lavish and opulent.'

'As is customary with Duke Jan,' observed Scharley.

They were passed by a brawny farm worker leading a buxom, ruddy-faced and fiery-eyed beauty into the bushes. Reynevan watched the couple with affection, hoping in his heart of hearts that they would find a discreet place that was also free of shit. His mind was preoccupied with the lingering thought of what the couple would soon be enjoying in the bushes and he felt a pleasant tingling sensation in his loins. *Never mind*, he thought, *never mind, only moments separate me from similar delights with Adèle.*

'This way.' Scharley led them between the booths of a blacksmith and an armourer with characteristic intuition. 'Tie your mounts up here, to the fence. And come this way, it's not so crowded.'

'Let's try to get nearer to the stand,' said Reynevan. 'If Adèle is here, she'll—'

His words were drowned out by fanfares.

'*Aux honneurs, seigneurs chevaliers et escuiers!*' boomed the marshal of the heralds after the fanfares had faded away. '*Aux honneurs! Aux honneurs!*'

Duke Jan's credo was to be modern. And European. Differing in this regard among Silesian Piasts, the Duke of Ziębice suffered from a provincial complex and bemoaned the fact that his duchy lay on the periphery of civilisation and culture beyond which there was nothing but Poland and Lithuania. Hence his insistence, irksome to those around him, on the use of French as the official language of *la jouste*.

The knights set their lances in the rests and rode at each other along the tilt accompanied by the thudding of hooves. One of them, as evidenced by the emblems on the caparison, depicting a mountain peak on a silver and red chequered pattern, was a member of the Hoberg family. The other knight was a Pole, judging by the Jelita coat of arms on his shield and the goat in the coat of arms on his modish helmet with a barred visor.

Duke Jan's European joust attracted great numbers of guests from Silesia and abroad. The space between the tiltyard and a specially fenced-off area was occupied by fabulously coloured knights and pages, including members of the most important Silesian families.

Aided by the mighty arms of Samson, Reynevan and Scharley climbed up onto a coal heap and then onto the roof of the blacksmith's shed. From there, Reynevan carefully inspected the now-close stand.

'By God,' he gasped very loudly. 'Adèle is there! Yes, as I live and breathe!'

'Which one is she?' asked Samson.

'The one in the green dress . . . Under the canopy . . . Beside—'

'Next to Duke Jan himself,' Scharley remarked. 'Beauteous, indeed. Why, Reinmar, I congratulate you on your taste. But I cannot congratulate you on your knowledge of the female soul. Sadly, this confirms my view that our Ziębice Odyssey was a misguided idea.'

'It can't be,' Reynevan assured himself. 'It can't be ... She ... She's a prisoner ...'

'Whose, I wonder?' Scharley shielded his eyes with his hand. 'Sitting next to the duke is Jan of Biberstein, Lord of Stolz Castle. On the far side of Biberstein is an elderly woman I don't know ...'

'Euphemia, the duke's older sister,' said Reynevan. 'Next to her ... Could it be Bolko Wołoszek?'

'The Lord of Głogówek, son of the Duke of Opole.' As usual, Scharley impressed them with his knowledge, rattling off a detailed list of the great and the good in attendance. 'The one person I can't see, Reinmar, is anyone who could be considered your Adèle's guard.'

'Right over there,' mumbled Reynevan, 'is Tristram of Rachenau. He's a relative of the Sterczas. As is Baruth, the one with the aurochs in his coat of arms. And there ... Oh! Dammit! It can't be!'

Scharley grabbed him firmly by the arm or Reynevan would have fallen from the roof.

'The sight of whom has shaken you so?' he asked coldly. 'I see that your goggling eyes are fixed on a wench with fair plaits. The one whom the young Lord Dohna and some Polish Rawicz are courting. Do you know her? Who might she be?'

'Nicolette,' Reynevan said softly. 'Fair Nicolette.'

The plan, which Reynevan had believed ingenious in its elegance and audacity, had failed utterly. Scharley had predicted it, but Reynevan couldn't be restrained.

Adjoining the tournament stand were makeshift constructions built from wooden frames with canvas stretched over them. The wealthier spectators spent the breaks in the joust there, entertaining one another with conversation, flirting and showing off their costumes. It was also a place for enjoying food and drink, and a constant stream of servants moved between the kitchen and the marquees, rolling barrels and carrying kegs and baskets. The idea of stealing up to the kitchen, mingling with the servants, grabbing a basket of rolls and heading towards one of the marquees seemed excellent to Reynevan. He was mistaken.

He only managed to reach the vestibule, where the products were stored to be distributed by the pages. Reynevan, single-mindedly carrying out his plan, put down a basket, slipped unnoticed out of the ranks of servants returning to the kitchen and sneaked behind the marquees. He drew a dagger to cut a viewing hole in the canvas. And it was then he was caught.

The grip of several pairs of strong hands immobilised him; one iron hand clenched him by the throat and another, just as powerful, prised the dagger from his fingers. He ended up inside the marquee full of knights much quicker than he had expected, although not quite in the way he had hoped.

He was shoved hard, fell over, and saw right in front of him some fashionable poulaines with incredibly long toes. He was jerked upright by Tristram of Rachenau, a relative of the Sterczas. He was accompanied by several Baruths – also related to the Sterczas – with black aurochs on their doublets. It couldn't have been worse for Reynevan.

'An assassin,' Rachenau introduced him. 'A killer, Your Grace. Reinmar of Bielawa.'

The knights surrounding the duke murmured menacingly.

Duke Jan Ziębice, a handsome and well-built man in his forties, was dressed in a tight black *justaucorps*, over which he wore a fashionably loose claret *houppelande* trimmed with sable. A heavy gold chain hung around his neck and on his head he sported a fashionable *chaperon turban* with a liripipe of Flemish muslin draped over one shoulder. The duke's dark hair was also cut according to the newest European styles and fashions – in a pudding bowl, two fingers above his ears, with a fringe at the front and shaved high at the back. The duke was shod, however, in red Polish poulaines with fashionable long toes, the same ones Reynevan had just admired from floor level.

The duke, Reynevan noted with a painful tightness of the throat and diaphragm, was arm-in-arm with Adèle of Stercza, who was wearing a gown of the most fashionable *vert d'emeraude*, with a train and slashed sleeves that reached the ground. A gold hairnet graced her tresses and a string of pearls encircled her neck above a cleavage boldly peeking out from a tight corset. The Burgundian was scrutinising Reynevan and her eyes were as cold as a serpent's.

Duke Jan took Reynevan's dagger from Tristram of Rachenau, examined it and then raised his eyes.

'And to think,' he said, 'that I didn't quite believe it when you were accused of those crimes, of the murders of those merchants. I didn't want to lend credence to it, yet here you are, caught red-handed as you tried to sneak up on me from behind with a knife in your hand. Do you hate me so much? Or perhaps somebody paid you. Or you are simply insane. Eh?'

'Your Grace ... I ... I'm no assassin. It's true that I sneaked up, but I ... I wished to—'

'Oh!' Duke Jan made a very ducal and very European gesture with his slender hand. 'I understand. You crept in here with a dagger to present me with a petition?'

'Yes! I mean no ... Your Grace! I am not guilty of anything! On the contrary, injustice has befallen me! I'm a victim, the victim of a conspiracy—'

'Oh, naturally,' pouted Jan of Ziębice. 'A conspiracy. I knew it.'

'Yes!' yelled Reynevan. 'Exactly! The Sterczas killed my brother! They murdered him!'

'You lie, varlet,' snapped Tristram of Rachenau. 'Don't accuse my kinsmen, I warn you.'

'The Sterczas killed Peterlin!' said Reynevan, struggling. 'If not with their own hands, then using hired thugs – Kunz Aulock, Stork of Gorgowice and Walter of Barby – scoundrels who are also after me! Your Grace, Duke Jan, Peterlin was your vassal – I demand justice!'

'It is I who demands!' yelled Rachenau. 'I – by the right of blood! That son of a dog killed Nicolaus of Stercza in Oleśnica!'

'Justice!' called one of the Baruths, probably Henryk, because the Baruths seldom christened their children otherwise. 'Duke Jan! A penalty for that murder!'

'That is a lie and a calumny!' yelled Reynevan. 'The Sterczas are guilty of murder! They accuse me to justify their actions. And from vengeance, for the love that binds me to Adèle!'

Duke Jan's face changed and Reynevan realised what a terrible blunder he had made. He looked at his lover's impassive face and slowly, very slowly began to understand.

'Adèle,' Jan of Ziębice spoke in total silence. 'What is he talking about?'

'He's lying, Jasiek,' the Burgundian said, smiling. 'There's nothing between us and there never has been. It's true that he tried to force his affections on me, but he left chastened, having gained nothing. Not even helped by the black magic he tried to beguile me with.'

'That's not true.' Reynevan had difficulty speaking with a lump in his throat. 'None of that is true. Adèle! Tell him . . . Tell him that you and I—'

Adèle tossed her head in a gesture he knew. She tossed it like that when she made love with him in her favourite position, sitting astride him. Her eyes flashed. He also knew that flash.

'Nothing of this kind would ever occur in Europe,' she said loudly, looking around. 'For a virtuous lady's honour to be insulted, and at a joust where that lady was only yesterday hailed *La Royne de la Beaulté et des Amours* in the presence of the knights of the tournament. And were something like that to occur in Europe, such a *mesdisant*, such a *mal-faiteur* would not remain unpunished for an instant.'

Tristram of Rachenau immediately understood the allusion and gave Reynevan a powerful punch to the back of the neck as Henryk of Baruth weighed in from the other side. Seeing that Duke Jan wasn't reacting, that he was looking elsewhere stony-faced, others leaped forward, including a Seidlitz or Kurzbach with fishes on a red field. Reynevan was punched in the eye socket and the world vanished in a great flash. He cowered beneath a hail of blows. Someone else joined in and Reynevan fell to his knees, struck on the arm with a club. He shielded his head and the club whacked him painfully over the fingers. He was hit hard in the kidneys and fell to the ground. As the kicks began to rain down, he curled up in a ball, protecting his head and stomach.

'Stop! Enough! Stop that at once!'

The kicks and blows ceased. Reynevan opened one eye.

Salvation came from the least expected quarter. His tormentors had been restrained by the menacing, dry, harsh voice and orders of a bony, elderly woman in a black dress and white wimple under a stiffly starched pillbox hat. Reynevan knew who it was. Euphemia, Duke Jan's older sister, the widow of Friedrich, Count of Oettingen, who had returned to her native Ziębice after her husband's death.

'In the Europe I know,' said Countess Euphemia, 'a man is not kicked when he is down. None of the European dukes I know would permit that, my noble brother.'

'He is culpable,' began Duke Jan. 'Wherefore—'

'I know of what he is culpable,' the countess interrupted him dryly. 'I hereby take him under my protection. *Mercy des dames.* For, I flatter myself, my knowledge of European tournament customs is no worse than that of the spouse of Lord Stercza present here.'

The last words were spoken with such emphasis and so scathingly that Duke Jan lowered his eyes and blushed all the way up his shaved nape. Adèle didn't lower her gaze, revealing not a trace of embarrassment, while the hatred emanating from her eyes was terrifying. But not to Countess Euphemia. Euphemia, rumour had it, had coped quickly and adroitly with Count Friedrich's lovers in Swabia. She didn't fear others; others feared her.

'M'Lord Marshal of the Court Borschnitz,' she said, beckoning imperiously. 'Please take Reinmar of Bielawa into custody. You will answer for him to me. With your head.'

'Yes, Madam.'

'Don't be hasty, noble sister,' said Jan of Ziębice. 'I know what *mercy des dames* means, but this is too important an accusation. The charges against this young man are too grave. Murder, black magic—'

'He will be held under arrest,' Euphemia cut him off. 'In the tower. Under the guard of Master Borschnitz. He will appear in court if anybody accuses him. I mean of anything serious.'

'Fie!' The duke waved a hand and vigorously tossed his liripipe over his shoulder. 'To hell with him. I have more important affairs here. Come on, sirs, the mêlée is about to begin. I won't spoil the tournament; I won't miss the mêlée. Come with me, Adèle. Before the fight begins, the knights must see the Queen of Beauty and Love on the grandstand.'

The Burgundian took hold of his proffered arm and picked up her train. Reynevan, who was being bound, fixed his gaze on her, hoping she would look back, give him a sign or signal with eye or hand. To say it was only a trick, a game, a ruse; that actually everything was still as it had been, that nothing had changed between them. He kept waiting until the last moment.

But to no avail.

Fanfares sounded, the crowd raised a thunderous ovation, the herald shouted his *laissez les aller* and *aux honneurs*. The mêlée began.

'Let's go,' instructed the esquire to whom the Marshal of the Court Borschnitz had given command of the escort. 'Don't try to resist, lad.'

'I'm not going to. What's the tower like here?'

'Is it your first time? Ha, I see it is. Pretty decent. For a tower.'

'Let's go, then.'

Reynevan tried not to look around, so as not to betray Scharley and Samson, who he was certain were hidden in the crowd observing him. In any case, Scharley was too wily an old fox to let himself be noticed.

But someone else had noticed Reynevan.

She had changed her hairstyle. Previously, near Brzeg, she had worn her hair in a thick plait. Now her straw-coloured locks were divided down the centre of her head into two plaits, coiled over her ears, topped with a gold headband. She was wearing a blue sleeveless dress and under it a white batiste chemise.

'M'lady,' said the esquire, clearing his throat and scratching his head beneath his hat. 'It is not allowed . . . It will get me into trouble . . .'

'I only want to exchange a few words with him,' she said, biting her lip comically and stamping her foot a little childishly. 'A few words, nothing more. Don't tell anyone about it and you'll have no trouble. Now turn around. And don't eavesdrop.'

When the esquire had complied, she narrowed her blue eyes and asked, 'Why are you in fetters and under guard this time, Aucassin? Beware! If you answer that it's because of love, I shall be very cross.'

'And yet,' he sighed, 'that's the truth. Generally speaking.'

'And more precisely?'

'Because of love and stupidity.'

'Oh! You're becoming more believable. But explain, please.'

'Were it not for my stupidity, I'd be in Hungary now.'

'I'll find out everything, anyhow,' she said and looked him straight in the eyes. 'Everything. Every detail. But I wouldn't like to see you on the scaffold.'

'I'm glad they didn't catch you, then.'

'They didn't have a chance.'

'M'lady.' The esquire turned around and coughed into his fist. 'Have mercy . . .'

'Farewell, Aucassin.'

'Farewell to you, Nicolette.'

Chapter Twenty

In which the old truth is confirmed once again that when all's said and done, you can always rely on old university friends.

'You know, Reynevan,' said Heinrich Hackeborn, 'it is generally believed that the source of all the misfortune that befalls you is that Frenchwoman, Adèle of Stercza.'

Reynevan didn't react to this very original statement. His lower back was itching and there was no way he could scratch it with both his hands tied at the wrists and his elbows held against his sides by a leather strap. Hooves clattered as the party's horses rode along the bumpy road. The bowmen were swaying drowsily in the saddle.

He had been locked up for three days in the tower of Ziębice Castle, but he was a long way from losing heart. For although he had been imprisoned, he wasn't being beaten and was fed every day, even if the rations were meagre and dull. He had got out of the habit of eating recently and was pleased to be back into it.

Sleep had been more difficult to come by, and not just because of the huge fleas infesting the straw. Each time he closed his eyes, he saw Peterlin's white, pockmarked face. Or Adèle and Jan of Ziębice, in various configurations. He didn't know which was worse.

The barred window in the thick wall offered a tiny patch of sky, but Reynevan hovered around the alcove, clutching the grating, full of hope that any moment he would hear Scharley climbing like a spider with a file in his teeth. Or watched the door, dreaming that any moment it would fly from its hinges under a blow of Samson's mighty shoulder. Justified faith in his friends' omnipotence was keeping his spirits up.

No rescue was forthcoming, however. Early in the morning of the fourth day, he was dragged from his cell, bound and put on a horse. He left Ziębice through the Paczków Gate, escorted by four mounted crossbowmen, an esquire and a knight in full armour with a shield bearing the eight-pointed star of the Hackeborns.

'Everybody says that humping that Frenchwoman was your downfall,' Heinrich Hackeborn went on.

Reynevan didn't reply that time, either, but he couldn't help nodding his head pensively.

Barely had they lost sight of the town's tower than the apparently gloomy and sickeningly officious Hackeborn cheered up and became animated and forthcoming, without any encouragement. Like every second German, he bore the given name Heinrich and was, it turned out, a relative of the powerful Hackeborns of Przewóz. He had arrived all of two years before from Thuringia, where his family's position in the service of the landgraves was deteriorating, and as a consequence they were becoming ever poorer. In Silesia, where the surname Hackeborn still meant something, Sir Heinrich was hoping for adventures and a career in the service of Jan of Ziębice. The former was meant to be provided by the great anti-Hussite crusade which was expected any day, and the latter by a favourable marriage. Heinrich Hackeborn confessed to Reynevan that he was in love with the gorgeous and spirited Jutta of Apolda, the daughter of Cup-Bearer Berthold Apolda, Lord of Schönau. Jutta, unfortunately, not only didn't return his affection, but took the liberty of mocking his advances. But never mind, the main thing was to persevere.

Although he didn't care a jot about Hackeborn's romantic adventures, Reynevan pretended to listen and nodded politely. There was no point being rude to his own escort, after all. When, after some time, the knight had exhausted the range of subjects bothering him and fell silent, Reynevan tried to doze, but with no luck. Either the image of Peterlin lying on the bier or Adèle with her calves on Duke Jan's shoulders kept appearing in front of his eyes.

They were in Służejów Forest, which was colourful and fragrant after the morning rain, when Sir Heinrich interrupted the silence. Without being asked, he revealed to Reynevan their destination – Stolz Castle, the seat of the powerful Lord Jan Biberstein. Reynevan's interest and anxiety grew in equal measure. He intended to question the garrulous knight but wasn't quick enough, for he smoothly changed the subject and launched into digressions about Adèle of Stercza and the problems the romance with her had caused Reynevan.

'Although everybody thinks that fucking her was your downfall,' continued Hackeborn, assuming an all-knowing expression, 'it's actually the other way around. Some people worked out that shafting the Frenchwoman actually saved your life.'

'I beg your pardon?'

'Duke Jan,' explained the knight, 'would have turned you over to the Sterczas without any qualms. Rachenau and Baruth were both exhorting him to. But what would that have meant? That Adèle was lying by denying it. That you did, in fact, bed her. Do you see? The duke didn't hand you over to be investigated regarding those murders you allegedly committed for the same reason – because he knew you'd sing about Adèle under torture. Understand?'

'A little.'

'A little!' Hackeborn laughed. 'That "little" will save your arse, chum. Rather than heading to the scaffold or the torture chamber, you're riding to Stolz Castle, because at the castle you can only talk to the walls about your erotic prowess in Adèle's bedchamber, and the walls there are thick. You'll do a bit of time, but you'll save your head and other members. In Stolz, no one can get their hands on you, not even the bishop or the Inquisition. The Bibersteins are powerful magnates, they aren't afraid of anyone, and no one will dare to fall foul of them. Yes, yes, Reynevan. It saved you that Duke Jan didn't want to admit that you had dallied with his new mistress before him. Understand? A lover whose exquisite little furrow has only been ploughed by her husband is almost a virgin, but one who has given herself to other paramours is a harlot. For after all, if Reinmar of Bielawa bedded her – anybody could have.'

'You're too kind. Many thanks.'

'Don't thank me. I told you that *amor* saved you. So see it like that.'

No, no, not entirely, thought Reynevan. *Not entirely.*

'I know what you're thinking,' said the knight, surprising him. 'That a corpse is even more discreet? That they're liable to poison you or quietly break your neck at Stolz. Not at all, if that's what you're thinking. Want to know why?'

'I do.'

'Jan of Biberstein himself suggested to the duke that you be discreetly imprisoned at Stolz, and the duke agreed at once. And now the best part: do you know why Biberstein was so quick to suggest it?'

'I have no idea.'

'But I do. Because a rumour was going around Ziębice that the duke's sister, Countess Euphemia, asked him, and the duke holds her in high esteem. Has done since they were children, it is said, which is why the countess is so important at the Ziębice court even though she has no position – I mean, what kind of countess is she? Her title's meaningless. She bore the Swabian Friedrich eleven children and when he died, they turfed her out of Oettingen, that's no secret. But in Ziębice she's a real lady, through and through.'

Reynevan had no intention of denying it.

'She wasn't the only one to approach Sir Jan Biberstein to intervene on your behalf,' continued Hackeborn a moment later. 'Want to know who else?'

'I do.'

'Biberstein's daughter, Katarzyna. She must be fond of you.'

'Is she the tall girl? With fair hair?'

'Don't play the fool. You know her. Rumour has it she saved you from your pursuers. Oh, how strangely entangled it has all become. Isn't this comedy of errors a veritable Tower of Fools?'

That's true, thought Reynevan. *A veritable Tower of Fools, a Narrenturm. And I . . . Scharley was right – I am the greatest fool of all. King of the chumps, marshal of the asses, grand prior of the order of pudding-heads.*

'You won't be imprisoned at Stolz for long,' Hackeborn continued cheerfully, 'if you display good sense. I happen to know that a great crusade against the Czech heretics is in prospect. If you take the vows and accept the cross, they'll release you to go and fight. And if you acquit yourself well in the battle against the Schism, they'll pardon your crimes.'

'There's one snag.'

'Namely?

'I don't want to fight.'

The knight turned around in the saddle and took a long look at him.

'And why would that be?' he asked with a sneer.

Reynevan didn't manage to answer. There was a shrill whistle and hiss and then a loud crack. Hackeborn choked and raised a hand to his throat to grasp the crossbow bolt that was sticking into his gorget. The knight spat blood copiously, tipped backwards and toppled from his horse. Reynevan saw his eyes, wide open and expressing blank astonishment.

Then things moved fast.

'It's a raaaaid!' yelled an esquire, jerking his sword from its scabbard. 'To aaaarms!'

There was a flash of fire, a terrible boom and a billow of smoke in the bushes. One of the servants' horses fell beneath him like a stone, pinning its rider to the ground. The other horses reared up, frightened by the explosion, including Reynevan's. With his arms tied together, Reynevan couldn't keep his balance and fell, striking the ground painfully with his hip.

Riders streamed out of the undergrowth. Even though he was

curled up on the sand, Reynevan recognised them right way.

'Kill them!' roared Kunz Aulock, brandishing his sword.

The Ziębice bowmen unleashed a salvo of crossbow bolts, but all three of them missed unforgivably. They tried to flee but were cut down by swords before they could. The esquire valiantly crossed swords with Kyrie-eleison, their horses snorting and dancing, blades clanging. Stork of Gorgowice put an end to the duel, thrusting a baselard into the esquire's back. The esquire stiffened and Kyrie-eleison finished him off with a thrust to the throat.

Deep in the dense forest, a frightened magpie screeched in alarm. The air was thick with the smell of black powder.

'Well, well,' said Kyrie-eleison, nudging the prone Reynevan with the point of his boot. 'Lord Bielawa. It's been a long time. Aren't you glad to see me?'

Reynevan was not.

'We've waited a long time for you,' Aulock complained, 'in the cold, the rain and great discomfort. But *finis coronat opus*. You're ours, Bielawa. And ready for use, so to speak, bound like a Christmas goose. Why, it just isn't your day.'

'Kunz, let me kick him in the teeth,' suggested one of the band. 'He almost poked my eye out in that inn near Brzeg, so I'll kick his teeth out now.'

'Drop it, Sybek,' snarled Kyrie-eleison. 'Control yourself. I'd rather you went and checked what that knight had in his saddlebags and purse. And you, Bielawa, what are you gawping at?'

'You killed my brother, Aulock.'

'Eh?'

'You killed my brother. In Balbinów. You'll swing for it.'

'Nonsense,' said Kyrie-eleison coldly. 'You must have landed on your head when you fell from that horse.'

'You killed my brother!'

'It's still nonsense, no matter how many times you repeat it.'

'You lie!'

Aulock stood over him and his visage expressed a dilemma: to kick or not to kick. He chose not to and turned away contemptuously. He took a few steps and stood over the horse killed by the gunshot.

'The Devil take me,' he said, nodding. 'Truly a nasty, deadly weapon, that handgonne of yours, Stork. Look at the hole it made in the mare. Large enough for a fist. It's verily a weapon of the future. It's progress!'

'Fuck progress,' Stork of Gorgowice replied sourly. 'I was aiming at the rider with that sodding pipe, not the horse. And not this rider – that one.'

'Never mind where you aimed, at least you hit a target. Hey, Walter, what are you doing there?'

'I'm finishing off the ones that are still breathing!' Walter of Barby shouted back. 'We've no need for witnesses, have we?'

'Make haste! Stork, Sybek, be quick, get Bielawa on a horse – the knight's castellan. And tie him up securely because he's a handful. Remember?'

Stork and Sybek remembered only too well, because before putting Reynevan in the saddle, they treated him to a series of shoves and vulgar insults. They tied his bound hands to the pommel and his calves to the stirrup leathers. As soon as Walter of Barby had finished off the wounded, the bodies of the Ziębice men were dragged into the bushes and the horses chased away. On Kyrie-eleison's command, they all galloped off. They rode hard, clearly wishing to put as much distance as they could between them and the scene of the raid and any potential pursuers. Reynevan bounced around in the saddle. Every breath he took pained him; his ribs hurt like hell. *It can't go on like this*, he thought preposterously, *I can't keep getting beaten like this.*

Kyrie-eleison urged his comrades with shouts and they galloped on. Never leaving the highway, they clearly preferred speed over stealth; they couldn't even trot through the dense woodland, much less gallop.

They arrived at a crossroads. And rode straight into a trap.

Riders, previously concealed, charged out at them from the

thicket from all directions. There were some twenty men, half of whom were wearing full suits of white armour. Kyrie-eleison and company had no chance whatsoever, but they put up fierce resistance, notwithstanding. Aulock was the first to fall from his horse, head cleaved open by a battleaxe. Walter of Barby tumbled beneath the horses' hooves, run through by a huge knight with the Polish Ogończyk on his shield. Stork was hit over the head with a mace. Sybek of Kobylagłowa was hacked to pieces. Blood splashed over Reynevan, who was cowering in the saddle.

'You're free, Comrade.'

Reynevan blinked. His head was swimming. Everything had happened much too quickly for his liking.

'Thanks, Bolko . . . I apologise . . . I mean Your Grace—'

'Never mind, never mind,' interrupted Bolko Wołoszek, heir to the Duke of Opole and Prudnik, Lord of Głogówek, cutting Reynevan's bonds with a cutlass. 'Don't stand on ceremony. In Prague, you were Reynevan to me and I was Bolko to you, whether drinking or brawling. Or when we shared a whore at a brothel in the Old Town to save money. Have you forgotten?'

'I have not.'

'Neither have I. As you see. One doesn't leave a college pal in the lurch. And Jan of Ziębice can kiss my arse. In any case, I'm happy to say we weren't slaughtering Ziębice men. Fortunately, we've avoided a diplomatic incident, because I must confess that as we lay in wait on the Stolz road, we were rather expecting an escort from Ziębice. And then this surprise. Reynevan, please meet my vice-starosta, Sir Krzych of Kościelec. Well then, Sir Krzych? Identified any of them? Any still alive?'

'It's Kunz Aulock and his company,' said the giant with the Ogończyk on his shield. 'But only one of them is still breathing – Stork of Gorgowice.'

'Well, well!' The Lord of Głogówek frowned and pursed his lips. 'Stork. And alive? Lead me to him.'

Wołoszek walked his horse where Sir Krzych led, looking down at the dead as he went.

'Sybek of Kobylagłowa,' he said. 'He cheated the noose more than once, but, as they say, it was only a matter of time. And this is Kunz Aulock. Dammit, he came from such a decent family. Walter of Barby. But if you live by the sword ... And who do we have here? Sir Stork?'

'Mercy,' mumbled Stork of Gorgowice, his bloodied face grimacing. 'Pardon ... For the love of God, sire—'

'No, Sir Stork,' Bolko Wołoszek replied coldly. 'Opole will soon be my new demesne, my duchy. The rape of an Opole townswoman is thus a very serious crime in my eyes. Too serious for a swift death. Pity we have such little time.'

The young duke stood up in the stirrups and looked around.

'Tie the scoundrel up,' he ordered. 'And drown him.'

'Where?' asked the Ogończyk in surprise. 'There's no water around here.'

'Over there in the ditch,' Wołoszek pointed, 'there's a puddle. A small one, admittedly, but big enough for his head.'

The Głogów and Opole knights dragged Stork, yelling and struggling in his bonds, to the ditch, turned him upside down and shoved his head into the puddle, holding him by the feet. The yelling became a furious gurgling. Reynevan turned his face away.

It lasted a very long time.

Krzych of Kościelec returned, accompanied by another knight, also a Pole, with the Nieczuja coat of arms.

'He swallowed all the water in the puddle, the knave,' said the Ogończyk cheerfully. 'It was the mud that choked him.'

'Time we were leaving, Your Grace,' added the Nieczuja.

'I concur,' Bolko Wołoszek agreed. 'Listen, Reynevan. You can't ride with me – I can't hide you in Głogówek, or in Opole or Niemodlin. Neither my father nor my uncle Bernard will want a feud with Ziębice, and they'll turn you over to Jan if he asks. And he will.'

'I know.'

'I know you know.' The young Piast squinted. 'But I'm not convinced you understand. Thus, I'll be blunt. Whatever direction you choose, avoid Ziębice. Avoid Ziębice, Comrade, I advise you as an old friend. Give the city and the duchy a wide berth. Believe me, there's nothing for you there. Perhaps there was, but not now. Is that clear?'

Reynevan nodded. It was clear to him, but he couldn't bring himself to admit it.

'Each will go his own way,' said the duke, tugging at the reins and turning his horse around. 'You're on your own.'

'Thanks again. I'm indebted to you, Bolko.'

'Think nothing of it,' said Wołoszek perfunctorily. 'Anything for an old university pal. Oh, those were the days, in Prague ... Farewell, Reinmar. *Bene vale.*'

'*Bene vale*, Bolko.'

Soon the sound of the Opole entourage had faded away, and Reynevan vanished into the birch wood on the dark bay castellan, until recently the property of Heinrich Hackeborn, the knight from Thuringia, who met his death in Silesia. It was now quiet at the crossroads; the magpies and jays had fallen silent and the orioles were singing again.

Barely an hour passed before the first fox began nipping at Kunz Aulock's face.

The events on the Stolz highway became – at least briefly – a sensation, a juicy bit of gossip, a popular subject of conversation and rumour. Duke Jan of Ziębice went around frowning for several days, and prying courtiers put it about that he was cross with his sister, Duchess Euphemia, irrationally blaming her for everything. A rumour was also circulating that Lady Adèle of Stercza's serving maid had her ears boxed for twittering and giggling when her lady was in no mood for laughter.

The Hackeborns of Przewóz announced that they would find young Heinrich's killers, no matter what. The gorgeous and spirited Jutta of Apolda, on the other hand, wasn't at all upset by the death of her suitor.

Young knights organised a hunt for the criminals, riding

from castle to castle amid a blowing of horns and a thumping of hooves, but the expedition was more of a picnic than a hunt.

Ziębice was visited by the Inquisition, but not even the nosiest busybodies managed to find out the nature of their business.

At the Church of Saint John the Baptist in Wrocław, Canon Otto Beess prayed zealously before the high altar and thanked God, his hands held together in prayer and his head resting on them.

In Księginice, a village near Lubin, Walter of Barby's senile, utterly decrepit mother thought about the approaching winter and the hunger that was sure to kill her in the early spring, now that she had been left without care or help.

There was much noisy conversation in the Bell Inn in Niemcza. Wolfher, Morold and Wittich Stercza, along with Dieter Haxt, Stefan Rotkirch and Jentsch of Knobelsdorf, yelled, swore and threatened, drinking tankard after tankard. The servants bringing the drinks cringed in terror hearing descriptions of the torture the revellers intended to inflict on a certain Reinmar of Bielawa in the not too distant future. Just before dawn, their mood was improved by an unexpectedly astute observation from Morold. *Every cloud has a silver lining*, stated Morold. *Since Kunz Aulock has gone to Hell, Tammo Stercza's thousand Rhenish guilders will remain in his pocket. Meaning in Sterzendorf.*

Four days later, the news also reached Sterzendorf.

Little Ofka of Baruth was very, very disgruntled. And very cross with the housekeeper. Ofka had never been fond of the housekeeper, for all too often, her mother made the housekeeper force her to do things she didn't like, in particular eating kasha and washing. But that day, the housekeeper had really got into Ofka's bad books – she had dragged her away from playing. The game consisted of dropping flat stones into fresh cowpats; owing to its joyful simplicity, the pastime had become popular among Ofka's peers, chiefly the offspring of the castle guard and domestic staff.

Having been torn away from her games, the little girl was

whingeing, sulking and doing her best to hinder the housekeeper in her work. She was taking such tiny steps out of spite that the housekeeper almost had to drag her. Ofka reacted with malevolent snorts at everything the housekeeper threatened her with because she didn't give a hoot about it. She'd had enough of translating Grandpa Tammo's speech, because his chamber smelled and he did, too. She didn't care that Uncle Apecz had just arrived at Sterzendorf with some extremely important news for Grandpa, and that when he finished, Grandpa Tammo would have lots to say, as usual, and of course, no one but she could understand what Grandpa Tammo was saying.

The high-born Ofka of Baruth didn't give a tinker's cuss about it. She only had one desire – to return to the castle embankment and drop flat stones onto cowpats.

The sounds coming from Grandpa's chamber could be heard from the staircase. The news Uncle Apecz was sharing must have been horrifying and highly unpleasant indeed, for Ofka had never heard grandpa yelling so loudly. Ever. Not even when he found out that the best stallion in the stud had got food poisoning and died.

'Vuaahha-vuaha-buhhauahhu-uuuaaha!' came the sound from the chamber. 'Hrrrrhurrr-hhhuh . . . Uaarr-raaah! O-o-oooo . . .'

Then the following sound:

'Bzppprrrr . . . Ppppprrrruuu . . .'

And then silence fell.

And soon after, Uncle Apecz left the chamber. He looked at Ofka for a long time, and at the housekeeper even longer.

'Please have some vittles prepared in the kitchen,' he finally said. 'Air the chamber. And summon a priest. In that order. I shall issue further orders after I've eaten.'

Seeing the housekeeper's perplexed expression, he added, 'A great deal will change here. A great deal.'

Chapter Twenty-One

In which the red-hooded goliard and the black wagon reappear, along with 500 grzywna. And all because Reynevan is chasing skirts again.

Around noon, the road was blocked by a long stretch of wind-blown trees lying in a row and extending deep into the forest. The barrier of splintered tree trunks, the mess of entangled boughs and the chaos of roots torn from the earth and seemingly contorted in agony truly reflected Reynevan's state of mind. The allegorical landscape had not only stopped him but made him think.

After parting from Duke Bolko Wołoszek, Reynevan had ridden south apathetically, towards banks of dark clouds. He had no idea why he had chosen that direction. Was it because Wołoszek had pointed towards it on parting? Or had he instinctively chosen a track taking him away from places and matters that aroused fear and aversion in him? Away from the Sterczas, Strzegom and Lord Laasan, Hayn of Czirne, the Świdnica Inquisition, Stolz Castle, Ziębice, Duke Jan . . .

And Adèle.

The wind was driving the clouds so low, they appeared to be snagging on the treetops beyond the windblown debris. Reynevan sighed.

Oh, how Duke Bolko's cold words had hurt, how they had stung his heart! There was nothing for him in Ziębice! God's wounds! Those words, perhaps because they were so brutally frank, so true, had hurt more than Adèle's cold and indifferent gaze, more than her cruel voice when she set the knights on him, more than the blows that fell on him because of her, more even than prison. There was nothing for him in Ziębice!

I have nothing anywhere, he thought, staring into the tangle of roots and branches. *Instead of running away, wouldn't it be better to return to Ziębice and find a way to meet my faithless lover face-to-face? To toss bitter reproach and cold contempt at her in person, and see the unworthy Adèle grow pale and confused, see her wring her hands, lower her gaze, see her mouth quiver. Yes, yes, let whatever will be, be, if only to see her shamed by the dishonour of her own betrayal . . .*

Like hell, said his good sense. *Reproach? Conscience? You ass! She would burst out laughing, order you beaten again and thrown into the tower. And then she would take Duke Jan to her bedchamber and fuck him so hard the very walls would shake. And there would be neither remorse nor regret. There would be laughter, because deriding that naive fool, Reinmar of Bielawa, would only spice up and inflame their erotic sport.*

Good sense, Reynevan noted utterly without being surprised, was speaking with Scharley's voice.

Heinrich Hackeborn's horse neighed and shook its head. *Scharley*, thought Reynevan, patting its neck, *Scharley and Samson remained in Ziębice. Or perhaps they set off for Hungary right after my arrest, pleased to have got rid of the problem at last? Scharley recently called friendship 'a great and beautiful thing'. But his words had sounded more genuine and sincere and less mocking on previous occasions when he declared that the only things that mattered to him were his own comfort, his own good and happiness, and the rest could go to hell. He said that, and, all in all . . .*

All in all, I'm less and less surprised at him.

Hackeborn's castellan neighed again. And something neighed back.

Reynevan jerked his head up just in time to see a rider at the edge of the forest.

An Amazon.

Nicolette, he thought in amazement, *Fair Nicolette! A grey mare, a fair plait, a grey mantle. It's her, without a doubt!*

Nicolette saw him at almost the same moment as he saw her. But in spite of his expectations, she didn't wave to him or cry out cheerfully and gaily. No, she reined her horse around and bolted. Reynevan didn't pause to think. He spurred the castellan and set off in pursuit at a gallop, around the edge of the downed trees. On the uneven ground, he risked the horse breaking a leg or breaking his own neck, but as usual, Reynevan didn't think. And neither did the horse.

As soon as he entered the forest, he knew he was mistaken about the Amazon. Firstly, the grey horse was not the fleet-hoofed thoroughbred mare he knew, but a bony, ungainly nag, galloping heavily and clumsily through the bracken. And the girl riding it could in no way be Fair Nicolette. Firstly, the bold and determined Nicolette – or Katarzyna of Biberstein, he corrected himself – wouldn't be riding in a lady's saddle. Secondly, she wouldn't be glancing back in panic or squealing so horrifyingly.

When it finally dawned on him that he was chasing a completely random girl through the forests like a moron or a pervert, it was already too late. The Amazon rode squealing into a clearing with Reynevan right behind her. He reined in his horse, but the skittish knightly steed couldn't be stopped.

A small entourage was milling about the clearing. Reynevan saw several pilgrims, a few Franciscan monks in brown habits, several crossbowmen, a fat sergeant and a wagon-and-two covered with a black, tarred canvas. An elderly gentleman on a black horse, in a beaver calpac and a cloak with a beaver collar, noticed Reynevan's arrival and pointed him out to the sergeant and the soldiers.

An Inquisitor, thought Reynevan fearfully, but realised his mistake when he remembered he'd already seen that wagon and that individual in the beaver calpac and collar. Dzierżka of Wirsing had identified him at the farmstead where she kept her herd. He was a tax collector.

Staring at the wagon covered in black canvas, he realised he'd also seen that conveyance on another occasion. When he recalled the circumstances, he wanted to turn tail immediately but wasn't quick enough. Before he managed to rein around the horse, which was stamping and tossing its head, the soldiers had galloped over and surrounded him, cutting off his escape into the trees. In the face of several drawn crossbows, Reynevan dropped the reins and raised his hands.

'I'm here by accident!' he called. 'By mistake! I have no ill intent.'

'Anyone could say that,' said the beaver-furred tax collector. He examined Reynevan with an unusually grim expression, so intently and suspiciously that Reynevan froze, expecting the worst and the inevitable. That the tax collector would recognise him.

'I say, I say! Lay off him. I know that young blade!'

Reynevan swallowed. It was definitely a day for renewing old friendships. For the man who called was the goliard he had met in the Raubritter's Kromolin hideout, the same one who had read the Hussite manifesto and later hidden in the cheese store with Reynevan; middle-aged, wearing a jerkin with a serrated edge and a red long-tailed cowl with curly locks of grizzled hair peeping out from under it.

'I know this youngster very well,' he said, riding over. 'He's from a noble family. His name is . . . Reinmar of Hagenau.'

'Perhaps a descendant of the famous poet?' asked the tax collector, his features softening somewhat.

'No.'

'But why is he pursuing us? Is he tracking us? Eh?'

'Tracking us?' The goliard snorted. 'Are you blind? Why, he rode out of the forest! Were he pursuing us, he would have been riding along the track, following our trail.'

'That makes sense. And you know each other, you say?'

'As sure as eggs is eggs,' the goliard confirmed cheerfully. 'After all, I know his name, and he mine. He knows I'm called Tybald Raabe. Go on, m'Lord Reinmar, what's my name?'

'Tybald Raabe.'

'See?'

In the face of such irrefutable proof, the tax collector cleared his throat, adjusted his beaver calpac and ordered the soldiers to stand down.

'Forgive me, sir, I was overly cautious – but I must be vigilant! I can't say more than that. Well, Lord Hagenau, you may—'

'Ride with us,' the goliard finished cheerfully after sending Reynevan a slight wink. 'We're going to Bardo. Together. The more the merrier . . . and the safer.'

The procession moved slowly, the bumpy forest track limiting the wagon's speed to one that the pedestrians – four pilgrims with staves and four Franciscans pulling a handcart – could easily match. All the pilgrims, to a man, had purple noses, empirically testifying to a love of strong drink and other sins of youth. The Franciscans were young.

'The pilgrims and Friars Minor are also headed for Bardo,' explained the goliard. 'To the holy Figure on the Mount, you know, Our Lady of Bardo—'

'I know,' interrupted Reynevan, checking if anyone was listening, especially the tax collector, who was riding beside the black wagon. 'I know, Master . . . Tybald Raabe. If, however, there's something I don't know—'

'Then that's how it must be,' the goliard interjected. 'Don't ask unnecessary questions, m'Lord Reinmar. And be Hagenau, not Bielawa. That'll be safer.'

'You were in Ziębice,' guessed Reynevan.

'I was. And I heard this and that . . . Enough to be amazed to see you here, in the Goleniowskie Forests, m'lord, because rumour had it you were imprisoned in the tower. Oh, what peccadilloes they attributed to you . . . How they gossiped . . . If I didn't know you, m'lord—'

'But you do.'

'Aye. And I'm kindly disposed to you. Which is why I say: ride with us. To Bardo . . . For God's sake – don't stare at her like that, m'lord! Isn't it enough that you chased her around the forest?'

When the maid riding at the head of the party looked back for the first time, Reynevan gasped. In amazement. And astonishment. At mistaking such plainness for Nicolette. For Katarzyna of Biberstein.

Her hair was, true enough, almost identical in colour, as fair as straw, the frequent result in Silesia of mixing the blood of a fair-haired father from Germany and a fair-haired mother from Poland. But there the similarities ended. Nicolette had skin like alabaster, while the girl's forehead and chin were dotted with pimples. Nicolette had eyes of cornflower blue, while the pimply girl's were dull, watery and still goggling like a frog's in terror. Her nose was too small and her lips too thin and pale. She had heard something about fashion and plucked her eyebrows, but with poor results; rather than looking fashionable, she looked idiotic. The impression was augmented by her costume – she was wearing a crude rabbit-fur cap and beneath her mantle a worn, grey gown of simple design made of poor, worn-out wool. Katarzyna of Biberstein probably dressed her serving girls better.

A plain Jane, thought Reynevan, *a poor plain Jane. All she lacks is pockmarks. But she has that to look forward to.*

The knight riding alongside the girl had already had the pox, the scars from which his short, grizzled beard couldn't hide. The trappings of the bay he was riding were very frayed and his mail shirt dated back to the Battle of Legnica. *A poor knight*, thought Reynevan, *like so many others. An impoverished vassus vassallorum. Delivering his daughter to a convent. Where else? Who would want a girl like her? Only the Poor Clares or Cistercians.*

'Stop gaping at her, m'lord,' hissed the goliard. 'It's indecorous.'

It was indeed. Reynevan sighed and looked away, devoting all his attention to the oaks and hornbeams growing at the side of the road. But it was already too late.

The goliard swore softly as the knight in the Legnica mail shirt reined in his horse and waited for them to catch up. His expression was very serious and very grim. His head was raised proudly and he was resting his fist on his hip, right beside his sword hilt.

Which was just as old-fashioned as his mail shirt.

'Sir Hartwig of Stietencron,' said Tybald Raabe after clearing his throat. 'Sir Reinmar of Hagenau.'

Sir Hartwig of Stietencron scrutinised Reynevan for a moment, but contrary to expectations didn't ask about his kinship with the famous poet.

'You frightened my daughter, my lord,' he announced haughtily, 'by chasing after her.'

'I beg forgiveness,' said Reynevan, bowing, feeling his cheeks burning. 'I was following her, for I . . . By mistake. I ask for your forgiveness. I shall also, if you permit, ask for hers on my knees—'

'Don't kneel,' the knight interrupted. 'Stay away from her. She is anxious. Shy. But a good child. I'm taking her to Bardo—'

'To the convent?'

'Why do you think that?' The knight frowned.

'For you both look most devout.' The goliard stepped in to save Reynevan from getting himself into more trouble.

Sir Hartwig of Stietencron leaned over from the saddle, hawked and spat, not at all devoutly and not at all chivalrously.

'Stay away from my daughter, Lord Hagenau,' he repeated. 'Completely and always. Understood?'

'Understood.'

'Very well. Good day.'

After about an hour's drive, the wagon got stuck in the mud, and the joint strength of all the foot travellers was required to pull it out. Naturally, neither the nobility – meaning Reynevan and Sir Hartwig – nor culture and art – represented by Tybald Raabe – stooped to manual labour. The incident made the beaver-furred tax collector extremely anxious and he ran around, cursing and issuing commands, looking around at the forest apprehensively. He had clearly noticed Reynevan watching him, for as soon as the conveyance was freed and the party set off, he considered it necessary to explain a few things.

'You should know that the load I'm transporting isn't just any old load,' he began, after riding his horse between Reynevan and the goliard.

Reynevan didn't comment. In any case, he knew only too well why the man was so concerned.

'I wouldn't reveal it to anyone else,' the tax collector said, lowering his voice and looking around somewhat timidly, 'but you're a nobleman, after all, from an honest family, with an honest look in your eyes. So I'll tell you, m'lord – we're carrying taxes.'

He paused again, waiting for a display of curiosity which was not forthcoming.

'A tax, passed by the Frankfurt Reichstag,' he continued. 'A special tax, levied in one payment, for the war against Czech heresy. Every man pays according to his wealth. A knight pays five guilders, a baron ten and clergymen five out of every hundred of their annual stipend. Do you see?'

'I do.'

'The coffer's pretty full, too, for in Ziębice I received funds not just from some minor baron, but from the Fugger family. It ought not to surprise you that I'm cautious – barely a week has passed since I was attacked. Not far from Rychbach, near the village of Lutom.'

Reynevan simply nodded.

'Robber knights. A truly impudent gang! Paszko Rymbaba himself was spotted. Verily, they would have murdered us, but fortunately Lord Seidlitz appeared with help and drove the scoundrels away. He received a wound in the skirmish, which sorely infuriated him. He swore he'd pay the Raubritters back and he will surely keep his word, for the Seidlitzes are unforgiving.'

Reynevan licked his lips, still nodding mechanically.

'Lord Seidlitz vowed in his fury that he would catch and torture them all more cruelly than even the Cieszyn Duke Noszak tortured the brigand Chrzan for killing his son, young Duke Přemysl. Noszak ordered him put on a red-hot copper horse and nipped his body with white-hot pliers and hooks . . . Remember? Ah, I see from your expression that you do.'

'Mhm.'

'So, it was fortunate that I could tell Lord Seidlitz who those robbers were. Wherever Rymbaba is, Kuno of Wittram and Notker of Weyrach won't be far behind. But others were there, too, and I also described them to Lord Seidlitz. A great big bruiser with a stupid face, demented, no doubt. A smaller individual, with a hooked nose – one look and you know: a blackguard. And also a whippersnapper, a youngster your age, the same physique as you, even a little similar to you, m'lord, in fact ... But no, what am I saying, you're a comely young man with a noble face, the spitting image of Saint Sebastian, while that one looked like a brute.

'Anyway, I was talking about them and Lord Seidlitz suddenly yells! Why, he knows those rascals, too, for his kinsman, Lord Guncelin of Laasan, is also after the hook-nose and the pipsqueak for a robbery they committed in Strzegom. Oh, these twists of fate ... And it gets better – you haven't heard anything yet. I'm just about to set off from Ziębice when my servant informs me that some characters are hanging around the wagon. So I lie in wait and what do I see? That hook-nose and that great simpleton! Can you believe it? What impudent scoundrels.'

The tax collector choked in indignation. Reynevan nodded and swallowed.

'So I ran as fast as I could to the town hall and submitted a report,' continued the tax collector. 'They've probably already been caught; the torturer is stretching them on the wheel in a dungeon as we speak. And do you see the scheme here? Those two scoundrels and that third one, the whippersnapper, were surely spying for the Raubritters and telling the gang who to waylay. I feared they were already lying in wait for me somewhere on the road. And my escort, as you see, is barely adequate! The bloody Ziębice knighthood prefers tournaments, banquets, and dances, blow them! So I'm afeared, for I want to live, and it would be a shame for this coffer containing more than five hundred grzywna to fall into those bandits' hands when it's meant for a holy cause.'

'Of course it would be a shame,' threw in the goliard. 'And the cause is both holy and good. Which is why I advised you, sir, to avoid the main roads and steal through the forest unseen, to reach Bardo in no time.'

'And may God bless us and keep us,' said the tax collector, raising his eyes to the heavens. 'And the patron saints of tax collectors, Adauctus and Matthew. And Our Lady of Bardo, who's famous for her miracles.'

'Amen, amen,' chimed in the pilgrims walking beside the wagon. 'Praise be the Blessed Virgin Mary, guardian and intercessor!'

'Amen!' called the Friars Minor in unison, walking on the other side.

'Amen,' added Sir Hartwig, and the plain Jane crossed herself.

'Amen,' said the tax collector, closing the subject. 'Bardo's a holy place, m'Lord Hagenau, clearly favoured by Our Lady. Did you know that she's said to have appeared again on Bardo Mount? And weeping again, as she was in the year 1400. Some say it is a harbinger of misfortune that will soon visit Bardo and the whole of Silesia. Others say the Blessed Virgin is weeping because faith is weakening and the Schism is spreading. The Hussites—'

'You never stop,' interrupted the goliard. 'You're always sniffing out Hussites and heresy. Could the Blessed Virgin Mary be weeping for other reasons altogether? Perhaps her tears fall because she sees priests engaged in simony, lecherous debauchery and thievery rather than praying and living in poverty, and the Church of Rome wielding power and spoiling to enter war and politics instead of serving the faithful? Not to mention apostasy and heresy, for what is acting contrary to the Gospels if not heresy? Perhaps Our Lady weeps at the sight of the holy sacraments turned into a conjuring trick at the hands of sinful priests. Perhaps she shares the outrage and sadness felt by many when they see the Pope, who is wealthier than the magnates, building the Church of Saint Peter not with his own money, but with the money of the impoverished faithful?'

'In sooth,' the tax collector said with a wry smile, 'harsh, harsh words, Master Raabe. But I would say that they could be applied to yourself, since you are not without sin, either. You talk like a politician, not to say a priest, rather than doing what befits you – busying yourself with lutes and pipes, rhymes and songs.'

'Rhymes and songs, you say?' Tybald Raabe untied his lute from the pommel. 'As you wish!'

The Holy Roman Popes
are Antichrists;
their power comes not from Christ,
but from the Antichrist
by Imperial order!

'A pox on that,' muttered the tax collector, glancing around. 'It was better when you were talking.'

Christ, through your wounds,
give us priests
to speak the truth,
to bury the Antichrist,
to lead us to You!
Poles, Germans,
Whatever your tongue,
if you doubt your speech
and your writings,
Wycliffe will tell the truth!

Will tell the truth . . . Reynevan, engrossed, repeated the words mechanically in his mind. *Where have I heard those words before?*

'You'll get into trouble one day for those rhymes, Master Raabe,' said the tax collector sourly. 'And it surprises me that you listen to it so calmly, Brothers.'

'The truth is often hidden in songs,' said one of the Franciscans with a smile. 'For the truth is the truth. It must not be distorted, it must be borne, though it hurts. And Wycliffe? Why, he went astray, but *libri sunt legendi, non comburendi.*'

'Wycliffe, may the Lord forgive him, was not the first,' added another. 'Our great brother and patron, the Pauper of Assisi, was

337

pained by what is discussed here. One cannot close one's eyes and turn one's head: evil is among us. Priests are drifting away from God, busying themselves with secular matters. Rather than living modestly, they are wealthier than dukes and barons—'

'Indeed, as the Gospel testifies,' added a third, his voice soft, 'Jesus said: *nolite possidere aurum neque argentum neque pecuniam in zonis vestris—*'

'And the words of Jesus cannot be changed or improved by anyone, not even the Pope,' interrupted the fat sergeant, clearing his throat. 'And if he does, then he's not the Pope, but the true Antichrist.'

'Aye,' called the oldest pilgrim, rubbing his nose. 'It is so!'

'Oh, by God!' said the tax collector crossly. 'Be quiet, all of you! What a company I've ended up in! Why, this is sinful talk indeed!'

'You'll be forgiven,' snorted the goliard, tuning his lute. 'After all, you're gathering taxes for a holy cause. Saints Adauctus and Matthew will intercede for you.'

'Did you mark how disdainfully he said that, Sir Reinmar?' asked the tax collector with evident irritation. 'In sooth, we all know that taxes are collected for worthy reasons, that they contribute to the common weal. That we must pay, because that is the order of things! Everybody knows it. And yet everyone hates tax collectors. They see me riding up and flee into the trees. They set dogs on me. They abuse me with profanities. And even those who pay look at me as though I were plague-ridden.'

'It's a hard life,' said the goliard, winking at Reynevan. 'Have you never desired to change it? Having so many opportunities?'

Tybald Raabe turned out to be a perspicacious and quick-witted fellow.

'Don't fidget in the saddle,' he said quietly to Reynevan, riding up very close. 'Put Ziębice out of your mind. Avoid Ziębice.'

'My friends—'

'You heard what the tax collector said,' interrupted the goliard. 'It's a noble thing to help one's friends, but your friends look like people who can cope by themselves. Nothing will happen to your friends in Ziębice, but that town will be your undoing. Ride with us to Bardo, m'Lord Reinmar, and I'll take you from there to Bohemia in person. Why are you staring so? Your brother was a close comrade of mine.'

'Close?'

'Very close. You'd be astonished how much we shared.'

'Nothing astonishes me now.'

'You'd be surprised.'

'If you and Peterlin really were comrades,' Reynevan said a moment later, 'you'll be happy to hear that his murderers have been punished. Kunz Aulock and his entire company are dead.'

'When you live by the sword, you die by the sword,' Tybald Raabe repeated the adage. 'Did they die by your hand, m'Lord Reinmar?'

'Never mind whose.' Reynevan blushed slightly, detecting a note of mockery in the goliard's voice. 'The main thing is they're dead, and Peterlin is avenged.'

Tybald Raabe said nothing for a long time and watched a raven flying over the treetops.

'I'm far from mourning Kyrie-eleison or bewailing Stork,' he said at length. 'May they burn in Hell, they deserve it. But they didn't murder Sir Piotr.'

'Who—' Reynevan spluttered. 'Who then?'

'Plenty would like to know.'

'The Sterczas? Or somebody they incited? Who? Speak!'

'Quiet, m'lord, quiet. Be discreet. Better for it not to reach the wrong ears. I can't tell you more than I heard myself—'

'And what did you hear?'

'That . . . dark forces are mixed up in it.'

Reynevan was silent for a while.

'Dark forces,' he repeated with a sneer. 'Yes, I've also heard that. Peterlin's rivals said it, that he prospered because the Devil helped him in return for selling his soul. And that the Devil would one day carry him off to Hell. Dark and devilish powers, indeed. And to think I considered you, Master Tybald Raabe, a serious and rational fellow.'

'Then I shall remain silent,' said the goliard, shrugging and turning his head away. 'I shan't say another word, m'lord, for fear of disappointing you even more.'

The party stopped for a break beneath a huge, ancient oak full of scampering squirrels. After unhitching the horses from the wagon, the company rested in the shelter of its branches. Soon, as Reynevan had expected, political discussions began again regarding the threat of Hussite heresy arriving from Bohemia and the great crusade that was meant to put an end to that heresy any day now. Typical though the subject was, however, the discussion didn't follow the usual course.

'War,' announced one of the Franciscans unexpectedly, rubbing his pate onto which a squirrel had just dropped an acorn. 'War is evil. For it is said: thou shalt not kill.'

'But in one's own defence?' asked the tax collector. 'Or in defence of one's property?'

'Or in defence of one's faith?'

'Or in defence of one's honour?' said Hartwig of Stietencron, jerking his head up. 'Foolish talk! Honour must be defended and insults are washed clean by blood!'

'Jesus didn't defend himself in Gethsemane,' the Franciscan replied quietly. 'And he made Peter sheathe his sword. Was that shameful?'

'And what does Augustin, a *doctor Ecclesiae*, write in *De civitate Dei*?' shouted one of the pilgrims, demonstrating unexpected scholarship given that the colour of his nose testified rather to other predilections. 'Why, we are discussing a just war. And what is more just than a war against heathenism and heresy? Isn't a war like that pleasing to God? Doesn't it please Him when someone kills His enemies?'

'And what do John Chrysostom and Isidore write?' called another polymath with a similarly blue-and-red nose. 'And Saint

Bernard of Clairvaux? He orders heretics, Moors and heathens killed! He calls them filthy swine. To kill such as them, he says, is not a sin – it glorifies God!'

'Who am I, may God be merciful,' said the Franciscan, putting his hands together in prayer, 'to contradict the saints and Doctors of the Church? Why, I'm not here to enter a dispute. I'm simply repeating the words of Christ on the Mount. He commanded us to love our neighbours and forgive those who trespass against us. To love our enemies and pray for them.'

'And Paul ordered the Ephesians,' added another of the monks, 'to arm themselves against Satan with love and faith, not with spears.'

'And God will also make love and faith vanquish, amen,' said the third Franciscan, crossing himself, 'and bring about reconciliation and *pax Dei* among Christians. For who benefits from the differences between us? The Infidel! Today, we are wrangling with the Czechs over the Word of God and the form of Communion. But what might happen tomorrow? Muhammad and crescent moons on churches!'

The oldest pilgrim snorted. 'Perhaps the scales will also fall from the Czechs' eyes, and they will disavow heresy. Perhaps hunger will help them with that! For the whole of Europe has joined the embargo and prohibited all trade and commerce with the Hussites. And they need arms and powder, salt and food! If it doesn't arrive, they will be weaponless and starving. When their bellies start rumbling, they'll surrender, you'll see.'

'War,' repeated the first Franciscan with emphasis, 'is evil. We've established that. And do you think that blockade accords with Christ's teachings? On the Mount, did Jesus entreat people to starve their neighbours? Passing over our religious differences, the Czechs are Christians, too. This embargo isn't right.'

'True, Brother,' interrupted Tybald Raabe, who was sprawled beneath the oak tree. 'It is not. Also true is that at times, such blockades can cut both ways. Let's hope this one doesn't cost Silesia as much as it does the Czechs.'

'It will be as God decrees,' said the first Franciscan.

For a long while, no one said anything.

The weather began to turn. Clouds, blown by the wind, darkened dangerously and the first drops of rain soon began to fall on hoods, mantles, horses' rumps and the black canvas covering the wagon. Reynevan moved closer to Tybald Raabe and they rode on, stirrup to stirrup.

'That was an interesting conversation,' he said quietly. 'I'm surprised you didn't summarise it all by reading the Four Articles of Prague, like you did in Kromolin. Is the tax collector aware of your opinions, I wonder?'

'He will be,' the goliard replied quietly, 'when the time comes. For as Ecclesiastes says, there is a time to keep silence, and a time to speak; a time to receive, and a time to lose; a time to keep, and a time to cast away; a time to love, and a time to hate; a time of war, and a time of peace. There is a time for everything.'

'This time, I agree with you completely.'

At the crossroads, among a bright birch wood, stood a stone penitential cross, one of Silesia's numerous reminders of crimes past and belated contrition. Directly opposite was a sandy highway, and dark forest tracks led in the other directions. The wind jerked the treetops and tossed dry leaves around. A fine rain was driving into their faces.

'There is a time for everything,' said Reynevan to Tybald Raabe, 'as Ecclesiastes reminds us. Now the time has come for me to say goodbye. I'm going back to Ziębice. Say nothing.'

The tax collector was watching them. As were the Friars Minor, the pilgrims, the soldiers, Hartwig of Stietencron and his daughter.

'I cannot abandon friends who may be in trouble,' continued Reynevan. 'It isn't right. Friendship is a great and wonderful thing.'

'Did I say anything?' asked the goliard.

'I'm going.'

'Go, then, m'lord,' he said. 'But if you happen to change your plans, if you prefer Bardo and the way to Bohemia, you'll easily catch up with us. We'll be riding slowly, and we mean to stop for a long break near Ścibor's Clearing. Will you remember it?'

'I shall.'

The farewell was perfunctory, the customary good wishes for happiness and divine *auxilia*. Reynevan reined his horse around. Seared into his memory was the look Stietencron's daughter gave him on parting. A childish, cow-eyed look, from watery eyes full of longing under badly plucked eyebrows.

What a fright, he thought as he galloped through the wind and the rain. *What a freak. But at least she can discern and appreciate a good-looking man.*

His horse had gone about a furlong before Reynevan thought it over and realised how stupid he was.

When he ran into them near a large oak, he wasn't even especially surprised.

'Oh! Oh!' yelled Scharley, reining in his prancing horse. 'God bless my soul! If it isn't our Reynevan!'

They dismounted and a moment later, Reynevan was groaning in the warm-hearted but rib-threatening embrace of Samson Honey-Eater.

'Well, I never,' said Scharley in a slightly altered voice. 'He escaped from the Ziębice assassins, and from Lord Biberstein and Stolz Castle. All credit to you. What a talented young man he is, Samson. He's barely been with me a fortnight, and see how much he's learned! He's become as crafty as a Dominican, the bugger!'

'He's travelling to Ziębice,' observed Samson, his cool tone tinged with a hint of emotion, 'which testifies conclusively against cunning. And good sense. Well, Reinmar?'

'I consider the Ziębice affair over,' said Reynevan, clenching his teeth. 'Nothing connects me to Ziębice now, or links me to the past. But I feared they had caught you there.'

'Them? Catch us?' said Scharley. 'You must be joking!'

'I'm glad to see you,' Reynevan said. 'I'm really delighted.'

'We'll have a good laugh when we share our stories, no doubt.'

The rain had grown stronger and the wind was tossing the trees around.

'Scharley,' said Samson. 'I don't think there's any point continuing to follow the trail. What we planned no longer has either purpose or sense. Reinmar is free, nothing is holding him back, so let's spur our horses and ride towards Opava and the Hungarian border. I suggest we leave Silesia and everything that's Silesian behind us. Including our desperate plans.'

'What plans?' asked Reynevan curiously.

'No matter. Scharley, what do you say? I advise abandoning our plans. And terminating the contract.'

'I don't understand what you're talking about.'

'Later, Reinmar. Scharley?'

The penitent cleared his throat loudly.

'Terminate the contract?' he said, parroting Samson.

'Indeed.'

Scharley was evidently fighting against himself.

'Night's falling,' he finally said, 'and the night will bring a solution. *La notte*, as they say in Italy, *porta la consiglia*. On condition, I shall add, that we spend the night in a warm, dry, safe place. To horse, lads, and follow me.'

'Where to?' Reynevan asked.

'You'll see.

It was almost dark when some fences and buildings loomed up in front of them. Dogs began to bark as they approached.

'What is it?' asked Samson apprehensively. 'Could it be—'

'It is Dębowiec,' interrupted Scharley. 'A grange belonging to the Cistercian monastery in Kamieniec. When I was locked away with the penitents, they sometimes made me work here as part of my punishment, which is why I know that it's a warm, dry place, perfect for a good night's sleep. And in the morning, we'll rustle up some grub.'

'I understand that the Cistercians know you, so when you ask them to put us up—'

'It's not as simple as that,' the penitent interrupted again. 'Tether the horses. We'll leave them here, in the forest. And you two follow me. On tiptoe.'

The Cistercian dogs had calmed down and were barking more quietly and unconvincingly when Scharley nimbly broke a plank in the wall of the barn. A moment later, they were in the dark, dry, warm interior, which smelled pleasantly of straw and hay. And soon, after climbing a ladder to the hayloft, they were burrowing into the hay.

'Let's get to sleep,' muttered Scharley, rustling. 'Pity to do it on an empty stomach, but I suggest we don't think about food until morning, then we can steal some provisions, if only a few. Reinmar – can you control your primitive urges . . . Reinmar?'

Reynevan was asleep.

Chapter Twenty-Two

In which it turns out that our heroes made a poor choice of where to sleep. It also confirms – although the details of the matter won't be revealed until much later – the famous truth that in historical times, even the tiniest incident may have historically significant consequences.

Reynevan, in spite of his fatigue, slept badly and restlessly. Before falling asleep, he thrashed around in the prickly, thistly hay and wriggled between Scharley and Samson, earning himself a few curses and shoves. Then he moaned in his sleep, seeing Peterlin pierced by many swords with blood flowing from his mouth. He sighed on seeing a naked Adèle of Stercza sitting astride Duke Jan of Ziębice, and moaned on seeing the duke stroking and squeezing her rhythmically bouncing breasts. Then, to his horror and despair, Adèle's place on the duke was taken by Fair Nicolette – Katarzyna of Biberstein – who rode the tireless Piast with no less energy and enthusiasm than Adèle. And with no less satisfaction at the climax.

Afterwards, there were half-naked lasses with hair flowing behind them, flying on brooms across a sky lit by the glow of fires, among flocks of cawing crows. A wallcreeper scurried over a building's façade, silently opening its beak, and a force of hooded knights galloped in the fields, yelling incomprehensibly. There was a *turris fulgurata*, a tower hit by lightning and falling apart, with a person falling from it. Another person was running over the snow, on fire, engulfed in flames. Then a battle, the roar of cannons, the firing of handgonnes, the thudding of hooves, the neighing of horses, the clanking of weapons, the cries . . .

He was awoken by the thudding of hooves, the neighing of horses, the clank of weapons and cries. Just in time, Samson covered Reynevan's mouth with a hand.

The courtyard of the grange was swarming with foot soldiers and riders.

'We've landed ourselves in it,' muttered Scharley, observing the parade ground through a slit between the planks. 'Like a hedgehog falling into shit.'

'Is it the search party from Ziębice? After me?' whispered Reynevan.

'It's worse,' Scharley replied. 'It's a bloody council, dammit. I can see a great crowd of people, some of them magnates and knights.'

'Let's do a runner while we can.'

'Regrettably,' Samson gestured with his head towards the sheepfold, 'it's too late. The whole area's staked out to stop the uninvited from entering. And I doubt they'll want to let anybody out, either. We woke up too late. It's a wonder we weren't roused by the smell, they've been roasting meat since dawn . . .'

Indeed, the smell of roast meat drifting from the courtyard was getting stronger and stronger.

'Those soldiers bear the bishop's livery,' said Reynevan, now looking through his own knothole. 'It might be the Inquisition.'

'Marvellous,' muttered Scharley. 'Fucking marvellous. Our only hope is if no one looks in here.'

'Regrettably,' repeated Samson, 'that's a vain hope, because they're heading here right now. Let's bury ourselves in the hay. If they find us, we'll pretend to be idiots.'

'Easy for you to say.'

Reynevan dug down through the hay to the planks that formed the ceiling of the space below the hayloft, found a crack and put his eye to it. He saw pikemen flooding into the barn and – to his growing alarm – searching it thoroughly, even plunging their glaives into sheaves of corn and the straw in hay-racks. One climbed the ladder, but contented himself with a cursory glance around rather than a full search.

'Praise and thanks,' whispered Scharley, 'to eternal soldierly "couldn't-give-a-fuckery".'

That wasn't the end of their troubles, unfortunately. Servants and monks poured in after the pikemen moved on to clear and sweep the dirt floor. Branches of fragrant fir were strewn around and benches hauled in. Tables were constructed from pine trestles and planks, then covered in canvas. Even before kegs and mugs had been brought in, Reynevan knew what was about to happen.

Some time passed before the magnates entered the barn. Their colourful clothes, gleaming armour, jewels, gold chains and buckles were incongruous in the squalid interior.

'A pox on it . . .' whispered Scharley, his eye also pressed against a crack. 'They've decided to hold a secret council in this very barn. It isn't just anyone, either – that's Konrad, Bishop of Wrocław, in person. And beside him is Ludwik, Duke of Brzeg and Legnica—'

'Quiet!' hissed Samson.

Reynevan had also recognised both Piasts. Konrad – for eight years Bishop of Wrocław – had a surprisingly knightly build, which was remarkable considering his love of drinking, gluttony and lechery. The credit was due no doubt to his robust constitution and healthy Piast blood, since other dignitaries who reached Konrad's age, even those who boozed less and whored more seldom, by then had bellies down to their knees, bags under their eyes and purple noses – if they still had noses. The forty-year-old Ludwik of Brzeg, however, resembled the King Arthur of miniatures – his long, wavy hair framed, like a halo, a face as sensitive as a poet's, yet still manly.

'Please sit down, noble lords,' said the bishop, his voice surprisingly resonant, like a young man's. 'Although it's a barn not a palace, please enjoy our hospitality, and we shall compensate for the simple vittles with Hungarian wine, easily as good as what you would drink at the court of King Sigismund in Buda. Which the royal chancellor, the honourable Master Schlick, will confirm – if, naturally, he shares that opinion.'

A very serious and wealthy-looking young man gave a bow. The coat of arms on his doublet showed a silver pile on a red field and three rings of reverse tincture.

'Kaspar Schlick,' whispered Scharley. 'Sigismund's personal secretary, confidant and advisor. A spectacular career for one so young . . .'

Reynevan pulled a straw from his nose, stifling a sneeze with a superhuman effort. Samson hissed in warning.

'I extend a particularly hearty welcome,' continued Bishop Konrad, 'to His Eminence Giordano Orsini, member of the Sacred College of Cardinals, now legate to His Holiness Pope Martin. I also welcome the representative of the State of the Teutonic Order, the noble Gottfried Rodenberg, the Vogt of Lipa. And I welcome our esteemed guests from Poland, Moravia and Bohemia. Welcome and please be seated.'

'They've even brought a fucking Teutonic Knight here,' muttered Scharley, trying to enlarge the hole in the floor with a knife. 'The Vogt of Lipa. Where is that? Must be Prussia. And who are those others? I see Sir Pûta of Častolovice . . . That broad-shouldered man with a black lion on a golden field is Albrecht of Kolditz, the Starosta of Świdnica . . . And the man with the Odrzywąs in his coat of arms must be one of the lords of Kravaře—'

'Be quiet,' hissed Samson. 'And stop whittling, or they'll discover us from splinters falling into their cups . . .'

Down below, cups were indeed being raised and toasts drunk. Chancellor Schlick praised the wine, but it wasn't clear if it was only out of diplomatic courtesy. The men sitting at the tables appeared to know one another, with a few exceptions.

'Who is your young companion, *Monsignore* Orsini?' Bishop Konrad asked, taking an interest.

'He's my secretary,' replied the papal legate, a small, grey-haired old man with a kindly smile. 'His name is Nicholaus of Cusa. I predict a great career for him in the service of our Church. *Vero*, he has rendered me a great service in my mission, for no one can invalidate heretical theories – especially Lollard and Hussite ones – like him. His Eminence the Bishop of Krakow can confirm.'

'The Bishop of Krakow ...' hissed Scharley. 'Bugger ... That's ...'

'Zbigniew Oleśnicki,' confirmed Samson in a whisper. 'In collusion with Konrad in Silesia. Dammit, we're in the shit. Be as quiet as mice, because if they discover us, we're done for.'

'If so,' continued Bishop Konrad below them, 'perhaps the Reverend Nicholaus of Cusa will begin? For that is precisely the purpose of our gathering: to put an end to the Hussite plague. While we eat and drink, let the young priest debunk the teachings of Huss. If you please, Reverend Cusa.'

The servants carried in a roast ox on a wooden board and placed it on the table. Daggers and knives flashed and began carving. Meanwhile, the young Nicholaus of Cusa stood up and addressed the gathering. And although his eyes shone at the sight of the roast, the young priest's voice didn't tremble.

'A spark is a small thing,' he gushed, 'but when it touches something dry, it can destroy walls, cities and great forests. Thus, bad teachings begin with one man and barely two or three listeners at first; but slowly the cancer spreads through the body, and as they say, one bad apple spoils the whole barrel. We should extinguish the spark as soon as it appears, and cut out the rotten flesh, and drive the lousy sheep from the flock, so that we will not perish ...'

'Cut out the rotten flesh,' repeated Bishop Konrad, tearing off with his teeth a hunk of beef, dripping grease and bloody juices. 'You speak well, very well, young Father Nicholaus. It's a matter of surgery! Iron, sharp iron, is the best medicine for the Hussite cancer. Cut it out! Slaughter the heretics, I say, slaughter them mercilessly!'

The men gathered at the table expressed their approval, mumbling with full mouths and waving the bones they were chewing on. The ox slowly transformed into a skeleton, and Nicholaus of

Cusa debunked in turn all the Hussite errors, revealing all the absurdities of Wycliffe's teachings: denying transubstantiation, repudiating the existence of purgatory, rejecting the cult of the saints and their images, renouncing auricular confession. He finally reached communion *sub utraque specie* and debunked that, too.

'Communion for the faithful should only be in the form of bread. For Matthew says: Give us this day our daily bread, and Luke says: He took bread, gave a blessing, broke it and gave it to them. Where is there a mention of wine? Verily, one and only one custom has been passed and confirmed by the Church: that the common man should receive communion under one kind. And that is sufficient for all believers!'

'Amen,' concluded Ludwik of Brzeg, licking his fingers.

'For all I care,' Bishop Konrad roared like a lion, tossing down a bone, 'the Hussites can receive it up the arse! Those whoresons want to rob me! They clamour for the absolute secularisation of Church property and for the evangelical poverty of the clergy, which means taking it from us and dividing it up among themselves. Oh, by the Passion of Christ, that cannot be! Over my dead body! But better over their heretical carcasses! May they perish!'

'For now, they live,' said Půta of Častolovice, the Starosta of Kłodzko, whom Reynevan and Scharley had seen scarcely five days before at the joust in Ziębice. 'For now, they are alive and well, not turning on each other as was predicted after Žižka's death.'

'The danger is growing, not diminishing,' thundered Albrecht of Kolditz, Starosta and Hetman of the Duchy of Wrocław-Świdnica. 'My spies report closer and closer collaboration between Prague and Korybut with Žižka's heirs. Lord Půta is right – there is much talk of joint crusades. Whoever expected a miracle after Žižka's death was mistaken.'

'Look,' said Kaspar Schlick, 'Prester John won't be arriving any time soon from India with thousands of horses and elephants to solve the matter of the Bohemian Schism on our behalf. We – and we alone – must put an end to it. King Sigismund sent me here for that very reason. We must know what we can realistically hope for in Silesia, Moravia, the Duchy of Opava and Poland. The latter, I hope, will soon be explained to us by His Eminence the Bishop of Krakow. After all, his intransigent stance regarding the Polish supporters of Wycliffism is known far and wide, and his presence here proves his support for the politics of the Holy Roman Emperor—'

'We know in Roma with what enthusiasm and devotion Bishop Zbigniew fights,' interrupted Giordano Orsini, 'and we shall not fail to reward it.'

'Thus,' asked Kaspar Schlick, 'may I assume that the Kingdom of Poland actively supports the policies and initiatives of King Sigismund?'

'I would be most glad to hear the answer to that question,' said the Teutonic Knight, Gottfried of Rodenberg, who was lounging at the table, 'and to learn when we can expect the active participation of the Polish army in the anti-Hussite crusade. I'd like to hear that from someone objective. So, please go on, *Monsignore* Orsini. We are all ears!'

'Indeed,' added Schlick, smiling, keeping his eyes on Bishop Oleśnicki. 'We are all ears. How went your mission at the court of Jogaila?'

'I spoke at length to King Władysław,' Orsini said in a somewhat sorrowful voice, 'but with little effect. On behalf of and with the authorisation of His Holiness, I gave the King of Poland a relic of no little importance – one of the nails that held our Saviour to the cross. *Vero*, if such a relic is incapable of inspiring a Christian monarch to join an anti-heretical crusade, then—'

'He is not a Christian monarch.' Bishop Konrad finished the sentence for the legate.

'You've noticed?' The Teutonic Knight grimaced scornfully. 'Better late than never!'

'So the true faith cannot count on Polish support?' asked Ludwik of Brzeg.

'The Kingdom of Poland and King Władysław,' said Bishop Oleśnicki, speaking for the first time, 'support the true faith and the Church of Peter using the best of all possible means – namely Peter's Pence. None of the kings represented here can say that about himself.'

'Bah!' Duke Ludwik waved a hand contemptuously. 'Say what you like, Jogaila's no bloody Christian. He's a neophyte with the Devil still lurking in him.'

'His heathenism,' Gottfried Rodenberg said, losing his temper, 'most clearly manifests itself in his fierce hatred towards the entire German nation, which is a mainstay of the Church, and in particular to us, the Knights Hospitaller of the Blessed Virgin Mary, *antemurale christianitatis*, who have defended the Catholic faith from pagans with our lives for two hundred years! And it is true that this Jogaila is a neophyte and an idolater, who, in order to oppress our Order, is liable to ally himself not just with the Hussites, but with Hell itself. Oh, verily, we were not meant to be debating today about how to convince Jogaila and Poland to join the crusade, but to return to the issue which we discussed at Epiphany in Pressburg two years ago: how to launch a crusade on Poland itself, and tear to pieces that misbegotten creation, that bastard Union of Horodło!'

'Your speech,' said Bishop Oleśnicki very coldly, 'is unworthy of somebody who considers himself the Bulwark of Christendom!'

'The fact is, Bishop,' interrupted Půta of Častolovice, 'that your king supports the Hussites both openly and secretly. We understand that by doing so, he holds the Teutonic Knights in check, and that he must do so is no surprise to me, frankly. But the results of such politics may turn out to be fatal for the whole of Christian Europe. You all know that.'

'We do, unfortunately,' confirmed Ludwik of Brzeg, 'and we can already see the consequences. Just look where the Poles are, where there are Polish coats of arms and Polish battle cries. Are

Jogaila's edicts, declarations and orders supporting the true faith? He's pulling the wool over our eyes, simple as that.'

'Meanwhile, lead, horses, arms, food and all kinds of goods pass endlessly into Bohemia from Poland,' added Albrecht of Kolditz gloomily. 'What then, Bishop? You send Peter's Pence, which you praise so much, to Rome down one road and powder and balls for Hussite cannons down another? Quite like your king, who, they say, runs with the hare and hunts with the hounds.'

'I also worry about certain matters,' admitted Bishop Oleśnicki a moment later. 'So help me God, I am making every effort to improve things, but it's a waste of breath to endlessly repeat the same counterarguments. Hear this, my lords: my presence here is the proof of the Kingdom of Poland's loyalty.'

'Which we value,' said Bishop Konrad, slapping a hand down on the table. 'But what is your Kingdom of Poland today? Are you it, honourable Bishop Oleśnicki? Or the Lithuanian Prince Witold? Or one of the aristocratic families? Who reigns in Poland? For it's certainly not King Władysław, a decrepit old man who is unable even to rule his own wife. Perhaps Sophia and her lovers are in charge.'

'*Vero, vero,*' Legate Orsini said sadly. 'It's a shame for such a king to be *cornuto*—'

'This is meant to be a serious gathering,' said the Bishop of Krakow with a frown, 'and we're wasting time gossiping like students in a brothel.'

'You will not deny that Sophia is cuckolding Jogaila and bringing shame on him,' Bishop Konrad said.

'I shall, because it is *vana rumoris*. Rumours spread and fuelled by Malbork.'

The Teutonic Knight got up from the table, red-faced and ready to make a rejoinder, but Kaspar Schlick restrained him with a rapid gesture.

'*Pax!*' he said firmly. 'Let us drop this subject, for we have graver ones to discuss. As I understand it, for the time being we cannot count on Polish armed support in the crusade, which is regrettable. But, by the shells of Saint James, see to it, Bishop Oleśnicki, that the points of the Treaty of Kežmarok and Jogaila's edicts from Trembowla and Wieluń are indeed respected. Those edicts are meant to close the borders and threaten to punish anyone who trades with the Hussites, yet goods and arms, as the Lord Starosta of Świdnica rightly observed, continue flowing into Bohemia from Poland—'

'I gave my word,' Oleśnicki interrupted impatiently, 'that I would do my utmost. And my promises are not hollow. Fraternising with Czech heretics will be punished in Poland; there are royal edicts, *iura sunt clara*. I shall, however, remind the Starosta and Hetman of Świdnica and the Right Reverend Bishop of Wrocław of the words of the Bible: "And why beholdest thou the mote that is in thy brother's eye, but considerest not the beam that is in thine own eye?" Half of Silesia trades with the Hussites and no one opposes it!'

'Honourable Father Oleśnicki, you are mistaken,' said Bishop Konrad, leaning across the table. 'I assure you; harsh measures have already been taken, not in the form of edicts and declarations, but some *defensores haereticorum* will experience first-hand what it means to consort with heretics. And the others will be quaking in their boots, I can assure you. Then the world will learn the difference between genuine and feigned action. Between a real fight for faith and pulling the wool over people's eyes.'

The bishop spoke so scathingly, with such bitter hatred in his voice, that Reynevan felt the hairs stand up on the back of his neck. His heart began to beat so hard, he was afraid the men below would hear. But they had other things on their minds. Once again, Kaspar Schlick dampened down the disputes and called for a calm, thorough discussion regarding the situation in Bohemia. The truculent bishops and nobles kept quiet and the previously silent Bohemians and Moravians spoke up. Neither Reynevan, Scharley or Samson knew any of them, but it was fairly obvious that they were lords from the circle of the Plzeň Landfriede and the Moravian nobility loyal to Sigismund, and loyal to Jan of Kravaře, the Lord of Jičín. It soon turned out that one of them was the famous Jan of Kravaře himself.

It was Jan of Kravaře, well built, black-haired and black-moustached, with a complexion that spoke of more time spent in the saddle than at table, who had most to say about the current situation in Bohemia. No one interrupted him. When he spoke, in a calm, impassive voice, everybody leaned forward and stared silently at the map of the Kingdom of Bohemia spread out over the table after the ox's skeleton had been removed. From above, the details of the map couldn't be seen, hence Reynevan had to rely on his imagination when the Lord of Jičín spoke of attacks on Polish strongholds, some more successful than others, and about campaigns in the west and the south.

'Oh, I really need a piss,' whispered Scharley. 'I can't hold it in . . .'

'Perhaps,' Samson whispered back, 'the thought that if they discover you the next time you piss you'll be hanging from a noose, will help you to hold on.'

Down below, they had begun to talk about the Duchy of Opava. Which sparked another quarrel.

'I consider Přemysl of Opava an unreliable ally,' declared Bishop Konrad.

'Why?' Kaspar Schlick raised his head. 'Because he has just married the sister of Sigismund Korybut, that thorn in our flesh? I assure you, gentlemen, that nothing will come of those family connections. The Jagiellonians are a rapacious family; they bicker more often than they cooperate. Přemysl of Opava will not ally with Sigismund Korybut simply because they are now brothers-in-law.'

'Přemysl is already allied,' countered the bishop. 'It happened in March, in Hlubočky. And in Olomouc, on Saint Urban's day. Indeed, Opava and the Moravian lords are quick to enter agreements with heretics. What do you say to that, Sir Jan of Kravaře?'

'Don't speak ill of either my father-in-law or the Moravian nobility,' snapped the Lord of Jičín. 'And know that thanks to the agreements between Hlubočky and Olomouc, we now have peace in Moravia.'

'But the Hussites have free trade routes from Poland.' Kaspar Schlick smiled superciliously. 'You understand very little of politics, Sir Jan.'

Jan of Kravaře's weather-beaten face flushed in anger. 'If Sigismund had supported us when Puchała marched on us, there would have been no need to negotiate.'

'Vain speculation.' Schlick shrugged. 'The main thing is that as a result of your negotiations, the Hussites now have free trade routes through Opava and Moravia, and are sacking and terrorising the entire region. It's they who have peace there, not you. You struck a lousy deal, Sir Jan—'

'Plundering raids are not just a Hussite speciality,' the Bishop of Wrocław interjected with an evil smile. 'I gave the heretics what for at Broumov and Trutnov in 1421. Czech corpses were piled six feet high and the sky was black from burnings. And whoever we didn't kill or burn we marked in the Silesian way – if you see a Czech without a nose, hand or foot, you can be certain they were taken during our glorious raid. Well, gentlemen, shall we repeat that enterprise? The year of 1425 is a holy year – perhaps we should honour it by wiping out the Hussites? I don't like needless talk, negotiating with rats or making peace with them! Well, Sir Albrecht? Sir Pûta? If each of you add two hundred lances and infantry with firearms to my forces, we'll teach the heretics some manners. The sky will blaze red from Trutnov to Hradec Králové. I promise—'

'Don't make promises,' interrupted Kaspar Schlick. 'And retain your enthusiasm for the appropriate moment. For the crusade. This is not about plundering raids. Or severing hands and feet, for King Sigismund has no need of handless and footless subjects. And His Holiness doesn't wish Czechs to be massacred, but to be returned to the bosom of the true Church. And the issue is not about murdering civilians, but destroying the Taborite–Orebite army thoroughly enough for them to agree to negotiate. Thus, let us get down to the matter at hand. What kind of force will Silesia field when the crusade is announced? Be exact.'

'You're more precise than a Jew,' said the bishop, smiling wryly. 'But if that is your wish, by all means: I myself shall field seventy lances with suitable infantry and firearms. Konrad Kantner, my brother, your future father-in-law, will field sixty mounted men. I know that Ludwik of Brzeg, present here, will do likewise. Ruprecht of Lubin and his brother Ludwik will muster forty. Bernard of Niemodlin ...'

Reynevan didn't even know when he'd nodded off. He was woken by a shove. It was dark.

'We're getting out of here,' muttered Samson.

'Have we been sleeping?'

'Soundly.'

'Is the council over?'

'For the present it is, but speak in a whisper – there are guards outside the barn.'

'Where's Scharley?'

'He's sneaked out to the horses. Now I'm going. And then you. Count to a hundred and walk through the courtyard. Take a sheaf of straw and walk slowly, with your head down, like a stable lad. Turn right after the last cottage and head into the trees. Got it?'

'Of course.'

And everything would have gone smoothly but for the fact that as he passed the last cottage, Reynevan heard his name.

A few soldiers were hanging around the field, but Reynevan slipped behind a shadowy awning, climbed on a bench and stood on tiptoes to peer into the room through the dirty oiled paper in the windows. In the poor lighting, he could make out three men talking. One was Konrad, Bishop of Wrocław.

'I am most grateful for the information, m'lord. It would have been difficult for us to obtain it ourselves. The merchants' greed is their undoing, and in commerce it's difficult to keep secrets, for there are too many go-betweens. Sooner or later, it comes out that somebody is trading with the Hussites. But it's much more difficult with nobility and burghers, they have to be wary of the Inquisition and know what befalls heretics and Hussite sympathisers. Without the help of Prague, we would never have picked up the trail of men like Albrecht of Bart or Piotr of Bielawa.'

The man sitting with his back to the window spoke with an accent Reynevan knew at once. He was a Czech.

'Piotr of Bielawa could keep a secret,' the Czech said. 'Even in Prague, few of us were aware of him. But you know what it's like: a fellow is cautious among foes, but tongues loosen among friends. Perhaps at this gathering of friends, some incautious word has slipped out about me, Bishop?'

'You offend me with such conjecture,' said Konrad proudly. 'I'm not a child. It is not without reason that this council is being held here in Dębowiec, out of the way. Furthermore, all those taking part here are true friends and allies. Even so, none of them saw you.'

'And such caution is creditable. For believe me, there are Hussite ears at Świdnica Castle, at Lord Kolditz's and at Lord Půta's in Kłodzko. I would also advise the utmost caution with regard to the Moravian lords here. No offence, but they are wont to change their loyalties. Sir Jan of Kravařě has plenty of kinsmen and relatives among the Hussites . . .'

The third man present spoke. He was sitting closest to the cresset and with his long, black hair and bird-like face, Reynevan thought he resembled a huge wallcreeper.

'We are cautious,' said the Wallcreeper. 'And vigilant. And we are capable of punishing treachery, believe me.'

'I do, I do,' snorted the Czech. 'Why wouldn't I, after what befell Piotr of Bielawa and Lord Bart and those other merchants Pfefferkorn, Neumarkt and Throst? A demon, an angel of vengeance, is abroad in Silesia, striking from a clear sky at high noon. People are frightened—'

'And so they should be,' the bishop interrupted calmly.

'And the results can be seen with the naked eye.' The Czech nodded. 'The Karkonosze passes are deserted, very few merchants travel to Bohemia. Our spies don't go on missions to Silesia as willingly as they once did, and the formerly clamorous emissaries from Hradec and Tábor have also quietened down somewhat. People talk, the matter becomes a rumour and grows like a snowball. Apparently, Piotr of Bielawa was cruelly stabbed to death. They say not even a sacred space could save Pfefferkorn, for he met his death in a church. Hanusz Throst made off at night, but the angel of vengeance kills not only at noon, but also in the darkness. And the fact that I've given you their names, Bishop, shows they are on my conscience.'

'I can hear your confession right now, if you want.'

'Thank you,' replied the Czech, who must have heard the mockery but ignored it. 'But I am, as you know, a Calixtine and Utraquist, so I do not acknowledge auricular confession.'

'That's your business and your loss,' Bishop Konrad commented coolly and a little disdainfully. 'I wasn't offering you a ritual but peace of mind, which doesn't depend on doctrine. It is your right to decline it, but then you'll have to cope with your conscience by yourself. But I will say that the deceased were at fault. They had sinned. And as Paul wrote to the Romans: "For the wages of sin is death."'

'Regarding sinners,' said the Wallcreeper, 'it is also written there as follows: "Let their table be made a snare, and a trap, and a stumbling block, and a recompense unto them."'

'Amen,' the Czech added. 'I regret that the angel or demon only watches over Silesia, for there's no shortage of sinners back home in Bohemia. Some of us there, in Golden Prague, pray morning and evening for certain sinners to be struck down by holy lightning or caught by a demon. If you want, I'll give you a list.'

'Why would you give us a list?' asked the Wallcreeper calmly. 'The people of whom we speak were guilty and deserved their punishment, and God punished them. Pfefferkorn was killed by a lessee, jealous of his wife, who then hanged himself from remorse. Piotr of Bielawa was killed in a rage by his brother, who is an insane magician and adulterer. Albrecht of Bart was killed by Jews out of envy, because he was wealthier than them. Several have been arrested and will confess under torture. The merchant Throst was killed by highwaymen; he liked to roam around at night and brought it on himself. The merchant Neumarkt—'

'Enough, enough,' the bishop said, waving a hand. 'Stop, don't bore our guest. We have a more important subject to discuss, so let's return to it – namely which of the Prague noblemen are ready to collaborate and negotiate.'

'Forgive my frankness,' said the Czech, after a moment's silence, 'but it would be better if Silesia were represented by one of the dukes. I know we need balance, but in Prague we've had so much trouble and strife thanks to radicals and zealots that the clergy provoke negative connotations in Bohemia—'

'Something is out of kilter, m'lord,' said Bishop Konrad, 'if you conflate Catholic clergymen with heretics.'

'Many consider,' continued the Czech, unperturbed, 'that zealotry is zealotry, the Roman kind being no better than the Taborite. Hence—'

Bishop Konrad cut him off harshly. 'I am King Sigismund's viceroy in Silesia and a Piast of royal blood. All the Silesian dukes and Silesian nobility accepted my leadership, electing me Landeshauptmann. I have borne that exacting duty from Saint Mark's Day, *Anno Domini* 1422, long enough for it to be known even in Bohemia.'

'All the same—'

'There is no "all the same".' The bishop cut him off again. 'I govern in Silesia. If you wish to negotiate, do so with me. Take it or leave it.'

The Czech was silent for a long time.

'Oh, Reverend,' he finally said, 'how you adore governing, meddling in politics, sticking your fingers into everything. Verily, it will be a dreadful blow for you when somebody finally snatches that power from your greedy paws. How will you survive? Can you imagine it? No politics! Nothing from Matins to Compline but prayers, penance, teaching and charity. How does that appeal to you, Bishop?'

'It clearly appeals to you,' the Piast declared haughtily, 'but as a wise cardinal once said, the barking of curs won't stop the caravan. This world is and will be ruled by Rome. I'd say that's how God wants it, but I won't take His name in vain. So I'll say that it is meet for power to be given to the most competent. And who, m'lord, is more competent than Rome? You, perhaps?'

'Some powerful king or emperor will come along,' said the Czech, not giving up, 'and then it will end—'

'It'll end in humble pie,' the bishop cut him off again, 'as it did at Canossa for King Heinrich IV when he demanded that the clergy, including Pope Gregory VII, stop meddling in politics and busy themselves only with prayer from Matins to Compline. That self-righteous prig stood in the snow for two days while Pope Gregory enjoyed the delights of the table and the renowned charms of Margravine Matilda. That should be a lesson to all, not to raise one's voice against the Church. We shall always rule, until the end of the world—'

'And even beyond,' interrupted the Wallcreeper scathingly. 'For even in the New Jerusalem, in a city of gold behind walls of jasper, someone must still wield power, after all.'

'Quite so,' snorted the bishop. 'Our enemies will endure penance, shame, snow and frozen heels. But for us a warm chamber, mulled Tuscan wine and a willing margravine in a feather bed.'

'At this very moment, in Bohemia,' said the Czech softly, 'the Orphans and Taborites are sharpening their blades, readying their flails and greasing the axes of their battle wagons. They'll soon be here, and they'll take everything from you. You'll lose your palaces, wine, margravines, power, and ultimately your reportedly competent heads. It will happen. I would say that God clearly wants it, but I won't take His name in vain. Instead, I say: let's do something about it. Let's take countermeasures.'

'I give my word that Holy Father Martin—'

'Oh, forget the Holy Father, King Sigismund, all the dukes of the Reich and the rest of that European shambles!' the Czech burst out. 'Another bevy of legates is already embezzling money collected for a crusade! For God's sake! You order us to wait until we reach some agreement, while death stares us in the face every day!'

'You cannot accuse us of idleness, m'lord,' said the Wallcreeper. 'We are taking action – you admitted as much yourself. We are praying zealously, our prayers are being heard, sinners are being punished. But there are many sinners and their numbers are ever growing. We are asking for further help from you.'

'You mean further names?'

Neither the bishop nor the Wallcreeper offered an answer, and the Czech was clearly not expecting one.

'We shall do everything in our power,' he said. 'We'll send lists of Hussite henchmen and merchants who trade with the Hussites. We'll give you names so you'll know who to pray for. Meanwhile, the demon is striking straight and true. An operation like that could serve us in Bohemia, too—'

'That would be more difficult,' Konrad said firmly. 'Who knows better than you that the Devil himself couldn't keep up with all the factions in Bohemia? That there's no way of guessing who is siding with and against whom, or if Monday's ally is still loyal on Tuesday. Pope Martin and King Sigismund want to negotiate with Hussites. Sensible ones – like you, for example. Do you think there was a shortage of volunteers to assassinate Žižka? We didn't agree to that course of action. The removal of certain individuals threatened chaos, complete anarchy. Neither the king nor the Pope wishes for that in Bohemia.'

'Talk like that to Legate Orsini, but spare me such platitudes,' snorted the Czech disdainfully. 'And apply your supposedly competent brain a little, Bishop. Think about common concerns.'

'Somebody is meant to die: your foe, whether political or personal. What does that have to do with us?'

'I told you,' the Czech ignored the mockery again, 'that both the Taborites and the Orphans are looking at Silesia greedily. Some of them want to convert you, others simply to rob and pillage. They'll set off any day now, they'll soon be here with fire and sword. Pope Martin, who desires Christian reconciliation, will pray for you in the distant Vatican. Sigismund, who wants a settlement, will froth at the mouth in far-off Buda. Albrecht the Austrian and the Bishop of Olomouc will sigh with relief that they're not being invaded. While here, the Taborites and the Orphans will be beheading you, burning you in barrels and impaling you—'

'Yes, yes.' The bishop waved a hand dismissively. 'Let it go, I can see it in paintings in every church in Wrocław. You want to convince me, if I understand right, that the sudden deaths of a few selected Taborites will save Silesia from invasion? From an apocalypse?'

'Perhaps it won't. But it'll delay it, at least.'

'Without obligations or pledges, who do you have in mind? Who ought to be removed? I meant – excuse the *lapsus linguae* – who are we to include in our prayers?'

'Bohuslav of Švamberk. Jan Hvězda of Vicemilice, the Hetman of Hradec. Also Jan Čapek of Sány and Ambrož, the former priest of the church of the Holy Spirit. Prokop the Shaven—'

'Not so fast,' the Wallcreeper instructed reproachfully. 'I'm writing them down. Please, though, m'lord, confine yourself to the area around Hradec Králové. We'd like a list of the active and radical Hussites from the regions of Náchod, Trutnov and Vízmburk.'

'Ha!' shouted the Czech. 'Are you planning something after all?'

'Quiet, m'lord.'

'I want to take some good news back to Prague—'

'And I'm telling you to be quiet.'

The Czech fell silent at a bad moment for Reynevan. Wanting at any cost to see his face, Reynevan was standing on tiptoes and shifting around on the bench. A rotten leg broke with a crack and Reynevan fell, knocking over some tools resting against the wall of the cottage with a clatter that was probably audible in Wrocław.

He sprang up immediately and bolted. He heard guards shouting not only behind him but also in front of him, exactly where he wanted to flee. He cut between two buildings, not noticing that the Wallcreeper had rushed out of the cottage.

'Spy! Sppyyyy! Follow him! Take him alive! Aliiive!'

A servant barred his way and Reynevan knocked him over. The next one seized him by the arm and he punched him in the face. With curses and shouts raining down on him, he cleared a fence, waded through sunflowers, nettles and burdock; the forest and safety were in his grasp, but his pursuers were close on his heels and more soldiers emerged from behind a hayrick. One was about to grab him when Scharley appeared out of nowhere and struck him in the side of the head with a large clay pot. Samson, armed with a plank torn from the fence, charged at the others. Holding the twelve-foot plank horizontally in front of him, the giant knocked three of them over with one blow, and gave the next two such a thwack they toppled over like logs and disappeared into the burdock. Samson shook the plank and roared like a lion, calling to mind his famous biblical namesake menacing the Philistines. The soldiers stopped for a moment, but only for a moment as reinforcements came running from the grange. Samson hurled the plank at the soldiers and beat a hasty retreat after Scharley and Reynevan.

They jumped into the saddle, urging their horses to a gallop with kicks and yells. They hurtled through a beech wood in a cloud of leaves and thrashing branches, then splashed through a puddle on the track and into a forest of tall trees.

'Don't stop!' yelled Scharley, risking a glance over his shoulder. 'Don't stop! They're after us!'

Reynevan looked back and saw the shapes of horsemen. He pressed himself to his horse's mane so as not to be swept from the saddle by the branches lashing him. Riding out of the thicket into thinner woodland, they urged their horses to a gallop. Scharley's chestnut was racing like a hurricane, pulling ahead. Reynevan urged his mount to go faster. It was very risky on the uneven ground, but the thought of being left behind didn't appeal to him.

When he looked back again, his heart froze and sank to the bottom of his stomach when he saw his pursuers – the silhouettes of horsemen with cloaks flowing out behind them like phantoms' wings. He heard a cry.

'*Adsumus! Adsumuuuus!*'

They rode as hard as they could. Heinrich Hackeborn's horse gave a sudden snort and Reynevan's heart dropped even lower. He pressed his face to the horse's mane and felt the animal leaping, jumping a hollow or a ditch on its own initiative.

'*Adsumuus!*' he heard behind him. '*Adsuuumuuuus!*'

'Into the ravine!' yelled Samson. 'Into the ravine, Scharley!'

Scharley immediately steered his galloping horse into the gully and the chestnut neighed, slipping on the carpet of leaves covering the hillside. Samson and Reynevan hurtled after him, also at full gallop. They raced over moss that muffled the thudding of hooves. Heinrich Hackeborn's horse snorted more loudly, several times in a row, as did Samson's, its chest flecked with foam. Scharley's chestnut wasn't betraying any signs of fatigue.

The winding sunken lane led them out into a clearing beyond which stood a hazel grove as dense as a primeval forest. They forced their way through until they could urge their snorting horses to a gallop again.

A short while later, Samson slowed and fell behind. As Reynevan did the same, Scharley looked back and reined his chestnut in.

'We must have . . .' he panted when they caught up with him, 'we must have lost them. What have you got us mixed up with this time, Reinmar?'

'Me?'

'Dammit! I saw those riders! I saw you cringe in fear at the sight of them! Who are they? Why were they shouting, "We are here!"?'

'I don't know, I swear—'

'Your oaths are of no use to me. Touch wood, whoever they were, we managed to—'

'Not yet,' said Samson, his voice sounding different. 'The danger isn't over yet. Look out. Look out!'

'What?'

'Something's approaching.'

'I can't hear anything!'

'But something comes. Something evil. Something very evil.'

Scharley reined his horse around, standing up in the stirrups to look around and straining his ears for whatever Samson had heard. Reynevan, on the contrary, was cowering in the saddle, terrified by the change in Samson's voice. Heinrich Hackeborn's horse snorted and stamped its hooves. Samson shouted. Reynevan yelled.

And then, from God knew where, a swarm of bats rained down on them from the murky sky.

They weren't ordinary bats. Twice as large as regular bats, they had unnaturally large heads, enormous ears, eyes like glowing coals and mouths full of sharp teeth. Their narrow wings whistled and cut like yataghans.

Reynevan waved his arms around frantically, pushing away the furiously attacking creatures. Yelling in terror and disgust, he tore off the ones that were clinging to his nape and hair. Some he knocked off, beating them away like balls. Others he caught and crushed, but the rest scratched his face, bit his hands and nipped his ears. Beside him, Scharley was slashing blindly with a sabre, splashing black bats' blood around. At least four were clinging to Scharley's head and Reynevan saw trickles of blood running down the penitent's forehead and cheeks. Samson fought in silence, crushing the creatures crawling all over him, grabbing several at a time. The horses were frantic, kicking and neighing in panic.

Scharley's sabre swished just above Reynevan's head, the blade brushing against his hair as he swept from it a huge, plump and unusually vicious beast.

'Flee!' roared the penitent. 'We have to get away! We can't stay here!'

Reynevan spurred his horse, also suddenly understanding. They weren't normal bats, but monsters conjured up by magic, which could only mean one thing – they had been sent by their pursuers, who would also soon appear. They set off at a gallop, not needing to spur their horses since the panicked steeds had shed their tiredness and were flying as though chased by wolves. They couldn't lose the bats, however, which were attacking, diving and falling on them relentlessly. It was hard to defend themselves at full speed. Only Scharley was winning, wielding his sabre and cutting down the huge creatures as he galloped with such skill he might have been born and spent his entire youth in Tatary.

But Reynevan, as usual, was more hapless than Jonah. The bats were biting all three of them, but it was Reynevan who was quite blinded when one of them clung to the hair on his forehead. The little monsters were attacking all three horses, but Reynevan's was the only one into whose ear a bat crawled. The horse thrashed around, whinnying frantically. Shaking its lowered head, it kicked and jerked its rump up with such force that Reynevan, still blinded, shot from the saddle like a stone from a catapult. Now free of its burden, the horse broke into a headlong gallop and would have fled into the forest had Samson not managed to seize its harness and rein it in. Scharley, meanwhile, jumped from the saddle with sabre raised and rushed among the juniper bushes where Reynevan was rolling in the tall grass with bats swarming over him like Saracens over an unsaddled paladin. Yelling terrible curses and vile insults, the penitent slashed with his sabre, splashing gore around. Beside him, Samson was fighting in the saddle with one hand and holding two struggling horses with the other. Only someone as strong as him could have pulled off a trick like that.

Reynevan, meanwhile, was the first to notice that fresh forces had entered the fray, perhaps because he was on his hands and knees when he observed the grass suddenly lie down flat on the ground, as though struck by a hurricane. He looked up to see, about twenty paces away, a man of gigantic stature. His hair was milk-white like an old man's, but his eyes flashed with fire. The old man was holding a staff, strange, gnarled and crooked, like a snake frozen in paroxysms of agony.

'Get down!' the old man thundered. 'And stay down!'

As Reynevan flattened himself on the ground, he felt a strange gale whistling over his head. He heard Scharley utter a stifled curse, followed by the sudden piercing squeal of the bats which had up until then been attacking in complete silence. The squeal was silenced as suddenly as it had begun. Reynevan heard and felt a hail of objects falling around him, thudding on the ground like ripe apples. He also felt a finer shower of tiny, dry things. He looked around. Dead bats were lying everywhere and an unceasing deluge of dead insects was falling from the branches of trees above.

'Matavermis . . .' he gasped. 'That was Matavermis . . .'

'Well, well,' said the old man. 'A scholar! Young, but knowledgeable. You can get up now.'

At second glance, the old man wasn't old at all. Although no youngster, either, Reynevan had no doubt that the white rime of his hair was less a sign of old age and more of the albinism that frequently occurred among mages. His great height also turned out to be a magically evoked effect, since the white-haired man resting on his staff was tall, but by no means unnaturally so.

Scharley approached, wading indifferently through the lifeless bats lying in the grass. Samson led the horses over. The white-haired man observed them for a moment – Samson in particular.

'Three men,' he said. 'Interesting. We were looking for two.'

Reynevan found out why he had used the plural before he could ask. Hooves thudded and the clearing was full of snorting horses.

'Greetings,' called down Notker of Weyrach. 'So, we meet. What a stroke of luck.'

'A stroke of luck indeed,' repeated Buko of Krossig, pushing his horse slightly against the penitent, with similar scorn in his voice. 'Especially since it's quite a different place than we'd planned!'

'You're unreliable, Master Scharley,' added Tassilo of Tresckow, lifting his hounskull. 'You don't keep your word. Which is disgraceful.'

'But he hasn't escaped punishment, I see,' snorted Kuno of Wittram. 'By the staff of Saint Gregory the Miracle-Worker! Just look how his ears have been nipped!'

'We ought to get out of here.' The white-haired man interrupted the scene playing out in front of the astonished Reynevan. 'The horsemen draw near. They are on our trail!'

'Didn't I say,' snorted Buko of Krossig, 'that we'd be rescuing them and saving their arses? Very well, let's ride. Master Huon? Those pursuers . . .'

'They aren't just anyone.' The mage held a bat up by a wing-tip and observed it, then transferred his gaze to Scharley and Samson. 'Yes, they aren't just anyone . . . I knew by the pricking of my thumbs. Well, well . . . You're fascinating, fascinating . . . One could say: show me your pursuers and I'll tell you who you are.'

'To hell with them,' called Paszko Rymbaba, reining his horse around. 'I don't give a fig! Let them come and we'll give them what for!'

'I don't think it'll be so easy,' replied the white-haired man.

'Neither do I,' said Buko, who was also examining the bats. 'Master Huon? Would you mind?'

The man addressed as Huon didn't reply. Instead, he raised his crooked staff and a fog as dense and white as smoke began to rise from the grass and ferns. In no time, the forest was completely engulfed by it.

'That old wizard,' muttered Notker of Weyrach. 'He gives me the shivers . . .'

'Huh!' Paszko snorted cheerfully. 'Not me, he doesn't.'

'Fog might not stop whoever's tracking us,' Reynevan found the courage to say. 'Not even magical fog.'

The mage turned around and looked Reynevan in the eyes.

'I know,' he said. 'I know, m'lord scholar. Which is why it's for horses, not men. So get yours out of here as soon as you can. If they smell the vapour, they'll go mad.'

'Let us ride, *comitiva*!' shouted Buko of Krossig.

Chapter Twenty-Three

In which matters take such a criminal turn that had Canon Otto Beess predicted it, he would have shaved Reynevan's head like a monk's and locked him up in a Cistercian monastery without further ado. And Reynevan begins to wonder if that alternative might not have been safer for him.

The charcoal burners and tar makers of the nearby village heading at dawn towards their place of work were alerted and alarmed by the noises coming from it. The more cowardly of them took to their heels at once. The more sensible hurried after them, realising correctly that there would be no work that day and they might get a beating to boot. Only a few of the more courageous men dared to steal close enough to the tar-burning pit to peep out cautiously from behind tree trunks and see in the clearing some fifteen horses and armed riders, six of whom were in full plate armour. The knights were gesticulating animatedly, shouting and cursing. Quarrelling knights were accustomed to taking out their anger and stress on peasants. While an angered nobleman might treat a peasant to a boot in the arse or a whip across the back, a furious knight might also reach for a sword, mace or battleaxe.

The charcoal burners fled. And alerted the village. Angry knights had also been known to burn down villages.

A fierce argument was indeed raging in the charcoal burners' clearing. Buko of Krossig was yelling so loudly that he frightened the horses being held by the pages. Paszko Rymbaba was gesticulating, Woldan of Osiny was fulminating and Kuno of Wittram was calling on the saints as his witnesses. Scharley was keeping fairly calm. Notker of Weyrach and Tassilo of Tresckow were trying to reconcile the feuding parties.

The white-haired mage was sitting on a nearby tree stump displaying contempt.

Reynevan now knew what the argument was about. Samson had filled him in as they fled their pursuers, and he was dumbfounded.

'I don't understand . . .' he said when he had calmed down. 'I don't understand why you decided to do something like that!'

Samson turned towards him. 'So you're saying that had it been one of us, you wouldn't have made any attempts to rescue us? Not even desperate ones?'

'No, of course not. But I don't understand how—'

'That's exactly what I'm trying to explain to you,' interjected the giant, quite forcefully for him. 'But you keep interrupting me with your outbursts of righteous indignation. Just listen. We found out they were taking you to Stolz Castle to kill you soon after. Scharley had spotted the tax collector's black wagon earlier, so when Notker of Weyrach unexpectedly happened along with his *comitiva*, the plan suggested itself.'

'To help them rob the tax collector in exchange for help in freeing me?'

'Couldn't have put it better myself. That was the agreement. And when Buko of Krossig found out about the venture, most probably because of someone's wagging tongue, he had to be included, too.'

'And now we're in it.'

'We are,' Samson calmly agreed.

They were. The discussion in the charcoal-burners' clearing was becoming so fierce that for some of the parties, Buko of Krossig in particular, words were no longer enough. The Raubritter walked over to Scharley and seized the front of his jerkin in both hands.

'Say it's been called off one more time,' he wheezed furiously, 'and you'll regret it. What are you telling me, vagrant? Perhaps you think that I have nothing better to do than waste time traipsing through forests hoping for some spoils. Don't tell me it was in vain, because my hands are itching to—'

'Calm down, Buko,' Notker of Weyrach said placatingly. 'Why resort to force before we've tried to work this out? But you, Master Scharley, if I may say so, have behaved poorly. It was agreed that you would track the tax collector from Ziębice, that you would inform us which route he would take and where he would stop. We waited for you. It was a collaborative venture. And what did you do?'

'When I asked for your help in Ziębice,' said Scharley, smoothing down his clothes, 'when I paid for that help with profitable information and an offer of assistance, what did you tell me? That you might help to free Reinmar of Hagenau – and I quote – "if we feel like it", but I won't even get a bent penny of the loot from the attack on the tax collector. Is that your idea of a collaborative venture?'

'It was about your companion. And freeing him—'

'And he is free. He freed himself, through his own inventiveness. It ought then to be clear that I no longer need your help.'

Weyrach folded his arms as the Raubritter knights started shouting again. Buko of Krossig silenced them with a vigorous gesture.

'This was all about saving his skin, wasn't it?' he asked through clenched teeth, pointing at Reynevan. 'And now that he's free, Master Scharley, are you telling us that the contract's null and void? Consider this, Master Scharley: if keeping your friend's skin intact is so dear to you, I can soon violate that intactness! So don't you dare tell me that the contract has been cancelled now that your companion is safe, since right here in this clearing, within my reach, the two of you are far from bloody safe!'

'Calm down.' Weyrach raised a hand. 'Restrain yourself, Buko. But you, Master Scharley, moderate your tone. Your companion is now liberated? Lucky you. You no longer need us, you say? We need you even less, know that. Begone, if that be your will – after first thanking us for the rescue. Had we not saved your arses last night, your troubles wouldn't have ended with sore ears. So before we part, simply tell us which way the tax collector and his wagon went and then begone, may the Devil take you.'

Scharley cleared his throat and bowed slightly, not to Buko and Weyrach, but towards the mage who was still sitting on the tree stump, looking on indifferently. 'I thank you for your help last night. Without mentioning that barely a week has passed since we saved the arses of Lords Rymbaba and Wittram near Lutom. Thus, we are even. Unfortunately, I do not know which way the tax collector went. We lost his party's trail in the afternoon of the day before yesterday. And since we met Reinmar just before dusk, we lost interest in the tax collector.'

'Restrain me!' yelled Buko of Krossig. 'Restrain me before I fucking kill him! Did you hear that? He lost the trail. He lost interest in the tax collector. He lost interest in a thousand fucking grzywna! *Our* thousand grzywna!'

'What thousand?' Reynevan blurted out without thinking. 'There wasn't a thousand. There was … only … five hundred …'

He very quickly understood what a grave error he had just committed.

Buko of Krossig drew his sword so swiftly that the grinding of the blade in the scabbard still hung in the air as the blade touched Reynevan's throat. Scharley had barely taken half a step before the blades of Weyrach and Tresckow – drawn just as quickly – met his chest. The blades of the remaining men stopped Samson and held him in check. All traces of rude good humour vanished as though blown away by the wind. The Raubritters' evil, cruel, narrowed eyes left no doubt that the weapons would be used. And used without the slightest scruple.

The mage sighed and shook his head, but his expression was blank.

'Hubert,' Buko of Krossig said slowly to one of the pages, 'take a strap, tie a noose in it and toss it over that branch. Don't move, Hagenau.'

'Don't move, Scharley,' Tresckow parroted as the other men's swords pushed harder against Samson's chest and throat.

Without removing the sword-point from Reynevan's throat, Buko moved closer and looked him in the eyes. 'So there wasn't a thousand, but five hundred grzywna on the tax collector's wagon. You knew it, so you also know which way it went. You have a simple choice, laddie: you either sing or swing.'

The Raubritters rode hard, forcing a frenzied pace. They didn't spare the horses. Whenever the terrain permitted, they spurred them on to a gallop and raced as fast as they could.

It transpired that Weyrach and Rymbaba knew the area and led them via shortcuts.

They had to slow when the final shortcut exited through the soggy marsh in the valley of the Budzówka, a left-bank tributary of the Kłodzko Nysa. Only then did Scharley, Samson and Reynevan have the chance to exchange a few words.

'Don't try anything stupid,' Scharley warned quietly. 'And don't try to get away. The two behind us have crossbows and are keeping a close watch on us. Better to ride obediently with them—'

'And take part in a robbery,' Reynevan finished with a sneer. 'Indeed, Scharley, knowing you has led me a long way. To become a brigand—'

'Let me remind you,' interrupted Samson, 'that we did this to save your life.'

'Canon Beess,' added Scharley, 'instructed me to guard and protect you—'

'And turn me into an outlaw?'

'It's thanks to you,' the penitent replied sharply, 'that we are heading for Ścibor's Clearing. It was you who revealed to Krossig where the tax collector would stop and he didn't even have to rough you up much. Had you resisted more resolutely, you would now be an honest hanged man with a clear conscience. I believe you'd have felt better about that—'

'A crime is always—'

Scharley snorted, looked away and spurred his horse.

Fog was rising from the bog as it sagged and squelched under the horses' hooves. Frogs croaked, bitterns boomed and wild geese gaggled. Ducks quacked anxiously and took off, splashing water. Something large, probably an elk, was cracking branches in the backwoods.

'What Scharley did,' said Samson, 'he did for you. You wrong him with your condemnation.'

'A crime . . .' Reynevan cleared his throat, 'is always a crime. Nothing can justify it.'

'Indeed?'

'Nothing. One cannot—'

'Do you know what, Reynevan?' For the first time, Samson manifested something like impatience. 'Go and play chess. That will be to your taste — black here, white there and all the fields square.'

'How do you know I was meant to be murdered at Stolz? Who told you?'

'A masked young woman, swathed tightly in a cloak, came to us at the inn during the night, escorted by armed servants. Does that surprise you?'

'No.'

Samson left it at that.

Even from a distance, it was apparent that there wasn't a living soul in Ścibor's Clearing. The Raubritters immediately gave up the stealthy approach they had planned and galloped into the clearing, thudding, stamping and yelling. Which only frightened some rooks feasting beside a fireplace ringed with stones.

The troop split up and ferreted about among the shacks. Buko of Krossig turned around in the saddle and fixed Reynevan with a dangerous look.

'Let him be,' Notker of Weyrach said. 'He wasn't lying. Somebody clearly made a stop here.'

'There was a wagon,' said Tassilo of Tresckow, riding closer. 'Look, wheel tracks.'

'The grass was dug up by horseshoes,' Paszko Rymbaba reported. 'There were plenty of horses!'

'The ash in the campfire is still hot,' announced Buko's page, Hubert, a fellow advanced in years. 'Mutton bones and pieces of turnip strewn around.'

'We're too late,' Woldan of Osiny concluded gloomily. 'The tax collector stopped here then moved on. We came too late.'

'Clearly,' snapped Buko. 'Assuming the youth didn't lie to us. For I don't like the look of him, that Hagenau. Who pursued you in the night, boy? Who set those bats on you? Who—'

'Drop it, Buko,' Weyrach interrupted again. 'You keep changing the subject. Go on, *comitiva*, ride around and search for tracks. We need to decide what to do next.'

The Raubritters split up again, some of them dismounting to search the huts. To Reynevan's slight surprise, Scharley joined in the hunt. The white-haired mage, however, ignoring the commotion, spread out a sheepskin, sat down on it and removed a loaf of bread, a strip of dried meat and a wineskin from his saddlebags.

'M'Lord Huon,' said Buko, frowning, 'don't you consider it meet to aid in the search?'

The mage took a sip of wine and a mouthful of bread.

'I do not.'

Weyrach snorted. Buko swore under his breath. Woldan of Osiny rode over.

'Difficult to glean anything from these tracks,' he said without being asked. 'All I know is that there were plenty of horses.'

'We knew that already,' said Buko, glaring at Reynevan evilly. 'But I'd rather know some details. Were there many men with the tax collector? And who were they? I'm talking to you, Hagenau!'

'A sergeant and five soldiers,' mumbled Reynevan. 'Aside from them—'

'Aye? Speak! And look me in the eye when I ask you a question!'

'Four Friars Minor . . .' Reynevan had already decided to refrain

from mentioning Tybald Raabe, and after a moment's consideration broadened his decision to omit Hartwig of Stietencron and
his plain daughter also. 'And four pilgrims.'

'Mendicant friars and pilgrims,' said Buko, his lip curled to
reveal his teeth. 'Riding iron-shod horses? Eh? Something doesn't
add—'

'He isn't lying.' Kuno Wittram trotted over and threw down
a piece of knotted cord at their feet. 'It's white,' he announced.
'Franciscan!'

'Bugger.' Notker of Weyrach frowned. 'What happened here?'

'Whatever happened, happened.' Buko slapped his hand
against his sword hilt. 'What do I care? I want to know where the
money is! Can anyone tell me? Master Huon of Sagar!'

'I am eating.'

Buko swore.

'Three paths lead from the clearing,' said Tassilo of Tresckow,
'and there are tracks on all of them. It's impossible to say which
way the tax collector went.'

'If he went anywhere,' Scharley said, emerging from the bushes.
'I believe he didn't. I believe he's still here.'

'How do you come to that conclusion?' Tassilo asked.

'By using my wits.'

Buko of Krossig swore crudely. Notker of Weyrach restrained
him with a gesture and looked pointedly at the penitent.

'Speak, Scharley. What have you found? What do you know?'

'You didn't want to give us a share of the spoils, gentlemen,' the
penitent said, raising his head imperiously, 'so don't make me into
a tracker. I know what I know. It's my business.'

'Just wait till I ...' Buko growled furiously, but Weyrach restrained him again.

'Not long since,' he said, 'neither the tax collector nor his
money interested you. And now suddenly you're wanting a share
of the loot. Something must have changed. I wonder what.'

'A great deal. If we're lucky enough to get our hands on the
loot now, it won't be by attacking a tax collector. Now we'll be

retrieving it by robbing the robbers. I'll gladly join in with that, because I judge it moral to rob stolen loot from robbers.'

'Be clearer,' Weyrach said.

'He can't,' said Tassilo of Tresckow. 'Everything *is* clear.'

The small lake hidden among the trees and surrounded by a swamp, though pretty, stirred feelings of unease and even anxiety. The surface was like pitch – black, still and undisturbed by any life. Although the tops of the spruces reflected in the water were swaying slightly in the wind, the surface sheen wasn't disturbed by the tiniest ripple. The only movement in the lake was caused by little bubbles of gas rising up from the depths through water thick with brown algae, slowly spreading and bursting on the oily, duckweed-covered surface, from which dry, forked trees stuck out like skeletal hands.

Reynevan shuddered. He had guessed what the penitent had discovered. *They're lying in the mud*, he thought, *at the very bottom of that black abyss. The tax collector. Tybald Raabe. The pimply Lady Stietencron with her plucked eyebrows. And who else?*

'Look,' pointed Scharley. 'There.'

The marsh sagged beneath them as their feet squeezed water out of the spongy carpet of moss.

'Somebody tried to cover the tracks,' Scharley said, 'but it's still clearly visible which way they dragged the bodies. Look here, there's blood on the leaves. And here. Blood everywhere.'

'That means . . .' Weyrach rubbed his chin. 'That someone—'

'That someone attacked the tax collector,' Scharley calmly finished his sentence, 'did away with him and his escort and sank the bodies here, in the lake, weighed down with stones from the campfire. If one were to examine the campfire carefully—'

'Very well,' Buko cut him off. 'And the money? What about the money? Does it mean . . .'

'It means,' Scharley looked at him with faint indulgence, 'exactly what you think. Assuming you think.'

'That the money was plundered?'

'Bravo.'

Buko said nothing for some time, all the while growing redder and redder.

'Fuck!' he finally roared. 'God! You see, but thunder not? It's come to this! Decency has collapsed, virtue has perished, goodness has died! They plunder, rob and steal everything! Everything! Thieves at every turn! Swine! Scoundrels! Knaves!'

'Rogues, by the cauldron of Saint Cecilia, rogues!' chimed in Kuno of Wittram. 'O Christ, why don't you put a plague on them!'

'They hold nothing sacred, the whoresons!' roared Rymbaba. 'Why, the money the tax collector was carrying was for a worthy cause!'

'Indeed. The bishop was collecting it for a war against the Hussites . . .'

'If that is so,' mumbled Woldan of Osiny, 'perhaps it's the Devil's work? The Devil is siding with the Hussites, so the heretics may have summoned his help. Or the Devil may have decided to spite the bishop himself . . . Jesus! The Devil, I tell you, was capering here – hellish forces were at play. Satan killed the tax collector and the others.'

'And what about the five hundred grzywna?' Buko frowned. 'Did he take it to Hell?'

'He did,' said Woldan. 'Or turned it into shit. There have been such cases.'

'He may have turned it into shit,' said Rymbaba, nodding. 'There's plenty of it over there, behind those huts.'

'The Devil may also have sunk the money in that pond,' added Wittram, pointing. 'It's no use to him.'

'Hmm . . .' muttered Buko. 'He may have sunk it, you say? Perhaps then—'

'Not a chance.' Hubert guessed at once what Buko was thinking and about whom. 'Not a chance! I'm not going in there for anything, sire.'

'I don't blame you,' said Tassilo of Tresckow. 'I don't like the look of that lake, either. Urgh! Never mind five hundred, not even five hundred *thousand* grzywna would get me in there.'

Something living in the lake must have heard him, because as though in confirmation, the tarry-black water of the lake churned up, effervesced and boiled with a thousand huge bubbles. A foul, disgusting stench erupted and permeated the air.

'Let's get out of here . . .' gasped Weyrach. 'Let's go . . .'

They left. In some haste. The boggy water squirted under their feet.

'The robbery of the tax collector,' declared Tassilo of Tresckow, 'if Scharley is not mistaken, judging from the tracks, happened last night or at dawn today. So if we apply ourselves a little, we might catch up with the robbers.'

'But do we know which way they went?' grunted Woldan of Osiny. 'Three paths lead away from the clearing. One towards the Bardo road. The second south, towards Kamieniec. And the third north, to Frankenstein. Before we set off after them, it would be worth knowing which of the three they took.'

'Indeed.' Notker of Weyrach cleared his throat pointedly, looked at Buko and gestured with his eyes at the white-haired magician sitting nearby and scrutinising Samson. 'Indeed, that would be worth knowing. I don't mean to be presumptuous, but perhaps one could use sorcery to that end, eh, Buko?'

The mage certainly heard but didn't even turn his head. Buko of Krossig ground out a curse.

'Master Huon of Sagar.'

'What?'

'We're searching for a trail. Perhaps you could help us?'

'No,' replied the magician disdainfully. 'I have no desire to.'

'You have no desire to? Then why did you sodding come with us?'

'For a breath of fresh air. And for some *gaudium*. I've had enough air but found no *gaudium*, so I'd gladly return home.'

'We missed the opportunity for plunder!'

'Well, that, if you don't mind me saying, *nihil ad me attinet*.'

'I support and feed you from plunder!'

'You? Indeed?'

Buko flushed furiously but said nothing. Tassilo of Tresckow cleared his throat softly and leaned over slightly towards Weyrach.

'What's the matter with that wizard?' he muttered. 'Does he actually serve Buko of Krossig or not?'

'He does,' Weyrach muttered in reply, 'but via Lady Krossig. Hush, don't say anything. It's a sensitive subject . . .'

'Is that the famous Huon of Sagar?' Reynevan asked Rymbaba in hushed tones.

Paszko nodded and opened his mouth. Unfortunately, Notker Weyrach had overheard.

'You are most inquisitive, m'Lord Hagenau,' he hissed, moving closer, 'which doesn't befit you or any one of your bizarre trio. All these difficulties are because of you. And you've given us bugger all help.'

'That might soon change,' said Reynevan, straightening up.

'Eh?'

'You want to know which way the men who robbed the tax collector went? I shall show you.'

If the Raubritters' astonishment was great, it would be hard to find an apt phrase to describe Scharley's and Samson's expressions. Even the word 'dumbfounded' sounds too weak. A flash of interest even appeared in Huon of Sagar's eyes. The albino, who until then had looked at everybody – with the exception of Samson – as though they weren't there, now turned the full weight of his attention on Reynevan.

'You showed us the way to this clearing under threat of the noose, Hagenau,' drawled Buko of Krossig. 'And now you help us willingly? Why the change?'

'That's my business.'

Tybald Raabe. Stietencron's ugly daughter. With their throats slit. At the bottom of the lake, in the mud. Black from the crayfish crawling all over them. And the leeches. And wriggling eels. And God knows what else.

'That's my business,' he repeated.

He didn't have to search long for what he needed. Rushes were growing in great tussocks at the edge of the swampy meadow. He added a stem of field mustard full of dry husks and tied up the bundle three times with a stalk of sedge in flower.

> *One, two, three*
> *Segge, Binse, Hederich*
> *Binde zu samene . . .*

'Very good,' said the mage with a smile. 'Bravo, young man. But I'm somewhat short of time and I'd like to return home as quickly as possible, so I'll take the liberty – no offence – of helping a little. Just enough, as the poet said, to get things going.'

He flourished his staff and described a quick circle with it.

'*Yassar!*' he intoned gutturally. '*Qadir al-rah!*'

The air trembled with the force of the spell, and one of the roads leading from Ścibor's Clearing became brighter, friendlier, more inviting. It happened almost immediately, much more quickly than when using only a talisman, and the glow emanating from the road was much steadier.

'That way.' Reynevan pointed, watching the Raubritters' open mouths. 'It's that way.'

'The road to Kamieniec.' Notker of Weyrach was the first to come to his senses. 'Lucky for us. And for you, too, Master Huon, for it's the same direction as your home, towards which you are hurrying. To horse, *comitiva!*'

'It's them,' reported Hubert, who had been sent ahead to scout, bringing his nervous horse under control. 'It's them, Sir Buko. They're riding in a column, slowly, along the highway towards Bardo. About twenty men, some heavily armed.'

'Twenty,' repeated Woldan of Osiny ponderously. 'Hmmm . . .'

'And what were you expecting?' said Weyrach, looking at him. 'Who did you think slaughtered and sank the tax collector and his entourage, not counting the Franciscans and the pilgrims? Eh? Tom Thumb?'

'The money?' Buko asked, getting to the point.

'There is a carriage.' Hubert scratched his ear. 'A strongbox . . .'

'Lucky for us. That's where they're carrying it. So follow them.'

'But are we certain,' asked Scharley, 'that they are the ones?'

'Master Scharley, when you say something . . .' Buko looked him up and down. 'I'd rather you'd say we can count on you and your comrades. Will you help?'

'And what will we receive of that recuperation?' Scharley looked up at the pine tops. 'What do you say to an equal share, Lord Krossig?'

'One share for the three of you.'

'Agreed.' The penitent did not haggle, but seeing the looks of Reynevan and Samson added quickly:

'But without fighting.'

Buko waved a hand, then unfastened a powerful battleaxe with a wide blade on a slightly curved helve. Reynevan saw Notker of Weyrach check that his morning star was rotating freely on its handle.

'Listen, *comitiva*,' said Buko. 'Although most of them are probably milksops, there are twenty of them, so we must act wisely. We'll proceed as follows: a furlong from here, I happen to know, the road crosses a bridge over a stream . . .'

Buko wasn't mistaken. The road indeed led over a small bridge, under which a stream flowed in a narrow but deep ravine hidden in a thicket of alder, noisily burbling over some boulders. Orioles sang and a woodpecker was drumming spiritedly on a tree trunk.

'I can't believe it,' said Reynevan, hidden behind some junipers. 'I can't believe it. I've become a brigand. I'm in an ambuscade . . .'

'Sssh,' muttered Scharley. 'They're coming.'

Buko of Krossig spat on his hand, gripped his battleaxe and lowered his visor.

'Beware,' he grunted as though from the bottom of a cooking pot. 'Hubert? Ready?'

'Ready, m'lord.'

'Everybody know what to do? Hagenau?'

'Yes, yes.'

Colours flashed and armour glistened among the light birch wood behind some maples on the far side of the gorge. They could hear singing. *They're singing* Dum iuventus floruit, thought Reynevan. *A hymn with words by Pierre de Blois. We also sang it in Prague . . .*

'They're cheerful, the varlets,' muttered Tassilo of Tresckow.

'I'm also cheerful when I rob somebody,' snapped Buko. 'Hubert! Attention! Prepare your crossbow!'

The singing stopped suddenly. A servant in a hood appeared by the bridge, carrying a lance crosswise over his saddle. Behind him rode another three, wearing kettle hats, mail shirts and iron rerebraces, with crossbows slung across their backs. They all rode slowly onto the bridge. Behind them came two knights armoured *cap à pied*, carrying lances set in holders by their stirrups. One of their shields displayed a coat of arms with a red step in a silver field.

'Kauffung,' muttered Tassilo again. 'What the hell?'

Iron-shod hooves thudded on the bridge as another three knights rode onto it. Behind them rattled a barrel-like carriage upholstered in claret canvas pulled by a pair of cobs. A strongbox, escorted by more crossbowmen in kettle hats.

'Wait,' muttered Buko. 'Not yet . . . Just let the carriage cross the bridge . . . Not yet . . . Now!'

A bowstring clanged and a bolt hissed. The horse under one of the lancers reared up, neighing piercingly, and fell down, knocking over one of the bowmen.

'Now!' roared Buko, spurring his horse. 'At them! Attack!'

Reynevan struck his horse with his heels and galloped out of the juniper bushes. Scharley rushed out after him.

A seething mass formed in front of the bridge as the battle

raged. Rymbaba and Wittram had struck the rearguard of the train from the right, and Weyrach and Woldan of Osiny from the left. The forest was filled with yelling, the squealing of horses, clanking, rattling and the thudding of iron on iron.

Buko of Krossig felled a servant carrying a lance and his horse with a blow of his battleaxe, and with a reverse swing carved open the head of a crossbowman trying to tighten his bow. Reynevan was spattered with blood and brain as he raced past. Buko twisted around in the saddle, stood up in the stirrups, smote powerfully, and his battleaxe cleaved open the spaulder of a knight with the step of the Kauffungs on his shield and almost cut off his arm. Tassilo of Tresckow flashed by at full gallop, knocking a page in a brigantine off his horse with a broad flourish of his sword. His way was blocked by an armoured man in a blue and white doublet, and they clashed with a clank of steel.

Reynevan had reached the carriage. The driver looked on in disbelief at the crossbow bolt sticking up to its fletching in his groin. Scharley leaped forward from the other side, knocking him off the box seat with a vigorous shove.

'Jump on,' he yelled. 'And whip up the horses!'

'Look out!'

Scharley ducked under his horse's neck. Had he delayed by a second, he would have been spitted on the lance held by a knight in full armour, with a black and gold chequerboard on his shield, charging from the bridge. The knight rammed Scharley's horse, dropped his lance and seized a mace hanging from a sling, but wasn't quick enough to smite the penitent on the crown. Notker of Weyrach came racing up at a gallop and slammed him over the sallet with his morning star with a great clang. As the knight swayed in the saddle, Weyrach took another swing and struck him again, this time in the middle of his cuirass, so hard that the spikes of the iron ball embedded in the metal, stuck fast. Weyrach released the handle and drew his sword.

'Whip them up!' he roared at Reynevan, who meanwhile had clambered onto the box. 'Ride on! Ride on!'

From the bridge, a wild squeal sounded as a stallion in a colourful caparison shattered the railing, tumbling into the ravine with its rider. Reynevan yelled at the top of his voice and lashed the horses with the reins. The cobs leaped forward, the strongbox swayed and bounced, and to Reynevan's great astonishment, a horrifying scream came from inside, behind a tightly sealed covering. There was no time for surprise, though. The horses galloped on and he had to struggle not to fall from the plank jumping about under his backside.

A heavily armed man without a helmet sprang out at a gallop from the right and tried to grab the horses by the harness. Tassilo of Tresckow caught up with him and smote him with his sword. Blood splashed onto the cob's flank.

'Riiiiide!'

Samson appeared from the left, armed only with a hazel withy, a weapon, as it turned out, entirely sufficient for the situation.

The cobs, lashed across the rumps, set off at such a gallop that Reynevan was literally pressed against the backrest of the box seat. Still squeaking, the strongbox jumped and rocked like a boat on a rough sea. Reynevan, to tell the truth, had never been on the sea and had only seen a boat in paintings, but had no doubt that they must rock just like that.

'Riiiiide!'

Huon of Sagar appeared on the road on a dancing black horse, pointed towards a track with his staff and galloped down it himself. Samson dashed after him, pulling Reynevan's horse behind him. Reynevan tugged on the reins and yelled at the pair.

The track was rutted. The strongbox bounced, rocked and squealed. The sounds of the battle faded behind him.

'It went quite well,' judged Buko of Krossig. 'Only two pages dead. Quite satisfactory. So far.'

Notker of Weyrach didn't reply, just panted heavily, massaging a hip. Blood was dripping from his codpiece and a thin trickle crept down his cuisse. Tassilo of Tresckow was panting beside him, examining his left arm. His vambrace was missing and his couter was hanging, half torn-off and attached by one flange, but his arm looked intact.

'And m'Lord Hagenau,' continued Buko, who looked unscathed, 'M'Lord Hagenau drove the wagon beautifully. He acquitted himself splendidly ... Oh, Hubert, are you in one piece? Ha, I see you're alive. Where are Woldan, Rymbaba and Wittram?'

'They're coming now.'

Kuno of Wittram removed his helmet and skullcap; his hair beneath it was curly and wet. The cut metal edges of the spaulder were sticking upright and the besague was completely bent.

'Help,' he called, gulping air like a fish. 'Woldan is wounded ...'

They dragged the wounded man from the saddle with difficulty, then pulled the severely dented, twisted and detached hounskull off his head.

'Christ ...' groaned Woldan. 'I took a nasty whack ... Kuno, have a look, is my eye gone?'

'No, no,' Wittram reassured him. 'You can't see because you're blinded by the blood ...'

Reynevan knelt down and immediately began to dress the wounds. Somebody was assisting him. He raised his head and met Huon of Sagar's grey eyes.

Rymbaba, standing beside him, grimaced in pain, rubbing a large dent on the side of his breastplate.

'My rib's broken, sure as anything,' he grunted. 'I'm fucking spitting blood, look.'

'Who gives a fucking shit what you're spitting,' said Buko of Krossig as he removed the armet from his head. 'Are they following us?'

'No ... We've knocked them about a bit ...'

'They'll soon be after us,' Buko said with conviction. 'Come on, we'll empty the carriage. Let's take the money and get out of here.'

He went over to the vehicle and tugged at the wicker door

trimmed with cloth. The door yielded, but only an inch, then closed again. It was apparent that somebody was holding it from the inside. Buko swore and tugged harder, eliciting a squeal from within.

'What's this?' said Rymbaba in amazement, grimacing. 'Squeaking money? Perhaps the tax collector accepted payment in mice?'

Buko gestured to him for help. The two of them tugged at the door with such force that it was torn right off, and along with it, the Raubritters pulled out the person holding it.

Reynevan gasped. And froze open-mouthed.

Because this time he had not the slightest doubt as to the person's identity.

Meanwhile, Buko and Rymbaba used knives to cut open the curtain and dragged a second girl from the fur-lined interior of the strongbox. Like the first, she was fair-haired, similarly dishevelled, dressed in a similar green *cotehardie* with white sleeves, perhaps just a little younger, shorter and plumper. It was the second, plumper one who was prone to squeal, and additionally began to sob when she was shoved onto the grass by Buko. The first one sat in silence, still gripping the carriage door and shielding herself with it as though it were a pavise.

'By the staff of Saint Dalmatius . . .' gasped Kuno of Wittram. 'What can this be?'

'Not what we wanted,' Tassilo stated to the point. 'Master Scharley was right. We ought first to have made certain of its contents and then robbed it.'

Buko of Krossig emerged from the strongbox. As he flung down some garments and effects he had removed from it, his face expressed only too clearly the results of the search. Anyone uncertain of what Buko had found was soon convinced by a volley of obscene oaths. The expected five hundred grzywna were not in the strongbox.

The girls drew close and hugged one another in fear. The taller one pulled her *cotehardie* all the way down to her ankles, noticing that Notker of Weyrach was staring lustfully at her shapely calves. The shorter one was snivelling.

Buko gnashed his teeth and gripped his knife hilt so tightly, his knuckles were white. His expression was furious, and he was certainly in two minds. Huon of Sagar noticed immediately.

'Time to face the truth,' he snorted. 'You've botched it, Buko. You all botched it. It's clearly not your day. Thus I advise you to head home. Quickly. Before another opportunity to make fools of yourselves arises.'

Buko swore, this time echoed by Weyrach, and Rymbaba, and Wittram, and even Woldan of Osiny through his dressing.

'What about the wenches?' Buko spoke as though only then noticing them. 'Do we slay them?'

'Or lay them?' Weyrach smiled lecherously. 'Master Huon is right to a degree that this day has indeed turned out lousy, so perhaps we could at least finish it on a pleasant note? We'll take the wenches, find a soft hayrick and take turns. What say you?'

Rymbaba and Wittram chuckled, but rather hesitantly. Woldan of Osiny groaned through the blood-soaked linen. Huon of Sagar shook his head.

Buko took a step towards the girls, who cowered and hugged each other more tightly. The younger of them sobbed.

Reynevan seized Samson, who was already gearing up to intervene, by the sleeve.

'Don't you dare,' he said.

'What?'

'Don't you dare touch her. Because the results might be disastrous for you. She's a noblewoman and not just any noblewoman at that – she's Katarzyna of Biberstein, the daughter of Jan of Biberstein, the Lord of Stolz.'

'Are you certain, Hagenau?' asked Buko of Krossig, interrupting the long and pregnant silence that followed his announcement. 'Perhaps you are mistaken?'

'He is not.' Tassilo of Tresckow lifted up and displayed a pouch with an embroidered coat of arms showing a red deer's antler on a field of gold he had taken from the strongbox.

'Indeed,' admitted Buko. 'The Bibersteins' arms. Which one is she?'

'The taller, older one.'

'Ha!' The Raubritter clutched his sides. 'Then we shall finish the day on a pleasant note indeed and make up for our losses. Hubert, tie her up and put her in front of you on your horse.'

'I predicted it,' Huon of Sagar said, spreading his arms. 'This day has given you a fresh chance to make fools of yourselves. Not for the first time do I wonder, Buko, whether you inherited your stupidity or acquired it.'

'And you,' said Buko, ignoring the sorcerer, stood over the younger one, who was cringing and had begun to snivel. 'You, lassie, wipe your nose and listen carefully. Sit here and wait for the pursuers. They might not have sent anyone after you, but they'll certainly come after Lady Biberstein. You'll tell the Lord of Stolz that the ransom for his young daughter will be ... five hundred grzywna, or precisely five hundred times three score Prague groschen: a trifle for Biberstein. Sir Jan will be notified of the means of payment. Do you understand? Look at me when I'm talking to you! Do you understand?'

The lass cringed even more but lifted her blue eyes towards Buko and nodded.

'Do you really consider this a good idea?' Tassilo of Tresckow asked seriously.

'Indeed. And that will suffice. We ride.'

Buko turned to face Scharley, Reynevan and Samson.

'You, however—'

'We,' Reynevan interrupted, 'would like to ride with you, m'Lord Buko.'

'I beg your pardon?'

'We would like to accompany you,' Reynevan, staring at Fair Nicolette, was paying no heed to Scharley's hissing or Samson's face. 'For safety. If you have nothing against it—'

'Who said I don't?' asked Buko.

'Well, don't,' said Notker of Weyrach pointedly. 'Why should you? Wouldn't it be better, given the circumstances, for them to be with us rather than behind us? They wanted, if I recall, to go to Hungary, so it's on their way . . .'

'Very well.' Buko nodded. 'You will ride with us. To horse, *comitiva*. Hubert, guard the girl . . . And you, m'Lord Huon, why are you pulling a face?'

'Think, Buko. Think.'

Chapter Twenty-Four

In which Reynevan, instead of going to Hungary, goes to Castle Bodak in the Golden Mountains. He doesn't know it, but he will only manage to leave there *in omnem ventum*.

They travelled along the road to Bardo, quickly at first, often looking back, but soon slowed. The horses were weary and the state of the riders was far from good. Woldan of Osiny, face badly cut by the dented helmet, wasn't the only man riding hunched over in the saddle, groaning. The others' injuries, although not as spectacular, were clearly making themselves felt. Notker of Weyrach was grunting and Tassilo of Tresckow was holding his elbow against his belly, trying to find a comfortable position. Kuno of Wittram, grimacing as though he'd drunk Marseilles vinegar, was calling on the saints in hushed tones. Paszko Rymbaba was feeling his side, cursing, spitting on his hand and looking at the saliva.

Of the Raubritters, only Buko appeared unharmed, or hadn't been beaten up as severely as the others, or withstood pain better. Finally, growing bored of having to stop and wait for his comrades lagging behind, Buko decided to abandon the road and ride through the woods instead. Hidden among the trees they could ride slowly, with no risk that a search party would catch them up.

Katarzyna of Biberstein – formerly Nicolette – did not make the slightest sound during the ride. Although her bound hands and position on Hubert's saddle must have tormented and distressed her, the girl wasn't moaning or uttering a word of complaint. She looked ahead apathetically, clearly resigned to her fate.

Reynevan made several secretive attempts to communicate, but to no avail – she avoided eye contact and pretended not to notice his gestures. At least up until the crossing.

They crossed the Nysa in the afternoon at a place that appeared shallow, but where the current was much more powerful than expected. Among the confusion, splashing, swearing and neighing of horses, Nicolette slid from the saddle and would have gone in were it not for Reynevan riding vigilantly beside her.

'Be brave,' he whispered into her ear, lifting her up and hugging her to himself. 'Be brave, Nicolette. I'll get you out of this . . .'

He found her small, slender hand and squeezed it. She reciprocated strongly. She smelled of mint and sweet flag.

'Hey!' yelled Buko. 'You! Hagenau! Leave her alone. Hubert!'

Samson rode over to Reynevan, took Nicolette from him, picked her up like a feather and placed her in front of Hubert.

'I'm not carrying her again, m'lord!' Hubert informed Buko. 'The giant can take over.'

Buko swore, but waved a resigned hand. Reynevan watched him with growing hatred. He didn't particularly believe in the man-eating aquatic monsters meant to live in the depths of the Nysa in the region of Bardo, but he would have given much for one of those monsters to emerge from the turbid river and devour the Raubritter and his blood-bay stallion.

'I have to honour you in one respect,' said Scharley, splashing beside him, in hushed tones. 'One could never grow bored in your company.'

'Scharley . . . I owe you . . .'

'You owe me a great deal, I don't deny it,' said the penitent, tugging at his reins. 'But if you mean to offer an explanation, drop it. I recognised her. You were gawping at her during the tournament in Ziębice, and later she warned us that they would be lying in wait for you at Stolz. I imagine you are indebted to her in other ways, too. Did anyone ever prophesy that women would be the end of you? Or am I the first?'

'Scharley—'

'Don't bother,' interrupted the penitent. 'I understand. You are indebted and infatuated, ergo we'll have to stick our necks out once again, and Hungary's a long way off. Too bad. I'd just ask you to do one thing: think before you act. Can you promise me that?'

'Scharley . . . I—'

'Beware, quiet. They're watching us. And spur your horse on or the current will take you!'

Towards the evening, they reached the foot of Reichenstein in the Golden Mountains, the north-west end of the border chain of Rychleby and Jeseníky. They planned to rest and refresh themselves in a settlement lying by the small River Bystra that flowed down from the mountains, but the peasants there proved to be inhospitable – by not allowing the Raubritters to steal from them. Arrows showered at the Raubritters from the palisade defending the entrance, and the determined faces of free peasants armed with pitchforks and bardiches, didn't invite them to demand hospitality from them. Who knows what would have happened in an ordinary situation, but now the injuries and fatigue were making themselves felt. Tassilo of Tresckow was the first to rein his horse around, followed by the usually quick-tempered Rymbaba, and Notker of Weyrach turned back without even tossing a coarse oath at the village.

'Damned churls,' Buko of Krossig said, catching them up. 'One ought, as my father did, to demolish their shacks and burn everything down to the ground at least once every five years. Otherwise they put on airs. Prosperity makes them conceited. And proud.'

It had become overcast. Smoke drifted over from the village. Dogs barked.

'The Black Forest's ahead of us,' Buko warned from the head of the line. 'Stay close together! Don't fall behind. Keep watch on the horses.'

The warning was treated seriously, because the Black Forest – a dense, wet complex of beeches, yews, alders and hornbeams – looked very grim. So grim it sent shivers down their spines. They felt at once an evil, slumbering somewhere in the thicket.

The horses snorted and tossed their heads.

And a bleached skeleton lying just at the side of the road didn't look at all out of place.

Samson muttered softly.

Nel mezzo del cammin di nostra vita
mi ritrovai per una selva oscura
ché la diritta via era smarrita . . .

'I can't get it out of my head, that Dante,' he explained, seeing Reynevan's look.

'It's extremely apt,' said Scharley with a shudder. 'A lovely wood, goes without saying . . . To ride here alone . . . After dark . . .'

'I advise against it,' said Huon of Sagar, riding over. 'I strongly advise against it.'

They rode up an ever-steeper hillside. The Black Forest ended, the beechwoods thinned out, limestone and gneiss grated under hooves, basalt clattered. Rocks with fantastic shapes grew out of the sides of the ravines. As dusk fell, it quickly grew dark as black clouds approached from the north in wave after wave.

Hubert took Nicolette from Samson on Buko's firm order. Furthermore, Buko, previously having ridden at the head, handed over the lead to Weyrach and Tresckow and remained close to the squire and the captive.

'Dammit . . .' muttered Reynevan to Scharley, who was riding alongside. 'I have to free her, but suspicions have clearly grown in his mind. He's guarding her and watching us the whole time . . . Why?'

'Perhaps,' Scharley replied quietly, and Reynevan realised in horror that it wasn't Scharley at all, 'perhaps he looked into your face? Which is a mirror of both your feelings and your plans.'

Reynevan swore under his breath. It was already quite dark, but it wasn't just the dusk that was to blame for his mistake. The white-haired mage had evidently used magic.

'Will you turn me in?' he asked point-blank.

'I shall not,' the magician replied after a moment. 'But should you try anything stupid, I'll stop you myself. You know I'm capable. So don't do anything stupid, and when we arrive, we shall see—'

'Arrive where?'

'Now it's my turn.'

'I beg your pardon?'

'My turn to ask a question. Why, don't you know the rules of the game? Didn't you play it at university? *Quaestiones de quodlibet*? You asked first. Now it's my turn. Who is the giant you call Samson?'

'My companion and comrade. And anyway, why don't you ask him yourself? Hidden behind a magical disguise, of course.'

'I've tried,' admitted the sorcerer without embarrassment, 'but he's cunning. He saw through it at once. Where did you come by him?'

'In a Benedictine monastery. But if it's *quodlibet*, it's my turn now. What is the celebrated Huon of Sagar doing in a *comitiva* with Buko of Krossig, a Silesian robber knight?'

'Have you heard of me?'

'Who hasn't heard of Huon of Sagar? And of Matavermis, the powerful spell that saved the fields by the Weser from locusts in the summer of 1412.'

'There weren't so many locusts,' Huon replied modestly. 'And regarding your question . . . Why, I provide myself with room and board and an existence at a decent level. With a certain amount of sacrifice, naturally.'

'Often regarding matters of the conscience?'

'Reinmar of Bielawa.' The sorcerer surprised Reynevan with his knowledge. 'The questions game isn't a debate about ethics.

But I shall answer: often, indeed. The conscience, however, is like the body – it can be toughened up. And it cuts both ways. Does the answer satisfy you?'

'So much so that I have no further questions.'

'Then I win.' Huon of Sagar spurred on his black horse. 'And regarding the maiden . . . Keep a cool head and don't do anything foolish. As I said, we shall see when we arrive. And we have almost arrived. In front of us is the Abyss. Farewell, then, for I have work to do.'

They had to stop. The road winding up the steep slope vanished in the rocky scree caused by the hillside subsiding and disappeared into the chasm. The chasm was full of grey fog which prevented them from guessing the actual depth. On the other side, lights flickered in the greyness, where vague shapes of buildings showed faintly.

'Dismount,' commanded Buko. 'Master Huon, if you would.'

'Hold the horses,' the mage said, standing at the edge of the precipice and raising his crooked staff. 'Firmly.'

He brandished the staff and shouted a spell that again sounded Arabic to Reynevan's ear, as it had in Ścibor's Clearing, but much longer, more intricate and complicated – in its intonation, too. The horses snorted and stepped back, stamping hard.

There was a frigid gust and abruptly, an icy chill fell over them. The cold stung their cheeks, creaked in their noses, made their eyes water and penetrated their throats when they breathed in. The temperature dropped so suddenly, it was as though they were inside a sphere that was sucking up all the cold from the world.

'Hold . . . the horses . . .' Buko covered his face with a sleeve. Woldan of Osiny groaned, holding his bandaged head. Reynevan felt his fingers gripping the reins going numb.

All the cold that the sorcerer had gathered from around him, which until then had only been palpable, suddenly became visible and took the form of a white glow billowing above the precipice.

The glow first sparkled with snowflakes and then turned a blinding white. There was a long-drawn-out, intensifying crack, a crunching crescendo which reached its climax in a glassy chord as plaintive as a bell.

'Well, I'll be—' began Rymbaba. And didn't finish his sentence.

A bridge lay across the precipice. A bridge of ice, sparkling and twinkling like a diamond.

'Onwards.' Huon of Sagar seized his horse tightly by the reins close to the bit. 'Let us cross.'

'Will it hold?' asked Notker. 'It won't break?'

'In time.' The mage shrugged. 'It's a very impermanent thing. Every moment of delay increases the risk.'

Notker of Weyrach asked no further questions and pulled his horse hurriedly after Huon. Kuno of Wittram stepped onto the bridge after him, then Rymbaba. Horseshoes jingled on the ice, echoing glassily.

Seeing that Hubert couldn't cope with both his horse and Katarzyna of Biberstein, Reynevan hurried to help, but was beaten to it by Samson, who picked up the young woman. Buko of Krossig kept close by, eyes attentive and hand on his sword hilt. *He smells a rat*, thought Reynevan. *He suspects us.*

The bridge, radiating cold, rang beneath the blows of hooves. Nicolette glanced down and groaned softly. Reynevan also looked down and swallowed. The fog covering the bottom of the ravine and the tops of spruces protruding from it were visible through the ice crystal.

'Swifter!' Huon of Sagar urged from the front, as though he knew what was about to happen.

The bridge creaked and began to whiten in front of their very eyes, losing its transparency. Spidery cracks ran in many places.

'Make haste, make bloody haste,' Tassilo of Tresckow, who was leading Woldan, urged Reynevan. The horses being led by Scharley at the rear of the column snorted. The animals were becoming increasingly skittish, shying and stamping. And with every stamp on the bridge, more cracks and fissures appeared. The construction creaked and groaned. The first chips broke off and plummeted downwards.

Reynevan finally found the courage to look beneath his feet and with immense relief saw rocks and boulders through the icy block. He had reached the far side. They all had.

The bridge cracked, creaked and emitted a glassy groan, then shattered with a boom and exploded into a million shining fragments, tumbling noiselessly into the foggy chasm. Reynevan gasped aloud in a chorus of other gasps.

''E always does that,' said Hubert in hushed tones. 'Master Huon, I mean. He just says it. There was nothing to fear, the bridge holds, it always collapses once the last man's over, never mind how many cross. Master Huon likes to frighten people.'

Scharley summarised Huon and his sense of humour with a well-chosen word. Reynevan looked around and saw a wall topped by crenellations, a gate with a rectangular watchtower over it, and a tower rising above it all.

'Bodak Castle,' explained Hubert. 'We're 'ome.'

'You have somewhat arduous access to your home,' observed Scharley. 'What do you do when magic lets you down? Sleep out in the open?'

'Not at all. There's another road over there, from Kłodzko. But that way's much longer; believe me, we'd have to ride until midnight that way ...'

While Scharley was talking to the squire, Reynevan was exchanging looks with Nicolette. The girl looked frightened, as though only now – on seeing the castle – did she understand the gravity of her situation. For the first time, Reynevan thought his glance brought her relief and solace. A glance that said: *Don't be afraid. And bear up. I'll get you out of here, I swear.*

The gate grated as it opened into a small courtyard. Buko of Krossig immediately swore at several servants, accusing them of idling, and drove them to work, ordering them to take care of the horses, armour, bathhouse, food and drink. He expected everything right away, briskly, at the double.

'Welcome, gentlemen,' said the Raubritter, 'to my *patrimonium*. To Castle Bodak.'

Formosa of Krossig must have been a beautiful woman once, for like most comely women she had changed with age into a hideous old hag. Her figure, once compared no doubt to a young birch tree, now brought to mind an old broomstick. Her skin, probably once resembling a peach's, was now dry and blotchy, stretched over her bones like leather on a shoemaker's last, causing her rather prominent nose to become horribly haggish. In Silesia, women were drowned in rivers and ponds as witches for much shorter and much less hooked noses.

Like most formerly beautiful women, Formosa of Krossig obstinately failed to notice or accept the fact that the springtime of her life was gone for ever, and that winter was coming. It was particularly noticeable in the way she dressed. Her entire costume, from the lurid pink slippers to the outlandish pillbox, the delicate white wimple, the muslin *couvrechef*, the clinging indigo dress, the pearl-encrusted girdle, the scarlet brocade *surcote* – everything would have been better suited to a younger woman.

On top of that, whenever she met a man, Formosa of Krossig instinctively became coquettish. The results were ghastly.

'You are most welcome.' She smiled at Scharley and Notker of Weyrach, flashing very yellowed teeth. 'I welcome you to my castle, gentlemen. You're finally home, Huon. I've missed you very, very much.'

Reynevan had managed to piece together a picture of the situation from snatches of conversations overheard during the journey, but it was far from complete. He did not know that Formosa of Pannewitz had been dowered with Bodak Castle when she married Otto of Krossig, an impoverished but proud descendant of Franconian *ministeriales*, for love. Or that Buko, her and Otto's son, was departing markedly from the truth by calling the castle his *patrimonium*. The word *matrimonium* would have been more accurate, although premature. Following the death of her husband, Formosa hadn't lost the property or roof over her head thanks to her family, the wealthy Pannewitzes of Silesia. And, supported by the Pannewitzes, she was the real lady of the castle for life.

Reynevan had also heard enough to guess at the relationship between Formosa and Huon of Sagar, but much too little to know that the sorcerer, pursued by the Inquisition of the Archbishop of Magdeburg, had fled to relatives in Silesia – the Sagars had an estate near Krosno dating all the way back to Bolesław the Bald. Somehow, Huon met Formosa, the sorcerer caught Formosa's fancy, and from then on had lived at the castle.

'I've missed you very much,' repeated Formosa, standing on the tips of her pink slippers and kissing the sorcerer's cheek. 'Get changed, my dear. And do come in, gentlemen, do come in . . .'

The wild boar on the Krossigs' coat of arms – next to something unrecognisable on the heraldic shield which was blackened with soot and covered in cobwebs – looked down from above the fireplace onto the large oak table in the middle of the hall. The walls were hung with animal skins and weapons, none of which looked serviceable. One of the walls was covered by a Flemish tapestry woven in Arras, portraying Abraham, Isaac and the ram caught in the bushes.

The *comitiva*, wearing gambesons marked with the indentions of armour, sat around the table. The mood, though initially rather gloomy, was somewhat improved by the arrival of a keg. And spoiled again by Formosa returning from the kitchen.

'Do my ears deceive me?' she asked menacingly, pointing at Nicolette. 'Buko! You've kidnapped the daughter of the Lord of Stolz?'

'I told that whoreson wizard not to say anything,' grunted Buko to Weyrach. 'Fucking conjurer, can't keep his trap shut for more than a second . . . I was just about to tell you, Mother. And explain everything. It happened like this—'

'I know how it happened,' interrupted Formosa, clearly well informed. 'You dolts! Wasted a week and somebody snatched the loot out from under your noses ... I'm not surprised by the youngsters. But you, Lord Weyrach, a mature, level-headed man ...'

She smiled at Notker, who lowered his eyes and swore under his breath. Buko was about to swear aloud, but Formosa wagged a threatening finger at him.

'And this idiot ends up kidnapping Jan of Biberstein's daughter,' she continued. 'Buko! Have you utterly lost your mind?'

'You might let us eat first, Mother,' said the Raubritter angrily. 'We're sitting here hungry and thirsty as if it's a wake. It's a shame in front of guests. Serve us with food and we'll talk about our interests afterwards.'

'The food is being prepared and they're bringing in the beverages. Don't teach me manners. Forgive us, gentle knights. And you, m'lord, I don't know ... Nor you, handsome young man ...'

'He asks to be called Scharley,' said Buko, remembering his responsibilities. 'And this stripling is Reinmar of Hagenau.'

'Ah. A descendant of the famous poet?'

'No.'

Huon of Sagar returned, having changed into a baggy *houppelande* with a large fur collar. It was obvious who enjoyed the grace and favour of the lady of the castle, for Huon immediately received a roast chicken, a dish of pierogis and a goblet of wine, served by Formosa herself. The sorcerer began to eat uninhibitedly, disdainfully ignoring the starved looks from the rest of the company. Fortunately, the others didn't have to wait long, either. To everyone's delight, a great dish of pork stewed with raisins was brought to the table, preceded by a delicious aroma. A second followed, piled with mutton seasoned with saffron, then a third, filled with a fricassee of various game meats, and finally pots of kasha. A few vats containing two-year mead and Hungarian wine were greeted with undiminished joy and immediately sampled.

The company began eating in dignified silence, interrupted only by the crunching of teeth and toasts being raised from time to time. Reynevan ate cautiously and in moderation – the previous month's escapades had already taught him the frightful effects of gluttony following a long period without food. He hoped that servants weren't usually neglected at Bodak and that Samson wouldn't be doomed to go without.

The meal lasted for some time. Finally, Buko of Krossig loosened his belt and belched.

'Now,' said Formosa, correctly guessing that this signalled the end of the first course, 'perhaps it's time to discuss our affairs. Although it seems to me there's nothing to talk about, for Biberstein's daughter is poor business.'

'Business, Mother,' said Buko, who had clearly gained some composure from the Hungarian wine, 'is my affair, with all due respect. It is I who work, I who bring goods to the castle. My efforts give food, drink and clothing to everybody here. I risk my life. If, one day, by the will of God, my day of reckoning arrives, you will see how frugal your lives will become. So do not gripe!'

'Just look.' Formosa turned to the Raubritters with arms akimbo. 'Just look how he struts, my youngest boy. Feeds and clothes me? Upon my word, I shall split my sides laughing. I'd look fine if I only relied on him. Fortunately, here in Bodak, there is a deep cellar, and in it chests. And in the chests, pipsqueak, is what your father and brothers put there, may the Lord keep them. They knew how to bring loot home. They didn't make asses of themselves. They didn't foolishly kidnap magnates' daughters. They knew what they were doing—'

'I also know what I'm doing! The Lord of Stolz will pay a ransom—'

'Not a chance!' Formosa cut him off. 'Biberstein? Pay? You fool! He'll give up on her, then seize you and exact revenge. Something similar happened in Lusatia. If you bothered to listen, you'd recall what befell Wolf Schlitter when he tried a similar antic with Fryderyk of Biberstein, Lord of Żary. And in what coin the master of Żary paid him back.'

'I heard about that,' Huon of Sagar confirmed indifferently, 'because the matter was trumpeted far and wide. Biberstein's men caught Wolf, stuck him with spears like an animal, then castrated and disembowelled him. There was a popular saying in Lusatia afterwards: the Wolf got away a few times and then found out how sharp the Deer's Antlers were—'

'As usual, m'Lord Sagar,' Buko cut in impatiently, 'you have heard everything and know everything. In the meantime, Sir Woldan is moaning in pain, Paszko Rymbaba is spitting blood and all our bones are aching, so perhaps, rather than reminiscing, you could prepare some kind of remedy? Why do you have a workshop in the tower, eh? Only to call forth the Devil?'

'Heed to whom you speak!' said Formosa, losing her temper, but the wizard gestured for her to be quiet.

'It is meet, indeed, to relieve suffering,' he said, rising from the table. 'Would Lord Reinmar of Hagenau like to help me?'

'Why, of course.' Reynevan also stood up. 'Naturally, m'Lord Sagar.'

They went out.

'Two wizards,' Buko grunted behind them. 'An old and a young. Devil's spawn ...'

The wizard's laboratory was located on the tower's highest – and definitely coldest – storey, and a large part of Kłodzko Valley would probably have been visible from the windows had dusk not fallen. Reynevan's expert eye noticed the workshop's modern equipment. Unlike old-fashioned mages and alchemists with predilections for workshops like junk rooms, full of all sorts of rubbish, modern wizards preferred workshops furnished and equipped spartanly, with only what was necessary. Apart from benefits in the form of tidiness and aesthetics, there was also the advantage that it made fleeing easier. Modern alchemists, threatened by the Inquisition, made their escape according to the principle *omnia mea mecum porto*, not looking back at the chattels they abandoned without remorse. Old-school mages defended to the end their stuffed crocodiles, dried sawfishes' snouts, homunculi, vipers in alcohol, bezoars and mandrakes – and ended up burned at the stake.

Huon of Sagar took a straw-covered demijohn from a chest and filled two goblets with a ruby-coloured liquid. It smelled of honey and sour cherries and so had to be *kirschwasser*.

'Sit down, Reinmar of Bielawa,' he said, pointing at a chair. 'Let's drink. I already have a large store of camphor unguent for bruises – it is, as you can guess, in great demand at Bodak. Probably only the potion for curing hangovers is used more often. I invited you here because I want to talk.'

Reynevan looked around. He admired Huon's alchemic equipment, which was pleasingly clean and well organised. He also liked the alembic and athanor, and the evenly arranged and neatly labelled flacons of philtres and elixirs. But he was most delighted by the library.

Abdul Alhazred's *Necronomicon* was open on a bookrest and clearly being read. Other sorcerer's grimoires Reynevan recognised were piled up on the table alongside medical and philosophical treatises. There were also, naturally, the *opera magna* of alchemic knowledge and some gems including the notorious *Red Dragon*.

'I feel honoured that the famous Huon of Sagar wishes to talk to me,' he said, sipping a little *kirschwasser*. 'Someone I could have expected to meet anywhere, but not—'

'But not at a Raubritter's castle,' finished Huon. 'Oh well, the fates have thus conspired. But I don't complain, actually. I have what I like here, namely peace and quiet and solitude. The Inquisition has probably forgotten about me, including the Reverend Gunter of Schwarzburg, Archbishop of Magdeburg, who was determined to reward me with execution for saving the country from locusts. I have a laboratory here, as you see. I experiment a little, write a little . . . Occasionally, for fresh air and recreation, I join Buko on a plundering raid. All in all . . .' The wizard heaved a deep sigh. 'All in all, it's not a bad life. Except . . .'

Reynevan politely restrained his curiosity, but Huon of Sagar was evidently in the mood to confide.

'You've seen what Formosa is like.' He grimaced. '*Exsiccatum est faenum, cecidit flos.* The woman's turned five and fifty, and rather than weakening, grumbling and being at death's door, the old mare endlessly demands that I service her, over and over, morning, noon and night, in more and more elaborate ways. I'm destroying my stomach and kidneys with sodding aphrodisiacs. But I have to keep the old cow satisfied. If I don't acquit myself in the bedchamber, I'll fall from grace and then Buko will turf me out.'

Reynevan made no comment again. The wizard scrutinised him keenly.

'For the time being, Buko of Krossig tolerates me,' he continued, 'but it would be unwise to underestimate him. He's a buffoon, indeed, but often so enterprising and ingenious in his evil inclinations it makes my flesh creep. He's sure to surprise us in the affair with Biberstein's daughter, I'm convinced of it, which is why I've decided to help you.'

'You, help me? Why?'

'Why? Because it doesn't suit me for Jan of Biberstein to lay siege here, nor for the Inquisition to renew its interest in me. Because I've heard nothing but good about your brother, Piotr of Bielawa. Because I was displeased by the bats that someone set on you and your companions in the Cistercian Forest. *Tandem* because Toledo *alma mater nostra est,* I don't want you to come to a sticky end, O confrater in the dark arts. And you may. There's something between you and Biberstein's daughter, you don't hide it. I don't know if it's an old affection or love at first sight, but I know that *amantes amentes.* On the way here, you were a hair's breadth from seizing her from the saddle and galloping off, which would have resulted in the two of you perishing in the Black Forest. Now, too, when matters are becoming complicated, you are ready to grab her around the waist and leap from the walls. Am I very wide of the mark?'

'Not really.'

'As I said,' the wizard smiled with the corners of his mouth, '*amantes amentes.* Yes, yes, life is a veritable Narrenturm. Do you know, incidentally, what day it is today? Or rather what night?'

'Not really. I've somewhat lost track of dates . . .'

'Never mind dates, calendars can be wrong. More importantly, today is the autumnal equinox. The *Aequinoctium autumnalis*.'

He stood up and slid out a carved oak bench more or less two ells wide and a little over one ell high from under the table and placed it by the door. He then took from a chest of drawers a labelled clay pot tied up with vellum.

'I keep quite a special ointment in this vessel,' he pointed. 'A *mescolanza* made according to classical ingredients. I wrote the recipe on the label, as you can see. *Solanum dulcamara, solanum niger*, aconitine, cinquefoil, poplar leaves, bat's blood, cowbane, red poppy seeds, purslane, wild celery . . . The only thing I changed is the fat. I replaced the fat melted from an unbaptised child as recommended by *The Grimorium Verum* with sunflower oil. It's cheaper and longer-lasting.'

'Is it . . .' Reynevan swallowed. 'What I think it is?'

'I never lock the laboratory door,' the wizard continued as though he hadn't heard the question, 'and there are no bars on the window. I'm putting the ointment here, on the table. You probably know how it's applied. I advise you to use it sparingly – it causes side effects.'

'But is it . . . safe?'

'Nothing is safe.' Huon of Sagar shrugged. 'Nothing. Everything is a theory. And as one of my friends says: *Grau, teurer Freund, ist alle Theorie* – all theory is grey.'

'But I—'

'Reinmar,' the magician interrupted coldly. 'Have some consideration. I've told and shown you enough already to be suspected of complicity. Don't expect any more. Very well, it's time we went. Let's take the camphor *unguentum* to rub on the maladies of our bruised robbers. Let us also take extract of *somniferum*. It alleviates the pain and puts one to sleep, for sleep heals and soothes, and as they say: *qui dormit non peccat*, he who sleeps doesn't sin. And doesn't interfere . . . Help me, Reinmar.'

Reynevan stood up and carelessly toppled over a small pile of books, quickly grabbing them to save them from falling. He straightened the book lying on the top, whose lengthy title inscription began *Bernardi Silvestri libri duo; quibus tituli Megacosmos et Microcosmos* ... Reynevan lost interest when his eye was caught by another incunable lying underneath, and by the wording of its title. He suddenly realised he had seen it before. Or rather, fragments of it.

He hurriedly shoved Bernardus Silvestris aside. And gasped.

DOCTOR EVANGELICUS
SUPER OMNES EVANGELISTAS
JOANNES WICLEPH ANGLICUS
DE BLASPHEMIA DE APOSTASIA
DE SYMONIA
DE POTESTATE PAPAE
DE COMPOSITIONE HOMINIS

Anglicus, *not* basilicus, he thought. Symonia, *not* sanctimonia. Papae, *not* papillae. The scorched sheet of paper from Powojowice. The manuscript Peterlin had ordered burned. It was John Wycliffe.

'Wycliffe,' he involuntarily repeated aloud. 'Wycliffe, who will tell a lie and tell the truth. Burned and disinterred—'

'I beg your pardon?' Huon of Sagar turned around holding two jars. 'Whom did they disinter?'

'They haven't yet,' Reynevan said, still somewhere else in his thoughts. 'It is to come. That's what the prophecy said. John Wycliffe, *doctor evangelicus*. A liar, because he was a heretic, but according to the goliard song, he's also the one who will tell the truth. Buried in Lutterworth, England. His remains will be dug up and burned, his ashes thrown into the River Swift and will flow to the seas. It will happen in three years.'

'Fascinating,' said Huon seriously. 'And other prophecies? The fate of Europe? Of the world? Of Christianity?'

'I'm sorry. Just Wycliffe.'

'Woeful. But it's better than nothing. They'll heave Wycliffe out of his grave, you say? In three years? Let's see if we can exploit that knowledge somehow. And since we're on the subject, why does Wycliffe . . . ? Oh . . . I beg your pardon. It's not my . . . Nowadays, one doesn't ask questions like that. Wycliffe, Waldhausen, Huss, Hieronim, Joachim . . . Dangerous reading matter, dangerous views, plenty of people have lost their lives because of them . . .'

Plenty of people, thought Reynevan. *Plenty, indeed. Oh, Peterlin, Peterlin.*

'Here – carry the flasks for me, and let's go.'

The company seated at table were now well in their cups and only Buko of Krossig and Scharley looked sober. The feasting had continued, for further dishes had been brought from the kitchen: wild boar sausage in beer, cervelat, Westphalian black pudding and plenty of bread.

Huon of Sagar rubbed ointment into the bruises and sprains and Reynevan changed Woldan of Osiny's dressing. Woldan's swollen face caused uproarious mirth when the bandages were removed. Woldan himself was less interested in his wounds than in the hounskull helmet, which had reputedly cost a whole four grzywna and which he had left in the forest. To the observation that the helmet was buckled, he replied that it could have been beaten out.

Woldan was also the only one to drink the elixir of poppy. Buko, after tasting it, poured the decoct onto the straw-covered floor and chided Huon for giving him the 'bitter shit'. The others did likewise. Thus, the hopes of sedating the Raubritters were dashed.

Formosa of Krossig hadn't stinted on the Hungarian wine and two-year mead, either, evinced by her flushed cheeks and slightly incoherent speech. When Reynevan and Huon returned, Formosa stopped sending seductive looks towards Weyrach and

Scharley and directed her attention instead towards Katarzyna, who, after eating a little, was sitting with head lowered.

'She's quite unlike a Biberstein,' she declared, eyeing the girl appraisingly. 'Quite unlike. Skinny waist, small behind. Since the Bibersteins married into the Pogarells, their daughters have been bigger-arsed. They also inherited snub noses from the Pogarells, and this one has a straight nose. She's tall, indeed, like Sędkowice women, and Sędkowice blood is also intermingled with the Bibersteins'. But Sędkowice women have dark eyes while hers are blue . . .'

Nicolette's lips began to tremble. Reynevan clenched his fists and teeth.

'The Devil take it!' Buko tossed a gnawed rib onto the table. 'What is she, a mare at a horse fair?'

'Quiet! I'm only looking, and if I find anything surprising, I comment. For example, she's not so young, must be approaching eighteen. Why then, I wonder, isn't she yet married? Flawed, perhaps?'

'What do I care for her flaws? Am I considering marriage with her?'

'That's not a bad idea.' Huon of Sagar looked up from his goblet. 'Marry her, Buko. *Raptus puellae* is a much less serious crime than kidnapping for ransom. Perhaps the Lord of Stolz will forgive you if you bow before him with her as your wedded wife. He couldn't very well break his son-in-law on the wheel.'

'Well, son?' Formosa smiled haggishly. 'What do you think?'

Buko looked first at her, then at the wizard, and his eyes were cold and evil. He said nothing and played with his goblet for a long time. The cup's distinctive shape betrayed its origin; the scenes from the life of Saint Adalbert engraved on the rim left no doubt. It was a chalice, probably stolen during the famous Whitsuntide raid on the custodian of the Głogów Collegiate.

'To that, m'Lord Sagar,' the Raubritter finally drawled, 'I'd gladly say: wed her yourself. But you may not, for you are a priest. Unless the Devil you serve has freed you of celibacy.'

'I could marry her,' Paszko Rymbaba, face flushed with wine, suddenly announced. 'I am fond of her.'

Tassilo and Wittram snorted and Woldan chortled. Notker of Weyrach looked on seriously, though his tone belied his expression.

'Absolutely,' he mocked. 'Wed her, Paszko. A connection with the Bibersteins is favourable.'

'Damn you,' burped Paszko. 'Am I their inferior? An impoverished nobleman? A *skartabellat*? Rymbaba *sum*! I'm a son and grandson of the Pakosławs. When we were lords in Greater Poland and Silesia, the Bibersteins were still in Lusatia, squatting with beavers in the mud, chewing bark from the trees and unable to utter a word in a human tongue. I'm wedding her and that's that – what is there to lose? All that's left is to send someone to my father. I cannot proceed without a paternal blessing . . .'

'There'll even be somebody to marry you,' Weyrach continued to mock. 'We hear that m'Lord Sagar is a priest. He could marry you right now. Couldn't he?'

The wizard didn't even look at him, appearing only to be interested in the Westphalian black pudding.

'It would be the done thing to ask the interested party,' he finally said, '*Matrimonium inter invitos non contrahitur* – marriage requires the agreement of both of the betrotheds.'

'The interested party,' snorted Weyrach, 'is silent, and *qui tacet, consentit* – silence gives consent. And we may ask the other parties, why not. I say, Tassilo? Do you wish to get hitched? Or perhaps you, Kuno? Woldan? And you, m'Lord Scharley, why so silent? One in, all in! Who else has the will to become, excuse the expression, a nupturient?'

'Perhaps you yourself?' Formosa of Krossig tilted her head. 'What? Sir Notker? For it's high time, I gather. Don't you want her for your wife? Doesn't she please you?'

'She does, to be sure.' The Raubritter smiled lecherously. 'But marriage is the tomb of love, for which reason I opt that we simply fuck her in turn.'

'It is time, I see,' said Formosa, standing up, 'for the ladies to leave the table in order not to hinder the gentlemen in their jokes and japes. Come, wench, you have no business here, either.'

Nicolette stood up meekly and walked away dragging her feet, stooping, head lowered, lips trembling and eyes shining with tears.

It was all a pretence, thought Reynevan, clenching his fists beneath the table. *All her daring, all her spirit, all her resolution was just deceit. How weak, frail, forlorn is the fair sex, how reliant on us men they are. How absolutely dependent on us.*

'Huon,' Formosa called back from the door. 'Don't make me wait too long.'

'I'm coming now.' The wizard stood up. 'I'm too exhausted by the idiotic chase through the forests to listen any longer to idiotic conversations. I wish the company a peaceful night.'

Buko of Krossig spat on the floor.

The departure of the sorcerer and the womenfolk was the sign for even more raucous merriment and heavy drinking. The *comitiva* roared for more wine and the wenches bringing the drinks suffered the routine pats, gropes, pinches and pokes and ran back to the kitchen flushed and sobbing.

'Let's wash down the food!'

'May we prosper!'

'Good health!'

'Cheers!'

Paszko Rymbaba and Kuno of Wittram, arms around each other's shoulders, began to sing. Weyrach and Tassilo of Tresckow joined in.

Meum est propositum in taberna mori,
ut sint vina proxima morientis ori;
Tunc cantabunt letius angelorum chori:
Sit Deus propitius huic potatori!

Buko of Krossig was hideously drunk. With each glass he

became – paradoxically – increasingly sober, from one toast to the next progressively gloomy, grim and pale. He sat glumly, clutching the chalice, keeping a close watch on Scharley through narrowed eyes.

Kuno of Wittram beat a rhythm on the table with his mug and Notker of Weyrach did likewise with the hilt of his misericord. Woldan of Osiny was rocking his bandaged head, mumbling incoherently. Rymbaba and Tresckow were roaring.

Bibit hera, bibit herus,
bibit miles, bibit clerus,
bibit ille, bibit illa,
bibit servus cum ancilla,
bibit velox, bibit piger,
bibit albus, bibit niger . . .

'Hoc! Hoc!'

'Buko, my brother!' Paszko staggered and fell on Buko's neck, wetting him with his whiskers. 'Good health! Let's make merry! Why, it's my damn betrothal to Lady Biberstein. I'm fond of her! Soon, by my troth, I'll invite you to the wedding and then the christening, and then we'll make merry!'

Hey, long live my dear pole
That fits just right in the hole . . .

'Be vigilant,' Scharley hissed at Reynevan, exploiting the opportunity to the full. 'I think we should soon make ourselves scarce.'

'I know,' Reynevan whispered back. 'If anything happens, flee with Samson. Don't wait for me . . . I must get the girl. And go to the tower . . .'

Buko shoved Rymbaba away, but Paszko went on.

'Don't worry, Buko! Why, Lady Formosa was right, you fucked up, kidnapping Biberstein's daughter. But I've solved that problem. Now she's my betrothed, soon my bride, it's cut and dried! Ha, ha, why, I'm rhyming like a poet. Buko! Let's drink! Let's make merry, hurrah, hurrah! Hey, long live my dear pole . . .'

Buko shoved him away again.

'I know you,' he said to Scharley. 'I thought so in Kromolin and now I'm certain of the place and the time. Although you were dressed in a Franciscan habit then, I know your face, and I recall where I saw you. In Wrocław town square, in the year 1418, on that memorable July Monday.'

Scharley didn't reply but looked boldly straight into the Raubritter's narrowed eyes. Buko turned the chalice over in his hands.

'And you,' he shifted his angry eyes towards Reynevan, 'Hagenau, or whatever you're truly called, the Devil knows who you are, perhaps a monk or a priest's bastard, perhaps Sir Jan of Biberstein also put you in the tower at Stolz for rebellion and sedition. I was suspicious of you as we rode. I saw the way you stared at the wench and thought you were looking for an opportunity to avenge yourself on Biberstein by stabbing his daughter. What with your revenge and my five hundred grzywna, I've had my eye on you. Before you drew your blade, your head would have left your shoulders.

'And now,' the Raubritter drawled, 'I look at your face and wonder whether I'm mistaken. Perhaps you weren't lying in wait for her, perhaps it was affection? Perhaps you want to rescue her, steal her from under my nose. So I ponder and the fury grows in me, wondering what kind of fool you take me for. My hand is itching to slit your throat, but I'm restraining myself. For the moment.'

'Perhaps,' Scharley's voice was absolutely calm, 'perhaps we could call it a night? The day was full of wearying attractions, we're all feeling it in our bones – why, just look, Sir Woldan has fallen asleep with his face in the sauce. I suggest we postpone further discussions *ad cras*.'

'Nothing will be postponed *ad cras*,' snapped Buko. 'I shall declare the banquet over in good time. Now drink, monk's son, bastard, when they fill your cup. And you, too, Hagenau. How do you know it's not your last drink? It's a long and perilous road to Hungary. Who knows if you'll get there? After all, as they say: a fellow doesn't know in the morning what the evening will bring.'

'Especially,' Notker of Weyrach added scathingly, 'considering that Lord Biberstein will have sent riders out. He must be simply furious at his daughter's kidnappers.'

'Didn't you mark what I said?' belched Paszko Rymbaba. 'Biberstein is a trifle. When I'm marrying his daughter. When—'

'Be quiet,' Weyrach interrupted him. 'You're drunk. Buko and I have found a better solution to the matter, a simpler method for dealing with Biberstein. So keep your absolutely redundant notions of marriage to yourself.'

'But I'm fond of her ... The betrothal ... And the bedding ceremony ... Hey, long live my dear—'

'Shut your trap,' Weyrach said.

Scharley tore his gaze away from Buko and looked at Tresckow.

'Do you, Sir Tassilo,' he calmly asked, 'approve of your companions' plan? Do you also consider it excellent?'

'I do,' replied Tresckow after a moment of silence. 'However much I regret it. But that's life. It's your bad luck that you complete the puzzle so well—'

'Very well, in fact.' Buko of Krossig interrupted him midsentence. 'Couldn't be better. The easiest to recognise among those who took part in the robbery are the ones without visors. Master Scharley. Lord Hagenau, who so dashingly drove the stolen carriage. And your giant servant isn't especially forgettable, either. They'll recognise those visages even on corpses. And they'll be identified, incidentally, as corpses. It will be revealed who robbed the train. Who kidnapped Biberstein's daughter—'

'And who murdered her?' Scharley finished calmly.

'And raped her.' Weyrach smiled lecherously. 'Let's not forget about the rape.'

Reynevan sprang up from the bench but immediately sat down again, pinned by Tresckow's powerful arm. At the same moment, Kuno of Wittram seized Scharley by the shoulders and

Buko pressed a misericord to the penitent's throat.

'Is this fitting?' mumbled Rymbaba. 'They came to our rescue—'

'We must,' Weyrach cut him off. 'Pick up your sword.'

A trickle of blood oozed down the penitent's neck from under the dagger's blade. In spite of that, Scharley's voice was calm.

'Your plan won't succeed. No one will believe you.'

'Oh, but they will,' Weyrach assured him. 'You'd be surprised what people believe.'

'You won't lead Biberstein up the garden path. Your heads will roll.'

'Why threaten me, monk's son?' Buko leaned over Scharley. 'When you won't live to see the dawn? You say Biberstein won't believe it? Perhaps. Will my head roll? God's will. But I shall still cut your throats. If only for *gaudium*, as that whoreson Sagar would say. I'll finish you off now, Hagenau, if only to annoy Sagar, because you are a comrade, another sorcerer. But you, Scharley, let's call it a settling of debts. Historical debts. For Wrocław, for 1418. The executioner beheaded the rebellion's other ringleaders in Wrocław town square; you'll meet your maker at Bodak, you bastard.'

'That's the second time you've called me a bastard, Buko.'

'I shall do it a third. Bastard! What will you do about it?'

Scharley didn't manage to answer. The door crashed open and Hubert entered. To be more precise, Samson Honey-Eater entered. Using Hubert to open the door.

In the complete silence that followed, broken only by the hooting of a tawny owl flying around the tower, Samson lifted the squire higher by his collar and trousers and threw him down at Buko's feet. Hubert groaned loudly as he hit the floor.

'This individual,' said Samson in the silence, 'tried to strangle me with some reins in the stable. He claims it was on your orders, Lord Krossig. Can you explain that, m'lord?'

Buko couldn't.

'Kill him!' he yelled. 'Kill the harlot's son! Have at him!'

Scharley freed himself from Wittram's grasp with a sinuous

movement and elbowed Tresckow in the throat. Tassilo wheezed and released Reynevan, who punched Rymbaba with clinical precision in his bruised side, right where it hurt. Paszko howled and doubled up. Scharley jumped at Buko and kicked him hard in the shin. Buko fell to his knees. Reynevan didn't see what happened next as Tassilo of Tresckow punched him powerfully in the nape of the neck and threw him onto the table. But he guessed, hearing the sound of a blow, the crunch of a nose breaking and a furious roar.

'Don't ever call me a bastard again, Krossig,' rang the penitent's clear voice.

As Tresckow grappled with Scharley, Reynevan tried to come to his aid but was unable to – Rymbaba, face twisted in pain, had grabbed him from behind and bent him over. As Weyrach and Kuno of Wittram fell on Samson, the giant seized a bench, pushed it into Weyrach's chest, shoved Kuno, then knocked them both over and pinned them down. Seeing Reynevan struggling and kicking in Rymbaba's bear hug, Samson dashed over and slapped Rymbaba in the ear with his open palm. Paszko scuttled sideways the length of the hall and slammed head first into the fireplace. Reynevan seized a tin vat from the table and clanged it down on Notker of Weyrach, who was trying to stand up.

'The girl, Reynevan!' yelled Scharley. 'Run!'

Buko of Krossig sprang up from the floor, roaring, with blood streaming from his smashed nose. He tore a bear spear from the wall, wound up and threw it at Scharley. The penitent nimbly dodged and the spear merely grazed his arm. And skewered Woldan of Osiny, who had just woken up and was rising from the table, completely disorientated. Woldan flew backwards, slammed against the Flemish tapestry and slid down it, his head lolling on the shaft protruding from his chest.

Buko bellowed even louder and lunged at Scharley with his bare hands, fingers splayed like a sparrowhawk's talons. Scharley warded him off with one outstretched hand and punched him in his broken nose with the other. Buko howled and fell to his knees.

Tresckow pounced on Scharley, Kuno of Wittram on Tresckow, Samson on Wittram, followed by Weyrach, Buko – streaming blood – and finally Hubert. They all struggled on the floor like a tableau of Laocoön and his sons. Reynevan saw none of that. He was racing up the steep steps of the tower.

He came upon her outside a low door, in a place lit by a torch in an iron basket. She didn't look at all surprised. It was as though she'd been waiting for him.

'Nicolette . . .'

'Aucassin.'

'I am come—'

He didn't manage to say why he was come for a powerful blow knocked him to the ground. He lifted himself up onto his elbows, was hit again and fell.

'I treat you with kindness,' panted Paszko Rymbaba, standing astride him. 'I treat you with kindness and you thump me in the ribs? In my broken ribs? You bastard!'

'Hey, you! Big fellow!'

Paszko turned around. And smiled in delight to see Katarzyna of Biberstein, the maiden he was fond of, to whom, he thought, he was already betrothed and with whom in his dreams he could already see himself coupled in the marriage bed. His dreams were a little premature, as it turned out.

His would-be fiancée jabbed him in the eye with the heel of her hand. As Paszko grabbed his face, the girl hoisted up her *cotehardie* for greater ease of movement and kicked him hard in the crotch. Her would-be fiancé curled up, breathed in with a whistle, then howled like a wolf and dropped to his knees, cupping the family jewels in both hands. Nicolette lifted her gown even higher, revealing a pair of shapely thighs, leaped up to kick him in the side of the head, then spun around and kicked him in the chest. Paszko Pakosławic Rymbaba pitched over onto the spiral staircase and tumbled down, head over heels.

Reynevan raised himself up to his knees. She stood over him, composed, not even breathing hard, breast barely heaving, with only her eyes, blazing like a leopard's, betraying any excitement. *She was pretending*, he thought, *only pretending to be afraid and intimidated. She hoodwinked everyone, myself included.*

'What now, Aucassin?'

'Upstairs. Quickly, Nicolette.'

She ran, bounding up the stairs like a mountain goat. He could barely keep up with her. *I'll have to make a thorough appraisal of my views regarding the weakness of the fair sex*, he thought.

Paszko Rymbaba tumbled all the way down to the bottom of the stairs and into the centre of the hall, almost under the table. He lay for a while, gasping for air like a carp in a net, then grunted, groaned and rocked his head back and forth, still holding his genitalia. Then he sat up.

There was no one in the hall, not counting Woldan's body with the bear spear plunged into his chest and Hubert, grimacing in pain, cradling one arm – clearly fractured – to his belly. The squire met Rymbaba's eyes and nodded towards the door leading to the courtyard. Needlessly, because Paszko had already heard the noise, shouts and regular thudding coming from that direction.

A terrified serving wench and boy looked into the hall, then fled as soon as they saw the knights. Paszko stood up, swore crudely, pulled down from the wall a large bardiche with a blackened blade and a shaft full of woodworm holes. For a while, he couldn't make up his mind. Although he was seething with evil desire to wreak revenge on Biberstein's beastly daughter, good sense told him he ought to help the *comitiva*.

Biberstein's daughter won't escape revenge, he thought, feeling his balls already beginning to swell, *since there's no way out of the tower. For the time being, I'll only punish her with haughty contempt. First, let the others pay.*

'Just you fucking wait!' he yelled, hobbling towards the courtyard and the sounds of battle. 'I'm coming for you!'

*

The door to the tower trembled from heavy blows. Scharley cursed.

'Hurry,' he yelled. 'Samson!'

Samson dragged two saddled horses from the stable. He growled menacingly at a servant who had jumped down from the hayloft. The servant fled, showing a clean pair of heels.

'This door won't hold for long,' said Scharley, dashing down the stone steps and wresting the reins from him. 'The gate, quickly!'

Samson saw another plank burst and splinter in the door they had locked, the only thing separating them from Buko and his comrades. They heard the clank of iron against stone and metal – it was obvious that the enraged Raubritters were trying to hack off the hinges. There was no time to lose. Samson looked around. The gate was held fast by a beam, additionally reinforced by a heavy padlock. Three bounds took the giant to a woodpile, where he wrenched a large axe from a tree stump, and he was back at the gate in another three bounds. He grunted, raised the axe and with extraordinary strength brought the butt down on the padlock.

'Harder!' yelled Scharley, glancing at the now-splintering door. 'Hit it harder!'

Samson hit it harder, making the entire gate and the watchtower above it shudder. The padlock, probably Nuremberg work, didn't yield, but the spikes supporting the beam came half out of the wall.

'Once again! Whack it!'

The Nuremberg padlock gave way under the next blow, the spikes were pulled out and the beam fell with a thud.

'Rub it under your arms,' said Reynevan, pulling his shirt down from his shoulders, then scooping up some ointment from the clay pot and demonstrating how to apply it. 'And on the back of your neck, like this. More, more ... Rub it in well ... Quickly, Nicolette. We don't have much time.'

The girl looked at him for a moment, disbelief fighting with admiration in her eyes. She didn't say a word, but reached for the ointment. Reynevan dragged the oaken bench into the centre of the room. He opened the window wide and a cold wind swept into the sorcerer's workshop. Nicolette shuddered.

'Don't go near the window,' he cautioned her. 'Better . . . not to look down.'

'Aucassin.' She stared at him intently. 'I understand we're fighting for our lives, but are you sure you know what you're doing?'

'Sit astride the bench, please. There's really no time to lose. Sit behind me.'

'I'd prefer to sit in front. Clasp me around the waist, tightly. Tighter . . .'

She was hot. She smelled of sweet flag and mint, which even the intense smell of Huon's *mescolanza* couldn't mask.

'Ready?' he asked.

'Ready. You won't let go of me? You won't let me fall?'

'I'd sooner die.'

'Don't die.' She sighed, turning her head back and briefly brushing her lips against Reynevan's. 'Don't die, please. Live. Cast the spell.'

Weh, weh, Windchen
Zum Fenster hinaus
In omnem ventum!
Hop out of the window
It won't touch a thing

The bench leaped up and shifted under them like a skittish horse. In spite of all her resolution, Nicolette was unable to suppress a cry of terror. Neither, indeed, was Reynevan. The bench rose two yards in the air and spun around like a furious spinning top. Huon's workshop blurred before their eyes. Nicolette pressed her fingers over Reynevan's arms entwined around her and squealed, more from eagerness than anxiety, he could have sworn.

Meanwhile, the bench shot straight through the window, into the cold, dark night. And immediately dived steeply down.

'Hold on!' yelled Reynevan. The rush of air pushed his words back into his throat. 'Hoooold oooon!'

'*You* hold on! Oh Jeeesuuus!'

'Aaaaaagh-aaaaaagh!'

Just as the Nuremberg padlock gave way and the beam thudded down, the door to the tower flew open and the Raubritters poured out onto the stone staircase. They were all armed and enraged and so blinded by bloodlust that Buko of Krossig, who was first across the threshold, stumbled on the steep steps and fell straight into a pile of muck. The others leaped on Samson and Scharley. Samson roared like a buffalo, fending the assailants off with wild swings of the axe. Scharley, also roaring, fought them off using a halberd he had found by the gate. But the advantage – and the combat skills – were with the Raubritters. Retreating before the venomous thrusts and treacherous slashes of swords, Samson and Scharley fell back.

Until they felt the hard resistance of a wall at their backs.

And then Reynevan flew past overhead.

Seeing the courtyard growing bigger and bigger, Reynevan yelled. As did Nicolette. Their screams, transformed by the suffocating wind into truly hellish howls, achieved a much better effect than their physical arrival. Save for Kuno of Wittram – who happened to glance skywards – none of the Raubritters had even noticed the riders on the flying bench. But the howling accomplished a literally devastating psychological effect. Weyrach dropped on all fours, Rymbaba cursed, yelled and flattened himself against the ground, and Tassilo of Tresckow tumbled down beside him, unconscious, the only victim of the air raid – the bench had caught him on the back of the head as it plummeted towards the courtyard. Kuno of Wittram crossed himself and crawled under a hay wain. Buko of Krossig cringed as the hem of Nicolette's *cotehardie* slashed him across the ear. The bench, meanwhile, shot upwards, accompanied by even louder screams from the flyers.

Notker of Weyrach stared open-mouthed as they flew away and was fortunate to glimpse Scharley out of the corner of his eye and dodge a halberd thrust at the last moment. He caught the shaft and they began to wrestle.

Samson discarded the axe, caught one of the horses by the reins and was about to grab the other when Buko lunged at him with a dagger. Samson dodged, but not quickly enough. The dagger cut open his sleeve. And his shoulder. Samson punched Buko in the teeth and sent him staggering towards the gate before he could stab him again.

Samson felt his shoulder and saw the blood on his hand.

'Now,' he said slowly and loudly, 'now you've really annoyed me.'

He walked to where Scharley and Weyrach were still fighting over the halberd shaft and punched Weyrach so hard that the old Raubritter turned a graceful somersault. As Paszko Rymbaba raised the bardiche to strike, Samson turned around and looked at him. Paszko took two rapid steps backwards.

Scharley caught the horses while Samson grabbed a round, wrought-iron buckler from a rack by the gate.

'Have at them!' yelled Buko, lifting a sword Wittram had dropped. 'Weyrach! Kuno! Paszko! Have at them! Oh, Jesus Christ . . .'

He had seen what Samson was doing. For Samson had taken hold of the buckler with the grip of a discus thrower and was whirling around like one. The buckler shot from his hand as though from a ballista, just missing Weyrach. It whistled across the entire courtyard and slammed into a corbel, shattering it. Weyrach swallowed. Samson, meanwhile, was taking another buckler from the stand.

'Jesus Christ . . .' gasped Buko, seeing the giant start to spin again. 'Take cover!'

'By the dugs of Saint Agatha!' yelled Kuno of Wittram. 'Every man for himself!'

The Raubritters bolted in different directions, it being

impossible to guess who Samson would throw the shield at. Rymbaba fled to the stable, Weyrach ducked behind a pile of firewood, Kuno of Wittram crawled under the hay wain again, and Tassilo of Tresckow – who was just coming around – flattened himself on the ground once more. In full flight, Buko of Krossig tore an old-fashioned elongated shield from the practice mannequin and covered his back with it as he fled.

Samson finished his spin standing on one leg in a classical pose worthy of a statue by Myron or Phidias. The buckler whistled towards its target and struck the shield on Krossig's back with a loud thud. The momentum propelled the Raubritter a distance of at least ten yards, where his progress was stopped by a wall. After a few seconds, he slid down to the ground.

Samson looked around. There was no one left to throw anything at.

'Over here!' yelled Scharley, now in the saddle, from the gate. 'Over here, Samson! To horse!'

The horse, although sturdy, slumped slightly beneath his weight. Samson patted it.

They set off at a gallop.

Chapter Twenty-Five

In which the talk is of love and death. Love is beautiful. Death is not.

One of Reynevan's Prague mentors had tried to prove that magical flights are subject to the mental control of a witch or wizard covered in flying ointment. The objects they fly on, however, whether brooms, pokers, shovels or whatever else, are just lifeless objects, inanimate matter, subject to the will of the magician and utterly dependent on their will.

There must have been something in that theory, since the bench carrying Reynevan and Nicolette, after soaring into the night sky to the height of Castle Bodak's battlements, circled around until Reynevan saw two horsemen – one of unmistakably impressive physique – leaving the castle. The bench glided gently after them, as though wanting to reassure him that neither of the horsemen racing along the Kłodzko road was seriously wounded and that they weren't being followed. And, as though sensing his relief, the bench described another circle around Bodak, then flew upwards into the sky, above the moonlit clouds.

It turned out that Huon of Sagar had also been right in his claim that 'all theory is grey', since the disquisitions of the Prague doctor about mental control were true only to a limited extent. A very limited extent. Having assured Reynevan that Scharley and Samson were safe, the flying bench completely stopped being dependent on his will. In particular, it wasn't Reynevan's will at all to fly so high that the moon appeared to be at arm's length, where it was so cold his and Nicolette's teeth began to chatter like

Spanish castanets. It was also far from Reynevan's will to fly in circles like a buzzard hunting for prey. His will had been to follow Samson and Scharley – but the flying bench didn't appear to give a toss about that.

Neither did Reynevan feel like studying the geography of Silesia from a bird's-eye view, so who knew how and under whose mental influence the item of furniture descended and flew northeast, above the slope of Reichenstein. Having passed the massifs of Javorník and Borůvková on their right, the bench soon flew over a town surrounded by a double wall bristling with towers, which could only have been Paczków. Then it carried them over the valley of a river that could only have been the Nysa. Soon the roofs of the towers of Otmuchów passed by beneath them. Here, however, the bench changed direction, made a big curve, returned to the Nysa and this time flew upstream, following the meandering ribbon, silver in the moonlight. Reynevan's heart beat faster for a moment, for it looked as though the bench planned to return to Bodak. But no, it suddenly turned and headed north, soaring over the lowlands. Soon, the monastery complex of Kamieniec flashed beneath them and Reynevan was once again alarmed. After all, Nicolette had also applied the flying *mescolanza* to herself and may also have been using her willpower to influence the flying bench. They might have been – which their trajectory appeared to be suggesting – flying straight towards Stolz, the Bibersteins' seat. Reynevan doubted he would be well received.

But the bench turned a little westwards and flew over some town or other. Reynevan was slowly losing his sense of direction and beginning not to recognise the scenery passing by under his eyes, which were watering from the wind.

They were not flying as high now, so they had stopped shaking and their teeth were no longer chattering. The bench was gliding smoothly and stably, without any aerobatics, and Nicolette's fingernails weren't digging into Reynevan's hands any more. He felt sure that the girl had relaxed a little. He was also breathing freely again, no longer being choked by the rush of air or the adrenaline.

They were flying beneath moonlit clouds. A chequerboard of forests and fields passed by below.

'Aucassin ...' she said, shouting over the wind. 'Do you know ... where we're ...'

He pulled her closer to his chest, knowing he should, that she was expecting it.

'No, Nicolette. I don't.'

He didn't. But he had his suspicions. Informed ones. And he wasn't even particularly astonished when a soft cry from the girl informed him that they had company.

The witch on their left, a woman in the prime of life wearing a married woman's cap, was flying on a broom, the rush of air blowing her sheepskin jerkin about. Moving a little closer, she greeted them with a raised hand. After a moment's hesitation, they waved back and she overtook them.

Two witches flying to their right didn't greet them and probably hadn't even noticed them, so absorbed were they with each other. They were very young, with plaits flying behind them, sitting astride a sleigh runner, one behind the other. They were kissing passionately and voraciously; it looked as though the one in front would break her neck trying to reach the mouth of the one behind. While the one behind was utterly preoccupied with the breasts of the one in front, which she had pulled out of her unbuttoned blouse.

Nicolette cleared her throat and coughed strangely, fidgeting on the bench as though wanting to move further away from Reynevan. He knew why she was doing it and was aware of his own excitement. The erotic scene wasn't to blame, or at least not that alone. Huon of Sagar had warned him about the side effects of the ointment and Reynevan remembered it had also been mentioned in Prague. All the specialists were in agreement that when rubbed into the skin, the flying ointment acted as a powerful aphrodisiac.

The sky was suddenly teeming with witches flying in a skein, the apex of which was vanishing somewhere among the luminescence of the clouds. The witches, *bonae feminae* (although there were also several wizards in the skein) were flying astride various objects, from classic brooms and pokers, to benches, shovels, pitchforks and fence posts. Myriad bats and night birds darted in front of and behind the flyers.

'Hey! Confrater! Greetings!'

He looked back. And, strangely, wasn't surprised.

The witch who had shouted to him was wearing a black pointed hat with her flame-red hair streaming out from under it. Her dirty-green woollen shawl fluttered behind her like a train. Flying beside her was the young witch with the foxy face who had made the prophesy. Bringing up the rear was the swarthy Jagna, rocking on a poker and none too sober, naturally.

Nicolette cleared her throat loudly and looked back. Reynevan shrugged and made an innocent face. The red-haired witch laughed. Jagna burped.

It was the night of the autumn equinox, called by common folk the Feast of the Ingathering, the magical start of the season of favourable winnowing winds. For witches and the Older Tribes it was Mabon, one of the year's eight sabbaths.

'Hey!' the ginger-haired witch suddenly screamed. 'Sisters! Confraters! Shall we have some fun?'

Reynevan wasn't in the mood for fun, all the more so because he had no idea what kind of fun it would be. But the bench was now clearly part of the flock and was doing what the flock did.

The squadron dived down towards the bright blaze of a campfire. Almost catching on the treetops, they flashed, whooping and shrieking, over a clearing and the campfire around which about a dozen men were seated. Reynevan saw them looking upwards and heard faint cries of excitement. Nicolette's fingernails dug into his flesh again.

The ginger-haired witch displayed the greatest audacity – howling like a she-wolf, she flew down so low that her broom threw up a shower of sparks from the campfire. Then all of them climbed steeply upwards, with the yells of the men by the fire hot on their heels. *If they had crossbows*, Reynevan shuddered, *who knows how the game might have ended.*

The skein began to descend towards a mountain rising up from a forest and itself covered in trees. It was definitely not Ślęza, however, contrary to Reynevan's conjecture. The mountain was too small to be Ślęza.

'That's Grochowa Mountain,' Nicolette said, surprising him. 'Near Frankenstein.'

Campfires were burning on the mountainsides, yellow, resinous flames were shooting up behind the trees, and a red glow was lighting up the magical mist lying in the valleys. Reynevan could hear shouting, singing, the squealing of flutes and pipes and the jangling of a tambourine.

Nicolette trembled at his side, and probably not just from the cold. He wasn't especially surprised – shivers were also running down his spine and he could barely swallow, for his heart was in his mouth.

A fiery-eyed, dishevelled creature with hair the colour of carrots landed beside them and got off its broom. Its sticklike fingers were armed with curved, six-inch talons. Close by, four gnomes in acorn-shaped caps were drowning each other out with their jabbering. They appeared to have all flown in on a large oar. A creature wearing something like an inside-out sheepskin that might have been its natural fur plodded past, dragging a baker's shovel behind it. A witch in a snow-white and a very immodestly unbuttoned shirt cast a hostile glance at them.

At first, during the flight, Reynevan had planned to escape immediately, and right after landing he was still wondering how to get away as quickly as possible, descend the mountain and vanish. Nothing came of it. They had landed in a throng which carried them away like a current. Any step in a different direction would have been conspicuous and aroused suspicion. He judged it would be better not to.

'Aucassin.' Nicolette cuddled up to him, clearly sensing what he was thinking. 'Do you know the saying: out of the frying pan into the fire?'

'Fear not,' he said, overcoming his constricted throat. 'Fear not, Nicolette. I won't let any harm come to you. I'll get you out of here. And I certainly won't abandon you.'

'I know,' she replied at once, so trustingly and warmly he immediately regained his courage and confidence – qualities that, to be frank, had almost utterly deserted him. He raised his head bravely and courteously offered the girl his arm, then looked around with a brave, even arrogant, expression.

They were overtaken by a hamadryad smelling of wet bark and passed a buck-toothed dwarf whose naked belly, shining like a watermelon, stuck out from beneath a short waistcoat. Reynevan had seen a similar dwarf before. In the cemetery in Wąwolnica, the night after Peterlin's funeral.

More flyers of both genders were landing on the soft slope beneath a cliff, their numbers constantly growing, slowly adding to the crush. Fortunately, the organisers had taken care of order and designated stewards were directing the arrivals to a clearing where they could deposit brooms and other flying equipment in a specially made enclosure. They had to wait in a queue for a while. Nicolette squeezed his arm harder when a thin creature in a shroud – smelling quite corpse-like – joined the queue behind them. In front of them were two rusalkas with hair full of dry ears of corn, stamping their little feet impatiently and nervously.

A moment later, a fat kobold took Reynevan's bench from him and gave him a receipt – a freshwater mussel shell with a magical ideogram and the Roman numeral CLXXIII painted on it.

'Look after it,' he snarled routinely. 'Don't lose it. I'm not going to search all over the place if you do.'

Nicolette cuddled tightly to him and squeezed his hand, this time for a more specific and obvious reason that Reynevan had also noticed.

They had suddenly become the centre of – by no means

well-disposed – attention. Several witches were staring at them evilly. Beside them, Formosa of Krossig would have seemed a pretty young thing and a rare beauty.

'Now, now,' croaked one, her ugliness distinguishing her even in such an assemblage. 'It must be true what they say – that you can buy flying ointment at every apothecary's in Świdnica! Now everyone flies: lizards, fishes and toads! Any moment now, and those Poor Clares from Strzelin will start flying here. Are we to put up with it, I ask? Who are they?'

'You're right!' said another hag, showing a single tooth. 'You're right, dear Madam Sprenger! They ought to say who they are! And who told them about the sabbath?'

'You're right, you're right, dear Madam Kramer!' croaked a third, bent double, with an impressive collection of hairy warts on her face. 'They ought! For they may be spies!'

'Shut your trap, you old cow,' said the red-haired witch in the black hat. 'Don't put on airs. I know these two. Will that suffice?'

Madams Kramer and Sprenger wanted to object and argue, but the red-haired witch cut short the discussion with a menacing shake of her clenched fist, and Jagna summed things up with a disdainful burp, loud and long, emerging from the very bottom of her guts. Then the adversaries became separated by a line of witches walking across the slope.

The young witch with the foxy face and the unhealthy complexion, the one who had prophesied in the wilderness, accompanied her sisters.

As before, a garland of verbena and clover rested on her fair hair. As before, her dark-circled eyes shone. And she was staring at Reynevan unceasingly.

'Others are also observing you,' said the red-haired witch, 'so to prevent further incidents, you must, as neophytes, come before the Domina. Then no one will dare to pester you. Follow me. Up to the top.'

'May I presume we'll be in no danger there?' asked Reynevan, clearing his throat.

The red-haired witch turned and fixed him with her green eyes.

'It's a bit late to be afraid,' she drawled. 'You needed caution when you were rubbing on the ointment and mounting the bench. I don't want to be overly nosy, confrater, but at our first meeting, I understood that you're the kind of person who always gets into trouble and ends up where he shouldn't. Though, as they say, it's none of my business. But are you in any danger from the Domina? That depends on what you conceal in your hearts. If it be anger and treachery—'

'No,' he retorted at once. 'I can assure you of that.'

'You have nothing to fear, then.' She smiled. 'Let's go.'

They passed campfires surrounded by groups of witches and other participants in the sabbath conversing, greeting new arrivals, making merry and arguing. Cups and bowls were being passed around, filled from cauldrons and vats, and the pleasant aroma of cider, perry and other fermented beverages floated up, mixing with smoke. Jagna was about to stop there, but the red-haired witch restrained her with a sharp word.

A huge fire roared on the peak of Grochowa Mountain, throwing up great flames; millions of sparks flew up into the black sky like fiery bees. Below the peak was a hollow, ending in a terrace. There, beneath a cauldron on a tripod, burned a smaller campfire with faint shimmering shapes around it. Several figures were standing on the slope beneath the terrace, clearly waiting for an audience.

As they approached and passed through the veil of steam belching from the cauldron, the indistinct shapes materialised into three women holding brooms decorated with ribbons and golden sickles. A heavily bearded and very tall man – made even taller by a fur cap with a set of forked stag's antlers attached to it – was busying himself near the cauldron. There was also another motionless, dark shape beyond the fire and steam.

'The Domina,' explained the red-haired witch, after they had joined the queue with the others, 'will most probably not ask you anything; we aren't customarily curious. If she does, remember to

434

address her as "Domna". Remember also that names aren't used at the sabbath, unless you're among friends. You are *joioza* and *bachelar* to everybody else.'

The petitioner preceding them was a young woman with a thick plait hanging down beyond her waist. Although very pretty, she was disabled and walked with a limp which was distinctive enough for Reynevan to diagnose congenital hip dislocation. She passed them, wiping away tears.

'It is impolite and unwelcome to stare here,' the red-haired witch reprimanded Reynevan. 'Go on. The Domina is waiting.'

Reynevan knew that the title of Domina – or Old Woman – belonged to the head witch, the leader of the flight and the sabbath's high priestess. So although he had hoped, in his heart of hearts, to see a woman slightly less repulsive than Sprenger, Kramer and the hags with them, he had still been expecting an old crone. What he hadn't expected was Medea. Circe. Herodias. A staggeringly attractive incarnation of mature womanhood.

Tall and well proportioned, her physique emanated authority, intuition and power. Her high forehead was decorated by a silver sickle, a blazing, horned crescent, and a gold ankh – *crux ansata* – hung around her neck. The line of her mouth spoke of determination, while her straight nose brought to mind Hera or Persephone from a Greek vase. Her serpentine cascades of jet-black hair tumbled down in splendid disarray, flowing over her shoulders to merge with the black of her cloak. Her gown, visible under her cloak, glistened in the light of the fire, shimmering in many shades: now white, now copper, now crimson.

There was wisdom, night and death in the Domina's eyes.

She recognised them at once.

'Toledo,' she said, and her voice was like the wind coming down from the mountains. 'Toledo and his noble-born *joioza*. Is it your first time among us? Welcome.'

'Our greetings,' said Reynevan, bowing.

Nicolette curtsied. 'Our greetings, Domna.'

'Do you have a request for me? Do you seek an intercession?'

'They want only to pay their respects,' the red-haired witch said behind them. 'To you, Domna, and the Great Triad.'

'I demur. Go in peace. Celebrate Mabon. Praise the name of the Mother of All.'

'*Magna Mater!* Praise her!' repeated the bearded man beside the Domina.

'Praise her!' chorused the three witches standing behind him, raising their brooms and gold crescents. 'Eia!'

Fire shot upwards. The cauldron belched steam.

This time, as they descended to the hollow between the peaks, Jagna refused to be held back and immediately strode towards the noisiest place with the strongest aroma of distilled drinks. She had soon pushed her way to the keg and was drinking apple brandy in great gulps. The red-haired witch didn't try to stop her, and willingly received the keg herself from a long-eared, shaggy creature almost identical to Hans Mein Igel, who had visited the camp of Reynevan and Zawisza the Black of Garbów a month before. Reynevan, taking a cup, considered how time had passed and what time had changed in his life. The drink was so strong it made his nose run.

The red-haired witch had many friends among the revellers, both humans and non-humans. Rusalkas, dryads and liskas greeted her effusively, and stout, ruddy-faced peasant women exchanged hugs and kisses. Women wearing dresses embroidered with gold and ornate capes, their faces partly concealed behind black satin masks, exchanged stiff, distinguished bows. Apple brandy, cider and slivovitz flowed profusely. They were being jostled around in the crush, so Reynevan put his arm around Nicolette. *She ought to be wearing a mask here*, he thought. *Katarzyna, daughter of Jan of Biberstein, the Lord of Stolz, ought to be masked like the other noblewomen.*

The revellers, now somewhat tipsy, began gossiping and backbiting.

'I saw her up there with the Domina.' The red-haired witch indicated with her eyes the cripple with the fair plait and face swollen from weeping, limping nearby. 'What's the matter with her?'

'It's an everyday thing, an everyday impairment.' The chubby miller's daughter shrugged her plump shoulders, still dusted with flour. 'She went to the Domina and the Domina declined her request. Told her to leave it to time and fate.'

'I know. I once asked her for something.'

'And?'

'Time brought what was needed.' The red-haired witch grinned ominously. 'But I took matters into my own hands a little.'

The witches shrieked with a laughter that made the hair on Reynevan's neck stand up. He was aware that the *bonae feminae* were observing him and he was angry with himself for standing rooted to the spot, looking like a frightened savage in front of so many beautiful eyes. He took a sip to give himself courage.

'Extraordinarily many . . .' he said after clearing his throat. 'Extraordinarily many members of the Older Tribes are present here . . .'

'Extraordinarily?'

He turned around. It was no wonder he hadn't heard any footsteps, for just behind his shoulder had stopped an alp; tall, dark-skinned, with pointed ears and hair as white as snow. Alps moved noiselessly.

'Extraordinarily, you say?' repeated the alp. 'Ha, perhaps you'll see the ordinary, lad. What you call "Old" may become the "New". Or the "Renewed". A time of change is approaching, and much will transform. Even what many – and even some of those here – thought unchangeable will change.'

'And they still think so,' said an individual Reynevan had least expected to encounter in this company, namely a priest with a tonsure, clearly taking personally the alp's scathing words. 'They still think so, for they know that some things will never return. You never enter the same river twice. You had your time, Master Alp, you've had your epoch, your era, even your eon. But what to do? *Omnia tempus habent et suis spatiis transeunt universa sub caelo.*

Everything has its time and hour, and what has passed will not return.'

'The order of the world will change,' the alp repeated stubbornly. 'Everything will be reformed. Turn your gaze to the south, to Bohemia. A spark fell there and a flame will be lit from it. Nature will be purged in that flame. Evil and sick things will flee from it. The change will come from the south, from Bohemia, marking the end of certain things and matters. In particular, that book you love to quote from will become nothing more than a collection of proverbs and adages.'

'Do not expect too much from the Czech Hussites,' the priest said, shaking his head. 'In some respects, they are holier than the Pope himself. The Czech reform will not go well for us, methinks.'

'The essence of the reform,' said one of the masked noblewomen in a clear voice, 'is that it changes apparently unchanging and unchangeable things. It opens a crack in an apparently inviolable structure, fractures a seemingly hard, unyielding monolith. And if something can be cracked, chipped or fractured ... it can also be demolished. The Czech Hussites will be a handful of water frozen in a rock. They will burst it.'

'They said the same about the Cathars!' someone shouted from the back.

'They were pebbles cast at the ramparts!'

A commotion began. Reynevan cringed, slightly frightened by the commotion he had caused. He felt a hand on his shoulder. He looked back and shuddered, seeing a tall, female creature, quite attractive, but with eyes glowing like phosphorous and green skin smelling of quince.

'Don't be afraid,' the creature said softly. 'I am only the Older Tribe. Ordinary extraordinariness.' More loudly, she said, 'Nothing can hold back the changes. Tomorrow will be different from Today, so different that people will stop believing in Yesterday. And Master Alp is right, advising you to look more often to the south. To Bohemia. Because the new will come from there. The Transformation will come from there.'

'Let me have my few doubts,' the priest said sardonically. 'War and death will come from there. And *tempus odii* – a time of hatred – will dawn.'

'And a time of vengeance,' added the lame girl with the flaxen plait in an evil voice.

'The better for us.' One of the witches rubbed her hands together. 'Things need shaking up!'

'Time and destiny,' the red-haired witch said pointedly. 'Let us count on time and on destiny.'

'Taking matters into our own hands, if possible,' added the miller's daughter.

'One way or another,' the alp said, straightening his thin body, 'I say it's the beginning of the end. The present order will fall. That cult hatched in Rome, that greedy, arrogantly rampant cult, stuffed with hatred, will tumble. Indeed, it's a wonder it has survived so long, when it is so senseless and unoriginal, to cap it all. The Father, the Son and the Spirit! An ordinary triad, of which there are legion.'

'As far as the Spirit goes,' said the priest, 'they were close to the truth. They just made a mistake with the sex.'

'They were not mistaken,' countered the green woman smelling of quince. 'They lied! Why, perhaps now, in the time of change, they will finally understand who was painted on their icons all those years. Perhaps it will finally dawn on them what the madonnas in their churches really represent.'

'Eia! *Magna Mater!*' chorused the witches. An explosion of wild music, the thudding of drums and songs from nearby campfires joined their cries. Nicolette clung to Reynevan.

'To the clearing!' screamed the red-haired witch. 'To the Circle!'

'Eia! To the Circle!'

'Listen!' shouted the shaman with the deer antlers on his head. 'Listen!'

The crowd gathered in the clearing murmured in excitement.

'Listen to the words of the Goddess, whose arms and thighs are wrapped around the universe!' called the shaman. 'Who, at the Beginning, divided the Waters from the Heavens and danced on them! From whose dance the wind was born, and from the wind the breath of life!'

'Eia!'

The Domina stood beside the shaman, holding her royal form proudly erect.

'Arise,' she screamed, spreading her cloak wide. 'Arise and come to me!'

'Eia! *Magna Mater!*'

'I am the beauty of the green earth,' said the Domina, and her voice was like the wind from the mountains. 'I am the white moon among a thousand stars, I am the secret of the waters. Come to me, for I am the spirit of nature. All things arise from me and all must return to me, before my visage, beloved by the gods and mortals.'

'Eiaaa!'

'I am Lilith, I am the first of the first, I am Astarte, Cybele, Hecate, I am Rigatona, Epona, Rhiannon, the Night Mare, the lover of the gale. Black are my wings, my feet are swifter than the wind, my hands sweeter than the morning dew. The lion knows not when I tread, the beast of the field and forest cannot comprehend my ways. For verily do I tell you: I am the Secret, I am Understanding and Knowledge.'

The fires roared and spat out tongues of flame. The crowd swayed with excitement.

'Worship me deep in your hearts and in the joy of the rite, make sacrifices of the act of love and bliss, because such sacrifices are dear to me. For I am the unsullied virgin and I am the lover of gods and demons, burning with desire. And verily do I say: as I was with you from the beginning, so you shall find me at the end.'

'Listen,' cried the shaman, 'to the words of the Goddess, whose arms and thighs are wrapped around the universe! Who divided the Waters from the Heavens at the Beginning and danced on them. Dance ye, too!'

'Eia! *Magna Mater!*'

With a sudden movement, the Domina cast her cloak from her bare shoulders. She entered the centre of the clearing with female attendants on either side.

The three of them stood, holding each other's hands with their arms extended behind them, faces outwards, backs inwards, as the Graces are occasionally portrayed in paintings.

'*Magna Mater!* Three times nine! Eia!'

Three more witches and three men joined them, linking hands to extend the circle. More came forward in response to their exhortation. Standing in the same positions, facing outwards, backs to the nine forming the centre, they created another circle. Immediately another circle was formed, then another, another and another, each with backs to the one before and larger than the last. While the *nexus* formed by the Domina and her company was encircled by a ring of no more than thirty people, there were at least three hundred in the final, outer circle. Reynevan and Nicolette, carried away by the frenzied throng, ended up in the penultimate circle. Next to Reynevan was one of the masked noblewomen. A strange creature in white squeezed Nicolette's hand.

'Eia!'

'*Magna Mater!*'

Another long-drawn-out cry and wild music sounding from God knew where gave the signal and the dance began, the circles starting to move and whirl. Each circle spun in the opposite direction from the ones adjacent. The sight itself made one dizzy, the hectic music and frenetic cries complementing the movement. The sabbath dissolved into a kaleidoscope of shapes before Reynevan's eyes, and his legs seemed not to touch the ground. He was losing consciousness.

'Eiaaa! Eiaaa!'

'Lilith, Astarte, Cybele!'

'Hecate!'

'Eiaaaa!'

He didn't know how long it lasted. He came to lying on the ground, among other people who were slowly getting to their feet. Nicolette was beside him – she hadn't let go of his hand.

The music played on, but the melody had changed, the frenzied and high-pitched monotonous accompaniment of the whirling dance replaced by ordinary pleasant and lively notes, in time with which the rising witches and wizards were beginning to hum, jiggle and cavort. At least, some did. Others didn't get up from the grass where they had fallen after the dance. Staying on the ground, they formed pairs – mostly, at least, for there were also threesomes and foursomes, and even larger configurations. Reynevan couldn't tear his eyes away, involuntarily licking his lips as he stared. He saw that Nicolette's face was flushed and not just from the glow of the campfire. She pulled him aside without a word, and when he turned his head back for another look, she scolded him.

'I know it's that ointment . . .' She cuddled up to him. 'The flying ointment excites them like that. But don't look at them. I'll be offended if you do.'

'Nicolette . . .' he squeezed her hand. 'Katarzyna—'

'I prefer being Nicolette,' she interrupted immediately. 'But I'd . . . I'd prefer to call you Reinmar. When I met you, you were – I don't deny it – my Aucassin, and you were in love. But not with me. Please don't say anything. Words aren't necessary.'

A flame from a nearby campfire leaped upwards and a cloud of sparks shot into the sky. The people dancing around it cried joyously.

'They are making such merriment,' he muttered, 'that they won't notice if we slip away. And I think it's time we did . . .'

She turned her face away and the glare of the fire danced on her cheeks.

'Why all the hurry?'

Before his amazement faded, he heard footsteps approaching.

'Sister and confrater.'

Before them stood the red-haired witch, holding by the hand the young oracle with the foxy face.

'We wish to talk to you.'

'Go on.'

'Eliszka, here, has finally decided to become a woman.' The red-haired witch laughed freely. 'I was explaining to her that it matters not with whom – there's no shortage of willing candidates here, after all – but she insists, like a stubborn ass, on one and no other. That means you, Toledo.'

The prophetess lowered her dark-ringed eyes. Reynevan swallowed.

'She's too shy and hesitant to ask outright,' continued the *bona femina*. 'She's also a little afraid, sister, that you might scratch her eyes out. And since the night is short and it's a waste of time running around the bushes, I'll ask directly: are you together? Are you his *joioza*? Is he your *bachelar*? Is he free or do you assert your right to him?'

'He is mine,' replied Nicolette, concisely and without hesitation, absolutely dumbfounding Reynevan.

'Then the matter is clear.' The red-haired witch nodded. 'Oh well, Eliszka, if you can't get what you want, you must . . . Come on, we'll find someone else. Farewell. Enjoy yourselves!'

'It's the ointment.' Nicolette squeezed his shoulder and her voice made him shudder. 'It's the fault of that ointment. Will you forgive me? For perhaps you desired her?' she said before he could cool down. 'Ha, I'm sure you did, because the ointment acts on you as it does . . . I know how it works. And I interfered, I got in your way. I didn't want her to have you. From pure jealousy. I took something away from you without promising anything in return. Like a dog in the manger.'

'Nicolette—'

'Let's sit down here,' she interrupted, pointing towards a small grotto in the mountainside. 'I haven't complained before, but with all these adventures I'm about to collapse.'

They sat down.

'My God,' she said, 'so much excitement . . . And to think, when I told the story of that chase by the Stobrawa, no one believed me; not Elisabeth, Anka nor Kaśka. And now? If I tell them about the kidnap, about our flight? About the witches' sabbath? I don't think . . .'

She cleared her throat.

'I don't think I'll tell them anything at all.'

'And rightly so,' he said, nodding. 'Quite apart from the incredible things we've seen and experienced, I wouldn't come out too well in the story, would I? From the ridiculous to the nefarious. I went from being a jester to a robber—'

'But not by your own will,' she interrupted him at once. 'And not as a consequence of your own deeds. Who ought to know that better than I? It was I who tracked down your comrades in Ziębice and disclosed to them that they'd imprison you at Stolz. I can imagine what happened next and know that it's all my fault.'

'It's not so simple.'

They sat for some time in silence, engrossed in the singing and gazing at the fires and the shapes dancing around them.

'Reinmar?'

'Yes.'

'What does Toledo mean? Why do they call you that?'

'There's a famous magical academy in Toledo, Castile,' he explained. 'It has become widespread in some circles to use it as a form of address for people who have studied magical arcana at universities, as opposed to those who have innate magical powers and to whom knowledge is passed down through the generations.'

'So you studied?'

'Yes, in Prague. But briefly and cursorily.'

'It was sufficient.' She touched his hand with some reluctance and then grasped it more boldly. 'You were clearly a diligent student. I never managed to thank you. You rescued me with courage – which I admire – and your talents. You saved me from . . . misfortune. Previously I'd only pitied you, been fascinated

by your story, which might be pulled straight from the pages of
Chrétien of Troyes or Hartmann of Aue. Now I admire you. You
are brave and wise, my Soaring Knight of the Flying Oak Bench.
I want you to be my knight, my magical Toledo. Mine and only
mine. Which is precisely why – from greedy and selfish envy – I
didn't want that girl to have you. I didn't want her to have you
even for a moment.'

'But you've rescued me more times than I have you,' he mumbled in embarrassment. 'It is I who am indebted to you, and I've
never thanked you, either. At least, not as I ought. But I vowed
that when I met you again, I'd bow before you . . .'

'Thank me in the way that you ought.' She cuddled up to him.
'And bow before me. I've dreamed that you would.'

'Nicolette—'

'Not like that. In another way.'

She stood up. Frenetic laughter drifted from the campfires.

Veni, veni, venias,
ne me mori, ne me mori facias!
Hyrca! Hyrce!
Nazaza!
Trillirivos! Trillirivos! Trillirivos!

She began to undress, slowly, unhurriedly, not lowering her eyes,
which were burning in the darkness. She unfastened her silver-
studded girdle and removed her *cotehardie*, which was split at the
side. Then she pulled off her woollen undertunic, beneath which all
that remained was a thin white *chemise*. She hesitated when she got
to the *chemise*. The signal was clear. He approached, touching her
gently. The blouse, he recognised at once, was made from cambric.

Pulchra tibi facies,
Oculorum acies,
Capillorum series;
O quam clara species!
Nazaza!

He cautiously assisted her, still more cautiously overcoming her instinctive resistance, her quiet, involuntary trepidation.

Once the cambric *chemise* was lying atop the other garments on the ground, he gasped, but Nicolette didn't let him feast his eyes for long. She pressed herself tightly against him, entwining him with her arms and searching for his mouth with hers. He complied. And what his eyes had been refused, he delighted in with his touch, paying homage with trembling fingers and hands.

He knelt down. Bowed at her feet. Worshipped her. Like Percival before the Holy Grail.

Rosa rubicundior,
Lilio candidior,
Omnibus formosior,
Semper, semper in te glorior!

She also knelt, hugging him closely to her.
'Forgive my lack of experience,' she whispered.

Nazaza! Nazaza! Nazaza!

Her lack of skill didn't hamper them. At all.

The voices and laughter of the dancers moved away a little, quietened down, and the passion in them calmed. Nicolette's arms trembled slightly and he felt the shaking of her legs wrapped around him. He also saw the flickering of her closed eyelids and her lower lip held between her teeth.

When she finally let him, he raised himself up and gazed upon her, the oval of her face like a painting by Campin, her neck like one of Parler's madonnas. And lower down, her modest, embarrassed *nuditas virtualis*, her small round breasts with nipples hard from desire. Her slim waist, her narrow hips. Her flat stomach. Her shyly clenched thighs, full, beautiful, worthy of the most elaborate compliments. Reynevan's intoxicated head was full of compliments and eloquence. For he was a polymath, a trouveur, and no lesser a lover – in his own opinion – than Tristan and Lancelot. He wanted to tell her she was *lilio candidior*, whiter than the lily, and *omnibus formosior*, comelier than all the others. He wanted to tell her she was *pulchra inter mulieres*. He wanted to tell her everything, but the words stuck in his tight throat.

She saw it. She knew. How could she not? For only in Reynevan's eyes, stupefied by happiness, was she a maiden, a trembling virgin who was embracing him, eyes closed and biting her lower lip in painful ecstasy. For any wise man – had there been one nearby – the matter was clear: she was no shy and inexperienced young lass, but rather a goddess proudly receiving the homage due to her. And goddesses know and see everything.

And do not expect homage in the form of words.

She pulled him onto her and the eternal rite began.

Nazaza! Nazaza! Nazaza!
Trillirivos!

In the clearing, the Domina's words hadn't fully got through to him. Her voice, like the wind coming down from the mountains, had been lost in the murmur of the throng, drowned in the cries, the singing, the music and the roar of the fire. Now, in the gentle fury of love, her words were returning resonantly, clearly. Emphatically. He heard them through the rushing sound of blood in his ears. But did he fully understand them?

I am the beauty of the green earth, I am Lilith, I am the first of the first, I am Astarte, Cybele, Hecate, I am Rigatona, Epona, Rhiannon, the Night Mare, the lover of the gale.

Worship me deep in your hearts and make sacrifices of the act of love and bliss, because such sacrifices are dear to me.

For I am the unsullied virgin and I am the lover of gods and demons, burning with desire. And verily do I say: as I was with you from the beginning, so you shall find me at the end.

They found Her at the end. Both of them.
The fires shot wild explosions of sparks into the sky.

'Please forgive me,' he said, looking at her back, 'for what happened. I oughtn't to have ... Forgive me.'

'I beg your pardon?' She turned to face him. 'For what am I to forgive you?'

'For what happened. I was unwise ... I forgot myself. I behaved badly—'

'Am I to understand,' she interrupted, 'that you regret it? Is that what you mean to say?'

'Yes ... No! No, that's not it ... But I ought ... Ought to have controlled ... I should have been more sensible—'

'So you *do* regret it,' she interrupted him again. 'You reproach yourself; you feel guilty. You feel with regret that a harm was done. In brief: you would give much for what we did to be undone. For me to be what I was.'

'Listen—'

'But I ...' She didn't want to listen. 'I ... I was prepared to follow you. Right away, as I am. To where you are going. To the end of the world. Just to be with you.'

'Lord Biberstein ...' he mumbled, lowering his gaze. 'Your father—'

'Naturally,' she interrupted again. 'My father will send men. And being hunted from two directions is too much for you.'

'Nicolette ... You misunderstood me.'

'You're mistaken. I did understand.'

'Nicolette—'

'Say nothing. Fall asleep. Sleep.'

She touched his lips with her hand, with a movement so fast it escaped his sight. He shuddered.

He thought he'd only fallen asleep for a moment. But yet, when he awoke on the cold ground, she was not by his side.

'Of course,' said the alp. 'Of course I remember her. But I'm sorry, I haven't seen her.'

The hamadryad accompanying him stood on tiptoe, whispered something into his ear and then hid behind his back.

'She's a little shy,' he explained, stroking her stiff hair. 'But she can help. Come with us.'

They set off downhill. The alp hummed to himself. The hama-dryad smelled of resin and wet poplar bark. Mabon night was coming to an end and dawn was breaking, heavy and murky with fog.

Among the small group of sabbath participants still talking on Grochowa Mountain, they found a female creature, the one with eyes glowing like phosphorous and green skin smelling of quince.

'Indeed,' nodded the Quince when asked. 'I saw the girl some time ago. She was descending towards Frankenstein among a group of women.'

'Wait.' The alp seized Reynevan by the shoulder. 'Slow down! And don't go that way. The mountain is ringed by Budzów Forest on that side, so you're bound to lose your way there. We'll lead you. We need to go that way, too. We have business there.'

'I'll come, too,' said Quince, 'and show you which way the girl went.'

'Thank you,' said Reynevan. 'I'm very grateful to you. We don't even know each other. But you're helping me . . .'

'We're accustomed to helping each other.' Quince turned around and pierced him with her phosphorous gaze. 'You were a pretty couple. And so few of us are left. If we don't help each other, we'll utterly die out.'

'Thank you.'

'But I wasn't thinking about you at all,' drawled the Quince.

They entered a ravine, the course of a dried-out stream with willows growing along it. A soft curse sounded from the mist in front of them, and a moment later they saw a woman sitting on a moss-covered boulder shaking stones from her slippers. Reynevan recognised her at once. She was the plump miller's daughter still bearing traces of flour, another participant in the debate around the cider keg.

'The fair-haired lass?' she mused. 'Aah, that noblewoman who was with you, Toledo? Of course I saw her. She went that way with a group, towards Frankenstein. Some time ago.'

'That way?'

'Indeed. Hold on, wait. I'm coming with you.'

'Because you have business there?'

'No. Because I live there.'

The miller's daughter was, to put it mildly, worse for wear. She walked sluggishly, hiccoughing, muttering and dragging her heels. She stopped annoyingly often to adjust her wardrobe. Inexplicably, she kept getting grit in her slippers and had to sit down and shake it out – and did it annoyingly slowly. The third time, Reynevan was ready to put the woman on his back and carry her, in order to speed things up.

'Could you do it a bit quicker, peasant woman?' the alp asked sweetly.

'Peasant woman yourself,' the miller's daughter snapped back. 'I'll be ready in a tick. Just have to . . . Hang on . . .'

She froze with the slipper in her hand. She lifted her head and listened intently.

'What is it?' asked the Quince. 'What . . .'

'Shh.' The alp raised a hand. 'I can hear something . . . Something's coming . . .'

The earth suddenly shook and rumbled as an entire herd of horses thundered out of the mist, all striking hooves, flowing manes and tails, bared teeth in foaming mouths and wild eyes. They barely managed to dodge behind some rocks. The horses flashed through at an impetuous gallop and vanished as quickly as they had appeared, the earth still trembling from the blows of their hooves.

Before they had recovered, another horse emerged from the fog. But unlike the others, this one bore a rider. A rider in a sallet, wearing full plate armour and a black cloak. The cloak, waving behind him in the gallop, was like the wings of a ghoul.

'*Adsumus! Adsuuumuuuus!*'

The knight reined in his horse. It reared up, flailed its front hooves in the air and neighed. And the knight drew a sword and charged at them.

The Quince screamed shrilly, and before the cry faded, she disintegrated – yes, that was the right word – disintegrated into a swarm of a million moths, which dispersed in the air and vanished. The hamadryad noiselessly took root, in a flash becoming slender and covering herself in bark and leaves. The miller's daughter and the alp, lacking equally cunning tricks, simply ran away. And Reynevan, naturally, followed them, running so quickly that he overtook them. *They've tracked me all the way here*, he thought feverishly.

'*Adsumus!*'

The black knight hacked the hamadryad in passing with his sword. It uttered a horrifying cry and spurted sap. The miller's daughter looked back, to her undoing. The knight knocked her down with his horse, cut her as she tried to stand, and hung from the saddle to hew her so hard that the blade crunched into her skull. The witch fell down, twisting and writhing in the dry grass.

The alp and Reynevan ran as fast as they could but had no chance against a galloping horse. The knight quickly caught up with them. They split up, the alp racing to the right, Reynevan to the left. The knight hurtled after the alp. A moment later, a scream came from the mist, signalling that the alp would not live to see the transformations or the Czech Hussites.

Reynevan ran at breakneck speed, panting and not looking back. The fog muffled the sounds, but he could still hear the thudding of hooves and neighing behind him – or thought he could.

He suddenly heard the stamping of hooves and the wheezing of a horse in front of him. He stopped, numb with terror, but before he could take any action, a dapple-grey mare with foam around its mouth bearing a short, stout woman in a man's doublet emerged from the fog. On seeing him, the woman brought her horse to a sliding stop and brushed away from her forehead a wind-blown fringe of flaxen hair.

'Lady Dzierżka ...' he groaned in amazement. 'Dzierżka of Wirsing ...'

'My kinsman?' The horse trader looked no less amazed. 'You? Here? Don't just bloody stand there! Give me your hand and hop up behind me!'

He seized her outstretched hand. But it was too late.

'*Adsuuumuuuus!*'

Dzierżka dismounted with astonishing grace and agility considering her rotund physique. Equally nimbly, she hauled a crossbow from her back and tossed it to Reynevan, then un-hitched another from her saddle.

'The horse!' she yelled, throwing him some bolts and a tool called a goat's foot lever used for nocking the bowstring. 'Aim at the horse!'

The black knight thundered at them with upraised sword and cloak flowing behind, so fast he was tossing up divots of turf. Reynevan's hands were shaking so much, the claw hooks of the lever wouldn't catch on the bowstring to pull it over the nut on the stock. He swore despairingly. It helped: the hooks held on and the bowstring caught the nut. He loaded a bolt with a trembling hand.

'Shoot!'

He shot. And missed. For against orders, he had aimed at the rider, not the horse. He saw the arrowhead send up sparks as it glanced off his steel spaulder. Dzierżka swore thunderously and obscenely, blew her hair out of her eyes, aimed and released the bowstring. The bolt hit the horse in the chest and penetrated deeply. The horse squealed, wheezed and tumbled forward onto its knees and face. The black knight fell from the saddle and rolled over, losing his helmet and sword. And began to rise.

Dzierżka swore again. Now both their hands were shaking, both kept missing with the lever, the bolts falling out of the grooves. And the black knight got to his feet, unhitched a huge morning star from his saddle and set off towards them with an unsteady gait. At the sight of his face, Reynevan stifled a cry, pressing his mouth to the crossbow's stock. The knight's face was white, practically silver, like a leper's. The eyes, ringed with blue and red, were wild and vacant and his teeth flashed between his drooling, foam-covered lips.

'*Adsuumuuuus!*'

Bowstrings clanged, quarrels hissed. Both hit, penetrating the armour with a loud crack up to the fletching – one through the bevor and the other through the breastplate. The knight wobbled, staggered heavily, but stayed on his feet, and to Reynevan's horror kept coming, yelling incomprehensibly, spitting the blood pouring from his mouth and swinging the morning star. Dzierżka swore and jumped aside, vainly trying to reload the crossbow. Knowing that she couldn't, she dodged the blow, tripped, fell down, and seeing the spiked ball coming for her, shielded her face and head with her arms.

Reynevan screamed and the scream saved her life. The knight turned to face him and Reynevan shot from close range, aiming at his belly. The quarrel went in up to the fletching again, penetrating the faulds with a dry crack. The force of impact was considerable and the arrowhead must have penetrated deep into his guts, but the knight still didn't fall. Instead, he staggered, regained his balance and moved swiftly towards Reynevan, roaring and raising the morning star to strike. Reynevan stepped back, trying to catch the bowstring with the goat's foot. He caught it and cocked the crossbow. And only then realised that he didn't have a quarrel. He caught his heel on a tussock and sat down on the ground, looking in horror at his approaching death – as pale as a ghost, wild-eyed, with foam and blood streaming from his mouth. He shielded himself with the crossbow.

'*Adsumus! Adsum—*'

Still half-lying, half-sitting, Dzierżka of Wirsing pressed the trigger of her crossbow and sent a bolt straight into the back of his head. The knight dropped the morning star, brandished his arms chaotically and fell like a log, making the ground shake. He fell half a step from Reynevan. Yet even with an iron quarrel and several inches of ash wood in his brain, he wasn't, astonishingly, quite dead. He went on rasping, shuddering and scraping the turf. He finally stopped moving.

Dzierżka continued to kneel for some time, supporting herself on straight arms. Then she vomited. And stood up. She cocked the crossbow and loaded the bolt. She walked over to the knight's snorting horse and aimed from close up. The bowstring clanged, the horse's head thudded limply against the ground and the rear legs kicked spasmodically.

'I love horses,' she said, looking Reynevan in the eyes, 'but in order to survive in this world, you sometimes have to sacrifice what you love. Remember that, kinsman. And next time, aim where I tell you.'

He nodded and stood up.

'You saved my life. And avenged your brother. To some degree.'

'Was it them . . . those riders . . . that killed Peterlin?'

'It was. Didn't you know? But this isn't the time for chit-chat, kinsman. We must flee before his comrades arrive.'

'They tracked me all the way here—'

'Not you,' countered Dzierżka unemotionally. 'Me. They were waiting for me in an ambuscade just outside Bardo, near Potworów. They broke up my herd and massacred the escort. Fourteen bodies are lying on the highway there. I'd have been among them, were it not for . . . That's enough talk!'

She put her fingers into her mouth and whistled. A moment later, hooves thudded on the ground and a dapple-grey mare trotted out of the mist. Dzierżka leaped into the saddle, once again astonishing Reynevan with her agility and the feline grace of her movements.

'Don't just stand there!'

He seized her hand and jumped onto the mare's rump behind her. The mare snorted and took small steps. Turning its head away, it recoiled from the corpse.

'Who . . . *what* was that?'

'A demon,' she replied, brushing some unruly hair from her

forehead. 'One of those that walk in darkness. I just wonder who the fuck informed on me ...'

'Hashshashin.'

'What?'

'Hashshashin,' he repeated. 'This one was under the influence of an intoxicating Arabian herbal substance called *hash'eesh*. You haven't heard of the Old Man of the Mountain? Of the assassins from the citadels of Alamut in Khurasan, Persia?'

'To hell with your Khurasan.' She turned around in the saddle. 'And your Persia. We are, if you still haven't got it, in Silesia, at the foot of Grochowa Mountain, a mile from Frankenstein. But, methinks, a lot doesn't get through to you. You're descending the slopes of Grochowa Mountain at dawn after the autumn equinox under the influence of the Devil knows what Arabian substance. But you ought to understand that our lives are in danger. So shut up and hold on, for I'll be riding hard!'

Dzierżka of Wirsing had exaggerated – fear had clouded her judgement. On the road and by the weed-covered verges lay only eight corpses, five of which belonged to the armed escort, defending themselves to the last. Almost half of the fourteen-man escort had survived, saving themselves by fleeing into the nearby trees. Of those, only one returned – a stableman who, being elderly, hadn't got far. And who was now, when the sun had risen higher in the sky, found in the undergrowth by knights riding along the highway from Frankenstein.

The knights – their train including pages and servants numbered twenty-one – were riding as if to war, in full white armour with pennants unfurled. Most of them had combat experience and had seen a thing or two in their lives. In spite of that, most of them still swallowed at the sight of the cruelly massacred bodies contorted on the sand, black with dried blood. And no one mocked the morbid paleness that crept into the faces of the more callow among them at the sight.

As the sun rose higher and the mist dispersed, its blaze

glistened on the clotted, ruby drops suspended like berries on the thistle and sagebrush verge. The sight didn't arouse any aesthetic or poetic association in any of the knights.

'They hacked them to pieces,' said Kunad of Neudeck, spitting. 'There was a bloodbath here, all right.'

'Headsman's blows,' agreed Wilhelm of Kauffung. 'Carnage.'

More of the surviving servants and stable boys emerged from the woods. Although pale and half-dazed with fear, they hadn't neglected their duties and were each leading several of the horses that had scattered during the attack.

Ramfold of Oppeln, the oldest of the knights, looked down from his saddle at a stableman, trembling with fear among the horsemen around him.

'Who attacked you? Speak, lad! Calm yourself. You survived. You're in no danger now.'

'God preserved us . . .' Panic was still swimming in the stableman's eyes. 'And Our Lady of Bardo—'

'You can pay for a Mass later. But speak now and tell us who attacked you?'

'How should I know? They attacked . . . They were in armour . . . In iron . . . Like you . . .'

'Knights!' a beanpole with the face of a monk bearing two crossed silver posts on a red shield said angrily. 'Knights attacking merchants on highways! Zounds, it's high time to put an end to these Raubritter practices and take some severe measures! Perhaps when a few heads roll, the lordlings from their little castles will come to their senses!'

'Amen to that,' said Wencel of Hartha, nodding inscrutably. 'Amen to that, m'Lord Runge.'

'But why were you attacked?' Oppeln reopened the enquiry. 'Were you carrying any valuables?'

'Why, no . . . Well, unless you count the horses . . .'

'Horses,' Hartha repeated pensively. 'A desirable thing, horses from Skałka. From Lady Dzierżka of Wirsing's stud . . . Lord, have mercy on her—'

He broke off, swallowed, unable to tear his eyes from the mutilated face of a woman lying on the sand in a horrifyingly unnatural position.

'That's not her.' The stableman blinked his vacant eyes. 'That's not Lady Dzierżka. That's the head groom's woman ... Him what's lying over there ... She rode with us from Kłodzko ...'

'They erred,' Kauffung stated coolly. 'They took the head groom's woman for Dzierżka.'

'They had to,' confirmed the stableman unemotionally. 'Because ...'

'Because what?'

'She looked more aristocratic.'

'Do you suggest, Sir Wilhelm,' said Oppeln, straightening up in the saddle, 'that it wasn't a robbery? That Lady Wirsing was—'

'Was the target? Yes. I'm certain of it.' Seeing the enquiring looks of the other knights, he added, 'Like Mikołaj Neumarkt and Fabian Pfefferkorn ... Like the others, who – contrary to prohibitions – were trading with ... with foreigners.'

'The robber knights are guilty,' Runge said emphatically. 'One cannot lend credence to foolish tales, rumours about plots and nocturnal demons. They've all been ordinary robberies.'

'The crimes may also have been committed by Jews,' said young Heinrich, called 'Starling' to distinguish him from the other Heinrichs in his family. 'To obtain Christian blood, you know, for matzah. Look at this one here, the poor wretch. I don't think there's a drop of blood left in him—'

'How could there be,' Wencel of Hartha glanced pityingly at the youngster, 'when his head is gone—'

'This atrocity might have been committed by those witches on broomsticks who fell on us last night by the campfire!' Gunter of Bischofsheim interrupted gloomily. 'By the skullcap of Saint Anthony! Indeed, the mystery is beginning to be solved! For I told you that Reinmar of Bielawa was among the she-devils – I recognised him! I am certain that Bielawa is a magician, and that he was making black magic in Oleśnica and casting spells on ladies. The gentlemen there can confirm it!'

'I know nothing,' muttered Ciołek Krompusz, looking at Benno Ebersbach. Both had also recognised Reynevan among the witches flying through the sky, but preferred not to reveal it.

'Aye, that is so.' Ebersbach cleared his throat. 'We seldom reside in Oleśnica. We pay no heed to gossip—'

'It's not gossip, but facts,' said Runge, looking at him. 'Bielawa was making magic. The wretch reportedly killed his own brother, like Cain, when the latter uncovered his devilish practices.'

'It is a certain thing,' said Eustachy of Rochow, nodding. 'Lord Reideburg, the Strzelin starosta, was talking about it. He received word of it from Wrocław, from the bishop himself. The young Reinmar of Bielawa had lost his mind from practising witchcraft. The Devil guides his hand, directs him towards misdeeds. He killed his own brother and those other merchants – why, he even tried to stab the Duke of Ziębice—'

'Verily he did,' confirmed Starling, 'and went to the tower for it. But he escaped. Doubtless with the Devil's aid.'

'If it's a devilish matter,' Kunad of Neudeck looked around with concern, 'let's ride from here with all haste before evil gets its claws into us—'

'Into us?' Ramfold of Oppeln patted the shield suspended from his saddle, above the coat of arms showing a silver pike pole and band with a red cross. 'Into us? Into this banner? Why, we have the cross, we are crusaders on our way to Bohemia with Bishop Konrad, to fight the heretics and defend God and religion! The Devil cannot draw near to us, for we are *milites Dei*, the Angelic Militia!'

'As the Angelic Militia,' observed Rochow, 'we have not only privileges, but also responsibilities.'

'What do you mean by that?'

'Lord Bischofsheim recognised Reinmar of Bielawa among the witches flying to their sabbath. We must inform the Holy

Office about it when we arrive at the rallying point for the crusade in Kłodzko.'

'Inform? Sir Eustachy! But we are knights!'

'Regarding witchcraft and heresy, denunciation does not stain knightly virtue.'

'It always does!'

'It does not!'

'It does,' stated Ramfold of Oppeln, 'but one must inform. And one will. But now, let us move on, gentlemen, to Kłodzko. The Angelic Militia must not be late at the rallying point.'

'It would be shameful,' confirmed Starling in his high voice, 'for the bishop's crusade to set off for Bohemia without us.'

'So we ride.' Kauffung reined his horse around. 'We're not needed here now, anyway – someone else will take care of the matter.'

Indeed, mounted soldiers of the Burgrave of Frankenstein were riding up the highway.

'Here we are.' Dzierżka of Wirsing reined in her horse and sighed deeply. Reynevan, pressed against her back, felt the sigh. 'This is the bridge over the River Budzówka, on the other side of which lies Frankenstein. On the left of the road is the Hospice of the Order of the Holy Sepulchre, Saint George's Church and the Narrenturm. On the right there are mills and dyers' huts. Further, across the bridge, is the Kłodzko Gate. Over there is the ducal castle, the town-hall tower and the Church of Saint Anne. Dismount.'

'Here?'

'Here. I have no intention of showing myself anywhere near the town. And you ought to think twice about it, kinsman.'

'Indeed I must.'

'As I suspected. Off you get.'

'What about you?'

'I don't have to.'

'I was asking which way you're heading.'

She blew a strand of hair away from her eyes and looked at him. He understood her look and didn't ask any more questions.

'Farewell, kinsman. We'll meet again.'

'Hopefully in better times.'

Chapter Twenty-Six

In which many old – though not necessarily good – friends meet in the town of Frankenstein.

Almost in the centre of the town square, between the pillory and the well, was a large puddle stinking of dung and foaming with horses' urine. A large flock of sparrows were splashing in it, while around it sat a group of filthy children busy messing around in the mud, splashing each other, making a racket and constructing sailing boats from bark.

'Aye, Reinmar,' said Scharley, finishing his soup, scraping the bottom of the bowl with a spoon. 'I must admit that your nocturnal flight impressed me. You flew like a veritable eagle. A king of flyers. Remember I prophesied that you would become an eagle, after the levitation with the witches in the forest? And you have. Though I don't think it was without Huon of Sagar's assistance, but still. I swear on my prick, laddie, you're making enormous progress in my care. Apply yourself a bit more and you'll be the next Merlin and build a Stonehenge for us here in Silesia, fit to put the English one to shame.'

Samson snorted.

'What about Lady Biberstein?' the penitent continued a moment later. 'Did you lead her safely to the gate of her father's castle?'

'Almost.' Reynevan clenched his jaw. He had looked for Nicolette – unsuccessfully – the entire morning, all over Frankenstein, peering into taverns, searching for her after the Mass outside Saint Anne's, at the Ziębice Gate and on the road leading to Stolz, asking people as he wandered through the Cloth Hall in the town square. And in the market hall, he had met – to his enormous joy and relief – Scharley and Samson.

'The girl's probably at home by now,' he added.

That's what he was hoping, at least. Stolz Castle was almost a mile from Frankenstein, the road to Ziębice and Opole was busy, and Katarzyna of Biberstein only had to say who she was for any merchant, knight or monk to help her get home. Thus Reynevan was almost certain that the girl had made it there safely. But it worried him that he hadn't taken her himself. That wasn't all he was worried about.

'Had it not been for you,' Samson appeared to read his mind, 'the lass wouldn't have got out of Castle Bodak alive. You rescued her.'

'And perhaps us, too,' said Scharley, licking the spoon. 'Old Biberstein must have sent out a search party, and we are quite close to the site of the robbery, much nearer than yesterday evening. If we are caught . . . Perhaps the maid, remembering the rescue, will intercede on our behalf and beg her dear father for our members to remain intact.'

'If she so wishes,' Samson observed soberly. 'And gets here in time.'

Reynevan didn't comment. He finished his soup.

'You also impressed me. At Bodak, you handled five armed Raubritter swashbucklers—'

'They were drunk.' Scharley grimaced. 'Had they been sober . . . But it's true that I watched the martial prowess of our very own Samson Honey-Eater with unalloyed admiration. If you'd only seen how he battered down the gate, Reinmar! Ha, in sooth, if Queen Jadwiga had somebody like that at the Wawel Gate, there'd be Habsburgs on the Polish throne now . . . In short: we owe our lives to him.'

'But, Scharley—'

'We're owe our lives to you, modest fellow. He also reunited us, Reinmar. When we had to choose at a crossroads, I was more in favour of Bardo, but Samson insisted on Frankenstein, claiming he had a presentiment. I usually ridicule such things, but in this case, when dealing with a supernatural creature, a visitor from the beyond—'

'You did what I suggested,' Samson cut him off, now quite unconcerned by the mockery. 'Which turned out to be a wise decision.'

'There's no denying it. Oh, Reinmar, how the sight of you in the Frankenstein town square gladdened me, framed against a slipper stall in the shadow of the town-hall tower. Have I told you how my—'

'You have.'

'—joy at seeing you,' the penitent wouldn't be interrupted, 'also inspired some minor corrections to my plans, about which I'd like to inform you. After your most recent exploits, particularly the adventure with Hayn of Czirne, the displays at the Ziębice joust and spilling the beans to Buko about the tax collector, I vowed that when we get to Hungary, I'd take you to the bridge over the Danube and kick your arse so hard you'd end up in the river. Today, overjoyed and moved, I am changing my plans. At least for the moment. I say, innkeeper! Ale! Look lively!'

They had to wait, as the innkeeper was in no particular hurry. Initially he was misled by Scharley's air and firm voice, but couldn't help noticing that earlier, when ordering soup, the guests had frantically totted up their resources, digging out coins from the bottoms of their pouches and deep in their pockets. The tavern in the arcades opposite the town hall was by no means busy, but the innkeeper had a high enough opinion of himself not to react with undue haste to the shouts of any old layabouts.

Reynevan sipped his beer, staring at the ragged children messing around in the yellow puddle between the pillory and the well.

'Children are the future of the nation,' said Scharley, catching his eye. 'Our future. And it doesn't look too promising. Firstly, it's thin. Secondly, it stinks repulsively.'

'Indeed,' Samson admitted. 'But something can be done.

Instead of carping, it can be taken care of. Washed. Fed. Educated. And the future is assured.'

'But who do you think should take care of it?'

'Not me.' The giant shrugged. 'It's nothing to do with me. I have no future in this world anyway.'

'Indeed. I'd forgotten.' Scharley tossed the hunk of bread he had dipped in the last of the soup to a dog hanging around nearby. The dog was so emaciated, it was bent in a bow. And it didn't chew the bread, but gulped it down like Jonah's whale.

'I wonder,' Reynevan pondered, 'if that cur has ever seen a bone?'

'Only if it's ever broken a leg,' said the penitent with a shrug. 'But, as Samson rightly says, it's nothing to do with me. I don't have a future here, either, and even if I did, it promises to be shittier than the future of those urchins and that mongrel. Right now, the land of the Magyars feels further away than Ultima Thule. This momentary idyll in the form of sleepy little Frankenstein, ale, bean soup and bread won't delude me. Any moment, Reynevan will meet some maid and it'll be business as usual. We'll have to run away again and finally end up hunkered down somewhere in the wilds. Or in some dreadful company.'

'Why, Scharley,' said Samson, also throwing the dog some bread, 'we are only a little over twenty miles from Opava, and from Opava to Hungary, it's about eighty miles all told. It isn't that much.'

'You studied the geography of the eastern marches of Europe in the beyond, I see.'

'I studied various things, but that's not the point. The point is to think positively.'

'I always think positively.' Scharley sipped his beer. 'Seldom is my optimism shaken. And then only by something serious. Something like, let's say, the prospect of a long journey with a total lack of cash. With two horses – one of which has founder – between three men. And the fact that one of us is injured. How is your arm, Samson?'

The giant didn't reply as he was busy with his beer, just moved his bandaged arm to show that it was in working order.

'I'm glad.' Scharley looked up at the sky. 'One problem less. But the others won't go away.'

'They will. At least partially.'

'What do you mean by that, dear Reinmar?'

'This time,' Reynevan raised his head proudly, 'not your – but my – connections will help us. I have friends in Frankenstein.'

'Do you mean some married woman or other, may I ask?' said Scharley with a straight face. 'A widow? A wealthy marriageable heiress? A nun? Or any other daughter of Eve?'

'Feeble jests. And vain fears. My friend here is the deacon of the Church of the Elevation of the Holy Cross. A Dominican.'

'Ha!' Scharley vigorously put his mug down on the bench. 'If so, I think I'd prefer another matron. My dear Reinmar, do you by any chance suffer from persistent headaches? Do you feel nauseous or dizzy? Are you seeing double?'

'I know what you mean,' said Reynevan, brandishing a hand. '*Domini canes*, dogs, just a pity they're rabid. At the Inquisition's beck and call. Predictable, sir, predictable. Furthermore, you ought to know that the deacon I refer to is indebted to me, greatly indebted. Peterlin, my brother, once helped him out of grave financial difficulties.'

'So you think that means something. What is this deacon called?'

'What, do you know them all?'

'I know plenty. What's his name?'

'Andrzej Kantor.'

'Financial difficulties appear to run in the family,' said the penitent a moment later. 'I've heard of Paweł Kantor, whom half of Silesia was chasing for debts and swindles. And Mateusz Kantor, a curate from Długołęka, was imprisoned with me in the Carmelite priory. He lost a ciborium and a thurible at dice. I dread to think what your deacon lost.'

'That's an old case.'

'You misunderstand me. I dread to think what he's lost lately.'

'I don't understand.'

'Oh, Reinmar, Reinmar. You've already met this Kantor, I presume?'

'I have indeed. But I still don't—'

'How much does he know? What did you tell him?'

'Practically nothing.'

'That's the first piece of good news. Thus let us pass both on this acquaintance and help from Dominicans. We'll find the necessary funds some other way.'

'I wonder how.'

'By selling this well-crafted jug, for example.'

'It's silver. Where did you get it?'

'I was walking around the market hall and looking at the stalls and it suddenly found itself in my pocket. It's a mystery.'

Reynevan gasped. Samson gazed into his mug, looking longingly at the remains of the froth. Scharley, however, was busy observing a knight beneath a nearby arcade who was vehemently dressing down a Jew. The knight was wearing a crimson chaperon and a rich doublet decorated on the front with a coat of arms portraying a millstone.

'I will leave behind me Silesia as such with but one regret,' said the penitent. 'Namely that five hundred grzywna the tax collector was carrying. Were it not for the circumstances, the money could have been ours. I confess I'm annoyed by the thought that a blockhead like Buko of Krossig got his hands on it, undeservedly and by accident. Or who knows, perhaps it was that Reichenbach who is presently abusing the Israelite? Or maybe one of those men by the leatherworker's booth?'

'There's a hell of a lot of knighthood and soldiery here today,' said Reynevan.

'Plenty. And look, more are arriving—'

The penitent broke off abruptly and sucked in air loudly. That very moment, the Raubritter Hayn of Czirne rode into the town square from Silver Mountain Street, which led from the dungeon gate.

Scharley, Samson and Reynevan didn't wait. They leaped up from the bench, meaning to steal away without being noticed. Too late. Hayn himself saw them, as did Fryczko of Nostitz, who was riding beside him, and the Italian Vitelozzo Gaetani. At the sight of Scharley, the latter's face, still swollen and disfigured by a fresh scar, paled in fury. The next second, the town square of Frankenstein resounded with yells and the thud of hooves. A moment later, Hayn vented his anger on the bench in the tavern, chopping it into matchwood with his battleaxe.

'After them!' he roared to his men. 'Give chase!'

'Over there!' yelled Gaetani. 'They went that way!'

Reynevan was running as fast as he could, barely keeping up with Samson. Scharley was leading, choosing the way, cunningly turning into a narrow lane and then weaving through gardens. The tactic appeared to be working – suddenly the rattle of hooves and shouts of the pursuers faded away. They rushed out into Lower Bath Street, its gutters full of soap suds, and turned towards the Ziębice Gate.

The Sterczas, chatting and lazily rocking in their saddles, with Knobelsdorf, Haxt and Rotkirch behind them, were riding up from the Ziębice Gate.

Reynevan stood transfixed.

'Bielawa!' bellowed Wolfher of Stercza. 'We have you, you son of a dog!'

Before the roar had died away, Reynevan, Scharley and Samson were now loping, panting heavily, through lanes, jumping over fences, dashing through gardens, getting tangled up in sheets drying on lines. Hearing the cries of Hayn's men from the left and the roars of the Sterczas behind them, they ran north towards the sound of the bell from the Dominican Church of the Elevation of the Holy Cross.

'M'Lord Reinmar! Here! This way!'

A little door opened in the wall and there stood Andrzej

Kantor, the deacon of the Dominican church. The priest indebted to the Bielawas.

'This way, this way! Make haste! There's no time to lose!'

Indeed, there wasn't. They ran into a narrow hallway, which, when Kantor closed the door, was plunged into gloom and gave off the smell of rotting rags. Reynevan knocked over some metal pots with an almighty crash and Samson tripped and fell over with a bang. Scharley had also run into something, for he swore violently.

'This way!' called Andrzej Kantor from somewhere ahead illuminated by a dim light. 'This way! Here! Here!'

Reynevan stumbled more than walked down the narrow staircase. He finally emerged into daylight, entering a tiny courtyard surrounded by walls covered in wild vines. Scharley ran out behind him and trod on a cat, which yowled shrilly. Before the cry had died out, a dozen men in black jerkins and round felt caps rushed out from both cloisters and flew at them.

One of them threw a sack over Reynevan's head and another tripped him up. He tumbled to the ground. He was pinned down and his arms twisted behind him. He felt a struggle beside him, heard furious panting, the sounds of blows and cries of pain, indicating that Scharley and Samson were putting up resistance.

'Has the Holy Office . . .' The shaking voice of Andrzej Kantor reached him. 'Has the Holy Office anticipated . . . a reward . . . even a tiny one . . . for the seizure of this heretic? The bishop's *significavit* doesn't mention it, but I . . . I have difficulties . . . I'm in great financial need . . . For which reason—'

'The *significavit* is an order, not a commercial contract,' an evil, grating voice admonished the deacon, 'and the chance to aid the Holy Inquisition is sufficient reward for every good Catholic. Which you are, are you not, Frater?'

'Kantor . . .' wheezed Reynevan, his mouth full of dust and hair from the sack. 'Kantooor! You whoreson! You papist dog! You sodomitic—'

He wasn't allowed to finish. He was struck on the head with

something hard and saw stars. A second blow caused intense pain and his fingers suddenly went numb. More blows followed. The pain made Reynevan cry out, the blood pounded in his ears and he lost consciousness.

He came to in almost complete darkness, his throat parched and his tongue dry. His head throbbed with a pain that spread through his temples, eyes and even teeth. He took a deep breath and almost choked, there was such a stench around him. As he moved, the compacted straw he was lying on rustled.

Nearby, someone was moaning horribly, someone else was coughing and grunting. He heard water trickling beside him. Reynevan licked his lips, which were covered in a sticky fur. He lifted his head and groaned from the thudding pain. He raised himself up more slowly and cautiously. A quick glance told him he was in a large cellar. In a dungeon. At the bottom of a deep stone well. And that he wasn't alone.

'You've come round,' Scharley stated. He was standing a few steps away and peeing into a bucket with a loud splashing sound.

Reynevan opened his mouth but was unable to utter a word.

'I'm glad you've come round,' said Scharley, fastening his trousers, 'because I have to inform you that regarding the bridge on the Danube, we're returning to my original plan.'

'Where ...' Reynevan finally croaked, swallowing with difficulty. 'Scharley ... Where ... are we?'

'In the temple of Saint Dymphna.'

'Where?'

'In a hospital for the deranged.'

'Where?'

'I'm telling you. In a madhouse. In the Narrenturm, the Tower of Fools.'

Chapter Twenty-Seven

In which, for quite some time, Reynevan and Scharley have peace, medical care, spiritual solace, regular meals and the company of unconventional men, with whom they can freely converse on fascinating subjects. In a word, they have what is usually on offer in a lunatic asylum.

'Jesus Christ be praised! Blessed be the name of Saint Dymphna.'

The inmates of the Tower of Fools reacted with a rustling of straw and incoherent, indistinct growls. The canon of the Holy Sepulchre played with a club, tapping it against his open left hand.

'You two are new to our divine flock,' he said to Reynevan and Scharley, 'and we give new people new names. And since today we are revering the holy martyrs Cornelius and Cyprian, then one will be Cornelius and the other Cyprian.'

Neither Cornelius nor Cyprian answered.

'I am the master of the hospital and guardian of the Tower,' continued the monk unemotionally. 'My name is Brother Tranquillus. *Nomen est omen*. At least until somebody annoys me. And it annoys me, please know, when somebody makes a racket, rants and raves, provokes disturbances and rows, dirties himself and the surroundings, uses vulgar words, blasphemes against God and the saints, doesn't pray and stops other people praying. And commit sins, generally speaking. We have various methods for dealing with sinners here. The oaken club. The pail of cold water. The iron cage. And the chain in the wall. Clear?'

'Clear,' answered Cornelius and Cyprian in unison.

'Thus, you will begin the treatment.' Brother Tranquillus yawned and examined his club, a well-worn and polished piece of oak wood. 'And if you successfully pray for the favour and intercession of Saint Dymphna, your lunacy and madness will leave you and, God willing, you will return, cured, to the healthy bosom of society. Dymphna is famed among the saints for her kindness, so your chances are good. But don't stop praying. Clear?'

'Clear.'

'Then God be with you.'

The canon of the Holy Sepulchre left, climbing up the creaking staircase that wound around the wall and ended somewhere high up at a door, a solid one judging by the sound of it opening and closing. Scarcely had the echo booming through the stone well died out than Scharley stood up.

'Well, brothers in torment,' he said cheerfully, 'greetings, whoever you are. It looks like we'll be spending some time together. Admittedly in prison, but still. So perhaps we could get to know each other?'

Just like an hour before, he was answered with clanking and the rustling of straw, snorting, a quiet curse and a few other words and sounds, mostly vulgar. But Scharley wasn't discouraged this time. He strode over to one of the straw pallets, of which a dozen or more were located by the tower's walls and around the ruined pillars and arcades dividing up the space. The darkness was slightly eased by light shining from above through some tiny windows at the very top of the tower. But Scharley's sight had become accommodated by now and some things could be seen.

'Good morrow! I am Scharley!'

'Oh, get thee gone,' snapped a fellow from his pallet. 'Pick on your own kind, madman. I'm of sound mind. Normal!'

Reynevan opened his mouth, quickly closed it and opened it again. For he saw what the man wanting to be regarded as sane was doing, which was the energetic manipulation of his genitalia. Scharley cleared his throat, shrugged and continued on his way, towards the next pallet. The person lying on it wasn't moving, if you didn't count a slight twitching and strange contractions of his face.

'Good morrow! I am Scharley . . .'

'Bbb . . . bbuub . . . bweh-bweeeh . . . Bweeeh . . .'

'As I thought. Let's move on, Reinmar. Good morrow! I am—'

'Stop! Look where you're treading, lunatic. On my drawings. Are you blind or what?'

Geometrical figures, graphs and columns of digits were scrawled in chalk on the rock-hard dirt floor among wisps of straw, being pored over by a grey-haired old man with a pate as shiny as an egg. Graphs, figures and digits also completely covered the wall above his pallet.

'Oh.' Scharley stepped back. 'Excuse me. I understand. How could I forget? *Noli turbare circulos meos.*'

The old man raised his head and grinned, showing blackened teeth. 'Scholars?'

'You could say that.'

'Then take your places by the pillar. The one with the omega carved upon it.'

They did so and made pallets for themselves out of straw at the foot of the pillar with the Greek letter scratched on it. They had barely completed the task when Brother Tranquillus appeared, this time in the company of several other monks in habits with a double cross. The guardians of Christ's tomb had brought a steaming cauldron, but only allowed the patients of the tower to approach it with their bowls after a choral rendition of the *Pater noster*, *Ave*, *Credo*, *Confiteor* and *Miserere*. Reynevan still hadn't grasped that this was the beginning of a ritual he would be observing for a long time. A very long time.

'The Tower of Fools,' he said, looking vacantly at the stuck-on remains of millet at the bottom of his bowl. 'In Frankenstein?'

'That is correct,' confirmed Scharley, picking his teeth with a straw. 'The tower is part of the Hospice of Saint George, run by

THE TOWER OF FOOLS

the canons of the Holy Sepulchre from Nysa. Outside the town walls, by the Kłodzko Gate.'

'I know. I walked beside it. Yesterday. I think it was yesterday . . . How did we end up here? Why do they take us for mentally ill?'

'Somebody must have analysed our recent antics.'The penitent snorted with laughter. 'No, my dear Cyprian, I was joking, we aren't so fortunate. It isn't just the Tower of Fools, it's also – temporarily – an Inquisition prison because the local Dominican gaol is being rebuilt. Frankenstein has two town prisons, one in the town hall and the other by the Crooked Tower, but they're always overcrowded. Which is why people arrested on the orders of the Holy Office are put here, in the Narrenturm.'

'That Tranquillus,' Reynevan went on, 'treats us as though we're insane.'

'Professional bias.'

'What about Samson?'

'What, what?' Scharley snorted. 'They looked at his face and let him go. Ironic, eh? They let him go, taking him for an idiot, and banged us up with the nutters. To be honest, I don't bear a grudge, I only blame myself. They wanted you, Cyprian, and no one else. The *significavit* only mentioned you. They locked me up because I resisted, broke a few noses, and a few kicks also found their targets. Had I kept calm, like Samson . . . Just between us,' he finished after a moment of silence, 'I'm pinning all my hopes on him, trusting he'll think of something and get us out. And fast. Otherwise . . . Otherwise, we might have problems.'

'With the Inquisition? But what will they accuse us of?'

'The problem isn't what they accuse us of.' Scharley's voice was extremely gloomy. 'The problem is what we confess to.'

Reynevan didn't need any explanation; he knew what it was all about. What they had overheard in the Cistercian grange meant death; death preceded by torture. No one could be allowed to find out that they knew. The pointed look the penitent directed at the Tower's other inmates didn't need any explanation, either. Reynevan also knew that the Inquisition customarily planted informers and agents provocateurs among its prisoners. Scharley, admittedly, had promised he would quickly unmask any spies, but recommended caution and secrecy with the other inmates, even those who appeared genuinely insane. He stressed that even they couldn't be confided in. There was nothing to be gained by them knowing anything or having any information, he said.

'People stretched on the rack talk,' he went on. 'They say a lot, reveal everything they know, mention every possible thing, for if they keep speaking they won't be tortured.'

Reynevan grew downhearted. So visibly that Scharley finally decided to cheer him up by slapping him on the back.

'Chin up, Cyprian,' he said, consoling him. 'They still haven't come for us.'

Reynevan grew even more downhearted and Scharley gave up. He didn't know that Reynevan wasn't at all worried that he would reveal the intrigue he had overheard at the grange. That he was a hundredfold more terrified by the thought that he would betray Katarzyna of Biberstein.

Having rested somewhat, the two residents of the billet at the omega made further acquaintances. With mixed results. Some of the Narrenturm's inmates didn't want to talk, still others couldn't, being in a state that the doctors of the Prague University termed – after the Salerno School – *dementia* or *debilitas*. Others were more forthcoming, but even they weren't too keen on revealing their personal details, hence Reynevan gave them suitable nicknames in his mind.

Their nearest neighbour was Tomasz Alpha, for he dwelt at the foot of a pillar marked with that Greek letter and had arrived at the Tower of Fools on the day of Saint Thomas of Aquinas, the seventh of March. He didn't reveal what he was in for or for how long, but nor did he give Reynevan the impression of being a lunatic. He called himself an inventor, but Scharley thought him a runaway monk on the basis of his speech mannerisms. Finding a hole in a monastery wall, he judged, didn't justify the appellation of true inventiveness.

Not far from Tomasz Alpha lived the Camaldolite, beneath the letter 'tau' and the inscription POENITEMINI scratched into the wall. He couldn't conceal his clericality as his hair still hadn't grown back over his tonsure. Nothing more was known about him, since – like a real brother from Camaldoli – he remained silent. And he bore the fasts that occurred extremely often in the Narrenturm like a true Camaldolite, without a murmur or a word of complaint.

Opposite him, two individuals who were ironically also neighbours on the outside, lived next to each other under the words LIBERA NOS DEUS NOSTER. Both denied being insane and regarded themselves as victims of deceitfully concocted intrigues. One, a town scribe, christened Bonaventure by the canons of the Holy Sepulchre on his first day, blamed his confinement on his wife, who was gladly making merry with her lover in the meanwhile. Bonaventure treated Reynevan and Scharley right at the start to a long disquisition about women, who he called base, perverse, lecherous, indecent, vile and treacherous by their very nature. The disquisition plunged Reynevan into dark recollections and even darker melancholy for a long time.

The other neighbour was nicknamed the Institor in Reynevan's mind, since he endlessly and loudly worried about his *institorium*, his rich and profitable stall in the town square. His children, he claimed, had taken away his liberty by denouncing him, with the goal of seizing the stall and the profits from it. Like Bonaventure, the Institor confessed to scientific interests – both of them dabbled in astrology and alchemy. Both fell strangely silent at the sound of the word 'Inquisition'.

One more citizen of Frankenstein who didn't conceal his identity had his pallet beneath the word ARSE. This was Nicolaus Koppirnig, a mason from a nearby village and an amateur astronomer, on top of that – sadly – a taciturn, uncommunicative and unsociable character.

Not far away, by the wall and set a little apart from the scientific enclave, sat Circulos Meos – Circulos for short – the man who had shouted at Scharley. He was sitting in a pile of straw like a pelican in its nest. The impression was heightened by his bald pate and large goitre. The fact he was not dead was proved by a foul smell, the flashing of his bald pate and his ceaseless, annoying scratching with chalk on the wall or dirt floor. It was explained that he wasn't, like Archimedes, a mechanic, that his graphs and figures served other purposes. Circulos had been put in the nuthouse for that reason.

There was a forbidding iron cage, used as a punishment cell, next to the pallet of Isaiah, a young, apathetic fellow, christened thus for endlessly quoting from that Old Testament book. The cage was empty, and Tomasz Alpha, who had been imprisoned for the longest, had never seen anybody put into it. Brother Tranquillus, declared Alpha, was indeed a calm and very forbearing monk. Until anybody annoyed him, of course.

The person who was soon to annoy Brother Tranquillus was Normal, who continued to ignore everybody. For during morning prayers, Normal devoted himself to his favourite activity – playing with his private parts. This had not escaped the eagle eyes of the canon of the Holy Sepulchre and Normal was given a sound beating with the oaken club, which, it turned out, wasn't just for show.

The days passed, marked by the boring rhythm of meals and prayer. The nights passed. The latter were a torment, owing both to the biting cold and the inmates' intolerable choral snoring. The days were more bearable. At least one could talk.

'Owing to anger and envy.' Circulos moved his goitre and blinked his suppurating eyes. 'I'm in here owing to human anger and the envy of my good-for-nothing friends. They hated me because I achieved what they failed to achieve.'

'Namely?' asked Scharley with interest.

'Why would I explain it to you laymen?' said Circulos, wiping chalky fingers on his smock. 'You wouldn't understand anyway.'

'Try us.'

'Well, if you will ...' Circulos cleared his throat, picked his nose and rubbed one heel against the other. 'I achieved no mean thing. I determined the precise date of the end of the world.'

'Would it be the year one thousand four hundred and twenty?' Scharley asked after a short, polite silence. 'In the month of February, on the Monday after Saint Scholastica's Day? Not especially original, if I may say so.'

'You insult me.' Circulos stuck out the rest of his belly. 'I'm not just some rabid millenarian or semi-literate mystic who parrots the chiliastic rubbish of fanatics. I researched the matter *sine ira et studio*, on the basis of academic sources and mathematic computations. Do you know the Book of Revelation?'

'Sketchily, but yes.'

'You recall that the lamb opened the seven seals, and John saw seven angels?'

'Absolutely.'

'And the number of the sealed was one hundred and forty-four thousand, and there were twenty-four elders, and two witnesses who were given the power of prophecy for one thousand two hundred and sixty days? When you add everything together and multiply the sum by eight – the number of letters in the word "Apollyon" – you get ... Oh, there's no point explaining it you, you wouldn't understand anyway. Suffice to say that the end of the world will occur in July. On the sixth of July, to be precise, *in octava Apostolorum Petri et Pauli*. On Friday. At noon.'

'Of what year?'

'The present, sacred one: 1425.'

'Yeees.' Scharley rubbed his chin. 'There is one snag, however ...'

'Namely?'

'It's September.'

'That's no proof,' said Circulos. He shrugged, then looked away and ostentatiously buried himself in the straw.

'I knew it was no use talking to dunces,' he snapped. 'Good day.'

Nicolaus Koppirnig, the mason from Frankenstein, wasn't talkative, but his coldness and brusqueness didn't discourage Scharley, who was fond of conversation.

'So you are an astronomer, then,' the penitent tried again. 'And you were put in the clink. Which confirms that watching the sky too closely doesn't pay for a good Catholic. But I'll put two and two together and get a different answer, sir. The conjunction of astronomy and gaol can only mean one thing: you questioned Ptolemy's theory. Am I right?'

'Right about what?' snapped Koppirnig. 'About conjunctions? You are. The rest, likewise. So I conclude you're the type that's always right. I've encountered people like you.'

'Certainly not like me.' The penitent smiled. 'But never mind. Do you think that Ptolemy was right? What is at the centre of the universe – the Earth or the Sun?'

Koppirnig said nothing for a long time.

'Whatever wants to be, can be,' he finally said, bitterly. 'How should I know? What sort of astronomer am I, what do I know? I withdraw everything, I confess to everything. I'll do whatever they tell me to do.'

'Aha.' Scharley beamed. 'So I was right! Astronomy clashed with theology? And you took fright?'

'What do you mean?' said Reynevan in astonishment. 'Astronomy is a science. What does theology have to do with it? Two and two is always four—'

'I thought so, too,' Koppirnig interrupted gloomily. 'But the reality is different.'

'I don't understand.'

'Reinmar, Reinmar.' Scharley smiled in pity. 'You're as naive as a child. Adding two and two doesn't contradict the Bible, which can't be said about the rotation of heavenly bodies. You can't prove that the Earth orbits a motionless Sun when it's written in the Bible that Joshua ordered the Sun to stand still. The Sun. Not the Earth. Therefore—'

'Therefore,' the mason interrupted even more gloomily, 'one must arm oneself with the instinct of self-preservation. Regarding the heavens, the astrolabe and telescope may err, but the Bible is infallible. The heavens—'

'He that sitteth upon the circle of the Earth,' Isaiah interrupted in mid-sentence, snatched from his lethargy by the sound of the word 'Bible', 'stretcheth out the heavens as a curtain, and spreadeth them out as a tent to dwell in.'

'Well, well.' Koppirnig nodded. 'He's a nutcase, but he knows.'

'Exactly,' said Scharley.

'Exactly what?' Koppirnig lost his temper. 'Are you so learned? I shall withdraw everything. I'll confirm anything they want, as long as they release me. That the Earth is flat and Jerusalem is its geometrical centre. That the Sun describes a circle around the Pope, who is the centre of the universe. I'll confess everything. Besides, perhaps they're right? Their bloody institution has existed for almost fifteen hundred years. For that reason alone, they can't be mistaken.'

'Since when,' Scharley squinted, 'have dates cured stupidity?'

'Oh, to Hell with you!' cried the mason angrily. 'Get tortured and burned at the stake yourself! I retract everything! I say: it does NOT move. *Eppur NON si muove!*'

After a moment's silence, he added bitterly, 'What do I know, anyway? What kind of astronomer am I? I'm a simple fellow.'

'Don't believe him, Master Scharley,' said Bonaventure, who had just awoken from a nap. 'He's saying that now because he fears the stake. Everybody in Frankenstein knows what kind of astronomer he is, because he's on his roof with his astrolabe every night, counting the stars. And he's not the only one in the family – all the Koppirnigs are stargazers. Even the youngest, little Nicolaus, who folk tease by saying his first word was "mama", his second "yum-yum" and his third "heliocentrism".'

The earlier dusk fell, the colder it became and the more the inmates were attracted by conversations and disputes. They talked
and talked and talked, sometimes to each other, and sometimes
to themselves.

'They'll squander my *institorium*, reduce it to nothing. They'll
ruin me. The youth of today!'

'And every woman, every single one, is a harlot. By deed or by
choice.'

'The Apocalypse will come, naught will remain. Absolutely
nothing. Why would I explain it you laymen?'

'I tell you, they'll finish us off sooner. The Inquisitor will come.
They'll torture us then burn us. And it serves us sinners right, for
we've offended against God.'

'Therefore as the fire devoureth the stubble, and the flame
consumeth the chaff, so their root shall be as rottenness, and their
blossom shall go up as dust: because they have cast away the Law
of the Lord of Hosts—'

'Hear that? He's a nutcase, but he knows.'

'Exactly.'

'The problem is,' said Koppirnig, lost in thought, 'we've done
too much thinking.'

'Quite, quite,' confirmed Tomasz Alpha. 'Hence we shall not
avoid punishment.'

'. . . And they shall be gathered together, as prisoners are gathered in the pit, and shall be shut up in the prison, and after many
days shall they be punished.'

'Hear that? He's a nutcase, but he knows.'

In the distance, by the wall, those suffering from *dementia* and
debilitas gibbered and blabbered. And alongside, on his pallet,
Normal was jerking off, grunting and groaning.

The weather grew even colder in October. And then, on the six-
teenth – a calendar that Scharley had drawn on the wall in chalk

stolen from Circulos allowed them to keep track – a familiar face appeared in the Narrenturm.

Their acquaintance was dragged into the Tower not by the canons of the Holy Sepulchre, but by soldiers in mail shirts and short quilted jerkins. He resisted, was hit a few times on the back of the neck and thrown down the stairs. He tumbled and ended up spreadeagled on the dirt floor. The inmates watched him lying there, and saw Frater Tranquillus approach him with his club.

'Today,' he said, first customarily greeting him in the name of Saint Dymphna, the patron and intercessor of the mentally ill, 'is Saint Gall's Day. But there've been so many Galls here, we won't have another one . . . Today is also the day of Saint Mommolem, so you will be called "Mommolem", brother. Clear?'

The man lying on the floor raised himself up on his elbows and stared at the canon of the Holy Sepulchre. For a moment, it looked as though he would comment in apt, succinct words. Tranquillus probably also expected that, because he raised his truncheon and took a step back to get a better swing. But the man only gnashed his teeth and muttered under his breath.

'Aye.' The canon of the Holy Sepulchre nodded. 'I understand. Farewell, Brother.'

The man on the ground sat up. Reynevan barely recognised him. The grey cloak and liripipe were gone, the silver clasp and chaperon lost. The tight doublet was covered in dust and plaster, split on both padded shoulders.

'Greetings.'

Urban Horn raised his head. His hair was dishevelled, he had a black eye and his lip was cut and swollen.

'Greetings, Reinmar,' he replied. 'You know, I'm not at all surprised to see you in the Narrenturm.'

'Are you in one piece? How do you feel?'

'Splendid. Simply excellent. No doubt there's sunlight streaming from my arse. Take a look and check, because it's hard for me to do it myself.'

He stood up and felt his sides. Massaged his lower back.

'They killed my dog,' he said coldly. 'Clubbed him to death. My Beelzebub. Do you remember Beelzebub?'

'I'm sorry.' Reynevan well remembered the mastiff's teeth an inch from his face. But he was genuinely sorry.

'I won't forgive them for it,' Horn said, gnashing his teeth. 'I'll get even with them. When I get out of here.'

'There may be a problem with that.'

'I know.'

During the introductions, Horn and Scharley scrutinised each other for a long time, squinting and biting their lips. It was clear that the two wily old foxes had met their match. It was so obvious that neither of them asked the other anything.

'Well then.' Horn looked around. 'Here we are. In Frankenstein, the hospital of the canons regular, the guardians of the tomb in Jerusalem. The Narrenturm. Tower of Fools.'

'Not only that.' Scharley squinted. 'Which you undoubtedly know, m'lord.'

'M'lord does undoubtedly know,' admitted Horn, 'for the Inquisition and the bishop's *significavit* put him here. Whatever you may think about the Holy Office, their prisons are usually tidy, spacious and clean. Even here, judging by the smell, they empty the piss pot now and again, and the inmates are quite presentable ... It's clear that the canons of the Holy Sepulchre take good care of them. What's the food like?'

'Rotten. But regular.'

'Not bad. The last madhouse I encountered was the Pazzeria in Florence near Santa Maria Nuova's. You ought to have seen the patients there! Starving, louse-infested, unshaven, dirty ... But here? I can see them paying a visit to court ... Not, perhaps, the imperial court, or the Wawel ... But somewhere like Wilno, let's say. I assure you, you could go as you are and wouldn't stand out unduly. Yeees ... I could have done much worse. If it wasn't for these nutcases here ... There aren't any maniacs among them, I trust. Nor, God save us, sodomites?'

'There are not,' Scharley reassured him. 'We're protected by Saint Dymphna. Just them, over there. They pass their days lying, jabbering and playing with their privates. Nothing special.'

'Splendid. Why, we'll be spending some time together. Maybe quite some time.'

'Perhaps less than you think.' The penitent smiled crookedly. 'We've been here since Saint Cornelius's Day, and we expect the Inquisitor anytime now. Who knows, perhaps it'll be today?'

'Not today,' Urban Horn calmly assured them. 'Nor tomorrow. The Inquisition has other matters to attend to.'

Although pressed, Horn only began explaining after lunch. Which, incidentally, he ate with relish. And didn't spurn the leftovers that Reynevan – who had lately been feeling bad and was losing his appetite – didn't eat.

'His Excellency, Konrad, Bishop of Wrocław,' explained Horn, scooping out the last groats from the bottom of the bowl with a finger, 'has attacked Hussite Bohemia. He and Sir Půta of Častolovice have attacked the Náchod and Trutnov regions.'

'A crusade?'

'No. A plundering raid.'

'But they're the same thing,' said Scharley.

'Ho ho,' snorted Horn. 'I was meaning to ask what you're in for, but I don't need to now.'

'Glad to hear it. What about that raid?'

'The pretext, if a pretext was at all necessary, was the alleged robbery by Hussites of a tax collector, apparently carried out on the thirteenth of September. More than one and a half thousand grzywna were reportedly stolen . . .'

'How much?'

'I said allegedly, apparently, reportedly. No one believes it. But the pretext suited the bishop, and he chose the moment well. He struck during the absence of the Hussite field army from Hradec

Králové. The bishop, it appears, has decent spies.'

'Aye, he probably does,' Scharley said without batting an eyelid. 'Go on. Master Horn? Speak, forget the nutters for now. You've plenty of time to have a good look at them later.'

Urban Horn tore his gaze away from Normal, who was indulging enthusiastically in self-abuse. And from one of the madmen who was attentively making a small ziggurat from his own excrement.

'Yeees ... Where was I? ... Oh, yes. Bishop Konrad and Sir Půta entered Bohemia via Levín and Homole. They ravaged and pillaged around Náchod, Trutnov and Vízmburk, burning down villages. They looted and murdered whoever fell into their clutches. They did spare children who fit under a horse's girth. Well, some of them.'

'And then?'

'Later ...'

The fire had died down to barely flickering flames over the pile of wood. The wood hadn't completely burned up because, firstly, it was a rainy day, and secondly, damp wood had been used so the heretic wouldn't burn too quickly but rather sizzled, giving him a suitable foretaste of the torment awaiting him in Hell. But they had gone too far and the excess of wet firewood meant that the rogue hadn't burned to death, but very quickly suffocated on the smoke before he even managed to scream much. Additionally, the corpse chained to the stake had more or less retained its human form. Bloody, partially charred flesh was still clinging to the skeleton in many places, the skin hanging in twisted strips, and the bones exposed here and there were more red than black. The head had been quite evenly roasted and the charred skin had sloughed off the skull; the teeth showing white in a mouth opened in a dying scream lent the whole scene a macabre appearance.

That appearance, paradoxically, compensated for the disappointment resulting from the short and not very painful torture in that it exerted a better psychological effect. The crowd that had been rounded up in the nearby village of Čechov and driven to the site of the auto-da-fé wouldn't have been shaken by the sight of some shapeless fried skin on a bonfire. However, seeing their recently alive preacher in the partly roasted, grinning corpse, the Czechs were totally distraught. The men were trembling, covering their eyes, the women were wailing and moaning, and the children were bawling wildly.

Konrad of Oleśnica, Bishop of Wrocław, straightened himself in the saddle so proudly and spiritedly that his armour creaked. He had at first meant to give a speech to the prisoners, a sermon intended to make the rabble aware of all the evils of heresy and warn them about the severe punishment awaiting dissenters from the faith. But he changed his mind and just looked on, pouting his lips. Why waste his breath? The Slavic rabble spoke poor German in any case. And the charred cadaver at the stake spoke more eloquently and emphatically about the punishment for heresy than he ever could. As did the corpses hacked and mutilated beyond recognition, piled onto a fire in the centre of the stubbled field. And the fire raging over the thatched roofs of the village. And the columns of smoke rising into the sky from other villages set alight along the Metuje River. And the horrifying cries from the stable where young women had been dragged for the enjoyment of Sir Půta of Častolovice's Kłodzko pikemen.

Father Miegerlin ranted and raged amid the crowd of Czechs. Aided by soldiers and accompanied by several Dominicans, the priest was hunting Hussites and their sympathisers. The list of names Miegerlin had received from Birkart of Grellenort was helping in the hunt, but the priest didn't consider Grellenort an authority, nor his list sacrosanct. Claiming that one could recognise a heretic by his eyes, ears and general expression, so far the priest had apprehended at least five times as many people as there were on the list. Some were murdered outright, others clapped in irons.

'What about them, Your Eminence?' asked Lorenz of Rohrau,

the marshal of the court bishop, riding up. 'What are your orders for them?'

'The same as for the previous ones.' Konrad of Oleśnica looked at him severely.

Seeing the crossbowmen and pikemen with harquebuses, the crowd of shackled Czechs began screaming horribly. Several men broke free of the crowd and bolted; mounted soldiers gave chase, caught up with them and hacked and stabbed them to death. Others bunched tightly together, knelt and fell to the ground. Men shielded women with their bodies, and mothers shielded their children.

The crossbowmen cranked up their weapons.

Oh well, thought Konrad, *there are no doubt some innocent people in the crowd, even good Catholics, perhaps, but God will know his flock. I'll go down in history as the defender of the true faith, the vanquisher of heresy. Posterity will speak my name with reverence. But that's for the future. As for today, will they finally appreciate me in Rome? Perhaps Wrocław will be granted an archdiocese and I shall become Archbishop of Silesia and an elector of the Holy Roman Empire. Perhaps it'll mark the end of that farce of the diocese being formally subordinate to the Polish Archbishop of Gniezno. Naturally, I'd rather go to Hell than accept a Polack as my superior – especially one who impudently demands that I receive his pastoral visitation! In Wrocław! A Pole in Wrocław! Never!* Nimmermehr!'

The first shots boomed, bowstrings clanged and people trying to flee the encirclement were cut down. The screams of the slaughtered rose into the air.

This will not go unnoticed in Rome, thought Bishop Konrad, calming his frightened horse, *they cannot ignore this. That here, in Silesia, on the marches of Europe and Christian civilisation, I, Konrad Piast of Oleśnica, hold the cross high. That I am a true* bellator Christi, defensor *and intercessor of Catholicism, and to heretics and apostates a* flagellum Dei – *a divine punishment and scourge.*

Shouts from the highway hidden behind the hill suddenly joined the cries of people being executed, and a moment later, a detachment of horsemen burst forth, galloping east, towards Levín. Wagons rattled after the horsemen and the waggoners yelled, standing up and mercilessly whipping the horses, trying to make them move faster. Lowing cattle were being driven behind the wagons, and behind them ran foot soldiers, yelling loudly. In the confusion, the bishop couldn't hear what they were yelling. But others could. The pikemen shooting the Czechs turned and fled to a man, following the mounted soldiers, the wagons and the infantry now filling the entire highway.

'Where are you going!' bellowed the bishop. 'Stop! What is the matter? What is happening?'

'Hussites!' yelled Otto of Borschnitz, reining his horse in beside them. 'Hussites, Father! The Hussites are coming! Hussite war wagons!'

'Nonsense! There is no field army in Hradec! The Hussites marched on Podještědí!'

'Not all of them! They're coming for us! Fleeee! Save yourself!'

'Stop!' roared Konrad, flushing. 'Stop, you cowards! Stand and fight! Fight, you dogs!'

'Save yourself!' bellowed Mikołaj Zedlitz, Starosta of Otmuchów, galloping beside him. 'Hussiiites! They're coming for us! Hussiiites!'

'Sir Půta and Lord Kolditz have already fled! Every man for himself!'

'Stop . . .' The bishop tried vainly to make his voice heard over the pandemonium. 'Noble knights! What are you—'

His horse was frantic beneath him and reared up. Lorenz of Rohrau seized it by the reins and brought it under control.

'We must flee!' he shouted. 'Reverend! We must save ourselves!'

Along the highway galloped more riders, bowmen and armoured troops, knights who only the day before had been boasting about their readiness to attack. And now they were fleeing in panic.

'Save yourselves, one and all!' yelled Tristram of Rachenau, speeding alongside. 'Ambrož is coming! Ambroož!'

'Christ, have mercy on us!' mumbled Father Miegerlin, running beside the bishop's horse. 'Save us, O Christ!'

A wagon full of spoils with a broken wheel was blocking the highway. It was pushed off and tipped over, and chests, trunks, barrels and other objects plundered from the villages being burned were scattered in the mud. When another wagon got stuck, and behind it another, the waggoners jumped off and fled on foot. The road was already strewn with spoils discarded by the foot soldiers. A moment later, the bishop saw discarded pavises, halberds, battleaxes, crossbows and even firearms among the bundles of loot. The unburdened pikemen ran so hard they were catching up with the horsemen and armoured men. Men who were falling behind wailed and yelled in panic. Cows lowed. Sheep bleated.

'Quicker, quicker, Reverend . . .' Lorenz of Rohrau urged him on, his voice shaking. 'We must save ourselves . . . We must save ourselves . . . We must reach Homole . . . And the border . . .'

In the centre of the highway, partly trampled into the ground, stained with cow shit, covered with bagels and pieces of broken pots, lay a standard with a large red cross. The sign of the crusade.

Konrad, Bishop of Wrocław, bit his lip. And spurred his horse. To the east. Towards Homole and the Levín Pass. *Save yourself while you can. As quick as you are able. Quickly. Because . . .*

'Ambrož is coming! Ambroooož!'

'Ambrož,' Scharley said, nodding, 'was the Hradec parish priest at the Church of the Holy Spirit. I've heard about him. He was at Žižka's side up until his death. He's a dangerous radical, a charismatic people's champion, a real rabble-rouser. Moderate Calixtines are scared stiff of him, because Ambrož regards moderation as a betrayal of the ideals of Huss and the Chalice. One nod from him and a thousand Taborite flails fall in behind him.'

'It's true,' Horn confirmed. 'Ambrož was already raging during the bishop's previous plundering raid in 1421. At that time, as you remember, it ended in a truce negotiated by Hynek Krušyna and Čeněk of Wartenberg with Bishop Konrad. The bloodthirsty priest called the two men traitors and procrastinators and the mob attacked them with flails. They barely escaped. Ever since, Ambrož has talked only about revenge ... Reinmar? What's the matter?'

'Nothing.'

'You look absent,' said Scharley. 'You're not ill, are you? Never mind. Let us return to the bishop's plundering raid, my dear Mommolem. What does it have to do with us?'

'The bishop caught plenty of Hussites,' explained Horn. 'They say he was catching people according to a list. Did I not say he had good spies?'

'You did,' replied Scharley. 'So, the Inquisition is busy wringing testimonies out of those captives. And so you think they won't have time for us for the present?'

'I don't think. I know.'

The conversation that had to happen took place that evening.

'Horn.'

'I'm listening to you, laddie, most attentively.'

'You don't have a dog now, no matter how it grieves you.'

'That cannot be denied.' Urban Horn's eyes narrowed.

Reynevan cleared his throat loudly to attract Scharley's attention, who was nearby playing chess with Tomasz Alpha using pieces formed from clay and bread.

'Neither will you find here,' he continued, 'any hollow, or humours, or fluids. In short, nothing that could protect you from the necessity of giving me answers to my questions. The same ones I asked you in Balbinów, in the stable of my murdered brother. Do you remember what I asked you?'

'I don't usually have problems with my memory.'

'Splendid. So giving me the answers you owe me shouldn't cause you any problems, either. I'm ready. Start talking.'

Urban Horn placed his hands under his neck and stretched, then looked Reynevan in the eyes.

'Well, well,' he said. 'How fierce. "Start talking." And if I don't, what then? What will happen if I don't answer your questions? Assuming, as I rightly believe, that I don't owe you anything? What then? If I may ask?'

'Then you may get a beating.' Reynevan glanced to see if Scharley was listening. 'Before you can say *credo in Deum patrem omnipotentem*.'

Horn said nothing for some time, continuing to lie with his fingers interlaced under his head.

'I've already said it didn't completely surprise me to see you here,' Horn finally replied. 'You blatantly ignored the warnings and advice of Canon Beess, mine also, which had to end badly for you. It's a miracle you're still alive. But you're in prison, laddie. If you haven't realised it yet, it's time you did: you're locked up in the Tower of Fools. And you're expecting – nay, demanding – from me answers to questions. You want information. And what, may I ask, do you mean to do with it? What do you expect? That they'll release you to celebrate the anniversary of the discovery of Saint Smaragdus's relics? That somebody will mercifully free you as a penance? No, Reinmar of Bielawa. You can expect the Inquisitor and an interrogation. Do you know what *strappado* is? How long do you think you'll last when they pull you up by your arms twisted behind your back? With a forty-pound weight hanging from your ankles? And burning torches held under your armpits? Well? How long do you think you'll last before you begin to sing? I'll tell you: before you can even say the *Veni Sancte Spiritus*.'

'Why was Peterlin killed? Who killed him?'

'You're as stubborn as a mule, laddie. Didn't you hear what I said? I won't tell you anything. Nothing you might reveal under torture. The game is too important and the stakes are too high.'

'What game?' Reynevan shouted. 'What stakes? I care nothing about your games! Your secrets haven't been secrets for a long time. The cause you serve is no longer a secret, either. What, do you think I can't put two and two together? Let me tell you, I don't give a damn about it. I don't give a fuck about conspiracies or religious disputes. Do you hear, Horn? I'm not asking you to turn in your accomplices, to betray any more hiding places where Joannes Wicleph Anglicus is buried. But I must, by the Devil, know why, how and by whose hand my brother died. And you will tell me. Even if I have to beat it out of you!'

'Oh! What a little rooster!'

'Get up. I'll give you a hiding.'

Horn stood. Swift, nimble, like a lynx.

'Take it easy,' he hissed. 'Take is easy, m'Lord Bielawa the younger. Let's keep calm. Anger mars beauty. You'll lose your looks. And your popularity with married women now famous throughout Silesia.'

Leaning back, Reynevan kicked Urban hard below the knee as he had seen Scharley do. Horn, astonished, dropped to his knees. But from that moment, Scharley's tactics began to fail Reynevan. Horn avoided the punch meant to break his nose with a slight but quick movement and Reynevan's fist only brushed his ear. Horn parried a wide and inaccurate left hook with his forearm, sprang nimbly up from his knees and jumped aside.

'Well, well.' He grinned. 'Who would have thought it? But since you want it so much, laddie . . . At your service.'

'Horn.' Scharley, without turning around, took Tomasz Alpha's bread knight with his bread queen. 'We're in prison, I know the custom, I won't get involved. But I swear that whatever you do to him I'll do to you twice over. Especially dislocations and fractures.'

Things moved quickly. Horn jumped at Reynevan like a cat, smoothly, gracefully, sinuously. Reynevan dodged the first blow and punched, even finding the target, but only once; all his other blows were parried or blocked. Horn struck just twice, very quickly. Both blows were accurate. Reynevan flew back and sat down hard on the dirt floor.

'Children,' said Tomasz Alpha, moving his king. 'Just like children.'

'Rook takes pawn,' said Scharley. 'Checkmate.'

Urban Horn stood over Reynevan, rubbing his cheek and ear.

'I don't want to return to this matter,' he said coldly. 'Ever.

But so you won't think we fought for nothing, I'll satisfy your curiosity somewhat and tell you a little. Something about your brother, Piotr. You want to know who killed him. Well, I don't know who, but I do know what. It's more than certain that your romance with Adèle of Stercza killed Piotr. Which was a pretext, an excellent pretext, that almost perfectly masked the real reasons. Don't tell me that's never occurred to you, since you know how to put two and two together.'

Reynevan wiped the blood from under his nose. He didn't answer. He licked his swelling lip.

'Reinmar,' added Horn. 'You look terrible. Sure you aren't feverish?'

Reynevan was cross for some time. With Horn – for obvious reasons. With Scharley – for not intervening and beating up Horn. With Koppirnig, for snoring, with Bonaventure for smelling, with Circulos, with Brother Tranquillus, with the Narrenturm and the whole world. With Adèle of Stercza, because she had behaved disgracefully towards him. With Katarzyna of Biberstein – because he had behaved hideously towards her.

To make matters worse, he felt ill. He had a cold and the shivers, was sleeping badly and waking up both wet with sweat and frozen.

He was tormented by dreams where he endlessly smelled Adèle's scent, her powder, her rouge, her lipstick and her henna by turns with the scent of Katarzyna, her femininity, her girl-ish sweat and the mint and sweet flag in her hair. His fingers and hands remembered the touches that returned to him in his dreams. And endlessly compared them.

He woke up covered in sweat. And while he was awake, he recalled his dreams and couldn't stop comparing.

His bad mood was made worse by Scharley and Horn, who since the fight had made friends and become chummy. The two old foxes often sat together at the sign of the omega for long conversations, obsessed with one topic, returning to it over and over. Even if they started somewhere else, they always came back to their prospects of getting out of clink.

'Who knows,' said Scharley softly, pensively biting a chipped thumbnail. 'Who knows, Horn. Perhaps we'll be lucky ... We have, as you can see, certain hopes ... Somebody on the outside—'

'Who is that?' Horn looked at him keenly. 'If one may know?'

'Know? What for? Do you know what *strappado* is? How long do you think you'd last when they pull you up by your—'

'Very well, skip it. I was wondering if you're pinning your hopes on Reinmar's beloved, Adèle of Stercza. Who is, rumour has it, enjoying great popularity and influence among the Silesian Piasts.'

'No,' countered Scharley, clearly amused by Reynevan's furious expression. 'It's not her we're pinning our hopes on. Our dear Reinmar is, indeed, popular with the fair sex, but there aren't any benefits from that, of course, beyond very fleeting carnal pleasures.'

'Yes, yes.' Horn appeared to have fallen into a reverie. 'It's not enough to be popular with the ladies, you have to be lucky with them, too. Have a way with them, if you'll excuse the euphemism. Then one has the chance to have not only worries and love's labour's lost, but also some benefits. In a situation like ours, for example ... Dammit, Reinmar, you really do look terrible.'

'... *Ecce enim veritatem dilexisti incerta et occulta sapientiae tuae manifestasti mihi. Asperges me hyssopo, et mundabor* ... Hey! I don't want to come and thump one of you! *Lavabis me* ... Oi! Don't yawn there! Yes, yes, Koppirnig, I'm talking to you! And you, Bonaventure, why are you rubbing yourself against the wall like a pig? During prayers? A little dignity, please! And I'd like to know whose feet stink. *Lavabis me et super nivem dealbabor. Auditui meo dabis gaudium* ... Saint Dymphna ... What's up with him again?'

'He's sick.'

Reynevan's back, which he was lying on, was painful. It surprised him to be recumbent, since he had only just been kneeling to pray. The floor was cold, the chill was radiating through the straw and he felt as though he were lying on ice. He was shaking with cold, trembling all over, and his teeth were chattering so much his jaw muscles hurt.

'Fellows! Why, his body's burning like Moloch's furnace!'

He wanted to protest. Couldn't they see he was frozen, trembling from the cold? He wanted to ask them to cover him with something, but he couldn't utter a single clearly articulated word through his chattering teeth.

'Lie still. Don't move.'

Somebody next to him was wheezing, coughing violently. *Circulos, it's probably Circulos coughing like that*, he thought, realising in sudden terror that even though the person coughing was only two steps away, all he could see of them was a vague blur. He blinked. It didn't help. He felt somebody wiping his forehead and face.

'Lie still,' said some mould on the wall in Scharley's voice. 'Lie still.'

He was covered, but didn't remember anybody covering him. But he had stopped shaking, and his teeth weren't chattering.

'You're sick.'

He wanted to say that he knew better – after all, *he* was a doctor, he'd studied medicine in Prague and could distinguish an illness from a passing chill and weakness. To his amazement, rather than intelligent speech, all that left his open mouth was a ghastly croaking. He was coughing violently, his throat sore and stinging. He strained and coughed again. And fainted from the effort.

He was delirious. He started dreaming. About Adèle and Katarzyna. He had the scents of powder, rouge, mint, henna and sweet flag in his nostrils. His fingers and hands remembered the touch, the softness, the hardness, the smoothness. When he closed his eyes, he saw the modest, embarrassed *nuditas virtualis* – the small round breasts with nipples hard from desire. The slim waist, the narrow hips. Her flat stomach. The thighs shyly clenched together . . .

Now he didn't know which was which.

He battled against the illness for two weeks, until All Saints' Day. Later, when he recovered, he found out that the crisis and critical stage had occurred around Saints Simon and Jude's Day, on the seventh day, as was standard. He also found out that Brother Tranquillus had supplied the herbal remedies and infusions that saved him, administered by Scharley and Horn who took turns to watch over him.

Chapter Twenty-Eight

In which our heroes are still – to use the words of the prophet Isaiah – *sedentes in tenebris*, meaning in common parlance that they're still locked up in the Narrenturm. Later, however, pressure is put on Reynevan using both arguments and instruments. And the Devil knows how it would have ended if it hadn't been for some university friends.

Nothing much changed in the two weeks that the illness erased from Reynevan's biography. It had grown even colder, which couldn't be called a phenomenon after All Souls' Day. Herring had begun to prevail in the bill of fare, reminding the inmates that Advent was coming. In principle, canon law instructed that fasting begin only four Sundays before Christmas, but the very devout – and the canons of the Holy Sepulchre were among those – began earlier.

Regarding other events, soon after Saint Ursula's Day, Nicolaus Koppirnig had had such an acute and persistent attack of carbuncles that they'd had to be lanced in the hospital *medicinarium*. After the operation, the astronomer had spent several days in the infirmary. He had talked so compellingly about the comfort and provender there that the remaining inmates of the tower had decided to have some of it. The rags and straw from Koppirnig's pallet had been divided up so that the other inmates might become infected. Indeed, soon after, the Institor and Bonaventure had come out in ulcers and pimples. But they weren't a patch on Koppirnig's carbuncles, and the canons of the Holy Sepulchre hadn't considered them worthy of operating on or hospitalisation.

Scharley, meanwhile, had managed to entice with scraps of food and tame a large rat which he'd named Martin in honour of the reigning Pope. The joke amused some of the Narrenturm's inmates, while others were outraged at Scharley and Horn when they'd baptised the rat and quipped: *Habemus papam*.

After Reynevan recovered his wits, little changed in the tower. Every evening they sat down and conversed, usually near Reynevan's pallet, who was still too weak to get up and was being fed on chicken soup specially supplied by the canons of the Holy Sepulchre. Thus, Urban Horn fed Reynevan and Scharley fed Martin the rat. Bonaventure scratched his ulcers and Koppirnig, the Institor, the Camaldolite and Isaiah listened. Tomasz Alpha ranted. And the topics – inspired by the rat – were the popes, popery and the famous Prophecy of the Popes of Saint Malachy, Archbishop of Armagh.

'You must admit,' said Tomasz Alpha, 'that the prophecy is very accurate, so accurate its veracity cannot be called into question. Malachy must have had a revelation, God himself must have spoken to him, revealing the fate of Christianity, including the names of the popes, from his contemporary Celestyn II to Peter the Roman, the one whose papacy would allegedly end in the destruction of Rome, the papacy, and the entire Christian faith. And so far, Malachy's prophecy has come true to the letter.'

'Only when stretched,' Scharley said, shoving a scrap of bread under Martin's whiskered snout. 'You can put on tight boots using the same principle. You just can't walk in them.'

'You're showing your ignorance. Malachy's prophecy correctly describes all the popes convincingly. Just take the recent Schisms: why, the one whom the prophecy calls the "Cosmedine moon" is the recently deceased Pedro de Luna, once cardinal deacon at Santa Maria's in Cosmedine who called himself Benedict XIII. After him, in Malachy's writings comes the *cubus de mixtione*, the "Cube of mixture" – and who's that if not the Roman Boniface IX, Pietro Tomacelli, who had a chequered band in his arms?'

'And the one called "Of a better star",' interrupted Bonaventure, scratching an ulcer on his calf, 'is of course Innocent VII, Cosimo de' Migliorati, who has a comet in his coat of arms. Isn't it?'

'Indeed, it is! And the next pope, called by Malachy the "Mariner of the black bridge", is clearly Gregory XII, Angelo Corraro, a Venetian. And the "Lash of the Sun"? Why, it's none other than the Cretan Peter Phillarges, Alexander V, made pope by the Council of Pisa, with the sun in his coat of arms. And the one called the "Stag of the Syren" in Malachy's prophecy—'

'Then shall the lame man leap as an hart, and the tongue of the dumb sing. For shall waters break out—'

'Quiet, Isaiah! For that stag is, is it not—'

'Who the hell is it?' snapped Scharley. 'I know, I know, you'll shoehorn Baldassarre Cossa, John XXIII, in here, like a foot into a tight poulaine. Yet he isn't a pope, but an antipope, who doesn't suit the list at all, moreover, having nothing in common with a stag or a syren. In other words, Malachy was talking nonsense there. As in many other places of that celebrated prophecy.'

'This is in poor taste, Master Scharley!' said Tomasz Alpha, growing annoyed. 'You oughtn't to treat prophecies like that! You should see what is indisputably true in it, and regard that as proof of the truth of the whole. The things you consider wrong can't be declared falsehoods, instead one must humbly acknowledge that being but a trifling mortal, one comprehends not the word of God, for it is incomprehensible. But time will prove the truth!'

'However much time passes, nothing can turn claptrap into the truth—'

'Here, Scharley, you are wrong,' Urban Horn interrupted with a smile. 'You seriously underestimate time.'

'You are profane,' said Circulos, who was listening from his pallet. 'You are ignoramuses. All of you. In truth, I listen and I hear: *stultus stulta loquitur.*'

Tomasz Alpha gestured at him with his head and twisted a finger against his forehead. Horn snorted and Scharley waved a dismissive hand.

The rat watched the incident with its wise, black eyes. Reynevan watched the rat. Koppirnig watched Reynevan.

'And what,' Koppirnig suddenly asked, 'do you say about the future of the papacy, Master Tomasz? What does Malachy say about that? Who will be the next pope, after Holy Father Martin?'

'The Stag of the Syren, probably,' sneered Scharley.

'Then shall the lame man leap as an hart—'

'I said be quiet, you nutcase! And I shall respond to you, Master Nicolaus: it will be the Catalonian. After the current Holy Father Martin, called the "Crown of the golden veil", Malachy mentions Barcelona.'

'The "Schism of the Barcelonas",' corrected Bonaventure, who was reassuring the weeping Isaiah. 'And that would mean Gil Sanchez Munoz y Carbon, the next schismatic after Luna, calling himself Clement VIII. This part of the prophecy is by no means discussing Martin V's successor.'

'Oh, indeed?' Scharley showed exaggerated surprise. 'By no means? What a relief.'

'If only the Roman popes are taken into consideration,' Tomasz Alpha concluded, 'the next one in Malachy's writings is the "Celestian she-wolf".'

'I knew we'd get there in the end,' snorted Horn. 'The *Curia Romana* has always been famous for its wolfish laws and customs, but a she-wolf on the Chair of Saint Peter? May God have mercy on us.'

'And a female to boot,' said Scharley. 'Again? Wasn't one Joan enough? And it was said that all the candidates would be more closely examined to see if they had balls.'

'They abandoned the examinations.' Horn winked at him. 'Because too many were eliminated.'

'Your jokes are inopportune,' frowned Tomasz Alpha, 'and what's more, smack of heresy.'

'I swear,' the Institor added gloomily. 'You blaspheme. Just like with that rat of yours—'

'Enough, enough,' Koppirnig quietened him with a gesture. 'Let us return to Malachy. Who'll be the next pope, then?'

'I checked and know,' Tomasz Alpha looked around proudly, 'that only one cardinal may be considered. Gabriel Condulmer. At one time the Bishop of Sienna. And Sienna, please note, has a she-wolf in its arms. This Condulmer – mark well my and Malachy's words – will be elected by the conclave after Pope Martin, may God give him a lengthy papacy.'

'It doesn't seem probable to me,' said Horn, shaking his head. 'There are more likely candidates, more well known, who are pursuing more brilliant careers. Albert Branda Castiglione and Giordano Orsini, both members of the College. Or Juan de Cervantes, cardinal at San Pietro in Vincoli. Or for example, Bartolomeo Capra, Archbishop of Milan.'

'The Camerlengo John of Palomar,' added Scharley. 'Gilles Charlier, Dean of Cambrai. Cardinal Juan de Torquemada. And finally, John Stojković of Ragusa. In my view and if I'm to be frank, Condulmer, about whom I know nothing, has meagre chances—'

'Malachy's Prophecy,' Tomasz Alpha cut off the discussion, 'is infallible.'

'Which one can't say about its interpreters,' replied Scharley.

The rat sniffed Scharley's bowl. Reynevan raised himself up with difficulty and leaned back against the wall.

'Oh, gentlemen, gentlemen,' he said with effort, wiping sweat from his forehead and stifling a cough. 'You're locked in a tower, in a sombre prison. No one knows what tomorrow will bring. Perhaps they'll take us away to be tortured and killed? And you're arguing about a pope who won't take office for six years . . .'

'How do you know it'll be six?' Tomasz Alpha choked.

'I don't. It just came to me.'

On Saint Martin's Eve, the tenth of November, by which time Reynevan was completely recovered, Isaiah and Normal were deemed healed and freed. They had previously been taken out several times to be examined. Whoever conducted the evaluations must have concluded that compulsive masturbation and communicating entirely by means of passages from the Book of Isaiah said nothing adverse about their mental health, for after all, the Pope had been known to quote the Book of Salvation and masturbation was a natural human act. Nicolaus Koppirnig had a different opinion about their releases.

'They are preparing the terrain for the Inquisitor,' he pronounced gloomily. 'They're removing the nutcases and loonies so that the Inquisitor won't have to waste time on them. They're leaving the cream. Meaning us.'

'I think so, too,' said Urban Horn.

Circulos overheard the conversation and moved soon after. He gathered up his straw and plodded, like a bald old pelican, to the opposite wall, where he made a new pallet, far from the others. Soon, the wall and floor were covered in hieroglyphics and ideograms. Signs of the zodiac, pentagrams and hexagrams predominated, but there were also spirals and tetrads, and the mother letters – Aleph, Mem and Shin – were a recurring feature. There was also something resembling the Tree of the Sephiroth.

'What do you say to that devil's work, gentlemen?' Tomasz Alpha nodded towards Circulos.

'The Inquisitor will take him first,' stated Bonaventure. 'Mark my words.'

'I doubt it,' said Scharley. 'I think, on the contrary, he'll soon be released. If they really are releasing the dimwits, then he fulfils the conditions perfectly.'

'I think you're wrong in his case,' countered Koppirnig.

Reynevan thought so, too.

Herring was the prevailing feature of the fast-time menu and soon even Martin the rat was eating it with visible reluctance. Reynevan, meanwhile, had made his decision.

Circulos paid no attention to him and didn't even notice when he approached while he was busy painting Solomon's Seal on the wall. Reynevan cleared his throat. Once, then again, louder. Circulos didn't turn his head.

'Get out of my light!'

Reynevan squatted down. On the circle surrounding the seal, Circulos had evenly scribbled the following words: AMASARAC, ASARADEL, AGLON, VACHEON and STIMULAMATON.

'What do you want?'

'I know those sigla and spells. I've heard about them.'

'Oh, yes?' Circulos only now looked at him, and said nothing for some time. 'And I've heard of spies. Begone, snake.'

He turned his back on Reynevan and resumed his scribbling. Reynevan cleared his throat and took a deep breath.

'*Clavis Salomonis . . .*'

Circulos froze. He remained motionless for a while, then slowly turned his head, causing his goitre to bob.

'*Speculum salvationis,*' he replied, his voice still suspicious and hesitant. 'Toledo?'

'*Alma mater nostra.*'

'*Veritas Domini?*'

'*Manet in saeculum.*'

'Amen.' Only then did Circulos grin to show the blackened stumps of his teeth and look around to check that no one was listening. 'Amen, young confrater. Which academy? Krakow?'

'Prague.'

'Mine was Bologna.' Circulos smiled even more broadly. 'Then Padua. And Montpellier. I also spent time in Prague . . . I knew doctors, masters, scholars . . . They didn't fail to remind me of that during my arrest, and the Inquisitor will want to know the details . . . But you, young confrater? What will the Defender of the Catholic faith hastening here want to learn from you? Who did you know in Prague?'

'I didn't know anyone.' Reynevan recalled Scharley's warning. 'I'm innocent. I ended up here by accident. It was a misunderstanding—'

'*Certes, Certes.*' Circulos waved a hand. 'Of course. If you are convincing in your saintly innocence, you'll get out alive,

God willing. You have a chance. Unlike me.'

'What do you—'

'I know what I'm saying.' Circulus cut him off. 'I am a recidivist. A *Haereticus relapsus*, understand? I won't endure the torture, I'll incriminate myself . . . The stake is a certainty. Which is why . . .'

He gestured towards the symbols on the wall.

'Which is why,' he repeated, 'I'm doing what I can, as you see.'

A day passed before Circulos revealed what he was doing. A day during which Scharley expressed his categoric disapproval of Reynevan's new friendship.

'I don't understand why you're wasting your time talking to that madman,' he concluded.

'Oh, leave him alone,' said Horn, siding unexpectedly with Reynevan. 'Let him talk to whoever he wants to. Perhaps he needs a change?'

Scharley waved a hand dismissively.

'Hey!' he shouted as Reynevan walked off. 'Don't forget! Eight and forty!'

'What?'

'The sum of the letters in the word "Apollyon" multiplied by the sum of the letters in the word "moron"!'

'I'm devising,' Circulos lowered his voice, looking around vigilantly, 'a plan to get out of here.'

'Using . . .' Reynevan also glanced around. 'Magic, correct?'

'There's no other way,' the old man stated unemotionally. 'At the very beginning, I tried bribery. They beat me. I tried to threaten them. They beat me again. I tried pretending to be a complete halfwit, but they weren't taken in. I would have feigned being possessed by the Devil, and if old Dobeneck, the Wrocław prior at Saint Adalbert, were still the Inquisitor, I might have succeeded. But that new, young one, he can't be fooled. What's left to me?'

'My question exactly: what?'

'Teleportation. Travelling through space.'

The following day, Circulos, glancing around vigilantly to check that no one was eavesdropping, introduced his plan to Reynevan, supporting it, of course, with a long lecture about the theories of sorcery and goetia. Teleportation, Reynevan learned, was quite possible, easy even, on condition, of course, that one sought the assistance of a suitable demon. Circulos revealed that there were several such demons, and that every decent book of spells offered its own kinds. Circulos's lengthy studies, Reynevan learned eventually, inclined him to follow the instructions of *The Grimorium Verum*. And *The Grimorium Verum* recommended the summoning of the demon Mersilde.

'But how to summon him?' Reynevan dared to ask. 'Without instruments, without an *Occultum*? The *Occultum* must meet a series of conditions, the creation of which in this filthy dungeon would—'

'Orthodoxy!' Circulos interrupted angrily. 'Doctrinairism! So harmful in empiricism, so narrow-minded! The *Occultum* is a trifle when one has an amulet. Am I right, Master Formalist? Of course I am. Ergo, here is the amulet. *Quod erat demonstrandum.* Just look.'

The amulet turned out to be an oval disc of malachite, more or less the size of a farthing, engraved with glyphs and symbols filled with gold, of which the most conspicuous were a serpent, a fish and a sun inside a triangle.

'It's the talisman of Mersilde,' Circulos said proudly. 'I smuggled it in here out of sight. Take a look. Go on.'

Reynevan held out a hand but quickly withdrew it. Faint traces of a dried-on, dark substance on the talisman betrayed its hiding place.

'I'm going to try tonight,' the old man said, unmoved by his reaction. 'Wish me fortune, young novice. Who knows, perhaps one day ...'

'I still have ...' Reynevan cleared his throat, 'a request.

I'm looking for answers . . . regarding a certain . . . incident . . .'

'Go on.'

He expounded the matter quickly but thoroughly. Circulos listened quietly and raptly, then began asking questions.

'What day was it? The precise date?'

'The last day of August. A Friday. An hour before Vespers.'

'Hmm . . . The Sun in the sign of the Virgin, which is Venus . . . The ruling dualistic phenomenon, in Chaldean: Shamas, in Hebrew: Hamaliel. The Moon, it looks from my calculations, was full . . . unfortunately . . . The hour of the Sun . . . could have been better, could have been worse . . . Just a moment.'

He brushed away the straw, rubbed the floor with his hand, scribbled some graphs and digits on it, added, multiplied and divided, mumbling something about ascendants, descendants, angles, epicycles, deferents and quincunxes. Finally, he raised his head and his goitre swayed comically.

'You mentioned that spells were used. Which ones?'

Reynevan began to quote them, trying his best to remember. It didn't take long.

'I know *The Arbatel*,' Circulos interrupted, waving a careless hand, 'although it's crudely muddled up in your recitation. It's a wonder it worked at all . . . And there were no tragic deaths? Never mind. Were there visions? A many-headed lion? A rider on a pale horse? A raven? A fiery serpent? No? Interesting. And you say that when Samson awoke . . . He wasn't himself, yes?'

'So he claimed. And there were certain . . . grounds for believing him. This is precisely what I'd like to find out – whether anything like that is even possible.'

Circulos said nothing for some time, rubbing one heel against the other. Then he cleared his nose.

'Space,' he said finally, pensively wiping a finger on his lap, 'is a perfectly organised whole and a splendid hierarchical order. It is an equilibrium between *generatio* and *corruptio*, birth and dying, creation and destruction. Space is, as Augustine teaches, *gradatio entium*, a ladder of existences, the visible and the invisible, the material and the immaterial. Space is also like a book—'

'I asked if it's possible.'

'Existence is not just *substantia*, existence is at the same time *accidens*, something that occurs unintentionally ... occasionally magically—'

'Is it possible or not?' interrupted Reynevan bluntly.

'Possible indeed.' The old man nodded and pouted his blue lips. 'Certainly, it is. In the given case, one must remember that any spell – even the most apparently trivial – requires a pact with a demon.'

'So it was a demon?'

'Or a *cacodaemon*.' Circulos shrugged his thin shoulders. 'Or something we give that name to symbolically. What precisely? I can't say. Plenty of individuals enter the darkness—'

'So the monastery simpleton entered the darkness,' asked Reynevan, 'and a *negotium perambulans* became incarnated in his corporeal body? They changed places?'

'Balance,' Circulos confirmed with a nod. 'Yin and yang. Or, if the Kabbalah means more to you, Kether and Malkuth. If a peak exists, then a trough must also.'

'But can it be reversed? Revoked? Can the exchange be repeated? So that he would return ...'

'I don't know.'

They sat for a moment in a silence disturbed only by Koppirnig's snoring, Bonaventure's hiccoughing, the gibbering of the lunatics, the murmur of voices conversing at the sign of the omega and the *Benedictus Dominus*, quietly rattled off by the Camaldolite.

'He,' said Reynevan finally, 'I mean Samson, calls himself the Wanderer.'

'Most apt.'

They were silent for some time.

'Such a *cacodaemon*,' Reynevan finally said, 'must certainly possess some ... superhuman powers ...'

'Are you wondering whether you can expect him to rescue

you?' asked Circulos, showing his perspicacity. 'And whether, now that he's free, he's forgotten about his captive companions? You wish to know if you can expect his help. Don't you?'

'I do.'

Circulos said nothing for a while.

'I wouldn't,' he finally declared with brutal frankness. 'Why should demons differ from people in that respect?'

It was their last conversation. Whether Circulos managed to activate the amulet smuggled in up his arse and summon the demon Mersilde would remain forever a secret. But beyond reasonable doubt, nothing came of the teleportation. The following morning, Circulos was still in the tower, lying on his back on his pallet, stiff, both hands pressed against his chest and fingers digging into his clothing.

'O Blessed Virgin Mary ...' grunted the Institor. 'Cover his face ...'

Scharley draped a bit of rag over the ghastly visage, contorted in a paroxysm of horror and pain, the twisted mouth, flecked with dried-on foam, the grinning teeth and the dull, glassily goggling eyes.

'Call Brother Tranquillus.'

'Oh, Christ ...' groaned Koppirnig. 'Look ...'

Martin the rat was lying belly-up nearby, convulsed in agony, its yellow teeth showing.

'The Devil broke his neck,' judged Bonaventure with a knowing expression, 'and took his soul to Hell.'

'Aye, no doubt,' the Institor replied, nodding. 'He painted devilish signs on the walls and got his comeuppance. The old wizard summoned up the Devil, to his own undoing.'

'An evil power, touch wood ...' said Bonaventure. 'We should rub out all those scribblings and pour holy water over them. Say a Mass before the Evil One gets his hooks into us. Call the monks ... What are you laughing at, Scharley, may I ask?'

'Have a guess.'

'Indeed,' yawned Urban Horn. 'It's laughable, the drivel you're talking. And your agitation. What are you getting excited about? Old Circulos has died, kicked the bucket, popped his clogs, shuffled off this mortal coil, gone to the Asphodel Meadows. May the soil lie lightly on him and may *lux perpetua* shine on him. And let it be the *finis*. I declare the mourning over. And the Devil? To Hell with the Devil.'

'Ooh, m'Lord Mommolem.' Tomasz Alpha shook his head. 'Don't make fun of the Devil, for his work is visible here. Who knows, perhaps he is still at large, hidden in the gloom. Hellish vapours hang over this place of death. Can you not smell them? What do you think that stench is if not brimstone? What gives off a smell like that?'

'Your britches.'

'If it wasn't the Devil,' said Bonaventure crossly, 'what do you think killed him?'

'His heart.' Reynevan spoke up, somewhat hesitantly. 'I've studied cases like this. His heart broke. A plethora occurred. An excess of bile carried in the pneuma caused a tumour, and a clog – or infarction – occurred. There was a *spasmus* and his *arteria pulmonalis* burst.'

'Do you hear?' said Scharley. 'Science has spoken. *Sine ira et studio. Causa finita*, everything is clear.'

'Is it?' Koppirnig suddenly spoke. 'And the rat? What killed the rat?'

'A rotten herring,' said Scharley.

The door slammed open above them, the stairs creaked and a barrel trundled down the steps.

'Praise the Lord! Your meal, brothers! Come on, time for prayers! And then bring your bowls for fish!'

Brother Tranquillus dismissed the request for holy water, a Mass and an exorcism over the deceased's pallet with a highly ambiguous shrug and a highly unambiguous twist of his finger to his temple. That fact greatly enlivened the post-prandial discussion, and bold theses and conjectures were put forward. According to the boldest, Brother Tranquillus was himself a heretic and a Devil worshipper, for only such a person withholds holy water and spiritual ministry from the faithful. Tomasz Alpha, Bonaventure and the Institor began to delve deeper into the subject, ignoring the fact that Scharley and Horn were in hysterics. Until – to general stupefaction – the most unlikely person joined the discussion: the Camaldolite.

'Holy water,' the young clergyman's voice was heard for the first time, 'would have availed you nothing if the Devil really did appear here. Holy water is powerless against the Devil. As I well know, for I have seen it, and am here because of it.'

After the excited hubbub had subsided and a deathly silence fallen, the Camaldolite went on.

'I am a deacon at the Church of the Assumption in Niemodlin and secretary to the Reverend Piotr Nikisch, the dean of the collegiate. The thing I shall tell you about occurred this year, in the month of August. Around noon, the Honourable Master Fabian Pfefferkorn, *mercator* and a distant relative of the dean, burst into the church. He was greatly agitated and demanded that the Reverend Nikisch listen to his confession forthwith. They began at once to shout at each other in the confessional, using words of a kind I may not utter. As a result, the Reverend did not absolve Master Pfefferkorn and Master Pfefferkorn went away, calling the Reverend all sorts of coarse names and blaspheming both against the faith and the Roman Church. When he passed me in the vestibule, he yelled: "May the Devil take you, you damned priests!" And the Devil appeared.'

'In the church?' Scharley asked.

'In the vestibule, by the very entrance. It descended from somewhere high up. Or rather flew down, for it was in the form of a bird – I speak the truth! – and soon it assumed a human form. It was holding a shining sword, like in a painting, and stabbed Master Pfefferkorn straight in the face with it. Blood splashed on the floor ... Master Pfefferkorn flapped his arms like a rag doll.'The deacon swallowed loudly. 'I scooped up some holy water from the stoup and flung it at the Devil. And what do you think happened? Nothing! It ran off it like water off a duck's back. The hell-fiend blinked and spat out what had entered his mouth. And looked at me. And I ... I am ashamed to admit it, I fainted out of fear. When the brothers brought me round it was all over. The Devil had disappeared and Master Pfefferkorn lay lifeless, his soul gone – no doubt carried off to Hell by the Evil One.

'But the Devil hadn't forgotten me, it took its revenge. No one believed what I had seen. They called me insane, saying I'd lost my wits. And when I told of the holy water, they silenced me, threatening me with punishments reserved for heresy and blasphemy. The affair got out and was dealt with in Wrocław itself, at the bishop's court. And the order came from Wrocław to silence me and lock me up as a madman. But I know what Dominican *in pace* is like. Would I let myself be buried alive? I fled from Niemodlin without a second thought. But they captured me near Henryków and put me in here.'

'Did you manage to catch a good look at the Devil?' Urban Horn asked in the hushed silence. 'Can you describe what it looked like?'

'It was tall.'The Camaldolite swallowed again. 'Slim ... Long, black hair, falling to his shoulders. Nose like a bird's beak and eyes like a bird's ... Most piercing. An evil smile. Devilish.'

'No horns?' called Bonaventure, visibly disappointed. 'No hooves? Didn't have a tail?'

'It did not.'

'Eeeeeh! What rot!'

Discussions about devils, devilishness and the Devil's doings wore on with varying intensity right up until the twenty-fourth of November. Right up to suppertime, to be precise, when Brother Tranquillus shared some news with the inmates after prayers.

'A happy day has dawned for us, my dears! We are being

honoured by a long-awaited visit to our diocese by the prior of the Wrocław Dominicans, the inspector of the Holy Office, *defensor et candor fidei catholicae*, the Right Reverend *Inquisitor a Sede Apostolica*. Some of those present – don't think I don't know – are afflicted with a different malady from what we usually treat here. His Excellency the Inquisitor will now take care of their health and well-being. And certainly cure them! For His Excellency the Inquisitor has ordered from the town hall a number of burly physicians and a range of medical instruments. Thus, prepare yourselves spiritually, dear brothers, for the treatment is about to begin.'

That day, the herring tasted even worse than usual. Furthermore, there was no conversation in the Narrenturm that evening. Silence reigned.

For the whole next day – it happened to be a Sunday, the last Sunday before Advent – the atmosphere in the Tower of Fools was very strained. The inmates listened out in the unsettling silence for every rattling from above. They finally began to react to them with symptoms of panic and nervous collapse. Nicolaus Koppirnig hid away in a corner. The Institor began to weep, curled up in a foetal position on his pallet. Bonaventure sat motionless, staring vacantly ahead. Tomasz Alpha trembled, buried in the straw. The Camaldolite prayed softly with his face turned to the wall.

'See?' Urban Horn finally burst out. 'See how it works? See what they're doing to us? Just look at them!'

'Are you surprised?' asked Scharley, squinting. 'Hand on your heart, Horn, are you surprised at them?'

'I see nonsense. What's happening here is the result of a planned, carefully prepared operation. The interrogations haven't yet started, but the Inquisition has already brought these men to the brink of mental collapse, made them into beasts cringing at the crack of a whip.'

'I repeat: are you surprised?'

'I am. Because one must fight back, not surrender!'

Scharley gave an evil grin.

'I trust you'll show us how it's done when the time comes.'

Urban Horn said nothing for a long time.

'I'm no hero,' he finally declared. 'I don't know what I'll do when I'm hauled out, when they begin tightening the screws and driving in the wedges. When they take the red-hot irons out of the fire. But I know one thing: it won't help me if I abase myself by weeping, sobbing and begging for mercy. You have to be tough with the Brother Inquisitors.'

'Indeed?'

'Yes, indeed. They are too used to people shaking with fear before them and shitting themselves at the very sight of them. These almighty lords of life and death love the power, grow drunk on the terror they sow. And who are they really? Nobodies, curs from the Dominican kennel, semi-literate, superstitious ignoramuses, deviants and cowards. Don't shake your head, Scharley, it's normal for satraps, tyrants and torturers – they are cowards, and their cowardice, when combined with absolute power, releases a bestiality in them that their victims' subservience and inaction only heightens. It's the same with the Inquisitors. Hidden behind their terrifying hoods are unremarkable cowards. And one must not prostrate oneself before them and beg for mercy, because that only results in even greater bestiality and cruelty on their part. You need to look them proudly in the eyes! Although it won't save us, I tell you, it might at least unsettle their feigned self-assurance. We can remind them of Konrad of Marburg!'

'Who?' asked Reynevan.

'Konrad of Marburg,' explained Scharley. 'The Inquisitor of the Rhineland, Thuringia and Hesse. When he nettled the Hesse nobility with his duplicity, entrapments and atrocities, they waylaid him and hacked him and his entire entourage to pieces. No one got out alive.'

'I vouch that every Inquisitor has that name and event permanently etched on his memory,' added Horn, standing up and walking towards the piss pot. 'So mark my advice!'

'What do you think of his advice?' mumbled Reynevan.

'Mine is different,' Scharley mumbled back. 'When they start on you in earnest, speak. Testify. Confess. Sing. Collaborate. And make a hero of yourself later, when you write your memoirs.'

Nicolaus Koppirnig was the first to be taken for questioning. The astronomer, who until then had been putting on a brave face, lost his head completely at the sight of the sturdy Inquisitor's lackeys. First, he made a desperate attempt to flee – with nowhere to run to. When he was caught, the poor wretch shouted, wept, kicked, struggled and wriggled like an eel in the thugs' arms. He achieved nothing by it, of course, except a sound beating. They smashed his nose, among other appendages, and his blubbering sounded amusingly nasal as he was carried out.

But no one laughed.

Koppirnig didn't return. When the following day the bruisers came for the Institor, he didn't make any violent scenes, but remained calm. He just wept and snivelled, resigned to his fate. But as they were picking him up, he soiled his trousers. Judging it a form of resistance, the bruisers gave him a severe beating before dragging him out.

The Institor didn't return, either.

The next one to go – the same day – was Bonaventure. Having utterly lost his mind out of fear, the municipal scribe began to berate the bruisers, shouting and threatening them with his connections. The bruisers, naturally, weren't afraid of his threats and didn't give a damn if he played piquet with the burgermeister, the parish priest, the master of the mint and the elder of the brewers' guild. Bonaventure was given a sound thrashing and dragged out.

He didn't return.

The fourth man on the Inquisitor's list was not, contrary to his own predictions, Tomasz Alpha, who spent the entire night by turns weeping and praying, but the Camaldolite. He offered no resistance, so the thugs didn't even have to touch him.

Murmuring a soft farewell to his fellow prisoners, the Niemodlin deacon crossed himself and walked towards the stairs with his head meekly bowed, but with a sure and calm step of which the first martyrs walking into Nero's or Diocletian's arenas wouldn't have been ashamed.

The Camaldolite didn't return.

'I'll be next,' said Urban Horn with gloomy conviction.

He was mistaken.

Reynevan was only certain of his fate the moment the door at the top boomed and the stairs, flooded with slanting rays of sunlight, thudded and creaked beneath the feet of the heavies, who this time were accompanied by Brother Tranquillus.

Reynevan stood up and squeezed Scharley's hand. The penitent returned the squeeze, very hard, and in his face Reynevan saw for the first time something resembling extremely grave concern. Urban Horn's expression spoke eloquently for itself.

'Take care, Brother,' he muttered, painfully crushing Reynevan's hand. 'Remember Konrad of Marburg.'

'And remember my advice, too,' added Scharley.

Reynevan remembered both, but it didn't make things any easier.

Perhaps his expression or some imprudent movement made the bruisers suddenly leap at him. One seized him by the collar. And very quickly released him, bending forward, swearing and rubbing his elbow.

'Easy does it,' admonished Brother Tranquillus firmly, lowering his club. 'Don't use force. This is, after all, a hospital, in spite of appearances. Understood?'

The lackeys grunted, nodding. The canon of the Holy Sepulchre directed Reynevan towards the stairs with his truncheon.

The crisp, cold air almost knocked him off his feet. When he breathed in, he wobbled and staggered, stunned, like after a gulp of aqua vitae on an empty stomach. He would probably have fallen, but the experienced bruisers caught him under the arms. And that was the end of his desperate plan to escape. Or of dying fighting. As they dragged him, all he could do was shuffle his feet.

He saw the hospice for the first time. The tower he was being escorted from formed a corner set between two walls. Several buildings, probably including the hospital and the *medicinarium*, clung to the opposite wall by the gate. The kitchen was also there, judging from the smells of cooking. There were a great many horses under an awning by the wall, stamping their hooves in puddles of urine. And soldiers were moving around everywhere. The Inquisitor, guessed Reynevan, had come with a sizeable escort.

Desperate, high-pitched screams were coming from the *medicinarium* up ahead. Reynevan thought he heard Bonaventure's voice. Tranquillus caught his eye and quietened him with a finger to his lips.

Half-dazed, he found himself in a brightly lit chamber inside the building. His trance was interrupted by a pain in his knees as he was thrown forward to kneel in front of a table, behind which were sitting three monks in habits: Brother Tranquillus and two Dominicans. He blinked and shook his head. The Dominican sitting in the middle spoke first, a thin man with a bald head dotted with liver spots inside the narrow garland of his tonsure. His voice was unpleasant. Slippery.

'Reinmar of Bielawa. Say the Lord's Prayer and *Ave*.'

He did. In a hushed and somewhat shaky voice. The Dominican, meanwhile, picked his nose, seemingly only interested in what was on his finger.

'Reinmar of Bielawa. The secular arm has serious delations and accusations against you, so we shall turn you over to the secular authorities for interrogation and trial. But first of all, the *causa fidei* must be assessed and settled. You are accused of practising witchcraft and heresy. Of professing and propagating things that are contrary to what the Holy Church professes and teaches. Do you admit your guilt?'

'I do not ...' Reynevan swallowed. 'I do not confess. I am innocent. And I am a good Christian.'

'Naturally, you think you are,' said the Dominican, curling his lips disdainfully, 'for you consider us evil and false. I ask you: do you deem or have you ever deemed as true a faith other than the one that the Roman Church requires us to believe in and preaches? Confess the truth!'

'I am speaking the truth. I believe what Rome teaches.'

'Because no doubt your heretical sect has a branch in Rome.'

'I'm not a heretic. I will swear!'

'On what? On my cross and the faith that you mock? I know your heretical tricks! Confess! When did you join the Hussites? Who inducted you into the sect? Who introduced you to the writings of Huss and Wycliffe? When and where did you accept communion *sub utraque*?'

'I have never—'

'Silence! Your lies offend God! Did you study in Prague? Do you have any Czech friends?'

'Yes, but—'

'So you admit it?'

'Yes, but not—'

'Silence! Write down: he confessed that he admits.'

'I didn't confess to or admit anything!'

'He withdraws his testimony.' The Dominican's mouth twisted in a grimace that was both cruel and cheerful. 'He has tangled himself up in his lies and deceit! That is all I need. I move for the use of torture, otherwise we shall not arrive at the truth.'

'Father Grzegorz,' the canon of the Holy Sepulchre cleared his throat hesitantly, 'instructed us to refrain from ... He wanted to question this man himself—'

'Waste of time!' snorted the thin monk. 'In any case, he'll be more talkative if he's softened up first.'

'I don't think there are any free stations at the moment. And both torturers are busy—'

'There is a boot nearby and tightening a few screws is a piece of cake. An assistant will manage. If necessary, I'll do it. Come on! Over here! Take him!'

Reynevan, almost dead with fear, found himself once more in the heavies' vice-like grip. He was hauled out and shoved into a side chamber. Before he understood the gravity and danger of his situation, he was already sitting in an oaken chair with his neck and hands in iron clasps, and a shaven-headed torturer in a leather apron was fitting a horrifying contraption to his left foot. The contraption resembled a metal-bound box; it was large, heavy and smelled of iron and rust. And also of old blood and decayed flesh, like a worn-out butcher's block.

'I'm innnoceeeent!' howled Reynevan. 'Innoceeeeeent!'

'Go on.' The bony Dominican beckoned the torturer. 'Do the necessary.'

The torturer stooped, something clanked metallically and something grated. Reynevan howled in pain, feeling the metal-edged boards squeezing and crushing his foot. He suddenly thought of the Institor and understood his behaviour. He was a hair's breadth from shitting his trousers.

'When did you join the Hussites? Who gave you the writings of Wycliffe? Where and from whom did you receive the heretical communion?'

The screws grated; the torturer grunted. Reynevan howled.

'Who is your accomplice? Who do you collude with from Bohemia? Where do you meet? Where are you hiding the heretical books, writings and postills? Where are the weapons hidden?'

'I'm innnoceeeent!' he howled.

'Tighter.'

'Brother,' said the canon of the Holy Sepulchre. 'Have some respect. Why, he's a nobleman—'

'You are taking the role of advocate a little too much to heart,' the thin Dominican scowled. 'You were meant to be quiet and not interfere, I'll remind you. Tighter.'

Reynevan almost choked screaming.

And just like in a fairy tale, somebody heard his cries and came to his aid.

That somebody, standing in the doorway, turned out to be a well-built Dominican aged around thirty. 'I asked you not to do that. You are guilty of overzealousness, Brother Arnulph. And – worse still – a lack of obedience.'

'I . . . Reverend . . . Forgive me—'

'Be gone. To the chapel. Pray, wait in humility, and perhaps you will feel the grace of revelation. You there, release the prisoner, at the double. And be off with you. Everybody!'

'Reverend Father—'

'I said everybody!'

The Inquisitor sat down at the table in the place vacated by Brother Arnulph and shifted a crucifix blocking his view a little to one side.

He pointed to the bench without a word. Reynevan stood up, groaned, grunted, hobbled over and sat down. The Dominican slipped his hands into the sleeves of his white habit and examined him for a long time from beneath bushy, menacingly joined eyebrows.

'Reinmar of Bielawa,' he finally said, 'you were born with a silver spoon in your mouth.'

Reynevan nodded to confirm that he knew, for it couldn't be denied.

'You're lucky I was passing,' repeated the Inquisitor. 'Another two or three turns of that screw . . . Do you know what would have happened?'

'I can imagine—'

'No. You can't, I assure you. Oh, Reynevan, Reynevan, how do we come to be meeting in a torture chamber! Although, to tell the truth, it could have been foreseen back at university. Debauched views, a fondness for revelry and drinking, not to mention wanton females . . . Bloody hell, back in Prague, when I used to see you at The Dragon in Celetná Street, I prophesied that you'd meet a sticky end, and that whoring would be your undoing.'

Reynevan said nothing, although he had thought and prophesied identically in Prague's Old Town, in all the scholars' favourite brothels in the backstreet behind the Churches of Saint Nicolaus and Valentine. Grzegorz Hejncze, undergraduate scholar – and soon after master – at the Department of Theology at Charles University was also a frequent and cheerful patron of those establishments. Reynevan would never have imagined that the enthusiastic reveller Grzegorz Hejncze would last in a priest's vestments, but evidently he had. *Lucky for me indeed*, he thought, massaging his wrists and left foot. Which – if not for his intervention – the boot would certainly have crushed into a bloody pulp by now.

In spite of the relief resulting from the miraculous rescue, panicky fear still kept his hair sticking up and his back bowed. He knew it wasn't over. The well-built, keen-eyed Dominican with the bushy eyebrows and angular jaw was not, in spite of appearances, by any means his mischievous companion from the drinking dens and brothels of Prague. He was – it was clear from the expressions and bows of the monks and torturers exiting the chamber – the superior, the prior. The fear-inspiring Inspector of the Holy Office, the *defensor et candor fidei catholicae*, the Right Reverend *Inquisitor a Sede Apostolica* for the entire diocese of Wrocław. Reynevan must not forget that. The gruesome boot stinking of rust and blood lay two paces away where the torturer had cast it down. The torturer could be summoned at any moment and the boot put back on. Reynevan had no illusions in this regard.

'But every cloud has a silver lining.' Grzegorz Hejncze interrupted the short silence. 'I hadn't planned to use torture on you, comrade. You wouldn't have borne any marks or cuts on your return to the tower. But now you'll return limping, painfully injured by the dreadful Inquisition, without arousing suspicion. And you ought *not* to arouse suspicion.'

Reynevan said nothing. In fact, all he understood of the speech was that he was going back to the tower. The other words were taking time to reach him, and when they did, they aroused once more the terror that had been briefly lulled.

'I shall take sustenance. Perhaps you are hungry? Would you like a herring?'

'No ... I'll decline ... the herring ...'

'I can't offer you anything else – it's a fast day, and in my position, I have to set an example.'

Hejncze clapped his hands together and issued some orders. Fast day or not, example or not, the fish he was brought were much fatter than the ones given to the Narrenturm's inmates. The Inquisitor murmured a short *Benedic Domine* and without further delay began to eat the herring accompanied by thick hunks of wholemeal bread to counteract the saltiness.

'Let's get down to business,' he began, without interrupting his meal. 'You're in deep water, comrade. Very deep water. I closed the investigation into your alleged sorcerer's workshop in Oleśnica, for I know you, I support progress in medicine, and the divine spirit blows where it will. Nothing, including progress in medicine, occurs without His will. Admittedly, the offence of *adulterium* sickens me, but I was not charged to prosecute it. As far as your other alleged secular crimes go, I choose not to believe in them. For I know you.'

Reynevan breathed out. Too soon.

'There remains, though, Reinmar, the *causa fidei*. The case of religion and the Catholic faith. For I cannot be sure you don't share the same views as your deceased brother regarding the question of *Unam Sanctam*, the authority and infallibility of the Pope, the sacraments, transubstantiation and communion *sub utraque specie*. As well as regarding the Bible for common folk, auricular confession and the existence of purgatory. And so on.'

Reynevan opened his mouth, but the Inquisitor quietened him with a gesture.

'I don't know,' he continued, spitting out a fishbone, 'whether, like your brother, you read Ockham, Huss and the rest, or whether, like your brother, you distribute the said literature in Silesia,

Neumark and Greater Poland. Nor do I know whether, following your brother's example, you give protection to Hussite emissaries and spies. In short: whether you are a heretic. I presume – and I have studied the case a little – that you aren't. I believe that you were simply entangled in the whole affair by "chance", if one can use that term to describe Adèle of Stercza's feminine charms. And your well-known weakness for such charms.'

'Grzegorz ...' Reynevan had difficulty forcing the words out of his constricted windpipe. 'I mean, please forgive me, Reverend Father ... I assure you, I have nothing to do with heresy. My brother also, I vouch, the victim of a crime—'

'I'd be wary about vouching for your brother,' interrupted Hejncze. 'You'd be surprised how many delations were justifiably issued against him. He would have been brought before the tribunal and turned in his accomplices. I trust you wouldn't have been among them.'

He threw down the herring's backbone and licked his fingers.

'Piotr of Bielawa's imprudent activities,' he continued, starting on another fish, 'were halted, not by justice, not by criminal proceedings, not by *poenitentia*, but by a crime, the perpetrators of which I'd like to see punished. As would you, yes? I see you would. So know that they will be and soon. That knowledge ought to help you to make the decision.'

'What ...' Reynevan swallowed. 'What decision?'

Hejncze crumbled a slice of bread in silence. He was torn out of his reverie by a cry from somewhere in the building, the desperate, horrible scream of a person suffering intense pain.

'From what I can hear,' the Inquisitor indicated with a movement of his head, 'Brother Arnulph must have prayed briefly and gone back to his work. A zealous fellow, very zealous. But it reminds me that I also have work to do. Hence, let us reach a conclusion.'

Reynevan cringed. And rightly so.

'My dear Reynevan, you've become embroiled in quite the scandal. You've been made a tool of. I sympathise. But since you are a tool, it would be a sin not to make use of you, particularly in a good cause and to the glory of God. You shall walk free. I shall release you from the tower, protect and defend you from the people who wish you harm. And that number has grown – your death is sought, from what I know, by the Sterczas; Duke Jan of Ziębice; Jan's lover, Adèle of Stercza; the Raubritter Buko of Krossig; and also – for reasons that are still unclear – Sir Jan of Biberstein. Why, there is reason indeed for you to fear for your life. But, as I said before, I shall take you under my protection. But not for nothing, naturally. You scratch my back . . . To *ut des*. Or rather: *ut facias*.'

The Inquisitor began to speak more quickly, as though reciting a text he'd learned. 'I shall arrange everything so that no suspicions will be aroused in Bohemia, where you will be going. In Bohemia, you will make contact with the Hussites, with the men I tell you to. You ought not to have difficulty making contact. After all, you're the brother of Piotr of Bielawa, who rendered great service to Hussitism, was a good Christian, a martyr for the cause, and was murdered by accursed papists.'

'Am I to be . . .' uttered Reynevan. 'Am I to be a spy?'

'*Ad maiorem.*' Hejncze shrugged. '*Dei gloriam.* Everyone should serve as he can.'

'But I am not fit . . . No, no. Grzegorz, not that. I won't consent. No.'

'Do you understand what the alternative is?' The Inquisitor looked him in the eyes.

The man being tortured howled from somewhere in the building, then screamed and choked on the scream. Even without that timely reminder, Reynevan suspected what the alternative was.

'You wouldn't believe what comes to light during painful confessions.' Hejncze confirmed his speculation. 'What secrets are revealed. Even bedroom secrets. During an investigation carried out by somebody as zealous as Brother Arnulph, for example, when a rascal confesses and says everything about himself, he begins to disclose information about others. Occasionally, it's even awkward to listen to testimonies of that kind, finding out who, with whom, when and how . . . And it often concerns clergymen. Or nuns. Or wives, believed to be faithful. Or marriageable maids, believed to be virtuous. By God, I think everybody has secrets like that. It must be terribly humiliating when the pain forces one to reveal them. To someone like Brother Arnulph. In the presence of torturers. Well, Reinmar? Do you have any secrets like that?'

'Don't treat me like this, Grzegorz.' Reynevan clenched his teeth. 'I understand everything.'

'I'm most glad. I truly am.'

The man being tortured screamed.

'Who are they torturing?' Anger helped Reynevan to overcome his fear. 'On your orders? Which of the men I was imprisoned with?'

'Interesting that you ask.' The Inquisitor raised his eyes. 'Because it is indeed a model illustration of my disquisitions. The town scribe was among the prisoners. Do you know who I mean? I see you do. Accused of heresy. The investigation soon revealed that the accusations were false and motivated by personal reasons, the denouncer being his wife's lover. I ordered the scribe released and the lover arrested, in order to check if he was only interested in ladies' charms. Imagine, at the very sight of the instruments, the adulterer confessed that she was not the first townswoman he had robbed under the pretext of romance. He gave somewhat confusing evidence, so some tools were employed to assist him. And then I heard a lot about other married women, from Świdnica, from Wrocław, from Walbrzych, about their immoral urges and inventive ways of satisfying them. And during a search, a satire defaming the Holy Father was found and a picture showing the Pope with devilish talons protruding from beneath his pontifical vestments. No doubt you've seen similar.'

'I have.'

'Where?'

'I don't remem—'

Reynevan choked and paled. Hejncze snorted.

'See how easy it is? I guarantee you that the *strappado* would refresh your memory. The fornicator couldn't remember at first who had given him the lampoon and picture of the Pope, but he soon recalled it. And as you can hear, Brother Arnulph is checking whether his memory isn't perhaps concealing any other interesting matters.'

'And you ...' Fear, paradoxically, lent Reynevan a desperate bravado. 'You enjoy it. You aren't the person I knew, Inquisitor. In Prague, you made fun of fanatics yourself! But today? What is this position to you? Still a profession or now a passion?'

Grzegorz Hejncze knitted his bushy eyebrows. 'In my position,' he said coldly, 'there oughtn't to be a difference. And there isn't.'

'Like hell.' Although Reynevan was trembling and his teeth were chattering, he went on, 'Tell me something more about the glory of God, about your lofty goal and holy zeal. Torture for the slightest suspicion, the slightest denunciation, the slightest word overheard or obtained through entrapment. Death by burning for admitting one's guilt under torture. Hussites lurking around every corner. And quite recently I heard a respected clergyman declaring bluntly that all he cares about is wealth and power, and if it wasn't for that, the Hussites could take communion using an enema, for all he cared. And if Peterlin hadn't been killed, you would have hauled him into a dungeon, tortured him, forced him to testify and probably burned him at the stake. And for what? For reading books?'

'That will do, Reinmar, that will do.' The Inquisitor grimaced. 'Calm yourself and don't be crude. In a moment, you're liable to threaten me with the fate of Konrad of Marburg.' A moment later, he said firmly, 'You'll go to Bohemia and do as I command. You will serve and thus save your skin. And at least partly atone for your brother's guilt. For your brother was guilty, and not of reading books.

'And don't accuse me of zealotry,' he continued. 'I am not

perturbed by books, even false and heretical ones. I believe that no books should be burned, and that even erroneous and misleading opinions may be respected. One may also observe, having some philosophical perspective, that there is no monopoly on the truth, for many truths once hailed as false are now considered true and vice versa. But the faith and religion I defend are not just theses and dogmas. The faith and religion I defend are the social order. When there ceases to be order, chaos and anarchy will ensue. Only malefactors desire chaos and anarchy. Thus, malefactors ought to be punished.

'In conclusion: Piotr of Bielawa and his comrade dissidents may freely read Wycliffe, Huss, Arnold of Brescia and Joachim of Fiore, but here my tolerance ends, Reinmar. I will not allow the Fraticelli and Picards to proliferate here. I shall strangle the likes of Wat Tyler and John Ball at birth, and crush emerging Žižkas.'

After a moment of silence, he added, 'The end justifies the means, and whoever isn't with me is against me. As John said, if a man abide not in Me, he is cast forth as a branch and is withered. And men gather them and cast them into the fire, and they are burned. Burned! Do you understand? I see that you do.'

The man being tortured hadn't screamed for a long time. He was probably confessing in a trembling voice to whatever Brother Arnulph demanded of him.

Hejncze stood up. 'You'll have a little time to think the matter over. I must leave for Wrocław forthwith. I'll tell you something: I thought I'd mainly be interrogating lunatics here, and to my surprise, I've uncovered a gem. One of your fellow prisoners, the priest from the Niemodlin Collegiate, saw with his own eyes and was able to describe a demon. The destruction that lays waste at noon, if you recall the relevant psalm. Thus, I must urgently attend to a certain minor confrontation. When I return, however, and I shall return soon – by Saint Lucy's Day at the latest – I shall bring a new resident to the Narrenturm. I once promised him I would and I always keep my word. You, Reinmar, mull it over well in the meantime. Weigh up the benefits and the draw-backs. When I return, I'd like to know your decision and hear a declaration. I'd like it to be the correct one, a declaration of loyal collaboration and service. Because if it isn't, by God, even though you are a varsity comrade, you will be to me a withered branch. I shall not deal with you directly. I shall hand you over to Brother Arnulph and leave you alone with him.

'Of course,' he added a moment later, 'after you have confessed to me personally what you were doing on Grochowa during the night of the autumn equinox. And who the woman you were seen with was. You will also confess to me, naturally, which clergyman joked about an enema. Farewell, Reynevan.'

He turned in the doorway. 'One more thing. Bernhard Roth, alias Urban Horn – give him my regards. And tell him there's no ...'

'... there's no time now to deal with you properly,' Reynevan repeated word for word. 'He would like to devote enough time and effort to you with Brother Arnulph as you indeed deserve. And he'll set about it immediately after his return, by Saint Lucy's Day at the latest. He advises you to organise the knowledge you have, since you will have to share that knowledge with the Holy Office.'

'The whoreson.' Urban Horn spat on the straw. 'He's softening me up. He's letting me ripen. He knows what he's doing. Did you tell him about Konrad of Marburg?'

'Tell him yourself.'

The surviving residents of the tower sat in silence, secluded in their pallets. Some were snoring, some weeping, some softly praying.

'What about me?' Reynevan said into the silence. 'What am I to do?'

'You think you have worries?' said Scharley, stretching. 'Horn has a painful interrogation in prospect. I – who knows what's worse? – might have to rot here for ever. In comparison, your problem is risible. The Inquisitor, your university pal, is giving you your freedom on a plate, as a gift—'

'As a gift?'

'I'll say! You'll sign an oath of loyalty and walk free.'

'As a spy?'

'There's no rose without a thorn.'

'But I don't want to. I'm disgusted by such a practice. My conscience won't permit it. I don't want—'

'Grit your teeth,' said Scharley with a shrug, 'and force yourself.'

'Horn?'

'Horn what?' He turned around suddenly. 'Want some advice? Some words of moral support? Then listen. Resistance is an innate trait of human nature. Resistance to base behaviour. Opposition to wickedness. A refusal to accept evil. They are innate, immanent human traits. Ergo, only individuals entirely bereft of humanity do not resist. Only blackguards become turncoats out of fear of torture.'

'So?'

'So,' said Horn, without even blinking an eye, arms folded on his chest, 'sign the loyalty oath and agree to collaborate. Go to Bohemia, as they command. And when you're there . . . Resist.'

'I don't understand—'

'You don't?' Scharley snorted. 'Really? Reinmar, our friend is preceding a very immoral offer with a lecture about moral and pure human nature. He suggests you become a so-called double agent and work for both sides: the Inquisition and the Hussites. After all, everybody already knows you're a Hussite emissary and spy, with the possible exception of those imbeciles moaning in the straw over there. Isn't that so, Urban Horn? Your advice to Reynevan sounds quite clever, but there's snag. Namely the Hussites. Like everybody who has dealt with espionage, they are already familiar with double agents. They know from experience that they are often triple agents. Therefore, any agents who show up should by no means be confided in. Quite the opposite – they should be hanged, after having first been forced to testify using torture. So you are preparing a sad fate for Reynevan with your advice, Urban Horn. Unless you give him a solid, trusted contact in Bohemia. Some secret password, something the Hussites will believe . . . But . . .'

'Go on.'

'You won't give him anything like that because you don't know if he's already signed a loyalty oath, or whether his university pal the Inquisitor hasn't already taught him how to spy for two sides.'

Horn didn't reply. He simply smiled. Wickedly, with just the corners of his mouth, without narrowing his ice-cold eyes.

'I have to get out of here,' said Reynevan quietly, standing in the middle of the prison. 'I have to leave this place. Otherwise I'll cause the downfall of Fair Nicolette, Katarzyna of Biberstein. I must escape from here. And I have a way.'

Scharley and Horn listened to the plan surprisingly calmly and waited, without interrupting, until Reynevan had finished. Only then did Horn snort with laughter, shake his head and walk away. Scharley was serious. Deadly serious, one might say.

'I can be sympathetic to the fact that you've lost your mind, but don't insult my intelligence, laddie.'

'The *Occultum* is still on the wall, Circulos's glyphs and sigla are still there. On top of that, look, I have his amulet – I managed to take it unseen. Circulos told me the activating spell and gave me the means of conjuration. I know a little something about evocations, I studied the practice . . . The chance is slender, I admit. But it's a chance! I don't understand your reserve, Scharley. Do you doubt the existence of magic? What about Huon of Sagar? And Samson? Why, Samson—'

'Samson is a fraud.' The penitent cut him off. 'A friendly, quite clever, pleasant companion, but a fraud and a charlatan nonetheless, like most people who invoke spells and witchcraft. The rest is insignificant. Reinmar, I don't doubt the existence of magic. I've seen enough not to doubt it. It's you that I doubt. I've seen you levitate and find roads, but as far as the flying bench goes, Sagar was certainly behind it – you couldn't have done that yourself. But you've a long way to go before becoming a real demon tamer, lad. You must know that. You must understand that hieroglyphics, pentagrams and hocus-pocus scribbled on walls by a moron are fit for nothing. And that sorry excuse for an amulet is a vulgar, shitty piece of junk. You must be aware of all that. Therefore, I repeat, don't insult my intelligence or your own.'

'I have no choice,' said Reynevan through clenched teeth. 'I have to try. It's my only chance.'

Scharley shrugged and rolled his eyes.

Circulos's *Occultum* looked worse than woeful, Reynevan had to admit. It was dirty, and all the magic books demanded immaculately clean sanctuaries. The Goetic Circle on the wall had been drawn crookedly, and the rules in the *Sacra Goetia* stressed the importance of precise drawing. Nor was Reynevan entirely certain regarding the correctness of the spells written inside the Circle.

The ceremony of evocation itself would have to take place not at midnight, as the grimoires laid down, but at dawn, since at midnight darkness prevented any activities in the tower. The black candles demanded for the ritual were out of the question – as were candles of any other colour. For obvious reasons, the madmen in the Narrenturm weren't given candles, cressets, lamps or any other means of starting a fire.

Actually, he thought bitterly as he began the ritual, *I only conform to the principles of the grimoires in one respect: a mage intending to evoke or invoke has to meet the condition of a suitably long period of abstinence from sexual intercourse. And for two months I have been an absolute, although unwilling, abstainer in this regard.*

Scharley and Horn observed him from a distance, keeping quiet. Tomasz Alpha was also quiet, mainly because he had been threatened with a beating should he in any way dare to disturb that silence.

Reynevan finished putting the *Occultum* in order and drew a magical circle around himself. He cleared his throat and spread his arms.

'Ermites!' he began melodiously, staring at the glyphs in the Goetic Circle. 'Poncor! Pagor! Anitor!'

Horn snorted quietly. Scharley only sighed.

'Aglon, Vaycheon, Stimulamaton! Ezphares, Olyaram, Irion! Mersilde! You, whose sight penetrates the abyss! *Te adoro, et te invoco!*'

Nothing happened.

'Esytion, Eryon, Onera! Mozm, Soter, Helomi!'

Reynevan licked his swollen lips. He put down the amulet decorated with the serpent, fish and sun in a triangle in the place where the deceased Circulos had repeated the words 'VENI MERSILDE'.

'Ostrata!' he said, beginning the activating spell. 'Terpandu! Ermas!' he intoned, bowing and modulating his voice as recommended by *Lemegeton, The Lesser Key of Solomon*. 'Pericatur! Beleuros!'

Scharley swore, catching Reynevan's attention. Barely believing his own eyes, Reynevan saw the words scribbled in the circle begin to glow with a phosphorescent light.

'By the seal of Basdathei! Mersilde! You, whose sight penetrates the abyss! Come! Zabaoth! Escwerchie! Astrachios, Asach, Asarca!'

The words in the circle burned ever brighter, the ghastly glare illuminating the walls, which began to vibrate perceptibly. Horn swore. Tomasz Alpha howled. One of the morons started yelling and weeping audibly. Scharley sprang to his feet, jumped at him and with a short punch to the temple knocked him down onto his pallet, where he fell silent.

'Bosmoletic, Jeysmy, Eth.' Reynevan leaned over and touched the centre of the pentagram with his forehead. Then, standing up straight, he reached for the polished, sharpened broken head of a nail. With a powerful jerk, he cut the skin on the pad of his thumb and pressed his bloody thumb to his forehead. He took a deep breath, aware that he was approaching the riskiest and most dangerous moment. When the blood was flowing sufficiently profusely, he painted a sign in the middle of the circle.

The secret, fearsome, forbidden sign of Scirlin.

'*Veni* Mersilde!' he cried, feeling the foundations of the Narrenturm begin to shake and tremble.

Tomasz Alpha howled again and fell silent as Scharley threatened him with a fist. The tower was shuddering visibly now.

'Taul!' evoked Reynevan, throatily and hoarsely, as the grimoires commanded. 'Varf! Pan!'

The Goetic Circle swelled with a more powerful brightness. The point on the wall it illuminated slowly stopped being just a spot of light and began to assume a shape. The shape of a human being. But not entirely a human being, for people didn't have such huge heads or such long arms. Nor such enormous horns, growing from a forehead vaulted like that of an ox.

The tower trembled, the imbeciles moaned at various pitches and Tomasz Alpha accompanied them in a loud voice. Horn sprang up.

'Enough!' he yelled, shouting over the din. 'Reynevan! Stop this! Stop this abomination, dammit! We'll all perish because of you!'

'Varf! Clemialh!'

The rest of the evocation's words stuck in his throat. The luminous form on the wall was now distinct enough to look at him with two great, snake-like eyes. He saw that the shape wasn't just looking, but holding out its arms. Reynevan shrieked with fear. The terror paralysed him.

'Seru . . . geath!' he gibbered, aware that he was mixing up the spell. 'Ariwh—'

Scharley jumped forward, seized him from behind by the throat, covered his mouth with his other hand and dragged Reynevan – now paralysed with fear – over the straw into the far corner, among the lunatics. Tomasz Alpha fled for the staircase, screaming horrifyingly for help. Horn, meanwhile – clearly in utter desperation – seized the piss bucket from the floor and flung its contents over everything: over the *Occultum*, the circle, the pentagram and the apparition emerging from the wall.

The roar that resounded made everybody cover their ears with their hands and cower on the dirt floor. Suddenly a great wind blew, whipping up a tornado of straw and dust which flew into their eyes, blinding them. The fire on the wall died down, quenched by clouds of foul-smelling steam, hissed and finally went out completely.

But it was not the end. For there was a great boom, a terrible boom, though not from the *Occultum* enveloped in stinking smoke, but from the door high up at the top of the stairs. Rubble showered down, a veritable hail of stone blocks in white clouds of plaster and mortar. Scharley caught Reynevan and dodged under the staircase with him. Just in time, for in front of their very eyes, a thick post from the door weighed down by a hinge plummeted and struck one of the panicked imbeciles straight in the head, splitting his skull like an apple.

A man fell from above in an avalanche of rubble, arms and legs splayed in the form of a cross.

Thoughts flashed through Reynevan's head. *The Narrenturm is falling apart. The* turris fulgurata, *the tower struck by lightning, is disintegrating. The poor, ridiculous fool is falling from the crumbling Tower of Fools, he's plummeting to his destruction. I am that fool, I'm falling, I'm tumbling to the bottom of the chasm. Destruction, chaos and disintegration, which I have caused. A fool and a madman, I have summoned a demon, I have opened the gates of Hell. I can smell the stench of hellish brimstone—'*

'It's gunpowder . . .' Scharley, huddled next to him, had guessed his thoughts. 'Somebody used gunpowder to blow up the door. . . Reinmar . . . Somebody—'

'We're being freed!' screamed Horn, scrambling from the rubble. 'It's a rescue! It's our Czech brothers! Hosanna!'

'Hey, boys!' screamed someone from above, from the opening

where the doors had been, daylight and frosty, fresh air streaming in. 'Get out! You're free!'

'Hosanna!' repeated Horn. 'Scharley, Reinmar! Get out and be quick! It's our boys! Czechs! We're free! Come on, at the double, to the stairs!'

He set off at a run, without waiting for them. Scharley followed. Reynevan glanced at the cooling, still steaming *Occultum*, at the imbeciles cowering in the straw. Then he rushed for the stairs, on the way stepping over the corpse of Tomasz Alpha who had been given not liberation but death by the explosion that destroyed the door.

'Hosanna!' Urban Horn could be heard greeting his liberators at the top of the stairs. 'Hosanna, Brothers! Greetings, Halada! By God, Raabe! Tybald Raabe! Is it you?'

'Horn?' asked Tybald Raabe in astonishment. 'You're alive?'

'By Christ, indeed! So you're not here because of me—'

'Not you,' said the Czech called Halada, who had a large red chalice on his chest. 'I'm glad to see you in one piece, Horn, and Father Ambrož will rejoice ... But we stormed Frankenstein because of them.'

'Them?'

'Them,' confirmed a giant in a quilted gambeson that made him look even bigger, pushing his way through the armed Czechs. 'Scharley. Reinmar. Greetings.'

'Samson ...' Reynevan felt a lump in his throat. 'Samson ... My friend! You didn't forget about us—'

'How could I forget two men like you.' Samson grinned.

Chapter Twenty-Nine

In which our heroes – although liberated from the Narrenturm – discover they are not as free as they'd like to be. They participate in historical events, burning down several villages and small towns. Then Samson saves what he can, and various other things happen, until finally, our heroes depart. Their path – to use the poet's metaphor – runs *in parte ove non è che luca*.

The snow lying on the roofs stung their eyes with its blinding whiteness. Reynevan staggered and would have fallen from the stairs if not for Samson's shoulder. The roar and boom of gun and cannon fire reached them from the hospice. The bell in the hospital church moaned painfully, and the bells of Frankenstein's churches tolled the alarm.

'Quickly!' yelled Halada. 'Towards the gate! And keep down – they're shooting!'

They were indeed shooting. A crossbow bolt whistled over their heads and split a plank. As they ran into the courtyard, hunched over, Reynevan tripped and fell to his knees in mud mixed with blood. The dead were lying near the gate and by the hospital: some canons of the Holy Sepulchre in habits, some lackeys and soldiers of the Inquisition, clearly abandoned by Grzegorz Hejncze.

'Quickly!' urged Tybald Raabe. 'To horse!'

'Here!' A Czech as black and sooty as a devil, wearing armour and holding a flaming torch, reined in his steed. 'Make haste, make haste!'

He swung and hurled the torch onto a thatched shed. The

torch rolled down the wet straw and hissed as it landed in the mud. The Czech swore.

The smell of fire and smoke surrounded them as flames shot up above the roofs of the stables, from where several Czechs were leading out stamping horses. More shots boomed, accompanied by roars and thuds from the fighting taking place near the church hospital. Men were firing crossbows and harquebuses at anything that moved, from the windows of the church tower and the chancel.

A canon of the Holy Sepulchre lay against the wall at the entrance to the burning *medicinarium*. It was Brother Tranquillus. His wet habit was smouldering and steaming, and he was holding his belly in both hands, blood streaming through his fingers. His eyes were open and staring straight ahead, but he probably couldn't see anything.

'Finish him off,' said Halada, pointing at him.

'No!' Reynevan stopped the Hussites with a high-pitched cry. 'No! Leave him.' Seeing their menacing looks, he added more quietly, 'He's dying . . . Let him die in peace.'

'Time is short anyway,' called the soot-covered horseman. 'No use wasting it on that half-corpse! Onwards, to horse!'

Reynevan, still half-asleep or in a trance, mounted the horse that was handed to him. Scharley – riding beside him – nudged him with his knee.

In front of him were Samson's broad shoulders and Urban Horn was on the opposite side from Scharley.

'Be careful who you support,' hissed Horn. 'They are Orphans from Hradec Králové. Don't fool around with them—'

'That was Brother Tranquillus—'

'I know who it was.'

They tumbled through the gate, straight into smoke. The hospital mill and outbuildings were burning, flames belching upwards. The bells were still tolling in the town and people teemed on the town walls.

They were joined by more riders, led by a moustachioed man in *cuir bouilli* and a mail hood.

'Over there,' the moustachioed man pointed at the church, 'the door to the vestibule's almost forced, and there'd have been plenty to loot! Brother Brázda – they were almost in!'

'Maybe, but those up there will soon realise how few of us there really are.' The man with the blackened face addressed as Brázda pointed at the town walls. 'Then they'll come out and finish us off even quicker. To horse, Brother Velek!'

They galloped away, splashing mud and melting snow. Reynevan's faculties had returned enough to enable him to count the Czechs: he calculated that a force of about twenty had stormed Frankenstein. He didn't know whether to admire their bravado or be surprised by the scale of the destruction wrought by such a tiny force – in addition to the hospital buildings and mill, the dyers' sheds on the banks of the Budzówka were ablaze, along with the sheds by the bridge and the barns just outside the Kłodzko Gate.

'Farewell!' The moustachioed man in *cuir bouilli* addressed as Velek turned around and shook a fist at the burghers gathered on the wall. 'Farewell, papists! We'll be back!'

The defenders responded with shots and yells. The yells were fierce and brave now that the town's citizens had managed to count the Hussites.

They rode at breakneck speed, not sparing a thought for the horses. Although it looked like sheer stupidity, it turned out to be part of the plan. Having covered a distance of almost half a mile at astonishing speed, they reached the snow-covered Owl Mountains and passed Silver Mountain, where five young Hussites and fresh horses were waiting for them in a forest ravine. Clothing and equipment were found for the former prisoners of the Narrenturm. A little time was also found for conversation.

'Samson? How did you find us?' Scharley asked.

'It wasn't so simple,' said the giant, tightening his horse's girth. 'After your arrest, you simply vanished. I did my best to find out where you'd been taken, but no one would talk to me. Fortunately, although they didn't talk *to* me, they talked in front of me quite freely. One rumour had it that they'd taken you to Świdnica, another that it was Wrocław. Then Master Tybald Raabe, our friend from Kromolin, happened along. It took me some time to persuade him to listen to me, because at first he took me for an imbecile.'

'Can we let that drop, Master Samson?' the goliard said with slight reproach. 'We've already discussed it. Why go back to it? And since you do look, forgive me, like a—'

'We all know what Samson looks like,' said Scharley, who was shortening his stirrup leathers alongside them. 'Just tell us what happened next.'

'Master Tybald Raabe was taken in by my appearance.' Samson's dopey face twisted into a smile. 'Like everyone else, he disdainfully refused to talk to me, but he was so indifferent to my presence that he talked in front of me. I quickly realised who Master Tybald Raabe was and made him understand that I knew. And how much I knew.'

'So it was, m'lord.' The goliard blushed, embarrassed. 'I was terrified then ... But it was all ... explained ...'

'It became clear that Master Tybald had friends,' Samson interrupted calmly, 'among the Hussites from Hradec Králové since he works for them as an intelligence agent and an emissary, as you've probably guessed.'

'What a coincidence.' Scharley grinned. 'And what an abundance of—'

'Scharley.' Urban Horn, standing behind his horse, cut him off. 'Drop it, will you?'

'Very well, very well. Go on, Samson. How did you find out where to look for us?'

'That is a curious thing. Several days ago, a slightly strange young man approached me in a tavern near Broumov. He made it clear he knew who I was. Unfortunately, at first he wasn't able to utter anything save the sentence – and I quote – "bring out the prisoners from the prison and them that sit in darkness out of the prison house".'

'Isaiah!' said Reynevan in amazement.

'Indeed. Chapter forty-two, verse seven.'

'That's beside the point. It was his nickname. And he led you to the Tower of Fools?'

'I wasn't that surprised, given the . . . unique manner in which he communicates.'

'And then,' Scharley said, 'a daring raid by the Hradec Hussites entered the Kłodzko region, rode all the way to Frankenstein – a good six miles over the border – burned down half the cottages outside the castle and seized the Hospice of the Holy Sepulchre and the Narrenturm. And all – if I understood it correctly – just for me and Reynevan. Master Tybald Raabe, I don't know how to thank you, indeed I don't.'

'The reasons will soon be made clear.' The goliard cleared his throat. 'Patience, m'lord.'

'Patience isn't one of my greatest virtues.'

'Then you will have to work a little on that virtue,' said Brázda, the commander of the troop, who had ridden up and come to a halt beside them. 'The reason we got you out of that plight will be explained when the time is right, and no sooner.'

Brázda, like most of the Czechs in the troop, had a chalice cut from red cloth sewn to his chest. But he was the only one to have pinned the Hussite emblem directly onto the coat of arms visible on his paltock.

'I am Brázda of Klinštejn, from the Ronovic family,' he said, confirming their guesses. 'And now we are done talking – time is short and this is enemy territory!'

'It's dangerous indeed to wear a chalice on your chest here,' Scharley agreed mockingly.

'On the contrary,' replied Brázda of Klinštejn. 'Such an emblem protects and defends.'

'Really?'

'You may have an opportunity to see for yourself, m'lord.'

One soon arose.

The troop rode swiftly through Silver Pass. Beyond it, in

the region of the village of Ebersdorf, they encountered a military detachment consisting of heavily armed cavalry and bowmen numbering at least thirty men, riding under a red standard decorated with a ram's head, the Haugwitzes' coat of arms.

And indeed, Brázda of Klinštejn was absolutely right. Haugwitz and his men stood their ground only until the moment they saw the sign of the Chalice, then the knights and the crossbowmen reined their horses around and rode away at a gallop, mud splashing from their hooves.

'What do you say about the sign of the Chalice now?' Brázda turned to face Scharley. 'Effective, isn't it?'

It couldn't be denied.

They galloped on, driving their horses unrelentingly. As they rode, they gulped down flakes of falling snow.

Reynevan felt certain they were heading to Bohemia, that after reaching the Ścinawa Valley they would turn upstream, towards the border, along a road leading straight to Broumov. He was surprised when the unit dashed through a hollow in the Table Mountains which loomed up blue to the south-west. He wasn't the only one surprised by the route.

'Where are we going?' Urban Horn shouted over the driving snow. 'I say! Halada! Sir Brázda!'

'Radkov!' Halada shouted back curtly.

'Why?'

'Ambrož!'

Radkov, which Reynevan was seeing for the first time, turned out to be a pleasant little town nestling at the foot of tree-covered mountains. Red roofs rose up behind the ring of town walls, above which towered a slender church spire. The sight would have put them in a cheerful mood were it not for the huge cloud of smoke swirling over the town.

Radkov had been the target of a raid.

*

The army gathered outside Radkov numbered a good thousand warriors, many of them infantry armed with various kinds of pole weapons, from simple spears to more sophisticated gisarmes. At least half the soldiers were equipped with crossbows and firearms. There was also artillery – a medium-sized bombard hidden behind a raisable shield aimed directly at the town gate, and trestle guns and cannons positioned in the gaps between pavises.

The army, though it looked dangerous, stood frozen to the spot and silent, as though entranced. The only things moving were the black dots of crows circling in the grey sky, and the cloud of smoke billowing above the town, here and there shot with red tongues of flame.

They trotted between the wagons. For the first time, Reynevan saw the famous Hussite battle wagons at close hand. He examined them with interest, admiring the clever construction of the lowered bulwarks made of solid planks, which could be raised if need be to turn the vehicle into a genuine bastion.

They were quickly recognised.

'Master Brázda,' said a Czech in half-armour and a fur cap, with the red chalice on his chest that appeared to be customary for the more senior ranks. 'The noble knight Brázda has finally deigned to join us with his elite noble cavalry. Well, better late than never.'

'I never thought it would go so smoothly,' replied Brázda of Klinštejn with a shrug. 'Is it all over? Have they surrendered?'

'Of course they surrendered. They have no one to defend them. We only had to burn down a few cottages and they began to parley. Now they're putting out fires, and the Reverend Ambrož is receiving their envoys. Thus, you must wait.'

'If we must, we must. Dismount, lads.'

They went on foot towards the Hussite army's staff, the only Czechs among them being Brázda, Halada and the moustachioed Velek Chrastický, accompanied by Urban Horn and Tybald Raabe.

They had arrived at the very end of the negotiations. The

Radkov emissaries had just left, the pale and very frightened burghers glancing back anxiously and crumpling their caps in their hands. It was clear from their expressions that they had achieved little.

'As is customary,' a Czech in a fur hat said quietly, 'the women-folk and children may leave at once. The men must buy themselves out in order to leave and pay a ransom for the town or it will be put to the torch. Furthermore—'

'All papist priests must be turned in,' finished Brázda, also clearly experienced in these matters. 'And all the fugitives from Bohemia. I needn't have hurried at all – it will be some time before the women come out and the ransom payment is collected. We won't be leaving here for a while.'

'Come before Ambrož.'

Reynevan recalled Scharley and Horn's conversation about the former parish priest from Hradec Králové. He remembered they had described him as a fanatic, extreme in his zealotry and ruthlessness even among the most radical Taborites. He thus expected to see a small, skinny, fiery-eyed tribune, brandishing his arms and proclaiming declarations, dripping with saliva and demagoguery. He saw instead a well-built man, economical in his movements, wearing a black costume resembling a habit but shorter, revealing high boots. He wore a beard as wide as a shovel that almost reached his belt, from which a sword hung. In spite of the sword, the Hussite priest appeared rather benign, jovial even. It might have been the high, bulging forehead, bushy eyebrows and magnificent beard making Ambrož resemble God the Father in a Byzantine icon.

'Master Brázda.' He greeted them warmly. 'Well, better late than never. The expedition, I see, has ended in success? Without loss? My compliments. And Brother Urban Horn? From what cloud has he fallen here?'

'From a black one,' replied Horn sourly. 'Thank you for the rescue, Brother Ambrož. It came not a moment too soon.'

'I'm glad.' Ambrož nodded. 'And others will be, too. We were already lamenting you when we heard the news. It's hard to escape the bishop's grasp. Indeed, easier for a mouse to escape a cat's. It was fortunate, as I didn't send the raid to Frankenstein for you.'

He shifted his gaze towards Reynevan, and Reynevan felt a cold spot between his shoulder blades. The priest said nothing for a long time.

'Young Sir Reinmar of Bielawa,' he finally said, 'the brother of Piotr of Bielawa, a virtuous Christian who did so much for the Chalice's cause, and who gave his life for it.'

Reynevan bowed without a word. Ambrož turned his head and stared long at Scharley. Scharley finally meekly lowered his eyes, but clearly only to be diplomatic.

'Master Scharley,' the parish priest from Hradec said at length, 'who doesn't abandon people in need. When Piotr of Bielawa died at the hands of vengeful papists, Master Scharley rescued his brother, heedless of the danger he was exposing himself to. Indeed, a rare example of honour for our times, and of friendship. The old Czech saying is apt: *v nouzi poznaš přítele* – a friend in need is a friend indeed. Meanwhile,' he continued, 'we hear that young Lord Reinmar shows clear evidence of brotherly love by professing his faith and bravely opposing papist errors and immoral deeds. Like every pious and virtuous fellow, he sympathises with the Chalice and spurns venal Rome like the Devil. You will receive your reward. You have already, in any case, Reinmar and Master Scharley. When Brother Tybald informed me that the Devil's spawn had cast you into a dungeon, I didn't hesitate for a moment.'

'Our thanks—'

'It's you who deserves our gratitude. For, thanks to you, the money with which that scoundrel and heretic the Bishop of Wrocław meant to buy our deaths will now serve our worthy cause. You will dig it up and give it to us righteous Christians, will you not?'

'The mon . . . The money? What money?' stammered Reinmar.

Scharley sighed quietly. Urban Horn coughed. Tybald Raabe cleared his throat. Ambrož's face hardened.

'Do you think to make a fool of me?'

Reynevan and Scharley shook their heads, and there was such childlike innocence in their eyes that the priest restrained himself. But only a little.

'Am I thus to understand,' he drawled, 'that it wasn't you who robbed the tax collector in aid of our cause? If it wasn't you, then somebody will have to explain himself. Master Raabe!'

'Why, I didn't say,' mumbled the goliard, 'that it was definitely they who robbed the tax collector. I said it was possible, that it was likely . . .'

Ambrož straightened up. His eyes blazed fiercely and his face flushed like a turkey's crop in the places not covered by his beard. For a moment, the Hradec parish priest looked not like God the Father, but like Zeus the Thunder-Wielder. Everyone cringed, expecting a bolt of lightning. But the priest quickly calmed down.

'You told me something quite different,' he finally said. 'Oh, you deluded me, Brother Tybald, you misled me so that I would send riders to storm Frankenstein, knowing I would not have done so otherwise!'

'*V nouzi*,' Scharley interrupted quietly, '*poznaš přítele*.'

Ambrož looked him up and down but said nothing. Then he addressed Reynevan and the goliard.

'I ought to have all of you tortured one after the other, my friends,' he snarled, 'since there's something fishy about this whole business with the tax collector and his money. And you all look suspicious to me. But in memory of Piotr of Bielawa, I shall not.' The priest's eyes bored into Reynevan. 'I shall get over the bishop's money – I was not fated to receive it. But our accounts are settled. Out of my sight. Get you gone and to Hell with you.'

'Reverend Brother.' Scharley cleared his throat. 'Passing over the misunderstandings . . . we were counting on—'

'On what?' Ambrož snorted into his beard. 'That I would

permit you to join us? That I would take you under my wing and escort you to Hradec? No, Master Scharley. You were imprisoned by the Inquisition and thus may have been turned by them. In short, you may be informers.'

'You insult us.'

'Better to insult you than my own good sense.'

The arrival of one of the Hussite commanders, an amiable fat man resembling a questor or a pork butcher, relieved the tension. 'Brother Ambrož—'

'What is it, Brother Hlušička?'

'The burghers have paid the ransom and are coming out, women and children first, as was agreed.'

'Brother Velek Chrastický,' Ambrož beckoned him, 'take the riders and patrol the perimeter of the town to prevent anyone fleeing. Everyone else, follow me. Everyone, I said. I charge Lord Brázda of Klinštejn with the temporary supervision of our ... guests. Onwards!'

A column of people was indeed emerging from the Radkov Gate, anxiously and reluctantly passing between a double file of Hussites bristling with blades. Ambrož and his staff stopped nearby, surveying the men coming out. Very carefully. Reynevan felt the hairs on the back of his neck stand up in anticipation of something dreadful.

'Brother Ambrož,' asked Hlušička, 'will you be giving a sermon?'

'To whom?' The priest shrugged. 'To that German rabble? They don't understand our speech, and I don't feel like talking in their tongue, for ... I say! Over there! Over there!'

His eyes flashed rapaciously like an eagle's and his face suddenly froze.

'Over there!' he roared, pointing. 'Over there! Seize them!'

He pointed at a woman muffled up in a mantle, carrying a child. The child was trying to break free and sobbing spasmodically. The soldiers parted the crowd with their pikestaffs, hauled the woman out of the crowd and tore off her mantle.

'That's no woman! It's a fellow dressed in a frock! A priest! A papist! A papist!'

'Bring him here.'

The priest was dragged over and thrown down onto his knees. He was trembling in fear and kept his head stubbornly bowed. He had to be forced to look Ambrož in the face. And then he closed his eyes tightly and his mouth moved in a silent prayer.

'Well, well,' said Ambrož, standing with arms akimbo. 'What faithful parishioners. To save their priest, they not only gave him a woman's shift, but an infant, too. What a sacrifice. Who would you be, papist scum?'

The priest screwed his eyes up even tighter.

'It is Mikołaj Megerlein,' said one of the peasants accompanying the Hussite staff. 'The local parish priest.'

The Hussites mumbled. Ambrož flushed, inhaling noisily.

'Father Megerlein,' he said in a slow, drawling voice. 'Well I never. What a stroke of luck. I've dreamed of such an encounter ever since the last bishop's raid on the Trutnov region. We were pinning our hopes on such an encounter. Brothers!' he said, straightening up. 'Take a look! Here is a cur of the Whore of Babylon! A murderous tool in the hands of the Bishop of Wrocław, he has bedevilled the true faith and condemned good Christians to torture and torment, and spilled innocent blood with his own hands at Vízmburk! God has given him up into our hands that we might punish evil and wrongdoing! Do you hear, you murdering papist? What, you close your eyes to the truth? Close your ears, like the deaf adder from the Bible? Ha, heretical swine, you do not know the Bible if you consider your wanton bishop, your venal Rome and your Antichrist Pope the only authorities. And your blasphemous gilded paintings! So I will teach you the word of God! The Apocalypse of John, fourteen, nine: "If any man worship the beast and his image, and receive his mark in his forehead, or in his hand, the same shall drink of the wine of the wrath of God! And shall be tormented with fire and brimstone!" Fire and brimstone, papist! Hey, over here! Take him and wrap him up, as we did the monks in Beroun and Prachatice!'

Several Hussites seized the parish priest. He saw what the other men were bringing and began to scream. He was struck in the face with an axe-handle, fell silent and went limp in the arms of the men holding him.

Samson struggled, but Scharley and Horn caught him at once. Seeing that two might be too few to restrain him, Halada rushed to help them.

'Be quiet,' hissed Scharley. 'By God, be quiet, Samson ...'

Samson turned his head and looked him in the eyes.

Four sheaves of straw were placed around Father Megerlein. After a moment's thought, two more were added, so that the priest's head was entirely covered in straw. Then he and the sheaves were bound tightly with a chain and the straw lit in several places.

Reynevan began to feel uncomfortable and turned away.

He heard a wild, inhuman roar, but didn't see the burning effigy run, stumbling, across the shallow snow through a double file of Hussites, who shoved it with their pikes and halberds. Or see it finally fall, rolling and thrashing around, smoking and throwing up sparks.

Burning straw does not generate enough heat to kill a person. But it does generate sufficient to transform them into something that barely resembles one. Something that thrashes around in convulsions and howls inhumanly, although it has no mouth. That must finally be quieted with merciful blows of club and axe.

The women in the crowd from Radkov moaned and the children wept. Another commotion occurred and a moment later another priest, a skinny old man, was dragged into Ambrož's presence and thrown down on his knees. This one was not in disguise. He was trembling like a leaf as Ambrož leaned over him.

'Another one? Who is this?'

'Father Straube.' The peasant informer hurried to offer his obsequious explanation. 'He was the previous parish priest. Before Megerlein ...'

'Aha. So a *priestus emeritus*. Well, old man, nearing the end of your earthly life, I see. Time to think about the eternal one? About renouncing your papist errors and sins? For you shall not be saved if you endure in them. You saw what was done to your confrater. Receive the Chalice, accept the Four Articles and you will be free, today and for ever.'

'M'lord!' the old man gibbered, cowering and placing his hands together. 'Good m'lord! Have mercy! How may I renounce my faith . . . After all, Peter . . . Before the cock crowed . . . I may not thus . . . Lord, have mercy . . . I cannot!'

'I understand.' Ambrož nodded. 'I do not approve, but I understand. Why, God looks down on us all. Let us be merciful. Brother Hlušička!'

'Yes, sir!'

'Let us be merciful. Without suffering.'

'Yes, sir!'

Hlušička went over to one of the Hussites and took a flail from him. And for the first time in his life, Reynevan saw the instrument that was already widely associated with the Hussites in action. Hlušička swung the flail, spun it around and struck Father Straube in the head as hard as he could. The man's skull split open like a clay pot, splashing blood and brains around.

Reynevan felt himself go weak at the knees. He saw Samson's pale face, saw Scharley and Urban Horn tightly gripping the giant's shoulders.

Brázda of Klinštejn couldn't take his eyes off the smouldering and smoking corpse of Megerlein, the parish priest.

'Miegerlin,' he said suddenly, rubbing his chin. 'Miegerlin. Not Megerlein.'

'What?'

'The damn priest who was with Bishop Konrad in the raid on Trutnov was called Miegerlin. And this one was Megerlein.'

'Meaning?'

'Meaning this priest was innocent.'

'Never mind,' Samson said in a flat voice. 'It's nothing serious. God will know. We'll leave it to Him.'

Ambrož turned around suddenly, fixed his eyes on Samson and stared at him for a long time. Then he looked at Reynevan and Scharley.

'Blessed are the poor in spirit,' he said. 'An angel sometimes speaks through the mouths of imbeciles. But keep watch over him. One day, someone might think the dimwit understands what he says. And that someone will be less forbearing than me and it will end badly. Both for him and for his masters. But all in all, the halfwit is right,' he added. 'God will judge, separate the wheat from the chaff and the guilty from the innocent. In any case, no papist priest is innocent. Every minion of Babylon is worthy of punishment. And the hand of a faithful Christian . . .'

His voice grew louder, thundering more and more mightily, rising above the soldiers' heads, soaring beyond the smoke still billowing even though the fires had been extinguished throughout the town, from which a long column of fugitives was still streaming after paying the ransom.

'The hand of a faithful Christian may not tremble when it chastises a sinner! For the world is the soil and the sons of the kingdom are the good seed, while the sons of Evil are weeds. Thus do I gather the weeds and burn them with fire, as it will be at the end of the world. The Son of Man shall send forth his angels, and they shall gather out of his kingdom all things that offend, and those who do iniquity, and shall cast them into a furnace of fire. There shall be a wailing and a gnashing of teeth.'

The crowd of Hussites yelled and bellowed, upraised halberds glistened and voulges, pitchforks and flails swayed.

'And the smoke of their torment,' thundered Ambrož, pointing at Radkov, 'the smoke of their torment ascendeth for ever and ever. And they have no rest, day nor night, those who worship the beast and his image, and whosoever receiveth the mark of his name!'

He turned around, a little calmer now.

'And you,' he said to Reynevan and Scharley, 'you now have the chance to convince me of your real intentions. You've seen what we do to papist clerics. I vouch that it is a trifle compared to what will befall the bishop's spies. We have no mercy for such as they, even if they be the brother of Piotr of Bielawa. Do you still beg for help? Do you wish to join me?'

'We are not spies,' Reynevan burst out. 'Your suspicions are offensive to us! And nor do we beg for your help! On the contrary, it's we who can help you! If only in memory of my brother, about whom much is said here, but with empty words! By all means, if you want, I shall prove to you that I am closer to you than to the Bishop of Wrocław. What will you say to the information that treachery is imminent? A conspiracy? A plot against people's lives? Yours, among others—'

Ambrož's eyes narrowed.

'Tell me who is in danger.'

Reynevan pretended not to see Scharley's desperate signs and expressions. 'I know of a plot aimed at killing the leaders of the Tábor. The following are to meet their deaths: Bohuslav of Švamberk and Jan Hvězda of Vicemilice . . .'

Ambrož's officers suddenly began to murmur. The priest didn't take his eyes off Reynevan.

'Fascinating information, indeed,' he finally said. 'Verily, young Lord Bielawa, it would be worth taking you to Hradec.'

While the Hussite army was busily engaged in pillaging the town of Radkov, Brázda of Klinštejn, Velek Chrastický and Oldřich Halada explained to Reynevan and Scharley what it was all about.

'Jan Hvězda of Vicemilice, Hetman of the Tábor,' said Brázda, 'departed this life on the last day of October, and his successor, Sir Bohuslav of Švamberk, expired less than a week ago.'

'Just don't say,' said Scharley, frowning, 'that they were both victims of assassins.'

'They both died of wounds sustained in battle. Hvězda took an arrow to the face at Mladá Vožice, on Saint Luke's Eve, and died soon afterwards. Sir Bohuslav was wounded during the battle for the Austrian town of Retz.'

'So they weren't assassinated,' said Scharley mockingly, 'but died natural deaths for a Hussite!'

'Not entirely. I'm telling you that both men died some time after sustaining wounds. Perhaps they would have pulled through had not somebody, let's say, given them poison? You must admit, it's a strange coincidence: two great Taborite leaders, both heirs of Žižka, dying one after the other, in the space of barely a month—'

'A sore loss for the Tábor,' Velek Chrastický interrupted, 'and for our foes so great an advantage that there have been suspicions of foul play . . . And now, after young Lord Bielawa's revelations, this must be thoroughly explained.'

'Indeed.' Scharley nodded, apparently serious. 'So much so that if the necessity arises, young Lord Bielawa will be tortured, since it is well known that nothing elicits explanations of suspicious matters better than red-hot iron.'

'Come, come.' Brázda smiled, but not very convincingly. 'No one is even thinking anything of the sort!'

'Why, Sir Reinmar is Sir Piotr's brother!' Oldřich Halada added, also not very convincingly. 'And Sir Piotr of Bielawa was one of us. And you are also ours, after all—'

'And as such free to go?' Urban Horn interrupted mockingly. 'They can, if they so wish, go wherever they want? Right now, for example?'

'Well . . .' stammered the hetman of the Hradec cavalry. 'How can I . . . No. They can't. I have other orders. For as you see . . .'

'Danger is all around.' Halada cleared his throat. 'We must . . . guard you closely . . .'

'Absolutely. You must.'

The matter was clear. Ambrož was no longer interested in them, but they were under the permanent observation and control of the Hussite forces. No one imposed anything on them; quite the opposite, they were treated like comrades. They were even armed and almost conscripted into Brázda's light cavalry, now number-ing over a hundred horse after being combined with the main forces. But they were undeniably under guard. At first, Scharley gnashed his teeth and swore under his breath, but finally let it slide.

But neither Scharley nor Reynevan intended to forget about the unresolved matter of the attack on the tax collector. Or drop it.

Although Tybald Raabe carefully avoided talking, he was finally pinned down. Or, to be precise, shoved up against a wagon.

'What was I supposed to do?' he said angrily when they finally let him speak. 'Master Samson pressed me – I had to come up with something! Do you think that without the rumour about the money, Ambrož would have sent men to break you out? Like hell! We'd have got damn all! So you ought to thank me, not shout at me! Had it not been for my idea, you'd still be locked up in the Narrenturm, waiting for the Inquisitor!'

'Your rumour could have cost us our lives,' Scharley said, 'if Ambrož had been more avaricious.'

'If, if! Blow that!' The goliard straightened the hood that Scharley had ruffled. 'Firstly, knowing in what esteem he held Master Piotr, I was certain he wouldn't harm young Master Re-inmar. Firstly. Secondly—'

'Yes?'

'I really did think …' Tybald Raabe cleared his throat several times. 'Let's face it … I was almost certain it was you who cleaned out the tax collector in Ścibor's Clearing.'

'So who did?' Scharley persisted.

'It wasn't you?'

'You, Brother, are asking for a kick in the arse. Very well, tell us how you managed to escape the attack.'

'How?' The goliard's countenance grew dark. 'At the double! And I didn't look back, though they were calling "Help!" behind me.'

'Listen and learn, Reinmar—'

'I am, every day,' Reynevan cut him off. 'And the others, Tybald? What happened to the others? To the tax collector? To the Franciscans? To Lord Stietencron? To his ... To his daughter?'

'I've already said, m'lord. I didn't look back. Don't ask me anything else.'

Reynevan didn't.

Dusk fell, but to Reynevan's astonishment, the army didn't pitch camp. Marching through the night, the Hussites reached the village of Ratno and illuminated the darkness by setting light to several cottages. The garrison of Ratno Castle ignored Ambrož's ultimatum, thus the decision to attack was taken in the glow of blazing cottages. The stronghold was defended desperately but fell before dawn. The defenders paid for their resistance – they were massacred.

The march resumed at dawn, and Reynevan had already realised that Ambrož's foray into the Kłodzko region was a retaliatory expedition, revenge for the plundering raids on Náchod and Trutnov in the autumn, for the massacres that the forces of Bishop Konrad and Půta of Častolovice had perpetrated at Vízmburk and in the villages on the River Metuje. After Radkov and Ratno, Ścinawa paid for Vízmburk and Metuje. Ścinawa belonged to Jan of Haugwitz and he had taken part in the bishop's 'crusade'. For that, Ścinawa was burned to the ground. The Church of Saint Barbara went up in flames two days before its patron's holiday. The parish priest managed to run away, saving his head from the flail in the process.

With the church burning behind him, Ambrož said Mass – since it was, as it turned out, Sunday. The Mass was a typical Hussite one, conducted under the open sky on an ordinary table. Ambrož didn't ungird his sword while celebrating it.

The Czechs prayed loudly. Samson, as motionless as an ancient statue, stood and watched the flaming straw roofs of beehives catching fire.

After the Mass, with the smoking ruins behind them, the

Hussites set off eastwards, passing through the depression between the snow-capped prominences of Holinec and Kopec,
arriving outside Wojbórz in the evening. It was an estate belonging to the Zeschau family. The ferocity with which the Hussites
attacked the village indicated that a member of that family must
also have been with the bishop at Vízmburk. Not a single cottage,
barn or shack survived.

'We are a good four miles from the border,' Urban Horn stated
loudly, 'and only a mile from Kłodzko. That smoke is visible from
afar and news spreads fast. We are putting our heads in the lion's
maw.'

They marched on. When the Hussite army left Wojbórz, a
detachment of knights numbering some hundred horse appeared
from the east. There were plenty of knights of the Order of Saint
John of Jerusalem in the detachment, suggesting the presence of
Haugwitzes, Muschens and Zeschaus. The detachment fled in
panic at the mere sight of the Hussites.

'Where's that lion, Brother Horn?' sneered Ambrož. 'Where's
that maw? Onwards, Christians! Onwards, Warriors of God!
Forward, maaarch!'

There was no doubt that the Hussites' goal was Bardo. Even if
Reynevan had harboured doubts – after all, Bardo was a large
town and perhaps too large a morsel even for someone like
Ambrož – they were quickly dispelled. The army stopped for
the night in a forest near Nysa and axes thudded until midnight
making spiked stakes reminiscent of the coat of arms of the
Ronovic family – logs with protruding side branches. Simple,
effective devices for climbing defensive walls.

'Are you going to storm it?' Scharley asked bluntly.

They were sitting around a steaming cauldron of pea
soup with the hetmans of Ambrož's cavalry, blowing on
spoons and eating up the contents of their bowls. They were
accompanied by Samson, who had been very quiet since
Radkov. Ambrož wasn't interested in the giant so he enjoyed

complete freedom, which he surprisingly made use of by enthusiastically helping in the field kitchen run by women and girls from Hradec Králové, gloomy, taciturn, stand-offish and nondescript.

'You're going to storm Bardo,' Scharley confirmed to himself when his question was acknowledged by slurping. 'Might you have some personal scores to settle there, too?

'Correct, Brother,' said Velek Chrastický, wiping his moustache. 'The Cistercians of Bardo tolled the bells and celebrated Masses for the thugs of Bishop Konrad who marched to Náchod in September, to sack, burn and murder women and children. We have to show him he can't get away with anything like that. We have to show him what terror means.'

'Furthermore,' Oldřich Halada added, licking his spoon, 'Silesia has imposed a trade blockade on us. We have to show we can break the embargo. We also have to give some heart to the merchants, intimidated by acts of terror, who trade with us. We must encourage the kin of the dead, showing them we will answer terror with terror and that the killers will not go unpunished. Right, younger Lord Bielawa?'

'The killers will not go unpunished,' Reynevan repeated dully. 'In this regard, I am with you, m'Lord Oldřich.'

'If you want to be one of us,' Halada corrected him without emphasis, 'you should say "brother", not "m'lord". And tomorrow you can show us who you are with, for every sword will come in handy. A fierce battle is promised.'

'Indeed.' Brázda of Klinštejn, silent up until then, nodded towards the town. 'They know what we have come here for, and they will defend it.'

'There are two Cistercian churches in Bardo, both very wealthy.' Urban Horn's voice was dripping with mockery. 'Having grown wealthy on pilgrims.'

'You reduce everything to mundanities, Horn,' snapped Velek Chrastický.

'That is how I am.'

*

The axes had stopped thudding in the camp, their sound replaced by the sharp, regular grinding of whetstones which sent shivers down Reynevan's spine. Ambrož's men were sharpening their blades.

'Stand facing me,' ordered Scharley, when they were alone. 'Show yourself. Ha. Haven't you sewn the Chalice on your chest yet? "I'm with you, I'm on your side" – what nonsense is that, Reinmar? Perhaps you've taken your role too much to heart?'

'What do you mean?'

'You know exactly what I mean. I won't reproach you for blurting out details about the altercation at the grange in Dębowiec in front of Ambrož. Who knows, perhaps it'll do us good if we remain under Hussite protection for a little while. But please remember that Hradec Králové is by no means our destination, just a stop on our way to Hungary, and that their Hussite cause is small beer and not worth a straw to us.'

'Their cause does mean something to me,' Reynevan protested coldly. 'Peterlin believed in what they believe in. That is sufficient for me, because I knew my brother and what kind of man he was. If Peterlin was devoted to their cause, it cannot be a bad cause. Quiet, quiet, I know what you want to say. I also saw what was done to the Radkov priests. But that changes nothing. Peterlin wouldn't have supported an evil cause. Peterlin knew what I know today: in every religion, among the people who believe in it and fight for it, there is one Francis of Assisi to a legion of Brother Arnulphs.'

'I can only guess who Brother Arnulph is,' the penitent said, shrugging, 'but I understand the metaphor, all the more so since it's not very original. There's something I don't understand, though – have you already given yourself to the Hussite faith? And now, like every neophyte, are you setting to work converting people? If so, then please restrain your proselytizing zeal because I'm absolutely the wrong person to try it on.'

'Undoubtedly.' Reynevan grimaced. 'You don't need converting, for you already have been.'

Scharley's eyes narrowed slightly. 'What do you mean by that?'

'The eighteenth of July, 1418,' said Reynevan after a moment's silence. 'Wrocław, the New Town. Bloody Monday. Canon Beess betrayed you with the watchword I gave you at the Carmelite priory, and Buko of Krossig recognised and unmasked you that night at Bodak. You took part – and willingly – in the Wrocław Uprising of July Anno Domini 1418. And what moved and provoked you then if not the deaths of Huss and Hieronim? Who did you stand up for if not for persecuted Beghards and Wycliffites? What were you defending if not the free right to communion under both kinds? Declaring yourselves as *iustitia popularis*, against what did you act, if not against the wealth and depravity of the clergy? What were you calling for in the streets if not for the reform of *in capite et in membris*? Scharley? What happened?'

'It was as it was,' the penitent replied a moment later. 'And it was seven years ago. It will certainly astonish you to hear this, but some people can learn from their mistakes.'

'At the beginning of our acquaintance,' said Reynevan, 'so long ago it feels as though centuries have passed, you regaled me, I recall, with the following adage: We were created in His image and likeness, but the Creator made sure there were individual features. I, Scharley, don't erase the past or forget about it. I shall return to Silesia to settle my scores and pay off all debts, with appropriate interest. Silesia is closer to Hradec Králové than Buda is—'

'And does the way Ambrož settle his scores appeal to you?' Scharley cut him off. 'Wasn't I right that he's a neophyte, Samson?'

'Not entirely.' Samson had approached so quietly that Reynevan hadn't noticed or heard him. 'Not entirely, Scharley. This is about something else, namely Katarzyna of Biberstein. I think our Reinmar has fallen in love again.'

*

Before the frosty dawn had risen, farewells had been said.

'Farewell, Reinmar.' Urban Horn shook Reynevan's hand. 'I'm off. Too many have seen my face here, and that is dangerous in my trade, which I intend to continue plying.'

'The Bishop of Wrocław knows about you now,' warned Reynevan. 'And the black-cloaked horsemen screaming "*Adsumus*" probably do, too.'

'It's time to hide and wait things out among kind-hearted people. So I shall first go to Głogówek, and then to Poland.'

'It isn't safe in Poland,' Reynevan said, 'given what we overheard in Dębowiec. Bishop Zbigniew Oleśnicki—'

'Poland,' interrupted Horn, 'isn't just Oleśnicki. Mark my words – Europe is about to change, and that's because of Poland. Farewell, laddie.'

'We shall no doubt meet again. Knowing you, you'll return to Silesia, as shall I. I still have a few things to sort out there.'

'Who knows, perhaps we'll sort them out together. But in order for that to happen, please accept my kind advice, Reinmar of Bielawa: don't summon any more demons.'

'I shan't.'

'My second piece of advice: if you're seriously thinking about collaborating in the future, learn to use a sword. And a dagger. And a crossbow.'

'I shall. Farewell, Horn.'

'Farewell, m'lord,' said Tybald Raabe, coming closer. 'It's time I went, too. I must work for the cause.'

'Look out for yourself.'

'That I shall.'

Although Reynevan was in fact ready to stand alongside the Hussites with weapon in hand, it was not to be. Ambroż had ordered he and Scharley to ride with his escort when the Hussite army crossed the Nysa through falling snow and mustered outside the town. Smoke was already drifting towards them from the north, where Brázda and Chrastický's horsemen had already burned down the mill and cottages outside the town as part of a sabotage operation.

Bardo was ready to defend itself, the walls teeming with soldiers, standards fluttering, men yelling. The bells of both Czech and German churches were tolling sonorously.

And outside the walls, nine blackened stakes stood in circles of charred remains and piles of ash. The wind carried the sour stench of burning flesh.

'Hussites,' explained one of the peasant informers, a dozen of whom were obsequiously accompanying Ambrož's army. 'Hussites, Czechs, Beghards and one Jew. As a warning. When they learned that you were coming, my noble lord, they took everyone out of the dungeon and burned them alive as a warning and show of contempt against heretics ... I mean, forgive me ... Against you ...'

Ambrož nodded. He didn't say a word. His face was set.

The Hussites quickly and efficiently occupied their positions. The infantry set up and braced pavises and barricades while the artillery was prepared. There was yelling and cursing from the walls, accompanied by the occasional roar of a cannon and some crossbow bolts. Frightened crows cawed and duelled in the sky and disorientated jackdaws flitted past.

Ambrož climbed up on a wagon.

'Virtuous Christians!' he shouted. 'Faithful Czechs!'

The army quietened down. Ambrož waited for complete silence.

'I saw before the altar,' he roared, pointing at the charred stakes and smouldering remains of fires, 'souls killed for the Word of God and for the witness they bore. And in a loud voice they called thus: How long, O holy and sacred Lord, will You refrain from judging or meting out punishment for our spilled blood to those who dwell in this land? I saw an angel standing in the sun! And he cried with a loud voice, saying to all the fowls that fly in the midst of Heaven: Come and gather yourselves together unto the supper of the great God; that ye may eat the flesh of kings, and the flesh of captains, and the flesh of mighty men, and the flesh of horses, and of them that sit on them! And I saw the Beast!'

From the walls rose an uproar; curses and insults flew. Ambrož raised a hand.

'Behold the divine birds above, showing us the way!' he cried. 'And behold, there, before us: the Beast! Behold, Babylon drunk with the blood of martyrs! Behold, the nest of sin and evil defamed by superstition, the lair of the Antichrist's servants!'

'Attack!' bellowed someone in the crowd of soldiers. 'Deeeaath!'

'For behold, the day is coming,' roared Ambrož, 'burning like a furnace; and all the arrogant and every evildoer will be chaff; and the day that is coming will set them ablaze so that it will leave them neither root nor branch!'

'Buuuurn them! Deeeaath! Have at him! Kill! Have at them!'

Ambrož raised both arms and the crowd immediately fell silent.

'God's work is awaiting you,' he called. 'A task we must undertake with a pure heart, after prayers! On your knees, faithful Christians! Let us pray!'

With a clanging and a grating, the army knelt behind the pavises and wooden barricades.

'*Otče náš,*' Ambrož began to thunder, 'who art in Heaven, hallowed be Thy name . . .'

'*Přijď tvé království!*' the kneeling army boomed in a single voice. 'Thy will be done! On Earth as it is in Heaven!'

Ambrož didn't put his hands together in prayer or lower his head. He looked at the walls of Bardo and hatred burned in his eyes. His teeth were bared like a wolf's and there was foam on his lips.

'And forgive us our trespasses,' he screamed, 'as we forgive those . . .'

One of the men kneeling in the front row, rather than forgiving, fired a handgonne. Shots were returned from the walls, a hail of bullets and bolts whistling through a burst of smoke from the battlements and striking the pavises.

'And lead us not into temptation!' The roar of the Hussites rose above the roar of the shots.

'But deliver us from evil!'

'Amen!' bellowed Ambrož. 'Amen! And now forward, faithful Czechs! *Vpřed, boží bojovníci!* Death to the Antichrist's lackeys! Kill the papists!'

'Have at them!'

Cannons and trestle guns spat fire and lead, harquebuses and hand cannons roared, crossbow bolts hissed, and a hail of lethal missiles swept the defenders from the wall. A second salvo, this time of burning projectiles, fell on the roofs of homesteads like fiery birds. A bombard spat fire from behind the raised wooden planking, enveloping the entire area in front of the gate in dense, stinking smoke. The gate couldn't withstand the fifty-pound stone ball and was reduced to matchwood. The attackers charged into the breach. Others climbed like ants up the spiked logs onto the wall. Bardo had been condemned to death, and the sentence was about to be carried out.

'Have at them! Kiiiilll!'

Wild, hair-raising shouts, moaning and yells.

Bardo was dying to the tolling of its bells. Mere moments after raising the alarm and issuing a call to arms, the bells now sounded like a desperate cry for help, which gradually became the fitful, quavering moaning of a dying man choking in his death throes. Finally, the bells fell silent, and almost at once, both bell towers were enveloped in black smoke as flames shot up into the sky like the soul of the dead town.

Because the town of Bardo had died. The raging conflagration was now a funeral pyre, and the screaming of the dying an epitaph.

Soon after, a column of fugitives began to file from the town: women, children and men whom the Hussites had permitted to leave. The fugitives were scrutinised by the peasant informers. Every so often, somebody was recognised, hauled out and slaughtered.

Before Reynevan's eyes, a peasant woman in a mantle indicated a young man to the Hussites. He was dragged from the line and when the hood was removed, his fashionably cut hair betrayed him as a knight. The peasant woman said something to Ambrož and Hlušička. Hlušička issued a short command. Flails rose and fell. The knight slumped to the ground, where he was stabbed with pitchforks and voulges.

The peasant woman removed her hood to reveal a thick, fair plait and walked away. Limping. Distinctively enough for Reynevan to diagnose a congenital dislocation of the hip. On parting, she sent him a knowing glance. She had recognised him, too.

Spoils were carried out from Bardo, a procession of Czechs loaded down with a variety of goods that had survived the hell of the fire and the clouds of smoke. The spoils were loaded onto wagons as cows and horses were driven out of the town.

At the very end of the procession Samson emerged from the burning town. He was black with soot, scorched in places, devoid of eyebrows and eyelashes. He was carrying a young cat, a creature with large, wild, terrified eyes, its black and white fur bristling. The cat was gripping Samson's sleeve tightly with its claws and opening its mouth silently every now and again.

Ambrož's face was set. Reynevan and Scharley said nothing. Samson came closer and stopped.

'I was thinking about saving the world yesterday evening,' he said very softly, 'and about saving humankind this morning. Ah well, one must cut one's cloth according to one's means and save what one can.'

After sacking Bardo, Ambrož's army returned to the west, towards Broumov, leaving a broad black track in the fresh white snow.

The cavalry was divided up. Some men rode at the head under

Brázda of Klinštejn's command, as the *předvoj* or advance guard. The rest, numbering thirty horse, came under the command of Oldřich Halada and formed the rearguard. Reynevan, Scharley and Samson ended up there.

Scharley whistled, Samson was quiet. Reynevan, riding alongside Halada, listened to his instructions, acquiring good habits and ridding himself of bad ones. The latter, Halada instructed quite sternly, included using the name 'Hussites', for only their enemies, papists and unfriendly people in general said that. One should instead say the 'true faithful', 'good Czechs' or 'Warriors of God'.

Reynevan nodded a little sleepily in the saddle and from time to time said he understood, which was not true. Snow was falling again and it was quickly becoming a blizzard.

Beyond the forest, at the crossroads near the ashes of Wojbórz, stood a stone penitential cross, one of Silesia's numerous reminders of crimes past and belated contrition. The day before, when Wojbórz was being put to the torch, Reynevan hadn't noticed the cross. But it had been evening, and snow was falling. Many things couldn't be noticed.

The arms of the cross were clover-shaped. Beside it stood two wagons, not war wagons but carts used for transporting goods. One was leaning far over to one side, resting on the hub of a wheel with a broken rim. Four men were trying in vain to lift the wagon up, so that two others could remove the broken wheel and put on the spare one.

'Help us!' called one. 'Brothers!'

'Empty the wagon!' yelled Halada. 'Make it lighter!'

'It isn't just the wheel,' shouted back the waggoner. 'We've broken the swingletree, we can't drive on! Someone must ride ahead and come back with a wagon! Then we'll transfer the goods—'

'To hell with the goods. Can't you see the snow falling? Do you want to be stuck here?'

'I'll lose the goods!'

'What about your life? Perhaps we're being followed—'

Halada's voice caught in his throat. Because he had spoken those words at a very bad time.

Horses snorted and a row of knights in full armour emerged from the forest. There were around thirty of them, most of them Knights Hospitaller.

They rode slowly, evenly, disciplined, none of the horses' muzzles breaking rank.

Another troop, just as strong, rode out from among the trees on the other side of the highway under the banner of the Haugwitzes' ram's head. Riding up en masse, the knights skilfully cut off the Orphans' escape route.

'We'll force our way through!' yelled one of the younger horsemen. 'Brother Oldřich! We'll force our way through!'

'How?' rasped Halada. 'Through lances? They'll stick us like pigs. Dismount and get behind the wagons! We'll sell our lives dearly!'

There was no time to lose. The knighthood surrounding them urged their horses to a trot, clanging shut the visors of their armets and lowering their lances. The Hussites dismounted and hid behind and beneath the wagons. Those who were left without a hiding place knelt with drawn crossbows. It turned out by a fortunate coincidence that in addition to stolen liturgical vessels, there were also weapons on the wagons, mainly pole arms. In no time at all, the Czechs had shared out halberds, partisans and gisarmes among themselves. Somebody shoved a pike with a blade as long and thin as an awl into Reynevan's hands.

'Make ready!' roared Halada. 'They are coming!'

'We're up to our necks in shit,' said Scharley, tightening and loading a crossbow. 'And I had so pinned my hopes on Hungary. I'd worked up a proper fucking appetite for some real *bográcsgulyás*.'

'For God and Saint George!'

The Knights Hospitaller and Haugwitzes spurred their horses to attack, charging the wagons with a roar.

'Now!' yelled Halada. 'Now! Fire! Have at them!'

Bowstrings twanged and a hail of bolts banged against shield and armour. Several horses tumbled; several riders fell. The others descended on the defenders. Long lances hit their targets and the crack of broken pikestaffs and cries of men being stabbed rose heavenwards. Reynevan was splashed with blood as one of the waggoners right beside him was run through, jerking convulsively. Close by, he saw one of Halada's dismounted riders struggling with a lance blade stuck into his chest, and watched a huge knight with the pike pole of the Oppelns on his shield lift another up on his lance and toss him, bleeding, onto the snow. He saw Scharley fire a crossbow, sending a bolt from close range into a lancer's throat, saw Halada destroy the helmet and head of another with a bardiche, and a third lancer, stabbed by two gisarmes, fall between the wagons and die, hacked and stabbed. A horse's head, muzzle foaming and teeth bared, loomed just above him. He saw the flash of a sword and instinctively lunged with the pike, puncturing something. Reynevan almost fell under the weight of the Knight Hospitaller he had stabbed as he swayed in the saddle. He pushed on the pikestaff and the knight arched backwards, calling on the saints in a high voice. But he didn't fall, supported by the high cantle. One of the Orphans helped Reynevan by striking the Knight Hospitaller with a halberd, flinging the knight from the saddle. Almost at the same moment, the Czech was struck in the head by a mace. The blow slammed the kettle hat into his throat and blood gushed from beneath it. Reynevan stabbed the attacker and, roaring curses, knocked him from the saddle. Beside him, another one fell from his horse, shot by Scharley. A third, slashed by a two-handed sword, slumped forward onto his horse's mane and splashed it with blood. There was suddenly more room around the wagons. The armoured men were falling back, fighting to control their panicked horses.

'Well done!' roared Oldřich Halada. 'Well done, Brothers! We gave them what for! Keep it up!'

They stood among blood and corpses. Reynevan noted with

horror that at most fifteen men were still alive, of whom only about ten remained upright. Most of those able to stand were bleeding from multiple wounds. He understood that they were only alive because the charging lancers had impeded each other and not all of them could reach the wagons, while those that had managed to approach had paid for the privilege, and dearly. The wagons were surrounded by a circle of corpses and wheezing, lacerated horses.

'Ready yourself,' rasped Halada. 'They will soon strike again . . .'

'Scharley?'

'I am alive.'

'Samson?'

The giant cleared his throat, wiping blood from his eyebrows that was oozing from a wound to his forehead. He was armed with a mace bristling with spikes and a pavise decorated by some self-taught artist with a lamb, a Host with diverging rays and the words: THE LORD OUR GOD.

'Ready yourself! They're coming!'

'We don't have a chance of surviving this,' said Scharley through his teeth.

'*Lasciate ogni speranza*,' agreed Samson calmly. 'It's fortunate, indeed, that I didn't bring that cat with me.'

Somebody handed Reynevan a harquebus – a brief pause had allowed the Orphans to load a few. He rested the barrel on the wagon, fastened the hook on the side and brought the hot fuse to the touch hole.

'Saiiint Geeeeorge!'

'*Gott mit uns!*'

The next charge came from all sides with a thudding of hooves. Harquebuses and handgonnes boomed and a crossbow salvo hissed through the air. And a moment later came long lances, spurting blood and the frenzied screams of men being stabbed. Samson saved Reynevan by shielding him with the pavise painted with the Host and the lamb. A moment later, the pavise saved

Scharley's life – the giant swung the enormous shield in one hand like a buckler, brushing away lance thrusts like dandelion fluff.

The Knights Hospitaller and Haugwitz knights forced their way between the wagons, standing up in their stirrups and hacking with swords and battleaxes, smiting with maces, amid yelling and clanging. The Hussites were falling. They were dying one after the other, shooting the lancers straight in the face with crossbows and handgonnes, thrusting and slicing with gisarmes and halberds, striking with maces and stabbing with pikes. The wounded crawled under the wagons and slashed the horses' lower legs, intensifying the confusion, chaos and commotion.

Halada jumped onto a wagon, sweeping a Knight Hospitaller from the saddle with a blow of a bardiche, then bent over double, stabbed by a thrust. Reynevan seized him and pulled him down. Two heavily armed men hovered over them, raising their swords. His life was saved again by Samson and his pavise. One of the knights, a Zedlitz, judging from the buckle on his shield, tumbled over with his horse, legs had been slashed. Scharley smote another, sitting on an armoured grey, with the bardiche dropped by Halada. His helmet split open and the knight bent forward, spattering his criniere with blood. At the same moment, somebody rode into Scharley and knocked him down with his horse. Reynevan stabbed the horseman hard with his pike, the point jamming in his plate armour. Reynevan released the shaft, turned around and cowered. There were knights everywhere, all around him a chaos of ghastly pointed hounskulls, a kaleidoscope of crosses and coats of arms on shields, a hurricane of flashing swords, a maelstrom of horses' teeth, chests and hooves. *The Narrenturm*, he thought feverishly, *it's still the Narrenturm, madness, lunacy and insanity.*

He slipped in the blood and fell over. Onto Scharley. Scharley was holding a crossbow. He looked at Reynevan and winked. And fired upwards. Straight into the belly of a horse towering over them. The horse squealed and kicked Reynevan in the side of the head. *It's over*, he thought.

'God heeeelp us!' he heard mutedly, paralysed by pain and weakness. 'Reeeeinforcements! Reeeeinforcements!'

'Rescue, Reinmar!' screamed Scharley, tugging him. 'Rescue! We're saved!'

Reynevan got up onto his hands and knees. The world continued to dance and float in front of his eyes, but the fact they were still alive couldn't be ignored. He blinked.

From the battlefield came a yelling and a clanging, where the Knights Hospitaller and Haugwitz knights had joined battle with the reinforcements, soldiers in full plate armour. The battle was short-lived – the highway to the west was already thundering with Brázda's galloping cavalry, yelling at the top of their voices, followed by Hussite infantry with upraised flails yelling even louder. On seeing them, the Knights Hospitaller and the Haugwitz forces fled, taking flight towards the trees individually and in small groups. The reinforcements were hot on their heels, slashing and hacking mercilessly, so loudly it echoed through the hills.

Reynevan sat down. Felt his head and sides. He was covered in blood, but not, it appeared, his own. Nearby, Samson, head bloodied, was resting against a wagon, still holding the pavise. Thick drops of blood were dripping from his ear onto his shoulder. Several Hussites were dragging themselves up from the ground. One was weeping. Another vomiting. One, pulling a strap with his teeth, was trying to staunch the blood gushing from the stump of a hacked-off arm.

'We're alive,' repeated Scharley. 'We're alive! Hi, Halada, do you—'

He broke off. Halada couldn't hear anything any more.

Brázda of Klinštejn rode over to the wagon, accompanied by the reinforcements. Although yelling and enlivened from the battle, they fell silent as the bloody mud began to squelch beneath their horses' hooves. Brázda took in the massacre and glanced at Halada's glazed eyes, but said nothing.

The commander of the reinforcements observed Reynevan,

squinting. He was evidently trying to recall where he'd seen him before. Reynevan recognised him at once and not just by the rose in his coat of arms – it was the Raubritter from Kromolin, the protector of Tybald Raabe, a Pole, Błażej Poraj Jakubowski.

The Czech who had been weeping lowered his head on his chest and died. In silence.

'I am astounded,' Jakubowski said finally. 'Look at these three. Hardly scratched. You're bloody lucky! Or some demon is watching over you!'

He didn't recognise them. It was actually no small wonder.

Although barely able to remain upright, Reynevan immediately set about tending to the wounded. Meanwhile, the Hussite infantry were finishing off and stripping the armour from the Knights Hospitaller and the Haugwitz lancers. As the dead were pulled from their armour, fist fights broke out over the spoils.

One of the knights lying beneath a wagon, seemingly as dead as the others, suddenly moved, his armour grating as he groaned from deep within his helmet. Reynevan approached, knelt down and lifted up the visor. They looked each other in the eyes for a long while.

'Go on . . .' rasped the knight. 'Finish me off, heretic. You killed my brother, now kill me. And may the Devil take you . . .'

'Wolfher of Stercza.'

'I hope you die, Reinmar of Bielawa.'

Two Hussites approached with bloody knives. Samson stood up and barred their way, and something in his eyes made them step back smartly.

'Finish me off,' repeated Wolfher of Stercza. 'Devil's spawn! What are you waiting for?'

'I didn't kill Nicolaus,' said Reynevan, 'as well you know. I am still not certain what role you played in Peterlin's murder. But know this, Stercza: I shall be back. And I shall get even with the guilty. Know it and tell the others. Reinmar of Bielawa will return to Silesia and demand that scores be settled. For everything.'

Wolfher's fierce expression softened, relaxed. Stercza had been acting tough, but only now did he understand that he had a chance of surviving. In spite of that, he said nothing and turned his head away.

Brázda's cavalry were returning from the pursuit and reconnaissance. Driven by its commanders, the infantry abandoned the stripping of the fallen and formed up in marching order. Scharley approached with three horses.

'We're setting off,' he said briefly. 'Samson, are you able to ride?'

'I am.'

An hour passed before they set off. Leaving behind them a penitentiary cross, one of Silesia's numerous mementoes of crimes past and belated contrition. Now, aside from the cross, the junction was also marked by a burial mound under which were buried Oldřich Halada and twenty-four Hussites, Orphans from Hradec Králové. Into the burial mound, Samson stuck the pavise with the lamb, chalice, Host with diverging rays and the inscription: BŮH PÁN NÁŠ – THE LORD OUR GOD.

Ambrož's army marched west, towards Broumov, leaving behind it a wide black strip of mud furrowed by wheels and churned up by boots. Reynevan turned around in the saddle and looked back.

'I shall return,' he said.

Scharley sighed. 'I was afraid you'd say that. Samson?'

'Yes.'

'You're muttering under your breath, in Italian to boot, so I presume it's Dante Alighieri again.'

'You presume right.'

'And no doubt it's a passage that applies to our situation? To wherever we are heading?'

'Indeed.'

'Hmm ... *Fuor de la queta* ... Would it be an imposition if I asked you to translate?'

'It wouldn't.'

From a quiet world into permanently trembling worlds,
Into a new domain, eternally dark.

On the western slope of Holinec, in a place with a good view of the valley and a marching army, a huge wallcreeper alighted on a spruce branch, shaking snow from the needles. It turned its head and its unmoving eye appeared to spot someone among the marchers.

The wallcreeper had probably finally seen what it wanted to see, because it opened its beak and croaked, and in the croak, there was a challenge. And a cruel threat.

The mountain was enveloped in the vague gloom of an overcast winter day.

Snow was falling again, covering their tracks.

END OF VOLUME ONE

Credits

Andrzej Sapkowski and Gollancz would like to thank everyone at Orion who worked on the publication of *The Tower of Fools* in the UK.

Editorial
Marcus Gipps
Brendan Durkin

Translator
David French

Copy editor
Lisa Rogers

Proofreader
Gabriella Nemeth

Audio
Paul Stark
Amber Bates

Contracts
Anne Goddard
Paul Bulos
Jake Alderson

Design
Lucie Stericker
Rabab Adams
Joanna Ridley
Nick May

Editorial Management
Charlie Panayiotou
Jane Hughes
Alice Davis

Finance
Jennifer Muchan
Jasdip Nandra
Afeera Ahmed
Elizabeth Beaumont
Sue Baker

Marketing
Lucy Cameron

Production
Paul Hussey

Publicity
Will O'Mullane

Sales
Laura Fletcher
Esther Waters
Victoria Laws
Rachael Hum
Ellie Kyrke-Smith
Frances Doyle
Georgina Cutler

Operations
Jo Jacobs
Sharon Willis
Lisa Pryde
Lucy Brem